EMPRESS
OF THE FALL
THE SUNSURGE QUARTET BOOK 1

DAVID HAIR

Jo Fletcher
BOOKS

First published in Great Britain in 2017
This edition published in 2018 by

Jo Fletcher Books
an imprint of
Quercus Editions Ltd
Carmelite House
50 Victoria Embankment
London EC4Y 0DZ

An Hachette UK company

A CIP catalogue record for this book is available
from the British Library.

PB ISBN 978-1-78429-098-6
EB ISBN 978-1-78429-100-6

10 9 8 7 6 5 4 3 2 1

Typeset by CC Book Production
Printed and bound in Great Britain by Clays Ltd, St Ives plc

Praise for David Hair

'Promises to recall epic fantasy's finest'
Tor.com on Mage's Blood

'For anyone looking for a new sprawling fantasy epic
to stick their teeth into, *Empress of the Fall* is an ultimately
satisfying journey into a fascinating and chaotic landscape'
ScFiNow on Empress of the Fall

'Modern epic fantasy at its best'
Fantasy Book Critic on Scarlet Tides

'Hair is adept at building characters as well as worlds,
and his attention to his female players is welcome
in a genre that too often excludes them'
Kirkus

'A tremendously exciting series'
Fantasy Book Critic on The Moontide Quartet

'Adult fantasy lovers who enjoy historical fiction
and intricate political plots will love this book . . . Epic'
Boho Mind on Empress of the Fall

'A truly epic feel'
Fantasy Review Barn on The Moontide Quartet

'A sprawling epic fantasy of grandiose proportions . . . with a hearty
taste of blood and gore, and plenty of vicious politics'
**Angela Oliver, author of Fellowship of the Ringtails
on Empress of the Fall**

'So epic, that it gets you so involved and is such an investment
in time and emotion, that there is a little sting of regret
that the ending had to come at all'
British Fantasy Society on the Moontide Quartet

'True epic fantasy. It has everything a fan could want'
A Bitter Draft on Mage's Blood

'Th

Also by David Hair

THE MOONTIDE QUARTET

Mage's Blood
Scarlet Tides
Unholy War
Ascendant's Rite

THE SUNSURGE QUARTET

Empress of the Fall
Prince of the Spear

THE RETURN OF RAVANA

The Pyre
The Adversaries
The Exile

This book is dedicated to my parents, Cliff and Biddy Hair. Always thoughtful, concerned, supportive and loving. Home has always been a sanctuary and the first place I gravitate to when things are tough, for some realism and perspective. I love you, and no matter where I travel, you're always with me inside.

TABLE OF CONTENTS

PART ONE

PART TWO

NOORIUM SEA

SCHLESS

ARGUNDY

RONDELMAR

NOROS

SILACIA

ESTELLAYNE

RIMONI

GULF OF J

GALLIA

GULF OF LANTRIS

OCEANUS

YUROS

URTE
c. 927

0   1000M

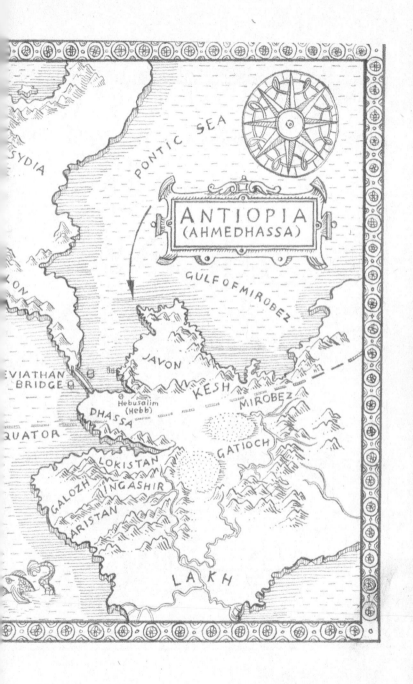

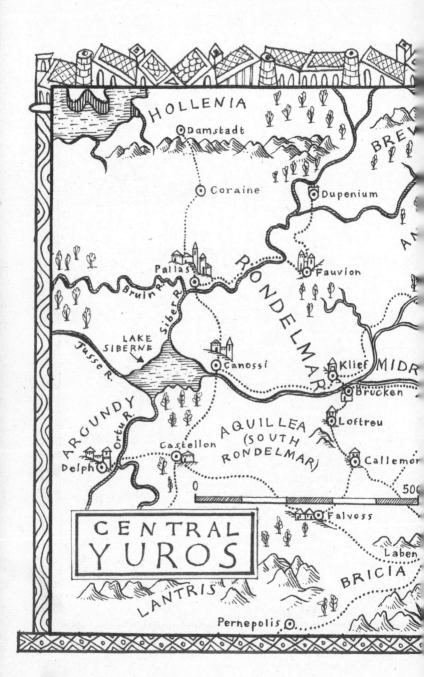

HOLLENIA

⊙ Damstadt

BREV

⊙ Coraine

⊙ Dupenium

Pallas ⊙

⊙ Fauvion

Bruin R.

RONDELMAR

Siber R.

Jusser R.

LAKE
SIBERNE

⊙ Canossi

Klief ⊙ MIDR

⊙ Brucken

A R G U N D Y

Ortur R.

Castellon ⊙

AQUILLEA
(SOUTH
RONDELMAR)

⊙ Loftreu

⊙ Callemor

Delph ⊙

0   500

⊙ Falvoss

C E N T R A L
Y U R O S

Laben

L A N T R I S

B R I C I A

Pernepolis ⊙

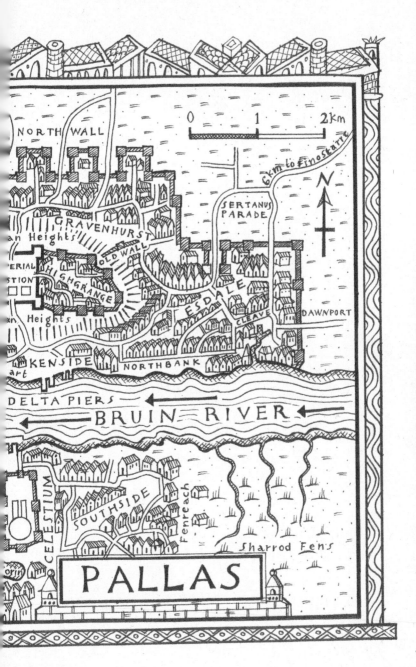

NORTH WALL

GRAVENHURST

an Heights

OLD WALL

PERIAL
STION

HIGHGRANGE

SERTANUS
PARADE

6km to Finoskairre

N

ESDALE

n Heights

CLEAVE

DAWNPORT

KENSIDE

NORTHBANK

art

DELTA PIERS

BRUIN RIVER

CELESTIUM

SOUTHSIDE

Fenreach

Sharrod Fens

orts

PALLAS

0   1   2km

THE GNOSTIC AFFINITY TABLE

STUDIES	EARTH (Element)	FIRE (Element)	AIR (Element)	WATER (Element)
THAUMATURGY [tangible/material]; the manipulation of inanimate matter	Earth-gnosis: find, manipulate and alter stone	Fire-gnosis: manipulate, survive and douse fire	Air-gnosis: fly, alter weather, and otherwise manipulate air	Water-gnosis: manipulate, purify, and breathe water
HERMETIC [tangible/unseen]; the manipulation of living matter	Sylvanism (Earth-linked): alter wood and plant material	Morphism (Fire-linked): alter the human form	Animism (Air-linked): control animals, take on their form and senses	Healing (Water-linked): restore flesh, and resist infection
SORCERY [intangible/ unseen]; the manipulation of spirit beings	Necromancy (Earth-linked): contact the dead, and remove life	Wizardry (Fire-linked): summon and control aetheric spirits	Divination (Air-linked): use aetheric spirits to predict outcomes	Clairvoyance (Water-linked): use aetheric spirits to 'scry' distant places
THEURGY [intangible/material]; the manipulation of mind and spirit	Spiritualism (Earth-linked): send one's spirit out of body	Mesmerism (Fire-linked): dominate or mislead another mind	Illusion (Air-linked): deceive another's senses	Mysticism (Water-linked): psychic linking to aid another mind

How to use the Table:

All magi have a primary affinity to a Study and/or to an Element. Most have an affinity to both, and many have a weaker secondary affinity.

Any affinity creates a blind spot to its antithesis, as follows:

FIRE	EARTH
AIR	WATER

THAUMATURGY	THEURGY
HERMETIC	SORCERY

Fire and Water are opposites
Air and Earth are opposites

Thaumaturgy and Sorcery are opposites
Hermetic and Theurgy are opposites

e.g. a Fire/Sorcery mage is strongest at wizardry (the intersection of Fire and Sorcery) and most vulnerable against Water-gnosis (the intersection of Water – the antithesis of Fire; and Thaumaturgy – the antithesis of Sorcery).

THE MOONTIDE CRUSADES
A Recounting of the Past

On the world of Urte there are two known continents. Yuros is cold and wet and the people are pale-skinned. Ahmedhassa (or 'Antiopia') is equatorial, largely arid, and heavily populated by dark-skinned peoples. These two great landmasses are divided by a raging sea; because of Urte's strong lunar cycle, massive tides make the sea impassable. Even though they were once one landmass until relatively recently, the two continents were unaware of each other.

That all changed some five hundred years ago.

The catalyst was a man called Corineus, who had gathered together a thousand religious pilgrims in Yuros. They consumed a fluid ('ambrosia') that imbued them with magical powers, which they called the *gnosis*. Half of the pilgrims died, including Corineus himself (apparently murdered by his 'sister' Corinea, who fled the scene). Of the remainder who survived the Ascendancy, three hundred, led by Sertain Sacrecour, set out to conquer the continent using their new gnostic powers; the magic of these 'Blessed Three Hundred' enabled them to destroy the Rimoni Empire with ease and establish their own regime: the Rondian Empire. They founded the 'Gnostic Keepers', an order of Ascendant magi dedicated to serving the empire and the gnosis. The Keepers encoded the recipe for the ambrosia into an artefact called the Scytale of Corineus to preserve its secret for the empire alone.

This event, known as *The Ascendancy of Corineus*, changed the world. The first magi, as they called themselves, found their children inherited their powers, though the gift was weakened if they didn't breed with other magi. As the magi multiplied, they claimed their own fiefdoms and spread their influence across Yuros.

Not all of the five hundred surviving Ascendants (the first magi) joined the Blessed Three Hundred in their conquest. A hundred men and women who abhorred violence and wanted no part in the overthrow of the Rimoni Empire departed into the wilds, led by Antonin Meiros. They settled in the southeastern corner of Yuros, where they formed a pacifist order of magi known as the Ordo Costruo.

The remaining hundred Ascendants at first appeared to have no magical power at all, but most had developed variations upon the gnosis, the most common being 'soul-drinking', whereby triggering the gnosis requires consumption of another mage's soul, and thereafter predation on human souls to renew their powers. These Souldrinkers (or 'Dokken') were declared heretics, but some eluded capture and remain a hidden threat to the magi.

Another dangerous variant, termed 'dwyma' or 'pandaemancy', involved the use of vast naturally-forming magical energies contained in a semi-aware 'genilocus' (spirits bound to a specific place). This was also declared a heresy and eradicated.

The magi used their new powers to explore beyond the known boundaries of the world. When the Ordo Costruo discovered northern Antiopia (or Ahmedhassa, as the native people call it), they discovered ancient societies very different to those in Yuros, but every bit as rich and varied. They came in the spirit of peace and soon established themselves in the northwestern corner of Antiopia, in the great city of Hebusalim. In the 700s, Antonin Meiros and his order commenced work on a massive bridge to link the two continents, and in doing so created the second great epoch-changing event of the age.

The Leviathan Bridge is three hundred miles long and perfectly straight. Because of limitations of both engineering and the gnosis, it rises from the waters only during the twelve-yearly super-low tide (the Moontide), and it remains passable for only two years of every twelve. After a hesitant start in 808, trade across the Bridge thrived and fortunes were made as a new breed of merchant-magi grew in influence. They ruled commerce for a century until, in 904, the Rondian Emperor Magnus Sacrecour, driven by greed, religious bigotry and racism, launched the First Crusade. Rondian legions headed by battle-magi seized the Bridge, pillaged Dhassa and occupied Hebusalim.

Most Easterners blamed Antonin Meiros, founder of the Ordo Costruo, as his magi could have prevented the attack – although it would have meant destroying the Bridge. At the end of the Moontide in 906, the Rondians retreated, leaving an occupation force in Hebusalim (which was subsequently withdrawn when its position became untenable).

Emperor Magnus didn't live to enjoy the spoils of his Crusade – he died in 909, which led to a palace coup: his second wife Lucia, acting on behalf of her child Constant, usurped the throne from Princess Natia, Magnus' daughter from his first marriage, and Natia's Argundian husband Ainar. Natia's fate is still unknown. The regime change led to uprisings in several regions, most notably Noros, which was quashed with difficulty, and in northern Coraine, the birthplace of Natia's mother.

Constant, under his iron-willed mother's guidance, was able to secure his reign, and in 916 he launched the Second Crusade, which penetrated deeper into Ahmedhassa and reaped a fresh harvest in plunder. The Rondians appointed a governor and established a permanent mission in Hebusalim. Constant came of age formally in 921, and had two children, Cordan and Coramore, but lost his wife Tarya to illness shortly thereafter.

The Third Crusade, launched in 928, was part of a Rondian strategy to seize the strategic region of Javon in northern Ahmedhassa as a staging point for permanent Occupation, to push beyond previous incursions and occupy hinterland territories, and to destroy the Leviathan Bridge while restoring the undersea isthmus upon which it was constructed, to enable permanent occupation of the East.

However, by now the East was prepared. Sultan Salim of Kesh had been building vast armies, and a mixed-blood Ordo Costruo mage, Emir Rashid Mubarak, had been secretly breeding Eastern magi, using captured Yurosi magi as broodmares and studs. Rashid had Antonin Meiros assassinated and the Rondian Second Army was lured into a trap at Shaliyah, deep in the deserts, where Salim's forces all but destroyed it. Meanwhile, a number of people discovered that the Scytale of Corineus was not safe in the cathedral vaults, but had been stolen by Noros magi during the Noros Revolt; they hid the priceless artefact when the Rondian Empire won. It was recovered, at enormous personal cost, by

DAVID HAIR

a young Noros mage, Alaron Mercer, who used it to found a new order
of Ascendant magi – the Merozain Bhaicara, or 'Brotherhood'.

In Junesse 930, as the Third Crusade ends, the Imperial Keepers are
preparing to destroy the Leviathan Bridge, unaware that the Merozain
Bhaicara are racing to stop them …

PART ONE

The Day the Emperor Died

Corineus

More than 500 years ago, in 379, a man died and his followers became the new gods of Yuros – the magi. They have ruled the western continent ever since, yet the name of he who died has been raised highest. Johan Corin – 'Corineus' – is now revered as a god made flesh, sent from Paradise Above to gather and empower his followers. He is said to have been the Son of Kore.

But he was just a man: dead people are always easier to deify than living ones.

ORDO COSTRUO COLLEGIATE, PONTUS, 927

The Celestium, Pallas, Rondelmar
Junesse 930
Final month of the Moontide

Kneeling is cruel, Ostevan Prelatus mused as he knelt in the holiest place in Yuros, mouthing prayers while staring at the massive rump of his superior. There were no seats, no cushions, just wooden leaning bars against which the thirty-two prelates of the Church of Kore could contemplate the infinite, while gazing upon the golden casket of Johan Corin – known to the world as Corineus the Saviour. *Prelates should be exempt.*

The Chamber of Humility, a circular subterranean room at the very centre of the cross-shaped Kore Cathedral, was open-roofed to the great dome above. The cathedral was the heart of the Celestium, the Holy City in Pallas, on the south bank of the Bruin River.

Though they were below ground, light poured through the stained glass of the windows in the dome, carving the dust-laden air into solid blocks of colour and setting the shadows to darker relief. Choirs sang, giving voice to the prayers of an empire.

The lesson of the chamber was that no living man meant more than this dead one – but it was an illusory lesson, for although the Celestium was a massive, glistening testimony to the power of the Church of Kore, it was forced to look up at the Imperial Bastion across the river. The first thing Grand Prelate Dominius Wurther, and all these other holy men saw as they opened their curtains each morning was a reminder that emperors stood higher than grand prelates.

I bet that cuts you to the quick, Dom, Ostevan thought.

He'd almost forgotten that prayers could end when, miraculously, they did. Wurther rose ponderously to his feet, backed away from the casket and left the chapel. His exit was the signal for the thirty-two prelates to do likewise. They rose as one, none meeting each others' eyes as they backed from the shrine.

Outside, Ennis, Wurther's secretary, was waiting. 'The Grand Prelate prays you will all adjourn to the amphitheatre to watch events in the East unfold,' Ennis announced.

Ostevan's eyes narrowed. It still hurt that he – who'd been Wurther's closest ally in his rise to the grand prelate's throne – had learned of this event only an hour ago.

It was approaching midday here in Pallas, but three thousand miles eastwards, over the Pontic Sea, it was already mid-afternoon, and the empire was preparing to destroy the Leviathan Bridge and change the world. Only a handful of men knew that Imperial magi planned to take the energy supporting the bridge and use it to raise the isthmus that had once linked Yuros and Antiopia. This incredible act of land-shaping was unprecedented, audacious and epoch-changing.

Clearly Wurther had known all along – and told no one, which said everything about Ostevan's current standing. He'd always been Wurther's man, helping propel him to the Pontifex's chair, but since 909, Ostevan's northern connections had been a liability.

And only one rump can fit on a throne, right, Dom? Especially one as large as yours.

4

Rodrigo Prelatus, an Estellan zealot, clutched Ostevan's sleeve as those prelates who were tied to the Imperial Sacrecour-Fasterius family shoved their way gracelessly to the exits. 'So how long have you know about this business with the Bridge?' the old Estellan wheezed. Like Ostevan, he wasn't one of the Imperial coterie, but there their similarities ended: Ostevan was – or had been, at least – an insider; Rodrigo, like the other provincial prelates, was a nobody.

'Longer than you, Padre.' Ostevan sniffed. 'Let's not keep his Holiness waiting, hmm?'

The clergy supposedly forsook their secular allegiances with their family names on entering the Church, but all were connected to powerful mage Houses and such allegiances were never truly put aside. Ostevan was a Jandreux of House Corani, and as Corani influence at court had waned, so too had his star.

He strode away, pausing briefly as he passed a mirror – vanity had always been his primary vice. Though in his mid-forties, he looked closer to thirty, with an admirably full head of dark, swishing hair, an elegant goatee and a cruelly handsome face, with intense eyes and full lips that had beguiled anyone he'd ever set out to ensnare – the fairer sex were his other main vice. In the Celestium, sins weren't so much forbidden as a secret currency.

The long walk to the amphitheatre took the prelates through the Mosaic Hall, where an earlier grand prelate had commanded a map of the world to be laid in coloured tiles and lit from within through gnostic artifice so that it glowed as they passed over it. Ostevan glanced at the two continents: Yuros, the western continent, was coloured in rich greens, while yellow tiles represented the eastern deserts of Antiopia, or Ahmedhassa, as the inhabitants called it. Golden models marked the great cities, with Pallas the most resplendent, presiding over an empire that directly ruled a third of the landmass and indirectly, the rest. As always, he looked first at the northwestern corner and found his home city of Coraine, then his gaze drifted to the east, over mountains, forests and plains, to Pontus.

Right now, everything revolved around Pontus and the Leviathan Bridge.

At their closest points, Yuros and Ahmedhassa were only three hundred miles apart, but the powerful tidal effects of the giant moon Luna made the seas impassable. The sunken isthmus that had once joined the two was long gone; but the Leviathan Bridge, running straight as a rod from Northpoint near Pontus all the way to Southpoint in coastal Ahmedhassa, had allowed trade between the two, and later, conquest – for the Yurosi, at least. And now the Rondian Empire planned to destroy the bridge and raise the isthmus again, to enable the permanent domination of both continents by Pallas.

A wonderful feat, thought Ostevan. *Shame it mostly benefits the stinking Sacrecours.*

He strode on, following the animated cloud of prelates, old men babbling like children, into a dimly lit amphitheatre built in the ancient Lantric style, with a circular stage overlooked by curved banks of seats. Ostevan sat away from the rest of his fellow prelates. This would be the Fasterius-Sacrecour alliance's crowning victory, the culmination of their triumph over the Ordo Costruo and an end to a troubling Third Crusade. There was much confusion over what was going on in Antiopia, with wild claims that the crusading Rondian armies had actually been defeated. But when the Leviathan Bridge collapsed and the isthmus rose from the sea, none would be able to deny Emperor Constant's triumph – well, Mater-Imperia Lucia's triumph, if truth be told; this was surely all the work of the Fasterius matriarch. Already the Sacrecour-Fasterius adherents were back-slapping and congratulating each other. Those like Ostevan, from lesser houses, were either sitting in isolation or trying desperately to pretend they were part of the inner circle.

How long before I need to join those cocksuckers?

'Brethren, pray be silent,' Dominius Wurther, Voice of God, Grand Prelate of Kore, boomed from his throne. 'The time has come.'

At his lordly gesture, a seer began to conjure images. His mind, linked to another seer on a windship over the Pontic Sea, half the world away, was able to translate everything his fellow mage saw onto the theatre stage. Even Ostevan forgot his vexations as the visions from Pontus began to unfold.

The gnostic image showed the deck of a windship, one of many hanging in the sky like insults to gravity. This one, the royal barge, was he largest ship in the windfleet. Far below was the Pontic Sea, with massive waves breaking ferociously upon a small island topped by a tall tower, Midpoint, which anchored the central point of the Bridge. Even amidst the heaving seas it looked impregnable, a testament to the mastery of the magi over nature. A beacon shone from the tip, bright as the sun, and Ostevan could see smaller windvessels circling it like midges. Running towards the tower-island from the southeast and on into the northwest was the mighty Leviathan Bridge: a line of darkness. But their eyes were drawn constantly to the Midpoint beacon, which was growing brighter and more intensely scarlet by the second.

Then suddenly beams of light flew in from four points of the compass, making visible the gnosis-currents linking Midpoint to its four satellite towers. The clergy gasped as the voice of Emperor Constant came through the gnostic link, hectoring his court about what a momentous moment this was.

'Here it comes,' someone muttered, and the beacon went brilliant crimson, painting the seas blood-red as it pulsed to a giant heartbeat.

Ostevan leaned forward, holding his breath.

A pillar of light burst from Midpoint Tower and carved the sky in twain – but quite unexpectedly, caught the windship next to the royal barge in its beam. For a second its shape was burned onto Ostevan's retinas . . . and then the windship ceased to exist.

The royal barge fell suddenly silent.

Then someone near the linking mage-priest cried out in anguish, and a babble of panic arose as the image began to flicker, jerking about in dizzying confusion. The watching prelates shouted in alarm as if they themselves were aboard that ship thousands of miles away. More light carved the skies, and another windship was blasted from existence.

What the Hel is going on? Ostevan rose to his feet as the vision ended in a burst of scarlet light, a momentary burst of transmitted agony leaving everyone watching reeling in shock. The amphitheatre plunged into shadow.

When the lamps were kindled, they revealed a sea of white faces dotted with black holes: eyes and mouths stretched open.

Ostevan sank back into his seat, staring, as the amphitheatre plunged momentarily into stunned silence. Then voices clamoured, demanding explanations, already seeking someone to blame; most directed their ire at the hapless young seer who'd been transmitting the images.

With an ashen face, Dominius Wurther rose ponderously to his feet and swept out of the door behind the throne, leaving the prelates in turmoil.

Ostevan was summoned an hour later, leaving his fellow prelates still milling about, demanding in vain that the flustered and frightened seer re-establish the link. Those with clairvoyance as an affinity tried to do the same, but they too failed. Others, Ostevan included, stared at the void in the middle of the room, waiting for sanity to reassert itself: surely, any moment now, the gnostic image of some palace dignitary would appear to reassure them that all was well, praising Emperor Constant for this great victory.

Instead of such reassurance, he was ordered to the grand prelate's chambers.

'Ostevan, my old friend,' Dominius said as he entered, 'come in.'

Ostevan kissed the Pontifex Band, noticing with a thrill of exultation that the office was empty but for them. Just as it used to be, when he was the brilliant young aide and Wurther his mentor.

Wurther looked sickly, his pallor relieved only by his bloodshot eyes. He'd changed from his richly adorned, heavy vestments to a simple grey cassock; Ostevan noted his armpits were already soaked in sweat.

'Dom, what is it?' Ostevan asked. 'Are you unwell?'

'Not I – what ails is this empire. It's confirmed: the emperor's dead.'

'Constant is dead? Kore take his soul,' Ostevan said insincerely. 'And Mater-Imperia Lucia?'

'Dead also,' Wurther whispered. 'Survivors are using relay-staves to send reports. We're still guessing what happened, but it looks like someone utilised those energies that were supposed to destroy the Bridge and turned them on the Imperial windfleet instead. Against such power, not even the most powerfully shielded windships could survive.'

'Who could do this – the Ordo Costruo?'

'Perhaps: they created the Bridge, after all. But we don't know . . .' Wurther's voice was anxious, but Ostevan recognised something in his eyes he'd not seen for a long time: the intense intellect that had plotted his irresistible rise to the Pontifex's Curule. The real Dominius Wurther, not the bumbling fool most saw, but the fiercely intelligent, cold-as-ice man he knew, was back. And his first act had been to recall the partner of his rise to glory.

So, my 'friend', just how desperate are you? he wondered.

'We must secure Mother Church,' Ostevan said, meaning, *We must secure our positions.*

'Of course,' Dominius said, understanding perfectly. 'Before she flew east, Lucia left the royal children in my care.'

Ostevan's eyebrows shot up. 'You have Prince Cordan and Princess Coramore?'

'Aye, I have the heirs – but they are nine and seven, too young to rule an empire, especially one that's been beheaded. The vassal-kingdoms will revolt unless we can immediately install a strong and united Regency Council.'

'Half the court went east, Dom – the Second Army has been destroyed, and the First Army – if it even still exists – is trapped in Ahmedhassa. The Crusade has been a disaster, and this empire faces a crisis of existence . . .'

Wurther wiped his slick brow. 'I know the armies of Rondelmar are severely weakened – but our vassal-states are in the same state. Lucia entrusted me with the task of keeping the heirs secure and the empire united – how she foresaw it, I don't know. But five centuries of Sacrecour rule could end tonight, unless we act swiftly.'

Ostevan stared. *Is he really going to remain true to the bloody Sacrecours? When we both know there's a better way?* He began his plea carefully. 'There is another faction, Dom, one which didn't send half its fighting men into the East, one which sits above the intrigues of the Great Houses: the Holy Church of Kore.' He reached across the table and seized Wurther's hand. 'Remember what we dreamed? A union of Bastion and Celestium? An Empire of Kore, ruled by a meritocracy of clergy, the best hearts and minds, dedicated to one Emperor-Pontifex.'

It had been a treasonous dream . . .

Wurther's mouth fell open, as it always did when his mind was racing, then he shook his head and pulled his hand away. 'Ostevan, I abandoned that dream years ago. The separation between Bastion and Celestium is necessary: no empire is eternal, and if our Emperor-Pontifex were to fall, then his Church would fall too. By standing free of the hurly-burly of politics, we preserve the Church against such calamity.'

Ostevan felt his hopes wither, but he knew when to obfuscate. *You timid fool*, he berated his former friend silently, but aloud he said, 'My dear friend, I merely test you. I'm yours to command, as always.'

Wurther looked at him steadily and for a moment Ostevan thought he'd snapped the last threads of trust between them. But then Wurther said, 'I summoned you, Ostevan, because you're the best man in a crisis I know. There's no time to waste – but I must know I can trust you *absolutely*. Put aside that old dream – it was always just a dream – and come back into the fold, my friend. I need you.'

Ostevan realised that without giving his unconditional support, he might not leave this room alive. So he kissed Wurther's ring again. 'I've always been yours to command, your Holiness.'

An hour later, alone in his quarters, Ostevan bent over a small bowl of water, conjuring the face of a man he'd not seen in the flesh for years, though they spoke weekly. Dirklan Setallius had grown older as all men did, even magi, but he remained a byword for unflinching pragmatism. His loyalty to House Corani was steadfast.

As is my own, Ostevan vowed.

Light blossomed in the water and Setallius' one-eyed visage appeared.

'My friend, drop everything!' Ostevan told the Corani spymaster. 'Finally, we have a chance to rectify the damage of 909.'

The Sett, Coraine, Northern Rondelmar
Junesse 930
Final month of the Moontide

Damage: that was the word Dirklan Setallius' mind always conjured when he remembered 909. No one who survived had done so unscathed.

Everyone had been wounded, whether physically, mentally or spiritually; that was the price of falling from the heights.

In 909 he'd been a senior Volsai, an Imperial Informer, or 'Owl', as people called them. A group of Corani had entered the academy together to redress the balance between supporters of Emperor Magnus, who'd married a Corani, and the long-entrenched Sacrecour-Fasterius agents. The new Corani Volsai's unspoken mission was to wrest control of the Owls.

In 909 they'd failed, utterly.

The Sacrecour counter-attack, when Magnus died and the Sacrecours swept the Corani from Pallas, had cost Setallius his left hand and left eye – and he'd counted himself lucky; most of his fellows had died, as had most of the Corani leadership. Three legions had been trapped and massacred; Arcanum students had been butchered in their dormitories. What still galled him was that the signs had been there, but no one believed Lucia Sacrecour could be so ruthless.

But now the witch is dead!

That thought lent purpose to his stride as he entered Corani Hall. The bells tolled, calling the magi and soldiery of Coraine to readiness, and all about him was bustle and confusion, though no one else knew if the bells signalled danger or celebration.

The crowds parted before him, something he'd become used to: he knew he cut a sinister figure with his left eye covered by a dark patch, long silver hair curtaining his scarred left cheeks and his black-gloved left hand – the lost flesh replaced by metal, fashioned to his own design. He strode through the hall to join Knight-Commander Solon Takwyth on the dais.

Takwyth was also a veteran of 909. Tall, lordly and steel-faced, he shone with belief today. He and Setallius had worked together to rebuild the Corani. He might be in his forties now, but he was bursting with energy. He saw this as destiny.

I don't believe in destiny, Setallius mused, *but I do believe in seizing chances.*

Takwyth raised a hand for quiet as Setallius scanned the room, seeking the patterns in the clusters of knights and battle-magi. The Falquists stood on the opposite side to the Jandreux, with the Sulpeters in between, as usual. Behind them was the faction that wasn't a faction: the lone wolves and dissidents and troublemakers, here in force. Every single man and woman was straining their ears.

It was those at the back Setallius felt most akin to. Most were the veterans of 909: men with haunted souls, like dead-eyed Jos Bortolin, the brothers Larik and Gryfflon Joyce, and Ril Endarion, who had been just twelve years old when his tutors at the Pallas Arcanum had tried to murder him in his sleep. These men were undoubtedly damaged by what they'd endured, but they were living legends among the Corani.

Setallius' ruminations were interrupted as Takwyth spoke. 'Men of Coraine, men of the North: hearken! I've much to say, and little time to say it. The chance has come for revenge – for 909, and for everything since.'

That got their attention.

For centuries, the Corani had been despised as the Pallacian nobility's country cousins, the butts of all their jokes – then, in 890, came their golden moment: Alitia Jandreux, eldest daughter of the Duke of Coraine, married Prince Magnus, the son of Emperor Hiltius. Suddenly the Corani were welcome at court.

The golden age was brief, though; four years later Alitia died in childbirth, leaving her husband with a daughter, Princess Natia. Though Natia was still the heir apparent, the northerners were worried: Magnus had betrothed the girl at birth to Ainar Borodium, son of the Duke of Argundy, in a plan to unite the two kingdoms, but Argundians had never been welcome in Pallas either, and now the Corani were tainted once again.

In 897 Prince Magnus remarried, to the ambitious and ruthless Lucia Fasterius, thinking to split the Sacrecour-Fasterius alliance. For a time the Corani breathed easy – but five years later Emperor Hiltius, now a widower, was murdered by persons unknown, and Magnus ascended to the throne, with Lucia at his side. Magnus publicly acknowledged Natia and Ainar as his heirs, and they were wed at the age of fourteen to great ceremony and rejoicing. The royal couple took the name Vereinen, which meant 'unity' in Argundian.

For a while it looked as if this compromise, and Magnus' grand plans for a Rondian-Argundian Empire, might have mollified his critics. His empress declared a programme of grand public works to honour her beloved husband.

And then the Fasterius clan struck.

When Emperor Magnus died mysteriously in 909, Lucia moved to secure the throne for her own son, Constant. Calling in her Sacrecour allies, she executed hundreds of alleged traitors, including Ainar Vereinen, then faced down the wrath of Argundy. Natia, just fifteen years old, was 'imprisoned', although it was an open secret among the Great Houses that she was dead. The Corani lost thousands of their fighting men: barracks were stormed in the dead of night and whole dynasties wiped out. Those few lucky or hardy enough to escape fled to their northern fastness, and to prevent total annihilation, the Duke of Coraine was forced to bend the knee.

That was twenty-one years ago, and those events haunted the Corani still.

'Knights of Coraine, stand for your Lady!' Solon Takwyth bellowed, and he stepped aside for a stooped, plain woman with small beady eyes and the close-cropped grey hair of widowhood: Radine Jandreux, Duchess of Coraine and Regent for her late-born grandson Yannoch.

'My knights,' she said, and though her voice was thin with age, there was no disguising her excitement, 'I have need of you. We have word out of Pallas, before the knowledge of our rivals.' She paused, and everyone present fell completely silent, straining to hear her next words. 'A great tragedy has occurred: the emperor and his Sainted Mother are dead!' Radine did not even try to contain her glee.

The entire room swallowed, gasping at the news, then low, vindictive cheers filled the air.

She held up a hand for silence. 'We must act swiftly to safeguard the realm,' the duchess said without the slightest trace of irony. History would be recording her words. 'Volsai Master Setallius has learned of six sites we must secure to prevent the Sacrecour cabal from reasserting control. Sir Solon has the list, and his orders are to seize them. I cannot predict what you will find, as our intelligence is incomplete, but my belief is that you will be securing the future of House Corani. I *know* you will do us proud!'

She allowed Takwyth to bend over her hand and fervently kiss her signet ring, then she hurried out, her train of clerks and advisors close behind.

The knight-commander waited until the duchess had disappeared, then turned back to the crowd. 'Her Grace might "know" that you slack-jawed drunkards are going to do her proud, but I bloody well don't! What I do know is that anyone who lets me down is going to find my boot up his arsehole!' He brandished a parchment. 'I have six locations, from a castle bordering the Sacrecour lands to a monastery in Tergatland, but one stands out and I'm taking that one myself. I want half of you with me, and the rest split over the other five locations.'

He rattled off names, assigning squads. As usual, his sycophants got the most important roles. 'And Sir Roginald Clef,' he concluded, turning to a grizzled veteran he disliked but couldn't ignore, 'you've got this monastery in Tergatland. Take Malthus Cayne, the Joyce brothers . . . and Ril Endarion. Every mage-knight in service must be in the air in twenty minutes!'

Setallius stepped forward. 'One of my people will accompany each mission, to coordinate our actions.' He rattled off some names, making a point of sending Basia de Sirou with Clef's group; her bond with Ril Endarion might be useful. Then he stepped back – he didn't much like Takwyth, but this was his show now.

Takwyth glowered about the room. 'Corani knights: this is our hour – may fortune smile upon you!' He strode out into the room, slapping shoulders, clasping hands, the consummate fighting man among his own.

Setallius stepped back into the shadows, assessing probabilities and considering implications, but in truth, this was a step into the unknown. It could as easily end in disaster as glory.

'C'mon, pooty-girl,' Ril Endarion murmured to his pegasus as he eased the bit into her mouth; Pearl, like every pegasus ever bred, was notoriously fussy – and right now all the mounts in the stable were skittish, alarmed by the bells and bustle; it was all stamping hooves, snorting and squealing and feathers flying. The Corani animagi bred pegasi as jousting beasts and taking Pearl into a real fight wasn't something Ril was looking forward to. The beasts were glamorous additions to a tourney field, but they weren't meant for war. All the venators belonged to the battle-magi though, and anyway, he'd never much cared for the ferocious flying reptiles.

Stablehands scurried throughout the huge stables making last-minute checks of gear as armoured mage-knights barked orders and mostly just got in the way as they shouted insults and encouragement to their neighbours. A swirl of court ladies added to the chaos, sallying amongst the men to wish good fortune to their current paramours. Ril glimpsed Lady Jenet Brunlye, the only woman he'd ever come close to marrying; she had her arm around her latest conquest, a knight of House Moravin barely out of the Arcanum. He winced and looked away.

'What's happening, d'ye think, sir?' young Malthus Cayne asked, tightening his helm before flipping up the visor.

'We're off to fleece some monks.' Ril grinned, washing Jenet from his mind with a swig from a wine-sack, then tossing it to big Gryfflon Joyce. 'Here, Gryff! You fly better drunk.'

'Rich, comin' from you,' Gryff sniffed, before draining the entire skin and carelessly throwing it to the ground. 'Rukkin' Hel, Larik, get a move on! You're only half-kitted!'

Gryff's skinny brother was standing with arms wide, aping the 'Corineus the Saviour' icons as his greaves were buckled on. 'Nearly done, nearly done,' he muttered. 'Thanks for not saving me a drink, fart-breath!'

Then Roginald Clef stomped up, annoyed at being given men he thoroughly disliked for a mission he knew nothing about. 'Get a move on!' he growled, his frown deepening as Basia de Sirou teetered through the confusion, her skeletal form encased in scab-red leathers. She was all angles, her delicate face set off by unfashionably short auburn hair. 'You too, Fantoche!'

'I'm ready, sir.' Basia barely even registered the nickname; 'puppet' was one of the milder insults these men had come up with over the years.

'You en't even dressed!' Larik snickered. 'Come on, Leggy, get some steel on!'

'Ladies don't wear tin, Larik. You know that.'

'Rich coming from someone who's no more a lady than the rest of us,' he muttered. 'And mostly made of tin anyway.'

Basia ignored him and joined Ril to finish buckling his armour herself. They'd both been orphaned in 909, and she'd only survived the attack on the Pallas Arcanum because of him. Two days trapped in a collapsed drain together, keeping each other alive, had forged bonds beyond love; they were closer than brother and sister.

'You up for this, Bas?' he murmured.

'Dirklan thinks so.' Setallius had made her artificial, gnostically powered limbs to replace her amputated legs – both crushed from the knee joint down – then persuaded her to join him in rebuilding the Corani Volsai. 'I'm just along to liaise; you boys can handle any fighting. Anyone who gets through you lot deserves my virtue.'

Ril snorted, then murmured, 'What's Dirk really up to?'

'Word came during the night and he's been with Radine's advisors ever since. I've no bloody idea what it's about. Hey, Bitch Lucia is dead! Our parents will be dancing in Paradise!'

Ril's mother, a Corani mage, had scandalously fallen pregnant to a rake in the Estellan Ambassador's entourage, which had left Ril in the strange position of growing up as the only bronze-skinned, black-haired mage-child in the pale blond north. That hadn't been easy, and after his parents had been murdered in Lucia's purge, he'd been raised as a Jandreux – no boon but a curse, as House Jandreux had run his estates into the ground to reimburse themselves for their 'generosity' in raising him.

Ril was now thirty-three years old, with little to his name but mounting debts. He'd been accounted one of the best swordsmen in the north for a decade, but time spared no one, not even magi, and his generation were now either ranking knights in the entourage of men like Solon Takwyth or Lord Sulpeter . . . or fading into obscurity.

'This could be the chance you need,' Basia whispered. 'What we're doing today *matters*, Ril.'

'You know, 909 was a long time ago, and I don't doubt some of our lot would have done the same thing given the chance,' Ril murmured. 'Twenty years is too long to hold a grudge, even for something like that. Sure, there are a dozen men I'd like to see dangling . . . Really, I'd settle for a little plunder to get me free of Radine's golden manacles.'

And if today yields no loot, I'm going to fly away . . .

'For my part, I'll never forgive them,' Basia said stiffly. 'Not if every Sacrecour was flayed before my eyes. I've never thought of you as a better person than me, Ril Endarion, but perhaps you are?'

Before he could answer, Takwyth and his bullyboys barged past.

'I hope that prick catches a blade in his belly,' Ril growled.

Takwyth had been the hero of the hour for getting a body of young Corani knights safely out of Pallas during the purge, but when he'd been given the task of rebuilding their military, he'd made it abundantly clear that his senior men would come from the Great Houses; there was no room for misfits like Ril. It didn't matter that he was a fearsome swordsman – advancement under Takwyth and Radine came through wealth, blood and sycophancy.

'Come on, let's go,' Basia murmured, teetering away to her mount. Watching her go, Ril reflected that she was the only person he'd really miss when he finally left this place.

Five minutes later, Ril was urging his pegasus higher as the six groups of winged riders fanned out across the skies. Roginald and Malthus were ahead of him, straining for purchase against the wind; Gryff and Larik were somewhere behind, vomiting every few minutes as the wine in their guts revolted against the awkward flying gait of their mounts. Basia's small wyvern alongside him didn't need much urging; the lightweight winged reptile had been bred for speed.

Once they'd reached altitude and Pearl was able to level out and glide on the wind currents, he pulled out his sapphire periapt; the gemstone began to pulse in time with his heartbeat, enhancing his gnostic energy as he reached out with his mind to Basia. *<Hey, who was Saint Balphus? Takky clearly didn't think it worth much.>*

<Saint Balphus is the patron of weavers,> Basia replied. *<Maybe there'll be some relics . . . or nice fabrics?>*

<Relics? Fabrics? I hope it's more than that – something yellow and metallic! And a gaggle of lonely nuns desperate for—>

<It's a monastery, not a convent, you idiot. But I'm sure some of the young novices will be hungry for company.>

He chuckled. <Come on, Fantoche, you must know more than that.>

<Only that there's something there the Church prizes.>

<It'll just be some dead saint's finger-bone.> He sighed. <So much for rich pickings . . .>

2

Saint Balphus Monastery

Rondelmar

Rondelmar is peopled by many diverse tribes united by the same tongue and racial stock: the Frandians. Conquered early by the Rimoni, they became loyal imperial subjects. Rondelmar's benevolent climate and resources fostered wealth and prosperity, but it is wrong to think of Rondelmar as one happy family. The Corani despise the Pallacians, the Dupeni loathe the Canossi, and they all hold the Aquilleans in mutual contempt. Only the dream of Empire holds them together.

ORDO COSTRUO COLLEGIATE, PONTUS, 724

Saint Balphus Monastery, Northwestern Rondelmar
Junesse 930
Final month of the Moontide

Four hours and almost two hundred miles out of Coraine, Ril Endarion, Malthus Cayne, Gryff and Larik Joyce and Basia de Sirou were trailing Roginald Clef through yet another cloudbank, swooping lower as the afternoon faded towards evening. Patchwork farms dotted the landscape, surrounded by rugged hills and forests. The joys of flight had given way to boredom, and Ril closed up with Basia and called to her, mind to mind.

<*Hey Basia, I've been thinking about the succession. Prince Cordan will become emperor, but he's only nine, so that means a Regency Council. Who'd lead that?*>

Basia's face was a pale blur a hundred feet to his right, but her voice crackled in his head. <*Garod Sacrecour, Lucia's nephew. He and Brylion Fasterius are still in Pallas.*>

Garod Sacrecour. Brylion Fasterius. The names brought back bad memories. *<I'd rather die than live in an empire ruled by those bastards.>*

<You're not the only one, Ril, but—>

Roginald Clef's anxious voice interrupted, calling, *<Enemy below!>*

They followed his gesturing arm, and saw seven winged shapes silhouetted against the fields thousands of feet below: venators. Their riders wore black-and-red quartered cloaks: Kirkegarde colours. The magi-knights of the Church were dangerous foes.

<What's going on?> Larik asked. *<It's just a monastery, right?>*

<Yes, but Setallius says it's important ...> Roginald replied, certainty draining from his voice. *<But they've beaten us here ...>* He looked ready to haul on his reins and back off.

He wasn't there in 909 ... Ril projected his mental voice into all of their minds: *<We have a mission. Stay high, and minimise your gnostic use. I don't want them to sense us.>*

He could almost hear Roginald sweating as he said, *<There's seven of them.>*

<Aye: one each and a spare. Load crossbows, everyone.>

Crossbows might not be a very knightly weapon, but they all knew how to use them. Ril glanced at Basia. *<Is this what Setallius expected?>*

<I told you, Dirklan didn't know any more than he said.>

Setallius mightn't know everything, but no one finessed the odds better. Ril suspected the real action was wherever Takwyth had gone; this was a sideshow. But they'd be expected to give their all – and after all, the Kirkegarde had been happy to help the Sacrecours in 909.

<Let's close up. Those 'saints' down there have misjudged their approach. We're still miles from the monastery but they've descended too soon and there's a low-altitude northerly down there. See how they're zigzagging? They're trying to tack into the wind like a windship would. They'll be exhausted. We'll hit them when they land.>

Gryff and Larik were grinning; they'd purged themselves and now they were ready for mayhem. Malthus Cayne, unimaginative oaf that he was, looked keen; Roginald Clef was jittery. The Kirkegarde fliers hadn't looked up yet, so Ril, somehow in charge now, took the squad lower, using the cloud cover to keep them hidden as they closed in.

Then he spotted their destination in the middle distance: a bulky brownstone building towering out of the lush fields, with a cluster of huts on one side.

<All right, here's what we'll do . . .>

They circled in the clouds while the Kirkegarde landed their venators near the monastery and a swarm of creamy-robed nuns emerged. *Which is weird, because this was supposed to be a monastery*, Ril thought. But there was no time to ponder that; he waited until the venators were all picketed, then signalled the attack.

They sent their mounts into a spiralling dive; twenty-one years of training and drilling but never seeing war boiling up inside. They'd been excluded from the Crusades; now they were desperate to show their prowess. Ril's heart pounded with exhilaration as he kindled gnostic fire on the end of his crossbow bolt and took aim, narrowing his eyes against the wind as and Pearl glided in with hooves poised to lash out.

<NOW!>

Ril's crossbow cracked and his bolt flew true, striking a Kirkegarde man in the back an instant before Pearl skimmed the crowd of nuns, then lashed out. Her hooves slammed into a venator, caving in its skull. Gnostic shields flared around the Kirkegarde knights; Gryff and Larik loosed their own bolts – and missed. Clef fared little better, catching a venator in the back and enraging it, but Basia's bolt slammed into another man's shields, ripped them apart and spun him round. She gave a faint *<Oh!>* through the mental link and quite obviously almost fainted.

But inside two seconds, the odds had dropped to six on five.

Pearl slammed her fore-hooves into the long serpent neck of another venator and broke its spine as Ril launched himself into the air, using kinetic gnosis to cartwheel groundwards, landing with blade drawn and immediately battering aside a lance-thrust from a Kirkegarde knight. He stepped inside the man's guard and stabbed, but – impressively, Ril admitted to himself – the man managed to get his own blade out and parried, then riposted, forcing Ril to spin away.

Then Gryfflon Joyce came flying through the air and cut the man in half with a massive two-handed kinesis-powered swing of his sword before ploughing into the field, gouging a massive wound in the earth and slamming head-first into a low wall. His gnostic shields flared madly, but he just lay there. For a moment Ril didn't think the shielding had been enough to save him, but at last he sensed a heartbeat and sighed in relief.

Five on four, though – much better!

'Rukkin' idiot!' Larik yelled at his brother, landing and shielding Gryff from mage-fire coming from the right, even as a torrent of flame all but engulfed Basia. Her shields kept the blaze at bay as the air turned to heat and smoke, though the effort was making her wobble on her unsteady legs. Heat and smoke washed over Ril and for a moment he couldn't breathe. Basia fired off her own blue bolts of energy into the murk, then Roginald Clef loomed out of the haze, shouting, 'Onwards, Corani!'

All very noble and heroic, no doubt. Ril called for Larik, then grabbed Basia's arm and they followed Clef. They burst out of the smoke into clean air to see nuns scattering, but the four remaining Kirkegarde had grouped together: one was a grandmaster, directing his three remaining men into a defensive shield about him.

All right, so now we're getting serious.

Clef reached the first of the churchmen and began hammering away at him. One of the other Kirkegarde, already wounded, with a crossbow bolt through his right bicep, went to his aid, an act of either commendable courage or reprehensible fanaticism, in Ril's eyes – but a bolt of light shot from Basia's hand and the wounded man spun and dropped.

Five on three. Ril flowed into the fight, forcing another of the Church knights to turn and face him. Their blades clashed; they thrust, parried and shoved, gnostic shields crackling in the air between them. As they probed at each other's defences, memories of his Arcanum tutors rose in Ril's mind: '*Every mage has an aura, a field of energy that can be used to sense the world around him. With it you can read an enemy's intentions, sense movement and instinctively counter an attack: that's called shielding. You can move objects – kinesis. Or you can kindle energy and kill with it – mage-bolts. Your gnostic aura is both armour and weapon.*'

Their blades slammed together again, then the Kirkegarde knight shoved with kinesis, forcing Ril away. Their shields, semi-visible pale blue spheres of gnostic energy flashing red as they caught blows and stabs of mage-fire, crackled between them. The Church knight was already panting and swaying, but Ril could sense Clef was faltering too, Basia was being driven back by the third defender and Larik was still some distance away.

Once the grandmaster joins the fray, we're in trouble . . .

Ril reached for more complex aspects of the gnosis: *'Every mage has options. If you're a thaumaturge, draw on the Elements: Fire, Earth, Water or Air. If you're a hermetic mage, change your body, or the world around you. If you're a theurgist, attack your enemy's mind. A sorcerer? Use the spirits. There are* always *options.'*

Ril's affinities were in Theurgy – messing with minds – and Air. He drew on the place where those two affinities intersected, weaving an illusory sword-arm over his real one, preparing for the moment when he could strike . . .

. . . then he lunged, pulling the illusion away from his arm so that his foe saw two blades. If the man had similar affinities, he'd see through the spell easily – but he didn't, and chose the wrong arm to parry. Ril's real longsword punched straight through his defences and the Kirkegarde went, '*Ooof!*' and stared, horrified, at the three feet of steel piercing his chest. Then he folded over with a groan.

Ril wrenched his blade out, vaguely sickened, and turned . . .

. . . as Roginald Clef fell for a sucker-thrust, blocking high as his man went low. The Corani knight jolted, grunting disbelievingly as he looked down at the sword in his groin, then the Kirkegarde, his face impassive, ripped upwards, cleaving steel like tin. Clef's guts spilled like writhing worms as he went down.

The grandmaster's face shone with righteous triumph as he strode through the line, heading for Ril, the man who'd killed Clef falling in behind him. 'Right, you Corani scum, let's see what else you've got,' he snarled, his shields strong and energy coursing through his blade: *pure-blood*-bright.

<*Larik!*> Ril shouted urgently, and then <*Pearl!*>

Basia was being battered backwards, but Larik stormed out of the smoke, hammering his blade at Basia's man, first high-high, then a feint and low. The man's shields flared strongly in the wrong place . . . and Larik drove his blade through the man's thigh. The Kirkegarde screamed and fell; the bloodied blade swept up and around and the man's head rolled to a stop three feet from his body.

Three on two . . .

But the Kirkegarde weren't backing off, which told Ril that this place was damned important after all. The man who'd killed Clef went for Larik, but the grandmaster came at Ril, who delivered a flurry of mage-bolts and one heavy blow that slammed against the grandmaster's sword like the ringing of the monastery bells. Pure-blood on pure-blood, knight and grandmaster—

Krang! The grandmaster's counter-blow smashed against Ril's blade and almost wrenched it from his hand. *Crunch!* The next blow hammered his shields, which flashed from pale blue through to deep scarlet, and got through enough to dent his hem. Ril staggered back, glassy-eyed, but still smashed the next blow away. He shook his head to clear it and circled back. From the corner of his eye he saw Basia send a mage-bolt at the grandmaster's back.

With a contemptuous backwards gesture, not even looking, the grandmaster replied with a blast of kinesis that sent Basia thirty feet through the air. She crashed back to the ground and skidded into the stone surround of a well, hitting it so hard half of the wall caved in. She bounced like a discarded doll and flopped dazedly on her side.

The grandmaster turned back to Ril. He looked to be in his fifties, old enough to have been involved in 909. 'Who sent you, Corani? How did you know to come here?'

'An Owl told me.'

The Grandmaster spat. 'Setallius.' He raised his sword, staring at Ril along the blade. 'I give you this chance to leave. It's the only one you'll get.'

Ril spun his own blade casually. 'Generous, but I have a mission. So I return the offer.'

'Don't you know who I am?' the Kirkegarde sneered.

Ril had never been terribly interested in heraldry, so the complex emblem the man wore on his tabard meant nothing. 'Not a clue, and I don't give a shit either. I only have one question: where were you in 909?'

'Esdale Barracks—' The grandmaster's eyes suddenly narrowed in understanding.

'Then you'll know why killing you won't trouble my conscience.'

'I'm amazed you have one. Do you know who the prisoner here is?'

Prisoner? Ril thought. 'Maybe I do.' *And maybe I don't . . .*

A few yards away, Larik and the other Kirkegarde were still bashing away at each other with reckless intensity. It wasn't the sort of fight that both would walk away from – but if Larik lost, he and Basia were sunk.

So best we just get on with this. 'Look, I could chat all day, but why delay the inevitable?' He lunged in, their blades belled and their shields flared again, but this time he drew on the double-edged blade of combat-divination. The grandmaster's sword began to blur, showing him the ghosts of intentions, the blows his foe *meant* to unleash, a split-second *before* he swung – which was great, but sometimes divination in combat could overload the senses and leave you *more* vulnerable, not less. Ril parried gracefully, arched his back away from a blast of energy and flitted from the knight's reach at the crucial point in a combination of blows designed to take his head off.

The grandmaster's frustration began to grow.

Then Larik took a blow through the side and staggered.

Oh Hel . . . Ril took a step back, pretending to lose concentration as he half-turned towards his falling friend. The grandmaster unleashed a huge killing stroke at Ril's neck—

—which Ril ghosted under as with his left hand he blasted a mage-bolt into the man's thigh, forcing his shields to coalesce low . . .

. . . and almost in the same motion, with his right hand, drove his gnosis-powered blade into the man's breastplate. The blade punched through in a sizzle of super-heated blood and meat, and the grand-master went down.

Ril twisted, too late to aid Larik . . .

. . . when a giant shadow swept over the last Church knight and two steel-shod hooves smashed down with force well beyond any mage's capacity to shield, at speed and without warning. The knight's helmet caved in as Pearl gave an almost human shriek of triumph. She reared over her fallen foe, then whinnied protectively at Larik.

Kore's Halo, I love you, pooty-girl . . .

Ril ran to Larik. The knight was ashen-faced. 'I'm fine, just need a healer,' he gasped. Dazed, he looked around for Basia. 'So could you perhaps wake her Ladyship?'

Those venators still living, unable to pull free from their pickets, were snapping and snarling impotently. All the Kirkegarde were dead, and so was Roginald Clef. In the distance, Ril could see the nuns fleeing back to their gates. He hurried to the fallen Basia. 'Fantoche?' he called urgently. Her eyes were glassy, her right arm limp. He patted her shoulder, which made her eyes bulge open. '*Rukka!* Don't touch me there!' she snarled. 'My collarbone's snapped, idiot—' Then her eyes rolled back into her skull and she fell sideways again.

'Shit!' He looked around. Malthus was also going to be out for some time. The nuns were mostly gone, but one of them was hobbling towards him. He straightened and went to meet her.

'Who are you?' she demanded. 'Why do you assail the knights of the Holy Church?'

He had to admire her cantankerous belligerence. 'Isn't this supposed to be a monastery?'

The nun, a thin woman with a paunch, surveyed the motionless, bloodied bodies scattered around as if she had all the time in the world. She had no gnostic aura, but her robe was of good thick wool, so perhaps she was in charge. 'I presume you're a Corani,' she observed. 'Why are you here?'

He took a guess. 'To collect the prisoner. Who are you?'

'I'm Abbess Jaratia of Saint Balphus *Abbey*. The old monastery was re-consecrated years ago. There are eighty souls in my care. Leave before you bring more dishonour on your House, Corani.'

Ril spotted a dispatch pouch hanging from the fallen grandmaster's belt. He plucked it from the corpse and found a sealed envelope inside, addressed to Abbess Jaratia herself. 'What's this?'

'That's the grand prelate's seal,' she said. 'Give it to me.'

'In a moment,' Ril said, opening it and pulling out a note scrawled on parchment.

Abbess Jaratia: the Grace of Kore be upon you. The time has come to end your vigil. Release your prisoner to the grandmaster, and cooperate fully. DW, Pontifex

It was accompanied by a small hourglass: an execution order.

DW, Pontifex – Grand Prelate Dominius Wurther . . . Holy Hel, what is this?

'Bring out this prisoner,' he said, 'or I'm going in.'

'No! And you will stay outside—'

'Sorry,' he said, 'I can't do that.'

'Our convent is forbidden to all unordained men – stay out, brigand, or be for ever accursed—'

She's playing for time . . . He went to go around her and she blocked him, shouting over her shoulder as loudly as she could, 'Secure the abbey and kill the prisoner!'

Kill the prisoner? He slammed a kinesis push into the abbess, sending her sprawling, then pelted towards the gates, already swinging closed, but he blasted them open, ignoring the nuns rolling around like skittles. A fat woman with immense shoulders roared like a bear and tried to tackle him; he hurled her aside with a blast of force, ignoring a bucket and hammer bouncing off his shields. He punched another nun blocking his way, and now most were fleeing – but a few were blocking some stairs leading from the courtyard, maybe to the tower he'd spotted. A bolt of blue light flew at him and as his shields solidified to repel it, he glimpsed one nun shrouded in gnostic shields of her own.

Another mage-bolt flashed at him. He re-engaged combat-divination and picked a course through ghosted futures of lancing mage-bolts, then engaged Air-gnosis and leaped skywards, arcing towards the foot of the tower, an inhuman leap that deposited him some ten yards from his foe: a handsome woman in the deep blue robes of an Anchorite: a mage-nun of Kore. A lethal burst of icy air and water flew from her hands, but he darted aside, closed the distance and sent an illusory bolt at the woman's legs while thrusting his longsword straight-armed at her chest. Her eyes bulged, her mouth formed an 'O' and she collapsed.

'The fearsome Ril Endarion, scourge of nuns,' he muttered sarcastically, but she'd been too dangerous to take lightly. Then a young woman's voice, crying out in fear, carried down the stairs of the windowless tower. He sprang to the staircase and used kinesis to leap up them five steps at a time. He barely checked himself at the top, bursting through the studded wooden door into a small, sparsely furnished chamber.

In the centre a hefty nun was straddling a girl with a flushed, frightened face, her thick, meaty fingers wrapped around the struggling girl's neck. The girl was kicking her legs and flailing her arms, but it was clear she had no idea how to fight off her assailant – so Ril smashed his sword-hilt onto the back of the nun's head and she collapsed sideways.

The girl beneath rolled into a ball, gasping and holding her battered throat. She had honey-gold hair and a pallid but pretty face. She looked no more than twenty.

Ril slammed the door closed and sealed it with gnosis energy, then looked around. The small cell had barred windows, a small pallet bed and a writing table. A chair had been broken in the struggle. There was no other obvious threat, so he gathered the young woman in his arms, scared she was going to go on choking until she expired. 'Hey, I've got you, I've got you,' he said soothingly. *Whoever* you *are, pretty girl* . . .

She kept on shaking, her face contorted with terror. Already her slender throat was bruising, and her chest was still heaving. 'It's all right, you're safe, I swear it,' he said, stroking her head. 'You're safe now.'

She looked at the fallen nun, the one who'd been throttling her, then buried her head in his chest again, as he thought furiously, *Who the Hel is she – and why has Dominius Wurther ordered her death?*

Finally she stopped gasping for breath, but she made no effort to move away. She stared up at him with hero-worship in her vivid sapphire eyes. 'You *rescued* me,' she panted. 'You *saved* me – like Celine and the White Knight!'

I suppose I did, he thought. *And she reads* The Fables. *But who is she?* 'At your service, my Lady . . . er?'

She missed his cues. 'I owe you my life,' she said, sounding as if she was reciting lines of a play. 'Everything I have is yours.'

He glanced around the room – everything she had didn't appear to amount to much more than a pile of small-clothes, a comb and a couple of books: a *Book of Kore* and *The Fables of Aradea*. The former was to be expected in a monastery – *no, an abbey* – but the latter looked out of place. He was about to ask for her name again when he heard stealthy footsteps on the stairs below.

'Sister Taddea?' someone called tremulously.

The girl pointed at the unconscious nun. 'Taddea's sleeping,' Ril called. 'Rukk off!' He heard whispering consternation, then the slap of sandals receding. Everything went quiet again.

If she's the prize we seek, I have to get her out, and make sure the others are safe.

She clutched his hand. 'Are you a good man, Sir Knight? Can I trust you?'

They weren't his two most favourite questions: *No* and *Maybe* were probably the most honest answers he could give. But she needed more, that was clear, and he had an almost overwhelming instinct to protect her right now. 'You can trust me,' he told her, and to his surprise, he found he actually meant it. *Damn, I thought I was over that heroic urge ...*

Her face had a guileless innocence that made him fear for her: she was like the delicate snowflakes who lasted barely a month at court before fleeing back to the pastoral home, usually with a full belly and their reputation in ruins. The deflowering of virgins was a competitive field in Coraine.

'Thank you,' she breathed. Her face was small and delicately structured, but her eyes had a steadiness that hinted that while she might not be worldly, she didn't lack for inner strength. She touched the badger sigil on his left breast, and said, 'You've come from my mother's people.'

She's Corani? He studied her face, seeking traces of family lineage, but coming up blank. 'I'm Ril Endarion, a knight in the service of Radine, the Duchess of Coraine.'

'I'm Lyra Vereinen,' she replied. When he looked at her blankly, she added, 'My mother was Princess Natia.'

'*Natia's daughter?*' he echoed as the whole world fell silent.

Holy Kore! Natia had a child? Ainar Borodium must have got her with child before they cut his head off—!

'My mother's dead,' Lyra said before he could ask. 'She took her own life after I was born – but she left me a letter, and her signet.' She pulled a necklace from round her neck, upon which a ring had been threaded. It certainly looked Imperial. 'I've been here all my life.'

Ril examined her aura and found a powerful Chain-rune. The spell preventing her from reaching her gnosis was too strong for him to easily break, and time was slipping away. Gnostic murmurs told him Larik and Basia were on their feet, but Gryff and Malthus were still down. They were a long way from safety, and more Kirkegarde could be coming.

'We must leave.' He went towards the door, but she didn't follow. 'My Lady?'

'They don't let me go outside except on Holy Days,' she said plaintively.

Holy Kore, what sort of life has she had? 'You're not a prisoner any more, Princess,' he told her. 'You're free now.' As he said those words, his mind was making mental leaps, each one more stunning than the last. 'Emperor Constant and his mother Lucia Fasterius are dead. Constant has children . . . but you're Natia's daughter, and she was Magnus' heir.' He paused, realising something quite stunning. 'You're the rightful Queen of Rondelmar . . . you're the Empress of Rondia!'

They shared a lot of disbelief and wonder.

It's like one of her rukking Fables . . .

The Palace of Tulips, Saint Agnetta's, near Pallas
Junesse 930
Final month of the Moontide

Solon Takwyth didn't like other men. Those who were kin were rivals, and those who weren't kin were enemies. It paid to remember these divisions in moments of uncertainty. Women were trophies, of course, chosen for breeding and connections, precious only for the status they gave and the children they provided . . . though he'd once been in love – truly in love – before she'd been snatched away.

Priests, though, were an unsettling breed, a strange paradox, a separate gender, emasculated and barren. They ought not to count at all, but infuriatingly, the world gave them status. Utterly unproductive yet so influential. They made no sense to him.

So when he burst into that final antechamber at Saint Agnetta's, the blood of three Imperial guards on his sword, he was neither pleased nor relieved to find a clergyman there, ally or not. 'Ostevan Prelatus! Why are you here?'

Ostevan bowed. 'You're late, Takky. Almost fatally late.' He pointed at the two men in Sacrecour livery sprawled on the floor with broken necks, surprised horror on their faces. 'A good thing I came myself.'

Takwyth knew Ostevan had sent the information that had brought him here – but that didn't mean he had to like him. The priest was altogether too self-regarding – a chaplain of boudoirs; a seducer of foolish wives, and too pretty to be a real man. If a knight looked like him, someone would break his nose in the practise yards.

'Are the royal children secured?' he demanded as Dirklan Setallius stalked into the chamber.

Ostevan bowed. 'They are indeed. Be nice; Radine wants them grateful for this "rescue".'

Takwyth started towards the doors, then turned back to the prelate. 'What have you gained from this, Priest? Wurther will have you excommunicated.'

'Wurther won't be long for this world, Solon. The Synod will be unanimous in voting for his removal, and I shall replace him.'

Takwyth sniffed. 'Well, I suppose you'd be as good as any.'

'Kind of you to say so. Please' – he gestured extravagantly – 'your prizes await.'

Takwyth left Ostevan and Setallius and entered the ornate nursery where Constant's children awaited him. Nine-year-old Cordan was standing stiff and formal as a young esquire, his sister Coramore, two years his junior, behind him. Both were in formal white and gold, wearing child-sized crowns. They had their father's pale skin, ginger-gold hair and weak chin.

'Prince, Princess; I'm Sir Solon Takwyth of House Corani and I'm here to protect you.'

DAVID HAIR

'We *had* protectors,' Cordan replied, gripping his sister's hand. 'You've killed them.'

He's frightened. The people who've warded him all his life are dead. But we've only got about ten more minutes before the Palace and the Church react, and we can't be trapped here.

'My Prince, Mater-Imperia Lucia entrusted your lives to Grand Prelate Wurther. He sought to misuse that trust. We must remove you to a place of safety.'

'House Sacrecour will protect me,' Cordan replied. 'My father's men—'

'They all went east, my Prince. There has been a terrible tragedy. Your father and grandmother are dead. I'm sorry to be the one to bring this news—'

Cordan flinched, and his sister gave a small gasp. 'Dead?' Both began to weep whilst standing stiff and formal, trying to be royal. It was somewhat touching, Solon supposed.

'I'm sorry,' he said, wondering, *What would happen if I just took a sword to these little rodents right now?*

War. That was the answer.

Then Ostevan Prelatus entered the nursery and the opportunity evaporated. The prelate had an odd expression on his face and he threw Takwyth a pitying look before going to Cordan and Coramore and kneeling before them. 'Prince, Princess,' he said in his mellifluous voice, 'will you accept the sanctuary we offer?'

'Osti!' Coramore exclaimed, and went to embrace him, but Cordan held her back.

'Cora – we're the emperor and empress now – be *dignified*.'

Takwyth repressed a grim smile. *Emperor and empress indeed . . .*

Ostevan drew the children to him, and they both burst into tears. 'What'll happen, Osti?' Cordan sobbed.

'A short journey, to a safe place. Then we'll see.'

The prelate bundled the royal children away while Takwyth's men hurried to return to their windcraft. He'd feared a counterblow, but none came; the skies were still clear as their craft rose into the air and caught the wind in their sails. By reflex he looked south, towards Pallas, some twenty miles down the Bruin River. He hated the place, but seeing it in the distance always set off a hunger inside him. To *really* matter, one had to matter *there*.

Ostevan joined Takwyth at the windship's rail as they pointed their prow north towards home. 'Well done, Takky. Mission accomplished.'

Takwyth kept his temper. Ostevan was a serpent who could bite in the blink of an eye. 'So, we have the heirs. A handpicked Regency Council might tilt things our way, but the Sacrecours still have teeth, priest. Many will flock to us, but many more will take up the arms of our enemies. Have we just given birth to a civil war?'

The prelate stroked his goatee. 'Perhaps ... but I have fresh tidings, from our other sorties. The tabula board has revealed pieces in play that we didn't suspect.'

Takwyth didn't play tabula; too many traps and tricks for his liking. 'What tidings?'

Ostevan arched an eyebrow. 'Have you ever been in love, Solon?'

'Talk plain, man,' he growled.

'I speak of love: a milky-soft mix of infatuation and lust – curable, but it can be deadly.'

'I've been married twice.'

'And you loved neither woman.'

Takwyth balled a fist. 'If you know so much, then you know my answer.'

'Indeed: you were in love with Natia Sacrecour. You were nineteen; she was fourteen and betrothed to another. You sent her poetry and dreamed of audacious rescues, but she still married Ainar. Weren't you in the honour guard which took her to her Argundian prince's bed?'

'*What of it, you silken arse-rag?*' Takwyth spat over the rail of the windship and watched the tiny white globule vanish into the gloom.

Ostevan smirked. 'You're still very touchy on the subject, Solon.'

'So? Natia's dead – *long* dead!'

'Yes, indeed. But it appears she had a daughter, who's very much alive.'

3

Ryneholt and the Stardancer

The Church of Kore

Corineus was sent by Kore to bring his people back to the one true religion. He gave unto his followers the gnosis, then conquered death itself and ascended into Heaven, to a seat at the right hand of the Father.

BOOK OF KORE

The Rondian cult of Kore, suppressed but never eradicated by the Rimoni, was used as the vehicle to justify the 'Blessed' Three Hundred's ruthless conquest of Yuros.

THE BLACK HISTORIES (ANONYMOUS), 776

Saint Balphus Abbey, Northern Rondelmar
Julsep 930
One month after the Moontide

Lyra Vereinen's life had been confined to the chapel, the refectory, the scullery, and on very rare occasions, the gardens behind Saint Balphus Abbey – and this cell, where she'd so nearly died. That didn't mean farewelling it was easy. It was all she knew: twenty years in a safe kind of Hel. Now the open world beckoned and all she could think of was how unprepared she was to face it.

Her mother had been fifteen years old in 909, when Lucia Fasterius had moved against her. Emperor Magnus had fathered a son on Lucia, but he'd continued to favour his elder daughter Natia over Constant as heir. None of them had suspected the peril they were in. When Magnus died, Lucia publicly blamed Prince Ainar of Argundy and had

34

him executed, though she contented herself with imprisoning Natia, who'd given birth to Lyra in her cell. Natia had killed herself a few months later, leaving her daughter no memory of her face.

I've always wanted to leave, but now the door's open and I'm scared to go.

She clutched her most beloved possession to her: her leather-bound edition of *The Fables of Aradea*, tales of crafty witches, gallant knights and beautiful princesses, their fates in the capricious hands of Aradea, the Queen of the Fey. The sacred *Book of Kore* gave her comfort, of course, but it was always to the *Fables* she turned when the loneliness and despair became too much. Tucked inside it was the one letter her mother had left. Brief, now blurred and faded, it said only who she was, and that her mother was *sorry*.

The only other token she had of her lineage was the ring on the chain around her neck.

Ril Endarion had left her alone for a few minutes to gather her possessions while he saw to his companions. Even this momentary separation frightened her. When he reappeared at the doorway, she was utterly relieved – and entranced.

She'd met men before: priests who came to inspect her once a year, wrinkled old men with tonsured grey hair, rheumy voices and cold, disdainful eyes. But Ril glowed with vitality, shining in her eyes with capability – and a hint of peril. He'd killed to save her. He was clearly older than her – much older, in his thirties, maybe, but that didn't deter her; rather, it felt like an antidote to her own innocence.

He called from the doorway, 'Milady, we've found a carriage and horses. Our flying steeds can't bear more than one person for any distance, and you've no experience of flight. But we have to go now. We're not safe if your enemies realise that we're here.'

'I understand.' She couldn't help staring: he had a wonderful exotic beauty to him. *Surely he has Southern blood.* His presence made her feel safe, but still the thought of leaving her room was overwhelming. 'I just need a moment. I've never left this convent in all my life.' She clutched the *Fables* in one hand and held out her other to him. 'Please, help me.'

His long-fingered, strong hand enclosed hers, giving her the strength to stand. 'Have you got everything?' he asked, eyeing her small leather bag doubtfully.

'All I have are three old dresses, a comb, an icon, two books and my signet ring.' She pointed to her *Book of Kore*. 'This was a gift to my mother from her father, Emperor Magnus.' Beside it lay her bronze Sacred Heart icon. 'And this faithful piece has been my object of worship all my life.' She put them into her bag.

Ril touched *The Fables of Aradea*. 'I've always preferred this to the holy book,' he said, handing it to her. 'I always wanted to be Sir Ryneholt and slay the draken.'

'And rescue the Stardancer,' she enthused. They shared a moment of connection unlike any she'd ever felt, and her heart swelled. 'Ryneholt was my hero! Until I met you,' she added, the words popping out of her mouth unchecked. She blushed instantly as something tightened about her heart. 'I'm only alive because of you.'

He looked a little uncomfortable at her earnest praise. 'I did what anyone would have done—'

'But it was you who broke through the door when Taddea tried to . . .' She clutched her breast, suddenly frightened again. 'What's waiting for me out there?'

'Safety, Milady.'

'But they'll try and kill me again, won't they?'

'I'll protect you.'

'Like Ryneholt?' she said, hopefully.

He licked his lips, then said lightly, 'Aye, I'll be your Ryneholt.' He hefted her leather bag containing her scanty possessions and led her to the door.

It was growing darker and more forbidding with each second. The fear was almost overwhelming – until she took his hand again. Her heart was thudding, but one thought filled her mind: *Ryneholt married the Stardancer.*

Ril doubted Lyra Vereinen was even aware of what she was doing, playing up to the protector in him, but it didn't diminish the effect she had on him. Part of it was due to her palpable naïveté – her fear and her hero-worship might just be momentary emotions, but he still couldn't help but shield her. If someone else came to kill her, they'd have to slay him first.

She lives in a fable. Coraine will be the death of her.

He'd outgrown such innocence years ago. Coraine might be just a provincial court, but it was big and ugly enough to strip away anyone's ideals. People thought of royal courts as places of honour and nobility, but in truth, they were more like dogfighting pits: noblemen prancing about in the newest fashions to show their status, gambling fortunes to bankrupt rivals, screwing each other's wives and sisters out of spite and seducing virginal debutantes to destroy their marital prospects, just for fun. They duelled and backstabbed, plotted and connived, lied and cheated – all to be one of the privileged few at the very top, feeding from the richest trenchers. He'd fought a long defeat in that arena all his adult life. He'd seen the worst in everyone – including himself.

Once he'd thought he was Ryneholt. Now he felt more like Ratsnipe, who stole Aradea's necklace and was turned into a blind vole for the crime. But finding Lyra was like finding the last fey princess. She'd somehow given him a glimpse of another world, somewhere inside Aradea's Mirror where life wasn't a sordid tangle of sleazy taverns and duelling circles, living hand to mouth while pretending he belonged or cared.

She's going to be eaten alive. Nothing in Aradea's Mirror is ever real. Radine and Takwyth would likely castrate him with blunt knives just for holding her hand, but he didn't want to let her go. *She needs me, and I need to be needed.*

'About bloody time!' Basia called as they arrived in the courtyard. She, Malthus, Larik and Gryff were all on their feet now, and they'd bound Clef's body to his pegasus. They couldn't fly home, not with Lyra among them, but pegasi could still gallop, and they'd found horses to pull the carriage. Basia held out Pearl's reins to Ril – then she finally noticed Lyra.

She glared pointedly at their clasped hands. 'Who the Hel is she?'

Excellent question, Ril thought dizzily. 'Basia, lads, gather round. You're not going to believe this, but I swear it's true. This is Lyra, and she's the reason we're here. *She's Natia Vereinen's daughter . . .*'

They clearly didn't wholly believe him, and he couldn't blame them for that – but time was pressing, so they fled the abbey as if the dogs of Hel were after them. Basia rode in the carriage with Lyra, while Ril sent messages arrowing through the aether, calling for aid.

A maniple of Corani cavalry – five hundred men on lathered, steaming horses – was waiting at a crossroad east of Coraine. Lyra Vereinen saw the relief on Ril Endarion's face and surmised that despite their assurances, they'd been scared. Then she saw a dozen winged creatures flash overhead, and soon after, everyone relaxed.

Her companion in the carriage was a strange woman: Basia de Sirou, who was like a character from a fable herself. She wore weird leather leggings and walked like a wading bird – but when Lyra asked, Basia told her she'd lost her legs in 909, when the Sacrecours had turned on the Corani. Her artificial limbs were empowered by the gnosis – Lyra had no idea it could even do things like that. She'd been mortified, but Basia had been kindness itself. 'Everyone asks, sooner or later. Dirklan Setallius made my legs himself.' The worship in her voice when she spoke of the Corani spymaster reminded Lyra of the way the nuns spoke of Kore.

It was amazing just to meet a woman who wasn't a nun. She told Basia all about herself, partly to convince the sceptical woman that she was truly Natia's daughter, but mostly because she'd been locked up alone so long that conversation was an opportunity not to be missed. She'd been born into captivity and raised knowing that she lived at all only through the intervention of the Gnostic Keepers. That circle of ancient and powerful magi had told Lucia Fasterius that she couldn't execute her, and the Mater-Imperia had respected – or feared – the Keepers enough to obey. Lyra had still been kept under a Chain-rune all her life, denied access to the gnosis. She supposed Lucia had wanted her kept ignorant and weak.

When the carriage drew to a halt and she saw so many knights arrayed to meet her, she couldn't help sucking in her breath in fear. Behind the armoured ranks was a large, ornate carriage with curtained windows. An old woman dressed in a fantasia of lace and autumn colours was alighting, wearing a tall conical headdress with a gauzy veil: a noblewoman's hennin.

'Look,' Basia said, 'Duchess Radine herself has come to greet you.'

This is where it all begins, Lyra realised as Basia helped her dismount. She looked at Ril, who nodded encouragingly, though his own expression was now grim, as if he were preparing to go into combat again.

Close up, the woman in the hennin was old and frail, with curling grey locks and a wrinkled, homely face. Basia whispered, 'Her Grace Radine Jandreux, widow of the Duke of Coraine and regent for her grandson Yannoch, who's still a child.' Lyra knew the name; it was Radine who had brokered the marriage between her grandmother, Alitia Jandreux, and Prince Magnus.

The Jandreux matriarch curtseyed, then seized her hand and kissed it. 'Lyra – Natia's child! What a miracle this is . . . you are the image of your mother, dear girl—'

'Hello, your Grace – er, Duchess Radine . . .' Lyra responded uncertainly, vague on the protocols and how she should act – she'd never been treated as anything but a prisoner until now. She went to curtsey, and Radine caught her by the hands.

'You bend the knee to no one, dearest!' She looked Lyra over intently, still gripping her hands. 'Dear Kore, I've waited all my life for this moment – even your voice has Natia's music! I knew in my heart that our dearest Natia could not be wholly lost to us – and here you are, her very image. Praise unto Kore – Rondelmar trembles at your advent!'

That didn't sound reassuring. 'What's to become of me?' Lyra whispered.

'Freedom, child: I promise you, you will walk free the rest of your days.' Radine studied her. 'Though of course, on the eternal tabula board of power, you are now a powerful piece.'

Perhaps Radine was trying to please her with such words, but they frightened Lyra. Her throat still bore the imprints of Sister Taddea's fingers. 'I'm not powerful. I can't imagine anyone weaker than me.'

'Dear girl, in tabula, the weakest piece is the queen – but to lose her is to lose the game. So conversely, she is the most powerful piece of all.'

Is that how she sees me? As her 'queen' in an endless game? 'But my mother's enemies . . .?'

'Are in chaos,' Radine declared. 'Though the Sacrecours are like a

39

DAVID HAIR

Lantric haedra – lop off its head and a dozen new ones sprout. These are dangerous days, my dear, but we will ensure that you secure your birthright.'

My birthright. Her mouth was suddenly dry – but with that fear came anger too: for all the damage caused by Mater-Imperia Lucia and her ambitions. *My birthright is a throne*, she thought, realising for the first time what that actually meant. It really was like one of *The Fables of Aradea*. Even that thought was frightening; all those tales of stolen thrones and perilous birthrights seldom ended well – even *Ryneholt and the Stardancer* was a tragedy.

'Lyra, my princess, pray join me in my carriage,' Radine invited. 'There is much to discuss.'

That discussion sounded daunting, but what choice was there? 'Of course, your Grace.'

'Call me Aunty, child. That's close enough to the truth.' Radine took her arm. Lyra sought a glimpse of Ril's face and took strength from that as she followed the duchess to her carriage. In seconds they were moving again.

Lyra endured Radine's silent regard, feeling skewered by the duchess' perceptive eyes. Finally Radine said, 'Well, your looks are entirely your mother's, dear. No one will doubt that you're Natia's child. We've known your mother to be dead for a long time, though no one formally admitted it – but we never suspected a child. How old are you, my dear? You must be twenty, but you look younger.'

Lyra swallowed. It was tempting to lie, but she feared Duchess Radine would see through any falsehood she tried to weave, so she whispered the truth. 'No, I'm nineteen.'

Radine's jaw dropped. 'But ... Oh, Kore's bollocks ... you're *not* Ainar's child?' She looked skywards as if chiding Kore Himself. 'Then who's your father?'

'I don't know,' Lyra admitted. 'No one said, and I never knew to ask – it was years and years before someone told me that a man was required to beget children. I never saw any man who wasn't an old priest until today.'

'Sweet Kore in Heaven! Did they teach you nothing?'

'Of course not – I learned my numbers and letters, Scripture and histories – but not about begetting until I first bled.' Lyra felt herself blushing and changed the subject: 'Sir Ril said I was the rightful empress – he said that Emperor Constant is dead?'

'The emperor has indeed perished, along with his mother. His children, Cordan and Coramore, still live, however: a snivelling pair of spit-dribblers aged nine and seven. Regardless, yours is the *rightful* claim: Magnus named *Natia* as his heir, not Constant, and you are the heir of that claim.'

'But won't the Sacrecours dispute it?'

'Perhaps. The emperor's uncle, Garod Sacrecour, is now head of his House and wishes very badly to be First Regent until Cordan turns sixteen.' Radine's face hardened. 'But the Sacrecours have lost most of their legions in the East: Pallas lies open, for those prepared to dare.'

'What will you do?'

'We'll act. Cordan and Coramore's claims have a further weakness: just as we snatched you to safety, so we have also captured them: we'll ensure they're no threat to you.'

'But they're just children—'

'And more dangerous than anyone else who draws breath,' Radine replied. 'Our people in the Celestium revealed just in time that the grand prelate despatched urgent messages to a number of sites within hours of learning of Constant's demise: it appears he'd been entrusted with orders to slay you if Constant died, as well as half a dozen well-connected political prisoners. We recovered most of them at the same time we rescued you.'

Lyra shuddered, once again feeling Sister Taddea's fingers around her throat. 'What will you do with the children?'

'That rather depends, my dear,' Radine replied. 'The empire is in shock. The Third Crusade has been defeated, a great many legions lost. There's a power void in Pallas, and unless someone can quickly restore unity, the empire will fragment: every man with a sword will think they can seize power, and the world we know will descend into a morass of treachery and murder. The people will suffer and thousands, maybe millions, will perish. But you can prevent that.'

'*Me?*'

'Yes: by being an empress *everyone* can rally around: the unifying claimant who preserves the whole by being brave enough to step forth!'

Lyra was remembering her mother's fate. 'I am the rightful heir,' she admitted. 'I've always known that, ever since I was old enough to read Mother's letter.'

'Of course you are. But is it something you want?'

'Yes,' Lyra said, a little surprised at her own vehemence, but her lineage was one of the few truths of her life. 'The Sacrecours murdered my father and caused my mother's death: I owe it to them to be what you want.'

'Excellent,' Radine replied. 'I did wonder if you would need some persuasion,' she admitted, 'but you've been locked away for a long time, dear, and a convent education cannot replace that which life provides. Without good counsel, any ruler struggles, but one not raised in the role . . .'

Lyra got Radine's message loud and clear. *I'm sure she's right, but she's also telling me who will really be in charge.* It reminded her of the little power struggles that had riddled the abbey: the petty rivalries and vicious gossip, the stigmatising and the self-aggrandisement. *If this is a tabula board, then I have seen it played after all. The board will be bigger, and there will be many more pieces, but it's the same game.* She took a deep breath. 'I will learn, from you.'

But not for long, she sensed. Radine was old, and she smelled of death.

'Good!' The duchess squeezed her hands, then searched her face. 'But I worry about who your father is. How could Natia get pregnant in a convent?'

'I don't know. Mother's letter never said, and no one told me.'

'Someone out there knows, and if they come forward—'

'If they are my father, won't they want me to be happy?'

'Possibly, but remember: your mother was in enemy hands. Your father is likely to be one of the Sacrecour cabal. If he reveals himself to Garod Sacrecour, it could destroy you.'

'I'm still of Natia's blood—'

'Of course, but it complicates matters.' Radine frowned, then asked,

'Would you be willing to state under a sacred oath that you're older than you really are, and the true daughter of Ainar and Natia?'

Lyra felt ill at the thought. Kore punished such falsehoods – the holy book was quite clear on that. 'But my real father will know I'm lying. And so will Kore.'

'Kore supports your cause, child – and unless your father can prove his claim, assuming he's still alive, he matters naught. He'd have to admit seducing or raping an imprisoned royal woman; that's not a crime many would willingly admit to. And once we're in Pallas, the machinery of state reverts to us. Imperial Legions, loyal to the Crown, become ours to command. Other Great Houses are eager to see the back of the Sacrecours. We'll have powerful friends, as well as enemies. We could silence anyone who besmirches your good name.'

'But my soul . . .'

Radine raised an eyebrow. 'Dear girl, fear not for your soul: you will have many years as empress to gain absolution. House Corani can put you on the throne: we just require your conviction that you should be there.'

Even if I must lie . . . Lyra swallowed, feeling sick, then nodded in assent.

'Excellent!' Radine radiated approval. 'Bravely done, child. But we must *never* speak of this question over your father again, you understand? Everything may depend on it.' Radine waited until she nodded again, then went on, 'Garod Sacrecour holds the Imperial Bastion in Pallas, but when the full news of Constant and Lucia's fall becomes widely known, his support will evaporate. Sixty legions marched East, and half of those were raised by the Sacrecours and their allies. Those are losses no faction can replace – but many of the Sacrecours' greatest rivals, like us, were banned from joining the Crusade and so are at full strength. Only we have a legitimate claimant to the throne, though, and there is *enormous* power in legitimacy: the God-given right to rule. Without it, any claimant must rule by fear, and that takes great will, comes at huge expense and causes immense suffering.'

'You said my involvement will prevent civil war?'

'Indeed – in truth, I think *only you* can avert such conflict.' Radine frowned, then added, 'Child, whenever someone plays Imperial Tabula, there are always casualties – there is no such thing in this world as a bloodless change of regime.'

Agree, Lyra realised, *and I'll be set on a path that ends either in a throne or an executioner's block.* And if she succeeded, others would fail, and pay the price. But she was her mother's daughter: this was her destiny. 'I'll do it,' she repeated.

'Bravo, my dear. Then we are agreed: you'll be our banner, and the North will march on Pallas. If we hesitate, others will unite against us.' Radine paused, and then asked quietly, 'What do you wish to do with the royal children?'

Lyra went to answer then stopped. Radine clearly wanted her to say, *'I'll leave that up to you, Aunty.'* And then they'll vanish, *and their fate will be on my conscience.*

To murder children was an *immense* sin – what would Corineus, looking down from Paradise, make of such an action? The Sacrecour children were also of the Royal Dynasty. In the *Fables*, killing princes and princesses was something only the wicked did, and such murders invariably had dire consequences.

'They are children, my niece and nephew – my *kin*. We can't kill them.' She searched for a solution. 'We'll make them swear fealty before the whole court.'

'Lyra . . .' Radine began, 'such promises will mean nothing if—'

'I *won't* murder children.'

'They wouldn't hesitate to do away with you.'

'Surely not? They're only nine and seven, yes? Are they killers already?'

'You know what I mean, Lyra. Garod's not one to be squeamish; he would have taken that decision. Even Wurther didn't hesitate, and he's Kore's representative on Urte.'

'Then I must be better than them. I'm a stranger to the people: if I'm to win their affection, it must be through acts of goodness and mercy, like Sasca of Rym—'

'Life is no book of *Fables*, girl,' Radine scolded. 'Making enemies fear you is far more important than having subjects love you—'

'Then we'll teach them respect – but not by murdering innocents,' Lyra said firmly. She fancied Radine was a little taken aback by her display of will – she was herself. *It's my mother, speaking through me*, she thought.

'Very well, Lyra. But they'll be compelled to fealty, and kept secure at all times.'

Kept secure . . . in other words, imprisoned, as I was. 'If that's the best we can do.'

'It's more than they deserve,' Radine muttered. She looked up, her expression inquisitorial. 'Did your gaolers ever mistreat you, Lyra?'

'Well, the food was dull, and I couldn't leave—'

'No, dear, that's not what I meant. Did they *bodily* mistreat you?'

'They were nuns!' Lyra protested.

'If you knew the complaints I receive of nuns and their ilk . . . Did they beat you, ill-use you physically? Are you still a virgin? You do know what I mean, yes?'

Lyra squirmed. 'Aunty, the nuns lived in fear of what would befall them if I was harmed. The only man I ever saw was one old priest who inspected me once a year. The Abbess told me that Lucia had ordered that I was to be "left to shrivel on the vine".'

Radine's face softened. 'Dear girl, what a Hel they made you endure! Isolation can drive a lesser soul to madness. That you remain so lucid, so *normal*, does you great credit.'

'I did have books and tutors, Aunty. I was taught from the *Histories* and the *Annals of Pallas* – and I was permitted to keep my mother's copy of the *Fables*. But it was lonely sometimes.'

'Were you taught the gnosis?'

'No. I suppose I must have it, but I've been under a Rune of the Chain from birth, to prevent anyone scrying me. So I've never used the gnosis, much less been taught it.'

'Dear Kore! We'll lift that Chain-rune as soon as you're safely in Coraine.'

And thus was the princess' magic restored . . . I'm actually living The Fables of Aradea *. . . That* thought emboldened Lyra to say, 'In the *Annals*, I read that all emperors have a champion. I'd like mine to be the knight who rescued me.'

'Ril Endarion?' Radine sounded *very* displeased. 'You'd best forget him.'

'Sir Ril saved my life—'

'I don't doubt it. But he's penniless.'

'But if he were in my service he wouldn't want for money—'

'No,' Radine said forcefully. 'You said you wanted my advice, well here is some: you must remain conspicuously chaste until you are wed, and that must be to a powerful and worthy man. There are Great Houses we must bind to us and some will demand the highest price: your virgin hand in marriage. Having any unmarried knight near you will damage your reputation, but most especially *that* one—'

'He saved my life—'

'For which he will be well rewarded, I promise you. I am proud that an orphan boy I took in and raised as my own has rescued you, but I know Ril's reputation. You *must* keep your distance, dear child.'

4

Suitors

The Imperial Dynasty

It is Kore who granted the Blessed Three Hundred dominion over Urte, and from their number, willingly and according to Kore's plan, did they elevate Mikal Sertain (who took the name Sertain Sacrecour) and his descendants to realise His will. Thus are we Sacrecours ordained to rule.

Lucia Sacrecour, Pallas, 903

Coraine, Northern Rondelmar
Julsep 930
One month after the Moontide

Like many Northern cities, Coraine had once been a Frandian hill fort: the local chieftain protected the farmers and foresters and in return, extracted goods and coin for the privilege. The Rimoni and their legions defeated then 'civilised' the Frandian 'barbarians', beginning the inevitable gentrification of the region, a gradual and uneven process involving whips and other physical coercions as much as gentler means. The Rimoni Empire fell, to be immediately supplanted by the Rondians, with their magi and sense of destiny, which accelerated the process of installing better roads, more focused agriculture and more people.

The Jandreux were one of several pure-blood magi families who settled in Coraine and claimed legal title – the Blessed Three Hundred usurped other people's land-rights all over the empire. The legion camp became the Jandreux fortress, the outer walls expanding to encompass strategic streams and wells. Archery fields, stables, a Beastarium and an Arcanum were added in due course, and the Jandreux and their related families became House Corani. This was the haven Lyra Vereinen was being taken to: the Corani stronghold known as the Sett.

Ril Endarion had visited his dead mother's rural estates only once, and never wanted to return. The peasants had viewed his southern skin with blatant hostility and the run-down property administered in his name by Radine's people had been depressing. The Sett was his true home.

Within hours of the return of the duchess and her knights, the castle was rife with speculation about the mystery woman they'd rescued, and the rumour mill started running even faster when Takwyth ordered the legions to prepare to march. Something big was definitely afoot.

Those in the know were forbidden to speak of it. Radine's people had closed ranks around Lyra, making it clear to Ril that his involvement, while 'appreciated', was over. The last time he'd seen Lyra, she'd looked like a doe surrounded by wolves: proud, but scared and friendless. Her face filled his thoughts, day and night. One of Radine's lackeys was tailing him, presumably to ensure he didn't flout her order to *'Stay away from the snowbud, boy. She's not for the likes of you'*. At first it had made him smile, but now it rankled.

'So what are you going to do?' Gryff asked. They were all drinking too much – or at least the brothers were; Ril and the drink had a long and troubled relationship, right now he was too busy brooding.

'I've got a few ideas.' Ril lifted the cup of ale, but barely wet his lips.

Ril had quickly learned that being the best swordsman at the Coraine Arcanum meant nothing when your skin was swarthy and your hair black, your purse empty and you had enemies in every major House in the North. Young noblemen wanted sycophants, not stroppy, truculent outsiders with neither gold, connections nor prospects. His legion stint brought out his inner rebel, and no family was going to let their daughter marry a young man so deep in debt. His prospects had evaporated before his eyes.

I should have gone South to Becchio and joined the mercenary legions years ago. The words were almost a mantra now, but the truth was, he'd been too proud to run away – and there was always another tournament, and prizes to alleviate his debts, for a time at least. It was hard to give up on dreams, or to turn away from the few people in his life, especially Basia, who'd endured and survived 909 with him. And somehow he was always falling in love with women as emotionally damaged as he: brief, tangled liaisons that always ended in recriminations.

He couldn't remember exactly when he met Larik and Gryff Joyce, just that he'd planned on getting stinking drunk that night but he'd run out of coin. The brothers knew who he was, and they'd stood him enough ale to float him all the way out to the gutter. Veterans of 909 always propped each other up, perhaps because few knew how to stand on their own two feet.

Gryff and Larik had been battle-magi with the Second Corani; the legion had to fight its way out of Pallas after seeing comrades slain or maimed by supposed allies, people they'd trained with, drunk with, begun to trust. Like many who survived that Hel-ish night, the Joyce brothers had never recovered. Most people just saw a pair of drunks – or *three* drunks, because after that meeting, Ril was almost always with them. He knew they were a bad influence, but he didn't care. They were friends.

It was only thanks to Basia that he *could* now stop after one beer these days. She'd saved his life – although drying out Fantoche's way hadn't been fun! – but he still had a reputation as a sot.

He put the cup down and looked around the Great Hall, which was filling up with high-spirited Corani; they had all been rejuvenated by the events of the past couple of days and speculation was rife: when and where would they march? What was happening in Pallas? And most of all: who was the young woman in Radine's guest chamber?

Ril sensed the atmosphere change as all eyes turned his way – because he was sitting in Solon Takwyth's chair. Larik and Gryff, who were *really* drunk, went on prattling away as a heavy hand fell on Ril's shoulder.

'Get up, Endarion,' said Takwyth. 'This is the high table.'

Ril brushed his hand away and stood. They were of a height, but Takwyth was heavier-built. It had been years since they'd last sparred, and they'd both taken a battering that day.

'Hey, Takky!' Ril slurred, 'I took it first – seems I get everywhere first these days.'

Takwyth scowled. 'Drunk, Endarion? Again?'

Esvald Berlond, at his side as always, glowered menacingly.

'Not too drunk to dance, Takky.' Ril winked.

Takwyth's eyes narrowed. 'Are you challenging me?'

Ril pulled a startled face. 'Good grief, no,' he exclaimed, with a broad hint of mockery, 'I just wish to *dance*, for the joy in my soul – for you see, I met the most wonderful maiden and she fills my heart with music!'

Takwyth ground his teeth and rumbled, 'Careful, Endarion.'

Ril spun around and grabbed the nearest woman – Basia, who was hurrying in to defuse whatever was going on – just as the musicians struck up the entrance march for Lady Radine. Ril let loose a mad guffaw and spun Basia into a furious two-step. 'Let's dance, Fantoche!'

She flung him off, crying, 'What's wrong with you, *idiot*?' and cracked him across the face with her right hand – she wasn't about to surrender her hard-won respect from the male magi, even for Ril. Around them, young knights hurled barbed comments. 'Piss off, before I smash your teeth out,' she growled more loudly.

He rubbed his cheek ruefully. 'Good point . . . well argued,' he slurred, and snatched up a full pitcher of red as he staggered towards the doors, spilling it all around him. He lurched forward, buffeted by snide back-slaps and shoves, just as Duchess Radine made her entrance.

'Sir Ril,' she fumed, '*what* are you doing?'

He bowed theatrically. 'Your Grace, I was just leaving, before I embarrass myself – or maybe after.' He bowed to her once again, then to the room, ignoring the bemused, contemptuous, disgusted or amused stares, and fled the room. No one followed him.

Perfect. He'd escaped his little shadow, who was stuck in the crowded Great Hall.

Ril picked up the pace as he took the back way through the infirmary, slipping through the apothecary's aromatic herb garden, past the postern gate and into the Lady's Bower, which was forbidden to men. A warm twilight glow lit the narrow paths; the heavy scents of the night-blooming flowers and the shimmer and hum of the nocturnal birds and their insect prey lent the evening a soft ease. The cooling air was refreshing after the smoky confines of the hall.

He smiled at the memory of Radine's outraged face, then sighed. Pretending to be drunk wasn't clever, but he couldn't think how else to escape the duchess' constant scrutiny – she would be outraged if she knew what he was really about. He looked up at the balcony; the lamps had yet to be lit in the room behind, but he was in no hurry: the world was beautiful tonight, with the sky streaked pink and gold, and the pitted face of Mater Luna taking on a silvery lustre as she shouldered responsibility for giving light from the fleeing sun.

Then a soft golden glow lit the windows overhead. Ril waited until he heard footsteps on the balcony twenty feet above, then used kinesis to spring over the railing, landing like a cat.

Lyra Vereinen went rigid in fright – then her smile bloomed, the stress and fear on her face falling away. To his relief, she'd clearly been wanting to see him.

'Good evening, Milady,' he said softly. 'My thanks for not screaming. Are you alone?'

She looked over her shoulder, then asked, 'Are you *allowed* to be here?'

'Not for a second. Yet here I am.'

She touched her hand to her mouth. 'Aunty Radine warned me about you.'

'She's just jealous that I'm too young for her.'

She giggled. 'I'm glad you're here. And surprised.'

'Surprised?'

'Radine said you'd have forgotten me by now.'

She has no artifice, and that's a beautiful thing. It also makes her so vulnerable . . . 'How could I forget you? I'm sorry to just appear like this, but it's the only way I could get to talk to you. I've asked to see you, many times, but Radine is guarding you closely.'

Lyra glanced over her shoulder. 'She's chosen companions for me – Lady Hilta, Lady Sedina and Lady Jenet. They're changing for dinner. I'm supposed to be doing the same.'

Of course Jenet's inveigled her way into the action, Ril thought ruefully. He studied Lyra's face: she was clearly anxious at being alone with a man, and no doubt Radine had blackened his character as much as she could – but there was also longing in Lyra's voice and eyes. *From convent to throne*, he thought. *Could anyone survive that journey?*

'I'll go, if you want, Milady,' he offered, meaning to reassure her that she had control here. Already coming here was beginning to feel foolish, fraught with peril. Perhaps he was more inebriated than he thought. 'I'm not here to make things hard for you.'

'Then why are you here, Sir Knight?' she asked with commendable directness.

He wasn't really sure himself any more. Most of his infatuations had begun something like this, following the lure of a pretty face, contriving a tryst. But this wasn't just a game, he belatedly reflected; this was about Empires. 'I'm just here to reassure myself that you're being well-treated – and given your due.'

'My *due*, sir?'

So, she's an innocent, but not silly. 'Radine wants to make you queen and empress,' he said. 'It's *your* birthright – not *hers*. She'll give you good advice, I'm sure – but crowns come with inherent rights and dues.'

'What sort of rights?'

'Within the limits of sensibility, to do whatever you like.'

She turned pink at the thought. 'Anything I like?' The gaze she turned his way was intense, and so transparent he was quite taken aback. *What if what I want is you?* that look asked. No doubt they'd told her she needed a protector, and clearly she had her own ideas about who that might be. Suddenly this little tryst had gone well past a momentary fascination, or even an idea of protecting her. It was about everything he might want in life. *I'm thirty-two, thirteen years her senior – that's not far off twice her age. And I'm penniless. I can wield a sword and a lance, but I have no followers, no soldiers, and my land is a debt-mill. My life has been frittered away on loss.* By now he ought to be a senior knight, even one of Radine's advisors, but she'd never wanted his advice or opinions, and small wonder.

So am I really just here to spite Takky and her?

But looking at Lyra, he couldn't deny the need to protect her – nor other, less selfless urges. But she was also the most dangerous person he could possibly set his sights upon.

But why should that prick Takwyth have everything his own way? And if this ruins me, what have I actually lost?

'Lyra, I swear that I am yours to command. I believe destiny guided me to your door in time to save you. I'm not some adventurer, following a passing fancy,' he added, though until a few seconds ago that was *exactly* what he was. 'What would you have of me?'

That turned out to be the perfect answer – he could see it in her eyes as they welled up, could feel in the grip of her hands. And her surprising maturity came through again, because what she asked for wasn't reassurances, but information: about the Sett and Coraine and Pallas, and about her family. Time flashed by as he told her about the Great Houses and their rivalries; the key players amongst the Corani, and what they might ask of her.

'Mostly, they'll want a figurehead who does as she's told and won't upset their plans.'

'Their plans and mine align,' she pointed out. 'Radine wants me to be empress, which is my birthright. It's perfect.' She spoke with a maturity that belied her convent upbringing, but it was still shot through with an innocence that worried him.

Do I have the right to ruin her fairy tale? He'd never seen himself as a trustworthy guide for innocent youth. *But who else will tell her the uglier truths?*

'Radine's plans won't stop there,' he said at last. 'She'll want you wed to a man of her choice and pregnant as quickly as possible. She'll tell you the Imperial Council is no place for you – that it's too boring, too complicated – and she'll shut you out of running your own realm. And most of all, she'll want blood. Has she told you about 909?'

'Yes, she has. She hates the Sacrecours, and especially the Fasterius family.'

'So does every Corani with a soul,' Ril growled. 'Kore knows, there are heads I would dearly love to see on spikes too, but war could *ruin* us – and put your own life at risk.'

'I'm sure Radine only wants what's best for the Corani,' Lyra said dutifully.

'Of course she does – she's devoted to this duchy. But she's old,

Lyra, and she's worried about her legacy. She's likely cursing that her grandson Yannoch, her only heir, is too young for you to marry. She has to trust in people like Takwyth and Setallius to see her intentions through, and to do that, she must bind them to you.'

'She's as much as told me that I'm to marry Sir Solon,' Lyra admitted, colouring.

The notion repulsed him, though he'd seen it coming a mile off. 'Is it what you want?'

'No,' she answered. Her eyes said: *I want you.*

'No good ever came of a bad marriage,' he quoted.

'That's from "The Tale of Chimaera",' she smiled. Then her intensity returned and she said, 'This must sound dreadfully forward, but I know that I have no time for second choices. I want to choose my husband myself, but I don't know how to tell Radine. She's like Abbess Jaratia – she makes me feel *helpless.*'

'You must learn the way things work here,' he told her. 'You'll need patience – but I'm sure you've got plenty of that, after all you've been through. You keep surprising me – how mature you are, for someone who's grown up in a convent.'

She pulled a strangely knowing face. 'Ril – can I call you Ril? A convent is a world in miniature. There is power, ambition, belief and doubt, betrayals, secrets, sin, love . . .' Her face went scarlet. 'I've seen a lot of things, and learned a lot about people there.'

She squeezed his hand tighter and his heart began to pound. As protective as he might feel, she was also young and lovely, and she was looking at him with worship in her eyes. It was a long time since anyone had done that . . .

Her face tilted to his, inviting, and he was halfway to her lips—

—when a woman called her name.

He kissed her anyway, because he was human, and for the moment she melted into him, her face all innocence and need and fear and filled with desires she barely understood.

Then he stood, kissed her hand and relinquished it, leaping from the balcony and landing gracefully an instant before Lady Hilta's voice said, 'Lyra? Are you alone? Goodness, you've not even changed yet!'

'I ... I ... er ... I got caught up in a daydream,' he heard Lyra stammer, but he was stealing away before anyone thought to look down.

He'd always wanted to be remembered. *How about as the fool who kissed an empress? 'Ril Endarion? Aye, that's his head on the spike, son. Let it be a lesson to ye!'*

Ril's kiss – so unexpected, so *heart-stopping* – sustained Lyra through a maddening evening of prattle about dresses and jewels and coronations and how heroic and handsome and worthy Sir Solon Takwyth was. She barely listened. Only one man existed for her now; in truth, since he'd rescued her. *I am the Stardancer and he is my Ryneholt. We are made for each other.*

That brief, wondrous embrace was like a sip of honeyed mead that left her craving more. His lips had tasted of sunlight and vigour; his breath was a caress on her skin. She felt lightheaded; she longed to see him again – but the world was refusing to heed her desires.

The next day took *aeons* to arrive, after a never-ending sleepless night of *wanting*. She knew *something* happened between men and women, but she still didn't understand what, exactly: it was only ever hinted at in the *Fables*, and not really explained by the nuns' explanations for her monthly bleeding. Knowing roughly what a man and woman needed to do *physically* to procreate didn't explain the *needing*, the *aching* . . .

But all dawn brought was another day of Radine's machinations. The duchess wanted to show Lyra the might of the Corani – but more importantly, she intended to reveal to the world the true identity of the girl she had rescued. The Northern nobles were all gathered below the ducal balcony, together with the city's most richest and most influential burghers. Orders were shouted: trumpets blared, drums rattled and horses clattered below as a great mass of soldiers started parading before their duchess and her guest.

Radine's shapeless body was hidden by the resplendent silk dress of Jandreux red and green; a bejewelled circlet and headdress covered her thinning grey hair. She looked *regal*.

But Lyra's own dress was something else entirely: an alarmingly ostentatious construction that would leave no one in any doubt whatsoever that they were looking at someone of enormous importance. The best tailors in Coraine had been working night and day to complete Radine's brief: it must be demure, but expensive, and unique in every way. She'd opened her own jewel case, providing ropes of creamy pearls, glittering diamonds and spinels and blood-red rubies. Thread of pure gold had been used to embroider the Sacred Heart into the bodice and cuffs of the high-necked, painfully narrow-waisted gown, which was practically impossible to breathe in. And most important of all was the heavy velvet fabric, of a rich purple – the hue forbidden to all but those of Sertain's royal line.

If Radine was regal, Lyra had been made to look *imperial* . . .

'Look,' said Radine proudly, 'here come your knights.'

Solon Takwyth, in open-faced helm and intricate gilded acid-etched armour, led the Corani knights. His strong, blockish face was staring fixedly up at her, filled with possessive pride.

'Solon is the greatest knight in the North,' Radine murmured. 'He rebuilt the Corani knighthood in the wake of Lucia's purges in 909.' Radine didn't add, 'He'll make a fine husband', but presumably that was taken as read. 'Solon's men worship him for his leadership and prowess. His skill and strength have kept our lands free.'

But he's so old, Lyra thought bleakly. Ril was older than her too, of course; he was *experienced*, as a potential husband should be, but with the vigour of youth, not like Sir Solon, who was *forty* already.

The knights rode in ranks according to seniority. She knew a few of the names now: Sir Oryn Levis' pudgy face looked up at her worshipfully, Sir Esvald Berlond regarded her with cold distance, young Malthus Cayne with awe. But there was only one face she *wanted* to see, and finally Ril Endarion clipped past, dipping his lance slightly when he caught her eye, and her lips tingled. To hear his voice again, to taste his kiss . . . that was what fuelled her dreams. She was grateful to Radine and everything she was doing to put her on the throne, but she refused to become 'The Queen of Icy Tears', the princess in the *Fables* forced to marry the Snow Lord, whose heart slowly turned to ice. Solon Takwyth wasn't the husband destiny wished her to have, she was certain of that.

Ril saved my life. He is my life.

The parade went on endlessly: after the knights came the legions, rank after rank of red-cloaked men with pale faces and narrow eyes, with their black-cloaked battle-magi riding beside them, all slamming fists to their hearts and saluting as they passed, while Radine burbled on about which legion came from where, and who had won what victories.

'How many more?' Lyra sighed.

'Not long now,' Radine said, with a hint of sympathy. 'We'll go to Corani Hall soon, and I'll introduce you to the most prominent families. We need them with us when we march on Pallas.'

'When will that be?'

'An excellent question! First, we must talk to the Imperial Council. They are currently governing, until a new emperor is named. Garod Sacrecour is trying to bully them into naming Cordan, but the council refuses while we hold the boy.'

'Who are the councillors?' Lyra asked, keen to learn more while Radine was being talkative.

'The Imperial Council is traditionally made up of the emperor, the treasurer, the grand prelate, the master-general and the arch-legate – Mater-Imperia Lucia usurped that latter role so that she could impose her will. The current Imperial Councillors are Calan Dubrayle, the Treasurer, Grand Prelate Dominius Wurther and Dravis Ryburn – he's a Sacrecour ally, and Knight-Princeps of the Inquisition – Constant made him Acting Master-General while Kaltus Korion was away leading the Third Crusade. And Arch-Legate Edreu Gestatium, Head of the Imperocracy – the empire's bureaucrats – has now reclaimed his seat.'

'Do they support us?'

'They are Sacrecour appointees to a man.'

'Then how can we hope for their help?'

Radine looked thoughtful. 'Because Sacrecour appointees or not, each man has risen to his position because he is a powerful person in his own right. None of them are entirely beholden to the Sacrecours, nor would it be easy to unseat them. It's far better to change their loyalties.'

'Do men change their loyalties so easily?'

'These do,' Radine purred. 'I know the key players quite well: Dubrayle and Wurther are both pragmatic – Wurther might be miffed that we stole

Constant's children from under his nose, but he'll get over it. Dubrayle thinks only of money, and right now, thanks to the débâcle that was the Third Crusade, the Corani may well be wealthier than our rivals. Ryburn's only a temporary factor. We'll be seeking a more *acceptable* Master-General' – she clearly meant Solon Takwyth – 'and as for Gestatium, well, I've always maintained good relations with the imperocrats.'

'Won't the Sacrecours be courting them too?'

'Of course, child: Garod is desperate for their help. Civil war is a distinct possibility, but no one really wants that. For one thing, we've got Cordan and Coramore, for another, Lucia and her idiot son bled the Treasury dry, and for the third: a Rondian civil war would allow vassal-states like Argundy and Noros the perfect opportunity to cede. We can't allow that.'

'Then what will happen?'

'Have you ever seen a pack of wild dogs, Lyra?'

Lyra wanted to shout, *I was locked up in a nunnery for nineteen years – I've seen nothing!* Instead, she just shook her head.

'Well, there's a lot of barking, but not much biting: most animals in the wild are far more scared of getting hurt than being dominated. They know instinctively that wounds turn septic and kill, so only the most determined will risk injury. Most often, it's not the biggest dog that wins, but the most determined.'

'So you're saying we must be the most determined dog?'

'Precisely. The throne is your *right* and we mustn't waver. We've got the only other legitimate contenders in captivity. Anyone standing against you will be an outsider – a mad dog – and that, the pack will not accept, so they will submit to us.'

'Then all we actually have to do is go to Pallas?'

The duchess laughed. 'Well, basically, yes. But we must get you there safely, and we must arrive looking like the only viable choice. We must create a spectacle that says: *This is your rightful ruler!* You must look like an empress, and you must be endorsed by Church and State. You must have the greatest knight in Koredom at your side. You must appear so saintly that Corineus Himself would polish your halo, and so rich that you could bathe in liquid gold.'

'I see.'

Radine noticed that the parade below was finally ending and led her inside, still lecturing: 'Then you understand why you must stop asking after Ril Endarion.' Lyra went crimson, but Radine didn't stop. 'I know that he saved your life – and no one denies his prowess in battle. In 909, when he was only twelve and had barely gained the gnosis, with courage and skill beyond his years he got Basia de Sirou and himself out of the Arcanum slaughter. But he's a drunkard now. He frequents whorehouses. He fights duels. He's penniless – no, he's *worse* than penniless – he owes hundreds of auros.'

'But—'

'There are no "buts", child. It's sad – and I'm fond of him, believe me: House Jandreux raised him; we sponsored him through the Arcanum and we still administer his lands – but he's made his own bed. He'll never amount to anything. You *must* forget him.'

'But surely you could cancel his debts, like the good king in—'

'Spare me the *Fables*, girl!' Radine snapped. 'I could cancel his debts to my house and give him a king's ransom in reward money and he'd *still* be underwater with a dozen other lenders. His well has run dry – all he sees in you is a chance for money.'

'He's not like that! He says—'

'You've spoken to him?' Radine asked sharply.

Lyra stammered. 'Just ... recently ...'

'Stop. Tell me no more.' Radine leaned in close, grabbed her hand and whispered, 'Ril Endarion is not to come near you ever again, my dear. I'm sorry to be direct, but I must impress this upon you: do *not* go near him. *Never* again!'

Lyra tried to pull her hand away, but the duchess wouldn't let go. 'This is *important*, Lyra: generations of Corani are ready to lay down their lives to ensure you sit on the Imperial Throne, as is your right. To risk that for an infatuation is selfish, immature and dangerous. I said you must have the greatest knight in Koredom at your side. I was being polite, but I will be clear now: you must have the greatest knight in Koredom *in your bed*. And that man is not Ril Endarion. Do you understand me, child?'

Lyra hung her head, though she seethed inside. 'Yes, Aunty Radine.'

5

The Clever People

The Writings of Corineus

Here's the irony: Johan Corin was a disaffected young nobleman from the country in the time of the Rimoni Empire. He left his home and oppressive father to speak against the empire and its tyranny. He railed against the very concept of empire, and spoke passionately for local self-determination – and yet what did his own followers do on gaining the power of the gnosis? They founded a new empire! Poor Johan must be spinning in his grave. And the reason so few of his original speeches are in circulation? Because the first emperor – his close friend Sertain – burned most of them!

THE BLACK HISTORIES (ANONYMOUS), 776

The Sett, Coraine, Northern Rondelmar
Julsep 930
One month after the Moontide

'There are four pillars of power,' Radine droned, as she led Lyra up Windspree, the tallest tower in the Sett. 'A ruler needs to exert control over *all* of them, or they're doomed to fail.'

While Lyra's education had been scant preparation for her new life, the behaviour of the nuns at Saint Balphus was certainly pertinent: their greed and jealousy, lies and pettiness – these things were universal, and she'd seen them in the nobles of Coraine in plenty. Today's meeting was, Radine pressed upon her, the most vital so far: she was to be presented via the gnosis to men hundreds of miles away: men whose opinions might very well decide her fate.

As they climbed, Radine said, 'You must control the military, that's obvious, but most men forget about the others pillars: money, philosophy – which includes religion, but is broader than that – and, of course, society.' She glanced at Lyra. 'Military power is easy to define, as is monetary power: the richest will always have the advantage.'

'Of course,' Lyra agreed, remembering Sister Ulfinia, the abbey's treasurer.

'But even a rich tyrant can't ignore the power of philosophy – of *belief*,' Radine went on. 'A ruler can't buy or bully everyone, not for ever – a bigger bully or a bigger purse can steal those followers away. You've got to make *believers* of people: believers in *you*.'

'In me?' The notion seemed preposterous.

'Oh, all *you* have to do is not be a gibbering idiot, child,' Radine said, condescendingly. 'It's the strength of the Corani, of me, Solon and Dirklan – that's what we need to make them believe in: If we can win over the clergy, all the better: the common muck believe that the sun rises and sets because Kore wills it – such are the cattle we rule, dear. They can be won over by a few pointed sermons. So tonight, child, we must win over both the money and the clergy.'

Lyra wondered if Radine knew how contemptuous of ordinary people she sounded. *She's like Abbess Jaratia: she believes her own world is all that matters.*

At the top of the stairs, Radine fished out a key, still lecturing. 'The other thing men are prone to forget is that those they rule must, to some degree, accept their ruler's *right* to do so. Not everyone can be coerced; some must be befriended, even charmed. Social skills are vital for any successful ruler. Even in the vastest of empires, you'll find only a few people at the very top, pulling the strings: they must also be won over.'

That sounded like the most daunting task of them all. Ever since she'd been rescued, Lyra had been immersed in nerve-wracking lessons in protocol, etiquette and social mores. They were never-ending. 'I'm doing my best,' she murmured.

'You're doing *splendidly*,' Radine said, in a patronising voice. 'And never forget: you have the advantage of *legitimacy*. Rondelmar has had hundreds of years of successful rule by the Sacrecours, which you now embody. A world without a Sacrecour on the throne is an unknown world, and the unknown scares people. Everyone fears civil war, but most – if not all, especially amongst the common herd – believe a Sacrecour ruler will prevent that suffering. But Lyra, remember: even legitimacy can be squandered by bad decisions. Follow my advice, and you will be empress. Say the simple things they want to hear tonight, defer to me if you get confused, and above all, *be brave*. These men are expecting to see a scared, unworldly girl. Show them that you're strong: show them you're a *Sacrecour*.'

But not too strong, Lyra inferred as Radine finally unlocked the door and led her inside the small circular chamber. Stone seats carved into the wall faced the summoning circle of silver set into the stone-flagged floor. Four narrow windows allowed the moonlight in.

The duchess made no effort to banish the darkness. 'Come, child.' She ushered Lyra into the circle, kindled the wards and then clasped Lyra's hands in hers to link her to the spell and enable her to join the communication. Radine had been true to her word, removing Lyra's Chain-rune, but so far she'd not experienced anything resembling the gnosis, though Radine had assured her that was normal for someone bound for so long. So she was completely in Radine's hands. Light like a glowing fog banked around the outside of the circle. Chillingly, faces formed and fell apart, and Lyra began to hear whispers, not through her ears but directly into her mind.

'What's happening—?' she asked anxiously.

'Spirits of the aether, made visible through the spell,' Radine replied, clearly unconcerned. 'We use them as a bridge between us and those with whom we wish to communicate.'

It was disconcerting to think these wraiths were once people. Lyra wondered if she would one day haunt a tower like this, a ghost drawn like a moth whenever one mage called another. Then a more substantial figure appeared on the far edge of the circle: the head and torso of a man sitting at a desk signing a parchment. He was dressed in drab colours, but his thinning brown hair was well cut and his cheeks newly clean-shaven: Imperial Treasurer Calan Dubrayle.

He greeted them in a matter-of-fact voice; 'Duchess Radine – I trust I'm on time?'

'As ever, Calan. May I present my ward, Lyra Vereinen?'

Dubrayle measured Lyra with a swift, searching glance. 'An honour, Milady. I rejoiced when I learned that you'd been freed.'

Whether he was being sincere or just polite, Lyra had no idea. 'Thank you, Lord Treasurer. Aunty Radine speaks highly of you,' she replied, as Radine had instructed. He and Radine seemed of a type: clever people, manipulators.

Another glowing shape, much larger, formed to Dubrayle's left and gradually resolved itself into a fat man in glittering clerical robes. Grand Prelate Wurther was a jowly man with straggling grey hair. He looked genial enough, but Lyra hadn't forgotten that but for Ril, his people would have executed her.

He peered at Radine over a gold goblet. 'Is that treacherous piece of shit with you, Radine?'

Radine *tsked*. 'Ostevan isn't here, Holiness. It's just Lyra and me.'

'Good.' Wurther turned to Lyra. 'Greetings, Milady. Congratulations on eluding your fate.'

Lyra was surprised at the sudden heat in her breast at the grand prelate's casual words. It must have shown because Radine seized her hand. 'It was a narrow escape, Dominius, and not yet a jesting matter.'

It never will be, Lyra thought furiously.

'My apologies,' Wurther drawled. 'Please understand, the orders were not of my choosing – but I was duty-bound to carry them out. It was nothing personal.'

Lyra bit her tongue. Grand Prelate Wurther was the living incarnation of Kore and Corineus on Urte; anyone who took sides against him risked driving the common people into the arms of their enemies. Radine had told her, 'He considers himself above us, but he knows he must pick a side if this mess is to be resolved. We must impress him, win him over. He's angry about Ostevan's betrayal, and I must be prepared to make sacrifices to win him to our cause.' By which she clearly meant to sacrifice the man who had risked his life to pass on the information that had resulted in Lyra's rescue.

'I understand duty,' Lyra said to Wurther, as evenly as she could.

Wurther gestured as if *he* was forgiving *her*.

'Your Grace, let's to business,' Dubrayle interjected. 'The situation is unstable here in Pallas. The Imperial Guard keep the peace, but the populace are unsettled. The Sacrecour-Fasterius faction control the city's food supplies and Garod Sacrecour is threatening to cut that lifeline.'

'Fortunately,' Wurther interjected, 'the Church has much agricultural land in the south, and will supply the shortfall.'

'At twice the price,' Dubrayle noted.

'Be thankful it's not tenfold. We're risking Garod's wrath.'

'He'd never move against the Church.'

'Not openly, but he's got patrols with blank shields riding the borders of our lands. The Kirkegarde are spread thinly, Calan, and our lands are widely spread.'

'Yes, you're quite the landlord,' Dubrayle observed.

'We are bequeathed land by heirless landowners all the time,' Wurther replied in a testy voice. 'We're not here to debate the Church's *legitimate* wealth.'

'We've much more to discuss than that,' Radine agreed. 'Gentlemen, take it as read that I know what Garod is doing. We also know that the Dukes of Klief, Canossi and Dupenium all fancy themselves as the next emperor – even the Aquilleans speak of uniting and marching north. But the reality is that two men will decide the fate of the empire: you two.'

Dubrayle looked away as if in modesty, while Wurther chuckled. 'At least you're prepared to admit it. Garod just tells us it's our duty to aid him.'

'Which, wisely, you've been cautious to do,' Radine acknowledged. 'You know the Corani have the manpower: our legions weren't depleted by the Crusade, and they are led by Solon Takwyth, whose reputation is unmatched. So we have wealth and power, and more importantly, our claimant has legitimacy: Natia Sacrecour was the daughter of Magnus and Alitia, the last rulers of the empire to be truly beloved of the people. Lyra is her daughter, raised in the bosom of the Church and freed into the hands of her kinfolk. This is a fable come true, the sort of thing commoners adore.'

Wurther grunted and scratched his belly. 'Lady Lyra, my faith rather forbids me from placing any store in "fables". I'm more interested in whether you have all your wits – Constant's children appear to.'

'What would you have me do, your Holiness? Recite poetry?' Lyra replied; Radine had suggested she display a little assertiveness, and a shy, winsome smile.

Wurther and Dubrayle reacted as if to a witty line in a play.

'Lyra is a young woman of intelligence,' Radine said, 'but she's not worldly: she'll need advisors, like yourselves. She is also, fortunately, *a woman*, so those who support her claim will have the opportunity to select the man she marries: the *real* ruler.'

The real ruler ... Lyra hid her annoyance as the two men nodded; this was a given.

'How do you feel about a dynastic marriage?' Dubrayle asked her.

'I know my duty,' Lyra replied, lowering her eyes demurely. 'Which woman of substance ever married for love?'

'I can name some,' Wurther rumbled, 'but few where it ended well. There are many consolations to a life of privilege, however.' He drained his goblet with a satisfied sigh. 'Do you harbour bitterness towards Mother Church, Lyra?'

'No!' Her reaction was instant, and genuine. 'Aunty Radine tells me that when a tyrant rules, even good men can be cornered into doing ill.'

Wurther didn't look like he believed her, but perhaps hearing her parrot Radine's words would emphasise the duchess' control over her. He and Dubrayle shared a look, then the treasurer said to Radine, 'If we did back you, your Grace, what would your next move be?'

Lyra heart leapt: this was the sort of phrase Radine had told her to listen for, an indication that these two men were prepared to *really* talk.

It was also her cue to leave. She rose to her feet. 'It isn't seemly for me to be involved in all these complicated negotiations – Aunty Radine tells me that a monarch shouldn't haggle, so if you will excuse me, I'll leave that up to you clever people.'

You clever people, she fumed as she left the tower alone. *How* wonderful *to be your puppet.*

*

Calan Dubrayle was the first to take his leave, an hour later. Radine Jandreux had been confident that the Imperial Treasurer would be her best chance of finding a supporter; he didn't give much away, but they'd always been like-minded.

Dominius Wurther was a different matter. The image of the treasurer faded, but the grand prelate remained. 'So, Radine,' he rumbled, 'you've done well out of Ostevan's treachery.'

'Not his *treachery*, Dominius, but his loyalty to the Corani,' Radine replied, 'and it's done now. I know you're angry at him, but I can't pretend that I don't celebrate his courage. But I also value *our* friendship, Dominius.'

They shared a look of understanding.

'All right,' Wurther growled. 'But that's not why I'm still here, Radine. You claim Lyra is Natia's daughter, and seeing her tonight removes any nagging doubt: she is undoubtedly her mother's daughter.'

Radine stiffened. Wurther would know, if anyone did, the rest of Lyra's provenance. 'You have questions, clearly.'

'Just one: *who's her Father?* Because it wasn't Ainar Borodium – he died more than a year before she was born.'

'Then you know who it is?'

Wurther studied her taut face. 'You do not?'

Impasse. Radine calculated fast. 'Dominius, it's important for Rondelmar that she is seen to be the son of Ainar and Natia – surely you see that?'

'I see it as a fiction ... but not one that is widely known.' He busied himself refilling his goblet, then admitted, 'The nuns of Saint Balphus know nothing, and nor did those at Saint Agnetta's, where Natia birthed Lyra, then died. Someone went to some considerable trouble to bury the truth.'

'Then I pray they did a thorough job,' Radine replied. 'Honestly, Dominius, even Lyra doesn't know. If you throw in with us, as I pray you will, then please tell me what you know.'

Wurther ruminated, then admitted, 'In truth, I don't know who her father is. Natia was held by the Sacrecours at Saint Agnetta's. She was reported dead, then the first whisper of a child reached our ears. Lyra was moved to Saint Balphus', which is administered through a Sacrecour bequest – I barely knew what went on in there. Who could have got to her? A Sacrecour knight? A sympathetic confessor? A gaoler?'

'I wish I knew,' Radine replied. 'I don't even know why Lucia Fasterius – never a great one for leniency, I think you'd agree – let Natia and then Lyra live?'

'The Gnostic Keepers intervened,' Wurther replied.

'Really? How do you know that?' Radine knew only what anyone else knew of the Gnostic Keepers: that they were Ascendant magi, charged with protecting the gnosis and guiding its use. There were only a few dozen, according to rumour.

'As Grand Prelate, I have a seat in their Inner Circle,' Wurther admitted. 'Natia and Lyra were direct descendants of the sacred Imperial line, so they were deemed sacrosanct.'

'So was Magnus,' Radine noted.

'Magnus broke one of the Gnostic Creeds.'

'What Creed?' Radine gasped. If that was true, it threw a whole new light on the events of 909. *Does this mean the Keepers sanctioned his death? And that they'll support Garod?*

Wurther sensed her fright and shook his head. 'I know the crime Magnus committed, but I'm forbidden to divulge it – it doesn't mean the Keepers favour Cordan over Lyra; they stood aside when Lucia struck, but they didn't aid her.'

Radine sought to work through the wider implications. 'The Keepers are sworn to uphold the gnosis, not the emperor. All I ask of them is that they remain neutral now.'

'And I'm sure they will,' Wurther told her. 'I'll remind them of that duty.' He smiled in satisfaction at this additional opportunity to put Radine in his debt. 'But I do wonder why Lyra's father hasn't come forward – if he's a Sacrecour, surely he'd want to discredit Lyra's claim?'

'I can think of many reasons,' Radine replied. 'Conflicting loyalties . . . The danger to his person such a claim would bring . . . Or maybe he's already dead? Perhaps he doesn't yet know? Maybe he plans to approach us once the girl is enthroned, to increase his reward? Perhaps he genuinely wants her to prosper . . . His silence would spare us many problems.'

'For you, maybe. It would be simpler if we were dealing with Cordan: his parentage is indisputable, and he's conveniently young.'

'He's also Constant *rukking* Sacrecour's very image. We don't need another weak-chinned dribble of spit on the throne. We need a strong hand.'

'Solon Takwyth, in other words? Can you control him?'

'Solon sees Natia in Lyra . . . he'll put her before all else. I trust that.'

Wurther contemplated her words. At last he sighed heavily. 'Very well. I'll say nothing of what I know, and I'll support the girl's claims. Maybe someone will come forward, maybe they won't. Let's see, shall we? But my silence will be *expensive*, Radine. On that you can depend.'

By the end of her second week, Lyra was starting to feel that the convent had offered more freedom than Radine's palace. The duchess, terrified of assassins getting to her prize, had her most trusted men guarding Lyra, so she had no privacy. The only place she could be alone was in Radine's private chapel, although soldiers still guarded the doors. The rote of prayer brought some degree of comfort too.

But today, the chapel wasn't empty. Someone had given Ril Endarion the keys.

'Good morning, your Highness,' he drawled as the door closed behind her, and she almost leaped out of her skin.

Then she burst into nervous, delighted laughter. 'Good morning, your Rilness,' she said playfully, torn between fright and exultation. All morning she'd been longing to be alone – but this was so much better than solitude.

He made a show of admiring her. Today she wore a long green velvet dress and a two-pronged hennin on her head that looked like bull horns; they made her feel strangely earthy and that mood was heightened at the sight of him. He looked gorgeous: freshly shaved, his black hair gleaming and his Southern skin wonderfully exotic amidst the pallor of the Corani.

'What were you going to pray for today?' he asked.

'That I'd see you, and look – Kore has already answered.' They walked towards each other and clasped hands, and she couldn't be bothered trying to find a clever, courtier's way to express all she wanted. She leaned into him, tilted her head and closed her eyes, praying he'd kiss her again.

He didn't disappoint; at the touch of his warm lips she melted. Her skin flushed hot as that earth-woman feeling swept over her. She drank in the taste of him, trembling in a turmoil of sinful desires as his tongue penetrated her mouth, a sweet, sensual invasion that left her breathless.

'Do we have long?' he murmured.

'Not enough.' She put her arms about him, feeling every part of her that touched him was aflame. Her throat felt parched as her heart thudded, pumping all the blood in her body to her loins. She knew just enough to be both appalled and curious – the Abbess used to smell her fingers each morning and any scent of bodily juices meant immersion in icy water. All the young nuns got that treatment, though it wasn't a complete deterrent, even for a pious girl like herself. *When someone does it to you, it's even better*, one of the less saintly girls had told her once, between dunkings. But mostly, the shaming was enough to dissuade her from exploration.

Regardless, she'd be tested for virginity on the eve of her marriage, even had her desires taken her so far, and she feared to test her relationship with Radine – or jeopardise her ascension to the throne.

'We shouldn't,' she murmured reluctantly. 'This is a church.'

'Then let's go somewhere else,' he said. 'There are gardens behind the chapel – no one ever goes there.'

His words set her pulse racing. She looked back at the locked front doors, knowing her guards were just outside. 'What if they come in and find me gone?'

'Have they ever interrupted you before? Don't worry.'

His hand on hers was reassuring, his eyes full of promises as he led her to a back door she'd not noticed. It led into a walled garden full of flowering bushes filling the air with their scent. They walked hand in hand, pausing every few steps to kiss again, until she was giddy in his strong arms, feeling hollowed out, as if he'd sucked the marrow from her bones. She felt light and unstable, her body a tangle of hot, tight aches and her mind spinning.

'I could do this all day,' she whispered in his ear.

'I think I would explode,' he muttered, and kissed her again.

'Have you ever been in love?' she dared to ask.

'I've been infatuated,' Ril answered, 'but looking back, I wasn't really ever in love. Love takes time, I think, and maybe I've always been too impatient to wait for it.'

'Were they prettier than me?'

'That wouldn't be possible,' he replied.

Love lends beauty: that was the moral of one of the stories in the *Fables*, and it must be right, because she felt beautiful when she was with him.

But in a few days she would have Solon Takwyth forced upon her. That thought was sobering enough to make her pull away.

'We should just walk,' she sighed.

Ril sucked in a gulp of the heavy air. 'Walk, yes, walk.' He led her down a narrow path, damp with rotting leaves, even though it was high summer. The hum of insects filled the air, and somewhere through the thick ivy that was consuming the trees, she heard a gurgle of running water. Though she knew there were high walls hemming them in, the foliage made the garden feel more like a vast forest.

Suddenly she saw a face peering through the trees and went rigid in fright – then she realised it was only a statue, of a severe-looking priest. They both laughed nervously, and went closer. The statue was grey and old, with dark lichen in the crevices giving it a strangely life-like appearance. It stood before a small pool that was slowly over-flowing into the wet soil around it. In the midst of the pool was a small, gnarled tree. It looked dead to Lyra, and she wondered why it hadn't been cut down.

Ril read the inscription at the base of the statue. 'Eloysius Sanctus. Never heard of him.'

Then Lyra heard a footstep behind them and she swallowed anxiously.

Ril patted her arm. 'Don't worry,' he said. 'I'd forgotten: our benefactor asked to speak with you.' He flashed the keys. 'Who did you think gave me these?'

A priest walked through the trees, a lean, smooth-looking man with liquid eyes and a sweeping of dark wavy hair who looked more like a courtier than a clergyman. 'Lady Lyra, Sir Ril,' he greeted them, without any hint of condemnation at their illicit tryst, 'I am Ostevan Prelatus. Welcome to Saint Eloy's Garden.' He kissed Lyra's hand flamboyantly. His voice was a melodious baritone. 'Milady, I wondered if I could have a private word?'

This was clearly his price for aiding them; Ril gave her a nod and drifted out of earshot. She felt a little annoyed at him, for the first time ever, for dropping this encounter on her, but she curtseyed her acquiescence.

Ostevan led her to the stone bench beside the pool and sat beside her, just out of reach, and his intense gaze made her uncomfortable. *He's going to ask something impossible of me*, she thought. Buying time to compose herself, she asked, 'Why is there a dead tree here?'

The prelate looked taken aback. 'It's a cutting grown from the Winter Tree and sacred to Saint Eloy, one of the forefathers of the Church of Kore. He gave up magic to serve Kore.'

She noticed he'd put special emphasis on the word 'magic' – that wasn't a word magi used much; they always spoke of *gnosis*.

When she asked what he meant, he frowned impatiently but explained, 'There was an early form of power called *dwyma* – the magic of life, they called it, and any practitioner was a "dwymancer". It was quite different to the gnosis. Saint Eloy had a vision that all dwymancers must renounce their sins and seek forgiveness in Kore, and he led them in doing so. The Celestium – the Holy City south of the river in Pallas – was built on the site of his abode, and this tree is a cutting from that very Winter Tree which sheltered his cave.'

'Dwyma? I've never hear of it—'

'It was declared heretical, Milady. The Church calls it "Pandaemancy", or literally, "the power of daemons". A pandaemancer's life is forfeit unless they take sanctuary in the name of Saint Eloy and renounce his gift. Otherwise they're executed.'

71

She shuddered, looking at the stark and somehow unnerving tree. 'Why do we keep it, when it's dead?'

'It's not – for reasons no one understands, the Winter Tree blooms in winter and dies back in summer.' Abruptly Ostevan dropped to his knees and seized her right hand. 'Lady, please, grant me a boon.'

Having an older man – especially one as lordly and charismatic as this one – begging at her knees had Lyra burning with embarrassment. 'What is it? I can't—'

'Lady Radine has reached some kind of accommodation with Wurther, hasn't she?'

'I suppose – um, yes, she spoke to him a few days ago.'

'Then I'll be dragged before the Church judiciary and stripped of my prelature,' he said. 'I know Radine's well and truly rukked me.'

Lyra was shocked, but before she could respond, Ril called, 'Mind your tongue, priest!'

Ostevan scowled, but didn't let go of her hand. 'Milady, my information saved your life – you're here because of me. Please, you must protect me—'

'I can't—'

'Of course you can,' he all but shouted. 'I risked my life for the Corani – and *this* is my thanks? I'm Radine's kinsman and she's double-dealing me with that hog Wurther! If they strip me of the prelature, they have the right to place me under a Chain-rune, and then I'll be helpless – it's akin to murder.'

Lyra felt for him, but he was alarming her. 'I don't know what I can do,' she started, but Ostevan was shaking his head.

'They're going to make you empress! Your voice *matters* – she'll listen to you!' His grip became painful but as she cried out, Ril was there to pull his hand away.

'Don't touch Milady again, Ostevan,' he warned.

'Get your hands off me, you lecher!' Ostevan hissed. Then he stopped himself and bowed his head, his face full of contrition. 'I'm sorry . . . I'm so sorry. I'm just upset. *Damned* upset!'

Lyra squirmed, but she started thinking. Perhaps, sometime in the future, something could be done? 'I'll fight for you,' she promised. 'I'll see you restored, Ostevan, I promise you. I know I owe you! I'll champion your return, I swear.'

The man was near to tears and she had to endure him kneeling at her feet and kissing her hem before he finally allowed Ril to lead him away. It was a relief to be alone: between Ostevan's wretchedness and her wanting of Ril, she could barely think straight.

While Ril and Ostevan were, she assumed, arguing in the chapel, she turned back to the pool, wondering if the water was drinkable. She bent and touched the surface with her fingertips ... and weirdly, something *noticed* her, which made no sense. Nothing had moved, but she felt as if the knots in the tree trunk were eyes, on the verge of opening. She was transfixed ...

Then the tree did open its eyes and she almost screamed – until she realised that it was just a big moth on the trunk, its papery wings fully six inches across, with big black eye-like markings that skewered her gaze. For a few moments, she couldn't breathe – and another one opened its wings, and another, and she realised there were dozens of them clinging to the bare branches.

Then in a waft of dry rustling, the moths all took to the air and fluttered around her. She spun about, spreading her arms, fear turning to delight as they settled on her dress – one even landed on her forehead, the hooked legs like a pin-prick on her skin, but she was too astounded to brush it off.

She looked down at the pool and saw a reflected face – at first she thought it was herself, but the angles were wrong, and the face had skin like bark and eyes like an owl.

Child, the air whispered. *Welcome.*

She stared as the pool *changed*. There was an image of a thin, pale hand – *her hand* – putting on a steel gauntlet with an eagle's-head motif on the back, then it burst into flame and she could feel the heat and smell the burning. She screamed aloud as the moths leaped into the air and swirled around her, but when she raised her hand to her face, expecting to see blackened skin, it was whole – and then the pain vanished, and she was reeling.

Ril sprinted back into the garden, shouting her name. He pulled her against his chest and she realised she was shaking. The moths had vanished into the shadows.

'What on Urte was that?' he demanded. 'Was it the gnosis? Have you gained it at last?' His eyes were full of alarm and hope, and she so wanted it to be true, but . . .

'No, no,' she said, the vision of the eagle's head, the gauntlet and the fire swirling around her head, then she wondered . . . *was it*? 'I don't know.' She clung to him, drawing courage.

Was it the gnosis? Was that what I felt? She'd been warned that disorienting things might happen to her when her mage-blood finally manifested, and that sometimes it could be quite complex, especially if her affinities were to Sorcery or Theurgy – but this felt *different*, not what had been described: there were no residual extra senses, no feeling that it had come from inside her – instead, she felt as if something had touched her, like a wind brushing her skin.

Then bells began chiming and she realised that they were out of time. They kissed hurriedly and she re-entered the chapel a few seconds before the doors swung open and her ladies, Hilta, Sedina and Jenet, swept in to take her to her next round of duties.

6

Heart of Empire

Gold and Wealth

What none of you seem to understand is that at any given time, the wealth of the empire is not simply the coins currently in the treasury vaults. The wealth of the empire is whatever we think it is. The price of gold is a function of our faith in the empire as an institution. In this sense, I am the 'High Priest of Money'.

CALAN DUBRAYLE, IMPERIAL TREASURER, PALLAS, 929

Hollenian Way, Northern Rondelmar
Augeite 930
Second month after the Moontide

The carriage rumbled south along the Hollenian Way, which was clogged not just with traders but soldiers too, as the Corani made their push for power. Lyra watched the passing crowds from her window, occasionally waving to those lining the road to catch a glimpse of her, as her procession passed by on the road to Pallas.

The fable she was living was nearing a climax: *I'm going to be Empress of Yuros. Or I'm going to be beheaded for daring to reach so high.*

She slept away as much of the interminable journey as she could. Their noble supporters offered hospitality, so each night Lyra was forced to exude happiness, confidence and gratitude, when really she just wanted to curl up in a soft bed and pine for Ril. She'd not even glimpsed him since that magical day in the chapel gardens; moths and kisses still haunted her dreams. The days passed and became weeks as they crawled south – until suddenly the carriage lurched to a halt and she heard joyous shouting.

It was just after midday. Radine was asleep opposite Lyra, her wizened face slack as she softly snored. Lyra shook her awake. 'We've stopped, Aunty.'

Tiredness made Radine look even older than she was, and twice as frail. But she brightened when she peered out the door. 'Come, let's stretch our legs,' she suggested.

When they disembarked, Lyra saw cheering soldiers and people lining the road. She waved to them as Radine led her to a small rise and then she caught her breath. The entire valley below was filled with buildings – roofs and walls and giant towers: Pallas, Jewel of the Empire, spread out before her eyes.

The Imperial capital was built around a confluence – the Aerflus – where two great rivers met: the Bruin, flowing from the east; and the Siber from the south. Radine pointed out the major sights: the Imperial Bastion dominated Pallas-Nord, the largest part of the city, sitting on top of Roidan Heights and housing the royal palace, the Imperocracy and the wealthiest noble families. The immense Place D'Accord at the eastern end of the Heights was dominated by a giant statue of Corineus the Saviour, visible even from here. Three-quarters of the populace lived on the north bank, in well-heeled areas like Nordale and Gravenhurst, at the various legion barracks in Esdale, or in the rough and lawless docklands like Tockburn-on-Water and Kenside.

On the west bank of the Aerflus was Emtori, founded by Argundian and Hollenian refugees, those who'd sided with the empire against their own people. 'There's money over there,' Radine sniffed, 'and Emtori docks service the river-trade from Lac Siberne and the south.'

'What's that?' Lyra pointed to a vast bulk on the south bank, adorned with golden domes and gleaming roof-tiles, reflected in the glimmering waters.

'That, child, is the Celestium, the Holy City, home of the Grand Prelate. And in its shadow you can see the Rymfort: it houses the senior Kirkegarde and the Inquisition. And outside' – her wave encompassed a sprawl of shanty housing outside the Holy City – 'that's Southside, the filthiest and most dangerous part of the whole city. Not that you'll ever have cause to go there.'

A hazy fog hung over the roofs and even from their knoll they couldn't avoid the stench of sewers and cooking smoke. The sight and stink of the city filled Lyra with foreboding: it looked alien, its own universe, too vast for a convent girl to rule.

Each cohort of legionaries marched to the top of the rise, cheering. Some had been in the Corani forces in Pallas when Magnus and Alitia were still alive; for others, this was their long-awaited chance for revenge on behalf of parents, aunts and uncles, siblings, cousins and friends.

An officer approached Radine with a message, which she read quickly, then turned to Lyra and flung her arms around her. 'Child, it's been confirmed: the Sacrecours have fled the city! There'll be no battle – this, my dear, is your procession to power. Welcome to your new home, Lyra.' Then she turned away, her eyes streaming and body shaking, and Lyra realised just how much tension Radine had been concealing. She got a glimpse of a younger woman, capable and ambitious and full of passion. 'I could almost wish they'd stayed to fight us,' the duchess breathed. 'I so wanted to see them die . . . But there's still time for that.'

Lyra was momentarily chilled, as if a placid pet had suddenly bared its teeth.

Radine must have caught something in her face. 'There must be justice for 909,' she said. 'They can't be allowed to just walk away.' Then she pursed her lips and wiped her eyes, and the fierceness faded behind her patient, calculating gaze. 'We'll enter via Draken Gate.' She stepped back, assessing Lyra. 'You must wear your purple gown, as an empress would. First impressions matter.'

They found a nearby house, owned by a gentleman farmer, and Lyra's ladies put her in the gown in which she'd been presented to the Corani nobility. They worked fast, Hilta cajoling the two younger women as Jenet worked on her hair and Sedina powdered her face and painted her lips. Finally, when Lyra was so wound up with tension and dread she could have run screaming from the room, Radine declared herself satisfied.

With venators circling overhead, their carriage followed the army into the city, through Draken Gate, under Actium's Hill and through Nordale along Sertain's Promenade, the northern passage into the heart of the city. The wide thoroughfare was jammed with Pallacian citizens waving flags in imperial purple, calling Lyra's name as if she were the answer to all their prayers. The noise pummelled her brain, blows that went on and on; her escort could barely contain the exuberant crowds. The three miles from the gates to the Bastion took most of the afternoon, and when she entered the Place D'Accord, it felt like the heavens themselves shook with the adulation. Above them all, the massive statue of Corineus watched serenely, glowing white and gold in the late sun.

So many nobles and dignitaries, bureaucrats and ambassadors of the vassal-states had come to greet her on this momentous occasion that her head was spinning: it was claustrophobic, dizzying and overwhelming – and when she waved to the presses of people jammed into the square, they wept as if Corineus himself had come again.

'They've been in dread of civil war,' Radine told her. 'Not only that, but they've been living hand to mouth – the Sacrecours blockaded the food supply. They see you as their redemption.'

It felt like a fearful responsibility, a great weight settling on her shoulders.

At the doors of the Imperial Bastion, her Imperial Councillors waited with Dirklan Setallius; the Coraine spymaster had flown in some days before to oversee the transition of power. The first man to greet her was Calan Dubrayle; his face showed the stress he was under, but he looked genuinely pleased to see Radine. 'Your Grace, you're a welcome sight,' he told her, a more fervent greeting than he'd given Lyra.

Grand Prelate Dominius Wurther was there too, lording over everyone like a big fat uncle, but Lyra had seen his merry eyes go cold and she wasn't fooled. The price for his cooperation had not been small; it included punishment for Ostevan Prelatus and the ceding of large tracts of land to the Church. More significantly, Church Law would henceforth overrule Civil Law within the Celestium, an unprecedented concession – and yet he still behaved as if he'd sacrificed everything to bring her here.

'Pallas rejoices, my dear girl,' he told her as she knelt and kissed his signet ring: he was the one person she must still kneel to, until she was crowned. 'Their beloved daughter has come to reside among them.'

The other two councillors were less fulsome in their welcome. Acting Master-General Dravis Ryburn, Knight-Princeps of the Inquisition, was well aware that he would shortly be ousted in favour of Solon Takwyth; he bowed with cold formality. And Arch-Legate Edreu Gestatium of the Imperocracy, grey-haired and fretting, was clearly worried that Radine would do as Mater-Imperia Lucia had and take his place; he relaxed only when Lyra assured him that he'd be keeping his place on her council.

Then she was ushered into the intimidating Imperial Bastion, with maze-like corridors that twisted and turned bewilderingly, until they opened into cavernous halls.

'The Sacrecour family fled Pallas as soon as news came that we'd marched,' Solon Takwyth told her as he escorted her through dusty corridors hung with torn tapestries and slashed paintings, past empty rooms or piles of broken furniture. 'They might have lost their nerve, but they took everything they could carry.'

'How can we ever live here?' Lyra wondered, looking around at the chaos.

'Don't worry; this was anticipated,' Radine reassured her. 'Half the contents of the Sett and a dozen other Corani castles are on their way south, and the carpenters and woodworkers are already busy at work. Dirklan tells me that Garod was afraid to take many of the imperial treasures lest they antagonise the Keepers. In a few weeks, you'll be amazed.' She took Lyra's arm possessively. 'Our first priority is to hold court daily, accepting pledges of support. This Holy Day you must attend a Service of Thanks and Praise in the royal chapel. You must be seen to be the pious and dutiful woman you are.'

Lyra swallowed and nodded dutifully. To her, this vast edifice of marble and stone pressed on her soul. Her mother Natia had been born here, but it was also where Natia's father and husband had been killed, and it was from here that her mother had been taken to exile and death

It felt like she was walking into a vast family mausoleum.

*

The next few days passed in a strange state of limbo. Lyra was uncrowned queen and empress, head of state – and yet not. She was exhausted, on the go all day, surrounded by the enforced company of her ever-growing coterie of ladies-in-waiting, assertive young magi noblewomen with hard, calculating eyes set like jewels in sculpted faces. Radine crammed her head with names and lineages and complicated kinships of magi and merchants, clergy and nobles. Every meeting she spoke the words Radine put in her mouth, then rushed off to the next costume change, with yet more perfume to cover her sweat and staleness; by the time she staggered to her bed, towards the middle of the night, she stank of tuberose and was too shattered to sleep.

She quickly realised she had none of the skills she needed, and that terrified her: she was awkward in public, lost without the prompts of the ever-vigilant duchess. Crowds made her claustrophobic and the guardsmen entrusted with her safety scared her: her mother had been torn down by such people. 'How did Constant ever deal with this?' she complained to Radine.

'He enjoyed it – you must learn to do the same,' the duchess replied, then her eyes would fall on someone else Lyra *simply must meet*, and off they went again.

Every morning, just before her first public event, and every evening before retiring to her rooms, Dirklan Setallius or Basia de Sirou would examine her mind for gnostic traces, evidence that someone had tried to beguile her with the gnosis. But they stressed that she was responsible for guarding her own mind – wards could protect her physically, because those could be affixed to something, but mental protections had to be rooted in her own aura, and would fall apart if not constantly adjusted. But they taught her simple mantras to protect her own mind – apparently simply silently chanting a factual, incontrovertible phrase like 'I am Lyra, I am Lyra' would leave someone attempting to manipulate her mind with nothing to grasp onto.

'Someone very powerful or very skilled can defeat any defence,' Dirklan told her, not very encouragingly, 'but I'm a pure-blood, and Basia's a half-blood: it would take an Ascendant to slip something past us – and all of those are either Keepers and sworn to serve the gnosis, or Merozains and they live in Ahmedhassa and are sworn to peace.'

Not once did Lyra lay eyes on Ril. Foolish or not, she was desperate to write to him, but scared Radine would find out. It was Ostevan Prelatus, unexpectedly, who was her saviour. When she asked for a confessor, it was he who arrived – until the grand prelate formally deposed him, he retained his rank and privileges – and despite the awkwardness of their encounter in Coraine, she found him perceptive and willing to help her. As a confessor, he won her over with his receptiveness, understanding and charm, and he passed her letters on to Ril, returning with professions of love and loyalty; sometimes that was the only thing keeping her going. But Radine wouldn't risk alienating Wurther by allowing Ostevan to stay. It was clear that the best she could do was soften his punishment.

Meanwhile, decisions about dress and jewellery were given as much weight and consideration as decisions of royal appointments. Solon Takwyth was formally raised to the Imperial Council and Dravis Ryburn was thanked for his service and returned to the Inquisition.

On the eve of the coronation, Lyra's dress was still being finished by an army of seamstresses, but she was fitted into a gown only marginally less ostentatious and taken by her suitor to promenade in the gardens to formalise the 'surprise' that would be announced after her coronation.

'We will be happy together,' Takwyth told her as they walked slowly through the Imperial Gardens. 'I adored your mother, and I see all her virtues in you.'

I'm a proxy for my mother, she realised. *It's her he thinks he's marrying.*

Half an hour with him felt like an eternity.

There was much more that had to happen: the virginity examination by a healer-mage nun included a search for gnostic traces, just to ensure no one had employed healing or morphic-gnosis to reinstate her virtue; Lyra had no idea that could even be done. Then, finally, she was permitted to spend the evening in prayer or to retire early to sleep.

She chose prayer. 'It'll be my last chance for solitude for some time,' she explained to Radine. 'I need to pray for strength to be a good empress . . .'

Lyra's ladies followed her to the chapel; Hilta, Sedina and Jenet looked resigned – they weren't the sort to enjoy long prayer sessions – and clearly expected to follow her into the dimly lit chapel.

'No,' she told them, 'thank you, dear friends, but I wish to pray alone tonight.' Each day she was becoming more accustomed to exerting authority.

'We're supposed to be with you at all times tonight,' Hilta argued.

'As I recall, you're supposed to ensure that I am given peace,' Lyra replied, 'and behold, I wish to be alone with my God.' She gestured into the empty chapel, aglow with many candles. 'This is the only entrance to the Royal Chapel.'

'But—'

'Hilta, thank you. You may wait out here.' She stepped through the doors closed it firmly in the face of the three women and turned the key.

The peace of the chapel settled over her as she made her way down the small central aisle and knelt in the front row, her view of the altar unobstructed. The Sacred Heart icon above the altar shone gold and scarlet. The serene face of Corineus, lovingly rendered in stained glass behind the altar, seemed to search her soul as she gazed up at Him. Night settled into the stones as the familiar words spilled from her devout lips.

> *'Father Kore, I beg Thee to lift my heart.*
> *May Your loving Son Corineus take my soul,*
> *Protect me from the wiles of the Accursed*
> *And lead me to Paradise.'*

She bowed her head, reflecting on all that had happened to her. She found it impossible not to see Destiny taking a hand: Kore had a plan for the world, as attested in the *Book of Kore*. How could she, a lowly nun, not only be raised to empress, but also find a knight-protector whom she adored, were it not destined? Surely it must be His plan?

It is recompense from Kore for all that was taken from my mother. That is why Father Kore is known as the Almighty Judge: it's why He bears the Scales of Justice in His right hand.

The third bell of night rang out, and as the echoes faded away, the vestry door opened and a priest emerged into the chapel. 'Milady,' he said, 'I'm told you desire a blessing?'

She rose to her feet, joy welling up inside her. 'Yes, I desire it very much.'

Thank Kore, for blessing this woman who loves You.

Three hours later, Dirklan Setallius took Lyra across the Aerflus by wind-sloop to keep her vigil in the Celestium. She'd emerged from the chapel to find her ladies asleep; they roused themselves to help her bathe and change into the traditional simple linen gown, to which they added a heavy blue velvet cloak; the midnight-till-dawn vigil would be chilly.

Setallius subjected her to a stern appraisal as the two-masted sloop turned in the winds for the approach to the far shore. 'Are you ready for this, Milady?' he asked, finally.

'I'm scared,' she confessed, 'but I want to *live*, Spymaster. I want more than just endless locked doors. If you think you're getting meek and obedient, though, you're wrong.'

He studied her intently, then the ghost of a smile touched his lips. 'Bravo. You are your mother's daughter.'

'You knew her?'

'For a time, and mostly from afar.' He looked up at the moon, his face wistful. 'Your mother was vivacious, charming and very deter-mined. Lucia feared her: she was the new belle of the court and the Mater-Imperia looked carping and dowdy beside her. You're not Natia – she grew up in the public eye and was confident in it – but I think you have her strength.'

'Her strength? She killed herself and left me with no one to protect me.' Lyra was surprised how much bitterness welled up in giving voice to long-harboured thoughts.

'Imprisonment would have destroyed Natia,' Setallius replied. He sounded more sympathetic than she'd expected. 'She was a social person; she thrived on company. To be locked up would have driven her to desperation. We can only guess what she went through before that.'

Does he know I'm not Ainar's? she wondered. *Probably – he's the Spymaster.* She didn't ask though; instead, she watched the Celestium draw closer. The white marble dome of the cathedral, set beneath a full moon that covered fully a fifth of the sky and lit from within through some feat of the gnosis, gleamed across the water. It was beautiful.

'The first Grand Prelate of Kore wanted his Holy City to outshine the Imperial Bastion,' Setallius commented. 'In the early days, priests were itinerant, speaking what was in their own heart, with no standard text to guide them. The first mage-priests, realising they could channel the superstitious fear the people felt towards the magi, wished to overawe the populace, so they corrected that. They built up their wealth and their own army – the Kirkegarde – and now the Church has more land and gold than anyone in Rondelmar, except perhaps the emperor. And of course, they wrote the *Book of Kore* to make sure everyone spoke as they wished.'

'Kore dictated the *Book of Kore* to Saint Balefeo Himself! And people give tithes to the Church so that we can give glory to Kore,' Lyra replied defensively. The nuns of Saint Balphus had lived in absolute poverty – and what would a *spy* know?

'You're not a prisoner of the Church any more, Lyra. Dominius Wurther is no friend to you – worse, he is a dangerous rival, and his prelates are every bit as cunning, venal and ruthless as any courtier. But here's the thing: in the minds of the people, Kore anointed the magi. While emperor and grand prelate see each other as rivals, the people demand that they stand together. So we dance around each other, keeping up appearances of unity whilst ruling different spheres.'

'The *Book of Kore* says "there must be separation of spiritual and secular power",' she quoted, 'and that "spiritual power is the greater, because it is eternal".'

Setallius grunted noncommittally. 'They would say that, wouldn't they?'

He's a cynic, she thought sadly. All at once she missed Ostevan's kindly reassurances, which were always rooted in faith. 'What happens tonight?' she asked. 'Will I be ... *safe*?'

'I believe so. I'll be close by. Don't be afraid – but do be alert.'

She bowed her head, then asked, 'Why can't I reach my gnosis?'

Setallius turned to face her and she realised that he'd removed his eyepatch. She was shocked to find that his sightless eye was a silver metal ball glittering with a faint blue light – but it seemed far from blind as it bored into her. 'You have an aura, Lyra: the potential of gnostic energy. It can take time to manifest itself actively. For a mage to be Chained before even gaining the gnosis is almost unheard of – there's no doubt it would result in difficulties in gaining power.'

'But how can I rule without it?'

'A ruler seldom needs to lift a finger. You're not a battle-mage. Your intellect and judgement are far more useful to you than a little gnosis.' He touched her shoulder gently. 'Lyra, I know you feel manipulated, and controlled, but we want you to be happy, as well as to prosper.'

She met his uncanny gaze, and for all he was a man who dealt in secrets and lies, she felt she could trust his loyalty. She clung to that as the sloop descended towards the Celestium and landed in a well-lit square where a small cluster of men in deep crimson cassocks awaited them. Setallius escorted her down the steps to Grand Prelate Wurther, awaiting her. She sank to her knees, as she still must, until her coronation.

'Welcome, child,' Wurther rumbled. 'Thank you, Dirklan, I'll take it from here.'

Setallius bowed, gave Lyra a reassuring look and retreated to the sloop. Wurther took Lyra's arm and introduced her to the prelates, chief among them his new heir-apparent, Rodrigo Prelatus, an Estellan with narrow, cunning eyes, who kissed her hand obsequiously. 'You are fair, dear lady. The people will love you.'

The next attendant to kiss Lyra's hand was a young woman, Lyra was startled to realise. 'My daughter Valetta, Abbess of Sancta Varina in Estellayne,' Rodrigo explained. 'In Estellayne a priest may wed.'

'An honour to meet you, my Empress,' Valetta said in a deep, resonant voice. She had a well-formed face, with the sort of full-lipped mouth that men seemed to drool over. Lyra found her oddly threatening, and was grateful when Wurther swept her onwards, leaving the rest of the welcoming committee behind.

He led her through a series of guarded portals and into a tunnel that opened into a large, circular walled space with a mound in the middle and a spindly brackenberry tree at the top, surrounded by a dozen or so smaller bushes. 'Welcome to the shrine of Saint Eloy,' Wurther boomed. 'You are looking upon the original Winter Tree itself.'

Lyra recalled the leafless sapling in Coraine; the grand prelate was clearly waiting for her to ask questions, so she said, 'Why is it called that?'

'It blooms in winter, Milady,' Wurther replied. He led her to the foot of the mound, which turned out to be a large rock with a cave-mouth in it. Hundreds of candles gave it a soft, warm light. The cave was sealed by a silver lattice-gate, but she could see a tunnel twisting downwards, out of sight; its walls were coated in a translucent golden paste that looked like dried honey. 'It's amber, the sap of the Winter Tree,' the grand prelate said. 'It seeps through the rock from the tree roots and solidifies as it flows down the walls.' He waved a hand in proprietary fashion. 'Welcome to the heart of Koredom.'

'Why is Saint Eloy so revered?'

'Because he gave up not only temporal power but his magic to dedicate his life to Kore, and some believe he saved the empire in doing so,' Wurther replied. 'He once said: "Set against eternity, our lives mean nothing": a good thing to reflect on before receiving a crown, Milady.'

She bowed her head. There was some kind of presence here, she was certain, and like the tree in Coraine, it felt benign to her. But Wurther appeared oblivious to it. He showed her a kneeling-stand before the silver gate.

'It's traditional to keep your vigil here, Lyra. The cave contains the bones of Eloy and his brethren. Once a year, the grand prelate is per-mitted to go inside and bring back a piece of amber, a gift for the Order of Eloysius.'

'What's it like inside?'

'Like no other place, Milady: the bones are mostly encased in amber now, and the walls can sometimes seem to glow. Animals don't enter it, nor insects. Even nature bows down before Kore.' The grand prelate laid a warm hand on her shoulder, as if trying for some kind of famil-iarity or rapport, and said, 'I'll go now and take the auspices.'

'What does that mean?'

Wurther chuckled, a cavernous sound. 'It's a tradition passed down from Rimoni times, when the Emperor was also the Pontifex, the Head Priest of the Sollan faith: I'm supposed to consult the stars on the eve of a coronation – superstitious clap-trap, of course, but it gives me something to do while you pray. And it's always helpful when the people believe that a new ruler's reign is to be blessed by good fortune.'

'Is mine?'

'Ha! My dear, the Rimoni believed that a reign begun in autumn is ill-omened, and we are on the cusp of Fall. Folk still sing an old rhyme about it:

> *"The King of Winter has a heart of ice,*
> *The King of Spring the ladies entice,*
> *The King of Summer loves wine and song*
> *And the King of Fall won't last very long."*

'That doesn't sound very hopeful,' Lyra said.

'Words like "King" and "Fall" never sound good together,' Wurther said whimsically. 'But don't fret, my dear: I'm sure I can find some good omens in the stars to balance things out.'

With that he wobbled away and vanished behind the doors to the garden, which clanged shut as the bells for midnight rang out. She knelt and for a time lost herself in prayer, asking for the strength and courage to go through all she must. Then she thought about Ril, and a warm glow flowed through her, sensual and comforting, and the cold vanished. She put a hand to her left breast, closed her eyes and bathed in memories of him.

The world was silent, the moon crept across the sky and stars glimmered coldly beyond. Then a faint breeze lifted her hair, there was a sharp *click* and the silver gate swung open. She threw a backwards look towards the Dome. She seemed to be alone, but this was an eerie place . . .

The faintly glowing amber had an allure she couldn't resist. She crept to the cave-mouth, feeling oddly safe as she stepped inside. She'd expected the floor to be wet, or slippery, but it was neither. A spiral stair descended, and in half a turn, the garden was gone and she was encased in a world of glowing honey-coloured sap. Two more turns brought her to a small chamber with an ash-filled hearth in the middle and a chimney-hole formed by the core of the stair, through which the Winter Tree could be seen, stark against the moon.

A dead man lay against the opposite wall, just bones and rags, and she glimpsed more bones half-covered in amber, yet she felt at peace. The air was like water, flowing through her garments and caressing her skin, and all the while the light shifted until half-formed faces coalesced in the amber walls, peering out at her. Despite this, she was filled with wonder, not fear. Saint Eloy was here, she was sure: he, and many others. Their eyes were heavy on her, penetrating deeply. She went down on her knees and murmured a prayer for their souls.

Sister, the air whispered.

Something wet spattered on her brow. She recoiled, and touched it: a drop of sap from the tree above. Without thinking, she wiped it off with her finger, then licked it off – it tasted sour and her throat caught a little, and for a time she floated in and out of dreams, wondering . . .

If they renounced their power, why does the tree bloom out of season?

Then she noticed that something had changed: right between her knees, a small leafy sprig had broken the soil. Carefully, she dug around it, then lifted it out and slipped it into her belt-pouch, trembling with excitement.

A distant hour-bell chimed, telling her that the night had somehow fled by. Imagining the uproar if Wurther returned to find her down here, she cast a final look around the chamber, touched her hand to her forehead in honour of the dead man on his eternal vigil, then hurried outside, exhilarated and scared.

Saint Eloy's people didn't renounce their powers. They preserved them, right under the noses of those who feared them most. She didn't know why this mattered to her, but the tiny sprig of life in her belt-pouch felt as precious as a child inside her. More than this it felt . . . *auspicious*.

Wurther returned at dawn, as promised, and gave Lyra into the care of Valetta, who was to take charge of her preparations this morning. As soon as Lyra was alone in her chamber, she wrapped the tiny Winter Tree sapling in wet cloth, then emptied out her jewellery casket and laid it carefully in the bottom, before replacing the ropes of pearls and chains of precious gems to cover it over. She was wary of the imperious Estellan nun, but she had no choice than to surrender herself into Valetta's hands. She was taken to the baths, scrubbed and rinsed in cold water before having to endure Valetta oiling and combing her hair while other nameless nuns came and went, all watching her with cold eyes. She remembered when noblewomen had come to her convent, and the mix of resentment and superiority she'd felt.

Rich women have everything but their souls, the sisters used to say. She wondered if these nuns saw her that way.

Soon after, a dozen of her own ladies-in-waiting arrived to fuss over her, but that didn't prevent Valetta from asking, 'Have you been *examined*, Milady?'

'The Abbess of Pallas-Nord examined me yester-eve,' Lyra said. She really didn't want to endure another round of having her nethers peered at. 'She brought her entire convent, I think.'

Hilta produced the certification of virginity, the ladies-in-waiting tittering behind their hands, but Valetta's sultry face was regally immune as she examined the papers attesting to Lyra's virtue. 'You must dress now, Milady. The hour approaches.'

The dressers bustled in and the machinery of royalty took over. Hairdressers were still working pearls into her braiding when Radine entered and seized her hands excitedly. 'My dear, you look *ravishing*! Has there ever been a more beautiful empress?'

While the courtiers all agreed that, no, there hadn't, Radine studied Lyra's face. 'You have made peace with your fate, yes, my dear? I'm so pleased. But you look tired.'

'The vigil – I've not slept all night, Aunty. But I feel full of energy.'

'That's good to hear.' She dropped her voice, leaning into Lyra's ear. 'I am immensely proud of you – and I know that Solon will make you happy, dearest. He will put you on a pedestal.'

Water and a light meal of fish and peas was served to sustain Lyra through the rigours to come: she wouldn't have the opportunity to eat again until the ceremonial seed and honey cake at the culmination of her coronation. She could feel her head clearing from its night-fog.

Finally Hilta rose to her feet. 'Milady, it is time.'

Lyra forced a nervous smile. It was indeed time: to become queen and empress.

Lyra's coach headed the traditional coronation parade. They left the Holy City and circled Lac Corin, where she tossed flowers into the man-made pool in supplication to Corineus, then wound through Greyspire, where the streets were lined three- and four-deep with cheering people. In the Rymfort, she took the salute of the Kirkegarde before re-entering the Celestium, to climb the steps at the head of her ladies and enter the vast glowing Dome, right on midday.

The journey flashed by her: afterwards, all she could recall were a few faces – weather-worn, hardship-lined, with unkempt greying hair and awestruck eyes, waving at her, somehow claiming her as something between goddess and victim. The ranks of the Kirkegarde on the parade ground in Rymfort were terrifying, the beasts stamping in unison, the officers saluting as one, banners dipping and rising, drums thundering. She felt tiny, a twig in a maelstrom, but the Corani knights formed an honour guard at the front of the cathedral and she was grateful for their presence. Even dull Sir Oryn Levis felt like a pillar of reassurance right now.

She entered the Dome between immense statues of Corineus and Sertain carved in marble and gold. They looked like they wanted to crush her. But she'd glimpsed Ril in the ranks of knights, and that gave her the courage to go on, pacing up the aisle alone in time to a single slow drumbeat, feeling the weight of all eyes on her, before kneeling on the lowest of the seven stairs leading to the Sacred Throne.

Dominius Wurther waited at the top. His mitre appeared to touch the ceiling. Her breath wasn't quite reaching her lungs, and the watching high nobles were like birds of prey. *But Ril is here . . .* She could do this.

Wurther hammered his giant crozier against the marble tiles, begin-ning the Rite of Crowning. 'Are you Lyra Vereinen, the natural offspring of Ainar Borodium and Natia Sacrecour?'

'I am,' she said, proudly and without hesitation, concealing the lie with assertion. She took the first step, and knelt again.

'Lyra Vereinen, are you of the Blessed Three Hundred, the founders of this Holy Rondian Empire, and a wielder of the sacred gnosis?'

'I am!' Another lie. She ascended to the second step and knelt again.

'Lyra Vereinen, do you love Kore and accept him as your only God?'

'I do!' It was a relief to speak a truth, finally.

'Lyra Vereinen, do you accept Corineus as your Saviour, and place your soul in his care?'

'I do!'

'Lyra Vereinen, are you the rightful heir to the throne of Rondelmar, and her Holy Rondian Empire?'

'I am!'

'Lyra Vereinen, are you of sound mind and whole body, and possessed of a fruitful womb?'

According to the healer-mystics who'd attended upon her earlier in the week, she was.

'I am!' She stepped onto the penultimate step and knelt. She could smell the wine-and-roasted-food reek of the grand prelate now, but mostly she was aware of the silence in the cathedral, and the way their words echoed through the cavernous space.

'Lyra Vereinen,' Wurther boomed, 'do you wish to serve your people as Queen of Rondelmar and Empress of the Holy Rondian Empire?'

'I do.'

'Then ascend, and kneel before your God and Saviour!'

She did as she was bidden, her nerves returning as she sank to her knees before the throne, the grand prelate and the immense, resplendent Sacred Heart icon above.

'As the golden dagger pierced His sacred heart,' Wurther intoned, 'the glory of the gnosis was revealed, a sacred flame kindled in the hearts of those faithful to Kore.'

'*WE ARE BLESSED!*' the congregation chanted.

'We, the descendants of those Blessed Ones, have accepted the charge of ruling Urte, until Kore returns.'

'*WE ARE BLESSED!*'

91

'Kore crowned Sertain Sacrecour His first emperor and set him upon his throne. I, Kore's Voice on Urte, offer myself as His avatar. Do you accept me as such, and permit me to crown this woman?'

'*WE DO! YOU ARE BLESSED!*'

'Lords and Ladies, descendants of the Blessed, here is a woman, Lyra Vereinen, born of Sertain's line and proclaimed rightful heir to the throne of Rondelmar. Do you wish her to become your Queen and Empress?'

Though it was all ritual, Lyra still found herself holding her breath fearfully, then the congregation thundered: '*WE DO! SHE IS BLESSED!*'

'Then Lyra Vereinen, raise your head.'

Wurther ushered forward a young page bearing a purple velvet pillow on which the Imperial Crown sat. Seeing it brought another tightening in her chest. It looked inhumanly heavy, like a collar or a yoke. Tears started in her eyes, and didn't stop as Wurther took the crown.

'I, Grand Prelate Dominius Wurther, by the grace of Kore His representative on Urte, do hereby crown you, Lyra Vereinen, as Queen of Rondelmar and Empress of the Holy Rondian Empire! Your body is now sacrosanct, and all who are joined in your body! Your possessions are now sacrosanct, and all those you take possession of in future! Your words are now sacrosanct, and holy to us! Hear me, People of Urte!'

'*WE HEAR! WE ARE BLESSED!*' the congregation thundered, then cheered and threw hats into the air as the crown was lowered onto Lyra's head. She managed to control her sobbing as Wurther brushed her cheek with his right hand, then offered his ring to kiss. She did so, then rose and he knelt and reciprocated: Crown and State, equals.

'You may sit now,' Wurther said kindly. 'We've saved you the best seat in the house.'

When she sat and looked out from her throne, she felt as if she could see far beyond the cathedral to the throng in the square, to those still in their homes, to the rolling green hills of Rondelmar and the mountains and rivers and plains of the vassal-states whose ambassadors waited below. Argundy, Hollenia, Noros, Bricia, Brevia and the rest – if she could hold them together. It was thrilling, frightening. *And Ril is here.* She managed to keep her face composed as the cheers washed over her.

Then came the First Blessings, the foremost of the congregation coming forward one by one to congratulate her, led by the Ducal Houses, those with blood-ties to the Sacrecours, titles to the provinces of Rondelmar and the greater vassal-states, in order of kinship to her. First to greet her was Sifrew, youngest brother of Duke Kurt Borodium, the new Duke of Argundy and kinsman of Ainar, her *supposed* father. That lie was prominent in her thoughts as she greeted this relative.

'Your Majesty, it brings Argundy great joy to see you seated upon this throne,' Sifrew said, his eyes shining. 'Your late parents will be singing in Paradise this night.'

'I'm proud to be kin to you,' she replied. 'I trust we will speak again soon.'

'I await your pleasure, my Queen.' In a low voice he added, 'There is nothing wrong with following your mother's example and marrying another Argundian.' He gave her a sly wink, making her smile.

After Sifrew came the Dukes of Hollenia, Midrea and Bricia; they saw her as someone they could charm, manipulate or bully, Radine said, but they were after advantages at home, not her throne, so those encounters were simple enough.

Then came the Lords of the Great Houses of Rondelmar, a different matter entirely. After the Imperial Council had declared for Lyra, the Great Houses had bowed to the threat of economic and military isolation, the lords of the Aquillean cities caving in first, followed by Klief and Canossi, leaving the Dupeni-Fasterius axis, the rump of Sacrecour power, isolated.

Now Radine led them forward: she might be wrinkled and frail, but today she was a triumphant little bird in full plumage. The other dukes ranged from dignified gravitas to truculent insouciance.

Then her most dangerous known enemy was standing before her.

She'd been surprised that Garod Sacrecour, Duke of Dupenium, had wanted to attend her coronation at all, but Setallius said he probably wanted to see her in person. He was a tall, rangy man, with long, unruly grey hair, clean-shaven in the Pallacian style. He had deep-set, hollow eyes and thin lips. Setallius said that his own powerbase was fragmenting: what was left of the Fasterius clan – conspicuous by their absence today – were demanding war, but Garod was refusing. His own interests were tied to trade and commerce; his family had lost too many legions in the East and war now would ruin him.

Crucially, he'd also loathed Lucia Fasterius; by attending, he was spitting on her grave.

'I swear allegiance to the Imperial Throne of Rondelmar, and to Lyra Vereinen Imperia, my Empress and Queen,' Garod intoned, his eyes boring into hers as he knelt. She saw jealousy, frustrated rage and lust too, which chilled her. This was the man who'd orchestrated the butchery of 909.

He'll not stay loyal for long, her instincts told her. But for now his pledge was enough.

Then the Imperial Councillors were called forth to take oath to serve her. Calan Dubrayle was dapper, business-like and precise, Edreu Gestatium formal but trembling with suppressed triumph. Then Dominius Wurther took the oath, speaking in a soft rumble as if he were giving a favourite granddaughter a Corineus Day gift. Then came the moment she had been dreading.

The congregation fell silent – did everyone know what was coming? – as Sir Solon Takwyth, Coraine's premier knight, climbed the stairs and knelt on the penultimate step. Red and white roses had been pinned to his breast above his gryphon-head heraldic blazon.

His voice boomed out, filling the cathedral to the vaulted rafters. 'Queen Lyra, as Knight-Commander of the Corani, I formally pledge allegiance to serve you as your Master-General! I will live and die for you! Obedience and Loyalty will be my watchwords, until I am dust and gone!'

'I accept your vow and pledge, Master-General.'

Takwyth kissed her signet ring, his big hands holding to hers, looking up at her. 'Milady,' he said, for her ears only, 'I have a boon to ask you.'

She stiffened and said, 'I pray, do not. Not here.'

His complexion coloured, but he set his jaw. 'There is no place better,' he muttered. She could sense Radine straining from her place on the bench to hear, and the weight of expectation. These people knew what was coming, and Takwyth knew they knew.

'There's no *worse* place, Solon.'

His eyes narrowed, calculating, then he raised his voice, speaking for all of the cathedral to hear. 'My Queen, I was a young knight of the Queen's Guard when your mother dwelled in Pallas twenty years ago. I served her faithfully and with honour, as I will you.'

The women in the congregation sighed audibly, and Lyra saw Radine's eyes glittering.

'All my life, I believed her line had endured. And here you sit, restored to us and her very image. You are Natia reborn!' He lifted his hands, clasped together, as if in supplication, when to Lyra it felt as if she were being cornered, in public, herded by hunting dogs. 'I cannot still my ardour, nor my tongue!' he shouted. 'Lyra, my Queen, will you consent to marry me?'

In the following silence, Lyra thought her heartbeat would break the windows, and shards of coloured glass would rain down. Anger got her through, and gave her the strength to reply.

'Sir Solon, I thank you – but I may not, for I am already married.'

Every mouth in the congregation flew wide open, like holes opening up in the universe. The sudden intake of breath drained the air of substance, leaving her barely able to breathe. But inside her heart, she could hear music.

'But you . . .' Solon Takwyth stammered, his composure breaking.

'My husband is here, alive and present.'

'*What?*' Radine was shuffling forward as swiftly as her tight ceremonial dress would permit. Her Imperial Councillors were staring, mystified. Only Dominius Wurther appeared to understand, for his lugubrious face had broken into a sly smile.

'My people,' Lyra shouted, 'please welcome to my side my husband, Sir Ril Endarion.'

Then she shut out the uproar and focused on Ril – *my Ryneholt* – as he sprang from the aisles, thrusting aside with easy grace those men who tried to confront him and bounding up the stairs. She rose, took his hands in hers and kissed him, the most wonderful kiss, and the perfect *Rukka te!* for Radine, Solon and all these manipulative bullies.

'I love you,' she breathed, drinking in his face.

The cathedral was in uproar, torn between wonder and shock. Radine was frozen at the bottom of the stairs, trembling and red-faced, but harder to behold was Solon Takwyth. His face had crumpled like screwed-up parchment, his dignity and his prestige shredded in one cruel instant, but she didn't feel more than fleeting pity.

'A queen cannot be married except by a prelate or crozier!' Radine shouted.

Ril brandished papers at her with mischievous defiance. 'Ostevan Prelatus married us last night, in sight of legal witnesses. The papers are legitimate, and the marriage consummated.'

Wurther's face became a whole lot less amicable, while Radine just gaped.

Then Solon Takwyth's right fist went smashing into Ril's face.

Ril went down in a heap, sprawled at the top of the stairs. He tried to get up, then sagged again, dazed. Lyra went to him, intent on shielding him from Takwyth's fury; the knight looked like a mask had been torn aside, revealing the raging desires behind his stony visage.

They both looked at the sword of office she'd presented him with only minutes before.

She remembered a gauntleted hand and flames burning her up, in an image in a pool.

The whole gathering went utterly silent, but there was no one present who didn't understand what had just happened here; Wurther's words, spoken as he crowned Lyra, still hung in the air:

Your body is now sacrosanct, and all who are joined in your body.

She half-expected to die, right now, but Takwyth's face cleared and the beast behind the mask receded. He tore the chain of the master-general from his neck and dropped it at her feet, unbuckled the sword of office and dropped it too, then tore off his family tabard and let it flutter; before simply turning and walking down the aisle. A few men tried to go to him, some to apprehend him, others perhaps to congratulate or even join him, but he growled something almost bestial and shoved them all aside, even his close comrade Esvald Berlond.

Wurther stepped to Lyra's side, whispering, 'Exile or Execution: those are your options, my Queen. He just struck a member of the royal family.'

She watched the knight walking away. 'Exile. I never want to see him again.' She looked down at Ril, who nodded in agreement, rubbing his chin ruefully, then they stood up.

Lyra looked at Radine, who had collapsed back into her seat and was gazing hopelessly into space, tears running down her cheeks. Sympathy touched Lyra, but she reminded herself that Radine had wanted Takwyth to wage war, to be her avenging angel for 909.

There'll be a different vision henceforth, Aunty.

Abruptly she felt stronger than ever before: these were the moments she'd been terrified of, and they were done, she was still standing, and through the warning she'd received through her vision in Coraine, war had been averted. The fires would not consume her.

Instead, she could face a future of her own choosing. She looked up at Ril, remembering the breathtaking moment on a lowly cot in the priest's room behind the chapel last night . . . the look on his face, the weight of him, the moment he pierced her, body and soul. The utter, absolute joy of feeling *whole*. It gave her the courage to turn to Wurther and lift her voice to fill the cathedral. 'Grand Prelate Wurther, you are commanded to perform another coronation.'

The clergyman looked at Setallius, then laughed hoarsely. 'Well played, Majesty. Your reign promises to be memorable.' He glanced at Radine, calculating, then turned to his aides. 'Bring forth the Prince-Consort's crown!'

Lyra glanced at Ril. They both understood this: she was the heir, not him. He would never have the title of emperor – but their eldest son would. He smiled, to tell her that this was more than enough, and as that small fear vanished she fell in love with him all over again.

Lyra was sitting with Ril when Radine swept in, Dirklan Setallius hot on her heels. The new empress and her consort had managed barely a moment together since they'd been escorted to the Celestium's royal suite for her next costume change, ready for the evening's coronation banquet. Her ladies had worked miracles on Ril too, producing any number of princely garments, accrued over the years from who knew where.

Radine glared, and the ladies-in-waiting fled, shutting the parlour doors – and no doubt immediately pressing their ears to it.

Lyra looked at Setallius first, and the spymaster returned her gaze enquiringly. *Yes*, Lyra replied silently, *I was already married when you came to take me to the Celestium.*

Setallius tilted his head in acknowledgement, a wry smile creasing his face, and she appreciated that.

But Radine looked as if she'd aged a decade or more. 'Lyra?' she croaked.

'Aunty Radine – how can I help?'

The old woman searched Lyra's face, then shrivelled up. Her voice was barely a whisper. 'All my life, I laboured to restore the Corani to Pallas and gain vengeance – *justice* – for 909. My own husband and I were captured that day – and then freed as an act of *contempt*.' Her voice was shaking and tears trickling down her cheeks. 'They made us walk out of the city while those *good Pallacians* pelted us with rotten fruit and worse, even piss and excrement! I have *burned* to answer the crimes of those days – that was all that sustained me! And now . . .'

There was no point telling her of the vision, no point trying to explain. Nothing would make it better in Radine's eyes. Lyra took her hands and let her weep, reminded of a discarded husk of an insect. She wondered if the old woman would even last a year without her lust for vengeance to animate her.

Ril looked at Setallius. 'Has Sir Solon gone?'

'I've got my people watching him,' Setallius replied. 'If he tries to rally support, I will know in moments. The commander of the Imperial Guard has been informed and his men are on alert. Any attempted coup will be dealt with immediately.' Then he raised a hand, clearly receiving a gnostic contact, and Lyra waited with bated breath.

If we go to war with each other, the rest of the Great Houses will tear us down . . . Unconsciously, her hand sought Ril's.

Then Setallius opened his good eye and even his deadpan voice hinted at relief. 'He's left the Bastion, on horseback, alone.'

They sat in tense silence, sweating. Through the windows came the ordinary sounds of the palace and the city beyond, minutes crawling by, until Setallius announced, 'Sir Solon has taken a ferry, heading south on the Siber. Apparently certain knights offered to go with him, but Sir Solon reminded them that they were first and foremost Corani. He told them to give their loyalty to their queen. There will be no insurrection.'

'Solon Takwyth is a byword for honour,' Radine mumbled in a desolate voice. 'I never believed he would turn on us. It's not in him. He always put Coraine first.'

'Lyra has still wed a Corani,' Ril reminded her, 'and someone you yourself raised—'

'Aye, as a son: the sort of son who rips his mother's heart out!' Radine snarled. She turned to Lyra. 'You lied to me, and you went behind my back! I'm beyond angry – and I am beyond frightened, too. This empire is in crisis, child: it needs strong leadership. You will rue this day when the blades come for you.'

'I'll protect her,' Ril said, in a strong and certain voice.

'*You?*' she spat. 'You! How can I trust anything you say?' Radine turned back to Lyra. 'And you, child? How can you rule without a strong man like Solon to guide you?'

'Ril and I will rule together,' Lyra answered firmly, 'with my councillors to guide me – just as you wanted. But Ril is the only man I could ever marry. He saved my life, and he is prepared to let me *live* it, something no one else was prepared to do. He is my love and now my husband, and we will rule as one.'

'But he has no more experience of leadership than you—!'

'But *you* do, Aunty, and Dirklan does. Wurther and Dubrayle do. And I will learn – I'm not a puppet: I have a mind and a heart of my own.'

Radine bared her yellowed teeth. 'And what about a sword-hand, girl: do you have one of those? The Sacrecour-Fasterius axis stands isolated! This is our chance, girl: let us march on Dupenium and Fauvion and do as they did in 909! *You must command it!*'

'No, Aunty! I will not!'

Lyra faced down Radine's blazing eyes until the old woman crumpled, shaking and weeping in rage for never-forgotten crimes and losses. Lyra felt so much sympathy – but she couldn't permit vengeance, not after she'd seen the relief on the faces of the ordinary Pallacians when they welcomed her, truly believing that the danger was over.

If it's between leaving one old lady heartbroken and destroying millions of lives, the choice is simple. 'There'll be no war, Aunty Radine. The empire can't survive it. You said so yourself.'

'If the empire survives by allowing murderers like Garod Sacrecour to profit from their crimes and laugh at us, it's not worth fighting for,' Radine rasped. 'If you knew the men and women who died that day, you'd know what you're really saying, Lyra – but you never even knew your mother and father. If they were watching you now, they'd die all over again.' She made one last appeal. 'Please, recall Solon – in a less senior role, if you must! But let him prosecute our righteous war on the Fasterius clan—'

'No,' Ril said firmly, 'no war, and Takwyth can go to Hel, the two-faced bastard. And I say this as one who *was* there in 909. I went through as much as anyone, and I'm telling you that you're wrong.'

His voice hinted at the personal cost of those words, and Lyra swallowed. *He's sacrificing revenge for love – for me . . .* Her heart chimed inside her.

Radine looked at Setallius, but seeing no signs of support, she sagged in defeat. It was like watching a soul leave a body. 'Must our pain be for ever?' she whispered. 'Will there never be justice for what they did? You *need* Solon, child – no one else in the north has his abilities in the field. Please, I beg you – recall him. He's far worthier of it than that lying snitch Ostevan, and you're willing enough to champion him!'

To Lyra's surprise, Setallius spoke against his duchess. 'Takwyth is like a man whose only tool is a hammer, and sees all problems as nails – only his tool is a sword. I believe the queen has done well to not marry him.'

Radine scowled. 'You actually endorse her farcical marriage, Dirklan? How dare you?'

'I didn't say that,' Setallius replied. 'Takwyth isn't the right man to rule an empire. To prosecute a war, yes – but that war isn't needed. We need to consolidate power and bind this empire together, not tear it down for vengeance.'

'If that's your belief, Dirklan Setallius, then you are no longer a man in whom I can place my faith. Consider your service at an end.' With a shuddering lurch, Radine stood and fixed Lyra with a piercing glare. 'As for you, I curse your marriage! I curse your womb! I curse your husband and I curse your happiness.'

She turned and shuffled away.

Lyra put her hand to her mouth, looking at Ril uncertainly.

'Don't fear,' he breathed. 'Curses are a fiction. There is no gnostic power that can do any of what she just said. She's just a bitter old woman.'

Lyra watched Radine vanish through the door, then looked at Setallius. 'I didn't expect your support, Spymaster. If you must leave Corani service, will you at least enter mine?' She looked at him hopefully. 'I have great need of you.'

The spymaster bowed. 'I am yours to command.' Lyra accepted a kiss on the hand, then Setallius asked, 'Might I have a word in private with your new husband?'

She swallowed, but saw no option than to acquiesce.

Ril could guess what was coming. He followed Setallius into a side-chamber filled with shoe-boxes – presumably preparing for the appropriate occasions of state – and closed the door. 'So, are you here to warn me or chastise me?' he asked.

Setallius didn't return his smile. His face was as grim as Ril had ever seen it. 'That depends, my Prince, on whether you're an opportunist who has snared a glittering prize, or a knight who has finally grown into a man, fit for the responsibilities he has usurped?'

Ril met the spymaster's one-eyed gaze, any flippant response dying on his lips. 'Fair enough,' he conceded. 'Of course I was aware of the benefits – but I didn't marry Lyra for those.' He turned to the window and stared out blindly at the night. 'When you see her, don't you just want to encase her in your strongest wards and keep her safe?'

'You've always been susceptible to vulnerable girls, Ril – my pardon, "Prince". But you also have a history of tiring of them swiftly once they've been "saved".'

'I know my faults, Dirk – but this is different.'

'How so? Because there's a crown involved?'

'No! A bloody crown is the last thing I want! But I saw the way Radine and Takwyth and the rest pushed her around – and you too, Spymaster. You all saw a tool for your ambitions, none of you saw *her*. She's young and bright and she sees the best in people; and she loves me, whether I deserve it or not. She *deserves* a chance to love.'

Setallius arched an eyebrow. 'And to be loved?'

Ril looked away. 'Do I love her? Honestly, I don't know. I always feel like this when a new romance begins – as if nothing could possibly go wrong. Will that become something more enduring? *I don't know!* But I swear this: Lyra will *never* not feel loved and protected and safe. I promise you that.'

Setallius sighed. 'I hope you're capable of keeping that promise.' He rubbed his chin, then added, 'What about the household knights? Because I tell you, you're *hated* in the barracks right now. Those men belong to Takwyth.'

'I'm every inch the fighting man Takwyth is,' Ril growled, 'and I should have been one of his commanders years ago. I'll not let this chance pass. And if Berlond thinks he'll be leading them, he can go to Hel. I'll not have Takky's lapdog guarding my back.'

'Very well, you'll get your chance,' Setallius conceded, then he added, 'For your ears only: I'm not entirely unhappy at what has come to pass, Ril. I've always believed there was a better man inside you. Prove me right, and I'll watch your back.'

Slowly, cautiously, they clasped hands.

When Ril returned to the chamber, Lyra looked up at him anxiously, but he bent over and whispered in her ear, 'I love you. You'll never know how much.'

She lit up like a candle, and shone through the remainder of the evening.

The next morning, the royal couple were still aglow in the aftermath of their first official night together. First order of the day was the parade through the streets of Pallas-Nord to the Bastion. They had bathed and been dressed in gorgeous fabrics so stiff with brocade and gems that Lyra felt as if she were wearing armour. Sustained by the warmth of his lovemaking, she took her husband by the hand and prepared to face the world.

They were about to leave when Lady Hilta announced Ostevan Prelatus.

'Your Majesties, you were both *magnificent* yesterday,' the clergyman gushed, but Lyra could sense his anxiety. Despite his role in the secret marriage, Wurther and Radine still ruled his fate, and their antipathy was deep. The grand prelate had made it abundantly clear to Lyra that his support for her would evaporate like steam if Ostevan was not punished for his breach of trust.

'Dear Ostevan,' Lyra said awkwardly. In the past couple of weeks she'd grown attached to him, and she felt guilty at her inability to have him forgiven. 'I shall always be in your debt. But you know the circumstances—'

'I do. But you promised you would seek to alleviate my punishment.'

'And I have,' Lyra told him. 'The grand prelate has agreed you will not face the Ecclesiastic Court. Instead, you are to be demoted to mitranus and exiled to a parish in Ventia.'

Ostevan's face was initially relieved, then it fell. 'But a mitranus is the lowest rank of mage-priest—'

Lyra held up a hand. 'But your gnosis remains yours,' she reminded him. 'Wurther sought to demote you to deacon so that your gnosis would be Chained, but I forbade that! Ostevan, *please*, know this: your exile will be brief, I swear. I believe we will be welcoming you back to the fold inside a few months.'

Ostevan bowed his head, resignation joining disappointment on his face. 'I shall suffer daily, until I am returned to your service, my Queen.'

'I'll never forget what you've done for us, my friend,' she said fervently. 'Neither of us will.'

The former prelate kissed her hands, and as he slipped away, she turned to Ril. 'We have to honour that promise. He's given up everything for us.'

Ril sniffed. 'Of course.'

'You don't like him.'

'I don't like the way he looks at you.'

'You're jealous of a *priest*?'

'Ha! If I told you all I've heard about him ...'

Ostevan was quite handsome, Lyra supposed, but he was a priest – they took vows of chastity. 'I'm sure it's just malicious gossip,' she said, 'and anyway, he's twice my age.' She took Ril's hand and placed it over her heart. 'You have no reason for jealousy of anyone, heart of my heart. You are everything to me.'

They were still kissing when the door opened again and Lady Hilta announced that their carriage was ready.

After the parade they held court. Ril was installed as Master-General, giving him Takwyth's place on the Imperial Council, and Dirklan Setallius was, unusually, elevated to the Council, in a special advisory role created for him. Lyra was pleased to see that neither Wurther, Dubrayle or Gestatium were happy about it; she hoped her new spymaster might see through their schemes better than she could.

And in between such weighty matters of empire, the nobility busied themselves aligning to the new state of affairs. Fresh faces flooded in, younger people sent in by their families to charm rulers their own age. In a matter of days, the court had inflated like a glistening bubble – all Ril and Lyra had to do was wave from a balcony and the watching crowds went into rapture.

There were endless banquets and lavish entertainments; Lyra's favourite was a Lantric masque in their honour, featuring performers wearing masks, their symbolism steeped in tradition. She laughed at Jest's droll advice, *tsked* wickedly at Beak's vulgarities, hissed and booed at treacherous Twoface and clasped her hands in her lap in fear for the star-crossed lovers Ironhelm and Heartface, until – thankfully! – they triumphed and found love.

They are Ril and me: Ironhelm and Heartface, eternal lovers. Our lives are in this masque.

PART TWO

PAGE TWO

PROLOGUE

The Masquerade (Heartface)

Ervyn Naxius

Ervyn Naxius is the only mage ever expelled from the Ordo Costruo. There is much evil that can be laid at his door – I've never wished a man ill, but should the rumours of his demise be true, I would shed no tear.

UNSUBSTANTIATED QUOTE OF ANTONIN MEIROS,
HEBUSALIM, 909

Veiterholt, Pontic Peninsula, Yuros
Janune 935
Four years and five months after the coronation of Empress Lyra

A woman with a ruined face, a mess of ridged scars and raw abrasions, opened a velvet box and took out a copper mask lacquered in exquisite detail. She raised it to her face and turned to the mirror. In the glass, Heartface peered back at her.

Alyssa Dulayne needed no one to explain the mask's meaning: Lantric plays, though today mostly performed by Rimoni gypsies, dated from before even the Rimoni Empire, when Lantris was the epicentre of Yurosi learning and culture. The same cast of nine appeared in every play, but no two performances were ever the same. Wit and improvisation were their essence as they wrung truths of the human condition from the melodramas enacted by the masked players.

Heartface was the Innocent, eternally seeking love and security in a perilous world. Liars and deceivers surrounded her, but if she remained virtuous and pious, she would find true love and redemption with faithful

DAVID HAIR

Ironhelm. For Alyssa, that meant only one man: Rashid Mubarak, Emir of Halli'kut. The man she'd failed, and who'd cast her aside.

Hold true, the mask promised, *and you will be redeemed.*

She *needed* that redemption. Once she'd been accounted the most beautiful woman in Ahmedhassa: tall and golden-haired, with a face that was indeed heart-shaped and flawless. Her body too had been perfect, and she'd taken that so much for granted – until Ramita Meiros ripped her apart in the final months of the Third Crusade.

She'd been on a mission for Rashid, and had found Ramita and the artefact she bore in a Zain monastery in Lokistan. The Zains might be sworn to peace, but Ramita certainly wasn't: somehow she'd transformed herself into a multi-armed horror from Lakh myth and gone into a berserk rage. She'd flayed Alyssa's back and broken her spine, her legs and arms, even pulled her scalp from her skull – and for all Alyssa was a pure-blood mage, the wounds refused to completely heal. She'd been tended in the monastery infirmary, then later by the Ordo Costruo, but not even the most powerful healing-gnosis could reverse the damage. Finally she'd been permitted to have the Chain-rune removed so she could use her own power – but a necrotising rot had set in and now her spine was bent over like a hunchbacked crone, her entire backbone visible through the remains of her skin. Her shoulders were twisted, she could scarcely use her left arm, and she couldn't walk without using kinesis and a stick to prop herself up. She was crippled, for all her years to come.

Rashid Mubarak had once been *proud* to be with her: the Keshi prince with the loveliest white woman in Ahmedhassa on his arm. But when he'd seen the ruin she'd become, he'd turned away. In public, he'd condemned her failure to complete her mission, but she saw deeper: he was sickened by the sight of her. For four long years she'd not seen Rashid, and she wanted him back with a need that transcended love or hate.

The desire to utterly destroy Ramita outweighed even that.

One day I'll stand straight and tall again. Men will worship me once more – and I'll disembowel everyone who ever stood against me – including Rashid, if he won't take me back.

That dream had brought her to the Veiterholt, twin fortresses built either side of Gydan's Cut, a giant gash in the land which ran a hundred miles across the Pontic Peninsula, making the tip of the peninsula an island. The Ordo Costruo had built a bridge across the Cut to link the two fortresses, testing their skills before they essayed the greater challenge of the Leviathan Bridge. It was accounted a wonder of the world.

She examined the mask, thinking of all it symbolised. The Master would not have given it to her by chance. Wearing it was a reminder and a promise of what had been and what could be.

Heartface will be redeemed, if she stays true.

She lowered it reluctantly, but kept her gaze on the figure the mirror revealed. It still shocked her that the twisted, ugly reflection was truly her. She swallowed a sob of loss, then turned away to begin the long, painful walk to join the gathering in the hall below.

Alyssa was last but one to arrive – no surprise, when a child could walk faster than her. Before she entered the gathering, she straightened her spine and carriage using kinesis and morphic-gnosis in a slow and agonising attempt to conceal her deformities – she'd be in excruciating pain and would burn through horrendous amounts of her energy, but it would hide her crooked shape for an hour or two.

Lamps were dotted about the walls of the stark circular space. The floor, a geometric mosaic about a central motif of a compass, was faded and broken in places. There were two doors but no windows, and the air was stale.

Seven masked faces turned to watch as she walked with grim stiffness into their midst, forcing herself not to moan with each step. The fortress was cold and they all wore thick dark robes, and their masks and cowls distorted height. They nodded mutely to each other, strangers, yet potential allies – if they agreed to the Master's proposal, perhaps anonymity would be lifted.

She instinctively looked for Ironhelm, wondering who he was, and found him walking towards her, equally interested. When he spoke, his voice was muffled; the glass in the eye-holes changed colour and shape. He could be anyone.

'Lady Heartface,' he said, speaking Rondian, as they'd been commanded to do. 'I suspect you and I are destined to become acquainted.' Clearly he too knew the Lantric tales.

'Heartface and Ironhelm don't always find the love they crave,' she replied, straining to sound calm when her broken body was *murdering* her.

'True,' tinkled a woman disguised as Tear, a sad, androgynous face with glistening ruby-tears flowing from the corner of one eye. 'I once saw a performance in which Heartface rebuffed Ironhelm and fell into vice. Beak rukked her up the arse on stage. Crassly entertaining for the peasants, I suppose.'

'I've only even seen High Theatre versions of the Lantric plays,' Alyssa replied haughtily.

Of the nine traditional roles, Ironhelm and Heartface were the lovers, Jest contributed humour and wisdom, Angelstar – a forbiddingly blank mask of white and gold – was the force of divine retribution, and Tear was the tragic one, his or her plight always miserable.

The dual-faced mask of treacherous Twoface stood alone; the man currently wearing it had already mastered the trick of standing so that whoever he was speaking to saw only half his face – either the kindly side, or the cruel one. Beak, the vulgar gossip and philanderer who was most often the cause of misery in the masques, was next to him – if Ironhelm failed to win Heartface, it was usually because Beak had led one or the other astray.

The eighth mask was Felix, the feline spirit of Luck, both good and bad, worn here by a plump man who reeked of perfume. He glided to Alyssa's side. 'They say these personae were the gods of a people who preceded the Lantric pantheon, Lady Heartface,' he said.

'I've heard that. But tonight, they are merely to protect our identities,' Alyssa replied. 'If one falls, they must not drag down the others. The Master told me this,' she added, to convey her intimacy with the Master's plans.

Oh yes, you might think you are insiders, but I'm at the heart *of this cabal . . .*

'Quite so, Heartface,' said a new voice. 'But there are other reasons for the masks.'

The Master had entered without fanfare. His voice, old and thin, had a hint of humour. He wore the ninth mask: that of the Puppeteer, who narrated the story and set the tone.

The eight masked men and women dropped to one knee in his honour, but the Puppeteer scolded merrily, 'My friends, that's not necessary.' He lifted his mask and smiled: his name was Ervyn Naxius and he was a piece of living history. Five hundred years ago, he'd been one of the first group of magi to gain the gnosis; he was likely the last original Ascendant mage still alive, with power beyond even a pure-blood.

Naxius fell out with the Ordo Costruo because of his research into the full possibilities of the gnosis – they'd charged him under the Gnostic Codes, claiming he'd breached every law they had, from deliberately infecting human subjects with daemons to pioneering the creation of reanimated corpses as slaves. He retaliated by betraying the Ordo Costruo to the empire, giving the Rondian Emperor control of the Leviathan Bridge and opening the way for the Crusades. Since then, he'd dropped from view, but his work had never ceased.

If he could deliver on his promises, no matter the price, he would become Alyssa's personal saviour. Nothing could be worse than living as she did now.

When Naxius met Alyssa's eyes, she felt her heart lighten. *You are my truest disciple*, his look said. Then he greeted the rest of the room. 'Welcome, my friends – welcome to the New Age.'

A faint, noncommittal murmur ran round the circle. Naxius laughed again. 'I know, I know, an outrageous claim, especially in the wake of the epoch-changing events of the Third Crusade. But in truth, that was just the beginning. History will say that the Third Crusade heralded us: it was just the fanfare before the play.'

Alyssa wished with every fibre that it be so.

'You'll be wondering who each other is,' Naxius continued, 'but for now, all you need know is that each of you is a powerful person in your own right. What unites you is this: you reached out for greatness, only to be thwarted – sometimes by a rival, and sometimes, Master Felix, by pure bad luck,' he chuckled, glancing at the man in the cat-mask.

'Acknowledged,' Felix responded. 'In my case, fortune certainly didn't smile.'

'Nor on me,' Beak put in, 'although in retrospect, I admit to making some unnecessary enemies – perhaps I put my beak in places it should not have gone.'

I came so close to grasping a prize beyond reckoning, Alyssa thought angrily. *Rashid blamed me, but it wasn't my fault.*

'You might be wondering if there's a message in the mask you've been given,' Naxius went on. 'The answer is yes, but not always the obvious one. You will all understand in time.'

More nods. More sideways glances. Alyssa looked at Ironhelm again, wondering.

'So,' Naxius went on, 'I have brought you here for several reasons. Hitherto you've had only my word; now you know you're not alone. The masks, as Heartface correctly deduced, are to preserve anonymity in case of misfortune, and we will continue to use them – but henceforth, should you agree to join me, we will act in concert.

'Second, you're here to hear my vision first-hand. You all know my broad philosophy: I am a researcher and explorer of the human condition and the nature of the world, most especially, the nature of power. In particular, I have come to appreciate the power of conflict: for this world is an arena of struggle. Species compete for habitat and the right to outbreed their competitors. The pretty song of a bird is really a boast about territory and strength. All species fight for food. Predators hunt prey. Even trees and plants compete, throttling each other as they seek a monopoly on sunlight and moisture. Nature itself is a battlefield.

'*Conflict is beautiful, my brethren.* In war we are revealed, our truths laid bare. In our struggle to master our homes, our places of commerce, our courts of justice and our battlefields, we become truly alive.'

'A world at war is a chancy place,' the obese man in the Felix mask put in.

'I agree,' Naxius replied. 'Open war is a means – not an end. That end is a *beginning* for us: a world where opposition to our agenda has been destroyed. You, my friends, are all but masters of your chosen fields; you were *so close* to ultimate mastery. My purpose is to give you the key, the final weapon you require to crush your enemies and cast them down so low that rising again is inconceivable. We may then remake the world to serve ourselves and those we deem worthy. I see a world where I am free to improve on nature without the trammels of so-called "morality" hindering me. Eggs must be broken to bake, my friends, and so too must society be broken, to be re-made anew. Once the war is over, we will rule in a peace of our choosing – one that is specifically of our choosing.'

Yes, thought Alyssa, *let it be so.*

'Since the Third Crusade, Lyra Vereinen's people have stabilised the West, and Sultan Salim has done the same in the East,' he went on. 'The Ordo Costruo have renewed control of the Bridge, and in so doing, they have all suppressed *your* opportunities to shine. They are your enemies, as they are mine – cast them down, and suddenly opportunities abound: we will each of us be free to do as nature intends: to predate upon the herd.'

Alyssa sensed approval around her, but also misgivings.

Angelstar spoke first, his voice melodic yet strong. 'Will we not come into conflict ourselves? My ambitions are not small: all of Yuros is my hunting ground.'

'Then already our Ahmedhassan friends are spared your wrath,' Naxius said with a smile. 'My friend, the Lantric philosophers spoke of four spheres in which a man may seek influence: the four pillars of power – the Warrior, the Philosopher, the Coiner and the Orator. A warrior seeks to dominate physically, but his understanding of the world of money or of ideas or loyalties is imperfect. Likewise, a philosopher caught up in the world of ideas is seldom either warrior or man of the people. Some can master two or more of these roles, but very few can master them all – Emperor Sertain, in Yuros and the Prophet Aluq-Ahmed, in Ahmedhassa, did, and perhaps a very few others. So, Friend Angelstar, your territory does not overlap with others here: it will bring you into *contact* with them, but not *conflict*.'

Angelstar bowed. 'Well argued, Master. I understand your reasoning.'

'Excellent. All discovery is preceded by a question.'

'Then I have another,' Jest said in his clever, urbane voice. 'A simple one to ask, if not to answer: why?'

Naxius' eyes narrowed. 'In terms you can all understand, Friend Jest? A simple answer: because Antonin Meiros and the Ordo Costruo restrained me, and I *do not* accept their right to do so.' He pulled a wry face. 'But it's deeper than that, of course: I am *centuries* old; my motivations are not those of a common man. Comfort, security, love, legacy – I've outgrown those. I have fought through the existential dread of facing eternity and made my peace with it: in fact, I intend to go on *for ever*, no matter the cost. I am purpose, and purpose only, my friends. I see a future ruled by an elite, and of course I wish to be one of them. It is natural evolution, that the mightiest accrue more and more to themselves, and I will not be left behind. When we are done, the world will belong to us, or we will have perished and failed. Evolve or die: that is the lesson of life, and I will not be another's prey!'

Seeing they were all hungry for the promised revelations that had drawn them here, he said, 'You each know what I want *from* you; now you want to see what I can do *for* you.'

There had been hints, but nothing tangible. Alyssa licked her lips in anticipation.

'Some of you have already encountered a new force on the tabula board of power: the Merozain Brotherhood. As you know, most magi can access three or four Studies strongly and a few more to a small extent; the rest are blind spots. The Merozains have discovered a unique skill: the ability to utilise every aspect of the gnosis, all sixteen Studies. This versatility of gnosis is an *extraordinary* advantage. Infuriatingly, magi of more than a few years' experience are so ingrained with their affinities they are incapable of retraining – I know this, for I have wrung every drop of knowledge from a captured Merozain and yet have failed to master it myself.'

Alyssa exclaimed, 'Yes, Master, give us a weapon against the Merozains!'

Naxius smiled. 'That is indeed part of my purpose. If the nine of us are to change the world, we need something even these Merozains cannot stand against. I have found us that edge.'

'Praise be,' Ironhelm breathed.

'During the Third Crusade,' Naxius said, 'I met a renegade Inquisitor who unlocked another path to power – he died, but I have enlarged on his work. And so: *behold!*'

The old man raised his hands, cackling with delight as all about him, light and dark kindled into life. Like the rest, Alyssa invoked gnostic sight to see and understand the energies, and what they saw filled the room with gasps of appreciation: traces of Fire-, Earth-, Water- and Air-gnosis shimmered alongside the runes and markings of necromancy, wizardry and the other sixteen Studies, all circling the Master's aura like stars in orbit.

'But you said the Merozain way eluded you?' Beak asked.

'I found a superior way, and one which requires no training!' Naxius announced. 'Better yet, I can give it to you too: Ascendant-level gnosis – and beyond – in *every* facet of the gnosis.'

Beyond Ascendant? Alyssa thought. *There is no 'beyond'.* 'How?' she demanded.

'Through the same means as I now have this power: daemonic possession.'

As one, they recoiled: daemons were known, and surrendering your mind to one, allowing it to possess you, was invariably fatal. You lost *everything*, becoming nothing more than a vessel for that daemon. The sense of disappointment Alyssa felt was sickening.

Is he possessed right now? she wondered. *Is this a trap set by a daemon?*

'Wait, my friends.' Naxius held up his hands. 'Those wizards among you, examine my aura: am I possessed? The taint will be clear if I am: daemons can't hide from gnostic sight.'

Alyssa looked, but her affinity to wizardry was poor. The fat man, Felix, examined him, then admitted, 'It's as Master Naxius says: there's no taint of possession. But how is this possible?'

'The "how" will become clear momentarily,' Naxius replied. 'Let me tell you first of the other benefits: I have unlimited mental and physical stamina. I need not sleep or eat and drink. I can heal almost any wound – indeed, I suspect I may be immune to age itself.' He gestured, and his age vanished, leaving a magnetically intense-looking man in his prime. 'And no, I am not possessed – *it is I possessing the daemon*.' They gasped at this extraordinary claim, but he went on, 'I can show you how. Do you desire to learn the secret, to become as I am?'

There was a pause as seven weighed up the risks against the gains, but for Alyssa, there was no question. *Like Heartface, I will risk everything for love.*

7

The Emir's Nephew

Crusades and Shihads

Since the failed Third Crusade, we have heard of many clergy preaching a Shihad of retribution. We, the Merozain Bhaicara, strongly counsel the Sultan of Kesh not to support this call. However much pain has been inflicted upon you, revenge must not be sought. Peace has to start somewhere.

MASTER PURAVAI, MEROZAIN BROTHERHOOD
LETTER TO SULTAN SALIM KABARAKHI OF KESH, 933

Halli'kut, Kesh, Antiopia
Safar (Febreux) 935

Family gatherings were wonderful, happy occasions, celebrations of kinship and love, or so Waqar Mubarak had been told. His family, however, was an ongoing feud, a morass of rivalries and jealousies.

Waqar was newly twenty, his thick glossy black hair framing a face the desirable colour of pale coffee, clearly delineating rank in a society where dark skin betrayed a life spent in the hard sun. It also hinted at his part-Rondian ancestry, which was both stigma and blessing; Rondelmar was a hated enemy, but he was of the exalted mage-blood. He and his sister Jehana had never quite resolved that dilemma.

The Mubarak family were currently arrayed on a lawn outside the family palace, overlooking Halli'kut, the greatest city of northern Kesh. Al-Qasr-Makhba – the Hawk's Lair – had been the setting for centuries of Mubarak adultery, duels, incest and murder, as far back as stories were told. Not all those stories were ancient, though.

'Look, it's here!' an excitable younger cousin shouted, and everyone peered up as a large windship swam into view. The dhou's triangular sails were pale blue and bore the insignia of the Ordo Costruo, the multi-racial mage order. For decades the order had been pariahs in the East, but since the defeat of the Third Crusade, those of the mage-blood were now – cautiously – being openly welcomed into the fold.

'How long has it been since you saw your mother?' Waqar's cousin Xoredh asked slyly. He had the Mubarak eyes, vivid green and penetrating as a cobra's stare. He was older than Waqar and closely allied with Attam, the emir's eldest son. They all bore the Mubarak stamp, though Attam was a muscular giant and Xoredh sly and smooth. They seldom missed an opportunity to belittle Waqar in the ongoing *harbadab*, the war of manners.

'Early last year, when I graduated as a mage,' Waqar replied calmly.

'I'm amazed a Mubarak could stay loyal to the Ordo Costruo after all they've done,' Xoredh murmured. 'Sakita is a family disgrace – I've heard Emir Rashid say so on many occasions.'

To belittle a relative offended the rules of harbadab, but one could repeat the words of the emir without breaking etiquette, so Waqar was forced to bite his tongue. Jehana scowled, and their older cousins smirked.

The dhou swooped in, landing struts extending from the hull. Now that magi were less stigmatised in the East, the number of windcraft was growing rapidly – seeing them in the skies above no longer sent commoners scurrying for shelter.

As the dhou touched ground, trumpets blared and Uncle Rashid stepped forward to greet his sister. He was tall and handsome, with piercing green eyes, and clad in all the finery of a great lord, but even dressed as a peasant he would have stood out. He had that undefinable quality that made the notion of demi-gods seem real.

My uncle, Waqar mused: *but to the rest of the world he is the Hero of the Crusade, the Victor of Shaliyah, and Saviour of the East. Oh, and Emir of Halli'kut, and Sardazam! Yes, First Advisor to Sultan Salim of Kesh himself!*

Waqar briefly squeezed his little sister's hand, preparing himself for an awkward homecoming. Jehana flicked an errant strand of hair from her face, squinting for a first glimpse of their mother as the walkway was lowered. 'There she is,' she murmured eagerly as an erect woman clad in the pale blue of the Ordo Costruo descended from the windship.

Both Sakita Mubarak and her younger brother Rashid had been born into the Ordo Costruo: three-quarter-bloods, both as Yurosi and magi. The siblings had been equally single-minded in their dedication to advancing themselves – until 904, and the First Crusade, when the Rondian Emperor marched his legions across the Leviathan Bridge, defying the Ordo Costruo to destroy their own creation and stop him. The Mubarak siblings felt distraught and betrayed – but while Sakita had eventually accepted the order's decision to surrender control of the Bridge rather than destroy it, Rashid hadn't. He began working in secret against both the order and the Crusaders, until the dawn of the Third Crusade, when he assassinated Antonin Meiros, head of the Ordo Costruo, captured most of the rest of the order's magi and led the armies of Northern Kesh in battle, winning great victories and the esteem of all the East. Now his name outranked all but Salim . . . and for some, even the Great Sultan came second to the emir.

Rashid had spirited his nephew and niece away when he openly broke with the order and raised them with his own family. He rarely allowed his elder sister to visit them.

I hope they can keep from killing each other, Waqar thought. Beside him, Jehana was bouncing with impatience. His feelings for his mother were ambiguous, but Jehana saw her as an idealistic heroine.

'Welcome to Halli'kut, Sister,' Rashid called. 'We rejoice at your coming!'

'You do me too much honour, Brother,' Sakita replied.

Rashid lowered his voice. 'I know, but it's expected,' he said drily. They kissed distantly, then Sakita greeted Rashid's seven wives impatiently, ignored Attam and Xoredh entirely and hurried to Waqar.

'My baby boy! Look at you!' She kissed him, her watery eyes drinking him in.

'Mother, I'm *twenty*,' Waqar muttered, keenly aware of his cousins' scrutiny. Her mother looked more Yurosi than ever, her hair cut short in a Western style that made her look out of place here.

'You're still my boy,' she whispered. 'Do they look after you? Do his sons bully you?'

Of course, he could have answered. Instead he said, 'I'm part of the family.'

'That's what worries me.'

Then she turned to Jehana, who flew to her mother's embrace. 'Mama, Mama!' she sobbed, suddenly a child again. Jehana was sixteen, skinny and ungainly, all angles and big green eyes, currently awash in tears. 'I've missed you so much!' she wailed, followed by, 'What have you done with your hair?'

Waqar watched awkwardly. The harbadab demanded more restraint, more composure, and though he might miss the time when such demonstrative affection was permitted, it wasn't *appropriate* any more. So he waited, more embarrassed than pleased, for the signal that they could all return to the shade for refreshment.

The other young men here had parents to protect them; he and Jehana had grown up isolated, perpetually the victims. Rashid's palace was a dangerous place where rote and ritual hid a quicksand of seething jealousy and colossal arrogance; any misstep in the elaborate game of harbadab could lead to ruin.

A man who cannot control his temper cannot control others, the *Kalistham* taught. Rashid demanded mastery of word and blade from his male heirs. The rewards were manifold, but it was a knife-edge.

I must survive and grow – for if I fall, who will protect Jehana?

Sakita and Waqar found a shaded cupola in the gardens to talk alone. The Crusaders had destroyed much of the palace, but thanks to the stalwart efforts of Rashid's Earth-magi it was almost fully repaired, unlike the city below, which was still largely in ruins. A vast tent-city beyond the old walls had sprung up at the end of the Crusade, nearly five years ago; it still stretched for miles. Even fifteen hundred feet above the plains, the stench was scarcely bearable.

'So, my son, does Rashid treat you well? Does he keep his promises?' Sakita asked. Having dispensed with her 'first impression' finery, she looked older than he remembered, with flecks of grey about her temples. As magi aged slowly and had many ways of concealing their years, it said a lot about her priorities; she always had lived for her research. She'd been here just a day and already had a blazing argument with Rashid; their voices had carried through the closed doors of the emir's private suite.

No one else dares raise their voice to him, Waqar thought, a little proud, mostly worried.

'All's well,' he lied. 'I've learned to ride and fight, and the gnosis, of course. My affinities are Theurgy and Earth, and the tutors say I'm exceptional at mysticism, especially at detecting gnostic traces. I've made friends among the magi at the Elimadrasa – that's what Rashid's people are calling an Arcanum – and I am mastering the harbadab.'

'No small challenge in such a place, I'm sure,' Sakita acknowledged. 'I am proud, my son: but tell me about the things that aren't so good.'

The things that aren't so good . . . Where do I start? 'Well, Attam can be unpleasant—'

'He's a mindless thug.'

'And Xoredh takes Attam's side—'

'He's leading that pig around by the nose, in other words.'

Yes, Waqar thought, but daren't say so. Words had a way of being heard, here. 'But I've made good friends – Uncle likes us to form groups of trusted people to live and fight alongside.'

'I've heard,' Sakita said dismissively. 'Waqar, things are hard for you here, I know, with no father to take your side – and I'm not here.'

He met her gaze. 'If you were here, things would be worse. You're not just estranged, Mother, you're *outcast.* I'm amazed Rashid even agreed to see you.'

Sakita's eyes narrowed. 'I have no illusions about my welcome here, but he still wants things of me. But I didn't come to cause you and Jehana upset: I want you to come back with me and join the Ordo Costruo. They'll admit you, because of me – and your father, of course.'

The offer wasn't a surprise; she'd made it before, but it still took him aback. He'd thought she'd given up on that campaign. But he was old enough now; it was his choice, not hers. 'Mother, I don't want to be a scholar. Rashid has promised me a place at court. There are things a nobleman must learn that only a royal court can teach.'

'Fornication and fighting,' Sakita sniffed. 'Even Attam can manage those.' She looked disgusted. 'I knew this would happen, but I hoped you might have higher aspirations.'

'Higher than being a noble in the court of the most illustrious man in history?'

'Ai! Courtiers are ten a penny! The Ordo Costruo is a legacy of greatness!'

A legacy of defeat while earning universal hatred, he nearly replied, but instead swallowed his words and said, 'Mother, the Ordo Costruo wouldn't let me near their precious Bridge, or anything important, not with my name.'

'They would eventually, once you earned their trust—'

'They still don't fully trust you!'

'I know people called Mubarak aren't popular in the Domus Costruo – why else do you think I took Placide's name?'

Placide Gentroi might be his father, but Waqar couldn't see himself as anything but a Mubarak. He barely remembered the man – he couldn't begin to imagine what his mother had ever seen in an eccentric Rondian obsessed with clouds. He'd died of a bad heart while Waqar was still a child – the gnosis could do incredible things, but congenital defects were mysteries still. 'Placide's dead,' he said bluntly, 'and if the Ordo Costruo don't know that you're loyal to them by now, Mother, they're blind.'

'I see their point of view, and understand – after all, would I trust the sister of a powerful enemy? But I'm true to my oaths – unlike Rashid, who betrayed his.' She took his hand. 'Come back with me, dearest. We need new blood, and there's so much we could teach you.'

He looked over the battlements at the city shimmering in the heat haze below. Halli'kut looked like a kicked-in ant-hill swarming with workers. The stench of raw sewage and rotting garbage tainted the air, which was filled with swirling flocks of vultures and crows that descended the moment anything stopped moving. The brown sludgy river was filled with washerwomen, their pegged-out clothes vast acres of colour.

'Rashid was quick enough to rebuild his own fortress,' Sakita commented, 'but his city still suffers. You should see Hebusalim, my son. Sultan Salim does his best, but outside a few fortunate places, children starve, often a few paces from an opulent palace like this.'

'The Eastern magi are aiding the rebuilding,' Waqar replied. 'Rashid's new mage order is working tirelessly!'

'Al-Norushan?' Sakita sneered. 'What "New Dawn"? Jackals pretending to be squirrels! Salim might have ordered the Hadishah mage-assassins to reform and start rebuilding the East, but we all know they're useless for anything except security and intimidation.'

'It's not as easy as you think,' Waqar protested, wishing this awkward conversation would end. 'It's good to see you, Mother,' he said, 'but I wish to stay here.'

'Your sister and I had this conversation earlier . . .'

His whole world lurched. 'But . . . Jehana's only sixteen – she's not yet completed her training at the Elimadrasa – you can't take her away!'

'I can and I am, and Rashid has agreed – probably because he sees her as just a scatty girl. And Jehana is eager to take up my offer, unlike my beloved son.'

He put his head in his hands. Jehana kept him sane. Even his closest friends couldn't make the world right the way she could. 'You're tearing our family apart.'

'No, I'm pulling it back together. If you came, it'd be whole.'

He tried to explain: that here, he could be a man: he could ride, shoot a dozen arrows and hit the target each time, fly windskiffs among the clouds, learn the sword. And since he'd turned eighteen, he was free to lie with the young women of the Scented Zenana – how could he give up all that for a quill and parchment amongst a mistrusting order of foreign magi?

Sakita read his answer in his face. 'One day you'll see beyond the glamour, Waqar.' Her eyes were wet, to his surprise.

'You don't understand. Living here is a dream come true,' he replied, with something like sincerity. 'Your magi order doesn't matter, not like being here does.'

'You foolish boy.' She dabbed at her eyes and composed herself.

'There's another reason I came here, Waqar. Something happened recently that's unnerved me – I've told Rashid, and now I'm telling you.'

He sensed genuine fear, which shocked him – his mother had always been fearless. *Is this why she wants me beside her? To protect her? Or be protected by her?* 'What happened?'

'Someone approached me last year,' Sakita answered. 'They used an intermediary to offer me a chance to "right my wrongs" – whoever it was believed I would resent the order for sidelining me. They knew a lot – too much – about me, and what I'm capable of, and that frightened me. So I broke off contact.'

'A year ago? But you're only just telling me now—?'

'Yes, because I thought the matter closed. Then a friend in the Ordo Costruo offered to divine my future and she was positive this unknown person was still circling me and mine.'

'But why would someone approach you, Mother? You're just a scholar.'

Sakita cast her eyes heavenwards. 'Give me strength. Listen, I might be your mother, but I'm also the greatest weather-mage alive – has that completely passed you by? I could call down a storm that would level this keep! I could pull snow from the mountains and dump it on my brother's proud head! It's my skills that have revitalised agriculture in the Hebb Valley! Certain people value that—'

'Oh.' He wasn't sure if she was boasting or telling the truth.

'Do you remember the Battle of Shaliyah, during the Third Crusade?'

'Of course, Mother! It turned the tide of the war. We lured the Rondians into the desert and then attacked during a … a … *giant sandstorm* …?' He stared at her.

'My apprentices conjured that sandstorm,' Sakita said, not with pride but bitterness. 'Rashid lured them away from the order and used them and all *my* knowledge, everything I'd taught them, for destruction. They broke their oaths as Builder-magi for him – and at the height of the battle, the strain of conjuring and controlling that storm killed them.'

Waqar swallowed. 'I had no idea …'

'That I'm not just a scribbling scholar? I could show you, if you joined the order. I could make you great.'

It was suddenly tempting, until he thought of the decades of training he'd doubtless need, years while his fighting skills atrophied and his social star plummeted, and that killed his enthusiasm. To go days without riding or flying? Nights without a supple body of his choosing beside him? He couldn't endure that. So he took the conversation back to this mysterious approach his mother had told him about. 'Who do you think was trying to tempt you, Mother?'

'Honestly, I don't know. I did wonder if it was Rashid. I think someone is probing the Ordo Costruo, testing our resolve. They think we're vulnerable after our losses during the Crusade, but we're still strong. I've heard stupid talk of a holy war across the Bridge at the next Moontide, but we won't let it happen.'

'Uncle Rashid knows that,' Waqar said. 'I've never heard him speak in favour of such a thing.' Though he'd heard Attam and Xoredh and many others within Rashid's court passionately advocate Shihad.

'A Convocation's been called to debate revenge upon Yuros.' Sakita sniffed. 'What kind of holy war will that be, when the Ordo Costruo control the only link between the two continents? Remember the fate of Constant and Lucia Sacrecour!'

'Rashid knows. And Sultan Salim wants peace.'

'Salim is just a man,' Sakita replied. 'My offer stands, Waqar. Please, come with Jehana and me back to Hebusalim. You really don't understand what you're refusing.'

'I can't, Mother. I belong here.'

She rose to her feet. 'Then Jehana and I will take our leave tomorrow.'

He stood, aghast. 'So soon? But you've barely got here! And Jehana and I—'

'I've outstayed my welcome already. And it's best if I take Jehana as quickly as possible, to settle her into her new Arcanum in plenty of time for mid-year exams.' She hugged him again, then left. Watching her walk away was an odd sensation, grief mixed with relief that he'd not have to face such awkward choices again. He liked to have his feet grounded, to feel certainty. Halli'kut might be a hard place to grow up, but at least he knew where he stood here.

*

Farewelling his mother was bad enough, but saying goodbye to Jehana was awful. Waqar got through it by keeping his back stiff and his eyes dry, knowing his cousins were watching like hawks for any trace of weakness. In the harbadab, for a man to shed tears over such a matter would be eternal disgrace.

Afterwards, the emir summoned him.

Walking with Uncle Rashid had always been an alarming thing. He'd craved a father-figure, someone to look up to after the death of his own; instead, he got a mage and a ruler. Rashid's brilliant emerald eyes could pick out a fault or weakness in moments; his briefest comment could cut to the bone.

Now Rashid paused beside a fountain and asked, 'So, Waqar, what did you make of your mother's warning?'

'She was worried,' Waqar replied carefully.

'Indeed. Overly so.' Rashid patted his shoulder. 'Such clandestine approaches happen all the time in the corridors of power, Nephew. But for Sakita, it was a new thing, so she made more of it than it warranted.' He walked on, adding, 'We discussed your future.'

'She asked me to join the Ordo Costruo.'

'I know. She had my blessing to ask – but I am glad you chose to stay.' He faced him, and there was nowhere to hide from that cool, analytical stare. 'Waqar, everything a man does must be for his family. All I am, all I do, is for Attam and Xoredh and my younger sons, and my nephews too. And of course, for my daughters, my nieces, my wives, and other kin – even Sakita. You know this, I hope.'

'Yes, Uncle.'

'There's a storm coming, Nephew, and to survive it will require each of us to be strong. I am prepared to do anything for my family; I expect the same of Attam, of Xoredh, and of you. I would spare you all if I could, but the truth is, I cannot. In the end, you boys – my sons and my nephews – are my legacy.'

The emir had never spoken like this to Waqar before; his words conjured hope in his breast.

'Ignorant clergy decried the Ordo Costruo magi as *ferang* devils, but my forebears saw opportunity,' Rashid went on. 'They saw what could be: to be sighted in the land of the blind. Marriages followed, and a new line was born: the Mubarak magi, the first legitimate gnosis-users of Keshi blood. That is your lineage, your legacy. If scholarship is your leaning, there is no better place than the Ordo Costruo, and I would understand.'

'I want to serve you, Uncle,' he said firmly. *No more talk of me leaving.*

'How would you serve me? Your tutors tell me you are well-liked, but they think you lack the hunter's instinct.'

Waqar flushed. 'If you mean that I'm not a brute or a backstabber, that's so – but I fight to win when it matters, Uncle. Silk and steel can both serve as weapons.'

'I see silk, yes. Steel . . .? Perhaps.' Rashid stroked his chin. 'I know you've been in conflict with Attam and Xoredh: doubtless they are the brute and the backstabber you refer to.' He raised a hand. 'Don't deny it; they're apt descriptions. But they have a quality you don't: ruthlessness.'

'I can learn that, Uncle.'

'One doesn't *learn* ruthlessness, Nephew; such traits we are born with.'

'Then what's the use of all the books of kingship you gave us? Sentorius and Makelli and al-Nuliem? How to be princes, to read words and deeds, to form courts and control them, to see hidden plots, to rule and lead. I've learned these lessons—'

'And if I send you to your mother and the Ordo Costruo?'

Does he want me to spy on the order? Waqar swallowed. 'I'll do whatever you wish, Uncle.'

Rashid shook his head. 'I wouldn't ask that of you, Nephew. Duplicity does not become you. And believe me, the Ordo Costruo is the hardest place to keep secrets in the whole of Urte.'

Yet you kept your betrayal secret for decades, Waqar reflected. 'I doubt I'd be very good at living a lie,' he admitted. 'But I'm loyal to you, and I've heard you say that trustworthy men are beyond price.'

'Truly. Very well, you shall accompany me to the Convocation next month. It's in Sagostabad: remember to dress for the heat.'

I'm going to Convocation! Waqar fell to one knee, his head bowed to hide his surprised, exultant grin. *This was the most perfect moment of his life.*

Sagostabad, Southern Kesh
Awwal (Martrois) 935

Sagostabad, chief city of the Sultanate of Kesh, was teeming with people, the Convocation adding hundreds of thousands of itinerants to the millions who lived there. At night the streets were jammed with sleepers unable to find a bed for let, and thousands more were arriving daily; not just from the Amteh heartlands of Kesh and Dhassa, but also from Mirobez, Gatioch, Lokistan, Khotri and even Lakh. The powerful brought giant entourages, and violence simmered at every intersection as rival groups blundered into each other. But reconciliations and treaties were also enacted, such was the power of a Convocation.

There were few places one could escape the clamour and the heat, but Waqar had been staring all day at the towers of the Yamas Masheed, the greatest dom-al'Ahm in Sagostabad, and had realised there was a haven up there – and a place to view the fermenting city.

The escape was meticulously planned by clever Tamir, and executed with military efficiency. Fatima flirted with the only guard close enough to hear them while Baneet broke the locks on the doors to the stairs. Then Lukadin extracted Fatima by pretending to be a Scriptualist, which he practically was anyway.

This is how we will rise at court, Waqar thought: *mine the vision, Tamir the planning, Lukadin and Baneet for strength and daring, and Fatima for her audacious charm.*

In a laughing mass the five of them climbed the spiral stairs, and reached the cupola of one of the four towers where the Godsingers came to chant. The sudden vista was spectacular; and as they admired the views, hundreds of feet below the takiya was already filling up with the devout, in readiness for the next lesson.

'We've got about an hour,' Waqar reminded them. 'You brought the arak, yes?'

Tamir produced the flask of liquor, smirking, 'Of course!'

'Here's the water,' big Baneet rumbled. 'I'll cool it: I've got a Water-affinity.'

'We squander our powers on chilling drinks,' Lukadin muttered.

Gnosis and religion were an odd mix, and Lukadin could be a volatile presence as he constantly debated the rights and wrongs of what they did with himself – and them. 'The gnosis must be used in service of Ahm, for Him to bless it.'

'We're not squandering, we're practising,' Fatima argued. 'Nothing wrong with that. You don't have to drink any, Lukadin. You can just disapprove.'

Lukadin mightn't like drinking, but being teased by Fatima was worse. 'Of course I'll have some. You can't leave me out. It's just, you know, Shaitan was the first brewer of alcohol—'

'And bless him for that,' Baneet chuckled.

Lukadin looked ready to flare up, so Waqar patted his shoulder. 'He's joking, Luka. We know what you're saying, and we agree, really. You're our conscience.'

'I thought I was,' said Tamir.

'You're the brains,' Fatima explained. 'I'm the face, of course. So pretty!' She threw a pose, though in truth she was more boyish than a beauty. 'Baneet is our spine, because he's so strong . . . and grumpy. Hey! Don't hit girls, Bani!' she exclaimed, rubbing her arm from a sly punch from the big youth.

'I don't see any girls,' Baneet teased, 'just a jabberer! You aren't the face, you're the mouth, the lungs' – he winked ostentatiously and finished with – 'and the fart from our behinds!'

Fatima punched his massive shoulder, hard.

'Double standards,' Lukadin pointed out with a laugh. 'Typical Fati!'

'Then who am I?' Waqar asked.

'That depends if this body is male or female,' Tamir said slyly. 'Does it need teats or danglies to complete it?'

'Don't be crass, Tamir!' Fatima scolded. 'You're our *soul*, Waqar. You are our immortal essence, and our reason to be. *You* are *Waqar Mubarak*!' She pretended to faint.

'Oh! *He's* Waqar Mubarak?' Tamir said in a stunned voice. 'The *real* Waqar Mubarak, nephew of the Demi-God?' He fell to his knees, using the same wide-eyed, incredulous voice that *everyone* used when they found out who he was. 'Please, tell your uncle I *must* meet him. I have important information that will *save* the world. It's vital! It's imperative! It's crucial! I must meet him! And would he like to buy some mangoes? Would you like some mangoes? Have you seen my daughter? Have you seen my daughter's mangoes? You're not married, are you? Anyway, what's another wife to a Mubarak?'

'Shut up!' Waqar tried to gag him as they all chipped in, chorusing the choicest pleas from the last banquet Rashid had hosted until they all fell about, laughing helplessly. The luxury of putting aside the harbadab and truly relaxing felt increasingly priceless these days.

He snatched the flask. 'One more word and this goes off the edge!'

'*Chod!* Everyone quiet!' Baneet exclaimed, and they all froze, until Waqar drew the flask back in and doled out the milky arak, then shared out nuts and dried fruit.

'Seriously, though, hasn't this Convocation been a bore?' Tamir asked.

'Of course it's a bore,' Fatima said. 'Old men droning on and on.'

As usual, Lukadin couldn't help but respond. 'I can't believe you all. Convocations are only called every four or five years – the Ayatu-Marja himself, the *head of the Amteh faith*, brings together all rulers to discuss the greatest questions of the day; and you say it's *boring*?'

'Well,' Fatima drawled, not fazed at all by Lukadin's passion, 'so far, it's been boring. And whatever decisions they reach won't become law.'

'Ha! Woe betide the ruler who neglects to follow the will of Convocation,' Lukadin exclaimed.

'And yet, it's been a bit . . . well . . .' Waqar started.

'Boring,' Tamir finished for him.

'It's been a disappointment,' Lukadin admitted. 'The old Ayatu-Marja keeps falling asleep, so everything said while he sleeps is wasted words. We've not even got to the big issues yet. And I swear, if you took all the speakers who claimed to have been at the Battle of Shaliyah, you'd have ten times the number who were actually there.'

Baneet scowled. 'That's because all the veterans of Shaliyah started wearing those red headscarves and crowing over anyone who wasn't there. Now everyone wears them.'

They nodded in unison. Life was one long frustration at the moment. They'd been too young for the Crusade, and in their world, deeds in battle were the highest social currency. It more than chafed their pride: it *burned*.

Waqar peered through the latticework. 'See, look below: on the left of the takiya? All those red scarves? Those're the Shihadis. On the right are the moderates – the Ja'arathi. They're wearing blue scarves.'

Fatima joined him at the rail, raking fingers through her boyishly short hair. She was one of a small but significant new breed of Eastern women: female magi who were as dangerous on the battlefield as any man, which gave them status other women couldn't aspire to – and left them as awkward presences in society, as men tried to work out where they should fit in. 'You know what I think?' She sounded as if she'd had a great revelation. 'Those red scarves make all those men look like they should be on blood-purdah.' She nudged Baneet, giggling. 'Imagine that: if men had monthly courses like women do!'

Lukadin's face went the same colour as the controversial scarves. 'The scarves mean they want *war* – a *just* war.'

'The last one was bad enough,' she said with a shudder. 'It left a horrible mess – and you keep telling me we won that one. Ahm help us if we lose!'

'It is right that we should exact retribution for what the Rondians did,' Baneet replied.

'That won't happen,' Tamir said. 'The Ordo Costruo won't let it happen again.'

'They let the Rondians cross for three Crusades,' Lukadin said angrily.

'But these new Zain magi who have joined the Ordo Costruo, the ones who killed the Rondian emperor? They've said that *no one*'s army crosses, ever again,' Tamir replied. They had all heard of the mysterious Zain magi, the 'Merozain Bhaicara' – Rashid had met with them and had come away shaken. But no one yet knew what they really wanted.

'They're Zains,' Lukadin said dismissively. 'Zains aren't warriors. They are weak by nature.'

'But these Zains are Ascendant magi, every one of them,' Waqar replied, 'and you know what that means. They're more powerful even than pure-bloods. I'm a three-quarter-blood – they'd wipe the floor with me!'

'The Merozain leaders slew the Rondian emperor and all of their court,' Tamir reminded them. 'Even Rashid wouldn't take them on.' He looked at Waqar. 'Would he?'

Waqar shook his head.

'Then those who want a war are idiots,' Fatima concluded. 'Isn't there enough to do rebuilding all our wrecked towns without wanting to drag everyone into another fight?'

Lukadin and Baneet frowned. Waqar guessed both would be wearing a red scarf by choice, while Tamir favoured the peace-making Ja'arathi. Clearly, so did Fatima. *Where do I stand? My friends have such strong views, but I can't make up my mind.* Clearly the Crusades had been evil, and not striking back felt demeaning, but the logistics were insurmountable. Rashid supported Salim's stance: peace for now, while they rebuilt and restored the lives of the common people. 'The Shihadi clerics can say what they want, but Salim won't go to war,' Waqar said.

'Leaving us for ever in the shadow of the Shaliyah veterans,' Lukadin sighed. 'If only we'd been born a few years earlier. Then we'd have been there . . .'

That was something they could all agree on as they finished their food and drink, revelling in the shade and each other's company. They'd been together for a decade, more than half their lives. There had been arguments and making up, a romance (Waqar and Fatima; his first taste of sex, and a vitriolic break-up), and the joys and trials of mastering the gnosis. Now even silences between them carried weight and meaning.

Finally they heard a clamour below, and a thumping noise. When they peered over the rail, they saw the prayer platform was crowded with men all looking up at the tower they were perched on. Waqar looked at Baneet. 'Hey, did you ward the door below?'

'Sure.'

'Well, I think you've locked out the Godsingers.'

Baneet's face dropped. *'Ya raabi!'* He lunged for the door, but Waqar grabbed him.

'Wait, Bani – it'll take ages to get them up here. That stair's only three foot wide!' He peered down at the shouting men and waved. Hundreds of men waved back, and a few shouted for him to get on with it. He grinned. 'Hey, how hard can all this singing be?'

Lukadin went pale. 'That's blasphemous!'

'Why?' Fatima asked.

'Because we're not Godsingers! And you're a *girl*!'

'I've got a better voice than you,' Fatima replied, 'and someone has to do it.'

'You know the songs, right?' Tamir said to Lukadin. 'We'll harmonise.'

Lukadin was aghast. 'But I'm only a trainee Scriptualist—'

'We are all trainees on Ahm's journey,' Tamir replied piously. Lukadin glared at him.

Waqar peered at the sea of faces below. 'Let's do it – come on Luka, lead us!'

Lukadin rolled his eyes, then in his best Godsinger wail, he began the call to prayer. The thundering on the door below stopped momentarily, then redoubled in fury, echoing up the stairwell, but to Waqar's joyous amazement, the crowd below, after some confusion, went down on their knees. In a few seconds the five of them were chanting every prayer Lukadin could remember. Then he spotted the black-robed imams making their way to the front of the takiya.

'Okay, okay, stop!' he said. 'The speakers are arriving. We're done.' He grinned about him and said, 'I guess we should go downstairs and . . . er . . . face the music.'

The maula of the dom-al'Ahm was waiting with a coterie of lesser clergy and a squad of armed guards, who thrust spears in their faces as they emerged from the stairwell door – but the weapons sparked off their gnostic shields and the soldiers' eyes went wide in fright.

As Waqar stepped forward to take responsibility, the maula glared at him. 'Waqar Mubarak,' he said. He didn't look at all intimidated. 'I thought as much.'

'Is there a problem, Maula—?'

'I am Ali Beyrami, Maula of the Yamas Masheed. This is a holy place, Prince Waqar, not a place for young people to blaspheme against Ahm.'

Not many high clergy were so blunt around his family. 'There was no mockery,' Waqar protested. 'We sang the proper words . . . well, as best we remembered them.'

The maula's flinty eyes bored into his. 'The songs of Ahm are reserved for the *Godsingers*, Prince, who spend years in rigorous training – and women may not sing the prayers at all.'

Fatima lifted her chin pugnaciously, but before she said anything inflammatory, Waqar said, 'We meant no offence – when the Godsingers didn't come up, we stepped in so that the prayers could go ahead.'

Ali Beyrami's beard jutted antagonistically. 'My Godsingers had specific verses to sing this evening. The lessons prepared by my imams hinged upon those verses.'

'Shihadi verses?' Tamir enquired. Songs of Shihad – holy war – were everywhere in Sagostabad right now.

Beyrami's eyes flashed. 'Do you think to criticise my choice in my own dom-al'Ahm?'

'There are too many fanatics.' Tamir's lack of stature had never prevented him from voicing his opinion.

'There are no "fanatics",' Beyrami countered, 'only men who love Ahm as he should be loved . . . and those who fall short. Do you fall short, Student?'

Waqar sensed his friends beginning to anger; *no one* talked to one of them like that. 'We sang because your Godsingers were *late*,' he insisted, to head off a fight. 'And now we're leaving.' *Try stopping us.*

As he and Beyrami locked horns, Waqar was a little impressed that the maula showed no fear . . . but neither did he. Then the tension ebbed as Beyrami backed down. 'Then we won't keep you, Prince Waqar,' he said with just a hint of condescension. 'I'm sure your noble uncle is anxious about you.'

Waqar didn't want to think about Rashid just then. He strode towards the exit, Beyrami and his coterie watching them. There was something distinctly unsettling about their demeanour.

Fanaticism. Tamir's right. Some people want war so badly they're beyond reason, and Ali Beyrami's one of them. It was uncomfortable facing a man so convinced of his faith that he would face up to a mage.

He knew I wouldn't touch him . . .

Waqar didn't feel comfortable again until the Yamas Masheed was five hundred yards away. He could tell they all felt relieved as they looked at each other a little sheepishly.

'Do you think we came across as a pack of irresponsible noble brats?' Tamir wondered.

'Definitely,' Baneet laughed.

'Phew. I was worried we'd made a positive impression somehow.'

'I hear you and your friends made trouble at the Yamas Masheed,' said Rashid Mubarak later that evening. Waqar found he wasn't surprised the news had flown so swiftly. Attam and Xoredh, lounging on the divans on Rashid's right, were grinning at Waqar's discomfort.

'We were just taking the view, Uncle. It was a misunderstanding.'

Rashid, Emir of Halli'kut and Hero of the Third Crusade, was seated cross-legged on a large cushion, facing Waqar across a low table that held an austere mix of dishes. Crystal wine glasses and a chilled bottle of Rondian wine were the only mark of his uncle's enormous wealth and reach.

'So you met Ali Beyrami,' Rashid said. 'What were your impressions?'

No lecture, Waqar thought with relief, then he concentrated on his report. 'He's a Shihadi, obviously – and unafraid to confront us. Most people are scared by our family name, or by the fact that we're all magi, but he wasn't, not at all.'

'He's all front,' Xoredh drawled. He feigned blowing a man over. 'A straw-giant.'

Rashid ignored him and looked speculatively at Waqar. 'Tell me, Nephew, what is your impression of the Convocation thus far?'

'Futile,' Waqar answered, knowing that his uncle respected forthright opinions – if they could be backed up with sound reasoning.

Rashid raised an eyebrow. 'Indeed? Explain.'

'It's futile because war on Yuros is impossible right now. Even if the Bridge were above the water, which it won't be until 940, when the next Moontide comes, Kesh and Dhassa aren't in any condition to fight. Irrigation has failed everywhere but in the Hebb and farmers are leaving their lands. The sultan is pouring money into aid, but corrupt officials spend it on themselves. Your own Hadishah have left to serve noblemen all over Kesh and Dhassa. Our armies have disbanded – many of our soldiers are now brigands. It would not take much to see Kesh and Dhassa come apart. Or so it seems to me, Uncle.'

The emir rewarded him with a nod. 'Your analysis is largely correct. The sultan's efforts to rebuild are failing and the central authority is floundering. The armies which won the war are now a danger to the very people they saved – but the Shihadi leaders are not blind: they know the situation. So why do they still clamour for Holy War?'

'Because our honour demands blood,' Xoredh put in, drawing a belligerent nod from Attam.

Rashid didn't dismiss the remark. 'Honour does demand it; that is a powerful imperative. But there are others.'

'Power and money?' Waqar suggested. 'If the Shihad is declared, then funds must be given to the generals, not the civic authorities – they can conscript and commandeer supplies and demand priority use of strategic buildings and bridges.'

'Correct,' Rashid answered. 'And you should none of you forget what a haven the army is for many men: place a nation on a war footing and all is simplified. Men will flock back to our banners the moment they are raised.'

'But if the generals don't deliver war, they will be cast down,' Xoredh mused. 'If Shihad is declared, battle must be joined, otherwise the men will turn on their generals.'

'Correct also,' Rashid remarked, making Xoredh sit straighter.

'But we're aligned with Salim,' Waqar protested, wondering if Rashid now favoured Shihad.

'I'm aligned to the greater good of Kesh, and so is Salim,' the emir said. 'The *Kalistham* demands that a man should always do what's right, and if what's right isn't possible, then he must make it possible.'

'Are you saying that it's right to make war on the Rondians?' Waqar asked.

'Are you saying that it's not?' Xoredh growled at Waqar. 'The *Kalistham* also says that the righteous man must bring the heathen to the faith, even against their will – suffering a heretic to live poisons society, Cousin.'

Xoredh must have new Scriptualist friends, Waqar thought. *He's never managed to remember a whole tract from the* Kalistham *before.* 'A ruler cannot allow priests to dictate his policies,' he countered. 'War now would be suicidal – who's going to feed the soldiers? Where's that food going to come from, and who's going to pay for it? Regardless, the Bridge is under the ocean, so it's a foolish discussion.'

'Wars require preparation,' Xoredh retorted. 'We can hardly have this debate a week before the next Moontide – and anyway, there are many places that deserve Shihad, not just Yuros.'

That stopped Waqar in his tracks. He'd not thought of that.

'Waqar, Xoredh is right,' Rashid interjected, 'Yuros isn't our only enemy. But you also are correct: Dhassa and Kesh are struggling and Salim is failing to set things right. In fact, many emirs and sheiks are usurping the tax rights, positioning themselves for independence. Unless something is done, Kesh and Dhassa will break into dozens, even hundreds of minor realms.'

Waqar had never heard Rashid sound so bleak. 'But how would a war help?'

'Wars can also *unify*, Nephew. Imagine if instead of pouring his money into rebuilding, Salim gave it to generals charged with building new armies to prosecute a war. With all the disparate parts of his realm *obliged* to contribute food, men and munitions, those armies would become the prime means of preserving unity.'

'But the last war almost ruined us—'

'Ai, Salim is spending gold like water, but Ahmedhassa is full of wealth beyond counting, Nephew, possessed by landed nobles who waste it on silk and statuary and opium and other nonsense, or worse, simply sit on it, when it should be put into making us strong again. A new war would free that money and bring us together.'

'But Salim's rebuilding projects are doing the same – or they should be—'

'But, crucially, they *aren't*, because rebuilding doesn't answer the need in our hearts for *justice*. Three times Yuros has invaded us and we *burn* to avenge that – no other cause will unite us more. We will *only* rebuild successfully if we do so under the aegis of war.'

'But Yuros is beyond our reach—'

Rashid smiled secretively. 'Wars can take many shapes and have many goals.'

It was exhilarating to be privy to such a discussion, but it made him worry for Sultan Salim, a man he truly believed in. 'Is this the advice you give the sultan?'

Even Attam realised that this was a daring question; he and Xoredh paused, waiting for their father's reaction.

'I serve Salim as his Sardazam: his First Advisor. I hope you know that I am also a man of my word. I may not always agree with him, but I obey: that's the loyalty owed all rulers.' Rashid looked at them each pointedly. 'Families also are based on such loyalty. We four are the future of the Mubaraks. Your loyalty is first and foremost to each other, even when we disagree.'

Waqar bowed, thinking, *Rashid might see me as family, but Attam and Xoredh surely don't.*

8

The Mollach Slave

Slavery

Slavery is a natural state that has existed from the dawn of time. Just as man is naturally superior to woman, so are some races naturally superior to others. It is right that lowly tasks are performed by the lowly, so that greater men may pursue more worthy endeavours.

REGIS KEVESTACK, EARL OF RELONNE, BRES 551

Dhassa, Antiopia
Awwal (Martrois) 935

'Lift up thine eyes, lift up thy soul
Raise your heart to Him Above
Kore my Armour, Kore my Sword'

The old hymn rose in ragged harmony from the line of men chained together and swinging their picks in rhythm at the rocky hillside. Their clothing was worn-out, their over-long hair and beards unkempt. Their skin, Yurosi-pale, was red and blistered, and many limped or bled. None looked upwards, despite the words they sang, because the only thing above them was the sun, beating them down as it travelled west, where they could no longer go.

Most were Rondian, former legionaries who'd been trapped deep in Kesh at the end of the Third Crusade five years ago. Deserted by their generals and magi, they'd been forced to surrender. Since then, forced labour had been their lives. Some still spoke of escape, but there was nowhere to go; their white skin marked them out as invaders. Hopes of prisoner exchange had long since vanished: the Rondian Emperor was dead, their captors told them gleefully, and the new empress didn't care. Few of them hoped for anything now.

Neither Valdyr Sarkany nor his comrades could conceive of a life without chains any more. The weak of body or mind had already perished, throwing themselves from cliffs or beneath wagon wheels, or hanging themselves in their cells.

Valdyr had decided he could live, even without hope.

A horn sounded, echoing through the desert air, and was taken up along the lines upon lines of black- and white-clad prisoners. Those in white fell to their knees and began a chant in praise of Aluq-Ahmed, the Eastern Prophet. The black-clad ones just slumped over their picks, panting and wheezing and spitting out rock dust. Then the overseers came through, cracking whips, and they all rose: the work day might be over, but there was still the slow trudge back to camp, the pitiful rations and the long hours of the night to endure: a nightmare without variance or end.

Valdyr had spent seventeen of his twenty-six years in captivity – twelve in a breeding-house, five in the slave-camps – after fighting like a Helkat to be allowed to join the Second Crusade, because his elder brother was going.

Why did Father let me go? he wondered for the thousandth time, and still he had no answer.

'Val,' the man next to him murmured. Arton, a stolid Rondian from Canossi, pointed at a pair of triangular-sailed windvessels above, heading up the valley. 'Keshi skiffs.'

'Fuck them,' Valdyr growled. Skiffs meant magi – Keshi magi, the scum bred by the breeding-houses he'd once had to endure.

'Looks like they're going to our camp,' Arton noted.

Valdyr hoped not. The last thing on Urte he wanted was one of *them* sniffing around. He'd long-since abandoned his real name, calling himself Valyn Timak to avoid such attention. He was the only Mollach in the camp and if he'd thought he could get away with it, he'd have pretended to be from somewhere else entirely. He'd discovered to his cost that it didn't pay to stand out here, especially not someone like him.

He scanned the slopes above. There was a line of archers positioned on the ridge above, Dhassan sentries who were bored silly having to watch chain-gangs breaking rocks all day. Sometimes a few men would take picks to their chains and attempt to escape, but no one had ever succeeded: the archers were too damned good. Sometimes they shot slaves just on suspicion, and let the prisoners haul the body around all day until they got back to camp.

'Perhaps there's news?' Arton still hoped that one day a Rondian ship might come for them. He was in his thirties, bitter for his lost life in Yuros – Valdyr had been chained to him for the last fifteen months. Parryn, the man on his right, never shut up . . . he'd had a strident singing voice and belligerent manner, until one of the Keshi overseers had cut his tongue out; now he mangled prayers to Kore all day long.

Valdyr couldn't think of any news that would matter to him. There was only this, until the day he fell down and couldn't get back up.

'Back to the road,' one of the overseers shouted in Rondian, and Valdyr's group of twenty struggled to their feet. The skin around their manacles was chafed and scarred, a thick ridge of hard flesh that had become numb to the metal.

Another chain-gang, their white robes marking their conversion to the Amteh faith, marched past, eating figs and singing in serene voices, *'Sal'Ahm, Sal'Ahm, miz merja hajji.'*

Parryn made a rattling sound and Arton, recognising his request for another hymn, chanted, *'Kore, I fly to you, on wings of song . . .'* and they all took it up.

One of the white-robed prisoners turned his head and tossed a couple of figs, which landed in the dust closest to Parryn. The mute fell on them and gobbled one down like a starving dog.

'Rukk off, you godless whores,' Arton snarled. 'Turncoats! Traitors!' His insults were taken up by those about him, including Parryn who started barking like a wild dog.

After three years, half the prisoners had succumbed to the Amteh Godspeakers – those who converted got better food, more water, prayer breaks and better living conditions. The genuinely devout (or better

EMPRESS OF THE FALL

actors) had even been allowed to become overseers; Valdyr suspected most were at least semi-sincere in their change of faith. But he could never do that: Kore was deeply entrenched in Mollachia: if he turned from his God, he would no longer know himself. So Valdyr was still clad in dark robes, still housed like an animal, still whipped for no reason. There was a perverse pride in defiance.

Parryn touched his knee, looking up at him like a miserable hound, and offered him the other fig, but he shook his head. 'It's yours, brother.' *I'm not going to eat something flung at me by a stinking Noorie-lover.*

Parryn's expression was piteously, almost comically, grateful. Arton put his hand on Valdyr's shoulder, but a Keshi overseer shouted, 'Move, you slugs!' and with a collective groan, the prisoners began the painful walk home.

The sun was a pale orange disc floating in the haze by the time Valdyr's gang reached the main camp. After relinquishing their picks, they were herded to the trenches to piss, then to the water troughs, where they were allowed two minutes to rinse the grime from their faces. Then Deko, a bald, bullnecked Vereloni overseer, stamped up. 'Sal'Ahm,' he said. 'Listen up.'

'Why? You going to sing a nasheed?' Arton sneered.

'Piss off back to your own people, traitor,' another man growled.

Deko sighed. 'An' I will, but first I have to tell you this: there's a Godspeaker up at the big house who wants to speak to anyone who knows about a battle-mage, one of them wot fucked off just before the First Army surrendered.'

'Well, we know they pissed off,' Arton grunted. 'The pricks didn't even look back!'

'The one they want was Mollachian,' Deko said. 'En't one of you lot a Mollach?'

All eyes turned to Valdyr. 'I'm a Mollach,' he admitted, because it was useless to deny it, but the attention set off a gnawing fear in his belly. *Dear Kore, don't let them find me ...* 'I don't know any magi,' he insisted, praying the man would just leave.

'This Godspeaker wants to speak to all Mollachs.' Deko turned to the guards. 'Unlock that one and bring him.' A heavily armed guard unlocked Valdyr's manacles, then hauled him to his feet. Deko grabbed his shoulder. 'You gonna give us grief, lad?'

Valdyr was over six foot now, and Arton had told him that when his face went hard, he could freeze a man's heart. *Would that I could. There'd be a trail of dead from here to Hebusalim.* But resisting was pointless. 'I'll come, but your men can keep their rukking hands to themselves.'

'Fair enough.' Deko lowered his voice. 'You know what a Hadishah is – a mage-assassin? There's one of them with the Godspeaker. I hope it's not trouble for you, boy.'

'Fuck you, convert.'

Deko pulled a martyred face. 'Sal'Ahm alaykum, Mollach.' He marched Valdyr up the rocky slope and into the administrative compound, where servants were shifting crates – more food was spilled here than Valdyr's gang ate in a week, and crows were already gobbling up what they could, squawking furiously.

Deko took him to a small door at the rear of the main house, where a dead-eyed Keshi robed in black met them. The Keshi bade Deko wait outside, then walked slowly around Valdyr. He looked about thirty, with a dark pockmarked face and a thick moustache and beard. 'What's your name, slave?' he asked, in accented Rondian.

'Valyn Timak.'

'You are Mollach? How old?'

'Twenty-one,' Valdyr lied. He was twenty-six, but any deception that might preserve his relative freedom was worth it.

The Keshi pulled a ruby pendant necklace from beneath his black robes. 'Know what this is?'

'Everyone knows what they are: it's a periapt.'

'Then what does it tell you about me?' the Keshi growled.

That you're magi and I should fear you, Valdyr inferred. Instead he said, 'That you had a Rondian parent.'

The Hadishah bared his teeth. 'Amusing,' he rasped, pulling the door open. 'Enter.' He pushed Valdyr ahead of him into a hallway hung with paintings and animal trophies. He heard the chatter of servants and even the tinkling laugh of a young woman, which set off a sudden,

EMPRESS OF THE FALL

entirely unexpected pang in his chest. Then the Hadishah called, 'My Lord?' and propelled him firmly into a room.

Three men were already inside: Bey, the commander of the camp, had an Amteh Godspeaker beside him, a grey-beard with a mild face who looked intently at Valdyr. Interest kindled in his eyes. 'We may have struck gold, my friend,' he said in Keshi to the third man, who was still looking out of the window, as if he didn't want to see Valdyr at all.

Or as if he feared what he might see. Then he turned, and Valdyr's chest emptied of air.

The man beside the window was tall, around six foot, strongly built and clearly Yurosian despite his Eastern garb and the Amteh trinkets he wore. His hair and beard were golden and his eyes bright blue. He looked in his early thirties, with a few laugh lines lending character to his frank, handsome face.

Valdyr's knees gave way and he fell to the floor, his eyes flooding with tears, because despite the years and the changes, he still knew Kyrik, his elder brother.

Valdyr stared at his brother across the table, his heart and mind churning. He didn't know what to do, what to think, what to say, for Kyrik had converted to the Amteh.

The sense of shame and betrayal poisoned all the joy he'd thought to have at this moment. Kyrik was one of *them*, a groveller to false prophets. He'd taken the soft way out while he, the younger brother who'd always been in awe of his older sibling, had stayed strong.

Kyrik had pulled him to his feet and tried to embrace him, but he'd hurled his older brother away, a small part of him amazed he could do that because he'd always been the little one. Kyrik was unhurt, but clearly shaken. He looked at Bey and the Godspeaker meaningfully, and the two Ahmedhassans left in silence, leaving the brothers alone.

How many years has it been?

Valdyr had been nine in 918; he didn't even have the gnosis, but Kyrik, his idol, though only sixteen himself, was going to war. He'd just graduated from what passed for an Arcanum in provincial Augenheim and been assigned to a Midrean legion – taking a military commission was often the only way a border-kingdom mage could be graduated, and it didn't seem a steep price to pay. After all, the First Crusade had been profitable for the magi houses, and virtually no one had been hurt. Eastern men were puny and weak, conventional wisdom said; no one thought there was any risk.

Valdyr begged and begged his father to let him go with Kyrik, to be his squire, and finally even stern Elgren Sarkany had relented. To the brothers, it was an incredible adventure to leave Mollachia and cross Verelon and Pontus, then to ride across the great Leviathan Bridge to a whole new world. They saw magical vistas: giant seas, massive coastal cliffs and vast deserts, all so different to the dirt-poor mountainous kingdom they called home.

Their legion had been assigned garrison duties in the Zhassi Valley and Kyrik, an Air-mage, was given a skiff and ordered to fly daily patrols. Valdyr, his brother's squire and a kind of honorary banner-man and mascot, had been permitted to join him when he was off-duty. The last time he'd seen his brother was after an apparent freak gust of wind had smashed their little windcraft into the sand, then four black-clad magi had overwhelmed them, disarming them with contemptuous ease – the Sarkanys were only quarter-bloods, Kyrik was barely trained and Valdyr hadn't yet gained the gnosis. Valdyr could still remember his disbelief when their captors unmasked, revealing Keshi faces with hook noses and black beards, all youthful, all magi.

How could a Keshi have the gnosis, the gift of Kore to Yuros? But the Keshi leader had laughed at his amazement. 'See, little boy: this gift, it does not come from your God at all.'

They expected death, but instead their captors had locked them in a Rune of the Chain, not just to bind Kyrik's gnosis but to prevent either of them from being scryed, then bundled them aboard the Keshi craft and taken them east, into a perfumed nightmare.

They'd not been spared out of mercy, but to breed more magi for the East. There were apparently many hidden camps in the mountains where all captured magi, men and women, were set to servicing Keshi 'volunteers'. Some of the women looked upon it as a divinely appointed mission, but in truth, it was rape, for both parties.

And I endured it for eight years, and worse things as well, while you took the easy way out, 'Brother'. When Kyrik tried again to talk to him, he turned his head away.

'Valdyr,' Kyrik said, 'please listen – I've looked for you unceasingly since the Third Crusade ended – they lost track of you in 930, when your breeding-house was raided by Javonesi magi – the Javonesi insisted you'd joined the First Army, and I hoped you'd made your way back to Mollachia. When I was finally allowed to write home, Father had heard nothing of your fate, so I realised you must either be dead or a prisoner. I've been to every camp in Kesh and Dhassa and now, *at last* . . . Brother, it's *really* you. I've found you—' Tears clogged his voice.

Valdyr stared at Kyrik's Eastern dress and choked out, 'Valdyr vagyok' – *I am Valdyr* – 'de nem batyam!' – *but you are not my brother.*

Kyrik's face twisted in pain. 'Val, I'm so sorry for what you've been through,' he replied in their native tongue.

'I've been in chains for five years,' Valdyr snarled. *'Five damned years!* When did you get out of the breeding-house? 921? So you've been free for nine years – and you're still here?'

'Then I was smart,' Kyrik snapped back. 'I tried to get you released as well, but they wouldn't, and when I finally persuaded Godspeaker Paruq to help find you, you'd vanished.'

'A *damned* Godspeaker?' Valdyr swore. 'Do you remember the day we left home? Father's Confessor anointed us with the sacred chrism and we swore to be true to Kore. We *swore!*'

'Paruq helped me find you—'

'In return for what? Your soul?'

'No, but if that was what I needed to pay, I would have!'

'Did you suck his cock to help persuade him?' Valdyr felt his fists bunching. 'Or did you put in extra shifts in the breeding-houses so you could father more magi for the Shihad?'

'No, I didn't. Don't be such a child.'

'A child? What would I know about being a child? I lost that chance while you were cosying up to your captors.' Valdyr stood. 'Take me back to my chains. I'd rather be with my real brothers, not a turncoat like you.'

Kyrik stood also, his expression pained. 'Valdyr, don't be stupid. I didn't search for you for five years only to let you go. I've come to take you home – to Mollachia.'

Home. The word hit Valdyr like a blow, conjuring visions of jagged white peaks, of ice-jammed rivers and black rock, of steam rising from hot pools, of men wrapped in furs, of women in brightly coloured headscarves dancing the harvest in. Of brilliant sunlight cutting through the mists like a reaper's scythe. Of wolves howling at dusk, their call haunting the valleys, and the bellow of the stags in mating season like distant thunder. Of incense and prayer in frigid chapels, and armoured warriors pledging their swords.

Then all he could see were memories of him and his brother: Kyrik leading midnight escapades into the woods, or teaching him to ride and swim. His first hunt, only seven years old and bewildered by it all, but still their laughter echoed through the pines. Kyrik, allowing him to pledge as his squire, and the chrism oil on his forehead as they knelt, swearing to the Crusade. How close they'd felt, and how proud he'd been.

He sank back to his chair, put his head in his hands and wept uncontrollably.

'He needs to be alone,' Kyrik Sarkany told Godspeaker Paruq, his Keshi fluent. He'd left Valdyr to his tears, understanding his younger brother's pain, though it was horrible to watch.

'He feels betrayed,' the Godspeaker observed. 'He's remained true to his faith in adversity.'

'Are you saying I'm weak?'

'No, my friend,' Paruq replied, 'you know I'm not. It takes greater strength to open your mind to another culture. You aren't weak.'

'That's not how Valdyr sees it.'

'Then you must open his eyes, otherwise your rift will never heal.'

'I believe you.' Kyrik rubbed tiredly at his brow, still shaken to have found his brother after so long a hunt. It hurt that he was so near, yet still out of reach. 'I just don't know what to do.'

'That's natural: these aren't light matters. First, let's get you both away from here. I have friends nearby who will provide for us. It will let him see past this place to what life now offers.'

Kyrik and Paruq had been friends ever since the Godspeaker had taken the rebellious young prisoner under his wing. Kyrik had been violently angry, assaulting guards and even the helpless women they sent into his cell, a self-destructive campaign to escape, or die trying. Paruq had understood; he'd listened, and talked frankly about Gods and Crusades and Shihads, about the damage of war and the way it mutilated society for generations – and about the need to reconcile and forgive, if one was to ever leave anger behind.

'What does life offer him now, Paruq?' Kyrik asked.

'Home, of course. I promised you I would get you home when he was found. Salim has said that low-blood magi must no longer be kept in bondage; that was a demand made by the Ordo Costruo, part of their price for aiding the rebuilding of Hebusalim, and we honour that pledge. You would be home already, had you not insisted on staying to find Valdyr.'

Kyrik ran fingers through his long blond hair. 'He's asked for the release of his fellow prisoners – the ones he was chained to. I said I'd see what I could do—'

'Sorry,' Paruq said, 'it was difficult enough gaining permission to release Valdyr. I've done all I can.'

Kyrik bowed his head. 'I know, and I can't thank you enough.'

Since his release into Paruq's care, Kyrik had even been permitted to use his gnosis, once he'd given his sworn word he would not escape. He'd been true to that oath – Mollachs took honour very seriously. It was through Paruq that he'd come to believe that all Gods were One God, and whether you called him Ahm or Kore or any other name didn't really matter. Now when he prayed, he felt an incredible inner stillness and sense of affirmation, something he'd never got in the forbidding churches of Mollachia. To him, praying among the Amteh was his portal to the One God.

'Father will hurl me from the battlements of Hegikaro when he finds I converted,' he sighed.

'I know how much your father means to you. Nobody needs to

know where your heart lies, my friend, nobody but Ahm. Remember that the Prophet initially concealed his faith from his own father, for the sake of peace in his family. Ahm knows you, Kyrik Sarkany. If you are unable to worship openly, then reconcile with your family and worship in your heart.'

'There are Shihadi Godspeakers who would stone you for those words.'

'Indeed – but they live in a fantasy world of absolutes and I live in the real world, with the rest of humanity.' Paruq stood. 'Let us go, whilst the twilight lingers. Your brother will be happier when he is away from here.'

As Kyrik entered the room where his brother still sat, he was struck again by how big and strong Valdyr looked, despite the privations of these last few years. His face was like a skull, his dark hair long and unkempt, his moustaches and beard halfway down his chest, making him look grimly fanatical. The boy he'd last seen thirteen years ago really was gone for ever.

'Val, we're going to take the skiff away from here. Will you come?'

His brother looked up, his eyes red-rimmed and hollow. 'Tell me one thing. Did you convert to help find me, or because you wanted ease?'

Oh Valdyr, that's the wrong question. I converted because I found truth.

But he couldn't say that, not yet, so he put on the courtly mask he'd cultivated while at Paruq's side, to deal with those victorious Keshi and Dhassan lords who wanted to crow at 'their' victory and humiliate the tamed *ferang*. 'I did what I had to, to survive and find you. That's all.'

'Is Kore still your Saviour and Redeemer?'

All Gods are one. 'Yes, Kore is still my Redeemer.'

Valdyr fixed him with a chilling stare. 'My brother would never lie about such things.'

Kyrik forced a wry smile. 'Your brother lied all the time! He lied about stealing from the kitchen, and late-night raids on the orchard. He lied about walking on the river when it froze. He lied about taking Father's bow to hunt beavers on the shores of Lake Droszt – and he even taught his younger brother how to lie just as convincingly.'

Valdyr's mouth twisted painfully. 'Father was never fooled. You wrote to him, you said?'

'I did, and he was overjoyed. He wanted me home as soon as possible, but I needed to find you first.' He watched that sink in, saw his brother's hands open and close, over and over. 'Brother, we can go home now. *Home*. And we'll never need to speak or think about the East ever again.'

Slowly, reluctantly, Valdyr opened his arms and embraced him. Then came the tears and the shaking. It was hours before they took to the air, and days before Valdyr could speak without breaking down.

9

The Queen's News

Corinea

The Ordo Costruo made wild claims in the wake of the Third Crusade, that a woman identifying herself as Corinea had been found. She claimed that Corineus was a Souldrinker, and that she saved the world by killing him. This is clearly a heresy, and one wonders at the motives of the Ordo Costruo in sponsoring her.

Fortunately, she died soon afterwards, and little more has been heard on the matter, but one wonders why it is that women are so prone to falsehood.

GRAND PRELATE DOMINIUS WURTHER, A NEW HERESY
(PAMPHLET), PALLAS, 932

Pallas, Rondelmar, Yuros
Martrois 935

The locals called the Imperial Bastion's northern portal 'Coldgate', for it faced the snow-chilled northerlies that prevailed right through winter and into early spring. They were easing now, though winter lingered in the frosty shade and old ice clung to the stonework. The Coldgate guards stayed close to the watch-room fire and passed visitors through with perfunctory briskness.

When the priest reached the head of the line, the guard looked twice at his papers, puzzled that the grandness of the title the papers proclaimed didn't match the man's garb. 'Er, good morrow, Comfateri,' he said cautiously. 'Where's your retinue?'

'There's only me, I'm afraid,' Ostevan replied. He pulled out his periapt and conjured a pulse of light in the gem to prove that he was indeed a mage. 'I trust I'm expected?'

'Of course – your name is on the lists ... but we expected ... a carriage?'

'I am a humble rural priest, recalled to the city as Confessor after the loss of poor Grafien,' Ostevan explained. 'Are my papers in order?'

'Yes, yes – please, pass on,' the soldier exclaimed, keen to end the awkward conversation.

Ostevan entered the narrow corridor beyond the gate, designed for defenders to pour burning pitch and rain arrows and crossbow bolts down on any attackers, and walked swiftly into Valcet Square, the parade ground before the Imperial Palace.

I'm back ...

Three colossal buildings faced him on the south side of the square: the barracks of the Imperial Guard at the east end and the offices of the Treasury and Imperocracy at the west. Between them, tallest and most beautiful, stood the Domus Imperium, the royal household, built in creamy gold and pink marble. Tall towers with lance-head roofs punctured the air and hundreds of banners, an elaborate heraldic code that revealed who was at court, flapped crisply in the cold breeze.

Ostevan scanned the banners cursorily as he sidestepped perambulating mage-nobles, scurrying functionaries and long-striding soldiers in Imperial purple and white. He took a side door into a small courtyard filled with life-size marble statues of every past emperor; the unlamented Constant had recently joined them.

How remarkable – they've managed to make the puny teatsucker look noble! He spat at the statue's base as he passed, then rapped on a wooden door. He heard shuffling feet, then an old monk opened it, stepped back and bowed low. 'My Lord,' he croaked, 'welcome back.'

'Not "Lord",' Ostevan said genially, 'simply Comfateri, Brother Junius.'

'Of course, Lord ... Comfateri. Let me show you to your rooms. They're tucked in behind the vestry, and you have your own herb garden too. Old Grafien loved his herbs.'

Junius fussed over him for a while until, pleading tiredness from the road, he was shown the door. Unpacking took little time – there had been *nothing* in Ventia he'd wanted to bring back – but he lingered over one item: a copper Lantric mask lacquered with a diamond pattern of red and green.

Hail, Master, he said silently, studying Jest's crafty visage. *I have arrived.*

He used Earth-gnosis to create a hidey-hole for the mask beneath the floor until he could find a more permanent place for it, then surveyed his new domain. His predecessor had few belongings, but he found himself rather taken with an ivory figurine of a bare-breasted winged woman, clearly Crusade plunder, so he placed it in front of his prayer-kneeler so that he'd at least have something to feast his eyes on while pretending to pray.

Then he went into the chapel, his new lair: a small, darksome place, the old stones black with age. A radiant porcelain statue of Corineus holding the dagger in his heart like a blessing from on high dominated the chamber. He made his unhurried way along the burial wall, examining the bronze plaques; behind them lay the decayed remains from centuries of Imperial rule: cousins and relatives, loyal generals and counsellors – anyone not worthy of a full sarcophagus in the catacombs below. Finally he found what he sought: a newer plaque, tucked into a low corner.

Radine Antaria Jandreux, Duchess of Coraine, d. 931.
The Soul of Coraine, beloved by all.
She dwells with Kore

To Ostevan's knowledge, Radine had died alone, still railing bitterly at the loss of Solon Takwyth and her plans of revenge for 909. Something had broken inside her after the coronation and marriage in 930; her health and her mind had collapsed.

I hope you suffered before you passed, you sour old bitch.

He went on into the Reliquary, a small side-chapel containing some supposed relics, the grave-goods of Corineus Himself, encased in a gold box surrounded by gleaming candles. Only the imperial family were permitted to pray here, so the small cloaked figure seated in the front row must be—

Empress Lyra Vereinen rose, smiling radiantly. 'Ostevan!'

He swept forward, smiled warmly and knelt, kissing the signet ring on her right hand. 'My Queen, my heart rejoices to see you.' *Dear Kore,* he thought, *she's become more rukkable than a harem of Eastern virgins!*

When he'd left Pallas, Lyra had been a thin, pallid girl, though possessed of a certain delicate prettiness. Nearly five years on, she'd lost her girlish naïveté, gained womanly dignity and filled out. His spies told him that her flashes of impetuous wilfulness had become tempered by sorrow and experience, that she'd tasted pain, encountered dashed hopes and suffered loss. It gave her a radiance that was positively *regal.* 'You look every inch an empress,' he said truthfully.

'Ostevan, you flatterer!' She took his hands, and her welcoming smile became sad. 'I'm sorry it's taken so long to recall you. I never knew when I made those rash promises that it would be so difficult.'

'I understand,' he replied. *I understand that you were weak and distracted, and you needed to keep Wurther happy,* he railed silently, keeping his face serene. *If I hadn't taken matters into my own hands, I'd still be in damned Ventia.*

But she noticed none of his inner rage as she sat and pulled him down beside her. 'You've not changed even a little, Ostevan,' she said. 'I hope I look as good as you when I reach fifty!'

'I'm not sure a beard would become you, Milady,' he quipped, and she giggled delightedly. As a pure-blood, he'd been well-preserved anyway; since he'd taken the daemon's embrace the real difficulty now was remembering to look his age.

'I trust you've kept up with events here?' she asked. 'I shall so rely on your advice.'

'Of course, your Majesty – you know how much I've hungered to return to your service.'

'Was Ventia truly awful? I so wanted you back, but Fate conspired against us.'

Wurther conspired, and Fate did as She was told, Ostevan thought. *I gave you the empire on a plate, and you sacrificed me to win Wurther's support.* For a time he'd thought she might find the wherewithal to recall him in defiance of Wurther, but as the months turned into years and his rage grew, he'd realised he'd have to do it all himself. His hatred for rural

Ventia was matched only by his loathing for those who'd allowed him to be sent there. But that bitterness was a boil to be lanced another day. 'How did our Grand Prelate react to my recall?'

'Very unhappily,' Lyra smiled, 'but it's time things didn't go entirely his way. Ostevan, I've missed you: it would have been a great comfort to have you here when . . .' Her voice faltered. 'You know what happened, don't you?'

'I do.' *Two miscarriages, no children, and the people whisper of 'Radine's Curse' and calculate the years until young Cordan comes of age. It's no more than you deserve.* 'My Queen, I wept when I heard. But I am sure you will be blessed in time. You must have patience.'

'Patience,' she echoed. 'So many things seem to demand it.' Then her face brightened. 'But your own patience has been rewarded and here you are: my new confessor! Though I have no idea how you persuaded poor Grafien to name you as his successor!'

It was one of the quirks of the Church that the incumbent Comfateri could name his own successor. Grafien had been an iron-willed tyrant; it had been a vast surprise to all that he'd named Ostevan as his successor, allowing him to return to Pallas.

Lyra leaned closer, unwittingly exposing her cleavage. 'How *did* you persuade him?'

I bit him and flooded his system with daemonic ichor, Ostevan recalled, enjoying the view. Blood was racing to his loins; Lyra's body had ripened delightfully but she was clearly still naïve in some ways. 'With faith and good hospitality,' he replied aloud.

'You always were a charmer,' Lyra twinkled. 'I'm so glad you're back. Is there anything I can do for you?'

Oh, the things you could do for me, he thought hungrily. Ever since the Master had changed him, Ostevan had been subject to increasingly lurid desires, fed to him by the daemon Abraxas. The urges could be almost overpowering when he was alone with a woman, but as Naxius had promised, he was still in control: Abraxas was a tap he could turn on or off. And though Lyra Vereinen might be in easy reach, she was the most scrutinised woman in Pallas. Giving in to such desires too soon was foolish. He would have to be . . . *patient*.

'Milady, being restored to your service is all I need at present,' he replied humbly.

'It's probably selfish of me to be so pleased that you're here, instead of in the Celestium where you belong,' Lyra said apologetically, utterly oblivious to how much he wanted to ram himself into her. 'But having you all to myself as my confessor will be wonderful, Ostevan.'

My dear girl, he thought, *you have no idea what you're wishing upon yourself . . .*

From her vantage facing south, Lyra could see all three parts of her capital: Pallas-Nord, Argundian-dominated Emtori on the west bank of the confluence, and the Celestium, glittering across the Bruin River to the south. The wealthy held the high ground, and the burghers, more than a million souls, were crammed into the lower slopes, vales and riversides. She knew there were places the City Watch were afraid to enter, like Kenside and Tockburn, but from her balcony, it was all a distant haze of grey stone buildings and red-brick tiled roofs, streets packed with carts and people, the blue-green rivers shimmering. Mansions encrusted the hills like gemstones and the Celestium stood stark and elegant above the squalor of Southside and Fenreach. This was Pallas the Mighty, heart of Yuros.

Her mind wasn't on the splendour of her realm, though, but the question of whether a missed bleeding meant she'd conceived again, which brought all the usual array of hopes and fears. If she was with child, it ended one domestic crisis and began another one. She and Ril had nothing to show for nearly five years of marriage except two traumatic miscarriages.

The first had almost destroyed her, because she'd been so full of hope and belief that Kore had given her the child they needed to seal their reign. That loss had sucked the joy from her marriage. Ril was still her hero, but his flaws were much more evident after that first setback. Even magi-healers didn't fully understand how bodies functioned; they blamed the miscarriage on him, at least to her face, but she suspected they really blamed her.

One miscarriage could be put down as misfortune. The second broke her heart. All of the court had advice, but when she finally conceived again, she was plagued with illness and the loss of that unborn child felt like the fulfilment of an long-known prophecy.

Must I go through all that again? She'd been procrastinating, knowing what she was in for once the pregnancy was announced. But this morning, during Unburdening, she'd told Ostevan – and how wonderful to have him back; it was three weeks now and it felt like he'd never left – and the Comfateri had advised her to tell the healers promptly, and place herself in their care. *He's right*, she decided, returning to her room and calling her maid. 'Geni!'

'Majesty?' Geni was a robust country girl with a cheerful, freckled face, a healer-mage born out of wedlock to a Jandreux grandee, chosen for the royal household for her attentiveness and good nature. 'Geni, I need to see the healers . . . my bleeding is a few days late.'

Geni gave a cautious smile. 'That's not unusual for you, Majesty.'

Lyra bowed her head in embarrassment. 'To be honest, I didn't actually bleed during these last two months. I think I'm in my third month of pregnancy.'

Geni's eyebrows shot up. 'You must see Domara!' she squeaked.

Lyra bit her lip. The moment she told her tyrannical royal midwife, her choices would be taken away; that was why she'd concealed her condition for so long – but her waist was visibly thickening now, had she permitted anyone to see her unclothed. She was running out of options. She would be placed into confinement, made to eat and drink what they told her, forbidden further congress with Ril lest it disturb the unborn, and even worse, forced to relinquish the reins of her realm. The constant scrutiny would intensify, and she hated that worst of all.

But if I don't tell them, they'll blame me if this pregnancy fails as well.

'I'm not sure I'm ready to face Domara,' she confessed, then she heard voices. 'Is that my next visitor? Lord Setallius, yes?' She'd come to rely upon her sessions with the spymaster, but he made Geni jittery. 'Show him in, then you can take the laundry down – and not a word to anyone yet, Geni.'

Geni curtseyed obediently and bustled away, avoiding even looking at Setallius.

There were deeper lines in the spymaster's face, and the curtain of hair that concealed the ruined left side of his face was paler – he would turn sixty this year, and even a mage wasn't immune to ageing. He was talking quietly to Basia as he entered; he'd appointed her Lyra's personal bodyguard, for she could accompany Lyra where it wasn't seemly for a man to go. They bowed, then Basia left and Setallius got down to business.

His first duty was to examine her aura for traces of hostile gnosis. Her own gnosis had never come, though she was assured her magical aura was fully formed. She'd learned the mental techniques anyone could use, but they were her only defence ... except for the dwyma, the secret only Setallius, Ril and Basia knew.

'All clear,' the spymaster told her, and she felt her usual tingle of relief – although he'd once told her that a more powerful mind than this could escape such detections. Fortunately, Dirklan Setallius was one of the most skilled pure-blood magi in all of Yuros.

'Now, I have a report from Sir Esvald Berlond. The peasants' revolt in rural Midrea has been suppressed and the ringleaders arrested,' he began.

Another revolt. The thought that there were people so desperate that they'd take up arms against the legions sickened her – but people were starving in the hinterlands; there just wasn't enough to go round. 'Who's being blamed?' she wondered, hating herself for asking.

'Your Council. Fate. Some rave about curses. Nothing coherent, Milady.' Setallius shrugged. 'The important thing is that there was nothing ideological or united in the unrest.'

'Nothing that comes back to Garod Sacrecour, then?'

'Nothing provable, Milady. In fact, I see different patterns.'

She sat up. 'What patterns?'

'It's rural lands, and the uprisings happen after the tax farmers have gone through.'

The tax farmers again. She pursed her lips unhappily. Two years ago, Calan Dubrayle and Edreu Gestatium had proposed a plan to collect tax by proxy, letting regional lords bid for the right to collect imperial tax in their lands. Dubrayle claimed it had saved her Treasury from penury – *saved her reign*, in other words – by alleviating some of the crippling debts the Crown owed the bankers. The cost so far was a score of minor insurrections.

'Have we done wrong in passing those laws?' she asked.

Setallius wrinkled his nose. 'It's not so straightforward, Milady. Dubrayle and Gestatium's purpose is to accumulate wealth for you, and they claim the tax-farming laws have been a success. Perhaps they have, but they don't include human suffering and increased threats to your security in their calculations.'

The laws had been passed when she'd been bedridden with the second miscarriage. Ril had been at the Council sessions, of course, but she knew her husband. He had many qualities, but legal intricacies were not his strength. 'Should we repeal them?'

'It's worth the discussion,' Setallius answered. 'Other places are teetering on the edge of rebellion: parts of Brevis and Hollenia, rural Ventia, even Mollachia . . . It wouldn't take much to tip them over the edge at the moment.'

'How did Constant deal with these stresses?'

Setallius snorted. 'These matters weren't stressful to him – the late emperor saw a peasants' revolt as just another opportunity for his legions to drill.'

Dear Kore, may I never become so callous, Lyra prayed. 'What else is happening, Dirklan?'

Much, it turned out: continued lawlessness in Rimoni and Silacia, which had fragmented into a confusion of baronies and city-states; the mercenaries alone appeared to be profiting from the current situation. Argundy continued to demand preferential concessions from her, playing on their 'kinship'. *At least the secret of my parentage remains unknown*, she reflected. No one had yet come forward claiming to be her real father.

'Meanwhile,' Setallius went on, 'Estellayne is in religious ferment – yet another person has apparently had a prophetic vision – and Noros and Bricia are rebuilding their military strength at speed. Nothing *immediately* alarming, but a stew of potential issues coming to the boil.'

'Thank you, Dirklan. It's good to have this understanding of what is transpiring before we go into full Council.' Lyra hesitated, wondering if she should say more . . .

'My Queen, are you well?' Setallius enquired, his one eye filled with knowing. 'You keep touching your midriff,' he added apologetically.

She pulled a face. 'Yes. I think I'm with child again.' She coughed. 'Erm, three months.'

He surprised her by giving her a warm, gentle look, full of sympathy, and – she was certain – genuine pleasure. 'Are you telling me, or telling the world?' he asked.

'Worse.' She smiled wanly. 'I'm about to tell Domara.'

Within the hour, Imperial Midwife Domara, a grey-haired woman with a face like a predatory bird, who didn't appear to have a maternal bone in her body, swept into the Royal Apartment, confirmed that Lyra had another child inside her and promptly put her to bed. Lyra let her head fall back to the pillow as the mechanism of Imperial childbirth gripped her yet again. Domara reminded her of the strictures, all the things she was now forbidden, and all the rites and ceremonies, religious and familial, that they would perform to ensure that this would be a successful gestation.

Lyra had hated it all both previous times, but if she rebelled, she would be trebly blamed for any failure. *Dear Kore, please just let this child be born safe and well!*

She cast her eyes among her retinue of ladies. 'Basia,' she called, 'I'm in good hands with Domara – could you do me a favour and find Ril? He needs to be here.'

Ril Endarion's gaze locked on the shape of Lero Falquist as the young knight circled him warily. He moved onto the balls of his feet, letting the younger man expend his energy while he waited for Lero to move his feet into a lunge . . .

'Ha!' Lero bellowed, the buckler in his left hand dropping as he swung into the blow. His blade only grazed Ril's gnostic shields, leaving a blur of sparks trailing in the air, as Ril darted right and thrust. The blunted tip of his weapon sliced through the shields and tapped Lero on the left shoulder. The men in the gallery boxes overlooking the small indoor

arena applauded. Ril came here every day he could get away, to practise with the other mage-knights – and to remind them who was their
commander. There were mage-knights from all over Rondelmar in his
service, but he kept a core of Corani around him; and it was them he
spent most time with.

'You did it again,' he told Lero now. 'When you attack, you drop
your buckler too low.'

Lero spun away, cursing. 'I can never reach you without over-stretching,'
he complained.

'It's the footwork: you've got to extend more when you strike, not
this halfway blow you've got into your system. *Commit to the blow!*'

Lero mopped at his brow and groaned. He was a Falquist, predisposed to believe himself the centre of the universe, but he was also a
diligent student.

They saluted each other, then Ril shouldered his practise blade and
walked on. He watched another pair duel before calling a break and
pointing out the flaws. 'Don't let the buckler creep too high – it's there
to protect your side, but if you let it block your vision, you're weakening your defences, not strengthening them.' The men he'd interrupted
nodded sullenly, but obeyed.

Four years he'd been doing this: training like a fiend, making damned
sure he was still the best – and that the men knew it – but he was still
at war with his own knights. He'd taken on all the senior men, Takwyth's cronies, in bouts that were a hair's-breadth from actual duels.
Limbs had been broken, blood had been shed. Lessons had been taught.

He'd made a particular point of beating Esvald Berlond, Jorden Falquist
and Rolven Sulpeter first off, to make the point. They still hated him,
of course, but the men beneath them had quickly realised that the
half-Estellan outsider could beat every one of them.

Taking down Takwyth's cronies was the first part of his plans; the
next was to befriend those who'd been like him, always on the outer,
seeking out those good enough to promote and giving them opportunities. Today, he felt he could trust maybe two-thirds of the men he
led – not bad, when four years ago it had been virtually none.

He heard a tinkle of feminine laughter and glanced up at a small group of women in courtly finery. Jenet Brunlye's merry, familiar laugh always pricked at his attention, bringing back memories. He saw her lively, intelligent face and rich red lips framed by long golden-brown tresses, her creamy skin amply displayed by a new low-cut red gown. Gold and diamonds glittered, no brighter than her eyes – somehow she always prospered. There was always another man who believed himself the only one. Their eyes met, and for a moment only he and she existed. Then he swallowed and looked away.

There's never a shortage of temptations here, old and new . . . The *Book of Kore* had much to say on the allure of sin, such as, *'Temptation lies within, not in that we behold'.*

Doesn't it ever?

Then Basia was tottering up to him, calling, 'Ril, you need to come.' Her anxious expression made him stiffen. 'What's happened?'

She bent in close and whispered, 'Lyra's with child again.'

Dear Kore. He looked skywards, a thousand hopes and fears thudding through his brain, then he tossed the blade to an attendant and strode back to the Domus Imperium, until he remembered himself and slowed his pace. 'Sorry Fantoche,' he murmured, softening the old nickname with a fond smile, 'I'll slow down.'

She hadn't changed all that much since Lyra's coronation, other than the crows' feet about her eyes and dark circles beneath them: being Lyra's bodyguard was a prestigious role, but always stressful. Thankfully, her vigilance had yet to be fully tested.

For himself, despite being in his late thirties now, with a few grey hairs about the temples of his black mane, he was probably in his physical prime. The demands of being the best knight of the realm had honed his natural strength and athleticism; he was lean and formidably muscular, the legacy of four years of sobriety and damned hard work.

'So,' he said, 'another child. Do we know when it was conceived?'

'She's three months in.'

Ril stared. 'Really?'

'Don't you know? She's your wife!'

Ril flushed. 'Woman's business.' He ran fingers through his hair. 'Three months? I guess she wanted to be sure. I don't think she could bear another miscarriage,' he confessed. 'And if it does happen, I'm done for.' Maybe not a written law, but infertility was grounds for putting him aside.

'I know. I'm sorry.' Basia forced a smile. 'This time, all may be well. She needs you, Ril.'

'Aye,' he said. He met Basia's eyes and knew she knew. Five years was a long time to live a lie – maybe if there'd been children, it would be different, but in the wake of the second miscarriage, something in him had rolled over and died. But despite this, he'd kept his promise to Setallius: he'd given up all his vices and thrown himself into being what Lyra needed, feigning love and desire – but despite all his fidelity and Lyra's adoration, he *didn't* love her.

Admire, yes, and more than ever. Her growth in maturity and judgement and her suitability as ruler was there for all to see. She still made mistakes, but her grasp of leadership improved with every law she debated, every issue she grappled with. Intellectually, she'd left him far behind. And her beauty was still waxing . . .

But in all other ways they'd disappointed each other. She had no interest in physical pursuits and feared exposing her lack of the gnosis, so she shunned riding or flying, pastimes he loved. Her passion was mental stimulus, but he couldn't keep up. There was little room for play and laughter, and increasingly they'd been throwing themselves into their separate domains; Lyra at court, he among the fighting men. They barely talked now.

Her prissy disapproval when he swore or blasphemed or criticised the Church rankled – she was too devout, too reliant on priests to tell her whether she did right or wrong. And now that snake Ostevan was back, and that troubled him too. And in the bedroom . . . they hadn't drifted apart, because they'd never really found each other.

Ril had been introduced to lovemaking by women who used their bodies with freedom, and they'd left him with desires that Lyra blanched at. She found his attempts to pleasure her with fingers or tongue degrading. Kisses and penetration were acceptable, but little else – and never vigorous and always beneath the covers. Lovemaking had become all about procreation, something they did in the phase of the moon when she was fertile. To her, it was still sinful. If there was some well of passion in her, he'd never found a way to uncap it.

With Jenet, he remembered hungrily, it was all about the pleasure. It was never dull.

'Boredom is a marriage-killer,' he used to tell Gryff and Larik, when he thought he'd never get married himself, and now he knew that was true. The biggest test came after the miscarriages, when the whispers began – *It's Endarion's fault – he's never fathered a bastard in all his years of whoring – his seed is thin, malformed. He must be put aside!* – and Larik and Gryff had reappeared, bottles in hand. His discipline slipped, just a little, as they laughed and joked about the old times, old flames and escapades. Temptations 'appeared' ... But this was Pallas, and there were eyes everywhere.

Kore help me, I've been strong ... To his shame, he realised that he wouldn't be unhappy if Lyra were forced to put him aside as infertile. *At least then I could live again* ...

'Ril,' Basia said gently, interrupting his gloomy reverie, 'I really believe that this time, everything will work out.'

He forced a grin. 'Of course it will! Third time is the charm, right?' But all the way up the stairs, his thoughts were of Jenet, and all that he'd given up for Lyra and House Corani.

When he entered the Royal Suite, though, he showed nothing but delight. He brushed through the congratulations and into the bedchamber, past that reptile Ostevan, to his wife's side. 'Lyra, my darling,' he said, kneeling and taking her hand. 'Well done.'

'All I did was lie there,' she said shyly.

Yes, and that's part of the problem. But he laughed dutifully. 'This time all will be well.'

'This time,' she agreed, her voice a mixture of hope and dread.

'It'll be a new start for us.' He kissed her belly, in accordance with tradition, and loudly said, 'May Kore bless us with a son!'

There was a resounding, '*KORE VENDEI!*', the traditional plea for Kore's blessing.

After that they accepted congratulations and well-wishes, until the crowd parted to allow two golden-haired figures, faces still plump with

163

puppy-fat, to approach. Ril disliked both of them: Cordan Sacrecour was sly, with a way of asking apparently childish questions that were designed to draw out unpleasant truths, while Coramore had a tongue snide beyond her years. Neither had gained the gnosis yet, but that couldn't be far away, especially in Cordan's case. They were Lyra's wards, and he knew people were speculating about what might transpire if Cordan attained manhood without Lyra producing an heir. He was almost fourteen now, with spots on his cheeks and the first hint of whiskers. His twelve-year-old sister had a puckered little mouth and piercing green eyes. They always left Ril feeling profoundly uneasy.

The royal children entered the bedchamber and made the correct obeisance. 'Congratulations, Aunty Lyra,' Cordan said, his voice high, piping. He was a fine singer, apparently.

Perhaps we should take his balls before they drop, like a Lantric castrato.

'We hope everything goes well *this time*,' Coramore added, making Lyra flinch.

'Thank you for your kind wishes,' she replied, extending her right hand so the children had to kiss it. 'It's so nice that we can be a family,' she added, with a hint of assertiveness.

Constant's children smiled fixedly.

'Let's have a portrait painted of the four of us,' Lyra suggested. 'That will give me something to do while I'm in confinement. Something lovely to hang on the wall, for the ages.'

'Lovely,' Cordan echoed while Coramore eyed Ril, clearly not wanting her image preserved with his for posterity.

'Won't we all be too busy?' Ril asked, no keener on the idea than the Sacrecour children. Then servants bearing platters of wine and food swept in, a goblet was pressed into his hand and by the time Ril turned back, the children had wandered off.

'Milady, I'm so pleased for you,' Jenet Brunlye said, gliding into the room, a gaggle of young women in her train. Ril caught his breath at the sight of her in her new red dress, and he wasn't the only one. He caught a whispered conversation between two young fops behind him.

'Sweet Kore's codpiece, I like the look of her!'

'She's Jenet Brunlye – the court slut. Play your cards right and you'll get to

enjoy every inch of her – but I warn you, she's damned expensive. Worth the cost though – you've never met a woman so enraptured with fornication—'

Ril closed his ears as her eyes brushed over him, and for the tiniest moment, they were alone in the universe once again. *Jenet, remember when . . .?*

They'd been of an age, ambitious, fresh from the Arcanum. He was still traumatised from the ordeals of 909 and she'd healed a part of his soul. He'd fallen for her totally, until he'd discovered that he wasn't the only one, just someone for her to practise her charms upon. As his star waned, so too did her interest in him – but somehow they'd gone through hatred and back to liking, coming to respect each other's ability to survive at court, without ever losing the cynicism their affair had engendered in each other. Most nights, his last thoughts were still of her.

Then Basia plucked at his sleeve. 'It's better if you keep your eyes on your wife alone, Ril dear. Don't give this rabble yet another chance to gossip.'

'He's a buffoon,' Cordan noted, watching Ril Endarion. 'He wasn't bred to this and it shows.'

Coramore sniggered. 'They're like the Fate-Cards: he's the Fool and Lyra's the Innocent. Lucia would've eaten them for breakfast.' They'd both been terrified of their grandmother, but enormously proud of her too.

The impromptu celebration of the Queen's conception was becoming increasingly loud and flirtatious. Cordan still didn't quite understand why men chased women, though he was beginning to find something *interesting* in Lady Jenet Brunlye's laughter. He always felt a little breathless when she was near.

'I don't dislike Lyra,' he commented. 'She'd make a perfectly service-able nun. But we're doomed to grow up watching her and her children rule while we die forgotten.'

'Just led out occasionally, like old horses, to show how benevolent and generous she is.' Coramore scowled. 'We have to escape somehow.'

'Exactly.' Cordan scowled back. 'When will Uncle Garod come for us?'

That question had been on their lips for nearly five years, but it remained unanswered. At first they'd been kept hidden, but since Duchess Radine of Coraine had died, they'd been permitted to attend court, under strong guard and confined to certain areas of the Bastion. Thanks to the miscarriages, Cordan was still next in line for the throne, and Lyra had begun summoning them for awkward conversations about how they were really all the same family.

No, Cordan thought viciously, *you're just a Corani-Argundian mongrel, and we'll see your head on a spike one day.*

Coramore nudged him and pointed out Ostevan Comfateri. 'Look who's back: the lizard who betrayed us. We'd be emperor and empress if not for him.'

Coramore's misunderstanding of her own place in the succession amused Cordan. When he took the throne, he wanted someone else entirely beside him. *Someone pretty, like Lady Jenet . . .*

Abruptly Cordan was sick of watching people celebrating a pregnancy that was going to ruin his life. 'Come on, let's go. Where's Mutthead?'

'Mutthead' was Sir Bruss Lamgren, a bald, bushy-bearded mage-knight whose job it was to follow the pair of them around. They cornered him and told him, 'We're bored now. We want to go.'

Lamgren grunted, put down his goblet and followed them out the door. He was, Cordan was convinced, stupid as cowshit, but he suspected he reported all their conversations to the one man he truly feared here: the Wraith, Dirklan Setallius.

They were halfway up the stairs when the dizziness struck him. All at once, Cordan was seeing triple and his bones seemed to be draining marrow. He gasped and clutched the railing to stop himself falling. In an instant Coramore was there, supporting him. 'Cordi? *Cordi—!*'

'Uh,' he moaned, bile rising up his throat like a flooding drain, then suddenly he was vomiting red wine and half-digested pastries over the stairs.

Mutthead grunted, 'You drunk, boy?'

'No!' he gasped, humiliated, 'I only had one cup. But I feel . . . *really* strange.'

'Help us!' Coramore demanded, cradling her brother against her, wiping his face with her sleeve and whispering, 'It's okay, it's okay.'

A pair of boot heels clicked on the stairs, then the Wraith himself was standing over him, his one cold eye staring into his face while he gripped Cordan's chin in his gauntleted left hand. 'Hold still, boy! Let me see—'

'What is it?' Coramore demanded, a note of hysteria in her voice. 'Have you *poisoned* him?'

'No, he's perfectly fine,' Setallius drawled. 'Congratulations, Cordan. You've just gained the gnosis.'

The gnosis . . . I've come into my powers! If he hadn't been passing out, Cordan would have swooned in joy.

Setallius summoned servants to help him to his room. 'Just keep drinking water and you'll come right in a few hours,' he told him. 'I'll notify the Keepers and they'll send someone to assess you. Then it'll be off to the Arcanum with you.'

Cordan couldn't tell if the Wraith was angry or pleased at this momentous change in his life.

When they were alone, he shared a look with Coramore, who was fighting to hold back tears; she dreaded being parted. They'd lived their entire lives together. 'You'll gain yours too, any day,' he told her, though she likely wouldn't for years.

'You'll go off to the Arcanum and leave me here to *die*,' she whimpered.

He tried to argue, but the nausea and an onrushing migraine put paid to that; instead he collapsed back into his pillow, the room swimming about him.

When he woke, Coramore was asleep in a chair, her thumb in her mouth and her hair a mess, and there was a woman sitting in the armchair beside the bed. His sudden thrill of fear was blended with confused wanting.

'Hush,' Lady Jenet Brunlye whispered. 'Be quiet. I don't have much time.' There was a nimbus of light around her.

Her aura, he realised. *I'm seeing her gnostic aura!*

Lady Jenet took his hand and pressed it to her lips. 'Don't be afraid, Cordan. I've come from your Uncle Garod. I'm here to help you. And you've gained the gnosis: how does it feel?'

His heart thrilled at her words. *She's come from Uncle Garod! I knew she was special!* Her hands on his made his whole body tingle. 'I feel strange,' he confessed. 'Dizzy.'

'That's normal: it'll pass as you learn to master it.'

He glanced around the room. 'How did you get past the guards?'

'I didn't come in that way.' Jenet caressed his cheek. 'Are you ambitious, Cordan?'

Her touch was like silk. He could scarcely breathe. 'I suppose, yes,' he stammered.

'And are you ready to learn the gnosis?'

'I can't wait!'

'It'll make a man of you,' Jenet whispered, her perfume washing over him as she bent close, so close she could have kissed him. 'It'll give you the power to seize your birthright.'

Cordan looked around, scared. Was this a trap set by sinister old Setallius? But his brain couldn't think beyond her enticing smell and touch.

'We're going to free you and Coramore soon,' she told him. 'Garod is preparing. Be ready.'

Cordan swallowed. 'But wouldn't that—?'

'Start a war? Perhaps. And would that be so wrong, when the cause is the overthrow of a usurper? Stay vigilant,' she whispered, her breath tickling his ear. 'And when the time comes, you and your sister must do exactly as I say.' She pressed her lips to his forehead, and then – thrillingly – to his lips. Then she was out of reach, vanishing behind a tapestry and gone, the click of a hidden latch the only sound.

Cordan lay back, trembling with desire, fear and ambition.

10

Homecoming

Mollachia

Our mission took us into a small kingdom wedged into the mountains bordering the vast Schlessen forests, peopled by a strange, superstitious people who claim to be born of the earth itself. They have been slow to accept Kore into their hearts, but I have hopes that they will come to know his love.

BROTHER DEVHRO, KORE MISSIONARY, MOLLACHIA, 713

Pontus and Sydia, Yuros
Aprafor 935

Seventeen years ago, Kyrik and Valdyr Sarkany had crossed the Pontic Sea, riding across the famous Leviathan Bridge, that incredible straight line of stone running three hundred miles to link Yuros to Antiopia. They'd believed they were destined for glory, a sixteen-year-old barely trained battle-mage and a nine-year-old boy with no gnosis at all. Looking back, Kyrik could barely believe their naïveté.

They returned on a trading-dhou, a Keshi windship piloted by a Keshi Air-mage, a young woman wrapped in a bekira-shroud. The small craft had a crew of just four, but it was a struggle to stay out of their way.

Since finding his brother, Kyrik's life had been a blur: Paruq had kept his promise, even commissioning passage back to Yuros for them. At the end of the Third Crusade, the Ordo Costruo had not just regained control of the Bridge but had unlocked new energies to command the sky above – there were stories of them unleashing lightning to destroy the Rondian Emperor's windfleet. Kyrik wasn't sure he believed that, but flying over the Pontic Sea was no longer something one did without permission from the order – and paying for the privilege.

They'd had to fly to Southpoint Tower, an immense pinnacle of shaped stone on the north coast of Dhassa, to have their cargo inspected. A metal panel had been fixed to the mast, enabling the tower magi to identify the vessel, but the magi had ignored the passengers.

'They've no real interest beyond the security of the Bridge,' Paruq had said. 'I suppose if the sultan came here they might look askance, but you're going home, and I'm just humble Paruq, the trader.'

Kyrik had found a perch in the prow which was draughty, but offered the best views. Valdyr had simply taken his six-foot frame into a corner, rolled into a blanket and closed his eyes. He still looked far from healthy; his body was all sinew, and his grey-slate eyes were cold as mountain peaks. It was hard to reconcile this grim, haunted man with the joyful boy he'd been.

'If you hoped to see the Bridge, my friend, you will be disappointed.' Paruq joined him, his cheeks ruddy from the wind. 'The seas are high, and the Bridge is far below the surface.'

'It's a Sunsurge year,' Kyrik pointed out, and at Paruq's questioning gaze, added, 'it's what we call the middle years between Moontides, when the seas are at their highest and the rainfall doubles. In Mollachia the snows are deepest in a Sunsurge winter.'

'During such years the wet seasons in Ahmedhassa are longer – a blessing.'

Kyrik laughed. 'The Sunsurge is a curse at home.'

Home. There was that word again. He could think of little else. Even Valdyr was excited, Kyrik thought, though his brother's emotions remained bottled up inside him. *Something damaged him badly. Was it the slave-camps or the breeding-house?* He prayed that being home and among his own people would heal his soul.

'So where will you set us down?' he asked Paruq. 'Pontus?' Pontus was at the southeast tip of Yuros; it would mean a long ride to Mollachia.

Paruq smiled. 'I think we can do better than that. How does the Bunavian Gap sound?'

Kyrik stared. 'Really? That would take hundreds of miles off our journey – but surely a Keshi craft isn't permitted so far into Yuros? And why would you even take us so far?'

Paruq chuckled. 'Your empire ignores Pontus and the East entirely, except during the Moontide. A trader is free to go anywhere he can make money. Keshi traders have been dealing with the Sydian tribes for some time.'

'The Sydians? But they're savages—'

'All men were savages once, even Mollachs,' Paruq chided. 'They are a primitive people, true, but open to change. And their horse-stock is incredible.'

'When did you become interested in horses?'

'I'm not. My interest is only to see you well on your way.'

The young pilot-mage chewed betel-leaf and sniffed powdered opium constantly to keep herself awake during the two days and nights it took to cross the sea. Despite being the only mage in the crew, she was very much the junior, barked at by the captain and snapped at if she fumbled a tack. When Kyrik finally realised that she was close to exhaustion, he helped recharge the keel – he hadn't the skill to pilot her craft, but he could at least do that.

They rested two nights in Pontus, which wasn't the bustling place he'd expected; Paruq told him it only filled up during the Moontide. But the city was still very diverse, with new Keshi and Dhassan quarters as well as areas peopled mostly by Rondians and other Western nations. Everyone was a trader, everything had a price, and there was a seedy air of avarice. Dhassan and Keshi whores, the discarded wives of soldiers, filled the streets, and the city watch didn't venture outside the central environs where the wealthy dwelt. Kyrik was glad to move on.

'I'm surprised how many Easterners live here,' he remarked to Paruq as their dhou rose into the air and tacked westwards.

'The Ordo Costruo have guaranteed no more Crusades will cross the Bridge. People are preparing for the next trading season, believing it will be safe.' Paruq frowned. 'I am not so sure: there are many old wounds to heal before anything like true peace can return.'

They left Pontus and followed the Imperial Road west, inland of the coastal ranges. The road was virtually empty, with just the occasional well-guarded caravan traversing the ancient trade-route; they were the only windvessel in the sky. A cold northerly forced them to wrap up tightly, and not just at night when they landed so that the strung-out pilot-mage could sleep.

'I saw snow on peaks to the north,' Valdyr commented the second night as they sat beside their campfire. 'It will have been a hard winter at home.'

'Ai,' Kyrik answered absently, making his brother frown.

'You're not in Kesh any more. "Ysh", Brother – remember?'

Mostly they'd been speaking Rondian to each other, the language of the legions and the slave-camps. They'd not heard their own language since they left Mollachia all those years ago. But now, Mollach words were stealing into their speech, a foretaste of home.

'Ysh,' Kyrik conceded, passing Valdyr a chicken leg. They shared a silent meal, Valdyr content with the silence, until finally, Kyrik said, 'I'm sorry.'

Valdyr glanced at him, but made no response. Mollach men weren't supposed ever to be sorry: *no regrets, no remorse*. Mollachia was too hard and unforgiving a place to waste energy on what might have been. You made your decision and lived – or died – with it.

He doesn't forgive me, and why should he? He never had a Paruq to rescue and guide him. He ran fingers through his blond hair, and unconsciously, Valdyr mirrored the gesture, combing his thick black mane away from his face. Their different colouring existed in many Mollach families: Mollachia had been settled first by the so-called Stonefolk, a Yothic people, the first race of western Yuros, then Andressans, led by Zlateyr the Archer, had moved into the valley. After initial warfare, the two groups, the fair and the dark, had put aside their differences, so the tales went.

Kyrik tapped his chin, seeking to spark a conversation. 'I suppose I shall have to grow moustaches, now we're returning home.' It was the custom in Mollachia to go clean-chinned in summer, bearded in winter, but luxuriant moustaches were prized year-round. Kyrik had been too young when he went on Crusade to grow either, and in Ahmedhassa, he'd gone clean-shaven. 'You'll have no problem – you have a pelt just like Father,' he told Valdyr, trying to raise a smile. *Having a pelt* was considered a masculine virtue in bitterly cold Mollachia.

Valdyr's face remained dour. 'You wrote to Father – when?'

'At the end of last year. He was well, but he spoke of tax debts.' Kyrik glanced towards the hold, where a small chest of bullion was secreted among his possessions. 'Paruq's given me money to help—'

'Why would a Keshi give you money?' Valdyr demanded.

'It's just a gift, nothing more, from one friend to another.'

Valdyr glowered at the Godspeaker, who was leading prayers for three of the crew while the pilot-girl cooked. 'What did you do when you were taken from the breeding-house?'

'Mostly, I learned. Paruq is a Godspeaker, welcome wherever he goes – so I was taken to Shaliyah and shown their holy places. He's taken me all over the East. He wanted me and the other Yurosi whose release he'd secured to be a bridge between East and West. He persuaded his superiors that there were benefits in giving a select group of Yurosi prisoners – those with influence in their homelands – an understanding of Eastern ways, so that when we returned to Yuros, we could speak against the Crusades. All the others have long since returned. I stayed on, looking for you.'

Valdyr looked up at him, his face haunted. 'Never trust them, Brother – especially not their filthy priests. I know what they're like when they get their claws into—' Suddenly Valdyr's mouth snapped shut; he hurled his chicken bone in the fire and stomped away.

Kyrik stared after him, thinking, *Did he just admit—? Oh Hel . . .*

The Bunavian Gap, Yuros
Febreux 935

The wind-dhou dropped through swirling clouds, lashed by a fierce northeasterly. The crew were hauling in the sails while Kyrik helped the pilot-mage adjust the tiller. The exhausted girl seemed to regard him as some kind of demi-god just for helping her. Her eyes were glazed and she was trembling constantly, but she still brought the craft down with practised skill.

Poor thing, how does she live like this? Arguing her rights had been fruitless: she was a woman and her place was to serve, according to the captain.

Even a few hundred feet above the ground, visibility was poor, just snatches of bare plains and an occasional tantalising glimpse of herds of horses. They were a week out of Pontus and had bypassed all the major cities of Verelon as they followed the Imperial Road into the west. Thantis, Cypinos and Spinitius were all behind them, as was Dusheim, westernmost of the Rondian fortress-cities. At the head of the Brekaellen Valley they tacked north against the prevailing winds. Kyrik was vaguely stunned that a Keshi windship could travel so freely in Yuros, but Paruq appeared to be right: as far as the Rondian Empire were concerned, there was nothing out here.

Then the dhou dropped below the clouds, and he caught his breath. They were above a vast Sydian camp, a city of painted tents. Huge pens of horses and cattle fringed the sea of canvas and leather. Gaggles of children sprinted this way and that, and the stench of smoke and waste hit him. Eerily, the wail of a Godsinger carried across the scene, coming from a stone cairn wound about in long white ribbons: a makeshift dom-al'Ahm.

Valdyr mouthed a curse, while Kyrik glanced toward Paruq. *The Keshi have sent missionaries into Sydia! Should I rejoice that some savages have found a faith? Or should I be deeply uneasy?*

Right now, he was somewhere between the two, especially when Valdyr turned to him and said, 'This is the beginning of the next great war.'

'It's just one tribe,' he countered. 'It may be the only one.'

'Really?' Valdyr stared coldly at Paruq and stomped to the other end of the dhou.

Kyrik was about to follow when he saw Paruq shake his head. He joined his mentor as the dhou extended its landing legs. 'You should have warned us – this is a shock, even to me. Amteh missionaries in Sydia?'

'If I'd left you in Pontus, you'd have had months on the road, and many dangers to face. Here, you are only a few weeks' ride from your borders. The other side of that coin is that you see our work here: peaceful missionary work.'

'If the Rondians knew of this . . .'

'Kore missionaries have been working the border tribes for centuries. Their skulls are usually mounted on spears to mark hunting territories.' Paruq patted his arm. 'We've lost a few ourselves, but the message of the *Kalistham* seems to resonate more here than the *Book of Kore*.'

'Which parts?'

Paruq smiled wryly. 'The *Book of Kore* describes Sydians as "the embodiment of bestial savagery". Those passages never go down well out here.'

'I can't imagine the Kore missionaries use them—'

'They don't – but we do. I've read the *Book of Kore* cover to cover. Know your enemy, Kyrik.'

'But *Sydians*? They screw publicly for entertainment! They keep slaves and marry multiple wives! They worship animal gods! They're *insane!*'

'Well, they're easing back on drinking and public fornication in return for better steel.'

'You were always a realistic idealist,' Kyrik replied, 'but they've been killing themselves with liquid poison while screwing in front of the campfires since the beginning of time. They'll never accept the Amteh – although I guess you're right: they'll always accept a better sword.'

'A good missionary knows what is solid and what is mutable. We've been converting heathens in Gatioch and Mirobez for centuries and believe me, the Sydians are gentle compared to them. And you know, getting rid of the public sexuality was the easy part,' Paruq chuckled. 'It turns out all a man really wants is to not have his penis size made public knowledge.'

Kyrik smiled at that, but it didn't erase his worry. As the dhou touched down, it was swamped by a sea of Sydian clansmen and women. While the men still wore the dun leathers he'd seen when he'd travelled east all those years ago, he saw that many of the women now favoured a colourful mantle that covered everything except the face.

Like a Keshi bekira-shroud, only in traditional colours and patterns.

The Sydians touched the windcraft reverently, until they saw the

Mollachs. They started crying, '*Rondian! Rondian!*' There was no welcome in the call.

Then the ramp was lowered and Paruq appeared at the top of it. The brothers watched uneasily as the tribesmen dropped to their knees, a wave of reverence extending into the middle distance, then they all stood expectantly.

Paruq recited a greeting in Sydian, and much to Kyrik's surprise, it was possible to follow it – there were many similarities to Mollach in the structure and linking words, and many nouns. It was a statement of greeting and introduction, then the Godspeaker turned to Kyrik and gestured for him to come forward. The Sydians stared up at him, then a grizzled Sydian warrior with bones in his braided hair and his bare chest painted with black and scarlet paste, bellowed out in Rondian, 'Why you bring pigs? Is they slave?'

'No, Nacelnik Thraan. This is no slave: this man is my friend.'

'*Nacelnik?*' Kyrik noted: another shared word, meaning 'headman' in Mollachia too.

'How can Rondian be friend to Amteh priest?' Thraan shouted.

'Not Rondian,' Paruq replied. 'This is Prince Kyrik Sarkany of Mollachia.'

'*Mollach?*' Thraan beetled his brow, then nodded slowly. 'Mollach is better. Mollach good.'

Mollachia had *never* been a password to acceptance in Kyrik's experience, but here somehow it was. Paruq led them down the ramp and they were engulfed by the crowds. The Sydians didn't do a lot of formality, just a mutual drop of the head and a hand-clasp. Thraan's giant paws were so leathery they felt like gauntlets.

'Welcome, Prince of Mollach,' the chief rumbled, and when they were eye to eye, he solemnly kissed both of Kyrik's cheeks. His breath was overpoweringly strong, as was his sour sweaty odour, like a great shaggy bear, but his eyes were clear and vigilant.

Kyrik was scared his brittle younger brother would misstep; Valdyr had a nervous air to him, despite towering above all but the biggest of the Sydian warriors. But he permitted Thraan's embrace with outward equanimity.

Then Thraan clapped Kyrik on the shoulder and said, 'Come, let us drink!'

Amidst a raucous cheer from his warriors, the brothers were led to the massive pavilion of the clan chief. Paruq, forbidden alcohol, went to confer with his missionaries. Kyrik felt like a twig in a river as they were swept inside and seated on firm leather cushions. The tent was of cured leather too, with a central fire-pit. Women and children were gathered around the fire, many of the women openly breastfeeding or changing swaddling: the noise never ceased, though everyone turned to stare curiously at the brothers. Thraan and his sons sat around them, studying them and speaking to each other in rapid Sydian. One of the women brought liquor – a clear fluid served in a thimble-sized cup carved from horn. It didn't really taste of anything, but it hit Kyrik like a punch to the nose and throat.

Thraan laughed and poured more. 'Is good? Ysh? Nii?'

They say 'ysh' and 'nii' ... Kyrik let his eyes drift, watching the faces. Sydians were uniformly black-haired, with an olive-bronze hue to their skin that wouldn't have been out of place in Dhassa. But their eyes were narrower, their cheekbones wider, and linguistically, they were very much of Yuros.

'We are Vlpa clan – Ve-yil-pah – is how you say,' Thraan told him. 'Vlpa, of Uffrykai tribe.' He pointed to a blazon on his tent walls. 'Fox-head, in Rondian.'

'Foxes are good luck in Mollachia, especially white ones,' Kyrik said in Mollach. He was having very little difficulty understanding, or being understood. *Handy ... but strange.*

'Nii, white fox is ghost, not good! Means bad snow, like this year.' Thraan jerked a thumb towards a line of white pelts hanging from a wire. 'Sunsurge, ysh?' He peered at Kyrik and asked, 'Why is Mollach friend to Amteh, eh?'

'He saved me, after I was captured on Crusade, and spared me. We became friends.'

'And you are going back to Mollach, Prince?'

'Ysh. We've been away a very long time.'

'Your father – he is Nacelnik, ysh?'

'Kirol, we say, our word for king. He is Kirol Elgren Sarkany.'

'He is descended of Zillitiya, ysh?'

Valdyr masked a startled snort by downing his drink, while Kyrik looked at the chief in surprise. 'Do you mean Zlateyr? I am honoured that you know the name of a Mollach hero!'

'A nacelnik knows the names of his forefathers! Zillitiya was an Uffrykai under-chief, many Moontides ago. He took many warriors – Vlpa included – into the mountains. He found Mollach.' Thraan raised his cup. 'Perhaps we are kin, ysh?'

'Perhaps we are!' Kyrik said, glancing at Valdyr warningly; his brother was looking far from happy with the notion. But what could have been an awkward moment was avoided when a dusky Sydian woman clad in the traditional leathers of the plains joined them.

Thraan made a respectful gesture, and introduced her. 'Kyrik and Valdyr Sarkany, this is Hajya, head of the Vlpa Sfera: our magi.'

Kyrik's throat went a little dry as he met the woman's world-wise eyes.

'Welcome to the Vlpa lands, Sarkany Lords.' She accepted a bone thimble, and he realised she alone among the women was drinking. Her voice had a husky sensuality, emphasised by her voluptuous grace of movement. 'You are mage, ysh?' she asked.

Kyrik nodded; he guessed she'd been observing his aura before approaching. 'Quarter-blood.'

'Strong,' Hajya approved, 'like me.'

I suppose to these people, quarter-blood is strong, Kyrik thought, meeting Hajya's brown eyes. Sydian women had a special kind of notoriety in Yuros: for many generations they'd been hurling themselves at Rondian magi, seeking to get with child, then disappearing back to their clan. The strength of the Sfera was often the strength of the clan.

'You and I must talk,' Hajya purred, all confident sensuality. She was perhaps his senior, handsome rather than pretty; her face had a leathery, lived-in quality, but with sparkling eyes and plump lips. 'Is seldom a fellow mage visits outside of the Moontide years.' She turned her gaze to Valdyr. 'Two is a great boon.'

Valdyr visibly cringed under her appraising stare; he threw back another shot of the liquor.

Kyrik suddenly felt like a slave on the block in the souks of Peroz; or a stud-beast at the cattle market. 'We can't stay long. We're journeying home to Mollachia, after many years away.'

'Since the last Crusade,' Thraan put in, and Kyrik let the misapprehension stand.

Hajya's eyes lingered on Kyrik with mercantile assessment. In her world, a passing mage was always an opportunity. 'Would you like a fertile young woman to enjoy during your stay?' she offered, as if proffering a great treat.

Valdyr's face went stiff, and Kyrik put a hand on his arm. 'That won't be necessary,' he replied, politely but firmly. He'd had his fill of such encounters; Valdyr's revulsion ran even deeper.

Hajya sighed regretfully, but raised her cup. 'May your lives be long and your children plentiful.'

They drank to that, and many other things as the evening wore on. A troupe of warriors brought in a spit-roasted bullock and platters of root vegetables cooked in spicy peppered gravy. There were songs, though – much to Kyrik's relief – none of the sexual displays travellers passing through Sydian always spoke of. Perhaps Paruq was right; they'd been overstated by those who wrote travel memoirs. But the liquor never stopped flowing. Then the drums started.

As the first of the drummers slapped the big hide-wrapped cylinders cradled on their knees, Hajya and a dozen other women rose to their feet with a sudden flex of their leg muscles, like deer springing into motion. All were Sfera, Kyrik realised from the periapts revealed as they shed the colourful bekira-robes to reveal thin leather shifts that barely covered chest and hips.

Valdyr threw him an alarmed look, and again he had to pat his younger brother's arm and shake his head, trusting in Paruq that this would be nothing that offended decency.

Bam-taka, bam-taka-taka, the drums went, and, '*Huy-huy*,' the men chanted as the women caught the rhythm in their hips, wriggling sinuously to the centre of the pavilion. Those watching clapped hands in time as they formed a circle, facing outwards, chests thrown forward, heads thrown back, black hair loose and flowing, bellies rippling and hips thrusting, then reversing the movement and throwing their heads forward so they were hunched beings with no faces, just curtains of black hair. Feet stamped and arms wove complex patterns, pulling aside the strands of hair to give glimpses of savagely grinning faces and rounded, fierce eyes. All the time the drums hammered away.

Kyrik found himself watching breathlessly, his eyes drawn first to the gyrating, thrusting hips, the flex of the thighs and the breasts straining at the leather shifts, and then the faces as they were revealed, then concealed again. The women spun and flowed about each other so that each in turn danced before the whole of the tent. Around him the men shouted and laughed, Thraan hurling comments with the rest of them, then the dance paused, each woman tossed her head and thrust out a hand into the crowd of watching men.

Hajya's hand was beckoning him, her face imperious, demanding.

She doesn't take no for an answer, Kyrik thought, but with Valdyr beside him, this wasn't something he could do, even had he not been over-whelmed by the alien nature of it all. He shook his head firmly.

Hajya's eyes flashed in contempt, then she chose another man and pulled him to her. Hands were grasped all around the circle of couples, each pair a rhythmic confrontation: arms touching, hips brushing, cheeks stroking cheeks, chests pressed then spinning away; the facial expressions challenging, demanding, in increasingly inti-mate movements.

Kyrik felt Valdyr rise abruptly and push his way through the crowd, but he was transfixed, watching Hajya with a big, graceful warrior with forked beard and plaited hair, who moved with her with prac-tised grace. He could see they had done this, and much more, all their lives.

Then the drums reached a crescendo and as they thudded into silence, the dancers froze. He found his mouth dry, his hair standing on end, as he stared over Hajya's partner's shoulder and into her eyes. She raised her chin, as if some kind of superiority had been established, then kissed the cheeks of her partner and gave up the floor.

The women were loudly applauded as they sat again and Thraan slapped Kyrik's shoulder. 'None of the Sfera may wed,' he shouted in

Kyrik's ear. 'Their bodies must always be open, to strengthen the clan. Hajya is strong: she has borne seven mage-children.' Then he noticed Valdyr's absence. 'Your brother, he don't like dance?'

Kyrik read disapproval in the question. 'The drink – it's strong. We've had none for years.'

'Aah!' Thraan laughed, slapping his shoulder again, 'it's strong, *ysh* – here, have more!'

When Kyrik was finally able to leave, several dances and innumerable drinks later, two of Thraan's sons had to help him.

Zillitiya . . . Zlateyr . . . I must ask Paruq, was Kyrik's final thought as he closed his eyes on the spinning world.

Sometime before dawn, Valdyr moaned and rolled over. He was sweating under a pile of blankets and his guts felt rotten from the rich meat and unaccustomed liquor. Moonlight still bathed the plains and the camp was silent, or as silent as such a large number of close-pressed humans could be. Outside his blankets the air was gelid and his breath frosted in clouds.

His gut rumbled again, and now his bladder was protesting too, so he rolled free, found the copper bowl in the corner, knelt and peed. His urine steamed hotly, the stench roiled his stomach further and he vomited into the bowl.

'That bad, eh?' Kyrik chuckled from the gloom. 'There's a godor outside the flap.'

Waste hole's a good description for Sydia, Valdyr thought as he found the foetid hole, uncovered it and emptied the bowl, then he crawled back to his blankets, chilled by his few seconds outside. He left the flap open to let the moonlight in, so he could see Kyrik.

'When do we leave?' he asked.

'As soon as we can,' Kyrik replied. 'But it's not so bad, really.'

'Not as bad as a slave-gang,' Valdyr conceded, massaging his temples, which had begun to throb. 'Sweet Kore, I've not drunk liquor in . . . I think during a Noorie festival two years ago, one of the overseers slipped me a flask of fenni for my work-gang, enough for one swallow each. Before that . . . Hel, I don't know.'

'I remember the Midrea IV rankers giving you beer in the evenings – I was so angry.'

'It didn't hurt me.'

'I suppose not.' Kyrik rubbed his eyes. 'Mother used to scold Father if he gave me wine at table, remember? "The boy's too young to become another drunkard!" she'd shout.'

Mother . . . Valdyr pictured a blonde woman with a sad, bitter voice. Dania D'Augene, last child of a bastard line of one of the oldest mage families of Midrea, now debt-crippled and landless. When rumour reached Mollachia that certain Houses were open to approaches from non-magi of wealth, Elgren Sarkany had gone into Augenheim with a purse of gems for her uncle, and brought her back to bleak, ice-bound Hegikaro. Dania had been fourteen and virginal. She'd had her gnosis Chained – allegedly with her consent – so that she wouldn't be a danger to her husband, and had eventually given the king two heirs, seven years apart. She'd died five winters later. Valdyr couldn't remember a day she didn't cry. She was small and skinny, capable of bird-like vibrancy and sudden fits of temper. She came alive in summer, but barely left her rooms in winter.

Mother, Mother, he thought sadly. *Father must have despised you – he spent all that money to bring the gnosis into the family, but all he got were two missing sons.*

'Hey, remember how we used to learn those Midrean harvest songs, to cheer her up?' Kyrik recalled. 'And all those lowland dances she tried to make us learn?'

'I remember – I remember I had to dance with skinny Sezkia Zhagy!'

'Hel, I'd forgotten her! *Egy csinosa barana!*'

'A "cute lamb"? Did you just call her a cute lamb?'

'It's what we called pretty girls, back then,' Kyrik laughed, then he said, 'Brother, the dancing last night? It was nothing – Paruq was right, those old travellers' stories about this place were exaggerated. And I'm not having that Sfera bitch telling *us* who to sleep with.'

Valdyr closed his eyes in relief. The thought of copulating for the breeding wants of yet another group of dark-skinned savages revolted him, even five years after escaping the breeding-house. *I don't think I'll ever want a woman again. That's the scar you left, Asiv . . .*

Collistein, Kedron Valley, Yuros
Martrois 935

Kyrik nudged his heels into the flanks of his mare and she jolted into motion once more, Valdyr following. There was no easy road into Mollachia, but the lowland route meant travelling the length of the Kedron Valley to Augenheim, then east along the banks of the Reztu, another four hundred miles. Instead, they'd headed for the Rondian fortress at Collistein; this was their second day of steadily slogging through the foothills of the Matra Ranges. Although the gorge trail into Mollachia would be blocked by snow now, there were windskiffs in Collistein. They were expensive, but they had funds.

They'd left the Vlpa clan after three nights, and it was a relief to go, in truth. For all he'd got along with Thraan, and the unsettling Hajya had kept her distance once she realised that he was sincere about not lying with a clanswoman, Valdyr's unease in the Sydian camp was almost palpable and Kyrik realised he had to get him out.

A low horn-blast from ahead wrenched Kyrik back to the present: the low grey clouds momentarily parted and he saw stone ramparts amidst the jagged stone ahead.

'Look! We're almost in Collistein!' He picked up the pace as rain began to sting his cheeks, and was grateful to reach the gates before the downpour really began. Seven bells tolled inside, marking the time; it might be the seventh hour since dawn but it was as dark as evening, and clearly not going to get any lighter.

'Halt!' the legionary standing sentry called. Collistein was primarily a legion camp, protecting mining operations. 'Names?' He eyed them suspiciously.

The brothers had debated giving false names, but Mollachia was part of the empire, and the Sarkany name might even open doors here. 'I'm Kyrik Sarkany of Mollachia, and this is my brother Valdyr, returned from Crusade.'

'Sarkany?' The sentry muttered something to his fellow, who hurried off. 'Wait here.'

There was nothing to be gained from doing otherwise, so Kyrik settled for dismounting, to give his aching muscles some respite. Valdyr followed suit, looking around warily. The sentry returned in a few minutes with a red-cloaked battle-mage, a balding man with a no-nonsense manner. He surveyed them, then came forward, extending a hand. 'Kyrik Sarkany, the son of King Elgren? I'm Secundus Url Rudman, of Midrea VII.'

'I'm Kyrik,' Kyrik confirmed. 'This is my brother Valdyr.'

'My men are confused,' Rudman said. 'We understood the Sarkany brothers had died in the Second Crusade? I take it you have proofs of your identity?'

'Of course,' Kyrik replied. He wiped the rain off his face and added, 'Inside perhaps?'

'Of course, come in,' Rudman replied, indicating the doors, while nodding to himself, possibly in response to an unseen communication from another mage. Suddenly the open gates began to look a little like a trap.

You're being paranoid, Kyrik told himself, *and anyway, we have no choice.*

He nudged his weary mare through the gatehouse into an empty courtyard beyond. He glimpsed open shutters and people watching, but most of his attention focused on the line of legionaries, a full cohort of twenty, standing in formation in the middle of the open space. They had javelins at the ready and their square shields deployed protectively: not a welcoming sight. He looked at Valdyr warningly and muttered, 'Don't do anything sudden.'

'I'll see those proofs now,' Rudman said.

Kyrik dismounted and handed over a thick envelope which contained the identification tokens he'd carried all through the Second Crusade, recovered by Paruq from the breeding-house. Rudman was studying them when a woman's crisp voice said, 'I'll see those.'

She had a stubborn-looking freckled face, short-cropped ginger hair and hazel eyes, and she strode into the courtyard like a man. Her green tunic had a badge of a stag in a ring of laurels. Rudman handed her the papers deferentially. 'Please, dismount,' she said to Valdyr. There was no direct threat in her voice, but her left hand was on her sword-hilt.

Valdyr complied reluctantly, then she turned to Kyrik. 'You're the elder brother, yes? We understood you both to be dead. It's been what, seventeen years?'

He smiled; perhaps charm would soften her attitude. 'It's been a while. You'd have been – what, four or five when we left on Crusade?'

'A little older,' she grunted. 'Where have you been?'

'We were captured and held by the Keshi until recently, when our release was secured.'

The woman's eyes narrowed. 'A prisoner of the Keshi,' she said appraisingly, clearly knowing what that implied. 'Were you ransomed?'

'No, released, through the agency of the Ordo Costruo.' It made a better tale than the truth. 'And you are—?'

She hesitated, then answered, 'Sacrista Delestre. My father is Lord Delestre of Augenheim. My brother Robear and I are his acknowledged bastards.' She gave his papers a cursory glance, then handed them back to Rudman. 'Documents are just paper – I must satisfy myself that you are who you claim myself.' She raised her right hand, kindling a faint gnosis-light at her fingertips. 'I am a theurgist, primarily a mesmerist: mental scanning is my forte. If you please?'

It was the moment of trust. Either he allowed her to enter his surface thoughts – knowing that if he did, he would have little recourse if she attacked him once inside his mental defences – or they took their chances trying to fight their way out.

We should have taken the long road. Valdyr was clearly no happier than he, but the reality was that they would just as likely faced a similar scene as they passed by Augenheim. *What choice do we have?*

He met Sacrista's eyes: greenish-brown eyes, the prettiest thing about her, and weighed her up. Women who could fight were rare, even among magi, but those who could were every bit as dangerous as a man. And they often held a grudge against every man who'd tried to prove them weak. She would have her own catalogue of those who'd tried to beat her in the arena, or assaulted her more privately. Sometimes her defences might not have been enough. There was a brittleness to her that spoke of violence and abuse endured and never forgiven.

Perhaps we have that in common. He nodded, and opened his mental shields.

Her face swelled to fill his consciousness; her eyes like giant moons bored into him intently. As always when gnosis-touched, he felt an intense sense of her, a sensation like being brushed with her sweat and musk in a salty, tangy rush; then she said, <*Yes, it's him.*>

With a searing jab of pain, his vision flashed pure white, then the darkness rushed in.

Hegikaro, Mollachia, Yuros
Martrois 935

Valdyr woke to a rattling sound, and the whole world lurched. Horses snorted, a gridline of square boxes of light flashed overhead and silver light stabbed his eyes painfully. He groaned and rolled over to escape the glare, and found Kyrik lying beside him on a wooden floor that was rocking backwards and forwards. His elder brother's face was vacant, his mouth open and eyes closed, but his chest rose and fell. Valdyr's own body was a mass of bruises and welts and deep throbbing pain. His nose was swollen – it felt broken – and a gash on his forehead had barely started scabbing over. He remembered trying to fight when light burst from Sacrista's hand, felling Kyrik, but Rudman had downed him with contemptuous ease.

He'd heard the battle-mage scoffing, 'He couldn't even engage his gnosis!' as the guardsmen had closed in and pummelled him halfway into the next life.

Then Sacrista was standing over him, reaching down and touching his cut forehead. <*Join your brother, Valdyr,*> she'd whispered, and slapped his mind into oblivion.

Now where are we? He peered through scrunched-up eyes and realised the boxes of light were actually the gaps in the bars of a cage, and then he saw a mast and furled sails. Horses whinnied as the floor below him lurched – they were being unloaded from a windship. The air was bitingly cold, and there were wolves howling in the distance, a sound he'd not heard since childhood. He pulled himself to his knees and looked around. The cage had been lowered onto a wagon hitched to two big, shaggy horses with feathered hooves: wain-horses. He hadn't seen a wain-horse in seventeen years. Legionaries in the Delestre livery were everywhere, but when he looked beyond them, the moonlight revealed a landscape that had haunted his dreams for two decades: Hegikaro Castle, perched on the shores of a glowing dish of reflected moonlight – Lake Droszt. The town huddling about the skirts of the castle was dotted by occasional dimly lit windows.

Mollachia . . . He blinked back tears. *We've come home.*

Her orange hair gleaming in the moonlight, Sacrista Delestre appeared above him, leaning from her saddle to peer into the cage. She made a gesture, and Kyrik jolted awake.

Valdyr's temper flashed. 'What are you doing? These are our lands! When Father sees—'

'Your father's dead,' Sacrista replied in a stony voice.

'What? No, he can't be . . .' Kyrik murmured. When he looked up at Sacrista, there was a childlike look of betrayal on his face. 'What happened to him?'

'He died earlier this year,' Sacrista replied. 'He owed debts to the banks in Augenheim, which my father purchased, along with the tax-farming rights to Mollachia. In all practical senses, your lands belong to us, at least for the term of our tax-farming contract.'

'How can that be?' Kyrik demanded. 'Free us, and we'll repay you in full!'

'With what?' Sacrista sniffed. 'I'm sorry, but business is business.'

'But I have money . . .' Kyrik hammered on the bars. 'Where are our travel bags?'

Sacrista smiled coldly. 'Bags? I remember no bags.'

'You're nothing but a stinking thief!' Valdyr snarled at Sacrista.

She snorted in amusement. 'Under the new Tax and Debt Law, you'll be locked up until your debts are repaid.'

Valdyr met Kyrik's gaze. None of this sounded right or just, or even legal.

Kyrik confirmed his suspicions, panting as he recovered his breath, 'You can't do this. I'm the rightful lord of Mollachia and can't be imprisoned over a tax debt. I have the right to oversee the payment of the debts—'

'That's for my brother and Governor Inoxion to decide. I'm just a soldier.' Sacrista's face had a touch of distaste as she mentioned the Governor.

Welcome home, the dark part of Valdyr's soul jeered. *See what you've been missing?*

'Listen, it's likely only for a time,' Sacrista told Kyrik, a touch of sympathy in her voice. 'Come summer, our tax-farming contract expires. You'll get your kingdom back then, and your freedom.' Then she sighed as if she were tired of their complaints, and signalled to the driver. The wagon lurched into motion, and carried the caged brothers home.

Kyrik fell asleep on the journey to Hegikaro, and awoke an unknowable time later, chained in a eighteen-foot-square stone cell. One wall was a steel grille onto a corridor. There was no bed, and just a bucket for bodily waste. The air was frozen and his breath steamed, but at least the chill dulled the stink of the piss-bucket. The only light came from a tiny hole high in one wall, closed off by a cross of steel imbedded in the bricks. Valdyr was chained to the opposite wall, unmoving. He didn't respond to Kyrik's calls.

Kyrik recognised the cell. They were in his father's dungeons.

He was still fighting the despair that tore at his belly, when a key rasped in the rusty lock and the door swung open. Sacrista Delestre led in a ginger-haired young man, presumably her brother Robear. With them was a purple-robed Imperial magistrate with a self-satisfied manner; his chain of rank identified him as the Rondian Governor.

Seeing the high-ranking official lit a flare of hope in his breast. 'Milord!' he gasped, 'you—'

'Be quiet, scum,' Robear Delestre said in an irritated whine; he gestured, and a kinesis-blow smashed across Kyrik's face, leaving him stunned. The Imperial Governor showed no reaction.

'So, are they who they claim, Lady Sacrista?' the man said, not even glancing at Kyrik. His leering eyes didn't leave Sacrista's chest.

Her lips thinned as she answered, 'Yes, they are, Governor Inoxion.'

'Well, that's a problem for you, isn't it?' the governor drawled.

'It needn't be,' Robear said. Unlike his sister, he had thick, surly lips, a big nose and was somewhat portly. 'Two blasts of mage-fire would solve the problem with ease.'

'No, it wouldn't,' Inoxion pointed out. 'They've been formally registered as passing through Collistein Gate and taken into your custody. That makes them legally alive and your responsibility. I'm not having them murdered on my watch.'

Kyrik looked up hopefully. Could this arrogant bureaucrat actually be on their side after all?

But Inoxion immediately dispelled that notion. 'If they die violently, I would be compelled to investigate. However, a non-violent passing – and a small consideration – might allow me to look the other way.' He patted Robear's back amiably. 'I'm sure it's not difficult to come up with something my healers can attest as beyond your control?'

You piece of shit . . .

Robear smiled, while Sacrista scowled; he was surprised to see unease on her face. 'I'm not comfortable with this,' she began. 'These are titled lords and—'

'Oh, Crista, don't be such a Squeam!' Robear chided. The grille opened untouched, he sauntered into the cell and stopped in front of Valdyr. 'Kore's Balls, look at the pelt on this one – hairy as a dog! It might keep him alive an extra night in this cold, don't you think, Sister?'

'What do you mean?'

Robear laughed. 'It'll get cold down here with no food or drink. I give them a month.'

Sacrista gaped. 'But that's no better than killing them – Governor Inoxion, you can't—'

'Are your sensibilities offended, Lady?' Inoxion smirked. 'I thought you as hard as a man?'

'Aye, but starving someone is also murder—'

'But the bodies will bear no marks of violence,' Robear told her in an 'explaining the joke' voice. 'It's perfect.' He ruffled her hair. 'We're not going to waste food on them, darling sister.'

Sacrista bunched her fists. 'We don't need to *kill* them at all – this isn't necessary – we can release them when we leave at the end of summer – in all honour, Robear—'

'What's honour?' Robear rolled his eyes. 'Crista, listen: these two fools returning home destroys the value of this investment. Father paid a fortune for the right to pillage this wretched hole. Estate-tax farming is only worthwhile in foreclosure, which means we can come in and take *everything*. That's what Father demands, and that's what we're here to do.'

'But—'

'Legally, we can't hold them, which leaves them free to find finance, and our return goes from "anything we can get" to "what the law requires", and that's not good enough. Right now, no one but us knows they're here, and that's the way it's going to stay.'

'But surely you must at least give them water? Dehydration is agony – that's torture—'

'Then it'll hasten the process,' Robear sniffed. 'I'll not argue about this. I spoke by relay-stave to Father, and he was adamant. We do it my way.'

Sacrista glared at him, then she whirled and stormed out.

'Is that your imperial justice?' Kyrik demanded – or tried to; the words came out in a sob.

Robear laughed. 'Imperial justice is the same as it's always been, Sarkany: fully paid up and transferable. Your father should have made better use of your mother's cunni, so he had more sons to defend him.'

'Don't you malign my mother—'

'I'll say what I like about a *prusi* who sold her cunni to a dirty old *prick* like your father. Much good having magi sons has done him, eh? Paid all that money, only for you to vanish when he needed you most.' Robear came and stood over Kyrik. 'How were the breeding-houses, Sarkany? Must've been tough, rukking Noories while real men fought. Must've been Hel.'

'You know *nothing*—'

'Don't I?' Robear's boot prodded Kyrik's groin. 'Poor little soldier.' He turned to go.

'Wait!' Kyrik called. 'Please, my father . . . What happened?'

'He drank himself into a stupor one night and never woke, or so I heard. The magistrate contacted my father in Augenheim and the rest, as the scribes would say, is written.'

Kyrik looked away. *Oh, Father. You never drank when you were young. The Kore priests spoke against it and you took their word to heart. But then your wife died and your sons left.* He hung his head, closed his eyes. When he opened them again, he and Valdyr were alone.

No one brought food or water at midday, or that evening, nor all the following days. The brothers gradually came to realise that the next time someone opened those doors, it would be to carry out their bodies for burial.

The first days were almost unbearable, as bad as anything Valdyr had endured in the slave-camps. The hunger and thirst was like being eaten from the inside, as if worms were consuming his throat and guts. Then came the cramping as tissues warred for fluid, the separate parts of the whole trying to preserve themselves.

He and Kyrik sang hymns to distract themselves. They tried talking, but their minds wandered; if anything of import was said, any great secrets spilled, they were erased within minutes. The ability to finish thoughts and sentences was lost and they lapsed into silence thinking they were still talking, imagining conversations with people drawn from the drying dregs of memory. Father came to them, roaring and raging at them to get up and fight. Mother danced through the tiny pool of moonlight, singing like a child. That was all bearable.

Visions of Asiv weren't.

'Kyrik. Wake.' Paruq's warm, husky voice drew Kyrik up from the dark depths and he opened his eyes and looked up at that well-loved face smiling down at him, telling him that no prayers go unheard, and that a Place Above awaited him. He could have wept in joy, but his tear-ducts were dry. His throat caught and he coughed weakly, blinking . . .

. . . and Paruq was gone. No, he'd never been here.

The silent darkness mocked the very thought of a Place Above.

In daylight, the few lucid moments brought only distant sounds of Rondian voices and boots on stone, and the harsh cawing of the crows. The moonlight waned as the month died. At night, the distant lonely music of the wolves rolled down from the peaks, and some nights Valdyr howled back at them, and in his delirium he ran with them, flowing across the snow, the scent of prey in his nostrils and the taste of blood in his mouth. He woke to find his tongue bitten and bloody.

Kyrik could feel his body growing light, as if he were about to rip his soul free from his body and go coursing out into the night. *Spiritualism*, he thought. *I'll leave my body here and go for help!* But he was under a Chain-rune, earthbound – Hel-bound. Outside the foetid cell, Mollachia called to him: home, the earth and the soil, the sea of trees and the endless mountains beyond. He grew calmer as the end came, saw fewer visions and delusions. He felt lucid again, and saw it in his brother as well. They exchanged long stares, searching each other out, truly seeing each other for the first time since they'd been reunited. They remembered that above all else, they were kin.

Words were impossible, because their bodies were atrophying from the inside out and they could no longer make intelligible sounds. *All I want to say is that I love you, Brother.*

Valdyr's eyes said that he knew.

Valdyr woke to find a man in a fox-head hat standing over him: a big, swarthy man with a giant bow of bone and wood, who grinned savagely. Behind him, a woman with a crescent moon tattoo muttered prayers to the sky, then touched his lips. *Brother*, she whispered, *come with us.*

The end was easy, a floating feeling as a multitude of ancestors lifted them up and carried them away, into the trees, upwards towards the snowy peaks, their ice-bladed peaks scarring the clouds as they passed.

We die.

We die.

The afterlife was fire.

Then came rebirth, by water.

Liquid touched Kyrik's cracked lips and burning mouth and forced itself down his throat. Fluid in places that had been parched was a new type of agony, reawakening his body with brutal sensations. If dehydration was like drifting away, rehydration was all cramps and churning guts, over and again, as he climbed back towards life.

When he could see again, he found himself staring into glinting eyes and a face he remembered: a craggy, lupine visage touched by frost. 'Dragan?' he whispered.

Dragan Zhagy, his father's best friend, had aged the Mollach way, becoming weather-beaten and bark-skinned, his long hair and moustaches drooping. He looked like something carved from the land, encased in steel and infused with unquenchable fire. His smile revealed long yellowed teeth. 'Kyrik,' he growled. 'Welcome back.' He put his hand to his heart. '*Vitae Sarkanum,*' he added: *long live the Draken.*

'I don't feel much like a draken right now, my friend,' Kyrik croaked.

Dragan bared his teeth again. 'All in time, my Lord.'

They were in a cave, icy walls melting from the radiated heat of a fire in a stony hearth. The air was smoky, but the worst was chimneyed into cracks in the roof and funnelled away. Kyrik remembered the place from his youth, a hunter's place lair at the headwaters of the Osiapa River. He looked around, and saw Valdyr lying under a blanket, his face aged and drawn, but his chest rising and falling.

Tears stung his eyes, and he sent prayers of thanks streaming to the One God Above.

We live.

11

In the Presence of Royalty

Messiahs

'Messiah' is a Dhassan word for a man sent by Ahm to save humanity from their wickedness. The Amteh believe there will only ever be two Messiahs, the first being the Prophet Aluq-Ahmed, who became spiritual and temporal ruler of all Dhassa and Kesh. The second Messiah will come at the End of All Days, when Ahm will descend and take the faithful to dwell with him eternally in Paradise.

ORDO COSTRUO, HEBUSALIM, 421

The false Messiahs who pop up every week, fermenting rebellion, are a plague upon our people. Let any who claim such status be put to death for their heresy!

GODSPEAKER ELIM, HEBUSALIM 809

Sagostabad, Kesh, Ahmedhassa
Thani (Aprafor) 935

Waqar left his friends below and retreated to the upper balconies to watch the court. He wasn't sure why Rashid had told him to make himself scarce, but no doubt that would become clear. He wasn't the only person up here: there were guards, and a couple of other men also watching proceedings, but no one approached him.

Making his way at the sultan's court had been harder than he'd expected: he was just one among a great many men scrabbling to be noticed. Some traded on their reputation as fighting men or – still rare, but becoming less so – on their power as a mage. Others had lineage or money, which opened all doors. There were many whose skill was to procure and facilitate – Attam's lusts were well-known, but Waqar had been a bit shocked to discover *noblemen* whose main function appeared to be to act as pimps. Xoredh liked opium, and there were plenty whose fortunes were tied to the poppy. Everyone with something to sell scrambled to make the right connections and tie themselves to a rising star.

Many latched onto Waqar as a potential benefactor because of his family name. From the moment he'd arrived here, he'd been beset with – well, *suitors*, sounding out his beliefs, opinion and desires. He'd opted for noncommittal caution: *A prince must listen to ten words for each one he utters*, the Rimoni philosopher Makelli wrote, so he'd done much more listening than talking. Tonight, standing above the crowds, he could clearly see the patterns woven by the red and blue scarves. The red-clad Shihadis clustered about the Maula of Sagostabad, Ali Beyrami, at one end of the hall, while most of those about the throne wore blue. But not everyone was sporting declarations of partisanship; some, like his uncle's people, were keeping their allegiances private – although Attam and Xoredh primarily mingled with the Shihadis.

Mostly, Waqar watched Sultan Salim, partly to learn, but also in hero-worship.

Salim Kabarakhi was either the first or third of his name, depending on which history one took as truth. The reigns of his grandfather and father had been disputed; his wasn't. He was still in his early thirties when he'd united Kesh and Dhassa under Shihad, in time for the Third Crusade, and the success of that war had cemented his rule. He was handsome and articulate, with a reputation for fairness, but when required to be strong, he'd crushed rebellious emirs and suppressed dissident Godspeakers with efficiency.

'What do you see, Prince Waqar?' said a voice at his elbow.

Waqar spun, alarmed that someone had got so close. The man was in his thirties, his face startlingly familiar. Waqar shot a glance at the throne below, where an identical man sat holding court. 'You're one of the sultan's impersonators—'

The man's mouth curved upwards. 'Or perhaps I'm Salim, and that fellow on the throne is the impersonator – we're all trained to deal with such scenarios.'

'Or maybe neither of you are Salim and he's still in Shaliyah?'

'Ah, but Sagostabad is where any leader of note must be right now.'

'What can I call you?' Waqar asked. 'If you're not the sultan, I have no idea what title to use.'

'Call me . . . Latif. How are you enjoying court life?'

Waqar sensed that 'Latif' wanted a genuine conversation, so he put aside the formality of the harbadab and admitted, 'It's very unsettling. Perhaps I expected more: I thought the court would be about talent, but there are men down there whose only skill is in witticisms.'

'Being witty is an underrated talent,' Latif deadpanned.

'Is it one that should earn a man a title?'

'I hear you, Prince. But we are drawn to those who can make us feel good, are we not? That's human nature. If we can work with someone, then things get done. A talented man's talents are useless if no one can abide him.'

'So is it better to appoint useless wastrels on the basis of a quip?'

'Not at all. But we are people, and therefore emotional, variable, frightened and insecure – and so too are our courts.'

Waqar was formulating his response when he heard a stir below. He and Latif looked down to see heads turning to the doors as a stir ran through the gathering.

Rondian magi . . . The Ordo Costruo are here!

The plump, grey-haired man in heavy sky-blue cloth was announced as Rene Cardien, the head of the Ordo Costruo; the shapely dark-skinned woman with pale hair at his side, Odessa D'Ark. The third name startled him—

Mother's here! No wonder Uncle told me to hide . . . Waqar felt a tremor of uncertainty as he stared at his mother, taking in every detail. She looked well, full of herself even, as if this moment vindicated her loyalty to the order. *Dear Mother,* he thought, frightened for her, *what are you doing here, of all places?*

In their train were a dozen more magi, men and women both, richly attired in Ordo Costruo sky-blue. They were all of mixed race, but most had Rondian pallor. Their entrance threw the whole room into confusion as the Shihadi, vocal haters of the West, were confronted with the embodiment of that hatred – but they reacted not in belligerence but fear. It was likely that the Ordo Costruo were, in raw gnostic power and in skill, the superior of even Rashid. Those around Salim looked at each other, unsure how to react; some hovered protectively, others edged away.

Then Waqar heard a surprised murmur wash through the hall as the newcomers made respectful homage to the sultan, briefly going down on one knee.

Salim's voice rang out. 'Greetings, honoured Magisters. Welcome to Sagostabad.'

Rene Cardien, obviously an old hand at dealing with Eastern courts, replied in fluent Keshi, 'Great Sultan, you honour us. We apologise for our unlooked-for appearance, but we heard disturbing rumours of renewed Shihad.'

Salim raised a hand to stop him. 'These are matters for the council chamber, not open forum.'

'No, they are matters for this room,' Sakita Mubarak replied in a loud voice.

Waqar flinched as the court gasped: *no one* contradicted a sultan, least of all a woman. The harbadab absolutely forbade it.

'Great Sultan,' she went on, 'the Ordo Costruo control the Leviathan Bridge. It will rise again in five years, but when it does, it will be closed to all but certified traders.' She glanced at the throng of red-scarved Shihadis. 'You can talk about Holy War all you like, but no soldier – of Yuros or Ahmedhassa – will cross the Bridge in the next Moontide.'

Waqar was impressed and angered, embarrassed and proud, all at once. But he doubted anyone would ever forgive his mother for this – or him, just for being her kin. His gnostic sight told him that every mage here was primed for instant violence, and even up here on the balcony, he felt scared to move.

Salim, however, had retained his composure. 'We know and understand your prohibition,' he said, masking any indignation he might feel at being dictated to in his own throne-hall. 'No one here fails to grasp the situation. Please, let us confer in private.'

Their point made, the Ordo Costruo magi allowed the sultan's counsellors to lead them out of the hall behind Salim. Only then were voices
raised, with the Shihadis shouting their outrage at this 'insult to all
of Kesh' and demanding instant redress. *Brave of you, now they're gone*,
Waqar thought. Attam and Xoredh were standing among the clergy,
making martial gestures, complaining of being 'held back' by the sultan's 'weakness'.

For himself, his mind swirled. *We are Keshi*, he thought, *we are* owed
redress. He agreed that talk of Shihad against Yuros was absurd, but
remembering that conversation with his uncle back in Halli'kut, he
knew the situation was far from simple.

Latif touched his arm. 'Prince Waqar, it's been a pleasure to meet
you. And your mother certainly knows how to make an entrance.' He
turned, then paused. 'I believe the sultan would like to meet you, if
you would be willing?'

Waqar bowed, heart thudding. 'Of course!'

'I should tell you, it is because Salim will wish to reach out to your
mother. He will see her as one who could aid him in promoting peace
and rebuilding the realm.'

'I'm used to my mother being the most important thing about me,'
Waqar admitted, wondering if the sultan actually approved of the Ordo
Costruo's appearance here. The implications were intriguing.

'There: a flash of wit and doors open,' Latif chuckled, wagging a
finger. 'At least you don't have to *impersonate* her.' They shared a smile.
'The next debate of the Convocation is at the end of this week. Join us
at dusk, outside the Royal Dom-al'Ahm, if you will.'

He left Waqar trembling at this offered chance to finally meet his
hero. What opportunities might follow?

'The Moon sometimes swings low,' the saying went. 'Catch it, and
you can ride to the stars.'

'Most of the Western magi left after meeting with Xoredh,' Tamir was
shouting above the din of the crowds. 'They reminded Xoredh that
the Pontic Sea was forbidden to any craft without a trading warrant.'

'What did Xoredh say?' Waqar shouted back. Xoredh as head of the

Keshi Al-Norushan mage order had met with the Rondians the day after they spoke to Salim.

'That he expected no more from the enemies of Kesh.'

Waqar appreciated the answer, but he still loathed Xoredh. He was nervous of the Builder-magi, too, and horribly conflicted about his mother being one of them, although he was looking forward to seeing her after tonight's interview with the sultan.

Before that however, was *this*: the biggest of the public debates of the Convocation. He and his friends had joined the thousands crammed into the square outside the main dom-al'Ahm. The usual markets had been cleared away and a throne dominated a dais erected at the west end of the square. From it, Ishaq, the Ayatu-Marja, supreme cleric of Ahm, held court. Before him the rival factions were squeezed together cheek by jowl and every speech was greeted with exchanges of insults and taunts, regional and personal, and constant pushing and shoving.

All week the debates had been heated, but today the most powerful speakers would take the stage, and His Supreme Holiness Ishaq was showing an attentiveness he'd not previously displayed. There were red scarves in plenty, but they were still in the minority. Sagostabad was the sultan's home, and his family, the Kabarakhis, had ruled the city for centuries. The local people adored him, and they were out in force today.

'They love Salim, these southerners,' Waqar shouted in Lukadin's ear. 'This is his city.'

All Waqar's friends were northerners; that was a far older rivalry. 'He's a victorious leader,' Lukadin conceded, 'so he can do no wrong in their eyes. But what of elsewhere?' Seated at the right of the Ayatu-Marja, Salim was the consummate Eastern ruler, brilliantly attired, handsome and urbane, the lines on his forehead lending him an aura of wisdom.

'Sagostabad is insulated from the suffering of the regions by its proximity to the wealth of the court,' Tamir added. 'They don't know how the rest of Ahmedhassa suffer.'

Only females of high rank could attend, which included Fatima, sweltering under her black bekira-shroud. She was pressed against Baneet's side – they'd begun sleeping with each other, something that afforded

Waqar the occasional flash of jealousy. Some part of him still thought of Fatima as 'his' – she'd have slapped him silly if he said so, of course.

The latest speaker, Faroukh of Maal, ended his speech with a plea for peace and those in blue scarves chanted Kabarakhi slogans. Then up stepped Ali Beyrami, the maula with whom Waqar had clashed earlier. He spoke with fury, denouncing all peace-making as weakness and a betrayal of the Prophet. 'Bring the Unbeliever to belief, or bring him to Death! Thus spake Aluq-Ahmed! The Unbeliever taints the air and pours venom in the water! Where there is Unbelief, the Believer knows no peace!' He pointed to the heavens. 'Twenty-five years and three Crusades and we know no peace because we allow the Unbeliever to live!'

There was much more like that, words of bitterness and revenge. Beyrami was, Waqar thought, a very angry man, and a frightening one, too. When he stood before the masses and screamed at them, there was no fear in his face, only hunger to subdue all who listened.

'He's a dangerous fanatic,' Tamir muttered, and Waqar agreed.

Beyrami's intensity had the reds and the blues on the verge of riot, and seeing this, the sultan gestured to the most senior of the clergy in his retinue. Jhiram Henayou, a locally born Ja'arathi clergyman considered heir-apparent to Ishaq for the throne of the Ayatu-Marja, rose to his feet and gradually a hush descended as he hobbled onto the speaking platform. He had a solemn face buried in a curly, grey beard, and his calm eyes seemed to say, 'Be at peace, for I am here'.

'Brothers in Faith,' he called, his gentler voice nevertheless cutting through the noise, 'is it not good to be here, in the heart of the Faith? Is it not good to be alive, when so many lost their lives only five years ago? We give thanks to Him Above the Skies for this gift!' He raised his hands, and those in blue scarves did the same. Those in red murmured, but none were so rude as to interrupt a blessing.

Then Godspeaker Jhiram looked down at the masses before him. 'Yet Maula Beyrami says we must scorn this gift and declare a new war! He says we must ask those who escaped death on the slopes of Ebensar, who survived the atrocities of Istabad and Halli'kut, Medishar and Bassaz, to jeopardise all they have once more! For revenge, he says, whilst quoting the *Kalistham*! But does not that same book say that revenge is the poison that slays our children? Does it not say that the unresolved feud is a cancer?'

More cheers, more blue scarves waving, beginning to overwhelm the red again.

'He's good,' Lukadin muttered, 'but wrong.'

'More than this,' the Godspeaker went on, 'my friend Ali Beyrami seems to forget that the Leviathan Bridge is closed to us: the Ordo Costruo *forbid us* the war my colleague so craves, and they have the power to do so! They were arrogant to remind us, yes – but are they wrong? Not only is this war that so many of you ardently want a waste of lives, it is also impossible to wage! You may as well declare war on the moon.'

'I would put them in their place!' bellowed Ali Beyrami.

'You would go up against the power that brought down the Sacrecours? I'm filled with admiration!' Jhiram said lightly, wringing an uneasy laugh from the crowd, then he put on a more serious face. 'My friends, there is, however, an enemy that we could declare war on, and indeed should. Some of them are even here today!'

A ripple of surprise ran through the crowd. *What does he mean?* Waqar wondered.

'*That enemy is Corruption!*' Jhiram roared, pointing his finger downwards, a sign of contempt. 'Our Great Sultan, Salim Kabarakhi of Sagostabad, has emptied the treasury, dispensing bullion as never before, yet not one coin in ten reaches the people – and *why*? Because of those who siphon the money into their own vaults and then cry poor! *They* are our enemies! *They* should be the target of our ire! *They* are why our children still go hungry!'

Beyrami raised a defiant fist. 'And "they" are all appointed by this regime!' he shouted, to the amusement of his followers, eliciting renewed waving among the reds.

Jhiram glanced at the throne, then raised a placating hand. 'Some, I admit, and our sultan knows their names – but others, not so – and some of them I see here, wearing scarves of red! They think a war will deflect us from investigation of their crimes!'

Both sides erupted with insults and raised fists.

Jhiram raised his arms skywards. 'I have one final thing to say, and it is this: those of you who clamour for war think it a panacea for our ills. It is not the cure you seek; it is merely *war*, which is to say: *bloodshed* and *suffering* and *destruction*. We must not go down that path. It leads to Shaitan! It leads to death and despair. We must take the hard road, of patience, diligence and good, honest, hard work. That has always been our greatest virtue. So it must remain.'

Waqar saw the Ayatu-Marja nodding as Jhiram took the applause. The sultan was clapping as well, his back straight, his demeanour calm and regal. Waqar compared them to the mouth-foaming rage of Beyrami and his people and felt that the debate had been won. The sultan raised a hand, requesting the right to speak and surely complete the victory for the peace faction—

—when Ishaq, the Ayatu-Marja, coughed painfully, and the whole square fell silent. An aide rushed to the holy man's side and gently patted his back, while another took his hand. There was a few moments of frantic hand-signalling, then the initial panic eased and the sultan sat back down, looking frustrated, as one of Ishaq's retinue announced, 'The Ayatu-Marja apologises, but he must rest! The Convocation will resume tomorrow, at four bells.' A crowd of servants helped the old man shuffle to his palanquin, to be carried back to his palace.

It was an anti-climactic way to end the day, and Waqar could sense the feeling of lost opportunity in the air as he followed Rashid's entourage through the press. He turned to Tamir. 'What did you think?'

'That Ishaq's coughing fit was awfully convenient for Ali Beyrami.'

'Ai, it was. I'd give anything to know what Salim was going to say.'

'No need,' Tamir grinned. 'You'll be meeting him shortly – just ask!'

The impersonator Latif was reading poetry when the door to the suite was flung open and the real Salim stormed through the doors, snatched up a glass of sharbat and glared at Latif. 'Damn the afreet who tickled Ishaq's throat!' he snapped, rolling his eyes reproachfully towards heaven. His voice drew more of his impersonators, all identically dressed, of the same stature and with identical hair, beards and even eyes.

This was perhaps the most unique household in all of Ahmedhassa; such was the threat of assassination that most royal lines used impersonators, but Salim currently had seven, and they all had to be kept completely up to date with every development, so that if they were sent to a banquet they knew everything that Salim knew, and what his views were. Four of the seven had a close but imperfect resemblance, used only in situations where the sultan was viewed from a distance, but the other three were virtually identical to him; Latif was one of those.

'We were minutes away from burying this debate: *a few minutes!* That's all I needed.' Salim struck the table. 'We've got so many more important matters to resolve than Beyrami's fantasy of a Shihad across three hundred miles of impassable sea!'

'Hear, hear,' the impersonators chorused.

'You don't think . . .?' Latif waggled his fingers in a meaningful way.

Salim stared. 'Gnosis? On the Ayatu-Marja? They wouldn't dare, Latif—'

'The Hadishah have fragmented since the Crusade ended. Most are now working for nobles and clergymen – I doubt it'd be a difficult spell.'

'Ai: Rashid could have done it himself,' another man put in.

'No, I refuse to believe it,' Salim exclaimed. 'Let us pray it was just itchy tonsils, Brothers. Latif, come: walk with me.'

Salim led Latif down a spiral stair to a windowless chamber below ground. It was cool and, most importantly, beneath enough stone that scrying was impossible. They sat on the benches informally, as equals.

'Brother, what do you make of this?'

Latif had for some time been Salim's main confidante. 'It could just be bad luck, and you'll carry the debate tomorrow. But if it was triggered by someone, then we're in real danger. We have Hadishah magi protecting us – but can we trust them? Can we trust Rashid?'

'Once Rashid was reviled as a part-afreet monster,' Rashid reminded him, 'and it was the people's fear of magi that ensured he had to accept a secondary role to me. Has the world changed enough that the people would trust a mage as ruler?'

Latif considered. 'Our victory in the Crusade has made him popular – *very* popular. The status of magi with Ahmedhassan blood is ambiguous now. In the *Kalistham*, afreet bow down to the Prophet, and clever Scripturalists are using those passages to legitimise the gnosis. If they succeed in swaying opinion, he may feel confident enough to move against you.'

'Ai, that is clear, but Rashid knows the Ordo Costruo are formidable, better than anyone. Yuros is beyond our reach, even if we did want war.'

'But is Yuros the real target here?' Latif asked. 'Once Shihad is declared, the man given the leadership of it can declare other targets; all he must do is prove a link to the overall goal. Gatioch, Mirobez, even Lakh – they are more realistic targets than Yuros.'

'They are – but what does Rashid want with war in the first place, Latif?'

'War gave him his greatest glory, Salim. He wants more of it.'

'But he's never spoken openly in favour of Shihad,' Salim observed.

'All the better to surprise us by changing tack at a vital moment. Ishaq *seems* to be on our side, but Beyrami's faction is large and dangerous. A split in the Faith would put *everything* at risk. Ishaq needs concord, not two giant factions at loggerheads. He might feel that a smaller, local Holy War might pull everyone back together.'

Salim scowled. 'That's plausible. Our strength is that most common men are struggling to rebuild their lives and don't want any kind of war. Our weakness is that we've been unable to help most of them in that rebuilding. But would a domestic war be enough to placate Beyrami?'

'I doubt it,' Latif replied. 'A Keshi might think of the Lakh as godless thieves, but he'll still do business with a Lakh trader. War against the Lakh doesn't speak to Keshi hearts. But mention Yuros and the hatred is visceral.'

'Then what of Javon?' Salim wondered. He was officially – though they'd never met – betrothed to a politically astute Javonesi noblewoman, daughter of the assassinated king. The marriage was delayed indefinitely, a ploy that left her as his ambassador in Javon, an arrangement that suited both parties. Thus far it had worked well.

'Javon does have a significant Yurosi population, but their borders are guarded by the Ordo Costruo: it'd be a difficult war to prosecute.' Latif scowled, then clicked his fingers. 'The only other place with a significant Rondian enclave is Hebusalim herself—'

'Not even Beyrami could sell that,' Salim exclaimed. 'And the Ordo Costruo are based there.'

Latif sighed. 'Ai, you're right. We're really none the wiser, are we?'

'We're not. So let's assume the worst. I'll force a decision from Ishaq tomorrow. And given the tensions here, I think it best if we split our household. I want you to take two others – you choose – and all the wives and children, and go to our summer palace in the hills.'

'I'd prefer to be here—'

'No, Latif, if something goes wrong, I want to know you at least are safe. Of all my brothers, you are the one best able to take over my role until my eldest comes of age. I need that of you.'

His sultan had never before singled him out for such lavish praise. 'As you command.'

'Thank you, Latif. I'm blessed to have such a man as you behind me. Now, I believe I have an appointment with young Waqar Mubarak. He is intelligent and pleasant, you said?'

'Is it wise to meet him at a time like this?'

'We'd be fools to let the opportunity to meet privately with Sakita Mubarak slip by, and that requires an intermediary like Waqar.'

'I've heard she's a disagreeable know-it-all,' Latif commented.

'Perhaps, but she's also a renowned mage – and perhaps Rashid's blind spot. She could be vital in maintaining his allegiance.' Salim laid a reassuring hand on Latif's shoulder. 'Make ready to leave. I've never felt so vulnerable in Sagostabad before.'

The sultan left to meet with Waqar Mubarak while Latif returned to the main lounge where the other six impersonators were chattering like anxious birds. All were loyal, he knew that, but some had more courage than others. He chose Halaam and Faizal, two of the staunchest, and briefed them, then left for the zenana.

As he strode through empty corridors towards the women's quarters, he felt a subtle change in the air. It wasn't a chill, more a creeping silence. The palace was a maze of long corridors and alcoves with seats and tables for courtiers to hold impromptu conversations. But as Latif paused at the head of one corridor, he thought he glimpsed someone in hooded robes vanishing into a barely lit alcove, and his unease crystallised. Every instinct said to back away. There were guardsmen at the major portals, but the closest was a hundred yards away and out of sight.

It could be nothing. It *should* be nothing. But it could be everything they dreaded.

He took a deep breath, then padded to the end of the corridor where the shrouded figure had vanished. There was no one, but his fear refused to subside. He crept to the next alcove, his heart in his mouth, and found an open door to a large throne-hall, one reserved for entertainments and dances. On the far side of the room, a grey-shrouded, masculine figure was standing in profile. He was wearing a strange mask of beaten copper that covered his forehead, eyes and nose but left the lower half of the face bare; it had a long beak, like a bird's, a foot long with a sharp point. His jawline was bearded, with a flash of dark lips and bared teeth.

In his left hand was a scimitar.

12

Dangerous Days

Mage Children

*A mage-child gains the gnosis during puberty, but of course their manifest supe-
riority is apparent well before then. We magi are as far above the common man
as lions are above cattle.*

LADY SARAE ROUX, PALLAS 839

Pallas, Rondelmar
Aprafor 935

'Let the Imperial Council come to order,' Ril Endarion announced formally. He'd actually read the pile of papers in front of him, which
would probably surprise the other counsellors. With Lyra confined, he
was having to chair the council, as well as staying on top of military
matters as Master-General. 'Gentlemen, we've a lot to talk about.'

'Of course,' Edreu Gestatium replied, sipping Dhassan coffee. Calan
Dubrayle gave no sign of having heard as he shuffled his own documents,
while the grand prelate sniffed his own coffee with the expression of
one who wishes it might somehow turn into mead. Dirklan Setallius,
at the foot of the table, rested his chin on his hand; as always, a subtle
air of menace hung about him.

'Think of every matter on the agenda as a crime,' Lyra had told Ril
earlier that morning as they'd gone through the business of the day;
she'd got that from Setallius. 'Solve the crime and pass sentence on the
guilty.' She might be stuck in the Confinement Suite, thickening at the
waist and suffering from morning sickness, but she was determined to

stay abreast of council matters. If she'd had the temerity to overrule her iron-willed midwife Domara, she'd have been here, but Ril scarcely blamed her for avoiding that confrontation.

Her confinement meant Ril also spent every night alone, despite the overt circling of certain ladies of court. He put that unwanted thought aside and turned to the first item of the day – the first crime: tax-farming. The treasurer opened the debate, bandying about words like 'recovery', 'confidence' and 'surplus', and of course Gestatium backed him up. Then Setallius countered with a catalogue of abuses by tax-farmers reported to the Crown, concluding that tax-farming was a false economy, cutting costs, but in the end saving nothing.

Dubrayle *harrumphed*, and provided tables of numbers. Setallius had tables too, but with vastly different conclusions. Wurther said smugly that his Church collected *tithes*, not taxes, and people competed to give the most. The other men glared him back to silence.

Lyra had discussed the core issue with him: Dubrayle's treasury received a steady but reduced upfront tax take, but the people hated it. 'The empress leans towards a repeal of the tax-farming laws,' Ril told them. 'Under Constant, tax was collected directly.'

Dubrayle looked tired and frustrated. 'But we don't have the resource any more—'

'Lyra believes taxation must be done accurately and fairly, no matter the cost.'

Dubrayle winced, but Gestatium leaned forward; he'd controlled tax collection before tax-farming was brought in. 'Does the empress sanction rebuilding the imperocratic tax bureau?' he asked, just as Lyra had predicted he would.

'Drive a wedge between Gestatium and Dubrayle on this and suddenly we've got the majority required, enough to start a review process,' Lyra had suggested. 'Crime solved!'

'I am authorised by the queen to add her vote to mine in this matter,' Ril told them. 'The motion is a full review, including rebuilding the tax bureau.'

The motion passed, four votes to Dubrayle's one – Setallius as an adviser couldn't vote.

Ril spent the rest of the morning solving other crimes, some of omission, some of deception. What stunned him most was the bare-faced cheek of his fellow councillors, usually Wurther or Dubrayle, both happy to propose a lengthy list of legal amendments, embedded amongst which were 'errors' that if not spotted would pervert the intent of the law – in their favour. Their attitude appeared to be that if the other councillors weren't sharp enough to spot them, they deserved the consequences. Ril was tempted to punch them both.

Evening was approaching before they reached the final two items. 'The seasonal riverreek outbreak has come early, and threatens to be the worst ever,' Setallius reported gravely. 'Another dozen cases have been reported in Pallas-Nord and five in Emtori – that's more than a hundred cases, with four deaths so far, and summer's not yet here.'

'Nasty business,' Wurther remarked. 'What are we doing about it?'

'Normal procedure is to encourage infected people to stay at home,' Setallius answered, 'but the mage-healers want to create quarantine houses for the sick, to better contain it.'

'They know their business,' Gestatium remarked. 'Most of the ware-house district is half-empty – house them there, perhaps?'

That sounded a little excessive to Ril. 'Riverreek is just a nasty cold, isn't it?'

'Spoken like a mage with superior immunities,' Setallius drawled. 'For the common burgher, riverreek can be a killer, and early onset is a bad sign.'

They agreed to quarantining, and an enhanced healing presence, then turned to the last item: border security. 'We have reports of fresh banditry across the Jusse and the Ortu,' Ril said. The rivers were the northern and eastern borders of Argundy, Rondelmar's biggest vassal-state – and most dangerous adversary.

'Real bandits, or pretend ones?' Setallius asked. 'I suspect the latter.'

'I believe they're testing us,' Ril said. 'But why now?'

The question went unanswered until Setallius said, 'If I may be so bold: they sense weakness.'

'Do they?' Ril asked warily. 'What kind of weaknesses?'

'Money. Unity. Will.' Setallius counted them on his fingers. 'Take your

DAVID HAIR

pick. They know Rondelmar was weakened by the Crusade and our armies haven't recovered. The vassal-states took horrific losses themselves, but they've never maintained as many legions as Rondelmar; their military strength is tied up in the noble Houses. They're watching rebellions break out over the tax-farming – things are unstable, so they're testing the limits.'

'Do they think we aren't willing to defend our borders?'

Dubrayle looked up. 'Are we? Wars cost money, far more than can be easily and quickly recouped. They're bad for business.' He then qualified that, adding, 'Most business.'

'They certainly seem to be bad for treasuries,' Wurther chuckled. He and Dubrayle shared a pricklish but tolerant look, longstanding colleagues and rivals.

'It seems to me,' Edreu Gestatium said in his prim voice, 'that we must make an example of someone. Remind the vassal-states that Rondian power is intact and that we're willing to use it.'

'How would you propose we do that?' Setallius enquired acerbically. 'Burn an Argundian border keep?'

'If that's what it'd take.'

'For a man who's never picked up a sword you're swift to suggest others do,' Ril grumbled. 'We can't just march across the Argundy border.'

'Tell that to the *tax-paying* Rondian farmers whose cattle and crops are being stolen or destroyed,' Dubrayle snapped.

Was any man ever so passionate about tax? Ril wondered. 'Then we find another way to impress the Argies,' Ril suggested, improvising now. 'Couldn't we have a few draken fly around the Delphic Pinnacle? Or challenge them to a drinking competition?' he added with a grin, then stopped, thunderstruck. 'That's it: we'll host a tourney.'

'A tourney?' Gestatium echoed. 'There's a jousting tournament circuit already; it's just amusement for rich young noblemen,' he sniffed. 'We don't have the money for *necessary* projects, let alone games.'

'Truth indeed,' Dubrayle agreed. 'Moving on, what if—?'

'*A tourney,*' Ril repeated. 'Didn't the Rimoni Emperors host games, with wild animals and swordfights and the like?'

'A Rimoni Ludus,' Wurther said with a chuckle. 'Those were the days:

210

gladiator displays, heretics against lions, chariot and horse races – they were mad, those Rimoni, but they knew how to put on a show. *Panem et Ludus*: Bread and Games: the twin pillars of their empire.'

'They used to cost a thousand auros or more to put on,' Gestatium put in. 'I've seen the records. Back then that was enough to buy a province . . . which is why they did it, of course! Public officials were voted into office back then, and such spectacles gained votes.'

'Thank Kore those days are gone,' Dubrayle muttered. 'Ridiculous waste. Now, moving—'

'Wait,' Setallius interrupted, surprising everyone, 'I find merit in this idea.'

They all stared. 'Dirklan?' Gestatium asked, worried he'd missed a jest.

'Listen,' Setallius said, 'we're trying to hold this empire together, but what do we actually *do* as an empire? We've been leaving our vassal-states and provinces to their own devices as long as the taxes flow. Garod Sacrecour is not the only one behaving as if Fauvion is his own kingdom – the Dukes of Canossi and Klief and the rest are doing the same. We need to bring them together and remind them that Pallas is the centre of the empire! A tourney could do just that: it will emphasise our continuing power. As Ril says: jousts, archery, pageantry, plays and entertainments: everything to bring people flocking in.'

Dubrayle was looking thoughtful, but Gestatium whined, 'Dirklan, the cost—'

'—will be far less than the long-term benefits,' the treasurer interjected, smoothly changing sides. 'We'd need loans from the major banks, obviously, but if I can't recover the outlay, I'm not doing my job properly. Meanwhile we demonstrate our prestige, and bring all of the vassal-state rulers together, under our thumbs.'

They all looked at Ril again, appraising expressions on their faces. *Trying to work out if I'm a lucky fool, or a secret genius*, he guessed. 'I do have my moments,' he told them.

'So what are the risks?' Gestatium wondered.

'That we bankrupt ourselves,' Setallius answered. 'That we provide a venue for the vassal-state lords to plot insurrection together. That we import rebellion from the provinces.' He glanced at Ril and added, 'And that the Imperial and Corani knights perform abysmally in the tourney, thus reducing instead of enhancing our prestige.'

'Pah,' Ril replied. 'We'll set the rules to suit ourselves. As for the rest, there is no gain without risk.' He rose to his feet, eager to get out into the fresh air and clear his head. 'I, for one, intend to be the victor.'

Maybe that will finally silence those who still doubt me.

Lyra found refuge in her one truly private place: the Winter Garden. She allowed a gardener in once a week, but for the most she allowed it to run wild. The garden was part of the small area where she could roam at will. There were only two entrances – Greengate, which was guarded, and the stairs from her balcony; though open to the skies, there were complex wards placed by past emperors and renewed by Setallius to prevent unwanted access from above.

The garden wasn't large, just a hundred yards long and barely thirty yards wide, and had been planted in what had been an old killing zone between the Bastion walls and one of the curtain walls that ringed the fortress. It faced south for the sunshine, and extended east – left – from the base of her stairs.

That morning she was feeling languorous, and lonely. The roses were blooming beautifully, filling the air with their rich scent. She'd slipped down after breakfast, clad – scandalously *un*-clad, really – in a white silk nightdress, a fine woollen dressing gown and thin slippers. Being so indecorous didn't trouble her – the garden could only be overlooked from her own private balcony, and no one else was permitted entry. The spring warmth seeped into her and sweat was dripping from her forehead and running from her neck and down into her cleavage. Four months into the pregnancy her belly was clearly swelling, as were her breasts, the skin tight and nipples tender. Since the morning sickness had eased off she'd noticed a return of appetite – and not just for food.

'Why can't my husband sleep with me?' she'd asked Domara that morning. 'I miss him.'

The nun-healer, a Sister of Kore, had looked down her sharp nose and said sternly, 'Physical congress is known to carry risk of miscarriage, my Queen. This is an attested fact.' She'd coloured heavily, lowered her voice. 'Any kind of . . . er . . . *stimulation* . . . carries risk.'

Both women had looked away, embarrassed.

I wonder why being forbidden something only makes the desire for it grow stronger? Because right now, the warm perfumed air had her feeling quite . . . *amorous.*

'I need a cold drink,' she decided, her skin tingling with want, and with shame for that want. She looked about guiltily, then took off her dressing gown. Clad in just the sweat-dampened nightdress, she followed the trickling sound of the fountain that fed the roots of her very own Winter Tree. She passed through the double row of old oaks to the pond where she'd planted the sapling from the shrine of Saint Eloy and knelt, careless of the dirt and leaf mould. She drank from her hands, feeling like a Fey Waif from the *Fables*: above her, the sapling spread its branches; it was several feet tall already, and covered in deep green thorny leaves and tart red berries, radiating an end-of-summer glow. Birds and insects trilled and thrummed about her.

She liked that *she* wasn't queen here, but she served one who *was* . . . She glanced around again, checking she really was alone, before holding out a hand and making a wish.

Aradea, she whispered with her mind, *show me Saint Balphus Abbey.*

A Blue Spindle butterfly fluttered about her and landed on her hand, then fluttered off as an eel rose from the bottom of the pool then wriggled away, leaving a vision forming in the swirling water: a tawny-skinned face with tresses of blackberry vines, teeth like a pike and moon-crater eyes. Lyra whispered a greeting and they stared at each other, then the face was gone, in its place a burnt-out, desolate building overgrown with vines.

The place where she'd grown up had been abandoned by the Church after she was taken. The ruins saddened her, to see her old cell smashed open to the sky. *You can never go back to the past*, the wind whispered. *Look ever forward.*

Then she saw a flash of something else: *a black-haired man dancing with a red-clad woman.* The image was too blurred to make out faces, but

213

the sight made her feel horribly insecure. Irked by it, she splashed the vision away, the air resounding to the slap of her hand in the water.

For four years, she'd been coming to the Winter Garden and opening herself to these little miracles. As the sapling grew, the place had become more and more like the chapel garden in Coraine or the shrine in the Celestium: a place of unexplained 'magic'. She knew the right name from a long-ago conversation with Ostevan, but whether she called it pandaemancy or dwyma was irrelevant; the power was a heresy. She could be *burned* for using it.

It frightened her – the Church would not lightly declare a power heretical – and she worried about what dabbling in it was doing to her soul, but she couldn't leave it alone. Her gnosis had never come – Setallius and Domara said that could happen, that sometimes a mage-born child simply failed to gain the power that was their birthright – but it scared her to be helpless, so she'd begun to explore this other thing.

In the early days of the gnosis, according to the histories, pandaemancers had been '*a threat to all good men*', but Saint Eloy had persuaded most to renounce their powers. The rest were given 'the judgement of Kore' – she'd seen a woodcut print of a women burning at the stake, the flames filled with diabolos from Hel. The depiction of her agony looked horribly realistic.

I'm not like her, she told herself fearfully. *Corineus is my Saviour and Kore my Lord.*

But she could do . . . *this* . . . now. She asked Aradea for light, and the water droplets in her hand glowed. She asked for cold, and the droplets, still glowing, froze. She cast the little diamonds of light back into the pool and watched them melt away, sensing Aradea watching through the eyes of the owls in the oaks above and the eel in the corner of the pool. Heresy or not, she felt safe here, and nowhere else.

Thank you, Father Kore, for creating such a place for me – and for the warning. She tried to recall which ladies favoured red this season. Just the thought of Ril with someone else made her stomach churn with jealousy, and anger at Domara's restrictions. She wanted Ril to be *here*, now – to prove he still loved her, on her body. It wasn't a frequent desire for her; the past few years had been an inner battle between her wish to please her husband – and her very real love of him and attraction to him – and the strictures she'd grown up with. The *Book of Kore* taught that pleasure was transitory, and obsession with the transitory imperilled the immortal soul. Marriage was for conception, the perpetuation of the line; the only love that *mattered* to true believers was the love of Kore. Ril didn't believe that.

Only Ostevan understood her struggle, and he was much more open-minded and forgiving than other confessors. She smiled, glad to have at least one person who understood her inner heart. And that reminded her that it must be time for her morning Unburdening. Smiling, she wandered back through the garden with her head full of earthly daydreams.

You cannot perceive all that I am, for I am a legion embodied in one man.

The words from the *Book of Kore* were meant to express the feeling of power of a true believer when unifying himself with the will of his Creator, Kore. But to Ostevan, they'd come to mean completely the opposite.

I have ten thousand eyes: the eyes of Abraxas.

He felt the daemon avidly peering through *his* eyes as he slipped into the queen's suite, greeting that naïve cowpat Geni with a smooth smile that made the maid's heart palpably pound. *Ugly lump.* He sent an impulse into the girl's brain, that she should be elsewhere, and glided into the queen's boudoir.

The bed was still unmade and he sniffed it, letting the fading aroma of Lyra's body tease his suppressed lusts. He collected hairs from her sheets, long strands from her scalp and shorter curling ones from her nethers, and swallowed them, then he licked the rim of her cup, tasting her dried spittle, imprinting her unique taste and feel in his memories, so that he could more precisely target her soul when the time came.

Then he joined Basia de Sirou on the balcony overlooking the Lyra's private garden. The Queen's Guardian was sitting on a stone seat, wincing in discomfort: she had unstrapped her artifice-legs and was massaging the stumps through her leggings. She sensed his presence and looked up, her narrow face going red. 'Ring before you enter, Comfateri,' she snapped, tugging at the harness until the stumps and artificial knee-joints were aligned. She tightened them and stood. 'What do you want?'

She'd be dead by now if I were an assassin. Which I will be one day. 'It's time for the Queen's Unburdening,' he reminded her. 'Why don't you go and relieve your bladder,' he added, his voice so bland only a master could have detected the indiscernible gnostic impulse implanted in the words. It was far beyond Basia de Sirou to resist; she rose obediently and teetered away.

He smiled, then peered down into the Winter Garden. The queen spent a lot of time down there, hidden from sight. Only with a personal invitation could anyone else enter, and despite the closeness he'd forged with her these past months, he'd not been invited – but no one had, he'd come to realise. This was her sanctuary, where she went to escape other people.

I must investigate, he told himself. *What's so fascinating in there?*

Abraxas was curious and unusually cautious, as if the daemon sensed something here that threatened it. *Intriguing.* Then another presence joined him in silent aetheric communion and he greeted the Puppeteer, Ervyn Naxius. <*Master, welcome.*>

The Master inclined his masked face. <*Brother Jest, how do our preparations progress?*>

<*Unimpeded and on schedule, Master. The riverreek we implanted in the city's water festers and spreads; the epidemic will soon take root. And the Prince-Consort believes the tourney to be his own idea.*>

<*Excellent.*> Naxius radiated approval.

<*It's almost too easy,*> Ostevan commented.

<*It may indeed prove simple,*> Naxius replied. <*Pallas is distracted by sideshows; in the confusion of our initial moves, they will turn one way then the other, following false trails and diffusing their defences . . . and then: in one night, Bastion and Celestium, the twin bulwarks of Empire, will be shattered . . .*>

<*But . . .?*> Ostevan wondered.

Naxius gave him an approving glance. <*Aye: 'But'. We're not just going up against a naïve empress and her adherents. We're going up against an empire. The magi built this realm from nothing: there will be hidden defences we don't yet suspect. We may be checked, if those defences are more potent than* we anticipate. We are an arrow in the dark, launched at a shrouded foe: we don't know what armour he wears beneath his cloak.>

<Then you do not expect us to prevail?> Ostevan said, a trifle dismayed.

<On the contrary, I expect that when the sun rises after our assault, the empress, her buffoons and the grand prelate will be corpses. I expect both Bastion and Celestium to be in our hands, and our puppets crowned – but even such an overwhelming success is only the first step, my friend. We will still be only a few predators among millions of cattle, and many of them have horns that can gore even such as we. Failure can't be discounted.>

<We won't fail,> Ostevan vowed.

<Good,> Naxius replied. <Doubt is the first seed of failure. Ensure all is ready: the tourney begins in a week's time.>

Ostevan bowed and Naxius started to withdraw from the link, then paused. <You hesitate, Brother Jest?>

Ostevan indicated the garden below. <The queen puzzles me, Master. Her aura is normal for an untutored mage, if unusually blank of affinity traces. I've never seen her use the gnosis, and she won't speak of it in Unburdening.>

<A woman unable to use her gnosis isn't that unusual,> Naxius replied. <Some mage-women are totally uninterested in the gnosis and put all their energies into domestic life, which is safe, comfortable and easy. The world of the gnosis can be perilous and not all born into it wish to be there. And the girl's a nun, when all's said and done.>

<Yes, but . . . it could be something more. I recall a conversation she and I had in Coraine in 930 . . . about dwyma.>

Naxius' mask twisted into a thoughtful expression. <Dwyma?> Ostevan was surprised to hear uncertainty, even apprehension. <Then that confirms my intentions for her. Our plans for Pallas are in motion and she's too visible a person to corrupt beforehand, but on the night that we strike, I want her given the seed of Abraxas – as a priority!> He turned to face Ostevan. <Stay close to her – observe only, for now, and keep me apprised of anything that confirms such abilities.>

With a swirl in the aether, the Master was gone.

His final words echoed in Ostevan's head. He looked about him: Geni and Basia were still absent, befuddled by his mental manipulations, and it was time for the queen's morning Unburdening: a perfect excuse to unlatch the gate and descend the spiral stairs into her Winter Garden. He banished Abraxas' presence to a low murmur at the back of his mind and extended his gnostic awareness, probing ahead as he stepped onto the green grass. Something stirred, a shadow at the edge of his perceptions, an echo just outside hearing. Wind rustled the leaves, here, where the air was sheltered from the outside breezes. The birds fell silent, but he could feel them watching him.

The sense of another power was elusive: unprovable – but it wouldn't leave him.

Then the queen stepped through the rose bushes, only a dozen feet ahead, wearing just a loose white nightgown stained by grass and dirt and unbuttoned below her creamy cleavage. Her fully erect nipples were barely covered, her hair was dishevelled and she looked flushed and dreamy. He stifled a growl in his throat as his member stiffened.

They stared at each other, her eyes going wide in panic – and, for the briefest instant, *desire*; he was utterly sure of it. Then he remembered himself and spun, exclaiming apologies and keeping his back turned as she threw on the dressing gown she carried under one arm.

'Ostevan, what are you doing here?' she demanded, her voice throaty and alarmed.

'I came for our Unburdening session and found your rooms empty,' he lied. 'I was concerned . . . I'm sorry if I've done wrong?'

She looked at him with big eyes, breathing hard. Despite the Master's admonishments about waiting still ringing in his ears, the desire to hurl her onto her back and possess her – *as she so clearly wants* – was almost irresistible. But his discipline held. 'Milady, I'll leave you at once.'

'No, wait,' she said. 'Just let me . . . prepare. We'll talk in the parlour.'

She's got no more defences than a child. I'm sure she doesn't have the gnosis at all . . .

In theory, that lack rendered her defenceless, but Naxius was right: she was the most scrutinised woman in Yuros. She must remain inviolate, lest Setallius or someone of his ilk perceive the threat. The Corani spymaster might be ageing, but he wasn't blind. She couldn't be touched . . . *not yet*. But that time would come.

So they returned to her parlour and he waited, as Lyra, Basia and Geni fussed over clothing her properly. The murmur of their voices through the door was followed by splashing water in a bowl and a quick-fire discussion about clothing and hair. When Lyra finally emerged, there was a hastiness to her appearance, a few loose tresses and an absence of powders and paints. To him that only added to her natural, unspoiled beauty.

When the time comes, I'm going to rukk her until she's a husk, he promised himself. Abraxas growled, a soul-shuddering sound that trembled through him. But Ostevan rose, bowed, and began the sacred blessings. She confessed to sins of impatience and short dealings with her attendants. He didn't press her deeply, skirting her obvious loneliness, which allayed her discomfort entirely, so that afterwards, she shyly bade him stay and take tea.

'I'm so sorry about earlier,' she babbled, 'I love to walk in the Winter Garden and I lost track of time.' She blushed again. 'I'm usually better dressed.'

'You gave body to the beauty of nature, my Queen,' he said with just enough lightness to ensure she wouldn't perceive him forward. 'A sylph of Lantris, come to life.'

She liked that, as he knew she would. 'I'm nothing special,' she insisted. 'There are many lovelier than I.' Then she asked, 'What do you know of the Winter Tree, Ostevan?'

Ahh . . . 'When Saint Eloy made the cave at the heart of the Celestium his home, the tree came to exhibit unusual traits, blooming in winter, withering in summer. And the sap turns to amber unusually swiftly. It's said that holding a piece of amber from the Winter Tree eases the coming of death. There is a small order of mage-healers, monks called the Eloysians, dedicated to travelling from village to village to bring succour to the dying, especially those in great pain. No one survives their ministry, as they call only upon those dying who have no chance of surviving.'

'What an awful thing.'

'Aye. What healer loses all their patients? And the amber does nothing the gnosis could not – but of course assisted suicide is a sin, while touching a sacred piece of amber is not. It fulfils a need in society, perhaps.' He met her eyes. 'There are hidden powers in this world, my Queen. The gnosis does not explain all.'

Her curiosity about the matter was changing his mind; maybe she had gained some kind of link to the dwyma. *Is our little Queen Lyra a heretic? And Naxius wants her enslaved . . .* What he knew of it suggested that an enslaved mind would be unable to reach the dwyma. *So Naxius wants her neutralised: is dwyma the one thing our Master fears? Intriguing. Maybe this is the weapon I can use against that old snake, if worst comes to worst . . .*

With that thought in mind, he turned the conversation back to her, seeking ways to increase her emotional dependence on him. 'My dear Queen, I have to ask,' he said, 'confinement can place strains on a marriage, for both husband and wife. How are you both bearing up?'

She dropped her eyes to her lap. 'It's hard. Why must we be kept so apart?'

'To protect the unborn: you know this. And you see Lord Ril every day – you don't lack his company—'

'Yes, but . . .' She wrung her hands unhappily. 'Some days we don't even talk.'

'That's not ideal,' Ostevan said cautiously. 'Communication is vital, Milady. And laughter. "Laughter is the heart of love", as the *Book of Kore* says.'

She looked up, eyes wide. 'You do understand – I knew you would. No one else sees it.'

Her dream life is unravelling . . . perfect. 'You fear he's bored?' Ostevan asked, in a 'you-can-tell-me-anything' voice, and when she nodded, asked, 'And yourself?'

Tears started in her eyes. 'I feel like I'm under siege. If this pregnancy goes wrong, I'll lose him, and he's the only one who makes me feel safe. I couldn't have endured these past four years without him!'

'Endured', he sneered inwardly. *Given every privilege and power, and you act as if you were made to swallow poison. I sacrificed everything for you, and you cannot even appreciate it!* Outwardly though, he was all calm and sympathy. 'Do you still love him?'

'I do!' she insisted, bunching her fists in her lap. 'I still do!'

'Still'. Methinks you protest too much, dear Lyra.

'But sometimes he wants more than I have,' she blurted, then flinched, pleading with her eyes that he *understand.* 'I don't know how to be everything he needs.'

Oh, this is better than I could have hoped, he mused, while giving her the sympathy she craved. 'A married couple are not always matched in all matters,' he told her. 'You blame yourself, but perhaps he's also not meeting *your* needs?'

Her eyes went round and she tried and failed to speak. That thought planted, he went on, 'I'm sure his heart remains true. These days, he's nothing like he *used* to be.'

There, Lyra . . . muse on what Ril used to be.

He left her trembling with fear for her marriage yet grateful for his comfort. She surrounded herself with much older men – *surrogate fathers?* – but spoke of intimate matters only to him, as confessor, and that was ideal. 'Until next time,' he said, kissing her hands and thinking how easy – and intoxicating – getting inside her defences would be when the time came.

The knights of Pallas spent weeks training with their winged steeds, practising for the Grand Tourney. There were all manner of flying beasts filling the skies: gryphons and hippogryphs, wyverns and giant birds, and even one or two perytons, although the winged deer were rare. And many pegasi of course, the heraldic steed of the Corani knights. Half the city clambered to the rooftops to watch the spectacle.

While the knights flew and the ladies of court gossiped, the appointed hour for the first phase of the Master's plan approached. Ostevan Comfateri's campaign began in his own chapel, where potential victims came daily, utterly oblivious to their peril.

'You must build up a network of enslaved souls to do your will,' the Master had told them. 'Blood-slaves, infected through your ichor, shed directly from your body to theirs. I leave the "how" to you, use morphic-gnosis to grow fangs, then pump ichor like venom – or use your cock if you are a man – but do remember: those you enslave will lose some of what makes them human: intellect will be suppressed and their baser instincts will rise to the surface, and they will exhibit signs of illness. So move carefully, lest you are detected through your slaves.'

Ostevan had selected his first victims some time ago, and could sense them outside his Unburdening Chancel, waiting their turn to see him. A steady stream of the pious had come in and out all afternoon, confessing pathetic sins that said more about their sanctimony than their spirituality. Finally, the second-last supplicant, a fat dowager seeking atonement for some pathetic misdemeanour, waddled out of the booth. Ostevan took a moment alone to rearrange his physiognomy. The daemon's ichor ran in his veins, but the purest ichor was stored in a reservoir next to his heart, from where it could be pumped into semen or into hollow canines in his mouth, for a purer form of infection.

Once his body was ready, he touched the lamp, signalling readiness for his next Unburdening. His chosen victim entered the chancel, a curtained room off the main chapel, screened not just with cloth but gnostic wards, to ensure privacy. She entered in a wash of perfume, her shapely form swaying. She'd been coming daily, confessing lurid sins of sensuous desire, all the time her eyes *suggesting* . . .

'Lady Jenet, how lovely to see you again – but surely it was only yesterday you were last here?' *And then, the time wasn't right . . . but it is now.*

He extended his senses, confirming that no one else lingered outside, then gave his full attention to the woman kneeling before him. Jenet Brunlye was a shrewd, attractive woman in her thirties. She fancied herself an intriguer, and had once been Ril Endarion's lover. He'd been dropping hints for some time that he liked what he saw in her.

'I rather think that I'm addicted to being with you, Comfateri,' Jenet replied, with a sly wink. 'You provide such *comfort.*'

'I'm flattered, Milady – but it's hardly proper to say such a thing.'

'Being "proper" bores me – I'm something of a rebel,' she answered, fluttering her eyelids.

No, you aren't, Ostevan thought. *You're exactly the opposite of a rebel, because everything you do reinforces the servitude of women.* Not that he cared. 'Really, Lady Jenet?'

'Most women are so conservative. *I* feel free to do whatever I want, with whomever I want.'

'Is this something for which you seek absolution? You don't seem terribly contrite.'

She leaned closer, her rich perfume wafting over him. 'Honestly, Comfateri? I'm not contrite. I've seen your intelligence, your wit, your charm ... I'm not immune to desire, Ostevan.' She put a hand on his thigh. 'I don't think you are either. I'm sure we can work together, in all sorts of ways.' She slipped from her kneeler, shuffled between his legs and unlaced his breeches.

Sink in your hooks, then play the line. He'd seen the game many times, played in many ways. This was far from subtle, but Jenet certainly knew her trade, teasing him cleverly, then taking his thickening cock in her mouth, looking up at him as if in worship as she sucked and licked, fingers working on the lower shaft while her lips and tongue tormented the head. Very soon he was gasping as he felt the inevitable begin. With a convulsive jerk, he went rigid and ejaculated in her mouth, the rawness of the sensation exquisite.

She licked her lips, and tittered, 'There, Comfateri – that's just a taster ... for both of us.'

He stroked her hair, waiting – then the ichor struck. Her eyes bulged as her body tried frantically to reject his seed; verdant darkness blossomed in her throat and spread like a stain beneath her skin, tendrils following her veins as she choked and coughed. He clamped his hands over her jaw to stop her from screaming, and with his mind he shut down any attempt to call for help with her gnosis. Her eyes were filled with betrayal—

—and then the daemon's mind latched onto hers, crushing Jenet Brunlye and sweeping her aside. In her place another intellect entered, full of hatred and barely restrained violence. The struggle was brief, then her eyes darkened and bled thin red tears.

'Master' – her voice was low, intense – 'how may I serve you?'

'Concentrate, Cordan,' Basia de Sirou admonished. Trying to teach the young Sacrecour heir was a trial, but for some reason Dirk Setallius had asked her to help the boy to attune his first periapt. Ordinary gems, amber and even some woods were used to enhance the efficacy of a mage's gnosis, sometimes even doubling the power, so getting a periapt right was no small thing. But Cordan had all the concentration of a kitten: he frowned and stared at the gem, and for a few moments, its light simmered – but he heard a bird at the window and looked away,

DAVID HAIR

and the light died. Basia had been with him for an hour now, but he'd not managed to keep it going for more than a few minutes.

'You need to keep it alight for at least six hours,' Basia told him *again*, ignoring his angry glare. 'It's not going to happen by itself, and no one else is going to do it.'

Cordan sighed and looked back towards the window. 'When does the tourney begin?'

'Properly, the day after tomorrow,' Basia replied. 'The commons have begun their archery and the like, but it's the jousting everyone's come to see, of course.'

'My Uncle Brylion Fasterius will win,' he declared confidently. 'He's a great and noble knight. I've seen him ride – he's *unstoppable*.'

Brylion Fasterius: 'great and noble'? she thought sourly. She pushed the gem in front of Cordan again. 'Come on. You're expected to have this attuned when classes resume next week.'

Cordan wrinkled his nose. 'If you weren't such a useless teacher, it'd be *easy*.' He glanced at Coramore, perched on a sofa reading a book of poetry, then down at Basia's artificial legs. 'Don't Northerners expose imperfect babies?' he jeered, thinking himself oh-so-clever.

'They leave them out to feed the wolves is what I heard,' Coramore tittered, looking up.

'I'm so glad that I'm physically perfect,' Cordan said, preening. 'A king must be, or he's denied the throne.' He gave Basia's legs a cruel look. 'Must be horrible, to be a cripple and know you'll never amount to anything.'

Basia felt her face harden. 'Actually, I was born with two legs.'

Coramore giggled. 'Did they fall off?'

'Did they sin, so you had to cut them off?' Cordan sniggered.

Basia straightened. 'Since you've asked, I was beside a well with three other girls, all normal, like me. I was thirteen, and had been at the Arcanum for just nine months. It was night time, and we'd slipped out to drink some wine we'd stolen.'

'You shouldn't have been drinking wine,' Coramore said primly. 'Did you fall and break your legs off?' She snapped her fingers vindictively. '*Snap! Snap!*'

224

'It was your own fault,' Cordan agreed.

Basia's eyes glazed over. 'Being outside when it started saved my life. We heard the first screams, and later I found that the knights – big brave *Sacrecour* mage-knights – had already begun cutting the throats of the sleeping students. We four girls were wondering what the screams meant when a horde of knights and students – senior *Sacrecour* students, forewarned and forearmed – burst in. They surrounded us, then raped us, several times. Then they held us over the rim of the well, cut our throats and dropped us in. I managed to arch away from the knife enough that it only opened my skin, and the man cutting me lost his grip – my blood was slippery, you see. I fell in, then Jenna was dropped on top and that almost killed me. I was floating down there and they could see I wasn't dead so they threw stones and mage-bolts, but I had just enough shielding to protect myself – though part of me wanted to die anyway.'

She looked up to find the two Sacrecour children staring, periapt and poetry forgotten.

'Then a very big knight came and shoved the students and lesser knights away. He saw me and laughed, made jokes I can't remember, and began a spell of some sort. I guessed this was the end, that all I'd done in escaping the knife was to give myself a few extra minutes of Hel. But then someone slammed into that giant brute above and slashed a blade across his face, then he whirled about and started hacking at anyone in reach, and two more bodies tumbled in – Sacrecour knights, slain by this mad Corani boy. Then they closed in on him, and he did the only thing he could – he leaped into the well too.'

'I don't care about any of this,' Cordan muttered, but he didn't look away. Coramore had looked slightly ill since the word 'raped' was spoken out loud.

Basia ignored Cordan and carried on, 'This Corani boy landed beside me with a splash and I grabbed onto him, and we both looked up, seeing the ring of silhouetted faces. They were howling abuse at my new comrade, and he yelled right back. Then the big knight reappeared and cast his spell, and collapsed the well on top of us.'

She swallowed a lump in her throat. So many years on, and the

memory was still raw. 'My knees and shins were crushed, and I should
have died – but that *amazing* boy, no older than I was, kept me alive
for three days without food, heat and sometimes even air – he had just
gained Air-affinity and I swear he found pockets of it where there were
none. He kept me talking when I drifted at Death's door. He got me free
of the rocks and pulled me through the drains and out to freedom. 909,
that was. That big, ugly brute still has the scar on his face – your hero,
Brylion Fasterius, raper of students and slayer of sleeping children.'

Cordan and Coramore stared wide-eyed. Then the prince said, '909
was a glorious victory.'

But Coramore asked, 'Who was the boy? Did he live?'

'He did,' Basia said, and for the first time a tear ran down her cheek.
'His name is Ril Endarion.' Then she rose stiffly and quietly walked away.

The prince and princess sat quietly for a few minutes. Coramore studied her older brother, looking for a reaction. That he'd been affected
by the crippled freak's tale was clear, and that *wouldn't* do. 'That was
all made-up,' she declared. 'I know for a fact that she was born with
no legs. None of that *happened*.'

'But in 909—'

'In 909 Father led our armies through the gates of Pallas and the
Corani *ran away*. That's all that happened – that's the truth of it.' She
took her brother's hand. 'These people are our *enemies*, brother. One
day we will banish them all, except those we behead. Then you'll be
emperor – and I'll be empress.'

He met her eyes and nodded sullenly. He picked up the gem, looked
at it, then threw it across the room. 'I wish I was riding in the tourney,'
he complained. 'I bet I'd win.'

Coramore looked up at him avidly. 'You're growing taller all the
time. One day you'll be as tall as Brylion!' Though in truth, even she
knew in her heart that her brother was small for his age – but their
father had been too, and he'd been *emperor*. And Cordan *had* changed:
before the gnosis he'd been listless, but now he burned with energy.

That will be me soon, too, she thought enviously.

Their door opened again and they caught a glimpse of their watch-dog,

Sir Bruss Lamgren, who admitted Jenet Brunlye. Cordan leaped eagerly to his feet. Coramore wasn't so pleased. Lady Jenet might be helping them, but she didn't have to like her.

'Good morrow, Highnesses,' the noblewoman purred, focusing her smile on Cordan. 'I trust you're well?'

'Very!' Cordan declared. 'I scored top in my last test.' He was looking at Lady Jenet with devotion, which made Coramore's mouth go sour.

'How wonderful,' Lady Jenet said, clapping her hands. 'You'll be graduating in record time, I'm sure.'

Coramore thought she looked wretched: her eyes were all bloodshot and her skin, beneath her powder, dry and flaking. Though Cordan hadn't appeared to have noticed such *ugliness*. 'Do you have news from Uncle Garod?' she asked bluntly, trying to forestall all the usual fawning.

'I do,' Jenet replied. 'He's coming to Pallas to free you and restore you to your rightful throne.' She bent closer, and Coramore winced: her breath was like rotting meat. 'The tourney will bring people from everywhere and all eyes will be upon it. No one will be watching you, except' – she glanced towards the door and smirked – 'the Mutthead.'

'Why can't you rescue us now?' Coramore demanded.

'Because this is about more than a rescue – this is a restoration, Princess. You wouldn't want the Imbecile Queen to escape, would you?'

'I want to see her head *roll*,' Cordan declared, 'along with all these Corani *liars!*'

Jenet stroked his cheek. 'What a wonderful king and emperor you will make, dear.'

Cordan gazed at Jenet Brunlye with his tongue almost hanging out. Coramore decided that she *hated* her. 'You look *sick*,' she said, to make sure Cordan noticed.

The noblewoman stared at her and for a moment, Coramore felt an intense sense of malice. 'Apologies, Highness. I'm battling a cold.' Jenet dropped her voice as footsteps approached. 'Be ready. The day is coming.' She whispered something in Cordan's ear, and he blushed.

'What did she say?' Coramore asked, when she was gone.

'Nothing,' Cordan replied, flushing hard. 'Nothing at all.'

13

Finostarre

Jousting

Jousting – the noble art of two men trying to knock each other off a horse with a stick – arose from the drills of the cavalry units maintained by the Rondian legions. Like all things frivolous, it was adopted by the royal courts and made into a spectacle. Over the years it's likely cost us more noble sons than real warfare.

LIVUS LIVIDIUS, KORE SCHOLAR, 823

Finostarre, near Pallas, Yuros
Aprafor 935

In the last weeks of Aprafor, the most renowned mage-knights in the Rondian Empire converged on the site of the Imperial Ludus: the village of Finostarre, four miles northeast of Pallas. The tourney was to be held on fields behind the Convent of Sainte-Lucia, named for the dead Mater-Imperia. On a bright and warm afternoon the royal household arrived in a caravan of carriages and wagons, and after the Imperial Guard swept the premises and surroundings for danger, Lyra and her ladies went for a walk in the manor gardens while servants unloaded the baggage.

'Wurther offered me rooms in the local convent,' Lyra was telling Hilta Pollanou. 'I think he was making a point – either way, I couldn't bear the thought – thank goodness Lord Crofton offered his manor!'

'How long was my Queen in the convent?' asked Medelie Aventour, a new lady-in-waiting; her family's strategically important estates bordered the Duchy of Fauvion.

'I was a Daughter of Kore for my first nineteen years.'

'That's almost as long as I've been alive,' Medelie noted, sounding faintly bored.

'Me too,' Lyra replied coolly, 'but they do say that youth isn't an accomplishment.' The subtle put-down got a titter of appreciation from the group, but Lyra regretted the cruelty immediately. *Her family sent her here, but they used to favour the Fasterius court. I should be making her welcome.* She sought to soften her words. 'But you wear it well, Mistress Medelie.' They shared a hollow smile and Medelie curtseyed, but there was little warmth in her eyes. More and more young men and women were being sent to Pallas now, hoping to progress in her court, which brought with it a whole new set of problems. And Medelie Aventour was wearing red, a colour Lyra mistrusted since her vision.

She turned her ear to the main conversation: the upcoming tourney, of course. Her ladies had lost the ability to speak of aught else.

'We'll prove that the greatest knights are the Corani,' young Lady Emali Kuipper exclaimed.

'Is the ability to knock people off their mounts with big sticks a sign of greatness?' Lyra asked, though secretly she was just as excited. 'It's a little barbaric, don't you think?'

'No, no, Milady,' Hilta replied, 'there's great skill involved—'

'—a knight must be brave, first and foremost,' Jenet put in, dabbing at her nose – she looked a little unwell, but was gamely carrying on. 'With a strong sword arm, proven in battle.'

'And wielding a mighty lance!' Medelie tittered. 'A natural rider, good in the saddle.'

That's all a little too risqué, Lyra thought. 'The best knights are also masters of the gentler arts, as I recall,' she said reprovingly.

'Indeed,' Hilta agreed. 'Mariat said that a knight was more than just a man on a horse: he must be a courtier, accomplished in dancing, verse and song, conversant with philosophy and the teachings of Kore and Corineus – and, of course, of unimpeachable honour.'

'There,' willowy Sedina Waycross exclaimed, 'you define the very soul of a Corani knight.'

'Do the knights of other Houses not have these qualities?' Emali asked innocently.

'I think it's well-known that the Sacrecours favoured knights of lesser quality,' Hilta declared.

'Why, can't they dance?' Sedina asked, all faux innocence.

'Dancing is about all they can do,' Medelie tittered. 'In truth, the only virtues the Sacrecour value are sycophancy and cock—' She paused deliberately, looking Lyra full in the face.

'—cock-fighting,' Sedina put in smoothly. 'They're addicted to it.'

Lyra wasn't amused: that had gone beyond the bounds of *risqué*. As they returned to the manor, she told Hilta, 'I don't want Lady Aventour's company tonight. She can eat alone.'

When she glanced at the miscreant, she thought Medelie knew exactly what she'd said and didn't give a fig. She almost rescinded the directive – *better to keep her under my eye* – but another hour in her company would be one too many.

Ostevan Comfateri took an early carriage and arrived in Finostarre an hour later in a mischievous mood. He found the Crofton Manor chapel and changed in the vestry, admiring his lean, sculpted body and the youthfulness he'd been subtly restoring to his face. Most would think him thirty – twenty years under his real age. Vanity appeased, he entered the small family chapel from the vestry door, finding it lit only by a large stained-glass rose window facing east. The morning sun was beautifully placed, penetrating the darkness with shafts of coloured light, so that the age-blackened gargoyles and saints looked alive.

Lyra Vereinen was already there, kneeling against the altar rail in the front row of the confined space; Basia de Sirou guarded the main doors. Ostevan hurried to greet the queen. 'Good morning, Majesty . . .?' His voice trailed off when he realised her face was streaked by tears. 'Milady? Are you well?'

The queen dabbed her eyes. 'Everything hurts! My back, my neck, my breasts . . . *everything* hurts, Ostevan. And Ril . . .' She glanced behind her. 'Basia, I wish for an Unburdening.'

Basia's eyes narrowed; she wasn't supposed to let her charge out of her sight unless it was within designated safe areas like Lyra's suite or garden – or with someone trusted. Officially, Ostevan was on the 'trusted' list, but Basia was Volsai, and she trusted no one. 'I won't listen,' she said testily. 'I just need to be able to see.'

'Unburdening is a sacred rite,' Ostevan reminded her, 'absolution given for confessed sins, in the safety of confidentiality.'

With a scowl, Basia left. Ostevan locked the door behind her, then returned to kneel beside the queen in the tiny chapel. He dispensed with the ritual Unburdening prayers before asking, 'What's really the matter, Lyra?'

Lyra glanced at the Sacred Heart icon above the altar. 'Isn't it strange that our holiest symbol is a knife stabbing a heart?' she said, before admitting, 'I'm afraid of losing my husband.'

'Tourneys can be dangerous,' he said, wilfully misunderstanding, 'but the finest knights are the least likely to take injury.'

'No, Osti – I mean that someone's trying to steal his heart away. I had a vision—'

'Divination-gnosis, Milady?'

'Something like that,' she replied evasively. 'He'll dance with a woman in red ... that was the warning.' She suppressed another sob. 'You know our marriage hasn't been perfect, but I *can't* lose him – we have a child to protect ...'

'Ril Endarion is well known for his protective nature,' Ostevan replied. 'And Milady, hard though it is to say, many marriages have survived infidelity.'

There, Lyra, let's see you deal with that notion.

She blinked back more tears. 'If I knew he'd been unfaithful, I could *never* lie with him again. I just couldn't bear it. The sin would taint us, and endanger our immortal souls.'

Sex, sin and salvation, Ostevan mused behind his carefully schooled expression of deep concern. *A wonderful brew.* A sudden idea came to him. 'Lyra, if you wish to keep his heart, you must fight for it.'

'How?' she flared. 'Would you have me flounce about like Sedina Way-cross with my bosom all but bare? Or take lessons from Jenet Brunlye?'

Oh my, she does have fangs after all, Ostevan thought, enchanted by her

231

flash of temper. Her cheeks were flushed, her eyes blazing: an intriguing glimpse of who she could become . . .

'Of course not,' he said, pitching his voice to soothe her, while still conveying anger at her situation. 'Lyra, you must *never* stoop to conquer – don't lower yourself to a rival's level. You're Ril's wife, and you carry his child. You love him. Remind him of that.'

'But I'm forbidden to be intimate with him—'

'Sister Domara is only a midwife – you're a queen.'

'But if I lose this child—'

'You won't.' He took Lyra's hands again, leaning closer. Inside him, Abraxas growled, but he quelled the lurid desires of the daemon. 'Frankly – and I speak despite my vocation – the Church knows little about such matters, but one thing I did learn while exiled in Ventia is that ordinary couples make love right through pregnancy and take no harm. '

She shot a look at the altar, almost as if expecting Kore to appear and condemn them both to Hel. The passion he'd let flow into his words had gripped her, though. 'So I should just ignore my confinement and go to him?'

'That's my advice. Think of it as a campaign of seduction.'

'But I don't know how to seduce anyone,' Lyra protested.

'He's your husband: that gives you all the advantages, Lyra. Be there when he needs you, concerned and willing. And you're beautiful, never forget that. Show him your belly, where his child is growing; tell him you need him.' He stroked her shoulder. 'He'll be unable to resist.'

She gave him a small, hopeful smile, then groaned. 'I don't think I can do it . . . This morning I could barely get out of bed. My back is killing me, and the skin on my breasts feels so tight it could rip . . . I feel *wretched*, Osti! I *hate* being pregnant – I'm fat and ugly and useless—'

'That's normal for the fourth month of pregnancy. Sister Domara will be able to help.'

'She just tells me to pray and be strong,' Lyra glowered.

Ostevan put on his best mask of concern. 'Well, in my lowly village in Ventia, I had to be many things: physician, apothecary, vetinarius. Are you willing to let an *old friend* help you?'

'What do you mean?'

'Well, I could give you some temporary ease, until Domara can be persuaded to be more sympathetic. A little massage, combined with healing-gnosis, and you'll be much improved.'

She wavered, doubtful. 'Um, I suppose . . .'

'Thank you for your trust,' he said warmly, unclasping her cloak and removing it. Beneath was a big, tent-like dress, typically dowdy.

Her mouth went round. 'But . . . *not here*! This a church—'

'Milady, before the magi, priests of Kore were also physicians, and temples were places of healing.' He dared a little mesmerism. '*Be calm, Lyra.* I'll just scoot in behind you and, *there* . . .'

While she was still caught up in his spell, he moved deftly, unbuttoning the back of her dress and pulling it open revealing her snowy-white back, while she gasped and caught the front of the garment, holding it to her chest. He was well versed in the old seduction technique: get your prey halfway undressed and the rest takes care of itself – but despite having Abraxas shrieking lustfully in his mind, what he wanted was to push the boundaries of trust between them, to forge a bond of greater intimacy.

But Lyra's base instincts were rebelling, despite the spell. 'Ostevan! I don't think—'

'*Hush*,' he told her, gentling her with a touch more mesmerism, 'we don't want to bring Basia in, now do we?' She flinched guiltily and tensed up, just as his fingertips found a knotted muscle and flooded it with warm healing-gnosis.

She gasped, and sagged against the railing. 'Ohhh . . .'

Breakthrough, he thought triumphantly. She'd been in genuine agony, and he'd given her the surcease her body craved. With strong, careful movements he spread that ease, working her back muscles from her hips to the nape of her neck and then up into the base of her skull, and every passing second saw her relax further, groaning with increasing abandon.

When he was done she sighed regretfully. 'That was *wonderful*. I feel like a new person.'

'Excellent. Now, let's see to your breasts.'

She coloured instantly, pulling the front of her opened dress tightly to her. 'But—'

233

He gently took her shoulder and pushed at her spine, straightening her back again. 'Lyra, I am your *physician* today, and breasts aren't *sexual*: they're *mammary glands*, and in need of attention, due to your pregnancy. Now, if you please?'

Gently but firmly, he removed the dress from her hands, while drawing her back against his chest. She sucked in a gasp as he cupped the underside of her mounds – *Damned right they're breasts*, he thought – and began to massage. She murmured some unconvincing protests, but the blissful sensation robbed her of the will to resist, all the while his resonant bedroom voice soothed and gentled her. 'We must prepare them for their role, and regular massage will help that. You should do this yourself every morning – with or without Domara's permission.'

'Uhhh,' Lyra moaned, sagging against him.

'And as for these,' he murmured in her ear, taking her nipples between his thumbs and forefingers, 'they are the conduits for your milk and require attention lest they become blocked. Massage them also, pinching them, gently at first, working up to the edge of what you can bear, like this.'

He did as he'd described, and Lyra groaned from the back of her throat, quivering and arching her back, her eyes closed. He could almost smell her cleft swelling. He marvelled again at just how guileless she was. Her mouth was right by his ear, her breath sweet and hot, each touch sending her deeper into an erotic trance.

Oh, my Queen, I could do anything *to you right now . . .*

What he chose was restraint. He removed his hands and drew up her dress again, enjoying one final look at her quivering breasts and engorged nipples and the tightly rounded swelling of her growing belly beneath. Her skin was flushed with pink, and her breath just a sigh as she looked at him with confused abandon on her face, like a virgin about to yield herself.

'I hope that helped,' he said brightly, taking her left arm and feeding it into a sleeve. 'Remember, every morning and evening, Milady.'

She looked up at the altar and went absolutely scarlet. 'Osti, we've *sinned!*' she gasped, her eyes round with disbelief at what she'd just allowed, then she faltered, 'Haven't we?'

'Because it gave you ease?' He used mesmerism again, the faintest touch: *Lyra, be calm.* 'You are I are very alike; we grew up in religious houses, and see pleasure as somehow sinful. But all we did was something any healer would have done. *We've nothing to feel guilty about.*' He sleeved her other arm, and calmly re-buttoned the back of her dress. 'Everything we did today was for your *ease* and *betterment.*'

'But you touched my breasts—'

'As any physician must occasionally do for a female patient. And if you also found it pleasurable, don't you think that's something your husband might appreciate knowing?'

She swallowed as she realised what he meant. 'Really? *Oh . . .*' They shared a look of such intimacy that he had no need of the gnosis to see her thoughts, which were all of how much better she felt now . . . and how *grateful.*

She knows she let her guard down, but I've given her ease and support and not taken advantage of her – and all in the name of bolstering her marriage. Of course, I'm now her greatest ally . . .

He carefully removed any traces of his manipulations from her aura with mystic-gnosis so there would be nothing for Basia or Setallius to find when they examined her next, then said, 'Now, Milady, are you ready to win back your husband?'

Her hesitant smile became emphatic. 'Yes, yes I am.' She bit her lip, and he watched her become herself again. 'We shouldn't do this again,' she said, without recrimination. 'It wasn't really proper . . . but it's not your fault, Ostevan. Domara's neglecting me.'

'Would you like me to speak to her, Majesty?'

'No, that's my duty.' Then her tones softened. 'Thank you, Ostevan. You risked our relationship, and your own standing, to help me. If there was any impropriety, the fault is mine.'

You're welcome, he thought mockingly. *You belong to me, Lyra. In time, I'll take all of you.*

Ril hunched over to reduce resistance as his pegasus swung into the wind. Lance held high, he nudged Pearl slightly to the right, trying to ignore the air buffeting the coloured metal target bolted to his left shoulder. He narrowed his eyes, seeking the starting-point for his next run. Hundreds of yards to the south, Gryfflon Joyce mirrored his movements.

The Imperial Ludus was to follow the rules of the jousting circuit: each bout was three passes, with points given for hits. Jousters had the kinesis-strength to stay mounted most of the time, but a strong, well-placed blow could unseat any knight – momentum and air-speed were a great leveller in aerial jousting – and unhorsed contestants lost the bout outright.

Ril had been training hard with his Corani knights: he was here to fight – and win. *I'm the lead actor*, he thought now, *and the stage is set.*

The first days of the Ludus were for the archery contests, running races and staff-fighting – *Entertainment for the mob, by the mob*, was Larik's view – but the knights ignored all that, too caught up in their own preparations in the skies overhead.

<Come about, pooty-girl,> Ril murmured, nudging Pearl with his mind as the pegasus reached the top of the run, then he cried, *<Now!>* as they dipped into a dive and accelerated, Ril couching his lance, shields blossoming as they shot towards a hoop of orange light hanging in the sky. There was a second one a hundred yards beyond; he corrected their trajectory as they burst through the first hoop, keeping to the right side of the line of light traced in the air to guide the jousters, ensuring they didn't collide mid-air. He saw Gryff's venator dropping into line and speeding towards them.

<Furl!> he shouted into Pearl's brain, and she folded her wings as Gryff and his beast, both encased in shimmering blue shield-light, shrieked towards them. Ril had maybe three seconds to align his lance with Gryff's target, and then – *Bam!* – their blunted lances battered into each other's gnostic shields and broke. Ril's leather strapping went taut and he almost jerked from the saddle as the impact buffeted him, but he held on grimly as Pearl reeled and dropped. For a second he thought they'd stall and plummet, then the pegasus spread her wings again and they caught the breeze.

He shouted his relief, then looking back, saw Gryff's venator gliding towards the ground for a fresh lance.

'There – nothing to it, pooty-girl,' he told Pearl, who'd done this as many times as he had. 'Well done, well done.' He pulled his helm off, relishing the wind in his hair.

It was a clear, cold autumnal day and he could see for miles. At least three dozen mage-knights were aloft and practising; he could see gryphons and hippogryphs, giant eagles and owls, perytons, alicorns and even a bat-like creature with garish wings. Each had different advantages – size, speed, obedience, courage, manoeuvrability, stamina – and flaws. 'I'd not trade you for any of them, Pearl,' he said, stroking her shoulder.

<Ril, another pass?> Gryff sent.

<No, I think we're done – I want Pearl to be fresh for tomorrow.> Ril sent his mount into a glide towards where Larik and Gryff were already waiting with their gear, landing at a graceful canter then trotting in. The pegasus was snorting and sweating; she needed watering and a good rub-down. A small crowd of stablehands surrounded them as Ril dismounted; they took his helm and unbolted his target before leading her away.

Ril grabbed a pitcher of water and re-joined his friends.

'Ril—' Larik smacked his arm, 'listen, you're looking good – but only to a point. You've got to spur Pearl into the impact; don't let her slow.'

'Yes, yes,' Ril replied absently; strangely, he was more relaxed now the tourney was practically here. Above him, Lero Falquist skimmed past, breaking his lance on the target of an Incognito, one of the low-blooded unaligned knights who frequented the tourney circuit, and sending the unnamed knight into the safety nets.

Ril broke off talking to applaud, then asked, 'Who am I fighting tomorrow?'

'*Argh!* Pay attention! Sir Wiltor Verden from Klief – he's a half-blood.'

'A half-blood? So why are you worried?'

'Because the speed of impact is almost eighty miles an hour and no shield can fully stop such a blow. Blood-rank doesn't matter here, Ril – it's all about speed and accuracy. You'll catch his lance in your eye if you're not careful,' Larik added irritably.

When Ril put aside his last-minutes nerves, he could see the tourney was turning out to be a great success. The Ludus had attracted massive crowds – although that brought its own problems, and the Imperial Guards were working hard to keep hostile contingents apart. The dour Argundians, fiery Estellans, truculent Hollenians, ill-disciplined Brevians and surly Andressans and Midreans all disliked each other and tempers were running high.

The biggest and most acrimonious groups were all Rondian, Ril noted: mutinous Aquilleans, duplicitous Canossi and arrogant Pallacians, all balling their fists at the slightest insult. But the biggest concern was the Dupeni group, led by Duke Garod Sacrecour himself, who'd come west, heavily guarded, to cheer on his knights.

Ril was itching to face those Dupeni *champions* . . .

Trumpets brayed, the vast crowd quietened and the heralds bawled out the names taking part in the next joust. The masses were still buzzing from the last clashes, reliving the spectacular fall and the victors' aerobatic celebrations. The hunger for more excitement filled the air.

'*IN THIS RUN, THE PRINCE-CONSORT, SIR RIL ENDARION*—'

Handkerchiefs waved – an insult in Estellayne, but a compliment everywhere else – and voices screamed. Ril felt a rush of adrenalin, the taste of glory and blood suddenly on his lips. He felt like a Rimoni slave-gladiator, ready to conquer or die.

'—*AND FACING HIM, SIR WILTOR VERDEN, THE GREEN KNIGHT!*'

Fewer cheers; Sir Wiltor was a half-blood known only to those who followed the tourney circuit. But as Larik kept pointing out, blood didn't matter so much here: a well-aimed lance could penetrate even a pure-blood's shields; technique, riding skill and the controlled rage of combat could count for more than raw gnostic power.

Ril mounted Pearl and as he steadied her, he noticed that Larik's hands on the reins were white-knuckled. 'Hey, relax, Larik, it's me,' Ril told him. 'Even you could flatten this guy.'

'"Even me"?' Larik sniffed. '*Thanks*. Remember: go in fast.'

'Uh-huh.' Ril yawned. If you gave an opponent too much respect, you became tentative. 'Let's get it done.' He lowered his helm onto his head and pushed up the visor. The roar of the crowd became muffled as he nudged Pearl into motion. The pegasus picked up his mood, trotting jauntily onto the parade ground before the royal box. Ril glanced sideways as Sir Wiltor appeared beside him, riding a golden-horned alicorn, a creature of Northern myth, similar to his own pegasus but lighter-built, with a single spiral horn protruding from between the eyes. Alicorns were a common heraldic beast in several Pallacian and Midrean Houses. This one was prancing with a mad look in the eye.

<*I trust your mount is under control, not in control?*> Ril sent to Wiltor, who was looking pale. *As well you might: jousting with royalty is a chancy business, and for you, pretty much a no-win contest,* Ril thought, feeling a little sorry for the man.

Then they were parading past Lyra's box and pausing to salute the empress, dipping their lances to her. Ril's was sporting ribbons in Lyra's imperial colours of purple and gold – he hadn't told her about the other token he'd found slipped into his helm during the night: a red ribbon. He'd almost thrown it away, but at the last minute tied it around his right forearm, beneath his undershirt. *For luck.*

Lyra's face was pale, her worry for him plain even at a distance. One hand rested on her swollen belly. He glanced about the royal box and found a few red dresses; including Jenet, and he decided the anonymous ribbon must be her token. The thought left him somewhere between edgy and energised ... then he noticed the new girl, Lady Medelie, was also in red.

And she looks like she'd be a pleasant handful ...

He told himself that looking wasn't a sin as he and his adversary took to the air. He barely saw the fields and streams, the woods, the village and convent spread out below like a child's playset. Stewards on board windskiffs guided them onto the approach path, marked by a corridor of gnostic-lamps hanging in the air, and as Pearl positioned herself, he was aware of Sir Wiltor mirroring his movement on the other side, almost half a mile away. They had to start simultaneously, so that they met in front of the main stand, and three times, Wiltor messed it up, which made Ril increasingly irritable. But finally Wiltor got it right and the Chief Marshall sent a blaze of red light skywards: the signal to attack.

<*Let's go!*> he told Pearl, nudging her left and couching his lance as

they dived. His temples thudded in time with his racing heart, rushing air stung his eyes and his lance wobbled crazily until his gnosis steadied it. They flashed through the approach circle and along the guideline . . .

. . . *closer, closer* . . . rukka! *It's* NOW!

At the last instant, Wiltor veered fractionally, weakening his own speed and spoiling his aim, and his lance passed harmlessly by Ril's shoulder – but his own pierced Wiltor's shields and struck the target on the Midrean knight's shoulder. The jolt was jarring; the lance snapped and Wiltor was hurled sideways in a crescendo of crashing metal and blue sparks from his gnostic shields. Ril barely noticed as he went flashing by, trying to right his mount and screaming in exultation. When he looked back, Wiltor was bouncing in the safety net and his alicorn was flapping away disdainfully.

Got you . . .

The sea of upturned faces below roared in approval, their excitement mirroring his own. He brought Pearl about, flipped up his visor and shouted triumphantly as he passed above them, then took the pegasus down in a rearing hind-legs landing and cantered to the Royal Box.

Lyra's face shone with frightened relief amidst the other ladies, all cheering and waving. He heard a chant from the stands too: *Prince of the Spear! Prince of the Spear!* That felt good.

A tankard of ale in one hand, he walked Pearl himself to cool her down after the brief but intense exertion. The wind in his hair felt good, the sweat on his brow well-earned, and the beer was nectar. Other competitors offered congratulations, some fulsomely, those of rival Houses more grudging. Then he saw Brylion Fasterius and his good mood wavered. The Sacrecour champion was a big man, scar-faced, rough-bearded and swaggering. When their eyes met, there was no respect, only appraisal, and a promise.

Let me meet him this week, Ril prayed silently. *Let me draw him!*

Then a red flare lit the evening sky and the next bout commenced above: an Argundian knight riding a peryton was up against an Incognito knight on a venator; the winged reptiles were ideal military mounts, but considered too slow to make good jousting beasts, so few knights flew them in tourneys. Ril's interest wasn't really pricked until something about the Incognito caught his eye – not the shield emblem, a fairly common white scales on black, a symbol of Justice; most knights who rode incognito were exiles who harboured a sense of being wronged and there were at least a dozen of them on the lists. But this man leaned into the impact, where most knights didn't have the nerve for that. His bulk and flying style looked familiar too – then came the clincher: just before he unseated the Argundian in a livid crash of gnostic sparks and crashing steel, he veered fractionally closer into the path of his foe, a risky manoeuvre that put more force into his blow, but risked taking the other man's lance in the chest or helm instead of the target. Ril had only ever known one man who habitually did that.

He stared as the man descended to the front of the stands. An Incognito wasn't obliged to remove his helm when receiving royal acclaim, and this one didn't as he knelt briefly before Lyra, then backed away, victory wreath in hand.

Ril licked his suddenly dry lips, passed Pearl's reins to a squire and re-joined Gryff and Larik. 'Takwyth's here,' he announced.

'Takky's here?' Larik exclaimed. 'What a bloody nerve.'

'Arrest him,' Gryff grunted.

Ril thought on that. 'We can't: he walked away. No court ever passed a verdict against him, so legally, unless I press charges now, he has the right to be here.'

'Then press charges,' Larik sniggered. 'Serve the prick right if you did.'

'And look like a coward before the whole empire? No, what we need is a plan to beat him.'

14

Masked Assassins

Hadishah

The Church of Kore claims that the Amteh are the only faith who have a sect dedicated to murdering non-worshippers – the feared 'Jackals of Ahm', the Hadishah. Somehow they contrive to overlook their own Holy Inquisition!

ANTONIN MEIROS, HEBUSALIM, 852

Sagostabad, Kesh, Ahmedhassa
Thani (Aprafor) 935

Waqar waited impatiently as the appointed time came and passed and the sultan still hadn't appeared. As instructed, he was standing outside the Royal Dom-al'Ahm, a small shrine set in the Walled Gardens of the palace. A brown-robed Godsinger had gone into the shrine earlier, but apart from that, the garden remained empty.

Salim has many calls on his time, Waqar reflected. *He's probably late to everything.*

Outside in the streets, the crowds were in ferment, mostly against the Ordo Costruo – even the Ja'arathi were indignant at seeing the sultan lectured in his own palace. Nonetheless, Shihadi promises to 'bring the Ordo Costruo to their knees' rang hollow. Unsurprisingly, the people of Sagostabad backed their native son, Salim, and red scarves were in the minority out there.

A bustle at the gates signalled the arrival of the sultan at last, and Waqar rose, trying to quell his nerves. Two guards remained at the entrance to the garden as the Keshi ruler approached. He was clad in green and gold silks, with a spotless white turban; Waqar could see somehow that he wasn't Latif, but whether he was the true sultan, he couldn't say.

'Prince Waqar, please, a bow suffices between friends,' the sultan said as Waqar went to prostrate himself. 'Apologies for my tardiness – something has arisen.'

Waqar got up hurriedly, his eyes downcast. 'Great Sultan, if now isn't a good time—'

'It's a security matter, and will be resolved swiftly.' The sultan sounded vexed. 'I'm eager to speak with one of our rising young men, and of course, with his illustrious mother.'

Rising young man, Waqar noted, and *illustrious mother*. The praise steadied him. 'My mother would be honoured to meet you, Great Sultan. She said to tell you that her words in the throne room were just politics.'

'Of course.' Salim smiled. 'Perhaps you and your mother might join me for spice-tea at the third bell of morning tomorrow, in the Mosaic Hall?'

'That would be an honour, Great Sultan.' Waqar realised with a start that he was fractionally taller than the other man – and he was *almost* certain that he was the real Salim, not another impersonator. *An impersonator lives a lie, but this man feels true.*

'Are you married, Prince Waqar?' Salim asked, and when Waqar shook his head, 'Engaged, surely, a catch like you?'

'I've only recently completed my gnostic training. I'm sure my uncle and my mother will have the matter well in hand, but I am content to attend court and learn its ways.'

'As well try to map the clouds,' Salim sighed. 'The court is always in motion, but if you can master the currents, it can be navigated.' He was about to say more when bells chimed all over the city, followed by the first wailing cry of the Godsingers—

—except, oddly, in the shrine beside them, which remained silent.

I thought I saw a Godsinger go inside . . . Waqar turned towards the dom-al'Ahm just as the air *shivered* and every bird in the gardens took to the wing. A grey-robed man appeared at the entrance to the shrine: his hands were gloved and his feet booted, and the only thing alleviating his monochrome attire was a lacquered mask of a handsome man wearing a steel helmet.

'Salim of Kesh, offer up your soul to Kore,' the masked man called in Rondian, his voice distorted by the mask. He was clearly a mage, because pale blue shields were distorting the air around him and lightning danced on his fingertips.

For a second the tableau froze, then Waqar conjured his own shields and whispered, 'Get behind me, Great Sultan!'

The masked man pulled a straight-bladed sword from beneath his robes and glided towards them. Waqar looked around frantically for the guardsmen, but he glimpsed two prone figures, and another dark-robed figure at the entrance. The lamps glinted off a masked face: they couldn't retreat that way.

'There's another gate, on the far side of the garden,' Salim said. He drew his own scimitar and thrust it into Waqar's hands. 'Stay calm,' he urged, then he faced the attacker. 'Who are you?'

'Ironhelm, the Knight of Virtue,' the man replied. He extended his blade towards Waqar. 'Go, boy. My quarrel is with your ruler.'

'Then your quarrel is with me,' Waqar replied bravely.

Ironhelm closed in, his sword extended before him, and lunged. They exchanged a hammering sequence of blows, then Waqar blocked a mesmeric attack that almost froze his brain. The masked man was clearly far stronger in the gnosis than he was. Then Salim hurled a dagger at the masked attacker and although it was deflected harmlessly, Ironhelm paused, and Waqar was able to disengage.

'Run!' he shouted to Salim, and together they pelted through the walled garden. Waqar blocked a mage-bolt from the attacker that almost knocked him sprawling, then ran into Salim's back as he stopped abruptly, thirty yards from the far gates. The sentries there were also lying in crumpled heaps, and standing over them was a tall feminine shape, also wearing a copper mask, this one a woman with a stylised heart-shape face, her rosy lips wistfully pursed, as if for love's first kiss. She spun a scimitar dextrously and went into a fighting crouch. 'Waqar,' her distorted voice purred in toneless Keshi, 'get out of here. We've come for Salim.'

Waqar responded by stepping in front of the sultan and kindling light in his hands. 'I'll die first!' he shouted, to drown the sudden realisation that he really *could* die here.

'HELP! HELP!' <*HELP!*> he screamed aloud and into the aether as Heartface advanced, her aura a bewildering swirl of light. From behind came the sound of boots on stone and he glanced back to see Ironhelm approaching. Where the third masked man was, Waqar had no idea.

He gripped his borrowed scimitar tight and prepared to sell his life dearly.

Sakita Mubarak had been given an apartment high on the eastern side of Sagostabad Palace facing away from the river; the stench of the slums reached up to clog the air, cooking-fire smoke wafting through her window morning and evening. It was an insult, of course – the best rooms were on the west side. 'For your protection,' Rashid told her. 'Threats have been made.'

Rene Cardien knew she and Rashid were far from friends, but the Arch-Magister of the Ordo Costruo had still thought she might be a bridge to new negotiations. He and Odessa had left the day before and she was dining alone, working on a paper concerning the differing temperature layers in a typical storm-cloud and how they interacted to produce winds, rain and hail. Her late husband Placide had been a genius at making sense of the sparse information, and diligent in creating new experiments to prove or disprove his theories. Most magi treated 'magic' as an art-form; to him – and to her, too – it was all science. They were like-minded and had grown somewhat fond of each other, but it had still been a shock when Antonin Meiros himself had called them both to his office and suggested they marry.

She couldn't say that she'd ever *loved* Placide, but she'd respected him, and they'd had two beautiful children. They'd made a real home of their apartment in the Arcanum complex, and their children, the whole point of the marriage, had sustained her through Placide's death.

Special children.

Her reverie evaporated as something clicked in the wall before her and a panel swung open.

She gaped foolishly, because she'd never even suspected there could be a secret passage here, but her shields kindled instinctively and she propelled a globe of gnosis-light into the darkness. It illuminated a grey-cloaked man in a lacquered copper mask: a leering cat wearing a wide-brimmed hat. She knew the mask: Felix, the Lantric masque character synonymous with Luck.

Felix gestured, and her light winked out. That little touch of power told her what she'd feared: that the intruder was formidably powerful. 'Sakita,' his voice said, distorted by the mask. He stepped towards her desk, spreading his hands.

Her heart thudding, she stood, kindled mage-fire in both hands. 'Who are you?'

'A messenger from a disappointed suitor.'

'*What?*'

'My Master propositioned you last year, but you refused him. I've come to renew his offer.'

'Then you're wasting your time. I don't want anything from him, or you.'

'Of course you do,' Felix purred. 'Estranged from your family, viewed with suspicion by your order, an outsider wherever you turn? We could give you a real family, Sakita.'

'You've got five seconds to leave before I splatter you over the wall.'

'I could even give you your mentor and lover back.'

Impossible, she thought. 'Four. You don't know who you're dealing with.'

Felix laughed. 'I know exactly who I'm dealing with, Sakita. I know all about you and your powers – even the things Rashid doesn't know.'

Surely he can't—? 'Three,' she cried, gathering her strength.

His voice changed. '*Twinkle? I've missed you. You look so sad and tired, Twinkle.*'

Dear Ahm, no one knows that's what Placide used to call me! 'Shut *up*! Two—'

'You're a lost soul, Twinkle. Let me bring you home—'

She blasted a storm of sky-blue mage-fire at the robed shape, a blast that ripped Felix's cloak apart and charred it to floating ash. The mask clattered to the floor amidst a haze of burning fabric, but no body fell: the cloak and mask had been empty. She went rigid in alarm when she should have moved, then twin daggers speared her calf and something slick and reptilian wrapped about her legs.

She shouted in horror as a crippling numbness took the feeling from her limbs and she toppled. The fangs released her, but only so the serpent could rear back for another strike. She tried to ward, but it was wrapped about her and her body was failing to respond.

<WAQAR!> she shouted to the heavens and the aether – then the serpent struck again.

Waqar's heart was hammering as Heartface's first blow slammed into his guard and a shower of sparks erupted where steel struck shielding, then he lashed out with his own blade, steel belled and the woman chuckled.

'Saluté, Prince! Have at thee!' she said, as if this were a theatre performance.

Waqar threw everything he had into a bolt of light, one that would have left an ordinary man's skull crisped to the bone and the brain cooked inside. But it died on her shields and the counter-blow slammed him backwards, a blast of kinesis like a giant fist.

'You don't have to die,' Heartface told him.

But Ironhelm had arrived now, and Salim, armed only with a dagger, placed his back to Waqar's while Waqar tried to extend his shields. <HELP!> he shouted again, broadcasting the call to any with the mind to listen, while parrying another flurry of blows. He had to find a place where he could protect Salim, and that meant downing one of these assailants. He chose the woman, assuming she'd be the lesser in combat.

'Ha!' he shouted, launching himself into his best combination: a high-low-high rain of blows meant to bewilder and open up the foe for a smashing kick to the knee, followed by a rapid killing blow. Her defences opened, he smashed a kick to her knee that bent it sideways – she should have been screaming and toppling . . .

Crunch.

A second kinesis-blow smashed him over backwards, hurling him against a tree trunk. He bounced and thudded to the ground, the air knocked from his lungs, leaving him flailing like a beached fish.

Heartface closed in, her scimitar trailing pure light along the edge. 'Stay down,' she warned as behind her, Ironhelm drove Salim backwards effortlessly, then skewered the sultan's right arm. The dagger fell to the turf.

'NO!' Waqar shouted, trying to rise, even as a voice cried out in his skull.

<WAQAR!> It was his mother, and she sounded desperate.

'Go to Mother, little boy,' Heartface told him. 'There's nothing you can do here.'

Behind her, Ironhelm hammered his left fist into the sultan's jaw and the ruler of all Kesh and Dhassa thudded bonelessly to the grass. Waqar shouted in dismay and launched himself at the masked woman—

—who slammed him straight back into the tree again, so hard the bark imprinted itself on his back and skull. Then the ground reared up at him and he pitched onto his face, tasting blood and dirt. Heartface appeared above him, reversing her blade and slamming the hilt through his paper-soft defences and into his temple. Salim's face flashed across the darkness and took everything away with its passing.

Even as Latif saw the masked man, someone grabbed his forearm and with terrifying strength, pulled him back out of sight. A hand clamped over his mouth and swallowed his startled gasp.

<Quiet!> a woman hissed into his skull.

All of the impersonators had been trained in combat, and those disciplines were enough to freeze him in place. Bony hands pulled him against the wall. 'Please, don't make a sound,' the woman whispered. Then boots clicked on the tiled hallway and Latif went still, though his mind was racing. *That's Halaam's room the masked man just left.*

The boots stopped, and he felt a tickling presence at the edge of his consciousness. The impersonators had also been trained in how to keep a mage from their mind; it was all about inner silence. He emptied his mind in an instant, fear sharpening his response, and the girl behind him – he was sure she was just a girl – joined his efforts. A cool, smooth emptiness radiated around them. A couple of steps came closer, but still he didn't move or even breathe.

The boots clicked away down the hall, towards Faizal's rooms.

He twisted his head and looked backwards and down at the girl behind him. She was tiny, just a pair of deep-set, intense hazel eyes peering through a bekira-shroud. The air about her tingled with gnostic shielding. He was quite literally inside her defences, but he was already certain she meant him no harm.

Unlike that masked man. 'Is Halaam . . . ?' he asked, heart in mouth.

'Too late,' she breathed.

'Faizal—?'

'Also too late. I'm only here to get you out. It's too late for everyone else in this wing.'

Is everyone murdered . . .? Lord Ahm, no—! 'What about the sultan?'

'You're not the real Salim? *Chotia!*' She gripped his sleeve. 'Then where is he?'

Hope flashed through his heart. 'He went to the dom-al'Ahm to meet Waqar Mubarak – we must find him—'

'Mubarak?' his rescuer spat. 'Is he behind this?'

'I don't know!' *Though why not? Rashid's so close to ultimate power already* . . . Latif's hands began to shake. 'We must raise the alarm. The intruder is only one man.'

'No, he's not,' the girl replied. 'There's at least one other – do you know the Lantric plays?'

'Of course.'

'I've seen Beak and Ironhelm. Your guards are all dead: if you shout, no one will come.'

'Who are they?'

'I don't know – I didn't see where they came from. But I've sensed their power, and they're stronger than anyone I've encountered.' Despite her youth, she obviously thought that was a momentous thing.

Oh, to be young and invulnerable again. 'Who are you? Where did you come from?'

'Call me Tarita. I've been pretending to be a servant.'

Tarita . . . that's not a southern name. But there was no time to press for more. 'The wives and children are in the zenana. We must get them out—'

'I'm supposed to rescue the sultan,' Tarita replied, wavering for the first time.

'And I'm not he. But the fastest way to the Walled Garden is through the zenana, and I know the way. Please – all the sultan's wives are there, and the children are in the nursery.' He swallowed, and added, 'My own wife and son are there.'

Tarita looked doubtful. 'You should just get out. They'll kill you if they can.'

'*My* life means *nothing* – it's the sultan who must be saved. Come, this way, there's a private entrance.' He pulled her in the opposite direction to the way the masked man – 'Beak', he guessed – had gone. He was grateful for his soft-soled slippers as they padded along the ghostly halls. All was silent – then he heard a door slam and a muffled cry. He froze, looking at Tarita. She shook her head. 'Keep moving.'

They traversed a hall into a gallery where three guardsmen lay unmoving in pools of blood, their own daggers lodged in their chests, fists locked around them. Their expressions were terrified. His gorge rose and he vomited. He'd seen violent death before, but he'd never become unused to it.

'Come on,' Tarita whispered, her voice flat. 'Which way now?'

He pointed towards the right. 'That way.' They darted from shadow to shadow down a long gallery, then climbed the steps winding upwards to a small door at the top. 'It's a servants' entrance, but we impersonators use it when we're in a hurry. We each have a key' – Latif patted his pocket and cursed – 'but I've lost mine—'

'It's okay,' Tarita whispered. She touched the door, pale light flickered around her fingers, the lock clicked and the door fell open. 'Wait here for me,' she told him.

'No,' he said, though his legs were shaking, 'I'm coming with you.'

'Then stay behind me.' She drew a small scimitar from beneath her robes. Her skinny hand looked scarcely strong enough to grip it, but she moved with practised grace.

She must be Hadishah . . . but which faction?

Together they crept along the dark servants' corridor and entered a hall. She conjured light in her hands and he pointed to the right.

'Those stairs lead to the pleasure rooms, and from there, on the far side, another flight goes up to a corridor leading to the Walled Garden.'

They ascended three flights and Tarita again used her gnosis to force the lock; the suppressed click echoed through his shredded nerves. But the zenana was utterly silent, which chilled his soul. Light kindled on the edge of Tarita's curved blade. 'How many people live here?'

'In the whole zenana? The sultan's six wives and eight children on the top floor, two above this. Four of us impersonators have wives, one level above us, and there are six children – one is my son. This is the pleasure level; there are only boudoirs and pools . . .'

'Twenty-four souls . . . And servants?'

Latif coloured. 'Oh yes, I forgot. Each of the wives has a maidservant and those with children have an ayah – so another twenty people.'

'Most of your type forget servants exist,' Tarita muttered. 'Stay behind me, and stay silent, no matter what we find. Our goal is the sultan. Everyone else is expendable.'

It wasn't a comforting thing to hear, but he couldn't fault her for it.

She slipped through the door and onto a balcony overlooking a central pool where the wives liked to relax in the midday heat. But a whirlwind had come through: a whirlwind with blades. Four of Salim's wives lay scattered like debris among the wreckage, their naked bodies sliced open like butchered carcasses. The pool was a cloudy scarlet.

Dear Ahm, take them unto you . . .

Tarita spotted the stair to the next level up. 'Come on,' she said, and Latif was both impressed and shamed by her courage. The air was thick with the stench of death as he followed her up steps slick with blood; an ayah was laying on her back on the top step, throat cut open. He grabbed the rails for strength. *My world is collapsing around me.*

Somehow he swallowed his terror and guided the young woman – she looked barely sixteen – through the slaughterhouse, past more bodies, more blood. Then he heard screaming: a woman's voice abruptly cut off, then another – his wife's voice, he was certain, a fading cry for mercy. It came from somewhere to the right. He choked back a wail of despair and broke into a run.

Umada had been chosen for him and marriage had never become

love: her body didn't move him and her company didn't please him. But together they'd made Juset, their beautiful son, and right now, they were the most precious things in creation. He had to find them . . .

Tarita caught him in a web of force and slammed him against the wall. She clamped her hand over his mouth and his eyes bulged as he struggled. Then he froze as the door to his own rooms opened and a grey-robed man emerged, his face concealed by a handsome helmed mask: 'Ironhelm', he guessed. His robes were dappled in scarlet and his blade was dripping.

Tears stung his eyes like acid, but he'd not heard his son's voice – it was just possible Juset was in the nursery; that thought kept him from panic. He let Tarita draw him further along the curved wall, out of the masked man's sight. Ironhelm's booted feet strode away.

As soon as the assassin was out of earshot, Latif ran for the door, pulled it open – then went stock-still, because he was far, far too late.

Umada was on the floor, bleeding her heart's-blood into a white snowcat pelt. The ayah was beside her, her skull mashed against a pillar as if she'd been hurled there by a giant. His son Juset, his neck broken to a ghastly angle but otherwise uninjured, lay in the middle of his mother's bed. Both women had been trying to shield him.

Latif sank to his knees. His heart almost exploded when Tarita touched his shoulder. 'I'm sorry,' she whispered. 'I'm so sorry.' Her pain sounded very real.

He somehow found the strength to go to his son and kiss his forehead and straighten his still-warm body. 'Is there anything you can do?' he asked, hoping against hope that she was a miraculous healer, one who could reunite soul and body. He'd have almost settled for a necromancer at that moment, just to see his son move again.

'No, Latif. I'm sorry. But we have to go now.'

'Can't . . .? I can't—'

'You'll do as I tell you,' Tarita said crisply. 'You at least will survive this, Lord.'

Such was the strength in her voice . . . Ah, yes, now he could feel her using mesmeric-gnosis to strengthen his will . . . It was a relief, in a way, to just surrender to her determination. He took one last look at his dead son and let his sorrow turn to hatred.

Who did this? he wondered. *Who are these people?*

They went back to the passage, Tarita leading the way, seeking the corridor to the Walled Garden. When they heard booted feet again, they hurled themselves behind a statue into a tiny niche. The footfalls echoed closer; they went rigid, close as lovers, as the assassin approached.

For a ghastly moment, Ironhelm's eye-slits seemed to look their way, then he strode past and was gone, the sound of his footsteps soon fading. Tarita emerged cautiously, then reached back and took Latif's hand. She pulled him behind her and headed for the garden.

Someone spoke, their voice carrying from above. A glass dome gave the zenana its natural light and Latif followed the sound to the railing overlooking the atrium. He had to swallow his despairing gasp as he saw what hung in that empty space.

Sultan Salim Kabarakhi, naked and bloodied, was suspended in the middle of the domed ceiling, rotating slowly. 'What do you want?' he begged, his voice broken, agonised. He was wheezing, as if through broken ribs. His handsome face was battered, his muscular body bruised and burned and the hair on his skull had been completely burned away.

A grey-robed figure appeared at the railing: Beak, his long sharp nose quivering as he laughed. 'What do we want? Why, everything and nothing, Great Sultan! Everything, because we want the world' – he made an expansive gesture – 'and nothing ... because you can't give it to us. You can only die.'

Latif choked back a shout and willed Tarita to act, but she was just staring, immobilised by the sight. *We must do something!* But his limbs remained locked as Beak raised his right hand, blue light coalescing about his fist. Salim didn't flinch as he turned in the air towards his killer.

A blast of that blue light flew.

Latif couldn't help it: rage and despair erupted from his throat as Salim was caught in a bolt of livid energy, jerking in a death spasm as he was engulfed, then plummeted, a blackened, broken thing that splashed into the bloody pool amidst his murdered wives.

Tarita swore, grabbed Latif's shoulder and dragged him away from the stairs as another bolt of light struck the very place he'd been standing a second before. 'Run!' she snarled, and threw him towards the left even as she faced right, already conjuring energy about her. He could not stop himself glancing over his shoulder: Ironhelm was storming around the curve of the passage. Blue light crackled in both directions; Tarita staggered and cried out as energy slammed into her shields – then a semi-transparent wall of force billowed from her own fingers and anchored to the walls on either side, catching the next bolts from Ironhelm. Latif backed away, and so did she. 'Find us a way out,' she snapped, her eyes on the advancing assassin.

A woman's voice called from above in Keshi, 'Who is it?'

'Two: an impersonator and a Hadishah,' Ironhelm answered as he reached Tarita's barrier and raked his blade, gleaming with purple energy, through the wall of force, then peeled the sides apart. Tarita and Latif turned and pelted towards the stair to the servants' quarters below. Latif could hear their hunters closing in. He reached for the door as Ironhelm appeared along the corridor, moving like an implacable force, batting aside Tarita's mage-bolts and conjuring a vortex of swirling purple light – necromantic-gnosis.

Latif yanked open the door, grabbed Tarita's collar and pulled, just as Beak came into view, hovering in mid-air above the central pool. He had a clear line of sight and his blast of fire *whooshed* towards them, but they were already tumbling through the door. Latif kicked it closed, and the heavy wood crashed closed on the flames, but Tarita was up and reinforcing the barrier with locking-wards anchored to the doorframe.

She didn't pause to see if it'd hold but shouted, 'Go!' and followed him down the tight spiral stairs even as a blow like thunder struck the door, sending dust filling the air as the plaster cracked and beams creaked alarmingly.

Latif heard a footfall high above and looked up to see a third assassin: a feminine shape in the mask like a pretty girl, peering down the stairwell. *Heartface*, he recalled. She saw him and it felt like her eyes had reached out and gripped his thoughts . . .

—then Tarita wrenched him from sight and Heartface's bindings fell apart.

With a defiant shout, Earth-gnosis thrummed from Tarita's hands, tearing at the stairs above and pulling them into a barrier to prevent Heartface from floating down the stairwell. The walls trembled and a dozen steel fastenings gave way. 'You'll bring the whole thing down!' Latif cried out, staggering onwards.

'Then run!' Tarita shrieked. Above them, somewhere in the wreckage, the door burst apart and boots stomped into the stairs; voices, male and female, crackled metallically. But Latif was at the bottom now, and pulling the door open. He stumbled through; Tarita sealed it behind them, then shoved him into motion again. The passage they found themselves in led past storage rooms jammed with furniture; enough to furnish a hundred princely homes. They were below ground, but there were high vents through which moonlight was streaming. Tarita looked around, then blasted the nearest vent open. The stone grille went flying off into the darkness with a crash.

'How can I get up—?' he began, but she'd already gripped his collar and was leaping, bringing him with her into the darkness – and just in time, for the warded door behind them shattered, blue light flashing beneath Latif's feet.

Then they were outside in a courtyard surrounded by buildings. A ball of fire burst from the hole; Tarita twisted and fired back at an indistinct shape that emerged, then she dragged Latif skywards again, cursing at him to *be still* as he clung on in terror, trying to stop his legs from kicking. They landed on the battlements as dark shapes came blurring towards them through the night. Tarita twisted in the air, then hurled Latif into space.

'*WHAAH*—?' he wailed as the darkness rushed past, and just before he hit the moat in a great splash he caught a glimpse of Tarita bringing up her light blade to parry a massive blow from Beak. His gaudy mask chilling in the darkness, he battered her sideways in a cascade of sparks – then Latif went under and came up clawing at the noisome water, winded and gasping and terrified. The giant face of Luna washed the cityscape in silver, lending the dozen crocodiles in the water an almost mystic quality as they surged towards him.

He thrashed for the outer shore, thanking Ahm and Salim that the sultan had installed metal rungs into the wall so that anyone unfortunate enough to fall in could at least *attempt* to climb out. He had just reached the lowest rung when the water boiled and a twenty-foot-long crocodile rose from below like a leaping salmon. He flew upwards, his hands and feet groping for the rungs, as the giant beast caught his longshirt and arrested his progress for a moment – then the fabric ripped and he hurtled onto the filthy bank. He lay on his back gasping as a windskiff soared overhead and mage-bolts flew, striking one of the two combatants on the battlements, but he couldn't say which. He flinched as someone – Tarita? – cried out in pain.

More shapes appeared on the battlements and the sound of combat grew. People were dying back there to enable his escape – and although all his reasons to live were lying dead back in the palace, something spurred him to run as if every afreet in Shaitan's Pit was on his trail.

For all he knew, they were.

Explosions lit up the walls as he made the first alley and dived into the maze of streets, the palace quickly vanishing behind him. At first he ran blindly, barely thinking, then his brain caught up, an avalanche of thoughts overwhelming him and driving him to his knees.

Salim is dead. My brother impersonators . . . my wife . . . my son . . . dear Ahm, you let them take Juset! For a time, his mind went numb under the sheer weight of it all.

The only thing that was clear, when he could think again, was that the world had no place for the impersonator of a murdered ruler.

15

The Vitezai Sarkanum

Magi Lineage

The descendants of the original magi inherited the mage-blood. The purer the bloodline, the greater the mage: do not mistake this for highborn elitism, but a reality of the gnosis.

However the pure-bloods are – probably because of that gnostic purity – notoriously infertile, which has driven the breeding, planned and incidental, of thousands of lower-blood magi lines whose still-substantial prowess holds the empire together.

ANNALS OF PALLAS, 847

Feher Szarvasfeld (White Stag Land), Mollachia
Martrois-Aprafor 935

The miracle of being alive gave the world a divine lustre – even a stony cave reeking of smoke and damp. The fleeting burst of sunlight flickering outside the cave-mouth was the gaze of angels; the wind was the breath of God; birdsong the joy of Life. The food was ambrosia.

We're not dead!

Kyrik and Valdyr had been here a fortnight or longer, but neither were ready to move on yet. They'd had to heal enough to eat more than broth, but when they could eat solids once more, the hot bread and spicy goulash tasted *divine*. They weren't out of danger – Hegikaro Castle was only thirty miles away – but the Rondians didn't appear to know about the cave, and they were far enough below ground to prevent scrying. Valdyr was asleep, his face still gaunt and drawn, but the brothers were getting stronger with every day.

'How did you get in without the Delestre soldiers realising?' Kyrik asked Janik, the hunter who was currently feeding him.

His benefactor grunted and said modestly, 'It was no great feat, Prince. This is our land. We knows its secrets.'

As the brothers were fading into unknowing, their rescuers had come up from below, silently removing one corner of the floor from beneath, then pulling them down into a lower floor of cells – 'one that prick Robear don't know about,' Janik said with a grin. They'd carried the Sarkanys out the way they came in: through the waste-water outflow from Hegikaro Castle.

'If we'd known you were there sooner, you'd have been out in no time,' Janik said now, 'but we din't know, not 'til a servant, one of ours, heard you singing that hymn, "On High" – your father's favourite. Thought it were a ghost.'

'I don't even remember that,' Kyrik admitted, then asked, 'So I presume those bastard Rondians are hunting us?'

'We've seen skiffs and patrols every day, but they'll not find us – we crossed the Osiapa seven times to get up here, and the snow's come down every night since – even their hunting dogs are useless to 'em.'

Kyrik thought about Robear and Sacrista Delestre, and the vile Governor Inoxion. *Paruq*, he thought, *you may decry vengeance, but I'll have their heads, if it's in my power.* 'I know I keep thanking you, Janik, and I won't stop. We owe you *everything*.'

'Just remember that when you're sitting on your father's throne,' Janik replied laconically. 'Meantime, you and your brother getting yourselves better is all the reward we need.'

The Sarkanys and their rescuers moved a week later, under cover of night. A fresh fall of deep snow filled the folds in the land, but beneath the trees the ground was largely bare and they made good time. Kyrik's gnosis was still imprisoned under Sacrista's Chain-rune, and he had no idea how they'd remove it – but that was a problem for another day.

Over the three-night journey they left the river valley and struck out through the highlands into Feher Szarvasfeld, or White Stag Land. Once they were enclosed on all sides by mountains, and Kyrik doubted anyone but a skiff-borne mage flying immediately overhead could detect them, he and Dragan decided they could risk day-time travel – the nights were dangerous up here, where winter still held the land in its treacherous grip. Only those who understood its secrets could survive this stark, forbidding place where deer bellowed mournfully and wolves howled, where ice encrusted the icethorns, which all but died in winter, only regenerating when the thaws came. That would be soon, but for now the icethorns were like blackened skeletons.

The brothers were still too weak to walk far, so they had to submit to being borne on stretchers. The bearers' breath steamed in clouds as they hauled Kyrik up yet another slope, towards a dense copse of trees. A few passes behind, Valdyr's carriers sweated and panted as they hauled their own fur-clad burden. Valdyr's face was thickly bearded, as was Kyrik's, and any exposed skin was greased with animal fat. He looked more like a sleeping bear than a man.

Dragan Zhagy and Tibor Siravhy blazed the path ahead of them; the Vitezai had established hidden camps through all the mountains against such times. Mollachia had never been a strongly united kingdom: every castle was its own fiefdom, and the king's influence was limited by his reach and his ability to lay siege to keeps quite as strong as his own. The Vitezai Sarkanum saw itself as the preserver of the True Way; it traced its history to the Mollachian folk-hero Zlateyr the Archer – but at times it too had been renegade, an outlawed group.

Zlateyr – or Zillitiya, Kyrik thought. *I never had a chance to ask Paruq.*

The idea that his national hero might have been Sydian, not Andressan, wouldn't upset him all that much, but as he was pretty sure Dragan, the *Gazda*, head of the Vitezai Sarkanum, wouldn't take the notion well, he had no intention of raising it. The Zhagy and Sarkany families went back a long way together; Dragan Zhagy was Kore-father for both brothers, entrusted with their upbringing should their father die.

Our lives are certainly in his hands now . . .

The brothers were set down beneath towering pines, on ground well-sheltered from the snow. The foresters kept the trails clear up here, allowing passage for those who braved the mountains – silver and grain were crucial for the kingdom's economy, but so too were furs and timber. The mountains were infested with wolves, bears and sabretooths and the weak or careless didn't last long out here, but the foresters were a hardy breed.

'Prince Kyrik, Prince Valdyr,' Tibor Siravhy called softly from ahead on the trail; no one shouted here in the heights where avalanches could take down entire hillsides. 'Come; see.' Behind him, Dragan was standing in the lee of an outcropping, gazing back down the valley.

Kyrik accepted big Merkus' help to get stiffly to his feet and gratefully thanked his bearers, then helped pull Valdyr upright. Together they staggered up to join the Vitezai leaders. Dragan had an air of menace about him: he was like a great, shaggy timber wolf, with leathery skin, lank grey hair and yellow teeth. Beside him, Tibor Siravhy was more like a hound; unusually for a Mollachian, he was clean-shaven, and kept his receding hair cropped short. Everything he did was tidy, efficient and understated. He greeted the Sarkany brothers with a deferential nod, then pointed southwards, down the valley. 'Rondian legionaries.'

Kyrik squinted and made out a string of dots far below: a century, perhaps: five cohorts of twenty. 'We were down there only this morning.' He strained his eyes and picked out a larger shape: a mounted man or woman.

'Are they scrying us?' Dragan asked.

'With the Chain-runes upon us, we can't tell,' Kyrik replied.

'Do the Chain-runes protect you from their scrying?' Tibor wondered.

Kyrik hadn't thought of that. 'Ysh, you're right; they've screwed themselves,' he said with a grin. 'They can't remove the Runes of Chain from a distance, and they can't penetrate their own spell.' The four of them shared a rare moment of levity.

'Then let's go on,' Dragan said, then patting Valdyr's arm, 'It's good to see you smile again, Little Draken.' He turned to Kyrik. 'More snow is coming. We're making for the Rahnti Mines, under Watcher's Peak. They're well-hidden, and the old tunnels go all the way through the mountain; they come out near Lake Jegto. The Rondians never come there.'

After another hour of climbing, the fugitives were led beneath a slick rock-face curtained by a grille of huge icicles and into a concealed cave mouth. Dragan smiled slyly as he indicated a stack of torches, each wrapped in oil-cloth. He sparked one to life with his tinder-stone, the flames lighting his craggy face, and handed it to Kyrik.

'Draken's fire, my Prince. May it spread through our land.'

Valdyr tottered wearily in his brother's wake as they clambered through the winding, uneven tunnels. The Rahnti Mines had been closed up before he was born, the seam of silver long mined out. The tunnels were harder work than the climb up the mountains; too narrow for stretchers, so the brothers had to walk, though there were many willing hands to aid them.

The past few days had been utterly draining, despite being constantly plied with food. No one recovered swiftly from starvation: muscle and flesh needed time as well as sustenance. Their bodies had been laid to waste like a torched grain-field: Valdyr's limbs felt hollow and he was hobbling within a few minutes. It took a while to notice that someone had his shoulder.

'Not long now, then we rest, my Prince,' said Nilasz, a rascally-looking man with ginger whiskers. 'You've grown tall, but I can manage.'

They came to a large chamber littered with broken mining equipment. A Sacred Heart had been carved into the wall. The brothers were gently helped to sit while others stuck torches into the rusted old wall mountings and doused the rest. They broke out cooking gear as the chamber filled up with men conversing cheerily, as if they hadn't spent days fighting their way across snow-covered wastes and through deserted mines.

Valdyr let his gaze rove over the men of the Vitezai Sarkanum. It had never been an order of noblemen, not like the Rondian knights; one had to be invited to join, and members kept their participation secret. Their mission was to keep Mollachia true to itself: *True to the People. True to Kore. True to the Land.* These men had all taken that vow; he half-recognised some from childhood memories: guardsmen of the keep, rangers and foresters. There was no badge, no uniform; only the *Gazda's* identity was made known to those that needed to know.

Valdyr accepted some thick broth and strips of dried meat with a smile and leaned against the wall, thankful to not be moving. He met

Kyrik's eyes and nodded; words weren't required – since the dungeons, even though he had no idea what they'd said to each other, they were brothers again.

And I'm bigger than him now – who'd have ever thought?

'What are you thinking, Brother?' Kyrik asked, slurping the hot broth.

'That it's good to hear our native tongue again.'

'It surely is.' Kyrik puffed out his cheeks wearily. 'Though I miss Keshi, in truth: there are so many words they have for things we don't – they can express nuances we can't in Mollach.'

Valdyr scowled. 'If we've not needed words for those things before, we don't need them now. Best forget it. We have bigger tasks ahead.' *A land to free from these Rondian thieves.*

To his relief, Kyrik nodded in agreement. 'Ysh, that life is behind me now.'

The next days were long and hard. There was no pursuit: Dragan's scouts reported that the legionaries had come nowhere near the entrance to the mines. But the tunnels weren't easy and Valdyr grew tired of being a burden.

Nilasz told him to stop apologising. 'In time you will carry us,' he said firmly.

Meaning the gnosis, Valdyr thought. *They can't defeat the Rondians without magi so they need Kyrik and me to kill Robear and Sacrista Delestre.* Which he'd gladly do, but he doubted it'd be that easy – especially as Kyrik was still Chained and his power remained elusive. That he would never gain the gnosis – it did sometimes happen, Kyrik had admitted – was a dread that haunted him; after all, he'd been Chained all his adult life, long before he'd come into it.

Beneath the earth, day and night no longer had meaning, and when they finally broke out of an iced-up chamber, they had to wrap gauze about their eyes to endure the daylight; though the sun was lost in glowing white clouds, the snow glittered across the wide valley and a distant flat expanse: the frozen Lake Jegto. Lightning played on the eastern heights and thunder rolled distantly. If there were birds here, they were silent.

The lake was still six miles away, but Dragan sent runners ahead, and before long other men returned, leading two ponies for Kyrik and Valdyr. By then they were so exhausted they had to be lashed into the saddle and led onwards. The ride passed for Valdyr in a slow haze, in which a fox-headed man and woman rode on either side of him, silently mocking his weakness.

They arrived at a small camp, just semi-permanent hide tents set on a headland above Jegto, where the lake fed the Magas River. The brothers were helped inside the largest pavilion, where fire-pits burned and the hide walls trapped the heat. Mead and stew were forced down their throats until they finally began to feel alertness return.

'Those ponies,' Kyrik said to Tibor, 'they looked Sydian . . .'

'Ysh,' Tibor replied, and jerked a finger. When Valdyr turned, he realised that the two squat figures in the corner of the tent weren't Mollachs but Sydians, an ancient man and woman, peering at him through narrow steppes eyes. Their grey hair was festooned with animal bones.

'They're from the Cuzhym clan, of the Uffrykai Tribe,' Tibor said. 'They're on some kind of pilgrimage; Kore only knows why. And ysh, it was their horses, so maybe you owe them something. Though in a while you might owe them even more.'

Valdyr frowned. 'What do you mean?'

'They claim they're Sfera – that's Sydian magi – and that they can free your magic.' Tibor shrugged. 'They've done no harm here, and healed some of our injured brothers.'

'Why would they help us?'

'Who knows? No doubt it'll come with a price.'

Doesn't everything? Valdyr reflected.

Kyrik and Valdyr were taken to meet the Sydian pilgrims the next morning, after a good night's sleep. The two old steppes-folk had their own pavilion, a small hide tent with faded markings similar to those they'd seen among the Vlpa. The brothers crawled inside as bidden and found the two ancients sitting cross-legged and draped in furs.

'Come in, come in,' they said in good Mollach. The old man climbed out from under his furs, and Kyrik was slightly alarmed to see that he was naked, his skin painted with lines and circles. His skin was leathery, his limbs skinny, but his belly was plump and his eyes were wolf-yellow. 'Disrobe, then lie down,' he growled.

'Ysh, lie down,' the women rasped. She was also naked, and of similar build.

Kyrik sensed care here, and trust. 'We're in their hands, Val,' he whispered. 'Let them do their work.' He started undressing carefully, leading the way.

Valdyr complied with a prudish look, and they lay down, side by side. The woman leered and cackled, but it sounded like harmless good humour. She came to kneel by Kyrik, while her – *husband? brother? cousin?* – knelt beside Valdyr. Each had a small cup of milky fluid that tasted of chalky mud. *Opium*, Kyrik recognised; he didn't care for the stuff, but he gave Valdyr a reassuring smile and drained it in one swallow.

The Sydian ancients chanted over them, and he wanted to berate them: *The gnosis isn't like this – it's knowledge, it's trained and precise, not your strange babble and painted runes*. But his tongue was too clumsy for speech. His body went numb and his thoughts scrambled, and that was his last rational moment for some time. He floated into nothing . . .

Scent returned: a rancid, earthy smell, like a woman's cleft, a powerful, fecund odour that reminded him of the breeding-houses. Then feeling returned to his toes, like a fire had been lit beneath them, and he began to sweat in rivulets as the heat spread. Then came taste, a sweet-and-sour berry tang that filled his mouth. The old woman swayed into view, calling to her gods: a litany of ancient names long-forgotten beyond the steppes. Her sagging breasts filled his sight and in his semi-dreamlike state, they repelled and fascinated him. Beside him, Valdyr was babbling in Keshi, screaming a name Kyrik didn't know; his black hair was plastered to his skull and his whole frame was shaking, and all the while a pressure was building, an all-over scratching and tearing, as if these aged Sfera magi had dug their fingernails into his skin and were slowly peeling it away. A burning smell filled his nostrils and seared his throat, then the woman kissed his forehead and numbness spread, an agonising balm like ice. A web of light flashed before his eyes. For a moment he saw piercing grey eyes – *Sacrista Delestre*

– then they were gone and so was the web, and he felt an incredible feeling of completion.

Beside him, Valdyr moaned and he turned his head, regarding his brother as their eyes met. Then Kyrik raised his hand and kindled blue light, the faintest wisp of it.

Ysh . . . I'm back! It felt momentous, a giant step back toward reclaiming his world.

When the web about him tore, Valdyr felt a stunning moment of clarity. *Can I—?*

He was standing atop an icy peak, but there was a fire-pit, cunningly set in a dip, and it was burning. Four figures were arrayed about it, dark shapes frozen sitting up in the snow. Empty eyes turned his way. The moon broke through the clouds, catching a white stag in its beam.

Can I . . .?

And then it was gone and he sagged backwards on the furs, groaning in despair.

When next Valdyr woke, there was light glimmering through the tent flaps and something rich and meaty was roasting. Flat, alien faces framed by braided white hair peered down at him. Thoughts were oozing sluggishly through his mind, unable to connect to each other; his only constant was Kyrik beside him, watching him with a wondering expression.

He drifted back into a reverie, wandering lost in a forest of thoughts until he found a clearing: there was a bowl in his hand, filled with steaming meat and gravy, a mounded roll of hot bread slowly soaking into it. Only when he took a mouthful and chewed, almost weeping at the taste that filled his senses, did he realise he was awake. Then he saw a cup of ale and swept it up, swallowed it fervently and savoured the dark, heavy brew, as filling as a meal in itself.

'It's good, isn't it?'

Valdyr turned and found that Kyrik was sitting propped up, also eating, and watching him intently. 'I've not had a good Mollach beer in . . . how long? I'd steal sips from Father's cup, that last year before we marched. So much better than the legion muck . . .'

Valdyr's eyes stung at the memory. 'So did it work? Do you have your gnosis back?'

'Ysh.' Kyrik kindled a spark of fire on his fingertips in satisfaction. 'You?'

'I felt like I touched it.' Valdyr grimaced in frustration. 'I know it's there, but I can't *reach* it – I was under a Chain-rune before I ever gained it so I have no idea what it even feels like.' He slapped the ground in frustration.

'Give it time,' Kyrik advised.

'We don't *have* time! These men expect something of us, Kyrik, and they expect it *now*—'

'No, Brother, Dragan understands. He's a patient man, and he'll make sure his men understand too.'

Understand that I'm useless, Valdyr thought morosely. He peered outside and saw daylight. 'How long did I sleep?'

'It's the next day, nothing more. Iztven and Ghili are outside.'

'They're the Sydians?'

'Ysh. I spoke to them earlier. They're old Sfera magi, past breeding, so they got the tribe's permission to leave to investigate the legend of a Sydian hero named Zillitiya. They're on what they call a dream-quest, following his footsteps as best they can.'

'Zillitiya?' Valdyr scratched his chin, remembering what the Vlpa had said. 'Like Zlateyr?' He sniffed. 'They've heard our tales and stolen them. But it's good they broke the Chain-rune, eh? Good for you, anyway.' *Please, Lord Kore, give me your gift – give me the gnosis!*

Kyrik looked around at his companions, sitting cross-legged on hide cushions in Dragan's tent: Valdyr, Dragan, Tibor and he had been joined by red-whiskered Nilasz and Rothgar Baredge, a hunter of the Stonefolk, the original Yothic people of the valley. There were still families in the highlands who'd never intermarried with Zlateyr's people.

Although the brothers were still mending, the Chain-rune had been broken a week back and spring was coming. It was time to make plans.

'So, Dragan, tell me everything,' Kyrik said, gesturing at the map spread before them.

'The Rondians brought two legions,' Dragan replied. 'Ten thousand men, with thirty battle-magi. One legion is Delestre men; the other is Imperial, put up by Ansel Inoxion, the Governor of Midrea. He and Robear Delestre are thick as thieves – and that is no metaphor: they've been robbing us blind. Inoxion is supposed to deal justice, but he's made it clear that Robear can do what he likes.'

'Inoxion is exploiting the Delestres,' Kyrik pointed out. 'In the dungeon, when they were negotiating to kill Valdyr and me, he was wringing concessions out of them.'

'Ysh,' Valdyr added, 'that prick was bargaining away our lives and they were kissing his arse – well, Robear, anyway. Sacrista wanted to slice his danglies off.'

'Perhaps we can exploit that,' Dragan said thoughtfully. 'The two legions don't mix at all: the Imperials are stationed in the western lowlands, near Lapisz, but they do nothing – it's the Delestre men who patrol and guard all the supply trains. They're spread all over too, not just in Hegikaro: Ujtabor on the road to the eastern silver mines, and even Rejezust, south of the river. They've also got most of the villages covered – they're spread pretty thin.'

'But there are barely a hundred thousand people in the valley,' Tibor noted.

Dragan agreed. 'That's true, and conventional wisdom is that only a tenth of the population can fight effectively; the rest are women and children, or too old. Mollachia's always been different, though; life is hard here and most adults can use a bow or spear effectively – but that's not the same thing as holding off a fully armoured legionary, let alone battle-magi.' He emptied his mug of beer and concluded, 'It won't be easy.'

'We're going to need help,' Kyrik said.

'Who'd help us?' Tibor asked. 'The Midreans won't, and no one else is close.'

'Some of my folk have Schlessen kin,' Rothgar Baredge suggested.

'Ni,' Nilasz replied, 'we're not having Bullheads here. Those *basznici* would never leave.'

'What are you calling my kin?' Rothgar drawled.

'Big hairy fuckers,' Nilasz replied truculently.

Kyrik waited for knives to come out, but Rothgar just grinned. 'Bigger, hairier fuckers than you, Ginger-balls.'

'That's what I'm saying. We don't want 'em around.' They both laughed.

'You two done playing?' Dragan asked. 'So, no Midreans, no Schlessen . . . what do you have in mind, Kyrik?'

'When Valdyr and I came west, we stopped with a clan of the Uffrykai – the Vlpa. They believe that they're our kin – through Zlateyr.' Kyrik noticed Valdyr looking away as the others stared at him in surprise, but he pressed on. 'They call him *Zillitiya*. Haven't you talked to Iztven and Ghili? Good Mollach names for Sydians, by the way. They're on a dream-quest to find Zillitiya's grave and they ended up *here*.'

'Are you saying Zlateyr was *Sydian*?' Dragan sounded disbelieving.

'No – I'm saying we can use their *belief*. If you'd like ten thousand archers to come to the aid of "Zillitiya's People" – well, perhaps it can be arranged? Iztven came here by journeying through the Bunavian Gap, then climbing into our lands along what he called the Sunrise Path.'

Dragan, Tibor, Nilasz and Rothgar exchanged interested looks. 'I know it,' Rothgar replied. 'A few years ago we found Schlessen hunters on the far side of Lake Jegto. They abandoned their hunt and never came back, but we tracked their route: a high trail from near the eastern tip of Lake Jegto, running due east.'

Kyrik tapped the map. 'If two old magi can cross it, then Sydian warriors certainly can. We could bring them into the valley without the Rondians knowing: unleash them at the right time and we could win this. They even have their own magi – Sfera, like Iztven and Ghili.'

'You really think they'll help us?' Rothgar wondered. 'Or will they turn into as big a problem as the Rondians?'

'They're plainsmen,' Kyrik answered. 'They won't want to stay. But they're interested in silver, so we may be able to pay them for their aid.' He looked around the circle, his gaze lingering on Valdyr. 'Anyone got any other suggestions?'

*

'So,' Kyrik said, 'I came to say goodbye . . . for now.'

Valdyr was staring out over frozen Jegto. The bleak, chilly view mirrored his mood. He grunted, 'I don't like farewells, Brother, I told you that. Just go.'

Kyrik wanted to talk though. He produced a forced grin and a pottery bottle. 'Palinka! It's from Dragan's people in Lapisz. It's very good. Try some.'

Kyrik always wants to talk. Silence is better. 'Sure. Leave me plenty: Tibor's threatening to teach me the sword and I'll need it to numb the pain.'

'You will.' Kyrik poured two tiny cups of the clear plum brandy, the drink Mollachs had been making for centuries, and they toasted awkwardly. 'Have you tasted this before, Val?'

'Of course! You were away at the Arcanum in Augenheim, and I stole a bottle. Six of us – I think Tomasz was the eldest; he was eleven – drank the whole lot. We were dousing the walls with vomit afterwards. When Father came home from the hunt, he thrashed us all.'

'Father was a hard man,' Kyrik recalled, 'but you couldn't fool him for a moment. Well, except those bastard Rondian money-lenders . . . he didn't see through them.' He exhaled heavily. 'I'll bring back warriors so we have a fighting chance.'

'Sydian warriors – heathen barbarians. I don't like this.'

'You said nothing at the meeting.'

'You're our rightful Lord, Kyrik; I'm "little brother". It's not my place.'

'We had a free discussion, an open meeting—'

'I'll not undermine you in front of Dragan!'

Kyrik let out a low breath. 'So you think I'm wrong.'

'Honestly, I don't know.' Valdyr put his head in his hands. 'Life is never simple.'

'Ysh,' Kyrik agreed wearily, 'especially with family. Paruq used to say, "Blood never runs clear."' He filled their cups again. 'And by that, Paruq meant the family of humanity. He said we're all kin.'

'When I was in the slave-gangs there was a centurion named Nalamead,' Valdyr replied. 'He used to show us the creatures around us – the vultures and the jackals; the desert foxes and cats; the goats and sand-deer; the birds and insects and snakes. He would point out how they each hunted and preyed upon the other. "That is us," he would say. "That is Man. We struggle, species against species, for the right to survive. Above honour and morality, the ultimate quest is for survival. That's what the Crusades were about, nothing else. There is the dark and the light: Kore is the light." Well, that's what Nalamead believed.'

Kyrik looked disgusted. 'He sounds like a bigot of the worst kind. That sort of thinking just begets more misery. This world is *immense*: there's room enough for *everyone* to live well, if only the greedy didn't steal the lion's share. Nalamead's bullshit is just an attempt to justify banditry.'

'Nalamead told us the world is a battleground, Kore against Shaitan, the proving place for the final battle. Those who ascend to Paradise become angels in the Army of Light; the rest are fodder for diabolos. That's what life is: that struggle. At least I know which Army I strive for.'

Kyrik sighed. 'I don't know where to begin.'

'What you mean is that you don't know how to argue against Truth.'

'That's not what I mean! If Paruq were here, he would show you the error in your thinking so much better than I ever could—'

'Well, I'm glad he's not, nor any of his Amteh scum.'

'You can't survive on hate, Brother. There are good men among the Amteh.'

And there was also Asiv, Valdyr thought, shuddering.

Kyrik fell silent, then tossed back another measure of palinka. 'We can't afford to be in conflict, Valdyr.'

'Then don't speak of these things. We have the Delestres to fight. If the Sydians want to help us, promise them everything and give them nothing: it's what Father would have done.'

'I know – but I've always wanted to be better than that old bastard.'

Valdyr stood. 'You need to leave, Kyrik. You've a long way to go.'

16

Son of Zillitiya

The Sydian Missions

The tribes of Sydia are benighted by ignorance, savagery and superstition, Great Sultan. They are crying out for the word of Ahm.

ALI BEYRAMI, MAULA OF SAGOSTABAD, 924

*Lake Jegto, Mollachia, Yuros
Aprafor 935*

'Again,' Tibor Siravhy said crisply. 'And keep your temper in check, my Prince.'

Valdyr Sarkany flexed his throbbing, leaden sword-arm and took his stance once more. The watching men exchanged comments, carefully out of his hearing. His breath was coming in great steaming rushes, billowing clouds in the chill air. Valdyr was taller and more strongly built than the lean Vitezai, but it still wasn't a fair fight. He'd been nine when he rode to war and even in the legion, they'd only given him a dagger. The sword in his hand now was the first he'd ever wielded; the simplest feints caught him out and the drills left his whole body screaming.

Kyrik had left a week ago; Jegto was beginning to thaw. The ice was steely-grey, reflecting the skies, and snow still encased the surrounding mountains. It was hard work, sparring on the lakeshore, but the two men flew into another bout – and yet again, Valdyr lost his self-control in the face of defeat. A right-left combination dragged his wooden blade out of line, and although Tibor declined to strike at his opened flank, Valdyr knew, and that was enough.

'Hah!' he shrieked, leaping in and thrashing about.

'Stop!' Tibor snapped. His blade stung Valdyr's wrist, numbing his grip, and his sword went spinning away.

'*Basznici!*' Valdyr bellowed. He dropped to his haunches, sweating and sore and angry with himself.

'Let's take a break,' Tibor offered, before striding away.

Valdyr could hardly blame the man – Tibor was a perfectionist who mastered his emotions at all times, while he'd always had a short temper. His playmates had feared him at times, something he'd been ashamed of even while Father proclaimed loudly, 'He's got the Draken in him!' That was Elgren Sarkany through and through.

He was still brooding when Dragan Zhagy's shadow fell over him. 'You need to fight more calmly,' the *Gazda* told him.

'Ysh, Dragan,' Valdyr muttered respectfully, 'I know that.'

'It's spring, Little Draken. We must raid while we can. Will you be ready to fight with us?'

The Rondians weren't mountainfolk and barely ventured abroad when snow covered the ground, but the thaw was underway and soon their wagons would roll through the valley, taking all the wealth of the harvest and the mines west, to Augenheim, leaving Mollachia to starve.

And here I am: a mage with no gnosis. A Prince of Mollachia who can't even use a sword.

'The gnosis will come when it's ready,' he said, praying this was so. 'I'll train harder, and perhaps that will bring other things too.' He looked east, to the high passes. 'How long will it take for Kyrik to return?'

Dragan grunted. 'Barring mischance, he should have found the Vlpa Tribe by now. If he can persuade them to help us, it'll still be weeks before he can return with aid. But we can't place all our hopes on that. We must still raid, my Prince.'

Valdyr picked up his practise blade again. 'Then I'd better let Tibor resume this humiliation.'

Dragan smiled, looking even more like a shaggy wolf. 'If it's any consolation, Tibor humiliates everyone ... except Rothgar, who's generously offered to humiliate you as well.'

The *Gazda* sauntered away and Valdyr looked around for Tibor . . . when a snowball hit him in the back of the head.

'Hey!' He clutched his head and spun around to see the miscreants: the two old Sydians, Iztven and Ghili, sitting like mounds of debris some twenty yards away. The old man was cackling toothlessly at him while the woman was rolling another ball.

'Why did you do that?' Valdyr demanded.

The crone snickered, then suddenly the ball in her hand flew, whizzing towards his face – though she'd not moved her arm at all. He threw up his hands and the snowball – more ice than snow and quite hard – smashed into his forearm. 'Ouch!' He glared at the pair indignantly, picked up the same ball and hurled it back.

It burst in a blue flash a few feet from them, obviously against gnostic shields, and he felt his skin chill. They were Sfera, of course, able to wield the gifts he'd failed to master. Then he suddenly understood what they were trying to do, and when the next snowballs flew, instead of dodging them he tried to believe a gesture – and the pulse of kinetic-gnosis it was meant to trigger – could stop a thrown missile.

Both snowballs hammered into his chest and burst apart. Then more came, more and more, until he screamed, 'Enough!' and sank to the ground. His body or soul or whatever just would not respond – nothing was coming, no spark, no extended perception, none of the sensations Kyrik had described. *Nothing.*

The two oldies creaked their way to their feet and shuffled towards him, faces serious, even sympathetic. He barely understood their thick accents: 'E ni . . . you no good.'

Ysh, I'm no damned good.

'Must feel,' the old woman added. 'Feel blow come, then shield.' She slapped his right temple. '*Feel!*'

'There's *nothing* to feel with,' he shouted, '*nothing!*'

Days passed in a numbing routine of muscle-straining blade-work. At least Valdyr was able to do that; after all, he'd spent more than half his life as a slave in the East. Swordplay required strength and endurance as well as skill: he had the physical attributes, and the rest was coming.

Soon he was sparring with the others and making progress, and that helped him control the rage that was always simmering inside him. Before long he could fall for a new trick without his temper snapping.

Iztven and Ghili didn't come near him again, and he felt both guilty and relieved; his shame at not being able to reach powers that should come naturally made him glad to avoid them. But Dragan and his men had believed they were rescuing a mage-prince, a leader who could shield them from enemy magic and defeat Arcanum-trained Rondian magi.

Without the gnosis, I have no right to lead.

He scarcely noticed the changes to the skies or the slow release of winter's grip.

Then Dragan, returned from a long trip, watched him drill, and when he was done, he called him aside. 'Prince Valdyr, I greet you,' he said, tapping his right fist to his heart.

'*Gazda* Dragan,' Valdyr replied, still panting from the bout.

'You've learned to fight, I see. Tibor praises your progress.'

'I still can't beat him,' Valdyr replied ruefully.

Dragan chuckled. 'No shame in that. But we're out of time, Little Draken. The mines will re-open soon, so it's time to move. Remember the cave at the Osiapa headwaters? From there we can raid into Bane-zust and Ujtabor. It's important that our men see the son of Elgren Sarkany fighting alongside them – but do you feel ready, my Prince?'

Dragan's words were deferential, but Valdyr could hear the impatience. *I can now hold a sword . . . but the gnosis eludes me.* It wasn't enough, he knew, but pride wouldn't let him beg for more time. 'I'm ready.'

Am I ready? It was Darkmoon: the face of Luna had vanished from the sky and the night was at its darkest, except for stars spanning the sky in a gentle east-west curve. The air among the pines was rich with new growth and hundreds of tiny streams laced every slope, providing an ever-present trickle of water. Even the rivers were moving again after months of icy stasis.

The Vitezai Sarkanum men slipped through the starlit gloom, woods-crafty and near silent. The ground beneath the trees was dirt and damp pine-needles, cushioning sound. Vision was poor, but the stars were bright enough here to make out the shape of the land, and to see detail if one focused. The Rondian cooking-fires in the camp lit their quarry.

They had moved into the Osiapa caves. Rondian patrols were more frequent here, but the lowlanders' woodcraft was poor and they were easily avoided. The air was markedly warmer and the whole forest was stirring: deer and hunting wolf packs were making their way to the uplands where the grass was beginning to sprout and birds were nesting, preparing for the first chicks of the new season. Mollachia was still forbidding, but the starkness was softening.

Tibor Siravhy was ten yards ahead of Valdyr, watching the Rondian camp like a hawk. Three dozen more lurked under cover, weapons blackened and metal covered, awaiting his signal. Then a gnarled brown hand touched Valdyr's forearm and Iztven's toothless smile filled his vision. 'Soon, ysh?'

'Ysh,' Valdyr replied.

To everyone's surprise, the Sfera had joined the raid, and despite their age they'd not slowed the group; using kinesis and Air-gnosis to leap obstacles, they easily kept up.

Ahead, Tibor gestured: a forward flicker, then a downward pat: *come in, keep low* ... They slithered into place. All had bows and boar-spears, except some of the bigger men who carried two-handed Schlessen zweihandles in back-scabbards; Valdyr himself had been given a zwei-handle by Dragan, who told him, 'This was your father's spare blade. His favourite hangs in Hegikaro Castle. One day a Sarkany will wield it again too.'

They all knew what they faced: Rondian legionaries were professional soldiers, trained to fight in formation, but they weren't bowmen by nature; archery required an investment in time that was prohibitive in a military that constantly rotated men. Dragan's plan was to strike hard and get out fast. Valdyr crawled to Tibor's side and peered over a fallen tree still half-buried in snow. The slope beyond fell away, black smears of earth and pine needles against unmelted ice. The stars glittered above in a cold, clear sky.

Dear Kore, let there be no magi below ...

Tibor whispered, 'Two sentries this side, left and right,' pointing out the guardsmen shuffling miserably back and forth. Valdyr reached back and loosened his zweihandle in its oiled scabbard as the longbowmen moved forward.

Tibor displayed two fingers and gestured forward, two longbows sang and the shafts whipped through the air and buried themselves into the torsos of the men below, who stiffened, staggered and slumped. One emitted a low moan, then a second shaft slammed in beside the first and he rolled over and went still. The other was already a silent mound.

Tibor climbed to his feet and led half their group down the slope. Another twenty Vitezai on the far side would move in when the attack began and the defenders were all facing away from them. The tents and the glowering embers of the dying campfires came into view through the thinning trees just as someone ahead shouted, 'Ware!'

The Vitezai broke into a run, pelting across the snowy ground, as a cluster of red-cloaks stumbled into view. Arrows flew, then the Vitezai Sarkanum roared aloud, '*Huy-huy! Razta!*' and stormed forward.

Someone in a red cloak lumbered into Valdyr's path; he raised his sword and blocked and their blades locked. He met the man's frightened blue eyes as he shoved, then someone stabbed a spear into the man's side, blood spouted from his mouth and he fell to the ground. The next Vitezai plunged his spear into the man's chest for good measure and Valdyr, quelling the urge to vomit, staggered onwards amidst his comrades-in-arms. A hurled torch caught a tent alight, then a legionary was in front of him, swinging a shortsword. Valdyr parried, swung, missed and over-balanced, but a woodsman slammed an axe into his foe's breastplate as he ran past. The Rondian staggered backwards and flames flared as he fell into a cooking-fire.

Valdyr was berating himself – he'd rukked up that last swing and it could have been him lying in the snow bleeding out – but he shook it off and ran on. A man emerged from a burning tent and he rammed his zweihandle at his belly, punching through leather and chain and ripping him open. Intestine squelched out in a spray of blood as the man screamed and fell backwards.

Valdyr wavered, paralysed by the ghastly sight, then anger surged. *Murdering Rondian kulfoldi!* He wrenched the bloody zweihandle out and hacked at the man's neck, once, twice, then the head flew and he fell onto the torso, roaring, 'Razta! Death!'

The blow that struck his flank and hurled him to the ground was neither arrow or spear but a blast of mage-fire that seared through furs, chain-mesh and steel; it foundered on the leather inner layer as it ran out of impetus: thank Kore Dragan had insisted on that added layer of protection. Valdyr groaned, and sagged dizzily.

Boots crunched from the direction of the blast and a male voice shouted in Rondian, a rallying call, The young man was wearing green silken robes, as if this were a summer's night in Bricia, but his face was a pale, taut mask of cold fury as he blasted away again, while arrows snapped and fell impotently away from his shields.

Sweet Kore, a battle-mage! Valdyr thought, but before he could react, a flurry of mage-bolts was smashing into the mage's shields and he spun away to face the new threat. Iztven and Ghili emerged from the forest: alien beings filled with menace, yellowy eyes glowing faintly, hunched and snarling like beasts. The Rondian sent gnosis-fire at them as the Vitezai and the remaining legionaries backed away, the mage-duel becoming an island in the swirl of the mêlée.

Valdyr realised the mage thought him dead. Scarcely believing his own stupidity, he began to creep forward. The trick to sneaking up on a mage, Kyrik had told him once, was to move silently and unseen: when a mage shielded, what he was doing was sensing movement and instinctively countering it with kinesis. While an arrow actually had more speed and force than a sword or dagger, it could be deflected or stopped with minimal exertion. Stopping a blow from a seven-pound blade required attention and equivalent counter-force. He just had to get close enough to swing.

The Rondian was fixed upon his new enemies, hurling a torrent of mage-bolts at the two Sfera – and any Vitezai who stumbled into his field of vision. As the pressure on him mounted, the shielding at his back visibly weakened as he focused his concentration on those in front of him.

Twelve yards . . . nine . . . seven . . .

Ghili faltered first: a fire-blast slammed into her shields and blew them away and she staggered towards Iztven, yowling as her furs ignited. The two Sfera tried to bundle their shields together, to cover each other, but the Rondian, sensing he was on top now, shouted triumphantly and hammered blast after blast into his foes.

Then Valdyr gripped his zweihandle like a lance and launched himself at the man's back. The blade went in with a wet crunch, plunged through ribs and organs and out again, erupting from his left breast. The Rondian gasped, his mouth fell open and he sagged, held upright on the steel.

Kore's Blood, I've killed him . . .

Then light flashed around the wound in the mage's back and he twisted, impaled though he was, and hurled blue fire at Valdyr's face. Valdyr jerked aside and the flames scorched past his eyes. In utter terror, Valdyr threw his weight forward and drove the man face-first into the snow-covered dirt, his blade sliding into the soil and pinning the Rondian to the ground. Then he drew his dagger and stabbed, over and over and over, until the man's back was just bloody ribbons of torn silk and ruined flesh.

When he looked up, there was a circle of Vitezai around him and all the Rondians he could see were dead, staring up at the starlit sky with empty eyes. He swayed, then planted his feet and pulled himself up using his buried sword. He wrenched it free and gasped for air. His hair was smouldering on one side and he still felt dazed, but he was also exhilarated.

'*HUY-HUY!*' the Vitezai cheered, and Nilasz was beside him a few seconds later, banging him on the back, then Dragan strode into the midst of the carnage, pumping his sword into the air and crying, '*SARKANY! SARKANY!*' The *Gazda* pulled Valdyr into a bear-hug.

Their cheers echoed through the clearing.

When Valdyr finally prised himself from their arms, he sought out the two Sydians. He was only alive because of them. They were sitting huddled together, smoking pipes and brushing wounds from their flesh with a pale white light – healing-gnosis, he guessed.

'Thank you,' he said fervently.

Ghili grinned toothlessly, and said, 'Son of Zillitiya.'

Valdyr swallowed. *Son of Zillitiya?* It sounded like more expectations, more demands he couldn't meet.

But there was no time for questions: there were supplies to plunder, and anything they didn't want, including a windskiff, they put to the torch. Their losses had been few – numbers and surprise had been in their favour – but there would be reprisals. They pulled out within the hour, leaving a massive bonfire raging behind them, and returned to their caves to escape the scrying eyes of their oppressors.

Before they left, Dragan pulled Valdyr aside and clasped his hand. 'Your father would be immensely proud of you today, Valdyr. I don't wish to test Fate, for your brother is a good man – but if the worst should come to be, Mollachia is in good hands with you.'

17

Ludus Imperium

Pregnancy Manifestation

I have always regarded 'pregnancy manifestation' as a tainting of the miracle of Corineus. Why should a mere human woman, solely by dint of bearing a mage's child, gain the gift of the gnosis? Would that only men could gain and wield our mighty power!

GRAND PRELATE HEFENIUS, PALLAS, 618

Pallas, Rondelmar
Maicin 935

Lyra was growing accustomed to crowds, but never to being crushed among them. The Royal Box at least gave her a little space to breathe, elevated above the masses pressed together in a noisy, sweaty, unwashed crowd below her. Even her ladies were jammed cheek by jowl on their benches.

But the box also meant she had to be seen; she could feel all those eyes on her, and so many remarks surely not meant to have reached her ears: everyone felt entitled to pass comment on her dress, her hair, her face, her belly, her demeanour ... Some of it was flattering, but much was cruel. But at least her back felt better now, no longer the agony she'd been enduring. Thinking of Ostevan's ministrations still flustered her a little, but surely that proved what a dear friend and ally he was, and she was fortunate to have him.

Presiding over the tourney also meant Lyra had to endure the company of her guest of honour, the Duke of Dupenium. Garod Sacrecour, seated to her right – and a little lower – slouched in his chair, his posture alternating between avid interest and utter boredom. They'd exhausted small-talk hours ago and Garod apparently had little interest in speaking to his own wife, a timid young waif called Marielle; instead, he spent most of the afternoon glaring into space, fidgeting until the next joust began. They were watching the third of the afternoon bouts; Ril's next encounter followed. She wasn't sure her already shredded nerves could take another round.

At every pass, Lyra's heartbeat crescendoed; she hated those where nothing was resolved, the blows missed or ineffectual, because it meant she'd have to endure the build-up all over again. She whispered to Basia, hovering behind her, 'Why are there no female battle-magi up there?'

'Because it's a stupid boys' game,' Basia sneered.

'Do you mean: it's stupid and a boys' game; or a game for stupid boys?'

'Yes.'

They shared an amused look, though she had to admit to being proud whenever the crowd started chanting for Ril: 'Prince of the Spear', they were calling him. Then another sickening collision in the air above drew her attention back to the event: a powerfully built Knight-Incognito had defeated an Aquillean champion, which saw many coins change hands, and not just in the Royal Box. This was the last Incognito remaining and she'd given up expecting him to remove his helm during the ceremonial presentations after his victories. As he left the arena, Hilta Pollanou plucked at Lyra's sleeve and in a low voice, said, 'Your Majesty, that Incognito – the one they're calling "The Wronged Man"? – people are saying it's Sir Solon Takwyth.'

Lyra caught her breath. 'Why would *he* attend? He's in exile!'

'*Voluntary* exile, Milady. Legally, he's free to return whenever he wishes.'

Shaken, Lyra stared after the man, but he was already lost in the crowds. 'What else are people saying?'

'That some Corani knights have visited his pavilion.'

The dangers were clear, and Lyra thanked Hilta. *I must speak to Setallius—*

Garod Sacrecour interrupted her thoughts. 'Your husband Prince Ril has done well to come so far through the tourney – you must be hoping he isn't eliminated before the choosing of the Regna d'Amore, Majesty.'

'Sorry – the what?'

'I forget, you're not familiar with tournament etiquette,' Garod said condescendingly. 'After this elimination round, the four remaining contestants each choose a woman as their "Paramour": their candidate to be Regna d'Amore, Queen of Love. The Regna d'Amore is chosen by acclamation at the Tourney Ball; she'll partner the victor at the banquet.'

Lyra threw an irritated glance at Hilta, who mouthed, *'I've told you this!'* She probably had.

'Why should this matter to me?' she asked Garod. 'Surely it's not fitting for me to be involved? I'd be accused of misusing my rank, considering it's so far above *everyone* else here.'

Garod winced, but his reply shocked her. 'It never stopped your mother.'

Lyra sat up. 'I beg your pardon?'

'Princess Natia was an enthusiast for the joust, Majesty – didn't you know? She was quite the one for lances and riding. Natia was named Regna d'Amore at every joust she attended, even though her husband was too young to compete. I danced with her myself after my victory at the Fauvion lists in 908.'

I danced with her myself . . . A sour taste filled Lyra's mouth. The following year, Garod had led the attacks on the Corani and captured her mother. Natia had been a Sacrecour prisoner for more than a year. *Dear Kore, did he rape her? Is this repulsive man my father? But if he is, wouldn't he have said so—?*

Then the fanfare blasted away all other thoughts as Ril and his pegasus Pearl pranced into the arena alongside a heavyset man riding a squat hippogryph, the favoured jousting steed of the Fauvion knights; the beast, part-eagle, part-horse, was entirely fierce-looking.

'My cousin's nephew, Sir Meryk Perqueton, of House Fasterius,' Garod commented. 'Would her Majesty care for a wager?'

The Fasterius knight was bigger and heavier than Ril, and his steed was much bulkier than Pearl. 'The *Book of Kore* doesn't encourage wagers, Duke Garod,' she replied, still seething at his two-edged comments about her mother – *quite the one for lances and riding, indeed.* 'But I have full confidence in my husband.'

'As you must,' Garod said, approval in his voice – which then turned sly. 'But tell me, if he triumphs and you won't permit yourself to be his Paramour – well, who will he choose? It's bound to cause gossip, after all, given his history.'

Lyra felt her cheeks go red. *Damn him . . . and I'm ugly when I blush too, or so this mob surrounding me keep whispering.* 'People change, your Grace. They mature; it's never too late,' she told him, sorely tempted to add, *for you.*

He appeared to get her unspoken message anyway, for his eyes narrowed and he looked away. She took that petty victory and returned her gaze to the arena, admiring her husband's *mature* beauty and trying not to think that these might be his last few minutes alive. But Ril looked excited, bursting with impatience and energy as he and Sir Meryk spurred away, Pearl moving sleekly, the hippogryph more ponderously. When it took to the air, it flew like an overfed duck, but its beak and fore-claws were formidable.

'Why is Ril doing this?' Lyra muttered in Hilta Pollanou's ear. 'He's the prince-consort – he didn't have to compete.'

'Because he's a man, with something to prove,' Hilta replied.

'Not to me.'

'Maybe to himself.'

Lyra clutched her belly protectively, thinking, *He could die up there in a split-second and leave me a widow.* Watching him these past few days had been torture, knowing every awful crunching sound could be a lance punching through her husband's heart. Even if he were only unseated, she was certain he'd miss the nets and be broken on the pitiless ground. There had been three deaths so far, and four other men crippled for life.

I fear for him so much – so surely I do still love him. She caught her breath at that thought and focused on the dot in the sky to her far left, now turning and diving towards the ring of fire before her as a red flare lit the brooding skies. She tensed as it drew closer and closer, Ril and Pearl growing in her sight, and now Meryk Perqueton entered her peripheral vision from the right, his hippogryph pealing a challenge as it bobbed in ungainly style towards the impact ring. Then all she saw were blurs, Ril flashing through the ring first because of his greater speed. The crash of impact echoed over the tourney field, the crowd roared and Hilta clutched her arm. Her eyelids flew open, her heart hammering at her ribs.

She followed Hilta's outstretched hand, and saw Ril and Pearl soaring over one end of the course, where the crowds were in pandemonium. Parqueton and his hippogryph were both tangled in separate parts of the safety nets, one roaring, the other shrieking. The air was full of thrown hats, twirling scarves and the thunderous roar of the people.

'ENDARION! ENDARION! PRINCE OF THE SPEAR! PRINCE OF THE SPEAR!'

'I don't know how much more I can take,' she whispered to Hilta as she rose to acclaim Ril. Pearl was flapping back towards the Royal Box. 'Thank Kore there's only one more day!'

Beside her, Duke Garod slumped in his seat. Then he turned to Lyra and said grudgingly, 'Congratulations, Majesty. Your prince lives to fight another day.'

That's all very well for him, she thought, *but I die and am reborn here every time he fights . . .*

Ril strode into the victors' arena, shoulder to shoulder with the other three remaining contenders. He'd barely had time to throw a bucket of water over his head after the bout, towel down and change. The others looked better groomed – or at least Brylion Fasterius and Elvero Salinas of Canossi did; like Ril, they were bareheaded. The fourth champion, the Incognito 'Wronged Man', still wore his helmet and visor, and he reeked of steel and sweat. By now many in the crowd had picked up the buzz of gossip about his identity.

The Royal Box filled Ril's eyes, and for a moment he just basked in the adulation, surely a measure of his rising popularity. Competing had been a risk, not just to life and limb, but more importantly, to his reputation – but by reaching the semi-finals, he'd sealed his position as the preeminent knight of Coraine. Rolven Sulpeter and Jorden Falquist had both fallen in the earlier round. Esvald Berlond's duties – he was in charge of security in Pallas in Ril's absence – had prevented him from competing, but in any event, he was no jouster.

Ril took the applause gratefully, drinking in the sea of faces, the waving hands, the dignified applause of the older folk and the rapturous fervour of the young. The lesser nobility and well-to-do had been permitted to leave the stands to surround the Royal Box, the better to view the Paramour ceremony. Guards strained to keep them contained as cheering filled the air.

'*ENDARION!*'

'*FASTERIUS!*'

'*SALINAS!*'

But here and there among the cacophony was an insidious call, mischievous, perhaps even seditious: 'Takwyth . . . *Takwyth—!*'

The Wronged Man gave no sign he heard as the four men came before the queen and went down on one knee.

A fanfare blew, and Lyra raised a hand, signalling quiet. The silence spread back through the crowd as everyone strained to hear how she would deal with this. Her voice was clear; she'd been well-tutored in how to be heard in large gatherings. 'Dear People,' she started, 'it's now time for the four champions to choose a Paramour, their choice for the Regna d'Amore. Our forefathers believed a man's worth to be embodied in martial prowess and a woman's in beauty. Who are we to question such time-honoured traditions?'

Ril smiled at Lyra's implicit criticism, and wondered who else noticed.

'So,' Lyra went on, 'I now call upon our four brave champions to come forward, take the coronets and pass them on to the Lady who is their chosen Paramour.'

The first victor that day, the handsome, southern-dark knight Elvero Salinas, son of the Duke of Canossi, strode forth and climbed the steps to kneel before Lyra and accept a gold filigree coronet. Brylion Fasterius followed, a hulking beast of a man with a scarred face. It gave Ril immense satisfaction that he'd put that scar there. The crowd strained to hear what Lyra said to the third man, the Incognito, but she stuck to formulaic words, and the anonymous knight's response was muffled. Then Ril accepted his coronet from his wife.

'I'm proud of you, Husband,' she said softly, though she looked tense and exhausted.

'You are of course my Paramour,' he said, meaning only to compliment her.

'Don't you dare pick me,' she said, her quiet voice firm.

'But—'

She dropped her voice lower, almost snarling. *'I am Empress – I will not be put in front of this crowd to be judged like some piece of horsemeat, especially not when I'm with child!'*

He was utterly taken aback by her anger, but he bowed his head and re-joined the other champions as they lined up facing the crowd, supposedly so they could assess the beauty of the women in the stalls. The crowd fell silent . . . and then dissolved into laughter as a lowborn woman ripped open her bodice and screeched, *'I'm yours, Prince Ril – just ten pfennig a poke!'* She jiggled her full breasts, then fled back into the depth of the press.

Ril opted for amused disdain.

'I believe in earlier days, the chosen Paramours were ours for the night,' Elvero Salinas remarked. 'There are tales of men sleeping through the finals, so worn out were they from their night-time exertions.'

Brylion guffawed and gave Ril a sly glance. 'Then it's a shame our empress is confined, eh? If I asked, would she refuse, do you think?'

'She'd spit in your face,' Ril growled.

Brylion snorted. 'I bet she'd like a real man to—'

The Wronged Man tapped the giant knight in the chest. 'You will not defame the queen.'

Brylion stared into the visor-slit. 'Don't overreach yourself, Takwyth,' he muttered.

It's not your place to defend my wife's honour, Takky, Ril thought, but before he could speak, Elvero Salinas was called forth to select his Paramour and the moment was lost. He watched as the Canossi heir walked back and forth, playing up to the drama, while turning his own mind to the choice he must make . . .

Jenet? But she looks unwell, and a lot of people know that before Lyra, Jenet and I used to be lovers. Sedina would be next choice for most ... Lady Emali is pretty and untainted ... Then his eyes were drawn to the new girl, from near Fauvion – Medelie Aventour, that was her name. She was laughing with Sedina, and her smile was beautiful as sunset. *She would make a good, neutral choice ... yes, her.*

As tradition demanded, Elvero used his scabbarded sword, the coronet dangling from the hilt, to select a blushing Lady Emali Kuipper. She looked overwhelmed. The women beside her helped settle the coronet, then she made her way to the front of the Royal Box and took Elvero's arm; the Estellan clasped his gauntlet over her small hand possessively and the crowd cheered approvingly.

Brylion Fasterius swaggered forward, and Ril noticed the women in the Royal Box visibly shrinking from him. The hulking knight didn't hesitate, though, extending his coronet to Sedina Waycross. Tradition forbade refusal, unless there was some grave issue – a great age differ- ence or a gulf in station – so Sedina had no grounds to decline. She ignored the pitying looks, feigning pleasure as she contrived to take Brylion's arm while maintaining a distance between them. Ril hoped she had the sense to make sure she and Brylion were never alone – the man was a brute, with a string of rape claims, as yet unproven, against him, but the Great Houses were notoriously untouchable.

'Let the Knight-Incognito come forth,' the herald called, 'and select his Paramour!'

The crowd went into a hush as the armoured man strode forward, his visored gaze turning left and right as he prowled once back and forth along the front of the stage. Then with a decisive gesture, he proffered his coronet ...

... to Medelie Aventour.

You prick, Ril thought.

He watched the young woman's lively smile brighten as the crowds gushed approval and the ladies about her feigned pleasure. She rose to her feet gracefully and placed the coronet on her dark tresses, then made her way down to the unnamed knight's side. Garod Sacrecour was frowning: the Aventour lands bordered his, no doubt he was uneasy that she was at court in Pallas. Lyra's face was unreadable.

Then it was Ril's turn. He stepped forth, his mind still unmade, gazing along the line ...

... and Jenet caught his eye, and for a moment all he could think was *how damned good it had been, she and him.* Two young aspirants in a treacherous court, practising the arts of love on each other while planning their campaigns, her to snare a duke or an earl, he to become knight-commander. *And why shouldn't we still be friends ...?*

It would be so easy, effortless ... *Lyra's confined, and I've got a suite to myself ...*

Without knowing how he'd got there, he was halfway up the stairs, his hand extended, and Jenet was rising and accepting the coronet with a satisfied little smile, one he knew so well ...

When Ril entered the ballroom that evening, it was already full and throbbing with sound. Jenet was on his arm, her presence so familiar it was as if the years since their relationship ended were a dream – yet here he was, Prince-Consort, the highest knight of the realm, and it felt inevitable that she was at his side.

And how inevitable the coming night felt, too ...

Jenet wore a full-length emerald gown with a high-peaked collar lined with ermine that set off her long golden-brown hair beautifully. She'd always had a business-like aspect to her face, a way of watching the world through narrowed eyes, but tonight she radiated triumph. Only he was close enough to see traces of a cold or some other ailment, but she was clearly determined to seize this chance to shine. The coronet glinted on her forehead and she looked cool and composed as they made their way through the press.

In another world, we would have wed long ago ... 'Are you pleased?' he murmured.

'Ril, dear boy, I've never stopped missing you. You've always been the best. It was just a shame: you know how it was – one must have more on one's plate than wine and love.' She glanced sideways at him. 'Did I treat you terribly badly?'

'You did,' he said, 'but maybe I'll let you make it up to me?'

They shared a secret look that tore years from his life.

As they approached the high table, Sir Oryn Levis intercepted them, stammering something complimentary to Jenet – she'd clearly given him a ride at some point in the past – then bent to Ril's ear. 'You know that the Incognito is Takwyth, Prince?'

'I've known for days,' Ril replied, seeking an escape; Lumpy was a bore at the best of times.

'The knights are saying, "Our Captain's back",' Levis rumbled, oblivious to Ril's inattention. He didn't look entirely unhappy; Levis was a born follower, and a Takwyth man to the core.

'Takky is yesterday's hero,' he told the knight, patted his arm and pulled Jenet with him through a crowd of well-wishers, accepting congratulations as he headed for the ordeal that would be the high table. Brylion Fasterius was already there with Sedina Waycross; Ril complimented Sedina – she was an attractive woman, if self-regarding and imprudent and currently rather pale – and ignored Brylion. He accepted a faint bow from Garod Sacrecour, kissed the hand of the duke's timid wife and greeted a group of ambassadors from the vassal-states, some of whom he actually liked. Jenet was perfect throughout – she'd mastered the arts of the courtier, especially when it came to witty small-talk. Ril contented himself with playing the triumphant champion, the man of action, confident of success. He laughed off the Canossi nobles' veiled comments about Elvero's renown and ignored the bellicose remarks about Brylion's might from the Sacrecour-Fasterius coterie.

'Hail, Prince of the Spear!' Avreu Bakti, Duke of Klief, greeted him. 'How do you fancy going head-to-head with the "Incognito"?' He winked at the last word.

All those in earshot hushed to hear Ril's reply, but the question was hardly a surprise and he was ready for it. 'An exile can always be exiled again – but why bother? I don't fear Yesterday's Man. Your health, Milords! I trust Pallas has made you feel welcome.'

'Like a well-paid whore,' put in Garod Sacrecour, already wine-soaked, loudly. Ril noticed that the other dukes had begun to distance themselves.

'We Corani have never had to pay for the favours of a lady, so I'm not sure what you mean,' Ril replied, watching to see who smiled:

everyone but Garod, as it turned out. 'To Pallas, our loving Mother,' he added, lifting his goblet and meeting Garod's eye, daring him to drink.

Garod scowled and joined the toast, then found an excuse to be elsewhere. Alexan Salinas, Duke of Canossi, a swarthy man with a distinctly southern caste to his face, inclined his head slyly. 'Lord Garod still smarts at the disrespect the Pallas mob showed when the news of Constant's death broke.'

'Sometimes it's hard for the lowborn to conceal their true feelings the way we noblemen can,' Ril replied, and Salinas snorted. 'I wish your son Elvero good fortune in the lists tomorrow,' Ril said, adding with a grin, 'Unless he faces me.'

Duke Salinas raised his cup. 'Elvero does the House of Canossi proud. As you do yours.'

And that, Lord Garod, is how to make friends – not snarking about the city you wish to rule.

Then the meal-chimes sounded and Ril led Jenet to the high table. He'd been placed opposite a big man in a green jacket and white tunic – Corani colours, but unadorned with a sigil. His head was covered by a lightly made helm blended with a Lantric mask: *Twoface*; half the face benign, the other sinister.

Twoface? Damned good choice for a two-faced prick, Takky!

Seated beside the masked knight, wearing a dowdy cream dress that did little justice to her beauty, was Medelie Aventour. Ril made a show of kissing her hand, then helped Jenet sit, before settling into his own chair. He remembered an altercation, five years ago . . . 'It seems I made the high table after all,' he told the masked man.

The Incognito considered him through the eye-slits, but said nothing.

'Oh, come on, sir,' Ril teased, 'we know who you are – won't the mask just get in the way of a good meal? Take it off: you're among friends.'

'I'll keep it on,' the knight rumbled, his voice muffled and distorted. 'I have my reasons.'

'Well, I'm sure we can have the left-overs sent to your room afterwards, so you can keep your strength up.'

Jenet whispered, *<You're being a prick!>* into his mind, in an amused voice.

<But it's fun – and I might provoke him; angry people say stupid things.>
<So do you, Ril darling, and you don't even have to be angry.>

He ignored that and turned to Medelie. 'You look lovely, Mistress Aventour. I trust you're enjoying life at court? Does it compare favourably with Fauvion?'

'Fauvion has always been rather provincial,' she replied smoothly. He found her hard to read; she had a formality and maturity that was hard to reconcile with the vivacity he'd admired earlier. 'My father believes our fortunes lie with Pallas.'

'Your family lands border the lands of the Earl of Fauvion, yes?'

'Yes, but Father also has estates in Tergatland, south of the Bruin.'

'Close to Saint Balphus Abbey?' he asked, suddenly a little more interested.

'Father once owned the monastery – it was bequeathed to the Church by my family.'

Ahh . . . I wonder what your father knew of the 'guest' there . . . He glanced at the masked man beside her, wondering if there was some message in Takwyth's selection. 'Did your family have any Corani connections?'

She glanced at Takwyth. 'Father had friends at court, prior to 909,' she answered carefully.

He was becoming intrigued, but then trumpets blared and Lyra entered the ballroom, resplendent in a golden gown fringed in purple, her train carried by four of her younger ladies. The room rose for her, even the large, sullen Sacrecour contingent. She read a short speech about consolidation of friendships among the elite of Rondelmar. 'We live in testing times,' she concluded. 'Only through unity can we prevail, and keep the empire strong.' It was simple stuff, easy to agree upon and therefore perfect for the event.

Everyone sat, and servants bearing heaped platters began to pour in. Here was all the bounty of the north: huge haunches of roasted pork and venison, game-birds drenched in honey or wine, mountains of root vegetables. Bread confections as tall as a man followed, and giant pitchers of wine. The gathering eagerly settled into the business of gorging on favourite dishes, getting drunk, groping serving girls and shouting across the tables at each other in disjointed conversations.

The high table was the only silent spot in the room; few of them were managing to keep up any kind of conversation. The awkwardness became pervasive, and it was a relief when the platters were finally taken away. Takwyth ate nothing, though he sipped wine by tilting his mask back an inch or so. Medelie looked nervous of speaking to him. Brylion, further down the table, was an uncouth presence, and Sedina was drinking steadily. Ril and Jenet were able to converse amiably with Elvero Salinas, who was a regular on the tourney circuit and full of wild anecdotes of derring-do in the skies, as well as tales of bad luck – lances that went astray, saddlery that broke on impact and flying mounts that died mid-flight. Lady Emali listened with bated breath, and Ril recognised all the signs of burgeoning infatuation.

Then it was time for the Acclamation of the Paramours. The four champions led them into the middle of the room as the musicians began an Estellan tarantella, a dance designed to show off the grace and beauty of the women, to better allow the crowd to select their Regna d'Amore.

To Ril, everything had an air of inevitability . . . Sedina was clearly drunk, and stumbled across the dancefloor, while Medelie looked over-awed by the occasion and underwhelmed by her partner – for all his prowess, Takwyth was no dancer. Emali initially looked to be the favour-ite, combining natural grace with a youthful sweetness, and Elvero was, inevitably, a masterful dancer. But Ril and Jenet had danced together many times – and in so many ways – that he knew they would triumph.

Then, quite unexpectedly, halfway through the tarantella, Medelie woke up. Perhaps some spirit of movement and music took possession of her, or maybe her true nature refused to hide. With a sudden and unexpected turn she spun away from her partner's hand and into the centre of the square, coming to a perfectly balanced pause, and the mood of the whole room changed. Every eye was now on her as she spun about Takwyth as if he were as wooden-limbed as Basia di Sirou. Every move was one of elegance and restrained passion. As the men retreated from the dancefloor, Ril knew he was staring, but no one would notice; there'd been a collective sucking-in of breath, and then an almost grateful gasp as the music reached its crescendo.

'Kore's Blood, that was a surprise,' Jenet muttered in Ril's ear as he led her from the floor. 'I wonder what other tricks she has up her sleeves?'

'You'd be the one to find out,' he muttered back.

There was only one choice of Regna d'Amore possible now, and the whole room rose to acclaim Lady Medelie. Ril joined the applause in perfunctory fashion. His mind was already questing ahead as his eyes met Jenet's. He already knew how good it was going to be, even though he could see that she was losing her battle with her cold. This close, even the candlelight couldn't conceal her bloodshot eyes and way her pale gums drew back from her teeth, making them look elongated, even dangerous, for an odd second.

Don't be foolish, he chided himself. *Jenet and I dreamed of being the stars of the court, and tonight we'll consummate that dream – and maybe make other plans. If anyone can see me through this maze of failed pregnancies and petty intrigues, she can.*

Feeling Lyra's eyes on him, he reached for the nearest goblet and drained it, then reached for another.

Midnight found Ril pacing his suite, unable to lie down, unable to sit and barely able to think. He felt feverish, flushed with too much wine, his pulse too fast, all his senses heightened. He knew he was caught up in the throes of lust and drunk, *really* drunk, for the first time in years. All his patient perseverance with Lyra felt tonight like a stupid, foolish waste of time.

Jenet and I should have begun this years ago, when I knew that Lyra was never going to be enough for me . . . When will she come?

The court had returned to Crofton Manor after the banquet, and he to his lonely suite. Lyra was at the far end of the floor, in Lady Crofton's confinement rooms, guarded by Basia and Geni and attended by Hilta, Sedina and Jenet. Doubtless Jenet would have to wait until everyone was asleep before she could come to him – but surely they were all snoring by now?

He'd washed and put on a clean tunic, and the gallon or more of water he'd downed to try and clear his head was beginning to work . . . so now all he could do was pace and fret. *Will I do this? Clearly I shouldn't . . . but will I?*

Then there was a faint knock and he almost tripped in his hurry to pull it open, reaching out to drag Jenet in and—

'*Lyra!*'

His wife looked at him quizzically, her hands on her swelling belly. She was clad in a red silk nightdress and slippers. Her blonde hair was unbound and she looked lovely in her unassuming way. 'Are you going to invite me in?'

'Yes – *yes!*' He managed a courtly bow, his mind whirling. 'I assumed you'd be asleep by now. Come in, come in!' He walked to the drink stand. 'Brandy?'

'No, thanks,' she replied, looking around. 'You have larger rooms than me.'

'It's Baron Crofton's own room – are you unwell? I can summon Domara—'

'No, please, not that draken-heart!' Lyra turned and seized his hand. 'I wanted to see my husband, but everyone seems to think that's a crime. So I have to sneak about like a thief just to be with you.'

He realised he was still looking at her vacantly, as if she might yet transform into the woman he had expected. *Dear Kore, what if Jenet knocks on my door now?* He went to the entrance and sealed it with a ward, then turned back to his wife. 'What is it? Is something wrong?'

'Yes,' she said quietly, with a look of determination on her face that was usually reserved for the council table. He'd never been able to reconcile her intellectual and moral courage and spirit with her physical and emotional timidity – but none of that mousiness was evident right now. 'There are all manner of things wrong, Ril. That man is here: *Solon Takwyth.* Setallius has his Volsai on high alert: they know where he's sleeping, and at the first sign that he's seeking to undermine us, we'll throw him in the dungeons.'

Ril blinked – this was as far from his tolerant wife as he'd ever seen. 'But Takwyth's the finest knight in Koredom – he says so himself,' he replied, trying for mirth he didn't feel.

'Dirklan says that "finest knight" doesn't mean "deadliest killer".

He's got people who can pierce wardings without a trace and turn sleepers into dead men. I'll not sit idly by and let another man take my child's future away.'

She's like a cornered vixen, Ril thought, almost unnerved by her intensity. But he approved; he'd come to think of her as passionless, but she clearly wasn't. 'No one will touch you, I swear.'

She looked up at him with a hint of her old hero-worship. She seemed to be wrestling with something, then she caught his hands in hers and pulled him to the sofa. 'Do you want to see something?' she asked shyly, and when he nodded, perplexed, she unknotted her dressing gown. The red silk nightgown was fitted, emphasising her tummy. 'Look! I'm having a baby.'

The abrupt change in the tone and subject threw him, but to his surprise, he found that it intrigued him too. He'd not been intrigued by his wife in a long time, so he didn't have to feign interest as he sat beside her, looking at her properly for the first time in quite a while. If anything, her face was thinner – but her breasts were growing larger and her belly was tight and firm as a melon. 'Is it . . . um . . . progressing well?'

She stroked the tight silk over her tummy and nodded. 'Domara the Draken says she can hear a heartbeat and that all signs point to healthy.' Her face was full of heightened hope and fear. 'The other two miscarriages happened earlier than this. And I feel . . . good, *really* good. Healthy and strong.' She sat up a little, gripped the hem of her nightgown and drew it up over her belly, then sank into the back of the sofa. 'See if you can feel him move. Sometimes I think I can.'

He stared at her stretched stomach, very white, with blue veins and silvery stretch marks. The tang of her body filled his nostrils too, an earthy, fecund aroma he found unexpectedly stirring – he'd been lusting all night, after all, even if not for her.

Did Kore send her here to keep me on the path of the righteous?

But Jenet's face still shone in his mind. 'Lyra, shouldn't you—?'

'Domara gave me an unguent for my belly,' she interrupted, 'but I still have stretchmarks. The skin's so tight it hurts. But the healers can magick them away afterwards.'

'Um, that's good, but should you be here? Didn't Domara say—?'

'Hush! Don't mention her again.' She took his hands and held them against her belly. 'Feel it – that's our baby, growing inside me. I'm so scared and happy, all at once.'

He stroked her skin as she leaned back, her eyes heavy-lidded and full of unexpected invitation. To his surprise he found his mouth going dry as she pulled the nightdress the rest of the way up, over her breasts. They looked ... *majestic*, the aureoles large and crimson, the nipples engorged. She looked up at him in a way he'd not seen since their first night together, and pulled his hand to her right nipple, purring deep in her throat, 'Pinch it, yes, like *that* ...' She sighed, leaned into him and whispered, 'Use your mouth, if you want to.'

She was as far from self-conscious, awkward Lyra as he'd ever seen her, and he had no inclination to do anything but explore this new person. He put his mouth to her breast as his fingers slid down her belly and between her thighs as they opened to him ...

They'd been drowsing in and out of sleep for some time. Lyra felt tired, but *affirmed*, in a way she'd never before felt. She'd followed an instinct tonight, somehow certain it would be dangerous to leave Ril alone when he'd spent the whole evening with his former lover. She'd been willing to risk the pain of rejection, and it had been worthwhile: tonight, the spiderwebs that kept them apart had been completely brushed away.

She hoped Kore understood, or had looked away – tonight had been all about pleasure, for maybe the first time in her life. His fingers inside her had been a guilty joy, and she'd wallowed in it as he took his time, enjoying each moment, this one, then the next, his mouth on her nipples *so wickedly good*, until a rare burst of pure release left her gasping. Then they'd left the sofa for the bed, and lying on her side, spooning with him as they were now, he'd entered her in a slow rush of silent tumult. He'd been gentle, yet strong, pliant yet dominant, and she'd adored it. She couldn't manage guilt in the aftermath of something so beautiful.

If that's a sin, no wonder Shaitan has so many slaves ...

He was sleeping now, cradling her, his body heat a soft furnace that soothed her aching back. When she began to overheat, she edged away and rolled over to watch him; his body, lit by the remaining candle stubs, that of a Lantric demi-god caught in dark marble. Perhaps he'd had wilder nights with Jenet Brunlye in the past, but she couldn't imagine they'd been more loving.

Kore made us, she reflected, *and it can't have been just to suffer.* She also thanked Kore for sending her Ostevan Comfateri – she still marvelled, blushing, at what he'd done, but she couldn't recall feeling uncomfortable, not after her initial surprise. He'd relieved her physical distress, but he'd also inspired her to this night. *Yes, it was daring, but nothing untoward really happened,* she told herself.

Then she heard bells chime midnight; she ought to go back to her own room before she was missed. The coming day was an important one and she needed some sleep. Setallius didn't think there was any impending threat, but it was possible her reign rested on the day to come – perhaps even on the outcome of a joust.

She managed to leave the bed without waking Ril. Donning her nightgown and backing away, she whispered, 'I pray I strengthened you, my love.' She crept towards the door – just as the handle turned in a faint glitter of sparks: Ril's wards were resisting someone's hand.

Lyra swallowed, then called softly, 'Who's there?'

The handle stopped moving. There was no other sound, but for a moment, Lyra felt a presence, ephemeral, and most definitely not benign. A cold malignancy enveloped her, a tentacle of thought that touched her with a smear of *vileness.*

Without conscious thought, she found herself gripping the door handle and trying to open it – but the wards held, and the challenge to them made Ril stir and then come suddenly awake. 'Lyra? What're you doing?'

She stared at the door. The presence was gone, so completely she couldn't be sure that she hadn't imagined it. She looked at the door in confusion, then back at him. 'I was just going back to my rooms, but the door wards . . .'

He sat up, rubbing his eyes. 'Just give me a moment and I'll—'

'No,' she said quickly, frightened of the darkness outside, 'I've changed my mind. I'll stay.'

'Who are the four finalists?' Cordan wondered. Finostarre was just four tantalising miles away, but he had to rely on others for news of the day's results.

Cordan talked of nothing else, which Coramore found irritating. 'Who cares?' she snapped. 'I hope they all killed each other. Where's Lady Brown-Nose?' While the Arcanum was on a break, the pair had been reunited in their usual suite in the Bastion, locked in and forgotten by the world – except for Lady Jenet, who'd visited every night of the tourney, always late at night.

Coramore yawned, but Cordan was fidgety. 'So: four champions left now,' he remarked. 'I hope Sir Brylion made it through,' he added, but not with the enthusiasm he might have shown before hearing Basia de Sirou's tale.

'Shut *up* about the stupid tournament. It's more important that Lady Brown-Nose comes.'

They were both tired and bored; their lessons had been suspended so even their tutors could attend the tourney. Cordan's gnosis had been Chained again – he told Coramore it was like someone had carved a void in his soul.

I wish I had my gnosis, Coramore brooded. *Then we wouldn't need rescuing.*

Then came the discreet knock on the door they'd been bursting for. The Mutthead unlocked the portal door and admitted Lady Jenet; both knight and lady had a similar sickly caste to their faces, the same unnatural pallor and bloodshot eyes. Jenet's black and white dress was wine-stained and she smelled of *men* when she swept up Cordan and Coramore in a hug.

Coramore disentangled herself. 'Ugh – don't touch me!'

Jenet's eyes slithered over her. 'You think it is easy for me to escape the lewd festivities of the usurper's court?' She looked frustrated, and cross. 'I serve as I can – I trust you'll remember my help once you are freed.'

'We will,' Cordan exclaimed, in a way Coramore profoundly disliked.

'What kept you?' she asked sharply.

'Duties. Arrangements.' Jenet bent closer. Her breath smelled like rotten plums. 'You have only one more day of captivity to endure – the next time I come, it will be to free you.'

'Why tomorrow?' Cordan whined. 'Why not now?'

'Because tomorrow, everyone here and in Finostarre will be blind-drunk,' Jenet whispered. 'It's the last evening of the tourney – no one will be vigilant. So give your captors no clues. Trust only those with this password: "Abraxas".'

'"Abraxas"?' Coramore wrinkled her nose. 'All right. But when tomorrow?'

'Two hours before dusk, as the final bouts begin. The palace will be virtually empty. I'll take you to a place of safety until the hue and cry dies down.'

'I thought we'd be going straight to Dupenium,' Cordan complained.

'It's too soon,' Jenet answered, looking irked at the ceaseless questions. 'That's the first place the Wraith will send his assassins. We must keep you hidden while we rally support – many people won't march until we give them proof that you are free and ready to take the throne. If we move too soon, it could still fail.'

'I'd rather die than kneel to that simpering Corani cow again,' Coramore declared. 'You better not let us down, Lady Jenet.' She saw the flash of anger on Jenet's face and thought, *Ha – my brother might be fooled by you, but I'm not.*

Cordan's face was shining at the prospect of escape, but his questions were all of the tourney. 'Who triumphed today? Who are the four champions – who meets tomorrow?'

'Brylion Fasterius, Ril Endarion, Elvero Salinas and an Incognito calling himself "The Wronged Man".'

'"The Wronged Man",' Cordan echoed. 'Do you know who he is? Tell me – or at least, tell me the draw?'

Jenet laughed and ruffled Cordan's hair. 'The Prince-Consort faces Brylion and the Incognito jousts against Sir Elvero tomorrow morning. The winners clash in the afternoon.'

Cordan's chest swelled. 'Uncle Brylion will *smash* Endarion.'

'No doubt,' Jenet said, straightening and smoothing her bodice. 'Rest well, my Lord, my Lady. Tomorrow, you'll be free.'

*

Ril rode into the arena with his head full of distractions. Last night had been unexpected, both that it happened at all, and that it had been so tender. Somehow, as if sensing their marriage was endangered, Lyra had come to him and – yes, she'd *seduced* him. Not with worldly wiles like Jenet; she'd been brave enough to risk refusal and trust in love. That touched him and warmed him still – but it didn't stop him being a basket of nerves as the carriage shuddered to a halt and he dismounted – but there were Larik and Gryff to greet him, and cheering hordes of Corani. Younger knights who'd not long served under Takwyth came forward to wish him luck. 'Smash that Fasterius arsehole,' was the prevailing message.

And so I must. I can't worry about Takky until I've dealt with Brylion.

Being enveloped by the tourney helped clear his mind, and as he allowed his retainers to arm him, he turned his thoughts to his foe: Sir Brylion Fasterius was taller and heavier than him, and didn't have the imagination to flinch on impact.

'Velocity by weight by angle equals impact force,' Gryff said. 'That's the riddle you must solve.'

Meaning: he thinks Brylion's going to flatten me.

By the time all was ready, though, so was he. Nothing else mattered now except the bout. The throb of expectation was palpable as the four champions rode beneath the safety nets into the arena and out into the parade ground. The four Paramours were seated in special thrones, with the Regna d'Amore highest, only a little below Lyra herself.

Ril barely glanced at them – then he noticed Jenet was missing. *She must have known that Lyra came to me . . . did it wound her feelings?* That was a strange thought – Jenet had always been careless and carefree in her relationships. But it was odd that she wasn't present today.

The four knights paused and dipped their lances for the empress, and Ril met his wife's eyes. Lyra looked tired, nervous and vulnerable, and her hands constantly returned to her belly, to *their* child, but she smiled with heart-warming courage, and his affection for her surged. He felt desperately afraid for her, and shame at what he so nearly did last night ran through him. Jenet's empty throne felt like an accusation. *Does Lyra guess what it means?*

'Well, who had a good night?' Brylion Fasterius rumbled. 'I'll tell you one thing, that Sedina Waycross knows how to suck cock. The perfect Corani slut.'

Ril couldn't tell if his boast was true or not. It was entirely possible that Sedina had been trapped, and forced to barter lesser humiliations to greater abuses.

Brylion turned to Elvero Salinas. 'What about you, Canossi? Did fair little Emali surrender her virtue?'

'Keep your lewd tongue inside your head, lest you lose it,' Elvero replied coolly.

'Big talk for someone who's never won a last-day bout,' Brylion sneered. 'What of you, Incognito?'

Takwyth's blank helm turned, but he said nothing.

Brylion sniggered as if he considered that a victory. 'And as for you, Prince Ril – is that wench you chaperoned as well-used as all say?'

Ril decided that Takwyth's cold silence worked for him too – then the trumpets thundered, they all took the acclaim of the Royal Box, and he and Brylion nudged their mounts forward to contest the first bout. Brylion looked arrogantly secure, riding a fierce-looking gryphon, the rear torso and limbs of a lion grafted to a massively enlarged eagle. Its raptor beak was shrilling, its taloned fore-legs raking at the ground. Gryphons were notoriously hard to master, but this one had more bulk than Pearl, and as much speed in the dive. Conventional wisdom was that a pegasus would always be too lightweight against a gryphon.

Velocity by weight by angle . . .

After taking the applause, the two knights trotted away to their own ends to finalise their preparations. 'I need water,' Ril declared. He was already boiling in his steel casing on this vividly bright spring morning. Gryff gave him a pitcher and he drank deeply.

'Too hot for you, Corani?' someone jeered from the packed watchers.

'What, is there a Fasterius in the crowd?' Ril exclaimed. 'Welcome, sir, and well met – tell me, does Brylion still fart as he spurs his mount? Is that the secret of his prowess?'

The crowd – mostly Pallacian, and more inclined to support him – laughed. The Fasterius man got halfway through a rude gesture then

DAVID HAIR

recalled that he was talking to the Prince-Consort. 'Sir Brylion is the greatest knight of Koredom,' he bellowed instead.

'He certainly has the worst breath in Koredom,' Ril responded. 'I can smell him from here – they say when he pisses, rivers turn rancid!'

More laughter. Crowds were easy, if they were ninety-five per cent predisposed to like you. The Fasterius man, wary of the locals packed around him, said, 'May Kore have mercy on you.'

'Kore wears my colours,' he retorted. 'He loves me well!'

Gryff and Larik were making last-second adjustments to his harness, getting the cinching right – he was damned if he'd be one of those jousters who tumbled out of the sky because his rig wasn't fitted properly. Then Brylion's squire trotted up with a bucket. 'Good sir,' the squire called, 'my master sends this receptacle, if your stomach's rebelling.'

More laughter, edged by partisan hostility. Ril made a show of taking the bucket and pretending to piss in it. 'In case your master's thirsty,' he shouted, playing to the gallery. There was more ribald laughter, and even the Fasterius squire smirked before running off.

'Watch the way the gryphon moves,' Larik warned, as he mounted. 'They bob when they fly. Many a man misses the mark because they fail to account for it.'

'But they're slow,' Gryff threw in. 'You'll have that advantage. Just aim true, lad.'

They looked up at Ril earnestly and he felt a sudden fondness for them both. They might not be noble of spirit, or even of good character – there were times when they'd been the worst of influences – but they cared about him, and they'd stood by him when others hadn't. He suddenly realised that they had a great deal of pride in him, too. 'I'll take him, lads. You'll see.'

They grinned and reached up to shake his hand, then the marshals signalled it was time to go. Ril lowered his visor, narrowing his world to this arena, this run, this opponent. There was time for five sharp breaths, then the ribbon rose and fell, Pearl cantered into the arena, wings spreading, picking up speed until she caught the breeze and they rose, the roar of the crowd falling away.

Ril's eyes fixed on the distant gryphon, five hundred yards away across the arena, as they circled, awaiting the signal to begin. Both hit their marks perfectly and the pennants dropped, the marshall blazed a red signal, Ril cried, '*Hee-yah!*' and Pearl dived for the circles.

Air ripped by them, deafening, and Pearl whinnied, flapping to increase their speed until he signalled for her to furl as they flashed through the approach circle. Brylion was powering towards him in rhythmic hops, that awkward flying gait Larik had noted. Ril lined up his lance-tip with the target on Brylion's shoulder, correcting as the distance shrank to nothing.

Crash!

As always, the impact happened before he was ready. Brylion's lance-tip grazed his target, while his own went wildly askew. He and Pearl were battered sideways and the pegasus shrieked in fright and unfurled her wings, almost ploughing into the nets – but then they were soaring again and the din of the crowd washed over them.

He patted Pearl heartily, though Brylion had won that pass. <*Good girl! Kore's balls, those gryphons are all over the place . . . but I think I get the rhythm now.*>

Neither needed a new lance so they stayed aloft and climbed back to their approaches. The marshall's voice, gnostically enhanced to carry across the fields, announced that Brylion had the points in that pass, and the arena below seethed with excitement. Ril put aside his annoyance at having been outmanoeuvred and reviewed the pass in his mind: *He made his gryphon furl later than I did, and that dropped him two feet . . . I have to allow for that.*

A minute later, he was taking Pearl into their second pass and urging her to full speed, the air whistling by as they flashed through the approach circle, perfectly aligned. He tapped out a rapid dance on Pearl's flanks, nudging her into a last-second shimmy that made her weave a tiny bit, almost imperceptible – unless you were the man flying straight at him, trying to aim a twenty-foot lance at a two-foot target.

He also engaged combat-divination, which even other diviners would have called suicidal. Being able to see potential blows was a boon in a mêlée, but in a joust, the speed of impact meant the lines of force emanating from the foe's lance altered so swiftly that nothing was gained – the information overload could even blind the diviner. But it wasn't Brylion's lance Ril was concerned with; it was trying to predict the exact place that his target would be – it turned out a gryphon's flight was more predictable than a shifting lance-tip . . .

They surged together, the potential points of impact narrowing as they converged in a blur he felt more than saw, lines of force twisting and swirling. The divination flashed images of death and victory over and over, and then it was all too late: the onrushing gryphon flapped, then furled, and Ril altered his aim to a space Brylion was even now dipping toward . . .

Crunch!

His lance splintered on Brylion's target even as Brylion's struck his own, making him spin. He gripped Pearl with clenched knees and kinesis as two straps snapped and the whole world whirled. Pearl's wings spread, desperately seeking purchase in the light breeze, and he clawed at his reins and hauled: the ground – the crowd – were feet away and flinching from his passage.

Then he was lifting above them again and the crowd screamed for joy. He looked backwards and saw a riderless gryphon clawing the air while the nets wrapped about a bulky, flailing knight.

YES!

<*You got him! You got him!*> Gryff was shouting above Larik's wordless howl of victory. <*You hit him, full and fair, middle of the target! Bravo, Brother!*>

He took care on his return flight to screech low over his fallen foe. *Eat your words, Fasterius, every one of those vile things you said* . . . Then he landed to the acclaim of the crowds as '*PRINCE OF THE SPEAR!*' resounded through the arena.

He stopped before the Royal Box, oblivious to everything except his pale, brave wife: *My only* Regna d'Amore . . .

Half an hour later, the Wronged Man and Elvero Canossi broke three lances on each other, but the third collision shattered Elvero's collarbone and the Incognito was declared the victor. The deciding bout would be the culmination of the Grand Tourney, the Ludus Imperium.

Takky and me . . . it feels like Fate.

18

The Sardazam

The Gnosis

A new interpretation of the gnosis is required. The Rondian magi thought them-selves appointed and empowered by their god to rule, but now I have come with magi of my own, and I do not bow to Kore but to Ahm. From whence then, comes this mighty gift?

RASHID MUBARAK, EMIR OF HALLI'KUT, 931

Sagostabad, Antiopia
Thani (Aprafor) 935

Waqar awoke to find his skull throbbing and soldiers everywhere, which was terrifying enough, but then the memory of *why* flooded his brain and he cried, '*SALIM!*' He thrashed about, his kinesis tossing grown men aside like toys, shouting the sultan's name, until someone quelled his gnosis with power of their own: a Hadishah man, he found out later. 'It's done, Prince Waqar,' the hard-faced man kept shouting at him, 'it's too late – it's done!'

'What's done?' he begged, then he remembered that desperate call. 'My mother—?'

'She lives,' the man replied, his voice odd, then someone gave Waqar something to drink, which he gulped down before realising what it was. His hearing faded, his vision blurred . . .

He woke again to find his friends around him, their faces pale and anxious. Tamir was biting his nails, Lukadin was pacing, and Baneet and Fatima were sitting on the bed beside him, waiting.

'Here, let me,' Fatima said, holding his temples and sending healing-gnosis tingling through her strong fingers, soothing away the pain. She kissed his forehead – there'd been a time when it was his lips, and he suddenly missed that – then went back to Baneet's side.

His head was clear enough to realise that he was in a healing suite and it was day-time. The air coming through the window was heavy with smoke and he could hear the low murmur of distant prayer from many throats. That didn't augur well for the questions he had to ask.

'Salim?' he whispered.

Lukadin's face was anguished. 'Dead. They're all dead: his whole household.'

They fell into appalled silence again.

Dear Ahm, why is the world still turning? Why is the sun still aflame? Waqar's eyes welled up with hot, stinging tears, and he let them fall, not ashamed to weep before his friends.

Tamir took up the narrative, dispassionately relating what they'd seen as they responded to the cries of alarm that arose suddenly from all over the palace. 'It's possible one of the impersonators and two of the wives escaped,' Tamir concluded, 'but some rooms were gutted by fire, so it's more likely their bones burned to ash.'

'Ahm take them,' Lukadin intoned.

'What of my mother?'

Fatima took his hand. 'She's been bitten by a snake – we don't know what kind, and the healers are at a loss.'

'If they save her, I'll give them gold from my own hands,' Waqar vowed. 'I must see her—'

'Next door,' said Baneet, but Fatima, the most expert of them, was shaking her head.

'There's nothing you can do. Her veins are all black beneath her skin, and her eyes are bleeding,' she said. 'It's not like any snakebite I've ever seen.'

'I must see her,' Waqar repeated, then the door was thrown open and Attam and Xoredh prowled into the chamber, followed by half a dozen magi of their coterie. Waqar's friends stood supportively around him as Xoredh wrinkled his nose in distaste.

'Well,' Xoredh sneered, 'the weakling has awakened. How did the sultan die when you still drew breath?'

'There was nothing anyone could do,' Waqar retorted.

'Nothing *you* could do,' Xoredh returned, 'but why did they spare you, I wonder?'

That question was haunting Waqar; he feared to examine it too closely.

'You would have done no better,' Fatima snapped, unwisely, for Attam turned and slammed her against the wall. She looked like a child in his grasp.

'Weak,' he said, blowing in her face. 'Weak like straw.'

Then Baneet gripped Attam's arm, a breach of the harbadab that could see him flogged, and the two giants eyed each other coldly. Attam was the taller, but not by much. Baneet's usually gentle face was like granite.

Xoredh separated them with a drawn dagger. 'He's not worth it, Attam. He's just a breeding-house mule.'

Attam wrenched free and shoved Baneet away, but he barely moved.

Waqar climbed dizzily to his feet. 'Leave us alone.'

Xoredh kissed his dagger, then sheathed it. 'Ai, let's not keep little Waqar – not when Father wants to see him, to find out how he failed to protect the sultan. I'd not want to be in his shoes.' He slapped Attam's shoulder and leered at Fatima. 'Come, I know a place where the girls aren't so ugly.' The two warrior-princes swaggered out and slammed the door behind them.

Waqar groaned as he wondered again, *Why was I spared?* Once he was sure his cousins were well gone, he described all he'd seen – the masked assassins, their deadly skill, the way they knew the layout of the palace intimately, how they'd trapped him and Salim – and most of all, the way Heartface had merely incapacitated him when she could so easily have taken his life.

'It's as if they were playing with me,' he concluded. 'They were so far beyond my skills that I was never a threat – and you know me, you've sparred with me – I'm not *that* bad!'

'Perhaps that's why they spared you?' Lukadin said. 'Perhaps they have their own honour code and won't kill the unworthy?'

'Flattering theory,' Tamir replied, winking at Waqar, 'but they had no compunction about killing dozens of guards and servants.'

'Killers don't have honour,' Fatima said, her mind still on Attam. 'They're like animals.'

'But Waqar's a prince, he *matters*,' Baneet put in, 'and servants and soldiers don't: not to people like that. Perhaps their targets – the people they were there to kill, not those who got in their way – were very specific.'

'Ai,' Tamir said, 'you don't just casually kill the nephew of Rashid Mubarak, especially if—'

'If what?' Waqar demanded.

Tamir dropped his voice to a bare whisper. 'Especially if Rashid arranged the attack.'

They looked at each other silently, and Waqar thought, *Let it not be so*.

'You said they spoke Rondian,' Lukadin noted. 'Surely they were Volsai from Yuros?'

'Many Dhassan and Keshi speak Rondian – we do,' Tamir pointed out. 'What could be easier than speaking Rondian during the raid to muddy the waters?'

'That's possible,' Waqar admitted. 'Don't forget that Mother was assailed too, perhaps by the same people. We can't jump to conclusions, but we must keep our eyes and ears open.'

They were churning over the possibilities while waiting for word on Sakita when a messenger summoned Waqar to the Sardazam's suite. Though he was desperate to see his mother, Waqar dutifully followed the messenger and was taken straight past a press of waiting suppli-cants, into Rashid's presence. His uncle sat before a massive wooden desk, writing with unhurried concentration. It was fully two minutes before he put the quill aside. His calmness in the wake of the calamity they'd been through was unbelievable. Waqar didn't know whether to be reassured by it, or worried.

'Nephew,' Rashid said finally. 'Sit. How do you fare?'

'I've just woken,' Waqar replied, sitting down. 'I have a headache.'

'Concussion,' Rashid said. 'Don't take it lightly – I've known men to

die of such blows. You should attend my physician when we're finished.'
He leaned forward. 'Describe what you saw.'

Waqar threw all his concentration into recalling the conversation
with Salim as accurately as he could, then described the attackers: 'One
was male, wearing a mask of a man in a steel helmet: he called himself
"Ironhelm". The other was a woman, with a female mask.'

'There were three attackers in all,' Rashid said, 'all wearing Lantric
masks. I've had the survivors describe them to our artists.' He pushed
three sheets of paper across the desk, each containing the labelled
sketch of a mask. He recognised Ironhelm and Heartface; the third
was labelled 'Beak'.

'Why Lantric masks, Uncle?'

'One of many things we don't know,' Rashid admitted. 'They spared
you, Nephew. Do you know why?'

Waqar swallowed. 'No, I don't.'

Rashid stood and began to pace, six steps one way, six back. 'The city
is in mourning, but there is also great anger – even the Ja'arathi are
roused: they are saying that Beyrami arranged this to clear the path for
war. The Shihadi refute that and blame the Ordo Costruo.' He paused,
looked down at Waqar. 'Others blame me.'

'But you weren't involved,' Waqar replied. He hadn't meant it to
sound like a question.

Rashid's eyes narrowed. 'No, I was not involved. Salim was our lord
and ruler. I have served him faithfully for my entire adult life. He and
I were aligned on all major matters.'

Including the Shihad? Waqar wondered silently.

Rashid saw his doubts. 'Nephew, I benefited either way, Shihad or
no Shihad. I was truly neutral – and I had no desire to see Salim's line
broken.'

'But who will rule us now?' Waqar asked. 'My friends told me the
nurseries were . . . a bloodbath.'

'They were. With one stroke, the Kabarakhi line is extinct. The seventeen Emirs of Kesh have been notified – most are already here. The
Convocation will select a new sultan.'

Waqar knew his history: only two dynasties had ever succeeded in unifying the thrones of Kesh: the prophet Aluq-Ahmed, and the Kaba-rakhis. Kesh could collapse into a dozen or more warring kingdoms if the Convocation didn't unite around a strong ruler.

Like you, Uncle . . . 'What will happen?'

'Unless a single emir emerges to command the allegiance of the rest, the kingdom will fragment again, which will destroy any chance of unity,' Rashid replied.

'Including a united Shihad,' Waqar said. 'So the Ja'arathi could also be culpable?'

Rashid made a gesture of approval. 'Yes, they could. There will be a public investigation, obviously. You'll be questioned, but I want you to do more: I wish you to join it.'

'*Me?* Why?'

'Because this crime was committed by magi, and only a mage can solve it. Both Shihadi and Ja'arathi insist on being involved in the investigation, and our family must also be represented. I can't spare Xoredh, and my senior Hadishah are hunting the killers or elsewhere engaged. I would take it on myself, had I the time, but I must see to the arrangements for the succession. You will be officially representing the household of Sultan Salim, not me.' Rashid's emerald eyes fixed on him. 'Waqar, I didn't – *I repeat: I did not* – instigate this attack. That there are people out there capable of such brutality and power frightens me. If they can penetrate our defences so easily, no one is safe. I need to know who they are – will you serve?'

He sounds genuine, Waqar decided. 'Of course, Uncle. What are my instructions?'

'Two-fold: first, publicly, you will find Rondian assassins guilty – for the investigation to find that Salim was killed by his own people would be *unacceptable*. But you must seek the true killers and reveal that information only to me.'

'Do you think the attack on Mother is related?'

'It may be so,' Rashid replied, clenching a fist. 'She is my sister, and what was done to her is a direct attack on me. *Remember that.* Learn everything you can – I want to know the truth!'

Waqar nodded, thinking, *This is my chance to shine.* The contemptuous battering he'd taken from Heartface still scared him, but he burned to prove that he'd not been weak, whatever Attam and Xoredh thought.

'The investigation starts tomorrow morning. The Shihadis and Ja'arathi have both sent magi to "help".' The contempt in Rashid's voice startled Waqar, until he remembered that such men would have been trained as Hadishah, then left the order. Rashid bowed his head, picked up his quill, then paused. 'Keep me apprised of Sakita's condition. Comfort her, and if you can, determine what ails her.'

'I won't let you down, Uncle.'

'I know.' Rashid handed him a warrant to enter the sultan's suite and the zenana, valid for a week. The interview was over.

Waqar left, harbouring a frightening thought. *What if the trail leads right back here?*

Waqar sat with his mother for hours, but she didn't wake and eventually he returned to his own bed and fell into a troubled slumber. Next morning found him outside the sultan's chambers, really wishing he didn't have to go through this.

His worries were confirmed immediately he went inside. The stench of burnt flesh was nauseating, but he contained his revulsion for the benefit of those awaiting him: a red-scarved man, thirty-ish with a greying beard and a hard face, and a blue-scarved younger, paler man with curling hair and a small goatee.

'Sal'Ahm, Prince Waqar,' the red-scarved man said. 'I'm Rhotan. Maula Beyrami sent me as his representative.'

'And I'm Iradhi, my Prince,' the young Ja'arathi added. 'With respect, I hope you have a strong stomach.' He indicated an inner door. 'This way, please.'

Waqar swallowed as a fresh waft of smoke and cooked meat met his nostrils. 'I'm ready,' he said, trying to pretend his gorge wasn't rising.

But when they entered the corridor that led to the private rooms of the sultan's harem and saw the carnage beyond, he realised that he was in no way prepared at all. At first all he could see were the blackened corpses, the frozen screams and the bulging eyes. His sight blurred, as if to protect him. He clenched his stomach muscles and locked up his throat, trying to breathe through his nose ... then vomited anyway, a helpless surge.

'You have not seen death before?' Iradhi enquired sympathetically.

'I'm fine,' Waqar panted. 'Let's get it over with.'

It got no better: the attackers had been swift, but they'd been savage. Some of the women and children had clearly tried to hide, but they'd been found, dragged into the light and despatched, most often by a mage-bolt to the head which left the faces burned to the bone. The blasts looked gratuitously powerful.

'I'm told you encountered the masked ones?' Rhotan asked.

'I did. Ironhelm and Heartface: a man and woman with skin colour hidden and voices distorted. They were the strongest magi I've ever encountered. They easily outclassed me.'

Rhotan didn't look like he thought that was much of a feat. 'They spoke Rondian?'

'They spoke both Rondian and Keshi.'

'And they spared you,' Iradhi noted, adding, 'thankfully! Why, do you think?'

I'm getting fed up of being asked that. 'I don't think they expected to see me – perhaps their instructions were to kill only Salim's household? They said several times that they only wanted Salim. They knew me by name and told me to go, and when I refused, they still didn't kill me.'

'You're a well-known person, Prince Waqar,' Iradhi said. 'Everyone knows you.'

'But we're told your meeting with the sultan was secret?' Rhotan added.

Waqar pursed his lips, wondering how much to reveal. 'Sultan Salim had asked to meet me, but we had barely time to greet one another when the attackers appeared.'

'It's clear that they must be Merozain monks or Ordo Costruo,' Rhotan stated, and Iradhi nodded in agreement.

'We know no such thing,' Waqar retorted. 'Quite apart from Sakita Mubarak being an Ordo Costruo mage and being attacked herself, what would they gain from this?'

'Revenge for the Crusade, of course,' Rhotan replied, 'and with respect,

Prince Waqar, it's not clear who attacked your mother. There were no witnesses, nothing was found at the scene—'

Waqar *tsked* impatiently. 'The Ordo Costruo had no quarrel with the sultan – if they wanted anyone's head, it was Rashid's. And why would they show *me* mercy?'

'Have three Crusades and millions of deaths taught you *nothing*?' Rhotan argued, barely respectful. 'They don't want peace, they just want to weaken us before the next Crusade—'

'The Ordo Costruo aren't the Rondian Empire!'

'Pah! Did you fight in the last Crusade? Have you ever bloodied a sword?'

'That's got nothing to do with it—'

'It's got *everything* to do with it. I was at Shaliyah,' Rhotan boasted. 'I *know* the Rondians! If they spared you, it was through arrogance or to confuse us. But my mind is clear.'

'The Rondians have their own Imperial assassins,' Iradhi added eagerly. 'The Volsai, yes? The Rondian Empress ordered this, have no doubt.'

The certainty Rhotan and Iradhi were showing rankled Waqar, but he remembered Rashid's instructions. 'Very well. I'll sign the report.'

But I'll not stop looking into it. I'll just do without these blind fools.

Rhotan and Iradhi snatched at the chance to leave. 'We'll report to the Sardazam immediately,' Rhotan declared and marched off, obviously aiming to claim the glory. Iradhi hovered a moment, torn: he clearly wanted to ingratiate himself with royalty, but the thought of Rhotan taking all the credit was too much and after a moment he ran after him.

Waqar was finally alone. Mercifully, someone had already taken down the sultan's badly burned body and laid him out in peaceful repose on a pallet. Salim was unrecognisable. Waqar meticulously sought traces of gnostic energy, examining every surface, from scorched pillars to burned cloth, blackened jewels to seared flesh.

Every mage had a distinctive gnostic trace – Fatima always said his was like tobacco, which was strange, as he didn't chew it. But as he worked, it became clear that the masked magi had *erased* their gnostic traces, which implied they feared they could be identified that way.

Does that make them well-known Hadishah? he wondered.

313

He also noticed the normal traces of spirits in the aether was absent, so someone had used wizardry or necromancy to erase them. Animagery had been employed to slay any animal or insect witnesses – in fact, Waqar discovered that *every* affinity had been employed, and that too was a clue; a group of three magi shouldn't have had such diverse skills.

Unless it really was the Merozains? But they're sworn to peace . . .

He renewed his efforts. Wiping away gnostic traces was difficult and time-consuming – surely they hadn't had the time to be so thorough? His combination of affinities made him quite skilled at reading traces, and he was sure if he persisted, he could gain some kind of insight . . .

Finally, he sensed something, at the very edge of his awareness: a buzzing, throbbing sensation like the echo of a wasp swarm. At first he thought he'd imagined it, then he found it on the crushed skull of a fallen servant – and there it was again, on the charred shoulder of one of Salim's wives, killed in an entirely different part of the zenana. Now he could recognise it, he found it in several other places, and that too was strange: so many different deaths had to have been at the hands of different assassins – but every trace he detected was identical.

Re-energised, he went to the Walled Garden and found the same 'swarm' where he'd been struck down. *Who are you people?* he wondered. *Why do you all have the same gnostic trace?*

At first Latif walked because he was too frightened to stop, darting down narrow alleys with no idea where he was or where he was going, knowing only that if he stopped, the masked ones would swoop down on him. He kept pressed close to the walls, huddling in empty doorways when he had to stop for breath. Crowds of youths jostled past, chanting for the Shihad, red ribbons tied to arms or around heads. Hard shoulders battered him aside and he cowered as they shouted, '*Shi–ha–di! Shi–ha–di! Death to Yuros! Shi–ha–di!*'

A nut-roaster's stall was smashed over as Latif wormed his way down a foetid alley, trying to avoid the rotting refuse piled against the walls. The rats were so bold they barely moved as he struggled by. He stumbled into another crowd and this time a burly arm shoved him up against a piss-reeking wall. Dark faces closed in. '*Hey, Skulker, where're you going?'* A fist hammered into his belly and he would have fallen if they'd not caught him – but that was only to line up more blows. *'Hey, Skulker, are you Ja'arathi?'*

He fought for air as the youths chanted, *'SHI–HA–DI!'* The man holding him jabbed fingers into his eyes at each syllable: *'SHI–HA–DI!'* The final jab became a bunched fist, and he reeled, tasting blood and snot.

'Stop,' Latif pleaded.

'Ooo, listen to the accent,' his assailant said. 'He talks like a harem girl!' As his mates laughed he pulled at Latif's clothing. 'Nice clothes – silks and embroidery! I think he's some rich man's bum-boy.'

'He's a Ja'arathi cocksucker!' another declared. 'Are you a cocksucker?' *Slap!* 'Huh? Do you suck cock for money?' *Slap!*

Latif slid down the wall as blows rained down on him, then someone shouted and the gang pelted off, the last youth grabbing his right hand and wrenching off his gold rings, then fleeing with the rest of his tormenters. Latif rolled into a ball, dry-retching.

Then something soft brushed at his face, snuffling, and he yelped in fright.

'No, Rani, leave him be,' a throaty voice called in Lakh from high above. Latif knew the southern tongue and he looked up, wiping blood from his face with his sleeve as a giant shape blocked out the night. A big sad eye amidst vast folds of grey skin peered down at him.

Ahm on high, an elephant, Latif thought dazedly, and looked higher to see a man with night-dark skin, broken yellow teeth and grey hair sprouting in all directions: the elephant's mahout. 'On, Rani,' the mahout told his beast.

'Where am I?' Latif called in Lakh. 'Please, ji!'

'You speak our tongue?' the man called down. 'Are you from Nishander?'

Nishander? The Lakh quarter in Sagostabad, where many Amteh-worshipping Lakh had settled. 'Ai . . . ai!'

The mahout hesitated, then lowered a rope ladder. 'Climb up, friend. I'm going home to Nishander myself.'

Thank Ahm . . . Latif stood painfully and climbed the short ladder until the mahout caught him under the armpit and heaved him up.

The man smelled strongly of sweat and betel-leaf and couldn't have been a day younger than fifty, but he had a strong arm. 'Perch behind me, *dosta*,' he instructed.

Friend, Latif translated silently. *What's 'thank you' again . . .?* 'Shukriya,' he panted.

'You shouldn't come through here alone,' the mahout reproached him as he sent his giant beast into motion down the narrow street. 'Not unless you are riding an elephant.'

'I got lost,' Latif said, which was something like the truth.

'Foolish,' the mahout said. 'I'm Sanjeep. And this is Rani, my queen. You are?'

Latif hesitated. His real name could be dangerous, but false names could be forgotten in the heat of the moment. He decided to use his real name, but lengthened the final syllable as a Lakh would, pronouncing it 'Lateef'.

'Sal'Ahm, Latif,' Sanjeep said. 'Praise Ahm that I came by when I did, yes?'

'I thank Ahm, and you.'

'And Rani! She and I work the building sites, hauling timber and stone, sunrise to sunset.'

Latif was too dazed to converse, and Sanjeep lapsed into silence. They crossed a square, paused for Rani to slurp water from the central fountain and expel a massive turd on the paving stones. As they swayed on, Latif saw a small boy swoop on the turd, grinning triumphantly; dried, that would keep a fire going a good long time. Passers-by frequently stroked the elephant's flanks as if for luck. At one cooking-stall Sanjeep threw down a coin, and a leaf plate filled with hot dumplings in a spicy brown gravy was placed on the end of Rani's trunk. She handed it carefully up to Sanjeep, who grinned. 'Kofta – you want to buy some? Very good kofta here.'

Latif shook his head. He had no coins, and now no rings either.

Sanjeep rubbed his chin. 'You look hungry, friend.' He sucked on his teeth, and as he tossed another coin down to the stallholder and called, 'One more!' Latif almost swooned in gratitude.

Rani took them deeper into the maze of buildings; she clearly knew her way home, and ten minutes later they entered a stable housing at least twenty elephants. Sanjeep backed Rani into a stall, then showed Latif how to wash and rub her down.

As Latif shovelled mashed feed into her feed-trough, Sanjeep said, 'Payment for giving you a ride, yes?' He was all affable slyness. 'Take better care in future, *dosta.*'

'I will,' Latif replied, clasping his hands before his chest in a gesture of thanks. He went to the stable doors, then stopped. It was fully night now, and he had no idea where to go. The city he'd grown up in and, in a way, had ruled, became more and more frightening. Then Sanjeep appeared beside him.

'You don't really live in Nishander, do you, Latif?'

'I just got here – and I've lost everything.' The dear face of Salim swam before his eyes. And his wife and son – and those awful, gloating murderers in their masks. 'I've nowhere to go.'

He only realised that he'd fallen to his knees in the mud when Sanjeep squatted down and clasped his hands, offering comfort as Latif wept until his eyes were raw, then the man drew him towards a pile of blankets in the corner of Rani's stall. He closed his eyes and shut it all out.

When next he was aware, Sanjeep was shaking his shoulder. 'Latif, wake up. Time to go.'

'Go?'

'Ai. You'll work for me, hmm? Just 'til you're back on your feet, eh?'

Latif's face was a swollen mess and his body ached down to his brittle bones, but he recognised the generosity of the offer. He allowed himself to be hauled upright and walked, blinking, into the dawn, seeking a new life.

'Mother?' Waqar whispered with voice and mind, but neither elicited any response. Sakita Mubarak looked like a corpse, but every few hours she'd wake, raving about voices and faces. Sometimes she called for Waqar or Jehana, or for their dead father Placide; other times she went into a frenzy and had to be restrained before she hurt herself or those tending her.

The Hadishah breeding programme was focused on martial skills; compared to the Rondian Arcanum system, there was no real system of training – often the 'teachers' had little more experience than their pupils. Female magi were expected to be healers, but few were even taught to read, despite their potential value; and they were always subservient to the few male healers, even when they were stronger and more skilled.

Ormutz, the chief healer tending Sakita, was far more concerned with ingratiating himself to a male Mubarak than healing a female one. He was only a quarter-blood and weaker than Fatima, though healing was far more about skill than raw power and at least he was experienced. But Ormutz was elsewhere that morning, telling Waqar self-importantly that he had *hundreds* of patients to oversee; he'd left Sakita in the care of a bony-faced nurse-mage in a full bekira-shroud called Nakti, whose sole skill appeared to be dabbing water on fevered brows.

'Did she wake in the night?' Waqar asked.

Nakti stiffened, a doe trapped by hunting dogs. 'Please, Great Prince, it was Nalimuz on duty during the night,' she muttered. 'I only just arrived.'

'Then where's this Nalimuz?'

'She's off-duty, Great Prince. Healer Ormutz will return soon.'

'When will the Ordo Costruo come?' he asked. He'd asked Rashid to request their aid, for although Sakita's wounds looked like snakebites, her room had been locked and warded and no snake had been found, just the residue of burnt cloth in front of her desk – and all their anti-venom spells were having no effect; she was slowly declining.

'I don't know,' Nakti bleated.

'Of course you don't,' he sighed bitterly. 'Why would you?' Nakti cringed and looked away. *She probably thinks I'll have her flogged if things go badly.* In truth, he felt sorry for her. She quivered in fright whenever a man passed by, and she had the unwashed smell of the very poor.

'Go and find food and drink,' he said, to give her some respite, and as she fled, he sat beside his mother and dribbled water between her cracked lips. Up close, her face and neck were a frightening mesh of black, bulging veins.

Then her head whipped around. '*Have you got more?*' she croaked.

His heart had leaped to his mouth but he gasped, 'Ai, just here.' He pulled a glass phial from his belt-purse and put it in her hand.

'Thank Ahm for a dutiful son!' Sakita tried to grasp it, but couldn't. 'You'll need to feed it to me.' She was getting worse: yesterday she'd got the stopper off herself.

The first morning after the attack, she'd awakened as soon as they were alone and recited a recipe, saying, 'Ormutz won't listen, but I know what I need.'

The recipe was odd and it took some potion-skill, but he'd always been a diligent student. He couldn't blame Ormutz for his doubts: with allium, argentum and bismuth, it was more poison than elixir – but Sakita insisted it was the only thing that could save her. 'Tell no one,' she'd whispered in his ear before going back to raving about snakes crawling through her skin. On the few occasions she'd been lucid enough to tell him what had happened, she'd been deliberately vague – to '*protect me*', *no doubt* . . . *Mother, I hope you know what you're doing.*

He hid the potion as Nakti returned with food and the chief healer, a man in his forties with a bald head and giant moustaches. She deposited her tray and cowered, while Ormutz sat beside Sakita. He examined her eyes, muttering.

'She's getting worse,' Waqar accused him. 'What are you doing to save her?'

'We're going to try leeches to get the poison from her veins,' Ormutz replied.

'But the blood-loss might kill her!'

'Not in the volume I propose. I'm confident it will help. Why don't you go and get some rest, Prince Waqar? Your mother is in good hands.'

'With respect, I'll stay,' Waqar replied, thinking, *Dear Ahm, he'll make her worse.*

'You are a true inspiration, Prince Waqar,' Ormutz smarmed, then he added, 'Please ensure she consumes nothing unless I personally have prescribed it, Prince. Foreign substances could jeopardise her recovery.'

'Of course,' Waqar replied. *Does he know about the elixir? No, if he did, he'd say something.*

'Then I wish you goodnight.' The healer left, clicking his fingers at Nakti to follow.

Waqar wondered if Jehana knew what had happened, and when the Ordo Costruo would send their healers, even whether Sakita's elixir was helping or harming her. His thoughts went around and around, leaving him disorientated and afraid and unable to do anything except grip her hand, his eyes fixed on her dark-veined, ravaged face as she slept.

I'm going to save you, Mother, he promised silently. *I swear I will.*

'Well, Nephew?' Rashid Mubarak enquired. 'How does my sister fare?' The leech-treatment had been going for two days now, but Waqar had seen no improvement.

'She's not good. Ormutz is a fool, and nothing he does helps.'

'But he tells me she's stabilising?'

Waqar couldn't believe how indifferent his uncle sounded. *But she was the family embarrassment,* he reminded himself. *Does he even want her to recover?* Then he chided himself for having such a thought. *My uncle is holding Kesh together in the wake of a horrific murder – he's under more pressure than anyone.*

'Shouldn't she be improving? When will the Ordo Costruo come? Does Jehana know what's happened?'

'We've sent messages to Hebusalim; I await their arrival, as you do.' Rashid rubbed his eyes – he looked like he'd been awake for days. 'How goes your investigation, Nephew?'

Waqar had made little progress, but he had some thoughts: 'As you said, Uncle, the official answer, that it was the Ordo Costruo, doesn't make sense. I believe the killers were very powerful magi, maybe even able to use all sixteen Gnostic Studies.'

'The Merozain Bhaicara?' Rashid raised an eyebrow. 'I have no love of them, but murder isn't their style. And they supported Salim's pacifism. Why do you think they're involved?'

'I didn't say I did. What I found were strange gnostic traces, all identical, even those of spells I'm sure were cast by different magi – but that's impossible, isn't it?'

Rashid's eyebrows lifted. 'Are you certain?'

Waqar had been going over that same question, knowing that the traces were deteriorating by the hour. 'Perhaps some kind of masking spell? A technique we don't know?'

'I suppose it's possible,' Rashid sighed. 'I admire your persistence, Nephew: but time is marching. Tend to your mother, and once she recovers, report back to me. I have a new task awaiting you.'

A new task. That should have enlivened him, but Waqar was exhausted, and all he wanted was to get back to his mother's side. 'Yes, Uncle,' he said, and hurried back to his rooms to fetch another draught of the elixir before returning to his mother's room. It was after meal-time and the wards were dimly lit, the patients settled for sleep. He made his way quietly, not wishing to disturb the sleeping – then he saw his mother's door was ajar, and a shadow was moving inside. He padded silently forward and looked inside, and his heart thudded: a black robed figure was bent over Sakita's withered frame.

'Who are you?' he demanded, pulling out his dagger.

19

The Wronged Man

The Mage-Knights

As the magi developed their skills in gnostic combat, it was natural that an elite would form, one restricted as much by wealth and attitude as mage-blood, one that prized martial prowess above all. They became the first mage-knights, obsessed with personal glory, too proud to serve as legion battle-magi, but deadly in single combat. For better or worse, they remain a potent part of the empire's military might.

PRIOR SHARDEN, KORE HISTORIAN, 698

Finostarre, Rondelmar, Yuros
Aprafor 935

If the point of being an Incognito was to be anonymous, the ploy had completely failed. When Ril and the Wronged Man entered the lists for the final bout that afternoon, the roar that went up was unmistakable.

'*TAKWYTH! TAKWYTH!*' echoed primarily from the Corani ranks, the men for whom Solon Takwyth had been a talisman for victory in the constant border skirmishes against Argundy and Hollenia. Although he was a pure-blood mage-noble, they'd always seen him as one of them: a career soldier. That Ril was now Master-General and Knight-Commander of Coraine hadn't eclipsed their affection for their former commander.

But what did surprise Ril was the response that rose from the Pallacian commoners, who were shouting, '*ENDARION!*' and '*PRINCE OF THE SPEAR!*'. The various chants swirled about the arena. Legion red was dominant, but there were purple pennants aplenty too: deep splashes of colour amid the sea of faces.

Pearl was in fine fettle, briskly prancing and showing no sign of fear of Takwyth's venator; the standard legion mount might be much bigger than a pegasus, but it was ungainly and far slower, especially on the ground, where it waddled like a duck – although Takwyth somehow contrived to ride it with grace.

Ril noticed Takwyth raising his hand to the legion men crying his name. His expression was hidden by the helm, but this had to mean much to him: a redemption, of sorts.

'They've got short memories,' Ril called. 'You're a disgraced exile.'

'They know why I left, and most would've done the same,' Takwyth replied. 'They can sense that your brief ascent is foundering, Endarion. Unrest is spreading through the provinces and vassal-states. You're blind to it in Pallas, but the people know; they want someone they trust to make things right.'

'You're wrong,' Ril replied, 'we're not foundering. Lyra's with child, and this tournament will reinforce our reign – especially after I flatten you this afternoon!'

'That won't happen,' Takwyth said, his voice devoid of doubt. 'You imagine you're in charge, but you're just a figurehead – a bad jest. You should hear how they laugh at your name in the provinces.'

'I wouldn't know; I don't go to the provinces. I'm too busy here, married to the woman who turned you down.'

Takwyth turned to face him, his voice suddenly earnest. 'Listen, Endarion, I never gave you the seniority you thought you merited, and perhaps I erred there. But there's a crisis coming – this riverreek epidemic, the confidence in Garod Sacrecour's demeanour, the unrest sweeping through the south – surely even you can feel enemies closing in?'

'Aye, and I'm looking at one right now—'

'Damn you, Ril; I'm *not* your enemy. I'm a sworn Corani – I want to serve my queen!'

Ril's temper flared. 'Go back into exile, Takwyth. Better yet, go to Hel!'

Trumpets brayed and as they turned from each other, Ril was angry, knowing he'd let Takwyth win the mind games. They reached the parade ground before the Royal Box and he looked up, focusing on Lyra's pale face. Beside her, Medelie Aventour was distant and watchful, her eyes flashing between him and Takwyth. Basia was a comforting presence, but when he looked for Jenet, she was missing again. *Perhaps her riverreek has worsened?* he thought. The gnosis helped, but magi could still get ill.

If she'd come to my door before Lyra . . . I came so close to falling . . .

'The man whose eye strays has already committed the sin,' Takwyth murmured as they approached the thrones and dropped to their knees. Ril shot him a venomous – and worried – look. *What does he know about it?*

He scarcely heard Lyra recite the rote words about bravery and honour, but he did listen as Medelie, as Regna d'Amore, exhorted them to fight with 'chivalric prowess'. She ended, 'May the best man prevail!' and as they parted, Takwyth's voice reached him, half sound, half sending: *'If you can see my lance, it can reach your eye-slit . . .'*

Before Ril could retort, the 'Wronged Man' spurred his venator towards his end of the arena.

Ril was still fuming as he cantered away, and Pearl had caught his skittishness. 'That prick thinks he can come back and everyone will just fall down at his feet,' he snapped as he re-joined his friends.

'Then beat him to his knees,' Gryff replied. 'But first: take a deep breath.' He linked minds with Pearl, using the gnosis to settle her.

'Whatever you want to say to Takky,' Larik added, 'you can say with a lance.'

Ril told himself that his friends were right, that he had to clear his head or he was going to end up severely embarrassed, badly injured or dead. *And I've never beaten him before.*

'What do we know about his previous bouts?'

'Well, luckily, one of us has watched them,' Larik replied drily. 'His style hasn't changed: he likes to come in low and drive upwards: velocity by—'

'By weight by cock-size,' Ril finished irritably. 'I know the drill—'

'He's only got a venator,' Gryfflon put in. 'They're slow and can't manoeuvre. Go in fast and jagged, hit him square while putting him off his blow and it'll be Brylion all over.'

Kore's Blood, I hope so . . .

They fiddled with his gear while he tried to imagine that it was all over, that he was being acclaimed champion and Takwyth was stretched on the ground. All the while his jitters grew; he barely heard the calls of encouragement. Other days he'd bantered with the crowd, but today he couldn't think of a single thing to say.

If you can see my lance, it can reach your eye-slit . . .

Then the marshalls signalled, the crowd exploded, and suddenly there was no more time for words or thoughts. The world shrank from complexity and confusion to a funnel of air and a target he must hit at the end of it. He climbed back into the saddle, patted Pearl and then spurred her into motion . . .

Cordan Sacrecour looked out through the barred window of their prison-suite, wishing he was four miles away in Finostarre. *I just want to be at the tourney,* he brooded. *Just to watch—*

'Cordan, are you ready?' Coramore called. All her clothes were packed into one of the two canvas saddlebags, but she kept adding trinkets and tokens, cheap girlish nothings that weighed the bag down ridiculously. His just had a few basics and was already strapped closed.

When I'm emperor, there will be tournaments in Pallas all the time—

'Cordan – someone's coming!'

Her words wrenched his mind back to the here and now and he took his sister's hand as the door wards flared, a key turned and the door opened. The Mutthead stood there, the sword in his right hand dripping blood.

Coramore squeaked in fear, as Jenet Brunlye appeared behind the giant knight, gesturing for the children to come. 'Abraxas,' she said, her odd password. She and Lamgren were both pale as ice, their eyeballs so bloodshot they almost glowed. Jenet held a knife that ran as thick with blood as Mutthead's blade.

'What's happening?' Cordan asked tremulously.

'Shh,' Jenet hissed. 'Gather your bags and come, children.'

But the two children were frozen by the naked ferocity on the faces of their 'rescuers': not just the blank, bloody stares and bared teeth, but the uniformity of their expressions, as if they were puppets painted by the same artist.

Suddenly this room felt like a sanctuary.

But even had they wanted, there was no turning back now. Jenet thrust Coramore's bags into her hands, so Cordan hefted his own. Then

Sir Bruss Lamgren hauled something into the room: a body, one of the guardsman, who'd been stabbed at least a dozen times.

Cordan looked at Coramore. *I don't think this is a good idea any more*, her eyes were saying.

'Come,' Jenet rasped, her face feverish. *'Come!'* She grabbed Coramore's arm and yanked her towards the door.

Cordan started to protest, then Bruss Lamgren's brutish visage turned his way. 'Move,' the knight boomed, looking at the boy like he was meat, and Cordan's protests died in his mouth.

The halls outside were empty but for the blood on the floor. Cordan glimpsed the maids' quarters through a half-open door: a pool of ruby-coloured fluid was soaking into a white dress and splattering a pale leg, toes down. *They've murdered the servants too, those who weren't given time off to attend the tourney . . .*

He grabbed Coramore's hand and held on tight as Jenet led them down the back stairs. There were no guards at the back door, but there were more streaks of blood on one wall. A carriage was waiting, and Jenet pushed them inside and shut the door. A figure in a black cloak and hood, wearing a Lantric mask of *Jest* was already sitting there.

'Who . . . who are you?' Cordan managed to bleat.

'A friend,' Jest replied, his voice melodious. 'One who can make you emperor.'

At the top of his run, Ril slammed his visor down, blanking an unwanted image of a lance-head punching through the grille. *I will prevail*, he told himself, over and over. Then the ribbon dropped, both jousters jammed their heels into the flanks of their steeds and Pearl began to pump her wings and pick up speed. Half a mile away, Takwyth's venator did the same.

Right, here we go . . .

But Takwyth was late to the first mark and they had to reset their approach. Ril doubted it was nerves, more likely a ploy to give him more time to worry. But the second time the red flare flashed across the sky, the crowd howled and Ril sent Pearl spiralling down towards the approach circle. He burst through the ring, perfectly aligned, and saw a big shape sweeping towards him.

Takwyth's lance was set high.

He's going to take my head off.

The stands on either side became a tunnel of darkness as they blurred towards each other, but at the last moment Ril remembered that damned phrase about lances finding visors and committed the cardinal sin—

—he flinched, pulled slightly right and unbalanced Pearl.

Takwyth's lance slammed into his target, a perfect hit, hammering Ril sideways, throwing them into a spin; but his harness held and they righted themselves a few feet above the nets and shot along the arena and climbed again. A marshall on a venator swooped in to see how he fared.

Rukka! He waved the man away. The first point went to Takwyth – but he was still on his steed, and still in the game. He took Pearl round and landed, seeking water, playing for time to regain his composure.

'The bastard!' he railed as Gryff grabbed Pearl and soothed her again. 'New cinches – new harness,' he shouted unnecessarily. 'Something almost gave!'

Yes, me! I flinched. It was the worst thing he could have done, and on the most important pass of his life. He ground his teeth, silently berating himself. Larik was babbling encouragement, but he wasn't listening; he just wanted to get back into the saddle and rectify this. He snatched the reins from Gryff, snapped something brusque at Larik and swung back onto Pearl's back. 'Not your fault, pooty-girl. You did well. It was me. My fault.'

This time, he goes down!

The second pass came around fast, the five minutes between vanishing – and that suited Ril fine – he didn't want to dwell on that last run. As the brazier lit, Pearl swirled and dropped, they ripped through the approach in the fastest dive he could remember, too fast to try and manoeuvre. But he was solid, and this time he didn't waver as the lances struck. The power of Takwyth's blow almost tore him from the saddle, but it was countered in the same instant by his own lance. Both poles broke as they thundered by, and he screamed in relief.

The crowd shrilled in appreciation, and he felt such a burst of relief and exhilaration he reeled in the saddle . . . but it wasn't enough: he was a full point behind. If he failed to unseat Takwyth in the final pass, he would lose.

I refuse to lose . . .

'Keep low, drive in on him,' Larik kept telling him. Gryff just slapped his shoulder greaves and yelled, 'Come on!' in his face. He barely noticed: the world had shrunk and all he could focus on was Takwyth now. Only this mattered. The interval was gone in a blink, and then he was stroking Pearl's flank, three hundred yards above the ground, and whispering, 'Come on, pooty-girl, you can do it.'

The brazier lit and they dived again, dipping into the approaches, shrieking between the long stands, at eye-level with the highest seats, slightly slower this time, as he dug in his left heel and kicked up under the right wing.

The crowd *ooo-ed* as Pearl flicked onto her side, wings out straight: pegasus and rider now flying sideways. It was a high-risk move, pulling his head and lance into the epicentre of the impact point, while shifting his target out of alignment. In the middle of the manoeuvre, Ril engaged combat-divination, hoping for the same result as the bout with Brylion Fasterius . . .

His vision blurred and lines of force streamed through his skull, nearly blinding him, because Takwyth also changed tactics, altering his venator's rhythm with a quick nudge of the knee, so that it lifted and then dipped before impact, bringing Takwyth into contact from above, not below, driving downwards with vicious force. Takwyth's lance followed Ril's target languidly, while Ril's divination-gnosis showed him too much; his sight blurred and he almost lost his aim . . .

Then his blow smashed home, even as Takwyth's lance pierced his shields, missed the target and crunched into his chest, almost punching through. Both lances broke, but the breastplate all but caved in, his lungs emptying as the world swirled and spun. Takwyth's blow killed most of Pearl's forward momentum and an instant later her hooves tangled in the nets and she spilled Ril from her back. He flew in a terrifying arc, the noise of the crowd buried beneath his beloved mount's scream, then he heard a sickening crunch, a moment before his kinesis prevented the ground from breaking his back. He rolled over and over, then hung there, winded and gasping, tangled in the net. All he could see was Pearl below him, her right wing shattered, and two legs broken.

NO! NO NO NO!

Takwyth's venator spread its wings as momentum took them over the Pallas end of the stalls, the Wronged Man already rising in his stirrups and punching the air.

Lyra whispered prayers to Kore as her husband was engulfed by marshals, animagi and other attendants. In the skies above, Takwyth's venator was arcing gracefully into a turn and flying back across the arena, the rider saluting the baying crowd.

Please Kore, let Ril be whole!

Once she was assured he was unscathed, she looked about her, measuring the reactions. Most of the men were groaning, apart from a few whoops from those who'd bet against the Prince-Consort. Her ladies were wailing theatrically, calling support and consolation to her. Basia was hurrying to Ril's side. Lyra wished etiquette permitted her to do the same. Beside her, Medelie Aventour was frozen, hand to mouth.

Then Takwyth's venator landed and the victor leaped from its back and strode towards the fallen Ril. He acknowledged the crowd in an understated way before offering Ril – sitting in the dirt – a consoling handshake. Ril endeared himself to no one by slapping it away.

'TAKWYTH!' the legion men chanted, then the commons took up the name also. He accepted a handshake from a marshall and then turned back towards the Royal Box, and suddenly Lyra felt something like the sensation Ril had described when jousting, of being alone in a tunnel with a foe bearing down on you. The victorious knight ascended the stairs, pausing to accept every handshake, then cast himself on one knee, still officially anonymous. That meant the herald was obliged to announce the victor as the 'Wronged Man'.

'Wronged', when you struck my husband.

But they'd not pressed charges, and she could hardly do so now. So she rose stiffly and let her voice ring out. 'Congratulations, Sir Knight – you are a worthy victor of the Ludus Imperium! The purse is yours, and the freedom of the city, as warranted under the statutes of the tourney—'

Freedom of the City – what the Hel possessed us to include that in the declaration?
The crowd roared approval.

'But an Incognito knight must reveal his name to claim the prize,' she added in a loud voice.

'You know my name, my Queen,' the helmed knight replied, his eyes shining through the grilled visor. 'I am your loyal knight.' He removed his helmet . . . and yes, it was him, Solon Takwyth, his head half-turned away so she only saw the right-hand side of his face. At first she thought that he looked just the same: the dour, inflexible features, the close-cropped hair a little greyer – then he turned to face her fully.

The crowd flinched, and so did she.

The left side of the former knight-commander's face was a dreadful sight, a horror-mask carved into flesh. Lyra couldn't say if it had been done with a brand or a hot knife, but the effect was of a pentagram, the sigil used by wizards to bind a daemon, and it covered the entire left side of his face. The symbol was so deeply burned into Takwyth's flesh that there were ridges covering his visage from the top of his skull to his jawline, permanently mottled in dark reds, purples and black, a stark contrast to the natural pallor of the right side. It reminded her chillingly of the mask of one of the more sinister characters of the Lantric Masques: *Twoface*, whose mask he'd worn to the ball the previous night. The flesh was clearly stiff and inflexible, but his left eye still shone amidst the darkened scar tissue as he looked up at her.

Dear Kore . . . Lyra contained her shock as best she could as she gasped, 'Sir Solon?'

'Yes, it is still me.' The voice was the same. 'I fell in with some bad men on my travels – when I called them "diabolos" they branded me with this sigil. They thought it a fine joke. Then they crucified me and left me to die. But I didn't oblige them.'

Oh my . . . 'Cannot the healers—?'

'Too late – a mage enchanted the branding iron with gnostic energy. I'll take this to the grave.' He shrugged as if this were of no moment and replaced his helm.

Lyra had tears in her eyes, despite her antipathy for him. *It happened in the exile I forced him into because I humiliated him . . . But he brought it on himself – dear Kore, did I do right?*

Only those in the Royal Box had got a proper look at his disfigurement; most were oblivious as they fervently proclaimed their champion. Which he was, so Lyra took the gold-leaf crown from the Chief Marshall and placed it on Takwyth's helmet. He kissed her hand and she flinched, then forced herself to stand firm.

Takwyth was permitted a brief speech, for which he kept his helmet on but his visor up, to minimise the impact of his disfigured face. Everyone fell quiet to hear the victor's words.

'I donate my purse to the veterans' fund,' Takwyth proclaimed first, and the veterans and legionaries and their families – almost half the commons – started screaming. The purse was probably less than a copper per family, but it was a grand gesture. 'And I thank all who supported me this week for their good wishes: this is your victory!'

Praise the crowd, and they'll love you for it, Lyra reflected; she'd done it herself at times these past years. It certainly worked for Takwyth today, for the noise redoubled.

Then, just as the tumult died down, he spun to face her, dropping to one knee again. 'My Queen, I am an exile who longs to return! I am a Corani knight whose loyalty to your Majesty has never faltered! All have seen today what I have to offer! I beg a boon of you, Majesty!'

You damnable man, she thought wretchedly. 'What boon, Sir Knight?' she asked, although she already knew his answer.

'Please, permit me to return to the Corani knights – in whatever capacity pleases you—'

The crowd took up his plea, deafening her, making the air throb with the pressure of their demand. This was politics as theatre and she felt trapped by it, for her refusal could turn things ugly. She glanced around, but there was no path out of his snare. Ril was still in the fields with Pearl and furious at his defeat; if she delegated this to him, she risked a decision made in anger.

'What role do you envisage, Sir Knight?' she asked, as the crowd hushed again.

It wasn't a random question but a memory of the convent: she'd once seen Abbess Jaratia confront an ambitious young nun who'd demanded advancement. The girl had overreached, and been cut down to size.

Overreach, Takky, she wished silently, *so that I can easily refuse . . .*

'My Queen, to be the least of your knights is an honour all men aspire to.' His words and gaze told her that he'd seen – and respected – the trap.

Damn you, she thought. *Then you shall be the least of my knights.*

Aloud, she said, 'Surely a place can be made for so worthy a champion.' It was the best she could salvage, she decided, as the Royal Box applauded and the more distant masses just assumed that all was well and started cheering again.

It was a relief to see Takwyth bow and back away. Her part in the proceedings was done; now it was time for the Regna d'Amore to fulfil her role, to walk the arena with the Victor, to unbuckle his armour and take charge of his comfort, then partner him for the Victory Ball. For a night, Medelie Aventour was queen. It was ceremonial, of course; servants would do the real work. But she and Takwyth would nevertheless be in close contact for many hours to come.

Lyra turned to the woman at her side and eyed her coldly. *I expect you'll enjoy it, you ambitious little chit.*

Medelie rose to her feet, her gaze trailing across the field to where Ril stood, then back to Solon. She looked a little unsteady after seeing her champion's ruined face, but then her expression became triumphant; she gave Lyra an almost vindictive look as she stepped to Takwyth's side and took his arm.

He is the Coming Man, her gesture said, *and he's mine.*

Then they waved to the crowds, and as the sun fell to the horizon, fresh cheers sent the birds streaming skywards in fright and the celebrations began. From now, the evening belonged to the Victor and his Regna, who descended to the ground and made their way before the crowd, winning hearts.

Lyra felt chilled by the sight of them, but at least it meant she was finally free to attend upon her husband. She hurried down the steps amidst her ladies and guards and started towards Ril and Basia, but Commander Barius of the Imperial Guard intercepted her, proffering a note. 'My Queen, Lord Setallius bid me give you this.'

The note read: *Incident at Imperial Palace: Sacrecour children gone. Get to safety. DS*

The Masquerade (Jest)

Strigoi

Mollachia is one of many places where the folklore includes the Unquiet Dead. In the tales, such beings rise from the grave to feed upon the living, reducing their victims to their own morbid state. Such tales predate the gnosis and therefore the Study of necromancy, which can make such legends real.

Can 'Unquiet Dead' occur spontaneously, or are these tales simply based on a misunderstanding of the process of post-mortem decay?

ARN HEDIS, KORE MISSIONARY, MOLLACHIA, 704

The Bastion, Pallas, Yuros
Maicin 935

Ostevan Comfateri, confessor to the Empress of Yuros, locked himself inside the Royal Chapel, then made his way down the aisles. The chapel had been the place of prayer for more than five hundred years of Rondian emperors, although given the longevity of the pure-blood magi, that meant only twelve men.

And one woman, Ostevan reflected: the thirteenth to wear the crown was the first of her gender: Lyra Vereinen, a convent-raised princess thrust onto the throne by House Corani, a highly unsuitable pretender with a disputed claim. But she'd been the compromise candidate in a unique time, the aftermath of the disastrous Third Crusade into Ahmedhassa. Emperor Constant Sacrecour had been slain, along with most of his court and almost half their legions; the remnants of the Sacrecour family had fled the capital, leaving Pallas open for those who dared to seize the moment.

House Corani had dared.

And my reward, Ostevan snarled inwardly, *was to be demoted and cast aside. Four years in an obscure rural parish when I'd been a prelate – all for the sin of divulging the information that got Lyra found and crowned!*

But he was back now, thanks to Master Naxius, his secret patron, and his master had called for a secret meeting. He left the main chapel and slipped into the alcove containing the centuries-old sarcophagus of Prince Vertonius, who'd drowned whilst drunk – he'd achieved nothing in his life, but he'd been royal, so *obviously* he merited a memorial in this holy place.

Outside, it was night-time and the Imperial Bastion was half-empty, the court and most of the servants still in Finostarre at the royal jousting tourney. The Bastion felt like a ghost-castle haunted by forgotten souls. Ostevan went to a small panel in the wall of the Vertonius shrine, unlocked it with a gesture and removed a bronze lacquered mask, the type used in the traditional plays from the southern city-states of Lantris. This mask represented 'Jest', the witty prankster whose tricks often propelled the narrative. It covered his face from forehead to chin with colourful diamond patterning; the Master had chosen it for him personally and it felt apt. He placed it over his face and it adhered to his skin without need of lacing. Without further ado, he sent his awareness out into the aether, seeking the Master.

To any observer, he would just be standing immobile, but his own experience was of a rush of movement, and then he was in a darkened room, standing in a circle of people, each, like him, robed anonymously, only their masks distinguishing them. He nodded vague greetings. Despite all he shared with these people, he had no more idea of who they were than they did his own identity.

To his left were *Ironhelm*, the Knight-Errant, and *Heartface*, the beautiful Innocenta. Many of the Lantric plays explored love through the pair, but he had no inkling from their demeanour whether the mask-wearers had such a relationship in real life. Beyond them was *Felix*, the cat-faced Spirit of Luck, and *Beak*, the Meddler.

To his right was tragic *Tear*, worn by a woman, and *Angelstar*, the force of Divine Retribution; and *Twoface*, sometimes benign, but more often treacherous. Only the Master wasn't present . . .

. . . and then he was, manifesting like a ghost between Felix and Tear. He wore the narrator's mask, the *Puppeteer* who steered the play. He was the only one they all knew: Ervyn Naxius, last of the original Ascendant magi: six hundred years old, and supremely powerful.

'Greetings, Master,' the eight masked men and women chorused.

'Welcome,' Naxius replied, his mask moving with his words as if it were his face, 'and well-met. It's five months now since we gathered in person at the Veiterholt and pledged ourselves to our shared purpose: to destroy the unwanted equilibrium in East and West and renew the conflicts that we have in the past found so beneficial. The plans we agreed that day are now in motion. East and West are plunged into crisis.'

The masked figures glanced at each other. They'd been working together, four in the East and four in the West.

Ostevan's own role had been crucial. *And it won't be over until I sit on the Pontifex's Curule in the Celestium.*

Naxius looked about the circle. 'Brethren of the West: report.'

Angelstar, Twoface and Tear gestured at Ostevan. 'Jest speaks for us,' Tear told the Master, and Ostevan inclined his head, accepting the charge, before addressing the circle. 'This very night, while the court of Pallas were at a tourney in nearby Finostarre, the royal children Cordan and Coramore, the rightful rulers of Yuros, were freed from imprisonment. Empress Lyra Vereinen is fearful: she dreads a palace coup, and quite rightly. We have agents placed in her palace and our position is strengthened by the return of the exiled knight Sir Solon Takwyth, which will divide her support, especially among the military. Meanwhile, we are spreading the riverreek disease, which mimics the symptoms of those we possess. Lyra's people think they're dealing with a growing health crisis; they have no idea of the true danger they're facing.'

'Excellent progress,' Naxius congratulated them. 'What happens next?'

'We will circulate the children's signet rings among the nobility of House Sacrecour and House Fasterius, proof that they are now free. When Duke Garod Sacrecour has mobilised his legions in Dupenium and Fauvion we will move on to central Rondelmar, Canossi and Klief, to rally support there. On the appointed day in the last week of Junesse – that's two months' time – we will strike.'

'I still think we must move more swiftly,' Tear put in, to Ostevan's irritation. 'Every day increases the likelihood of the empress recovering the royal children.'

'We've discussed this already, Lady Tear,' Angelstar rasped irritably. 'Armies can't mobilise overnight. The preparation time is too short already – and we need the riverreek outbreak to spread to fully mask our activities, and for Takwyth's return to split the Corani knights and leave the queen exposed.'

Tear bowed her head in acquiescence and Twoface took up the narrative. 'When we strike, it will be at both Bastion and Celestium. Cordan will be swept into the city by Garod's legions.'

'And Grand Prelate Wurther will be deposed and a better candidate will take his place,' Ostevan finished. *A much better candidate.*

'And the queen will be brought to me,' Naxius said firmly.

The four western Masks bowed, though Ostevan felt a touch of vexation. He had Lyra Vereinen wrapped around his little finger, and if she really was a pandaemancer, the first known wielder of that heretical magic in centuries, then it would be such a *waste* to give her to Naxius. *I could make far better use of her . . .*

Naxius had turned to the four Easterners. 'There you have it, my friends. Two months. Is that sufficient time for your own plans? I want the hammers to fall on the same day on both continents. I want those who oppose us thrown into confusion, truly believing the world is coming to an end.'

Ironhelm stepped forward. 'Ai, we too have made great progress, even more than our Western brethren. They might not be aware, being ignorant of all beyond their own lands; but we have slain the pacifist Sultan Salim of Kesh and a new ruler is being selected: our candidate, one who will plunge the continent into a great war.'

'Is this a war that you are prepared for?' Naxius asked.

'Ai, well prepared: the time has come for Ahmedhassa to emulate Yuros and be united beneath a great mage-ruler. It is time for a Gnostic Emperor to rule the East and lead her to her Destiny.'

Ostevan wondered where Ironhelm figured in the list of potential emperors ... and what he thought the East's 'Destiny' might be. *The Kalistham speaks of One Kingdom of Ahm*, he recalled. *All very interesting, but with the Leviathan Bridge and the Ordo Costruo preventing future Crusades, it's of little moment to us.*

'And your own next steps?' Naxius asked the Easterners.

'To crown our sultan and declare Shihad – holy war – against a single enemy. Internal union is our goal: one Ahmedhassa, united beneath our chosen ruler. We will achieve this in two months. The Shihad will be launched in the last week of Akhira.'

The four Easterners bowed in unison to Naxius.

We argue openly, while they speak with one voice, Ostevan noted, *and they see this as a virtue*. To him, it was a deep cultural difference between the two peoples. *Our divisions and disputes are our strength: we argue and reach compromises; together, we find better ways. They just grovel and resent; the ruler imagines he has unquestioned support right up until the moment he is knifed in the back.*

The Master sounded pleased, though. 'It is heartening to us all to learn of each other's progress. But be aware, all of you: as I told Brother Jest recently, what we are attempting is akin to an arrow shot at a silhouetted victim. We can see their shape, we have some idea of their vulnerable points – but we do not see their hidden defences. Expect the unexpected: hidden armour and concealed weapons. It is said that no plan survives contact with the enemy, and our plans have only just begun to unfold. You are still only partway through phase one. Go, complete your tasks.'

They all bowed and vanished one by one. Ostevan was last to leave, hoping for some private words with the Master. The Puppeteer turned to him expectantly.

'Master,' Ostevan began, 'I have concerns over some of my colleagues.'

Naxius' masked face went still. 'Elaborate,' he said tersely.

'I have suspicions over the identities of two of my colleagues, and if I am correct, they have quite divided loyalties concerning Empress Lyra Vereinen.'

'Whereas your own feelings are clear?' Naxius enquired, gently ironic.

'Totally clear,' Ostevan insisted. 'On the appointed day, let me be the one who takes her – I'm closest to her.'

'Are you sure of that?'

'Yes, Master: she is clay in my hands. And if she really is a dwymancer . . . We mustn't infect her, but *seduce* her to our cause—'

'No, Brother Jest,' Naxius interjected firmly, 'I want her *enslaved*. The goal you claimed when I first brought you into the cabal was the Celestium – leave the young queen to Twoface and Tear. They will bring her to me.'

Ostevan bowed his head sullenly. 'What if one of them betrays us?'

'Then Abraxas will destroy them.'

'But we control the power of Abraxas, don't we?' Ostevan asked, suddenly alarmed. Could this gift he'd been given be taken away?

'You do . . . but do you think that if you act against the will of Abraxas, you will still be able to draw upon His might? I wouldn't recommend you find out.' Naxius pulled a wry face. 'Brother Jest . . . *Ostevan* . . . don't be concerned. Your brethren will play their part, or pay the price.'

Ostevan bowed his head. 'I merely express my worries, Master.'

'I'm sure,' Naxius drawled. 'Ostevan, all of us share a vision of a world ruled by ourselves, untrammelled by conscience and constraints. We will burn the Gnostic Laws and research *anything* we desire – we will create anything that is possible to be made, so long as it serves us. That is our shared vision, is it not?'

Yes, thought Ostevan, *yes, yes, yes!*

'Your fellow conspirators want the same thing, Ostevan – for different reasons, of course, but the vision is the same, as is their hatred of those in power. Because I don't *control* you, I need to trust that your vision is my vision. You and the rest of my "Masquerade" are those I've chosen to trust.'

'But I'm the most untrustworthy person I know,' Ostevan quipped, not really jesting at all.

'It is your cynicism and duplicity that I trust most about you, Brother Jest.'

Ostevan returned the Jest mask to its hiding place and swept the alcove of gnostic traces – although he believed the place was long-forgotten, it was vital that no one suspected that he might be up to anything but his duties. His conversation with the Master confirmed what he'd already worked out, but it had left him disturbed. To gain access to Ascendant-level gnosis and all sixteen Studies, he'd allowed the 'daemon' Abraxas a pathway to his soul, but thanks to Naxius, he wasn't possessed, not in the usual sense of the word – he wasn't the daemon's puppet; his body and intellect weren't being exploited while his soul was tormented – and it wasn't going to be over in a few days. The effect was permanent, and he was in control.

But he *was* noticing a subtle loss of autonomy: gauzy mental threads were now constantly tugging at him; the presence of Abraxas was subtly warping his nature. The daemon wanted the vicarious thrill of living through its host. It wanted *lust* and *savagery*, and it was adept at planting in his head urges that Ostevan hadn't been prone to before.

And sometimes, one has to give in to them.

He adjourned to his private office and waited for the appointed time, when the door opened and a plump young woman in a dun habit entered. She was clearly petrified. He bade her close the door, then stand before him. The young nun, a plain girl with fat fingers and dimples, was shaking already, and sweating in rivulets.

He spoke in his most soothing voice. 'Sister Hanetta, do you know why you're here?' He knew his own reputation: the handsome, charming politician-priest, intimate with the empress and the ladies of court. Being the official absolver of sins in the Bastion, he knew all their secrets – and he also knew what they whispered about him, that he had no aversion to sampling the flesh of the prettiest of his congregation.

Sister Hanetta plainly didn't want to express her suspicions. 'I don't know,' she said weakly. She was a simple Daughter of Kore: a human nun, without the gnosis – a nothing, in the greater schemes of life, and that suited his purpose perfectly.

He got up and walked around the desk. She watched him approach with pitiful trepidation, trying to follow him with her eyes as he walked around behind her, lowered her cowl and pulled it down to her shoulders. Her hair was a typical northern blonde and greasy to the touch as he lifted it from the nape of her neck. She gave a martyred whimper.

'Dear Kore, I'm not going to *misuse* you, Hanetta.'

'Oh,' she breathed, her voice at first relieved, then wary. 'Then what do you—?'

'*This*.' He engaged morphic-gnosis and two-inch hollow canines speared from between his lips; he yanked her head sideways and plunged them into her throat. Ichor welled up and jetted into the wound, as pleasurable as any orgasm, while she gasped in pain, struggling helplessly in his iron grip. Then the next assault started on her, from within, and she fell writhing to the floor. He grabbed the desk for support until his own rapture had passed, and then watched the greenish-black veins of daemonic ichor spreading from the gaping wound on her neck. She writhed at his feet, howling soundlessly as her mind and body succumbed.

'Was that good for you too?' he asked her prostrate form. As he poured himself a brandy, her eyes overflowed with tears of blood, carmine snot ran from her nose and reddened spittle from her mouth. He wasn't concerned; the riverreek disease that was plaguing northern Rondelmar had the same symptoms.

An illness to mask a deeper corruption – poetic, really.

Hanetta stood with a new poise and dignity and smoothed her clothing.

'Who am I?' he asked her.

'You are my Master.' There was no sign of rebellion or emotion at what had befallen her: although Hanetta was still a presence inside her body, she wasn't in control any more.

'You are now mine,' he told her. 'I can enter your mind and sense what you sense. You can contact me in return, should you see something that imperils me. You may act on my behalf, but your only desire is to please me.'

'Yes, Master. What do you require?'

Not all of those he'd thus infected became so pliable so fast – sometimes it could take an hour or more to completely subdue a victim – but the more corrupt or spiritless ones usually succumbed quickly.

'Go down into the city and volunteer at one of the new riverreek quarantine areas. Once inside, you'll find others like yourself. When you get someone alone, bite them, as I have bitten you – your body will provide the means. Spread your condition and make new servants for me. Be a Shepherd to them. Preserve and multiply your herd – but don't permit them to attack others yet. I require discretion for now. Understand?' When she nodded, he added, 'You have a passive form of the gnosis now; it will make you resilient and enhance your strength and endurance. It only functions internally: you can resist fire but not manipulate it; you can heal yourself, but not others. Conceal this power, lest it draw attention.'

He used healing-gnosis to smooth the bite wound away and remove any traces of blood. 'Finally,' he added, 'avoid prolonged exposure to sunlight: it resists and may even sterilise the ichor I have implanted in you. You'll find those you infect avoid sunlight instinctively – it causes them discomfort, as it will you.' He assessed her one last time, still finding only obedience, and ordered, 'Go. Multiply. And await my command.'

When she was gone, he sipped his brandy, calculating. He had dozens of slaves like her, and every day they created more. There was a descending level of power, of course: those annointed by Naxius, the eight Masks, had the power of an Ascendant mage and access to the complete spectrum of the gnosis. Those they infected with ichor, like Sister Hanetta or Lady Jenet Brunlye, were enhanced, and his to dominate and enslave; he thought of them as his shepherds. But those they infected, or those he simply fed his blood, were little more than mindless herd animals – kine, though possessed of subhuman savagery when unleashed.

This is the world we will create, the nine of us: we will rule over a world of shepherds and kine.

And the eight Masks will become seven, then six, until eventually, it's just me. Because I think I know how to kill even you, Ervyn Naxius . . . But it requires the queen . . . uninfected, yet eating out of my hands . . .

Reluctantly, he thrust that particular plan to the back of his mind again, for he had something else to prepare: a very special meeting with a group of disaffected prelates. Of course, he wouldn't be able to bite them.

But a very special liquor would be served . . .

20

A Proposal of Alliance

The Fate of the Dead

As a butterfly leaves the chrysalis, so do our souls leave our bodies at 'death'. For a time they linger, farewelling all they have known and loved, before passing on into the vast beyond, on a journey into the infinite. All we strive for in our lives are but dreams. Only the infinite matters.

THE BOOK OF KORE

The Soul is Energy . . . and like all energy, available to be harnessed.

ERVYN NAXIUS, PONTUS, 873

Western Sydian Plains, Yuros
Aprafor 935

Kyrik Sarkany, wrapped in illusion, crouched down in a sea of long, coarse grass and gazed eastwards, where a group of horsemen had appeared. They were still just dark shapes, too far away to discern detail. He'd be able to give them the slip easily, but with luck, he mightn't need to. He was hoping that when they were close enough to identify, he'd see a distinctive fox-head emblazoned on their quivers.

Almost a month had passed since he'd left his brother Valdyr behind on the shores of Lake Jegto. He'd found the high pass the Sydian Sfera Iztven and Ghili had used, Hajnal Palya, *the Sunrise Path*, easily enough, though it had entailed a long trudge due east through the Arkadaly Ranges, then a hard climb to a knife-edged ridge followed by a slithering descent through heavily wooded slopes to the forest floor. All the way he'd been assessing the ease of return. A strong, fit man could do it, and his horse too, if he were a skilled rider.

In the forest he'd spent two weeks evading Schlessen hunting parties: big men in furs with blond hair and brutish features. He'd had to bypass an unexpected village deep in the woods, a wooden palisade enclosing dozens of buxom women and squalling children. The Schlessen were a forest people, and in Rondian eyes, the epitome of the barbarian: brutal, savage and uncivilised, with strange codes of honour. He'd heard of the occasional Schlessen mage, usually offspring from the legion camps, but generally the Schlessens were too proud to do as the Sydians did and whore their women to get the gnosis.

Kyrik was pleased his woodcraft skills had returned so quickly – in Mollachia, hunting was the noblemen's sport and the common man's sustenance, and Elgren Sarkany had been adamant that his sons should be able to survive in the wilds. Kyrik had spent a week alone in Feher Szarvasfeld when he was twelve, trapping otters in the streams and playing a deadly game of hide and seek with a lone wolf. He'd skinned the beast himself and used its pelt as a rug.

Perhaps Robear Delestre is standing on it now, he thought, crouching lower, disturbed by the way the riders appeared to be heading straight for his hiding place. The undulating ground meant their path should have taken them well south of his position. He strained his eyes, and now he could make out twelve men and a woman with a shock of black hair and an easy riding style. Her weathered face was stern, her thick lips pursed, as she led them straight to him.

He chuckled, stood up and waved.

'Hail, Hajya,' he called. 'I'm impressed that you found me.'

The head of the Vlpa clan magi didn't return his smile. 'Torzo, our diviner, foresaw your return some weeks ago – and I can smell you a mile away.'

She probably could, he decided, remembering that she was an animage. 'Did he divine why I'm here?'

'No, but I sense I won't like it.' She weighed him up as if pondering having her archers shoot him.

It wasn't an encouraging welcome, but Kyrik wasn't about to turn

343

around now – and he could see they had a spare horse, so he doubted she intended to do away with him just yet. 'Shall we see what Thraan says?'

The Sfera woman grunted, then gestured to the spare mount. 'Can you ride?'

It was a double-edged question; Kyrik had refused to 'ride' any of their women when he'd been the tribe's guest, declining to strengthen their pool of magi.

'I've ridden all over Ahmedhassa,' he answered.

She sniffed. 'This isn't Ahmedhassa. I hope you can keep up.'

In minutes, they were pounding eastwards, back towards the Vlpa lands.

They reached the Vlpa camp at nightfall, which surprised Kyrik, as they were far from the normal migratory routes, the complex cycle of grazing and moving laid down by centuries of tradition and warfare. To leave the usual paths risked all manner of dangers, from blundering into rival tribes to running afoul of the Rondian border legions patrolling these regions.

But there was no outward sign of disaster evident as Kyrik followed Hajya and her men to the pavilion of the clan chief, the nacelnik Thraan, who was waiting for them with his eldest sons, light furs draped over their shoulders, big chests bare in the warmer air of spring.

'Hail Thraan,' Hajya greeted her chief. 'Joy to this reunion.'

The nacelnik kissed both her cheeks, listened to her whispering in his ear, then strode towards Kyrik. 'Draken Lord,' he boomed, 'welcome back.' He looked into Kyrik's eyes intently and murmured, 'The Sfera saw your coming, but not your purpose. I will hear you, ysh? Come, let us drink and talk.'

Kyrik's pack was whisked away, presumably to a tent of his own, and he was led into the pavilion. The wives and children quickly absented themselves, but they were joined by Hajya, and Missef, the clan shaman, not a mage but a priest, the intercessor with their gods. Kyrik had thought the man half-mad when they'd last met.

The fifth member of this exclusive gathering arrived as Kyrik was about to sit: Paruq Rakinissi. Kyrik greeted his Ahmedhassan guardian and mentor with joy. 'Paruq – I wasn't sure you'd still be here.'

The Amteh Godspeaker's gentle eyes lit up. 'My friend, welcome back.' At Thraan's gesture, he joined them. Missef, who viewed Kyrik and Hajya with suspicion, exuded even more hostility towards Paruq.

Shaman versus Godspeaker, Kyrik reflected: *That's a war only one can survive . . .*

Thraan bade them all sit, waited until food and liquor had been handed round, then turned to Kyrik. 'So, Prince: you return to us, and Hajya says that it is in great need, so much that she went to find you.'

Kyrik took a sip of the fiery liquor and tried to order his thoughts. 'I do come in need, Chief Thraan, but do not mistake me for a beggar, for I'm not weak. And what I propose will strengthen both our peoples.'

Thraan waved a casual hand. 'Speak on.'

Kyrik explained the situation in Mollachia: the new tax-farming laws, his father's debts, and how the Delestre family had misused their authority to take so much more. 'They have more soldiers than we can deal with,' he confessed. 'Two legions, with battle-magi. Without aid, we will be crushed.'

'Of what concern is that to the Vlpa?' Missef sniffed.

'My belief is that the people of Mollachia and your clan are akin. Thraan himself spoke of this during my last visit' – Thraan looked pleased to have his words remembered – 'and we agreed that the Saga of Zlateyr, the central myth of Mollachia, has many similarities with the tale of Zillitiya of the Uffrykai, the tribe of which you Vlpa are a clan. We have similar languages, foods and drinks – even names.'

'Your "Zlateyr" – he is Zillitiya of the Uffrykai, this is clear to me,' Thraan rumbled. 'We are kin to the mountain folk from long ago.'

'We are one people to the other tribes of the steppes,' Missef sniffed, 'yet still they make war on us.'

'Missef is right,' Hajya put in. 'Would we aid a clan of the Jergathai, or the Kolvahani? They too are our kin, and more recently than the time of Zillitiya.'

'If it advantaged us,' Thraan rumbled. 'I would hear more, friend Kyrik.'

Kyrik raised a cup to Thraan. 'Thank you, Nacelnik. I have explained the plight of my people, but when I was last here, you spoke of your own problems. And now I find you well west of where I understood your customary trails to be – do you need men to defend your territories? When my people secure our lands, I would be in a position to aid you.'

'Promises,' Missef sneered, earning another nod from Hajya.

Thraan silenced them both with a scowl, then his face turned rueful. 'The Vlpa are not in the habit of seeking aid, any more than a Mollach prince,' he told Kyrik. 'But the Uffrykai, the great people of which we are but a part, are also being pressed: the larger eastern tribes are steadily constricting our traditional hunting and grazing lands. A bloodletting is coming. We are sharpening our blades, readying for a clan war.'

Kyrik watched Thraan's face carefully, but he also kept his eye on the others. He knew Missef and Hajya didn't like each other, though they were apparently united against him, but their expressions during Thraan's narrative became bleak, which told him that while both rejected change, change was coming for them. It gave him hope.

'Last month,' Thraan went on, 'we were betrayed: the High Chief of the Uffrykai bent the knee to the High Chief of the Jergathai and gave tribute. Many of his clan chiefs followed his lead – but we Vlpa do not placate thieves, and there is bad blood between ourselves and the Jergathai. Extra tribute was demanded of me, and I refused. We are now cast adrift. We are thirty thousand souls, barred from our pastures to the north. Our migration routes have been severed. We must seek new pastures.'

Kyrik stared into the crackling fire and in his mind's eye, the tribal dance of seasons on the plains of Sydia turned into a bloody waltz.

Unexpectedly, because he'd been so silent Kyrik had almost forgotten he was there, Paruq spoke up. 'My mission here has fallen on receptive ears, in part through the plight of the clan, I know this. But Keshi steel can't preserve this tribe.'

Kyrik shot his mentor a glance; there was a message in his words.

'We must pay the tribute,' Missef intoned in a defeated voice. 'We cannot stand alone. To wander south into Verelon or west into the Kedron or the Brekaellen is to provoke the Rondian Empire. Our only hope lies in a return to our traditional place on the Wheel of Seasons.'

He fixed Kyrik with an unfriendly eye. 'We don't need *pleaders* who will weaken us further.'

Kyrik took that without flinching. He glanced sideways at Hajya. Her dark eyes were more reserved than the shaman's. She'd clearly supported Thraan's refusal to bend the knee.

Everyone here needs something. There has to be a solution that suits us all.

He'd intended to simply ask for Vlpa warriors in return for the promise of silver from the mines, but there was a bigger offer available, if he had the courage to make it. He looked at Paruq, who give him a tiny nod.

'Nacelnik Thraan,' Kyrik began, 'I am a king, yet a pauper. But there is wealth in Mollachia. We have silver mines, large forests and rare furs. We have some pasture too, much of it underused.' He looked the clan chief in the eye. 'We could offer refuge to even so great a people as the Vlpa.'

He heard the intake of breath from Missef and Hajya, but he kept his eyes on Thraan. The man wasn't, as he liked to project, a bluff, hearty barbarian. He was a strong, thoughtful leader of a proud, independent tribe. And though Hajya was a mage and Missef spoke for their gods, Thraan was the leader here.

Though the big nacelnik gave little away, there was something in his face that suggested interest. 'But you told us you don't control your lands?' he replied.

'Not currently,' Kyrik admitted. 'But a large warband of Vlpa horsemen could do much to redress that.'

'Ah,' Thraan mused, 'this takes shape to me now.'

'You can't be serious, Nacelnik Thraan,' Missef exclaimed. 'These Mollachs are Kore-kneelers, of the same ilk as the slavers who plague our lands! They're worse than the Amteh, if that can be believed,' he concluded, glaring at Paruq.

'Ysh, Mollachia is for Kore,' Kyrik conceded, because it was fruitless to deny it. 'That faith has deep roots in our kingdom – most of us have never met non-Kore worshippers, and may not react well. But we are also pragmatists who do not hesitate to break a scripture here and there in the name of survival.'

347

Paruq threw him a faintly amused smirk, but Hajya caught that look and asked, 'What faith do *you* profess, Kyrik of Mollachia?' Her light tone belied the intensity in her eyes.

Kyrik glanced again at Paruq, because his notions of faith had been shaped by his mentor, but they didn't entirely follow his creed. 'I have read the holy texts of both Ahm and Kore and in truth, I see little difference. The heart of both is very similar: one God, a set of near-identical virtues and sins, and a common belief in Paradise.'

'Stone religions, city religions, divorced from the lands and the seasons,' Missef sneered. 'Book religions! Lawyers' religions!' He spat into the fire. 'Our people are losing their True Faith—'

'Peace, Missef,' Thraan grunted. 'The Old Gods will always be first among the Vlpa.' He turned back to Kyrik. 'Would your Mollachia refuse our aid because we are – what is your word: heathens?'

'No,' Kyrik replied, hoping he was right. 'If we reach agreement, I will honour that treaty, I promise you.'

'*Western* promises,' Hajya sniffed. 'What are they worth?'

'Men of the Empire – *vassals, I think they are called* – tend to forget their promises once they have what they want,' Missef snarled. 'We give you men, you get what you want, then you close your fortress gates and send us away. We're not fools. And even if we were to aid you, what if we fail? What are we left with then?'

'A good point,' Thraan agreed. 'But I confess, this interests me.' He turned to Missef and Hajya, his face becoming decisive. 'I hear your objections, but you suffer from smallness of vision.' He raised a hand to their objections. 'Your minds are tied to the Wheel of Seasons still: the trek north as the snows retreat, foaling in the spring, summers among the Uffrykai, selling and buying bloodstock, then the slow retreat as the snows return until we are here in the south. *For the Vlpa, that time is over*: our tribe have turned their backs on this clan, and we on them. We must trust now to legends: to a hero who *forsook the old ways* and sought a new life! You, Missef: how do you not see it as a sign when a *Son of Zillitiya* comes among us? And you, Hajya, who claims to be able to see the paths before us – how can you *not* see that this path is the answer we have prayed for?'

Kyrik schooled himself to stillness, staring at a very satisfied-looking Paruq, as Missef and Hajya's faces crumbled into disbelief and defeat.

Thraan turned back to Kyrik. 'In my mind, this is decided,' the nacelnik rumbled. 'But you too must *commit*, Kyrik of Mollachia. We are putting our future in your hands. You must put your future into ours.'

'I've explained that we have little, but I can have a contract drawn against future revenue, a legal commitment—' Kyrik began.

Thraan cut him off with a gesture. 'You have something of greater worth to us,' he said in his gruff voice. 'You have your sack. You have your manhood.'

Holy Kore, does everything here come back to this lust for gnostic blood? 'Would you have me lay with every woman in the tribe?' Kyrik asked incredulously.

Thraan guffawed, while Missef and Hajya listened with sick expressions. 'No, just one,' the chieftain replied. 'You must take a Vlpa bride to be your queen in Mollachia: the new homeland of Clan Vlpa.'

Kyrik sat back, his momentary sense of triumph evaporating. To commit to such a thing, to make a part-Sydian his heir, was to break all manner of unspoken expectations, more than he could enumerate. *A Sydian bride! And thirty thousand at her back!* He wished Valdyr was here, or Dragan. What would they think? What would his dead father think, and all his forebears?

'Thraan, I hear you,' he protested, 'but I swore to my father before I left Mollachia that I would marry a mage, as he did. I'm pledged to maintain or strengthen my gnostic bloodline. The mage-blood is sacred to Kore – this is important to my people. So I *must* marry a mage.' He didn't look at Hajya. 'I know that your Sfera magi are forbidden marriage, so we are at an impasse.'

Missef made a chopping gesture. 'There,' he exclaimed, 'this cannot happen, Thraan. It is better we die than break our sacred traditions. Send the Mollach on his way. Everything he talks of will destroy our way of life!'

Hajya chimed in on Missef's side, 'Tradition forbids this, Nacelnik.'

Kyrik wavered. *Am I being too dogmatic here? Should I compromise on this?* But before he could speak, Thraan, who'd been glowering into the fire, looked up intently at Hajya. 'You still suffer from smallness of vision, Sfera-leader. You are thinking of *us and them*. But in the act of marriage, we become they and they us. The union I propose might weaken the Sfera, but it strengthens the clan. If tradition forbids it, then tradition must bend the knee to *survival*.'

'But Nacelnik, I— no – *no!* We are a plains-people – we can't live in mountains! We are free as we are – better to die free than shuffle into a stone prison—'

'Are you free?' Paruq asked, 'or trapped by a cycle of seasonal migration that prevents you from ever building something that lasts?'

'We don't need things that last,' Hajya squalled. 'Life is transitory—'

'If life is transitory, then so too is tradition,' Paruq observed.

Kyrik forestalled her retort by raising his hand. 'I will marry one of your Sfera, if there is someone suitable.'

Hajya whirled on him. 'Ha! He who would not dance on his last visit will now deign to *buy* one of us in his desperation? Well, we of the Sfera don't want him! We know his type – the sort who despise brown skin – the sort who despise *women!*'

'Not so,' Kyrik flared, the memory of all the women of the breeding-houses in his mind. 'That is so far from the truth I can barely express it, you ignorant *kurva!*'

'Don't call me a bitch,' she snarled, light kindling at her fingers.

'*Enough!*' Thraan bellowed, slamming a log into the fire so that it burst into sparks. '*Silence! I am still master of this hearth!*'

Kyrik bowed his head, muttering an apology, annoyed at losing his temper. Hajya bowed her head also. 'Nacelnik, I serve you, as ever,' she said in a sulky voice. 'I will abide by your decision. There are several of our young women who might be "suitable", and—'

Kyrik raised a hand, his mind racing. 'Wait! If I am to marry, it must be to someone who is, as much as possible, my equal: both my people and yours must feel that the union carries equal weight in both camps. A naïve young woman of weak blood will not suffice as Queen of Mollachia. If I am to marry, it must be to a woman roughly my age, whole of body and able to bear children, and a quarter-blood, no less. I must have a *partner*, not a handmaid.'

The men around him stared, their faces somewhere between bemusement and considering. 'What?' he asked. 'Is equality such a novel idea?' An equal marriage was something he'd debated long into the night with Paruq, and it made perfect sense in these circumstances. His mentor was smiling, and even Thraan grinned.

But Hajya climbed to her feet. 'An "equal"?' she growled. 'Since when has *marriage* ever been of equals?' She spat in the fire and stalked out.

'I will agree these terms,' Thraan called to her back.

'Do what you damned well like,' she snarled, then she was gone, apparently having sucked the air out with her, because Kyrik was suddenly breathless.

'Have I missed something?' he asked.

Thraan chuckled. 'Friend Kyrik, the only woman in this tribe who meets your need is Hajya herself.'

21

Death to Rondelmar

The Magi

The first magi were unequivocally the spawn of Shaitan, white devils sent to plague the faithful. But now we find that magi born in part of Keshi and Dhassan stock fought for Ahmedhassa in the Third Crusade! What are we to think any more?

GODSPEAKER YAMEED UMAFI, 117TH CONVOCATION,

SAGOSTABAD, 935

Sagostabad, Kesh, Ahmedhassa
Jumada (Maicin) 935

The black-robed figure standing over Waqar's mother whirled. It was his mother's nurse, Nakti. Her eyes were twinkling with gnosis-light as she cursed and gestured. The door behind Waqar slammed shut and she raised her other hand like a barrier. He tried to launch himself at her and found his face slamming into a wall of air. He rebounded and came up into a fighting crouch.

'Prince Waqar,' she whispered urgently, 'I'm trying to help her!'

'Get away from my mother!'

Sakita opened her eyes, raising her hand feebly. 'Peace, son. She's . . . friend.'

Though he doubted his mother would know, he paused. Nakti backed from the cot, letting Waqar approach. He didn't take his eyes from the girl as he bent over Sakita. 'Mother? What's she doing?'

'Just examining me,' Sakita wheezed. 'And taking messages.'

'What messages?' He stared at the girl, seeing her properly for the first time; normally he didn't notice servants. Her bird-like skull was accentuated by severely tied-back hair, a long nose and deep-set eyes. 'Take off the bekira-shroud, "Nakti".'

She threw him a challenging, wholly un-servile look. 'Why?'

'To make sure you aren't armed.'

'Very well.' She shrugged off the enveloping garment, revealing a twig-thin body with a high bosom, clad in a sweat-stained smock and leggings. She reeked of last week's perspiration and had ugly boils on her face. No weapons, but there was a chain on her right wrist containing a piece of amber: a periapt, by its glow.

'Why are you here?' he demanded.

She considered, then said, 'I work for people representing the Javon throne.'

'*Javon?*' The northernmost kingdom of Ahmedhassa was a curious place where an Ahmedhassan people called the Jhafi co-existed with Rimoni from Southern Yuros who had migrated after the Leviathan Bridge opened. The Rimoni had brought new crops that thrived in conditions similar to their native lands, as well as legions of well-trained fighting men. After some conflict they had assimilated passably well with the Jhafi. 'What's a Jhafi doing here?'

'Javon is home to many Yurosi,' Nakti replied. 'We're an easy target for an anti-Yurosi holy war.'

She was right, but she barely looked old enough to have completed Arcanum training, let alone be entrusted with a spying mission. 'How old are you?'

'I'm old enough to wander around your court for the whole Convocation unnoticed,' she replied in an irritatingly superior tone.

'You're no courtier,' he retorted. Her speech patterns, her dirty nails and ripe odour, her body language all betrayed a menial background.

'I didn't say I was disguised as a princess,' she sniffed. 'I was just another maid in a dirty shift, scrubbing the floor – conveniently below the notice of the likes of you.'

She had to be a mage-bastard, or maybe she gained the power bearing a mage's child, though she looked barely old enough for that. But

353

her tale rang true. *Who better to infiltrate a palace than a mage in servant's garb?* 'Can you prove your tale?'

'My masters can. I can arrange a meeting?'

Is she trying to lure me to an ambush? he wondered. But as a mystic, reading people was his forte, and though he sensed secrets, he didn't sense malice. 'You've not said why you're in my mother's rooms?'

'I'm here to find out who murdered the sultan – then I heard about your mother.'

Everyone permitted into the palace was examined by Hadishah agents, even servants – if she'd circumvented that, she knew her business. And her gnostic shields were strong; he doubted he could defeat her easily. And perhaps she really was a potential ally.

'Is Nakti your real name?' he asked, sheathing his dagger.

'No. You may call me Tarita.'

It was a northern name, common enough. 'Tell me what you've learned.'

'That the same people who killed the sultan attacked your mother,' she replied, echoing his own suspicion. She was about to say more, but then they heard footsteps approaching. In a flash she'd pulled her bekira-shroud over her head. She whispered, 'Beside the Elephant Fountain, soon as you can get away.' Then she dropped to her haunches, grabbed her straw brush and began sweeping.

A moment later Healer Ormutz hurried in, looking exhausted, his tunic bloodstained. 'Sal'Ahm, my Prince. I'm sorry for my appearance; a noblewoman went into labour this morning and we had to cut the baby from her womb.' He noticed the girl on the floor and said, 'Go home, girl. Your shift is over.'

'Tarita' scuttled crab-like out the door as Ormutz bent over Sakita. She opened her eyes blindly, then convulsed, back arching and limbs going rigid. Waqar ran to help, holding his mother down to stop her hurting herself, but she subsided swiftly, gurgling as she sagged into the sheets. She smelled awful, as if she was rotting from the inside.

'What's wrong with her?' Waqar demanded, frightened that she was dying *right now*.

'We ... we're still ... we don't know ...' The healer was clearly frightened for his career should his patient die. 'We're *trying*, my Prince!'

Waqar's anger dissipated. He sensed the man really was doing all he could – and if he was the best healer in the city, then his mother was in deep trouble. 'One of my friends is a healer: perhaps she can help?' When Ormutz nodded eagerly – probably at the thought of having someone else to blame – Waqar sent a gnostic call to Fatima; she was of stronger blood than Ormutz, even if she had less experience.

Once she was ensconced with Ormutz, he left them to it and went to find Tarita.

When he reached the Elephant Fountain, near the Southern Gates of the palace complex, there was no sign of Tarita, so he sat down to wait – at which point a sweeper-girl he'd completely failed to notice waddled on her haunches to the end of the bench and whispered, 'Sal'Ahm.'

'Oh!' he exclaimed. *She might as well have been invisible*, he realised, embarrassed. 'I didn't see you. Will you sit?'

She ignored the offer, instead squatting at a nearby drain, pulling the filthy mulch out with her bare hands and patting it about the roots of a bush. 'I'll stay down here. Princes and servants don't sit as equals,' she reminded him.

She had a slightly stiff-backed way of moving, he noticed, as if she'd not fully recovered from an injury. And she stank, well past the point of disguise in his view. 'Can't you at least wash occasionally?' he muttered.

'You know, nothing deters rape like a bad smell and fresh pus,' she said lightly. 'I've been in contact with my master and he wants to meet you. We know that you examined the murder scenes; we'd like to know what you found, especially as the investigation officially closed well before you stopped looking.'

That told him that she had been watching him for some time – and apparently all that took was to look like a servant. He'd always considered himself observant, but he was fast revising that opinion. 'Who do you think is behind this?'

'Well, I don't think they were Hadishah: they were too competent.'

He had to smile at that. 'Volsai? Ordo Costruo? Merozain? Javonesi spies?'

She grinned, and her teeth were better than he'd expected. She was clearly younger than him, but there was something about her that suggested she'd packed much into her years. 'Unlikely, no, no and no. There were four of them, each wearing these strange masks. Lantric, ai?'

'Ai, but our people saw only three—'

'Your mother mentioned a "Felix" mask, so with Ironhelm, Beak and Heartface, that's four. Perhaps I could learn more if you allowed me into the royal suite?'

'They're cleaning it tomorrow.'

'Then best we do it tonight.'

Meeting her alone after dark would be a leap of faith, but Waqar was inclined to trust her.

'This way,' Waqar murmured as he opened the deserted royal suite from the inside and slipped Tarita in through an unguarded servants' entrance. She was dressed as three hours before, and in the confined space smelled even worse. He took her into the living quarters – the bodies were all gone: the funerals of all but the real Salim had taken place three days after the assassinations. Salim's state funeral was scheduled for two days' time.

He decided not to tell her about the strange gnostic traces he'd found – she was too much of an unknown still – so he let her examine the scorch-marks and bloodstains and draw her own conclusions. The gnostic traces had broken down by now anyway.

'Take me to the Walled Garden,' she said eventually, sounding disappointed.

As they made their way through the silent halls, he asked, 'How did you gain the gnosis? Through birth, or pregnancy?' A woman pregnant to a mage sometimes gained the gnosis; she'd be roughly half as powerful as her child.

'Perhaps,' she said evasively. 'Show me where you were attacked.'

The garden was empty, but the trees were filled with squalling birds, the 'evening chorus', as the poets generously called the cacophony. Waqar showed Tarita where he'd fought Ironhelm and Heartface and she hunkered down and sniffed the place like a hound. 'Too much time has passed,' she muttered.

He took her back to where he'd waited for Salim and a memory resurfaced. 'There was a Godsinger who arrived before Salim – but no one sang from the dom-al'Ahm tower that evening.'

Tarita's eyes glinted with interest. 'Describe him.'

Waqar's mystic-gnosis aided memory and he quickly pictured the moment: 'Brown robes. I couldn't see a face.'

Tarita peered towards the dom-al'Ahm. 'Let's look inside.'

'But you're a woman,' he protested. Men and women *never* used the same shrines.

She ignored him, but at least she slipped off her sandals before going in. 'Look,' she said, pointing to a brown robe lying against a wall, 'that must have been his.' She picked it up and buried her face in it, then passed it to Waqar. 'What do you get?'

Tentatively he sniffed, using nose and gnosis. 'It's his: Ironhelm. But the trace is fading; it wasn't a possession he had long or treasured.'

She looked dispirited – then Waqar had an inspiration and took her to the door where Beak had appeared briefly, then vanished. 'He killed two guards, then entered the zenana,' he told Tarita. 'He must have thought Ironhelm and Heartface could easily deal with Salim and me. Correctly,' he admitted ruefully.

Tarita perked up, though. 'This is a public place – it's possible they didn't return here to erase their traces . . .' She cast about, her eyes turning amber – animagery-gnosis, Waqar guessed. 'What we need is . . . Yes!' A grey-green gecko emerged from a crack in the stonework and crawled into Tarita's hand. 'These fellows are able to remember things for a little while,' she told him.

She reached out and seized Waqar's hand, cradling the gecko in her other, bathing it in soft golden light. Waqar's sight blurred and he was swept into a vision of what she was drawing from the gecko's memories: a warped image of a masked face, an instant before light blazed and the gecko fled for the cracks in the stone.

Then the image withered and he opened his eyes. Tarita was cradling the shrivelled remains of the gecko. 'Such spells are too much for them,' she whispered regretfully. 'Did you see it?'

He was still reeling, and aware that she'd shown daunting skill for one so young. 'I saw Beak,' he told her, 'and below the mask, his beard was braided – that's a Gatti custom. I doubt many of Gatioch blood were in the Hadishah.'

'Perhaps not. But it could also be a disguise. My master might be able to trace such a one though. Will you meet him? Tomorrow or the next day, perhaps?'

He hesitated, then nodded. 'How can I contact you again?'

She looked at him carefully, as if weighing him up, then bent and pulled a tiny copper ring from one of her little toes. It was badly worn and utterly worthless. 'I've had this since I was twelve and never before taken it off. Use this and you'll reach me from almost anywhere in Kesh.'

Then she folded over into the shuffling creature no one ever noticed and scurried from sight, leaving him alone in the empty palace. He was about to call out when Tamir's mental voice filled his head. <*Waqar, where are you? It's your mother*—>

He forgot Tarita, conjured light to show his way and ran.

Waqar found Lukadin waiting at the doors to let him in. 'Thank Ahm, you're here,' his friend exclaimed. 'She's been calling for you.'

They hurried to Sakita's room, where he found Fatima hunched over his mother, holding her hand and mopping her brow. Tamir was watching from the window, biting his nails; Baneet stood beside the door like a statue. Sakita looked worse than ever: one side of her face was lifeless and drooping, her left arm twisted up like a claw. He fell to her side, gripping her shoulder. '*Mother?*'

She didn't react, but she was still breathing.

He almost broke down as he pulled out the latest vial of elixir and tipped it down her throat, scared he was just pouring more poison into her venom-stricken body. The fang wounds on her calf wept continually. She smelled of sweat and piss and decay.

'Shh— Son?' she slurred. She looked like a corpse, but her eyes were desperately trying to focus.

'Mother—' He grabbed her hand.

'Th ... p'shun ... no work,' she muttered. 'Voish ... Eee ... ting me ... up.'

What's she saying? 'Hush, don't try to talk.' He clasped her hand and forced a mental link. *<Mother?>*

She drew heavily on the link. *<God oh God ... I'm losing, Son. I thought I could fight it, but I can't ...>*

<You can – you must! The Ordo Costruo will come; they'll save you—>

<Too late ... too fast! No one I trusted – the Order, the court ... Spies everywhere. Jehana knows ... But you wouldn't leave Rashid. I wasn't sure ...>

She wasn't sure she could trust me, Waqar realised, mortified. *<Mother, you can tell me anything – I love you, I love Jehana – your secrets are safe with me—>*

<Trust no one,> she began, then her eyes bulged. *<No! He's here, Waqar – Abraxas is here ...>*

<Abraxas? Who's that?>

She looked at him fiercely, her mind trying to spill words into his as her wards flared at the edge of their link, protecting them. Beyond, he sensed something immense, like a wall of eyes and mouths and ears, an amorphous blob of faces a thousand times his size; and he quailed before it.

Is that Abraxas?

<Waqar,> she tried to send, *<You ... Jehana ... unique ...>*

Then the sea of faces outside her shields struck and he felt it engulf her as she cast him from the link. In his mind's eye he was falling as a wave of bloody flesh crushed his mother, mouths latching on and tearing her apart ...

Suddenly he was back in the room, holding her hand, as Fatima tried to pour healing energy into her and Tamir shouted for help. Ormutz thundered in, another healer and several nurses hurtling along in his wake.

He tried to re-open the link, crying, *<Mother—?>* but there was no response; all he sensed was that immense, hideous thing in the aether; then she convulsed, a slow, agonised ripple of every muscle in her body locking, then unlocking ... and she sagged, a limp pile, her head falling towards him, both eyes now open and empty.

*

Waqar sat alone beneath the Elephant Fountain, hoping Tarita would reappear. It was after midnight, the air still warm and dusty, and he was just another shadow on a moonlight-streaked night.

'*I wasn't sure*', she'd said – of *him*. She hadn't trusted her own son. *Because I stayed with Rashid . . .*

But she'd tried to tell him everything in the end. *Then something –* '*Abraxas*', *maybe? – stopped her.* His mind kept trying to unpick her final words: 'You . . . Jehana . . . unique—' *But how are Jehana and I unique?*

And how does this relate to Salim's murder? Why did the masked ones spare me? Why did they only poison Mother when they slaughtered Salim and all his household? And why finish her off now?

The night gave him no answers, and neither did the dawn.

Two days later, Waqar, in the second rank of princes, stood on the balcony overlooking the giant square where the Convocation had met, where Salim had made his final public speech. Today it seethed with men and women clothed in white, their faces ash-smeared, wailing and screaming for Ahm to send justice.

In front of him, Attam and Xoredh puffed out their chests, barely able to restrain themselves from joining in the chants. '*DEATH TO RON-DELMAR!*' rolled across the square, waves of sound beating at the walls of the city. '*SHIHAD! DEATH TO YUROS! SHIHAD!*'

Rashid Mubarak, the Sardazam, presided, looking relaxed and masterful, as if this great victory for the Shihadi faction was everything he wanted. Red scarves had washed the square scarlet; the Ja'arathi blue had vanished. The city had been seething since Salim died, waiting for this chance to vent all its grief and rage.

The real assassins must be laughing their heads off, Waqar brooded.

This was only the beginning of a momentous week. Tomorrow the Convocation would begin the search for a new sultan. The Ayatu-Marja would be nominally in charge, but it was the Sardazam who set the agenda. Already it was clear that only the most suicidal of the emirs would stand against Rashid if he wanted the title.

Waqar had been denied even the comfort of a memorial for his mother. Rashid had permitted emissaries of the Ordo Costruo to collect her body and take it by windship to their cemetery in Hebusalim. They'd claimed no one had told them that Sakita was unwell, so someone was lying, but Waqar was scared to ask who. Either way, his mother's body was borne away on the winds and he felt utterly empty.

The next morning, as the Convocation began, a note was left for him, in a sealed envelope. It gave directions to a meeting place in the city, later that day. With no desire to watch the Convocation unfold, he took Tamir and Fatima – they were best able to blend into a market-place – and headed for the rendezvous.

'I could blast your face off in half a second,' Waqar warned the man in the plain dun clothes and checked headscarf, who'd introduced himself as Qasr, Keshi for hawk. Qasr didn't look at all perturbed by this threat. He had a mild, plump face and a shaven scalp. He spoke Keshi well, with a Yurosi flavour. 'You're in no danger from me, Prince Waqar.'

Tarita had instructed Waqar to stop at the third fruit vendors' stall on the eastern edge of the Mahdi-al'Edher Souk, south of the river, and pick up an orange during the chiming of the fourth bell. He'd worn plain clothes Tamir had found; they were unpleasantly dirty but they'd worked; no one looked twice as he left by a back gate among a gaggle of servants, tailed by his two friends. He'd been nervously glancing about as he made his way through the crowds, wondering if that man in brown was following him, or that woman in the bekira-shroud . . . He got lost for a time in backstreets piled with refuse and stinking of urine; this was a side to the city he'd barely known existed. Crippled beggars and prematurely aged faces stared as he passed; a badly beaten youth lying against a wall groaned for help while surly house-guards brandished their cudgels and berated him. Desperate-looking vendors were selling the most pitiful of wares: precarious lives barely clinging on, fading, failing. The stench left him feeling polluted. He wondered how anyone could stand it.

But he saw smiles and laughter too: madcap children racing through the squares after balls or each other; wizened women chattering, men playing games on blankets in the shade. Dust-caked labourers digging ditches were singing cheerily; a tall girl with a platter of sweetcakes balanced on her head swayed through the press, graceful as a gazelle. The chatter and hum of bargaining, news and gossip was everywhere.

Somehow he'd regained his bearings and reached the appointed stall in time. 'Qasr' introduced himself and now Waqar, unsure if Tamir and Fatima had kept up, had to decide whether to trust the man.

'This way, Prince Waqar,' Qasr said, indicating an unmarked door in a grubby wall. 'If you please? I swear, you are in no danger here.'

This is a waste of time if I don't take a few risks, Waqar decided. *I'll trust Tamir and Fatima to find me*. He followed Qasr up some stairs to a sparsely furnished apartment. A young man with a mincing gait brought tea as they settled into chairs and studied each other.

Qasr looked considerably older than Waqar, and his eyes held a lively intelligence. 'So, I represent Javon, but I'm not Javonesi. I'm from Estellayne, in the west of Yuros – I was a mercenary in the Third Crusade and when my legion changed sides during the Javonesi conflict, we were permitted to settle.'

Waqar knew things were complex in Javon, and that sounded plausible to him. 'Wasn't there a Javonesi princess Salim was betrothed to but never actually married?' he asked.

'Exactly: the engagement gave him some influence in Javon, and provided some reciprocal benefits. His death changes everything. Tarita and I were here to monitor the Convocation, but Salim's assassination altered our mission. We wish to know who killed Salim – we need to assess the danger to Javon.'

This aligned with what Tarita had said, but he asked, 'How can a Yurosi function as a spy in the East?'

Qasr said, 'I'm what we Yurosi call a "spymaster". The noble houses in Yuros and Ahmedhassa employ people like us. It's my duty to maintain a network of informants. Most of my sources do little more than pass on a bit of knowledge in return for coin while going about their normal lives, unaware even of where that information goes. Their "handlers" – the collectors of that information – have handlers themselves, in a pyramid that leads to people like me, so perhaps a few hundred people are involved in the whole of the known world: a small, dangerous universe.'

'So my Uncle Rashid has a spymaster?'

'Of course – but that's far too big a morsel for this little chat. Let's stay focused: who are these masked magi and why did they kill Salim? Why did they spare you? Where and when will they strike again? To know that, we have to understand who they are and what they want.'

Tarita surely had already told her master about the man with Gatti braids, so instead he revealed what he'd learned about the strange gnostic trace he'd found. He didn't mention Abraxas – he could do that later, if Qasr proved trustworthy. But he did show him the sketches of the masks Rashid had given him.

'Beak, Ironhelm and Heartface – who was a woman.' Waqar looked up. 'Do you know of Alyssa Dulayne?'

Qasr leaned forward. 'Of course.'

'Do you know where she is?'

'I've not known for some time. Do you think it was her?'

'I felt like "Heartface" knew me personally – Alyssa's the only Rondian woman I've ever met.'

'But if the masked woman wasn't Rondian?'

'Then she could be anyone. But Heartface had the right stature.'

'Alyssa Dulayne was crippled by the Merozains, left disfigured, broken,' Qasr replied. 'I have this on good authority. Did you know that?'

'No!' Alyssa had been beautifully, tall and willowy: vanity personified. 'The *Merozains* did that to her? What happened to peace and love?'

'The wounds were sustained in combat, I understand,' Qasr replied. 'I've heard the best healers couldn't cure her and she's now a deformed hunchback, not seen publicly since. Interesting, though; I'll make enquiries. I'm already asking about a Hadishah with Gatti braids – I don't hold out great hope of finding him, but whatever we learn, I'll pass on. And thank you for your intriguing information about the gnostic auras.'

He stood, and Waqar followed suit. He sensed no threat. 'Some advice, if you're to dip your toes in my world, Prince Waqar,' Qasr said. 'Be very careful what questions you ask, and whether you truly want to know the answers to them.'

The more Waqar thought on those words, the more ominous they sounded.

The new Convocation went as predicted: everyone was happy to blame the Rondians for Salim's death, especially Ali Beyrami's Shihadi fanatics. Young men clamoured for a new Shihad, attacking any who disagreed in bloody street clashes. Meanwhile, the emirs united to eulogise the man who stood above them all, and unanimously elected Rashid Mubarak as their new sultan. He would be Kesh's first mage-born supreme leader, and if anyone was disquieted to be setting one of Shaitan's Afreet as their overlord, no one had the courage to say so in public.

Attam and Xoredh were ahead of Waqar in every ritual and ceremony and they never failed to emphasise it. Waqar's days were filled with such events and his friends began to feel like strangers, his old life a fond memory. The masked assassins were pushed from his thoughts and even his mother's loss receded to a dull ache.

'I have a task for you, Nephew,' Rashid said, drawing him away from the others.

'I am yours to command, Uncle, as ever.'

'Excellent. I need you to fly south. There are great events afoot and all of my kin must play a part. Are you aware that since the First Crusade, we in the East have been building windships? We kept them secret until the last Crusade, and we have built many more since.'

This didn't come as a huge surprise. Rashid went on, 'It might surprise you to learn that I've been building far more than even Sultan Salim knew: right now we have almost ten thousand windships under construction.'

Waqar blinked. *'Ten thousand?'* He wouldn't have thought there were enough trees in Ahmedhassa for so many.

Rashid smiled at his shock. 'We have created ship-building sites in the wildernesses, wherever there is timber, and we have been dealing with Yurosi traders – on the black market, everything is for sale. When the Shihad is launched, we will rule the air.'

Waqar felt his jaw drop. With such massive windship resources, everything changed. Yuros might still be out of reach, for the Ordo Costruo controlled the skies over the Leviathan Bridge, but suddenly anywhere in Ahmedhassa was in reach . . .

'Then it's really war?'

'Shihad has been ordained. It's my duty to execute it.'

Something in Rashid's poise reminded Waqar of a hooded cobra, ready to strike. 'Is it Javon? Or Lakh?'

'In truth, you'll have to wait and see. I'm sending you to Lokistan, to the largest of our ship-building bases. You're to take command of that fleet and ensure it's ready to fly by the end of Akhira.'

'*So soon?*' Waqar was astounded. 'That's only six or seven weeks away—'

'Soon by your reckoning,' Rashid replied, 'but some of us have been waiting a lifetime for this moment, and preparing for almost as long. My commander there is Saarif Ibram – be guided by him.'

The name rang bells: 'Saarif Ibram? Isn't he just a merchant?'

'He's a man of many talents.' Rashid stood. 'You may take your friends with you, as protectors and advisors. Ensure they too learn from the experience.'

Waqar bowed, then hesitated. 'Must we go to war?'

Rashid's face turned flinty, but he didn't censure him. 'Waqar, I pardon your questioning, for I know you grieve for your mother, my sister. I too grieve. But look around you: Kesh is in ruins. If we do nothing, our homeland will disintegrate into chaos.'

'But war is what has done this, Uncle!'

'Ai, war has ruined us – but war now *unites* us. That is the energy it brings. The emirs will stand together – provided I give them someone to conquer. To alleviate the suffering of generations to come, *our* generation must take the hard choices.'

Next morning, Waqar flew south, those words ringing in his ears.

22

The Archer's Test

Knowledge and Power

So this skinny prick says, 'Knowledge is the only true power.' I'd had a few, so I bloodied his pointy nose. Next day I had to skip the bloody district: turns out he was the earl's son. Should'a known, I guess!

JERZI SNYTT, VERELONI CRIMINAL, 627

Sagostabad, Kesh, Ahmedhassa
Jumada (Maicin) 935

Latif, once a sultan's impersonator, flexed his bleeding fingers and hefted another load of bricks still hot from the kiln. He was beyond exhaustion, utterly wrapped up in the mind-numbing, bone-deep ache of labour. All round him was haze and dust and half-naked men with their heads wrapped in filthy scarves, as his was, so they could breath. They were sun-blackened, skin-and-bone wraiths drifting through the smoke, in one of row upon row of building sites, each merging with the next like a giant quarry. His eyes were filled with grit and dried clay clogged his hair. His shoulders ached from the yoke he bore.

Behind him, Sanjeep was guiding Rani as she pulled another load of fresh bricks. It might be only a month since the old mahout had rescued him but it felt like a lifetime: living in the stables, washing as best he could every evening in a bucket and sleeping in bug-infested straw. The only respite came on Jome, holy day; mornings were spent at the dom-al'Ahm, of course, but in the afternoon they could rest.

The next Jome was days away, but even so, prayer dominated their free time. The Amteh prayed six times a day: at dawn, mid-morning, midday, mid-afternoon, dusk and late evening. Not all the labourers were devout, but all appreciated the break. This morning a new campaign of Shihadi hectoring had begun, the Amteh clergy now reminding their flock that the Lakh were godless infidels. This worried Sanjeep and his fellow displaced Lakh: the Nishander district already suffered enough rampages by Keshi youths without adding extra provocation.

And Rashid Mubarak, Emir of Halli'kut, was now Sultan of all Kesh.

That was inevitable, Latif reflected. The change in ruler didn't make him at all inclined to return to the palace and identify himself. If Rashid had been behind the murders, then he'd have Latif silenced, and even if he hadn't, who needed the impersonator of a dead sultan? And what if the masked magi heard that he'd survived?

No, better I forget that life as if it never was.

'Latif,' Sanjeep called, tossing a water-bottle, 'drink – you look done in.'

The sheer weariness of back-breaking labour was exacerbated by not enough food or water. Every day someone died, from collapsed walls or other accidents, or sheer exhaustion. Latif could feel the spectral hand of death reaching out for him, but he was too numb to care. He completed another load, then the wail of the Godsingers rose from a distant tower, calling the men of the Prophet to worship, and he sagged in relief. 'Ahm be praised!'

'Indeed, my friend,' the old Lakh mahout said, slapping his shoulders.

They joined the lines filing into the dom-al'Ahm and knelt in ranks on the takiya beneath the gaze of a stern Godspeaker and his retinue of Scriptualists. This was familiar territory for Latif, who'd thought to be a Scriptualist before being plucked from his scribe's family and placed in Salim's retinue as a nine-year-old. He feared discovery still, despite his dishevelled appearance, so he kept his head low.

'The Blessings of the Prophet be upon you all,' the Godspeaker called, before rattling through the ritual prayers of the day in perfunctory style. Latif used the time to give his tortured body some respite. Then came the lesson. 'The Prophet Aluq-Ahmed was many things, brethren,' the Godspeaker started, 'a holy man, a ruler, a scholar, a seer. With the holy hand of Ahm upon Him, He united Kesh in the name

367

of the one true God. The old idols and blasphemies were expunged, burned away like chaff. He then confronted the defining question of His time: should He be content that His people were saved, though idolatry and evil thrived beyond the borders of His lands? Should He be callous to the plight of those born in heathen lands, doomed to die having never known the Word of Ahm? Would it be right to shed blood in bringing the Word to the Lost? These questions He put to all the wise men of Kesh, in the first Convocation of the Faith: asking, "Can a war ever be holy?"

'The answer they reached was that a war commanded by Ahm and waged in His name is indeed *holy*: it is *wrong* to allow evil to thrive beyond one's borders, for that evil will grow and threaten the physical and spiritual wellbeing of your own people. It is *wrong* to let an ignorant man condemn himself to Shaitan's Pit when he can be redeemed. If first he must be disarmed, then disarm him: just as a wild horse must be tamed before it is ridden, so must the barbarian be tamed before he can be taught.

'The new Kesh, united under Sultan Rashid Mubarak I, has pledged Shihad against all heathen nations, *in perpetuity*. We know who our enemies are: *they are the enemies of Ahm*. Whether they are worshippers of devils or false gods, they are *the enemies of the Faith*. Whether they dwell in the south of Lakh or in godless Gatti and Mirobez or far-flung Javon and Yuros, they are our enemies. *We are a people at war!*'

Perpetual untargeted Shihad . . . Latif shivered. *A licence for Rashid's favoured generals to take all they want and more, for ever.*

But no one here saw it like that; the Godspeaker had paused as every man cheered and shook his fists in the air, proclaiming 'Death to the Yurosi!' with blithe, careless righteousness.

It seemed wise to do the same.

No wonder Salim failed to quell this message. It's so simple: we tried to reason, but the Shihadi just rabble-roused. But if you promise blood you must deliver . . .

After the lesson, red scarves were handed out and Latif took one, because they all did. It would keep the dust from his mouth.

Somehow, Latif endured, the mindless routine of labour, eating, praying and sleeping allowing him to forget his old life. It saved him from embracing the hand of death, as others sometimes did, when the deep, swift Tigrates River flowed through the city and there were a hundred other ways to die readily at hand. He teetered on the edge of despair, then slowly trudged back towards life, losing himself in another impersonation: of someone he could have been, had not Salim's agents taken him into the royal household all those years ago.

Then, without warning, everything changed again.

Sanjeep and Latif returned from mid-morning prayer to find a blackrobed man with hawkish features stroking Rani's trunk. He was clearly a warrior; his scimitar-hilt was in plain sight, a strung bow in a tooled leather sheath hung on his back, beside a quiver of arrows.

To Latif's trained eye, he was much more. He wore a gem that was likely a periapt, and there were certain tattoos on his wrists.

Hadishah.

'This elephant – is it yours?' the man demanded of Sanjeep.

'Ai, sahib,' Sanjeep replied anxiously.

'How old?'

'Twenty-four years old, sahib. Female. She cannot breed any more. I have ownership branding for her, sahib,' Sanjeep added. Among the elephant owners, beast and master had identical brands. 'I can show you.'

The Hadishah sniffed indifferently. 'You are the mahout? How old are you?'

'Fifty-seven, sahib,' Sanjeep replied.

'And you are Amteh?'

'Ai, sahib! All my life! Ask anyone, they will—'

'Quiet, old man.' The Hadishah looked Rani up and down. 'Is she trained for war?'

'No, sahib. She is a working elephant only.'

'But she can be trained,' the Hadishah insisted.

Latif guessed where this was going, and so did Sanjeep. 'If I were there to guide her, sahib,' Sanjeep said plaintively. Without Rani, he'd have nothing. 'She needs my hand, otherwise she—'

'Silence,' the Hadishah snapped, and Sanjeep almost swallowed his tongue.

The old Lakh fell to his knees. 'Sahib, Rani is my whole world.'

The Hadishah gestured brusquely. 'The elephant is now mine, Lakh. So are you.'

'But sahib, I have contracts with the—'

'I'll deal with that.' The Hadishah looked at Latif, his eye running over him from head to foot and back, no recognition in his eyes. 'Get lost, wretch. I don't need you.'

Sanjeep looked at Latif apologetically.

For Latif, two futures opened up: one of them a short, miserable life choking on brick-dust until it clogged his lungs and killed him. The other possibility was so unlikely as to barely exist ... but he snatched at it. In war, elephants bore a castle of wicker and hide to protect three crew: the mahout, a spearman and an archer. Latif had seen them many times – and all the impersonators had been trained in the basic skills of war. 'I can shoot, sahib,' he told the Hadishah. 'And I can help with Rani.'

The Hadishah pulled the bow from his back-sheath. 'Show me.'

Latif gulped, but took the weapon and an arrow.

The Hadishah looked around. 'See that pillar?' he said, pointing to a piece of timber some fifty paces away. 'Hit it.' He looked Latif in the eye. 'Miss, and I'll have you flogged for lying.'

The nearby workers and the overseer stopped to watch as Latif nocked the arrow and measured the distance. It'd been months since he'd last practised, on an idyllic morning before the Convocation. His wife and son had been watching, and while he could barely recall his wife's face, his son's was vivid in his memory, wide-eyed and filled with hero-worship.

Stay relaxed. Draw, pull, sight and release; let it flow, all one movement ...

That was the secret: to not allow yourself time to waver and doubt. The movement came to him easily, the bow sang and the shaft buried itself in the pillar, left and low of where he'd aimed, but still a hit. He stared at the quivering shaft as his future morphed again.

'Very well,' the Hadishah said. 'You come too. I am Ashmak. You are both now soldiers of the Shihad and I am your new master.'

Oh, the irony, Latif thought. *Salim, what must you be thinking, watching in Paradise? And Rashid, if you knew, how you would laugh!*

'Our possessions are at the stables, Lord,' Sanjeep said, his voice disbelieving.

'Is there aught of value? No? Then forget them. You will be furnished with uniforms and equipment at my barracks.' Ashmak clapped his hands. 'Come!'

Latif seized Rani's guide-rope while Sanjeep clambered nimbly up to the howdah. Ashmak peered upwards, then grunted and settled into a walk beside Latif as they left the worksite.

'Where did you learn to shoot?' he asked, his voice faintly curious.

'I was an archer in the Third Crusade,' Latif replied, which wasn't far from the truth. 'I was at Shaliyah, then Ardijah and Riverdown.'

'Salim's own army?' Ashmak grimaced in remembrance. 'You were fortunate. The late sultan was careful with his men. I was in the north, where Rashid Mubarak burned through soldiers like tinder. What are you called?'

'Latif,' he replied, deliberately dropping the Lakh pronunciation. He was tired of that lie, and he needed to keep things simple around a Hadishah man.

'Then you're not Lakh?' Ashmak stared, and his eyes glowed faintly. Latif realised in alarm that the Hadishah man meant to probe his mind and immediately blanked it, as he'd been taught. Ashmak frowned. 'Where did you learn to do that?'

Latif swallowed, but he couldn't see what else he could have done. The impersonators had been taught how to wall up their minds so that any mage probing them would destroy their sanity before they unlocked Salim's secrets – but he needed another explanation: 'There was a Hadishah man attached to my satabam who taught us, in case Rondian magi attacked him through us.'

'Smart thinking,' Ashmak said grudgingly. 'So why are you working among the Lakh if you're Keshi?'

'I'm a mongrel,' Latif replied. 'Keshi raised me, but I have Lakh blood also.'

'I don't care if you're half-dog,' Ashmak said, 'as long as you can shoot. You belong to me now.'

The Hadishah led them to a compound east of the city and once inside he flicked his finger at Sanjeep, indicating he should climb down. Guardsmen closed in. Their leather breastplates were embossed with jackal heads. Latif stood beside the older man, looking about warily. No one looked very welcoming.

Ashmak clicked his fingers. 'Follow,' he said, turning on his heels, and they hurried after him into a sweltering smithy filled with fires and hammering sounds. Latif had no idea what was happening, but Sanjeep stopped at the door. 'No, sahib!'

The soldiers seized them and forced them to their knees. Latif struggled in bewilderment, but he stood no chance in his weakened state. 'These are runaway Lakh slaves,' Ashmak announced. 'I found them, and claim them. Brand them with my sigil, and the elephant too.'

Branding? Dear Ahm!

The guards subdued him easily and a red-hot piece of metal was jammed into his skin. He screamed and doubled over, howling on and on, even after a wet compress smelling of herbs was jammed against the wound. He'd pissed himself, though he didn't realise until minutes after. He couldn't watch as they did the same to Sanjeep. The old mahout wailed and sobbed before the brand was even applied, the sound redoubling as the metal seared his skin. The cooked meat smell made Latif vomit.

When he could finally see straight, he saw Ashmak dictating to a slave with a scribing board. 'Burn their clothes and shave their heads, then equip them. Arrange for a battlefield howdah. Training begins tomorrow morning.'

As his consciousness faded again, Latif thought, *I'll be dead by nightfall . . .* For vast minutes there was nothing but the throbbing pain, then he blacked out again. He had to be revived twice more before he could hold down the water given by a sympathetic-looking Keshi servant in dirty whites.

'Drink deep, boy,' he said softly. 'Then try and rest.'

Latif could feel tears on his face. 'Sweet Ahm, it hurts!'

'I know. We've all been branded – it's so he doesn't have to pay us.'

'It's *illegal* – they can't *do* this!'

'Shihad is declared, my friend,' the servant said. 'The army does what it likes.'

23

The Abduction

Nurturing the Bloodlines

The gift of the gnosis is carried in bloodlines, and the strength of our empire lies in the strength of our magi. Therefore it is the duty of every mage to breed. Be fruitful, and cover the empire.

GRAND PRELATE RODAS, PALLAS, 684

The exhortation by Rodas for magi to breed willy-nilly was one of several irrational utterances during his sorry reign as Arch-Prelate. Of course magi must breed – but the core power of this empire lies in the pure-blooded magi, and they must seek to contain the bloodlines to themselves. Mixed-blood liaisons are to be discouraged.

GRAND PRELATE PETRON, PALLAS, 722

Pallas, Rondelmar, Yuros
Aprafor–Maicin 935

Empress Lyra Vereinen clung to her husband's arm as her windship landed in a courtyard of the Imperial Bastion. The swift vessel had brought them directly from the post-tourney revels in Finostarre; while the local innkeepers and whoremongers sought to extract every last coin from the revellers, Lyra's Imperial Council was gathering to discuss the latest threat to her reign.

Pallas seemed oblivious, night settling over her like a star-spangled shroud.

Until the child in her belly could be born, Lyra's heir was Cordan Sacrecour, and after him, Cordan's younger sister Coramore, the children of the late Emperor Constant, her mother's half-brother. While she held Cordan and Coramore, the old Sacrecour regime – House Dupeni – had been unable to move against her.

During the final bout of the tourney someone had stolen the Sacrecour children and the threat of insurrection now hung over her neck like an executioner's axe.

'Thank Kore you're with me,' she murmured to Ril as they walked through the small group of officials gathered to meet them and headed for the council chambers. The many unknowns swirled inside, but the innate protectiveness of her prince-consort was a comfort. *We're in this together*, she thought, drawing calm from his strong features and confident stride. His Estellan colouring was unique in the palace; his black hair and olive complexion made his the most beautiful face in Koredom to her. A few weeks ago – *no, it was just a few days ago!* – she'd feared she was losing him; last night they'd put that behind them. In truth, he'd been her shield from the moment he'd smashed into her cell in the convent and saved her from being murdered, and he was still the centre of her life: husband, lover and father of her unborn child. *I won't let this fear crush me, not when he's here.*

She walked slowly into the meeting room, aware she was becoming ungainly as she entered her fifth month of pregnancy. She surveyed her waiting councillors silently, wondering if any of them were behind this outrage. *Grand Prelate Wurther, you are the obvious suspect.* The Corani had stolen the children from under Wurther's nose, and her too. But for the audacity of Ostevan, her confessor, and Ril's courage, Cordan would be Emperor-elect and she would be lying in an unmarked grave – and no doubt Wurther would have profited handsomely.

There are questions I could ask him, but could I trust the answers? She met the grand prelate's bow of greeting, then shifted her gaze around the room.

Edreu Gestatium, the head of the Imperocracy, the empire's bureaucratic service, stood next to Wurther. He was a man of details and dust; she could picture him involved in any number of conspiracies. Beside him was Treasurer Calan Dubrayle. She'd thought him fully on her side, having given him his head on rebalancing the treasury, but he probably had his price too.

Next to him was Dirklan Setallius, and the thought of him as an enemy worried her sick. The spymaster knew *everything* . . . but he was also Corani, and to the death, after all he'd been through in 909.

Their guest counsellor for this meeting, Esvald Berlond, was the Corani Knight-Commander and deputy to Ril as Master-General. He'd been in charge of security here in Pallas while the court was away: the children had been taken on his watch. Yes, Berlond was Corani through and through, but he'd been fiercely loyal to Ril's predecessor and rival, Solon Takwyth, who'd dramatically returned from exile and that very day won the tourney she'd arranged, defeating Ril in the final bout.

'Sit, please,' she invited them. 'We all know why we're here. Tell me what we know, Lord Setallius.'

The spymaster, a sinister figure with his long silver hair, gloved metal hand and black eyepatch, looked around the room as if deciding how much to reveal. 'About three hours ago, late afternoon, while the entire court was four miles away at Finostarre, two people entered the suite here in the Bastion where Cordan and Coramore Sacrecour were held. One was Sir Bruss Lamgren, a trusted knight of Coraine who'd been appointed their guard; the other was a senior lady-in-waiting, Lady Jenet Brunlye. Lamgren appears to have slain three servants and the two guardsmen watching the door, then he and Lady Brunlye used the gnostic key Lamgren had been entrusted with to release the royal children. The children appear to have departed willingly. The four of them left by a rear exit, by carriage, we believe. The palace was almost empty, and no one has seen them since.'

'Lady Jenet complained of illness and left this morning for the Bastion,' Lyra said. 'We all saw her at breakfast in Finostarre.'

'Lamgren also had riverreek – that's why he didn't compete at the tourney, or so he claimed,' Setallius noted. 'We've got thousands of people sick in Emtori and Fisheart. It feels like half of Pallas has the riverreek this season.'

'What are you doing to find the children?' Ril demanded.

'There's a manhunt, obviously – I've got the Imperial Guard going door to door, but the children are probably already out of the city,' Setallius replied. 'My contacts in Dupenium, Fauvion and the major towns of Eastern Rondelmar are watching for signs that they've shown up in the court of Garod Sacrecour or one of his allies.'

'Is Duke Garod mobilising?' Berlond asked.

'The Sacrecours are never far from full mobilisation,' Setallius replied. 'None of the Great Houses are. But there's no immediate signs of a march on Pallas. Obviously we'll be deploying legions on the roads east.'

'If the children are seen in Dupenium or Fauvion, it's open war,' Ril said. 'Someone, somewhere, is moving those children to wherever they believe will be the best place to announce them to the world.'

Setallius agreed. 'It can only be a matter of time. But it might not be immediate: we know how the Sacrecour-Fasterius alliance will react to this, but what of the Canossi, and the Aquilleans to the south? They're far from committed to Cordan's cause; they may require proofs that Cordan is free – and a viable ruler – before moving. They don't like us any more than Garod, but no less either. I believe there's a window of time in which we can recover the children, perhaps up to three months.'

Three months . . . Lyra clutched Ril's hand while covering her belly. *Dear Kore, is that all the time we have?* 'What else can we do?' she asked, hearing fear in her voice.

'We must set a bounty on their heads,' Gestatium suggested. 'Enough to make the most ardent Sacrecour change his colours.'

'Nobles of Great Houses don't break ranks,' Calan Dubrayle replied in a clipped, faintly bored voice. 'It won't work.'

'Great Houses have servants who see more than their lords suspect. And most Houses are riddled with infighting,' Gestatium countered, and Setallius nodded in agreement as he went on. 'There'll be someone who sees something, and has a price.'

'Perhaps the children were snatched by a neutral, an opportunist seeking a ransom?' Wurther asked.

'No one's neutral about the throne except the Church,' Ril drawled. 'You lost them once – did you take them back?'

'No,' Wurther scoffed, 'I am the Voice of Kore and I cannot lie: I don't have the royal children, and I wouldn't harbour them. The Church is a voice for peace and prosperity in Rondelmar.'

Lyra wished she could believe that, but Wurther had been cornered into supporting her claim in 930 and she was certain he still resented it. 'What of Sir Solon Takwyth's return?' she asked. 'A coincidence?'

'I don't believe in coincidences,' Wurther said.

'That's because you're a merchant of superstition,' Dubrayle sniffed. 'It profits you to claim that everything that happens serves some divine purpose.'

The grand prelate chuckled. 'You're a soulless man, Calan.' He turned back to Lyra. 'If you want my opinion, Takwyth's return is very much part of this. The tournament was an integral part of extricating those children from a place they'd not normally be. Where did the idea come from?'

They all turned to Ril, who coloured – then his eyes went round. 'Jenet Brunlye! I was talking with her one day, just an idle conversation, not long before the council meeting where I suggested the tourney, and she said she loved them ... I think that made the idea pop into my head during the meeting.'

Lyra's hand went to her mouth, trying to forget that Jenet and Ril had been lovers once – and that until a few days ago, she'd suspected the relationship to have resumed. 'But that would mean she's been working against us for *months*!'

Setallius said ruefully, 'I've had suspicions about her at times, but no proof.'

'If you harboured suspicions, why wasn't she questioned?' Gestatium snapped.

'When suspicions are all we have, it's better to give people a little rope and see if they hang themselves.'

'In other words, you risked your queen's life,' Wurther accused.

'If I acted on every suspicion and rumour, the streets would be empty and the cells full,' Setallius retorted. 'Lyra, I believe Takwyth saw an opportunity in the tourney – but only to get himself back here to Pallas. He's being watched, obviously, but I don't think he's the immediate threat.' The spymaster glanced at Esvald Berlond. 'You will respect the privacy of the meeting room, obviously, Sir Esvald? I will know to whom I should talk if I suddenly find that Takwyth hears what we discuss.'

The surly-faced knight snorted. 'Of course. I'm not a fool, Setallius.'

Lyra sighed. 'I trust you all. Follow him, see who he talks to. And Sir

Esvald, put the Corani legions in and around Pallas into full mobilisation. Lord Dubrayle, find the funds to do so. Lord Gestatium, you have highly placed officials in every court: cooperate with Lord Setallius on keeping me informed. Dirklan, your task is to find those children.' She paused, fearing for her soul, then said firmly, 'They will stand trial if they have committed treason of their own volition.'

They all looked at her.

Yes, I'm that frightened and angry: this is an attack on my unborn child!

'What are we facing here?' Calan Dubrayle asked. 'A general uprising doesn't happen at the drop of a hat. There's been simmering rural unrest for some years now, for economic reasons, but we've not see a large-scale movement towards revolt. Except for Garod Sacrecour, the dukes are broadly content with their lot – in fact, the tax-farming legislation has them closer aligned with us than the previous regime.'

Lyra looked to Setallius, who said, 'Broadly, rulers face four threats: assassination, palace coup, revolt or revolution. Revolution sees a complete change, not just of regime, but mode of governance – a change to clerical rule, for example. A revolt is an uprising against the ruler, with the goal of replacing them with another from the same ruling class. Both require widespread unrest to succeed and I see no evidence that we're facing either.'

'Nor I,' Dubrayle added. 'Money moves – or fails to move – when such events occur. I'd be aware if something like that was potentially building up.'

'Then that means assassination or coup,' Wurther put in. 'If this were "just" an assassination, the goal would be to replace the ruler with their heir – but Cordan *is* Lyra's heir, so why kidnap him? Why not just strike at Lyra directly and let the laws of succession do the rest?'

'To keep him safe until his succession is confirmed?' Setallius suggested. 'The kidnappers would know that Cordan wouldn't be safe, were Lyra to be murdered.' He glanced at Lyra. 'Apologies for discussing your demise so freely, my Queen.' The faint levity in his voice made Lyra smile for the first time that night.

'Don't let my longevity restrain your theorising, Dirklan,' she replied lightly.

The spymaster's mouth twitched, then he grew serious again. 'The other real possibility is a palace coup: in such an attack, the knives come out for the leadership but don't tend to touch the people on the street – well, not until afterwards, if at all. There's a bloodletting and a change of regime, but for most, life goes on. That's what happened in 909 when the Sacrecours ousted the Corani. They've done this before.'

'A coup requires key people to either aid it or stand aside,' Dubrayle added. He looked Lyra in the eyes. 'You have my full support, Majesty, and I would hope that of everyone here.'

There was a supportive rumble about the table, and each man pledged again to try and find those responsible. Praying they were honest, Lyra accepted their aid with thanks, though she took little comfort from it. Someone out there was holding those children against her as a threat, and the fear of what might be done to them – and to her own child – left her nauseous.

'Find them,' she urged as the meeting broke up. 'Bring them back.' She gestured to Setallius to stay with her and Ril. As soon as they were alone, she squeezed Ril's hand, then said, 'Dirklan, last night – so, before the final day of the tourney and these events – we were in Finostarre, at the tournament. Late that night, I visited my husband's rooms, and I stayed the night—'

'Excellent,' Setallius said. 'I find this whole confinement business a nonsense.'

Lyra smiled at that; her midwife had been making her live like a nun to protect the unborn child. 'I wasn't after your *approval*, Dirklan! The thing is, around midnight I went to leave just as someone *outside the door* tried the door handle. But Ril had used a locking-spell, so they couldn't get in.'

'You never said—' Ril exclaimed.

'You were exhausted – and whoever it was left,' Lyra explained. 'But before they went, I think they used the gnosis to try and force my hand, maybe believing that my touch might remove the locking-spell ... I understand that it's common for such spells to be created with certain people immune – isn't that how I can come and go from my rooms without Basia unlocking every door for me?'

'You're correct,' Setallius told her. 'What else did you sense?'

'Only that they *hated* me . . . and an odd buzzing sensation.'

'Buzzing?' Setallius stroked his chin. 'You may have sensed the gnostic trace of the other person. Every mage has their own unique trace. Can you think who it might be?' he asked, looking at Ril.

Ril bit his lower lip. 'No.'

It hurt Lyra to realise that she didn't *quite* believe his denial, even though they'd made love last night so tenderly . . . but Ril did have a past. 'Is it possible some past flame might have sought you out that night?'

Ril looked down and muttered, 'Jenet Brunlye, you mean? Well, she was in Finostarre, in the same building that night . . . I swear, I've not had *any* relations with her, not for *years* before you and I married, Lyra.'

'I'm sure . . . I know . . .' she answered, squeezing his hands, then she looked at Setallius. 'Lady Brunlye didn't depart Finostarre until the morning of the final bouts – but if it was her, why risk exposure just before the abduction?'

'"Abduction"?' Ril snorted. 'I'm sure they had their bags packed and ready!'

'Perhaps it was murder, not seduction, on this visitor's mind?' Setallius said. He tapped the table. 'I'll consider it. I have some ideas of my own . . .'

As Sir Solon Takwyth entered the knights' hall in the Imperial Bastion, a feeling of rightness settled upon his shoulders like a mantle. The knights of Coraine were almost all here to welcome his return.

'Milord!' Esvald Berlond burst out, his battle-hardened features restored to boyhood by his excitement. More than anyone, he'd kept Takwyth's memory alive among the knights while Ril Endarion had tried to win them over. *Pretend you're Endarion's man all you like,* he'd remind them; *but Solon will return one day.*

And he was right, Takwyth reflected, as man after man dropped to one knee – men from all the titled northern families: Sulpeters, Falquists, and all the rest.

And all of them stared at his horribly disfigured face. The whole left side had been branded, the flesh left a mottled mess of scar tissue and dead flesh.

'Who did this to you?' someone asked as they all stood.

He told the story so they could all hear it: the capture and torture, the escape. It made a good tale, and it reinforced his prowess: in agony from the branding, he'd nevertheless got free and wreaked bloody revenge.

I'm still the best, that tale reminded them, as did beating Endarion at the tourney.

'Yes, it's ugly,' he said, pitching his voice to fill the hall, 'but it's done. I've made my peace with it.'

'Must've hurt like buggery,' old Thom Cransford marvelled.

'Wouldn't know, Thom – I've not your experience of buggery,' he called back, earning a general laugh and then clasping the old warrior to him to show it was all in jest. 'Didn't feel it, Thom – I'm a Corani, with snow for skin and ice for blood.'

They liked that, too. He made a point of circulating, making sure he shook every hand, then took the senior men into a private room and broke out the brandy. The toasts were for their ears only. 'You know I would give my life for the Corani,' he told them. 'You know that the North comes first: that will never change. But five years in the Rimoni Wars down South taught me many things, chief of those being that Southern men are not to be trusted, not with your back, nor with your gold, nor with your woman. Rimoni ... Silacian ... *Estellan* ... they're all scum.'

They knew *exactly* who he meant.

'Our queen has my loyalty, but she hasn't married well,' Takwyth told *his* commanders. 'It's not disloyal to hate the half-Estellan fornicator who seduced her. It's not a betrayal of her, to bring Endarion down.'

Somewhere in Rondelmar
Maicin 935

'Cora?' Cordan Sacrecour whispered through the crack beneath the door. '*Cora?*'

No one answered. He pressed his face to the floor and tried not to cry again. The plastered stone room had nothing but a bed-pallet and a piss-pot, a water jug, a pile of books and a lute. Hours of raging and shouting had drawn no response and food was delivered only when he genuinely slept. He had no idea how many days had passed. He'd had to wash using the water jug, and smashing it elicited nothing but a fresh ewer next time he slept.

But the next time he woke, he wasn't alone: a man robed in black wearing a Lantric mask was sitting in a chair beside the door. It was Jest, the prankster, and Cordan was almost sure it was the same man who'd 'rescued' them from the Bastion.

'Greetings, my Prince,' the man said, his voice muffled. 'We must talk.'

Cordan scrabbled upright, rubbing his eyes, ashamed at his disarray – and angry, because this man had caused it. 'What do you want?' he demanded.

'Only what is best for you, my Prince.'

'Then why are you locking me up? Where's Cora? If you've hurt her, I'll . . .' His voice trailed off as he tried to imagine what he would actually do. Something *hideous*.

'Prince Cordan, I assure that this is entirely necessary. Lyra Vereinen has every resource of the Crown seeking you. We can't take chances, my Prince; not until the day comes when you may ride openly into Pallas.'

'Is Cora safe?'

'Of course, and she sends her love. She understands, and is willing to endure these privations.' Jest's dark eyes glinted through the mask. 'Believe me, the best thing you can do now is read, practise your music and pray. When the time comes, you'll need to be rested and ready.'

'*When?*'

'It's best you don't know. There's much to be done, but it'll be soon, I promise.'

'Who are you?'

'Again, best you don't know. For now, be assured that all that is being done is with your interests at heart. You will be emperor, Cordan. By the end of Junesse, you will be crowned.'

24

Sacred Union

Goddess of Love and Madness

Mater Lune is the Sollan Goddess of the Moon; in their mythology she is part of many thematically linked notions: love, insanity, fertility, poetry and music; the tides, of course, and the seasons. Whilst the goddess is clearly a myth, these entwined themes are highly instructive.

ORDO COSTRUO ARCANUM

Western Sydian Plans, Yuros
Maicin 935

The call of a Godsinger rose at dawn, wailing out across the valley in Eastern Sydia where Clan Vlpa was encamped, protecting their herds during the foaling season. There was an air of uncertainty that an outsider like Kyrik could sense: foaling usually happened well north of their current camp, in valleys where the snows had retreated and the lush spring growth could support the new stock until they were strong enough to continue the migration north.

But this year, the Vlpa were in new territory at the mouth of the Bunavian Gap, too close to where the Rondians patrolled, on arid plains where the grasses grew tougher and shorter. They couldn't stay here more than a few months, and if they tried to go north, they'd find the trails eaten out.

They're committed, in other words, Kyrik reflected, as he sipped from his water-flask. *It's Mollachia or perish.* He looked about him, soaking up the daily routines of the huge camp. Riders still herded and hunted and worked the livestock. The women milked the cattle, washed the clothing, tended the fires and prepared the meals. Children ran naked through the tents, playing vast, endless chasing games, or stood just staring at him, the only white man most had ever seen. The young men practised archery and fought; the girls squabbled and giggled. And amidst all that, preparations were being made for a trek, and for a very particular marriage, one that touched them all. *Tonight*, Kyrik thought, a little unsteadily, *everything changes . . .*

He was sitting at the mouth of his tent amidst dozens of fox pelts: Vlpa tradition was for a groom to gift his bride a fox-fur coat. Hunting the pelts was supposed to be time the groom spent with his closest male kin, getting advice on entering the tribe fully as a married man. But Kyrik had no kin here, so he'd hunted alone, using the gnosis as much as the bow: at least she'd have plenty of pelts.

Then the alien wail of the Amteh Godsinger rose again over the sea of tents and he was again reminded of all that was in flux. Drawn by the thought of hearing Paruq speak for what might be the last time, he went to listen. The morning was changeable, light cloud scudding across the skies, driven by a fresh northeasterly. Some four dozen converts were gathering beside a small river where they'd built a little dom-al'Ahm from wood and hide daubed white. The carefully chosen lesson that morning was of forgiveness and tolerance of differences.

He waited until Paruq had dismissed the gathering, then greeted him.

'Sal'Ahm, friend Kyrik! How are you this auspicious morning?'

'It's "auspicious", is it?' Kyrik grinned, knowing Paruq had nothing but disdain for auspices and omens.

'Well, in truth, I haven't consulted the stars, but the sunrise was pretty.' Paruq clapped Kyrik on the shoulder. 'What brings you here?'

'A few final words, if you have the time. I need advice . . . or at least to know you don't think I've gone insane.'

'You know I've always tried to reserve judgement on that point.'

Kyrik chuckled. 'This migration is madness, eh? What was I think-ing? Once his marriage to Hajya had been agreed, he and Thraan had worked out a plan. As soon as possible, five thousand riders would depart with Kyrik, the most that could be spared and still keep the tribe secure. The rest of the tribe – twenty-five thousand souls, plus their herds – would follow as swiftly as they could.

'And even should we defeat the Rondians – which I must believe we can, despite all logic – then I still have to get the clan settled in Mollachia without antagonising the whole of my people,' Kyrik concluded. Another thought occurred to him. 'What are you going to do, Paruq? Will you stay with the Vlpa and come to Mollachia?'

Although having his friend join the migration appealed, he knew there would be no welcome for a Godspeaker in Mollachia. But Paruq shook his head. 'My mandate is to seek converts on the Sydian plains. When Clan Vlpa leave this region, I won't be joining them. I'm sure it's for the best.'

Kyrik exhaled, a little relieved. 'Paruq, I have a question. Do you know what happened to Valdyr in the breeding-houses? He's clearly traumatised – I mean, it was bad for all of us, but ... well, you know what I mean.'

Paruq looked troubled. 'The breeding-houses are an abomination, and he was very young. But I'm not aware of him being singled out. He did have a special tutor—'

'Who?'

Paruq frowned. 'Asiv Fariddan, a man I've not met. People say he was very clever – one of the few Hadishah with a gift for scholarship. A half-blood, born in Gatioch. Very senior in the breeding-houses, I understand.'

'Is it possible he *abused* Valdyr?'

Paruq's face tightened in anguish. 'I couldn't say – and nor could I refute it.'

'Dear Kore, if that's what happened, I'll kill this Asiv Fariddan, I swear—'

Paruq placed a hand on Kyrik's forearm. 'Peace, my friend. This is all supposition. There may be other explanations for your brother's inner pain. I'll make enquiries.'

'Thank you – but please, be discreet. I can't let it get out that such a thing happened to Valdyr – it would destroy him. I wish I could reach him, but he's always hiding inside himself—'

'That would be consistent with abuse,' Paruq admitted, 'but there are many forms of abuse. The breeding-houses were dreadful, but they're a fact of life, I fear.'

'I am forever grateful that you took me away from that,' Kyrik said. 'Though I do wonder if I will someday meet a half-Keshi who calls me "Father".'

Paruq smiled sadly. 'Perhaps one day you will.'

Kyrik's wedding day passed in ritual. The shaman, Missef, clearly resented the union, but he nonetheless led the group of young acolytes in undressing Kyrik and painting him in red swirling symbols with stylised fox-heads at the centre. The shaman's pavilion was smoky with some kind of drug that left his head spinning. His hair was caked in a buttery jelly and spiked into a strange crest and he was hung with necklaces of bones, all the while prayers were chanted over him. The Stallion God, Amazar, unsurprisingly associated with male virility and hunting, was invoked constantly. The words blurred and the dreamlike unreality grew as the hours drifted by, until finally he was draped in a full-length cloak of furs and led outside.

When he emerged from the hide tent, the cacophony stunned him, as did the sea of faces. He hadn't realised, secluded in Missef's pavilion, that all through the afternoon a festival atmosphere had been building. Everyone who had a musical instrument was blowing or hitting or strumming it, and everyone else was caterwauling at the top of their lungs. The noise was like a physical blow that staggered him, sweeping away all his complacency. Then he was hoisted aloft and carried, lying on his back, through a sea of people. This was suddenly very real, and he felt utterly unprepared.

Ahm be with me, he thought, but his God felt a very long way away.

Tribesmen wearing animal skins and masks poured out of the crowd, seized him and bore him aloft towards a central bonfire whose heat permeated the camp. Luna, rising in the East as the sun fled, was full and very bright. The rhythmic, pounding chanting enveloped him and he felt like he was adrift in a sea of half-naked men, many wearing animal masks, especially of the fox. But when they carried him to the fire, a great conflagration radiating intense heat, he saw a sea of woman on the far side, similarly masked, many naked to the waist, dancing and stamping their feet. Everyone seemed to inhabit some middle place between the kingdoms of man and animal, where base needs and desires ruled. He realised that this wasn't an ordinary marriage, which Paruq had told him was normally a small, dignified affair: this was ceremony and ritual, the union of a king – the Sun-Father's avatar – and a Sfera-mage, a Daughter of the Moon. It was at once uncharted territory and rich with tradition: Missef had spent all week creating the rituals to be performed tonight.

Kyrik had no idea what was going to happen.

The masses of bared flesh, the masks and the fires all boded ill, in his view. It was disturbingly pagan: heat, virility, fertility, blood, and all the time the sheer power of the drums vibrated through him, loosening his joints and making his legs quiver. As the men lowered him to his feet facing the fire, he felt utterly drained already, and realised he was shivering with apprehension.

Missef was waiting in a fox-mask and cloak and nothing else, but Kyrik barely noticed him, because on the far side of the fire, a group of woman had just borne someone in on their shoulders, someone lying flat as if they were a corpse, draped entirely in a white cloth – the colour of death in Eastern cultures, but meaning purity in the West. It'd been freshly speckled in animal blood. When they set her down, she planted her feet firmly and raised her hands skywards.

They'd told him to mirror her movements, so he did the same. The drums hammered and she spun left and so did he, keeping the fire between them. He remembered her dance the first time he'd come to the camp, the challenge she'd laid down and the contempt she'd exuded when he'd refused that challenge. This time he accepted, mimicking her movements as best he could, rolling his hips as she did, gyrating from the hips and the shoulders, though imperfectly, always a step behind. He saw her eyes catch the firelight as she stared at him across the flames.

This time he was dancing.

Reel her in, he'd been told, *bring her to the shaman*, so now he over-stepped with each movement, each time coming a little closer, until the fire only partly obscured her and he could see flashes of her muscular calves and arms. But she was drawing it out, letting him get a little closer, then swaying away – until he suddenly threw in a kinesis leap, making the watchers roar in wonder, and though she did the same, suddenly she was within reach and he grasped her shoulder . . .

. . . just as she spun back into his grasp, as if she'd been intending to be caught all along, and unexpectedly he was staring into her face, just inches away. Hajya was breathing heavily, her breath meaty and hot, but not unpleasant. She too was sweating from the heat of the flames, perspiration running into her thick brows, heat flushing her leathery cheeks. The moon tattoos of her Sfera rank had been renewed and gleamed black; her hair was a black cloud tumbling down her back, a stark contrast to the blood-dappled white cloak; her deep brown eyes stared intensely into his own blue eyes. She was naked beneath her cloak, just as he was naked beneath his.

'Well?' he panted, his voice low, 'what now?'

'Thrice around the fire, side by side, but not touching, then we kneel to the shaman,' she told him. 'There, he will offer me to you.'

Kyrik licked his dry lips. 'And then?'

'You take me . . . or not.' She looked him in the eye.

He felt his back stiffen. 'Will this involve one of your ceremonial mating rituals that everyone tells me no longer happen here?'

'What do you think?' She gestured regally. 'Walk with me.'

So he did, watching her out of the corner of his eye as he fell into slow step with her, thinking that she wasn't beautiful, but she was striking, compelling, impossible to ignore. Right now, he didn't feel like her equal at all.

'Will he also offer me to you?' he asked as they moved in time to the slow boom of the drums and the rhythmic clapping of the endless sea of onlookers.

'Of course not. A wife is just a possession. You and your "equality",' she sneered.

'We will be equals,' he vowed. 'You'll see. And for the record, I'm no keener than you about this – but it must be done.'

'Well you're going to have get keen, aren't you?' She laughed. 'I hope you Western magi know how to fake an erection, hmm?'

For the thousandth time he wondered what he was getting himself into. But he managed to match her stride as they walked around the fire, then suddenly the three circles had gone in a flash and they were standing before Missef. Kyrik inhaled deeply, trying to find his equilibrium. He'd always known that when he married, it would be a family alliance to help secure the kingdom. He'd just never imagined it might be to a Sfera witch . . .

Just be grateful and thankful, he told himself. *The fight to free Mollachia begins here.*

The ceremony felt brief, as if all were impatient to see it done, but he suspected that was because his mind was wandering ahead, failing to hold onto the now in anticipating the next moment. In no time at all their hands were being ritually tied together and blessings spoke over them. Red paste was daubed on their foreheads and Amazar entreated to fill his loins. The Stallion God's female counterpart, Ponya, was invoked as well, and Hajya's cheeks were painted with mare's blood. A ring was placed on the third finger of her left hand: a concession to Rondian customs.

'You are given leave to become one,' Missef told them, before turning to Hajya.

'Do you accept this man?' he asked.

Her chin lifted. 'I accept him.' Her voice was truculent.

'And you?' Missef asked, his tone distant, almost bitter as he addressed Kyrik.

He swallowed. 'I accept.'

The crowd broke their silence to whoop and ululate, a deafening shriek that went on and on as they were led before the bonfire and shown to the clan. If this had been a purely Sydian high-ceremony wedding, he would now lower her to the earth and plough her. But – *Thank Kore!* – he'd negotiated a compromise and instead, they made their way to a specially constructed marital tent, her steady, intimidating gaze locked on him as they walked slowly and carefully, their hands still tied together – and every few steps, someone would stop one or the other and force liquor into their mouths that burned his throat and heated his belly.

Then the tent flap was being opened for them and they were inside, and alone. Outside, huge cheers resounded and the hammering of the drums, still so alien to him, struck up again. In Mollachia, as in Rondelmar, music was slow, stately and elegant among the rich, jaunty and melodic in the low taverns. In the East it was all unnatural tones, complex rules and strange techniques. This was more primal, more dangerous. It pounded in time with his heart, faster and faster.

Then the flap was pulled aside behind him and a gaggle of beast-masked young women spilled into the tent. He jabbed an angry finger at them: '*Out!*'

'No, they stay,' Hajya snapped. 'There must be witnesses.'

'The agreement was that we would have *privacy!*' He took a step towards the girls and they all tilted their masked heads upwards, defiant and unmoving. 'Are they your daughters or something?' he asked in exasperation.

Hajya laughed a little shrilly, a single crack in her armour. 'No. They are my sisters of the Sfera, here to ensure that you can uphold your part of the bargain.'

He looked at her and saw that she intended him to crack or crumble. *Will everything be a battle between us?* he wondered. 'Very well. When we have freed Mollachia, we will marry again, with Kore rites, and you will see how such ceremonies are done among *civilised* people. For now, this will do.' He unbuttoned his fur cloak and tossed it aside, facing her naked, sweating rivers.

The girls tittered, somewhat appreciatively, somewhat mockingly. He decided they were under orders from Hajya: he knew he was nothing to laugh at physically.

Hajya cast off her bloodied white robe and faced him. Her body was heavy, voluptuous, the scars of her pregnancies clear on her belly and in the small roll of waist fat around her muscled torso. Her breasts were large, her pubis thick with black hair: a lived-in body – but when she turned and swayed towards the pile of furs, her muscle tone was obvious.

'Come then,' she said, turning to face him. 'What do you have, Mollach?'

The watching women, now silent, leaned forward, avid. Outside, the drums hammered on.

He let his temper feed his energies. With a little training and concentration, a mage could control his bodily reactions. There was nothing about Hajya that he found unattractive, and in truth, the challenge she presented was far more interesting and enticing than some statuesque court beauty. He barely needed to feed in energy, already feeling his blood pounding in his loins, his member stiffening and swelling. The girls made throaty noises, still giggling, but no longer with mockery.

Hajya sniffed as if unimpressed, then dropped to her knees, facing away. 'Let me know when you're done.'

Anger made him harder. He knelt, gripped her hips, flipped her onto her back and pulled her legs open as she struggled, scratched and hissed. But instead of taking her then, he gripped her buttocks and kissed her belly, then slid lower, licking the lips of her cleft. She stiffened in surprise, and then in understanding: the battle-lines had been redrawn. The girls sucked in their breath and bent closer.

I'll make you want me, his angry side snarled, even as he bent to teasing her into submission. It took time, but having the women here worked against her: alone, she might have resisted, but she too had her role: the bride was expected to show her own inner heat. If she was unreasonably unresponsive, it was she who would lose face.

And he did know what he was doing.

His tongue probed her, followed her, left her nowhere to flee, and she began to gyrate her hips as she wept fluids rich with her musk. He worked her harder, until she began to pant and stiffen, until she moaned and her back arched, quivering.

While she was still in the throes of that moment, he raised himself over her and drove in, her eyes opened wide as fear and defiance blended with lust and she cried out, convulsing again as he pushed himself all the way in and lowered himself fully onto her, panting in her ear as she moaned into his.

He waited until she was moving against him, then he began to thrust rhythmically, withholding his own climax until he forced another from her, then finally releasing himself in a series of powerful thrusts as she clung to him, hips rising to meet him, her breasts pressed to his chest and her mouth wide open.

He stayed inside her, propped himself above her face and waited until her face relaxed and her eyes met his. 'Are you now my wife?' he asked her.

'I am your wife,' she said grudgingly. She jerked her heads at the masked girls, and they left. Outside, the cheers renewed and the drums roared.

He stayed on her, and in her, murmuring, 'Thank you.'

She looked up at him quizzically. 'You don't need to thank a possession for performing its function.'

'Equals, remember.' He bent his face to hers. 'Kiss me.'

She scowled, then reluctantly closed her eyes, and pushed out her lips. Her hesitation didn't surprise him; a kiss was far more intimate than what they'd done. Sex was a bodily function, but a kiss could be made something spiritual.

He took his time, learning her taste and texture, and didn't let up until their tongues were slithering against each other and her eyes had opened again. At last he pulled himself out of her and rolled away to pour drinks. When he rolled back onto his side, she matched his posture, facing him, a measure of interest in her face that hadn't been there before. She sipped her liquor and admitted, 'I've underestimated you.'

He wrinkled his nose. 'Why? Because we had good sex?'

She chuckled throatily. 'There's nothing wrong with good sex, *Husband*.' She pulled a face. 'And it was *good*, ysh. No, I meant, I didn't think you had the balls or the brains to make your mad idea work. But you convinced Thraan, and he's no fool. You bargained well. Your plans for the migration are . . . plausible, realistic. I can't fault them, as yet. You make me believe it can be done.'

'And yet?' he asked, raising an eyebrow.

'And yet . . . the problems are multitude, and may be insurmountable. To migrate a whole people into a kingdom and defeat a Rondian occupier? Most would call that impossible. But sometimes belief must come before reason, and be raised higher. Sometimes, the heart must lead the head. We, the Vlpa clan, have taken irrevocable steps. We are committed now – I recognise that. For the head of the Sfera to now express doubts would be to undermine my own people's safety.'

'What are you saying?'

'That whatever doubts I harbour will not be seen by my people. I will tell them to you, and you will hear me and we will resolve them. But what my people will see is a man and a woman moving forward together.'

He put his drink down and took a deep breath, then looked up, admiration swelling in his chest. 'Then I've underestimated you too. That's more than I had hoped.' He met her dark gaze. 'And so are you.'

She loosed another deep, throaty laugh. 'You're not so bad either, Kyrik Sarkany. But it takes more than one good tumble to win me over entirely. In my life I have had my free pick of men. More than a hundred, I think. Does that intimidate you?'

Kyrik thought about the breeding-house and shook his head. 'How about *two* good tumbles?'

She laughed again and crawled towards him, shoved him on his back, spilled liquor on his chest and straddled him. 'More than two. I'm thinking a higher number. I'm difficult to please.'

In the two days after the wedding, the Vlpa warriors Kyrik would be taking into Mollachia completed their preparations. Thraan and Missef would be leading the migration, while Brazko, Thraan's eldest son, would be joining Kyrik in the vanguard entrusted with defeating the Rondians and clearing the way for the tribe's arrival. Kyrik was trying to insist that Hajya stay with the clan, but that argument was still raging on.

The Sydians had no concept of honeymoon; the morning after his wedding, Kyrik washed himself in the river, nursing a heavy hangover – just like the other men, who started coming up to him to give their names and explain their kinship. He was Vlpa now, though his status was still uncertain: he was husband to their Sfera-leader, not a king – Thraan was their nacelnik, and his sons after him. Here, that wasn't a problem, not to him, but it would be something to worry about when they were in Mollachia.

By day, Hajya was as good as her word: supportive, constructive, and clever. By night they mated hungrily, both caught up in the novelty of learning a new body. He found the element of contest lifting him to fresh exertions – not just at night, but in preparing for the trek as well. When they argued, they did so privately, and then made up. His body was battered, his manhood ached and his pubic bone was bruised, but it felt good to have such a lover: a true mother of earth and sky, an equal, in his eyes at least, even if she remained sceptical.

He was beside the river when Paruq's voice broke through his reverie and he looked up gladly. 'Paruq – Sal'Ahm. I keep worrying I'll not get to say farewell.'

'I'd not let you leave without my blessing, my friend.' The Godspeaker sat beside him, and clapped him on the shoulder. 'How's married life?'

'It's war – no, that's unfair. It's an arm-wrestle.' Kyrik ran his fingers through his hair. 'You know, I *like* her. I like her a lot. I didn't expect that.'

Paruq smiled broadly. 'This is very good: a happy marriage is the strong, resilient sole of a man's feet. Great journeys require such a thing.' He clapped Kyrik on the shoulder. 'I rejoice for you.'

'Sal'Ahm, Paruq – and thank you for everything. You took a broken young man and set him back on his feet. And I don't think she would've agreed to this alliance without your timely involvement in the debate.'

Paruq stood, and Kyrik rose with him. 'You'll face many problems, friend Kyrik. The road; the battle; settling the Vlpa in Mollachia – but no one is more capable of defeating these obstacles than you.'

Kyrik fought tears as they embraced. 'May we meet again.'

'As Ahm wills,' Paruq replied. 'All is unto Him.'

The next morning, Kyrik left for Mollachia with five thousand warriors and half the Sfera, including Hajya, who insisted on accompanying him. She cited something called 'equality', to clinch the argument.

25

The Knowledge Trade

Sorcery: Divination

People misunderstand divination. It does not read the future: it predicts it. But it does so using the knowledge of the spirits, who see the vast patterns that we, with our singular perspectives, can only guess at.

GILDEROY VARDIUS, SORCERER, PALLAS, 846

Sagostabad, Kesh, Ahmedhassa
Jumada (Maicin) 935

Tarita Alhani sat in a half-barrel tub in her room, enjoying the blissful touch of hot water while using healing-gnosis to smooth the ugly boils from her face and body. It felt glorious to be clean, wonderful to be soaking up the rose-scented oils, and bliss to be able to stop hiding her true self behind stinks and sores.

Paradise will involve a lot of bathing, she decided, *assuming Ahm is merciful and I get so far.* She rather feared that Ahm would have to be a lot more relaxed about sin than the *Kalistham* suggested for her to make it, though.

Her body betrayed her history: scars pitted the entire line of her spine where healers had opened up her back to reach the spinal cord in a bid to heal her paralysis. They'd failed, and the scars would never fade – but other means had been found to restore her movement.

The door opened, and Emilio of the curly black hair and mincing walk sauntered in with a plate of steaming spice-cakes and a glass of wine. 'Are you clean yet, darling?' he asked, in Rondian. 'Dear Gods, you stank!'

'The perfect disguise,' she replied in his tongue, grinning. She stretched luxuriantly; knowing even shapely breasts like hers held no sway with Emilio, an unabashed frocio, a lover of other men. A shame, because she'd not had a man for a long time and he was very pretty. 'It even drove off Prince Waqar, sadly.'

'A handsome boy,' Emilio recalled appreciatively. 'Too good for a stinking dirt-caste girl like you.'

'Go rukk yourself,' she laughed, '—just leave the tray behind!'

Emilio left with a disdainful sniff to go back to his cooking. He was replaced by 'Qasr', whose real name was Capolio, once a mercenary battle-mage from southern Estellayne, now a senior member of Javon's royal intelligence-gatherers. He stole a cake as he sat beside her tub, no more interested in her body than Emilio. He was her master, mentor and guide in what he called 'the Knowledge Trade'.

'I may have a clue to the man you seek,' Capolio said. 'You were right: a part-Gatti mage is a rarity, but an Ordo Costruo source tells me one of their men went exploring in Gatioch twenty years before the First Crusade. He impregnated a Gatti noblewoman, but never stayed. It's possible our man is descended of her.'

'How does this help?'

'Because since the Third Crusade, the records of various breeding-houses have been traded on the black market and the Ordo Costruo have been gobbling them up – naturally, as so many of their people were captured and forced to breed. Many wish to trace and reclaim their progeny. I've requested access and they've agreed. Tomorrow you fly to Hebusalim.'

'Me?'

'Why not? I have matters to deal with here. And Emilio is a better cook than you.'

'And more to your taste in the bedroom. I wish I had a handler who liked handling *me*,' she grumbled. 'Anyway, Hebusalim is hundreds of miles away—'

'And good practise. Flying is about experience. You can't get that in a bathtub.'

'I've had all sorts of experiences in a bathtub.' She finished her wine, gobbled down the last spice-cake and stood. 'A towel, slave!'

Capolio laughed and handed her a drying-cloth. As he picked up the tray, he added, 'Join me in my study. I've got something to show you.'

Twenty minutes later, clad in blissfully clean clothing, her long hair oiled and combed and her feet in slippers, she padded into Capolio's austere office.

'Behold!' he said, holding up his hand. A sparrow was perched on it. 'Meet Scevalux.'

'Fancy name for a sparrow,' she commented.

'*Rukka-te*,' the sparrow chirruped.

Her eyebrows lifted. 'Nasty mouth on it, too.'

The bird went to speak again and Capolio shushed it with a gesture. It pecked at him viciously, but a globe of pale light appeared, confining it. Capolio placed the sparrow on the table beside a small saucer of silvery fluid. The sparrow looked at the liquid and tried to back away.

'Is that a minor daemon?' Tarita asked. She'd been a mage for only five years: she had power to burn, but her education into the esoterica of the gnosis was limited.

'Yes: just intelligent enough to possess a name and little else.'

'*I heard that*,' the sparrow trilled irritably.

'And that liquid – it's what Sakita Mubarak had me brewing?' Tarita guessed.

'Exactly: allium, argentum and bismuth, basically. A puzzling mix – it's essentially inert – but watch.' He turned to the table and waved a hand. 'Scevalux, I command you to bathe in the fluid in the saucer.'

'*Don't want*,' Scevalux answered, trying to hop away from the saucer, but the ball of light encasing it rolled it back towards the saucer, taking the increasingly frantic sparrow with it. '*No! No! Don't want! Please – no!*'

Tarita stared as the ball of light with the sparrow floating in it was deposited in the fluid. Capolio dissipated the globe, the bird fell into the fluid and vented an almost human shriek. It tried to launch itself into the air, but as it did, a shadow burst from its mouth, swirled about, then vanished. The bird's wings gave out and it struck the floor and rolled about, dazed.

'What just happened?' Tarita asked, staring.

'The potion banished the daemon is what happened,' Capolio said.

'This isn't altogether surprising – we know argentum can disrupt certain spirit-based gnosis. Bismuth is added to certain inks for marking out magic circles. Allium is, well, garlic: it stinks, and more, it has some place in folklore concerning banishment of spirits.' He picked up the dazed sparrow and soothed it, then released it out of the window.

'Are you saying Sakita was possessed?' Tarita asked.

'She certainly thought so, perhaps by the snake-bite you described, perhaps by another means. Realising what she was fighting but not knowing the specifics, she sought a general "cure-all". Given the toxic properties of the argentum and bismuth, it was both bizarre and dangerous, but perhaps she was unable to banish it with wizardry.' He produced another vial. 'I've brewed more. Take this, and if you have the chance, get it further analysed. There may be other properties I've not detected.'

Tarita spent the day preparing for her journey, then joined Capolio and Emilio for the evening meal; there were just the three of them tonight, as the four other agents on their mission were embedded in the royal household. She enjoyed their company; there was a wonderful freedom to speaking as an equal with such worldly, amiable people and she was learning so much, every day.

There were three ways to gain the gnosis. First, and most common, one could be born to it if one or both parents were magi. Second, a woman bearing a child to a mage could gain the power, generally half the strength of her child. The most unusual way was by drinking *ambrosia*, the secret potion that bequeathed what the Rondians called 'Ascendancy': raw gnostic power greater than even a pure-blood mage.

Tarita had been a maid and just sixteen years old when she was left paralysed and facing a brief future of pain and misery. But her mistress, Elena Anborn, had somehow contrived to get Tarita the ambrosia. She'd survived the dose, then she'd had to learn healing-gnosis to repair her own spine – only someone inside the damaged body could sense exactly what was needed. No one had expected her to take to the gnosis so swiftly – she quickly outstripped all expectations, even as she relearned how to walk and move. She'd overheard words like 'prodigy' spoken when they thought she slept. Within two years she was better than any other ordinary mage of her age, in skill and power. Then Elena sent her to the Merozain monks, and her life had changed again.

She'd not been required to become Zain herself – thankfully, because all that calmness and virtue really wasn't her way – but she'd been granted the opportunity to learn the gnosis *their* way: instead of finding her affinities, the areas of the gnosis which would normally come naturally to her, she was young enough and new enough to the gnosis to follow the Merozain process, giving her access to all sixteen Gnostic Studies. Even the Merozains had been surprised at her swift success.

She was barely two months out of the monastery and this was her first assignment for Capolio – the Convocation had created the necessity, so she hadn't had the luxury of being eased in. But after all she'd survived, she couldn't conceive of failure.

'Where's Prince Waqar?' she wondered. 'He's gone, and nobody knows where.'

'"Nobody" includes me,' Capolio admitted. 'He left during the night and I don't have spare hands to trace him.' Being part of a fledgling spy network was vexing to him, though in truth he had far more resource than when just a mercenary. 'I'll keep my ear to the ground.'

'Attam and Xoredh might know,' she suggested.

'Perhaps I should seduce one of them?' Emilio wondered, winking at Capolio.

'Attam's a brute,' Tarita told him. 'I had a narrow escape from him once.'

'I'm sure he says the same of you,' Emilio replied. 'Anyway, I was thinking more of Xoredh. He looks like a broadminded man, and he's got a wicked swagger.'

'You're not going near either,' Capolio said firmly. 'They're both dangerous. I think Rashid is grooming Xoredh to be his next spymaster.'

'They're both *evil*,' Tarita agreed. 'Stay away, Emilio. Don't even joke about it.'

Capolio raised his goblet. 'To our newest recruit. You've done well, my girl. I know it doesn't feel like it, but you've exceeded expectations. May your journey north bring further success.'

She was gone before dawn, her skiff rising unseen over Sagostabad in the predawn sky, and by sunrise, she was far over the northern horizon.

26

A Vanishing Trail

Theurgy

Just as the more subtle and precise longsword replaced the broadsword as the weapon of choice among the Pallas courtiers, so Theurgy, with its ability to manipulate hearts and minds, is the preferred gnostic weapon in Pallas. The poisonous whisper is applauded there, while an honest act is scorned.

AINAR BORODIUM, DUKE OF ARGUNDY, 926

Imperial Bastion, Pallas
Maicin 935

Four days wasn't long, but for Ril the days after the kidnapping of the Sacrecour children felt like a lifetime. Every morning he woke from bad dreams, haunted by pale ginger-haired children who were implacable and unstoppable daemons, ripping through walls and smashing down barriers as they prowled towards Lyra. Then, just when he thought himself safe, Lyra would transform into Jenet and cut his throat . . .

He didn't need a dream-reader to interpret *those* dreams.

Then there was the suspense of waiting . . . But this morning, he awakened determined to do *something*. Leaving Lyra to the benevolent tyranny of her midwife, he took himself off to Valcet Square, thinking to work out his frustrations with some swordsmanship practise. The square was almost empty, which was unusual, but he'd assigned half the Corani mage-knights to Setallius as hunters, should there be strong leads for finding the missing children. Rumours were circulating like wildfire: that they'd been seen in Fauvion, Dupenium, Klief, Canossi, and all points besides.

He and Gryfflon Joyce sparred for an hour or so, then, sweating and breathing heavily, they sauntered back to the armoury to return the practise blades and mail – only to find the armoury packed with twenty or more Corani, reciting prayers around a thick-stemmed candle.

Ril glanced at Gryff. The prayers were for remembrance. He leaned against the wall to watch and wait. When the prayer finished, Sir Oryn Levis – the Lump – lumbered to the fore. 'Morning, your Grace,' he muttered uncertainly, glancing to his left for guidance, and when Ril followed his eyes, he saw a man wearing a chainmail coif that covered his head: Takwyth. Their eyes met, then Takwyth dropped the coif and turned, exposing his disfigured face.

It was the first time Ril had encountered Takwyth since the tourney final and his dramatic recall to Corani service.

'Your Grace,' Takwyth said coldly. The Corani knights were all armed and armoured, and there were none of the smiles and friendliness Ril had become used to from these men over the past four years. It was as if all his efforts to win them over had never happened; even those he'd considered friends, like young Lero Falquist, were staring at him blankly.

'Who were you remembering?' Ril asked. 'You could have used the Royal Chapel – you had only to ask.'

'Ah ... Sir Bruss Lamgren,' Levis stammered, again looking to Takwyth, despite his own seniority.

Ril stiffened. 'Sir Bruss Lamgren *kidnapped* the Sacrecour children.'

'Bruss Lamgren was one of ours,' Takwyth replied. 'We Corani acknowledge our dead.'

'He was likely a traitor,' Ril snapped.

'That's unproven,' Takwyth countered. 'It appears to us that he was duped by your *good friend* Lady Brunlye.'

They stared at each other as Ril wondered how far he could push this. Gryff was visibly sweating still, but no longer from the sparring. Rulers had died because they lost the command of their knights. *And I'm losing these men.* There was a cold watchfulness in the air, a palpable sense that he was more than unwelcome.

He wondered how secure Takwyth felt – but right now, it was twenty on two, and extracting himself felt much the better part of valour. Takwyth had done nothing wrong, nothing *provable*.

Does a strong ruler wait for 'provable'? he wondered.

'I'm sure our investigations will bring clarity,' was the best rejoinder he could find.

Takwyth paused just long enough to relish his control of the moment, then said, 'If there is anything I can do to assist your investigations, I'm eager to help. We all are.'

I'm not going to enlist your aid when I half-suspect you're involved, Ril thought, but he could hardly say that aloud, not to these men, so he acknowledged Takwyth with a nod and walked through the men to divest himself of his armour, forcing them by proximity to bow their heads and step aside. With studied courtliness, Takwyth marshalled the knights and took them away. It felt like mockery.

'It's wonderful to be so loved by my men,' Ril sighed. In truth, he was quite disturbed – he'd spent five years trying to win these people around, but in five minutes Takwyth had them eating out of his hand.

'They don't know you as I do,' Gryff chuckled, trying for levity. 'If they did, they'd show far more outright hatred.'

Squires helped them out of the armour and they took themselves off to the palace bath, a ground floor complex in the Rimoni style, with tepid running water. Then Gryff left to find his brother and Ril sought out Setallius for an update.

Outside the spymaster's office, Basia rose to meet him, her pencil-thin body clad in her usual tight leathers – most unladylike, and entirely in character. Her auburn hair had been freshly cropped and she moved with an awkward grace, the result of her legs being gnostic-artefacts from the knee down. He was a little surprised to find her – she was Lyra's bodyguard and should be with the queen.

'Where's Dirk?' he asked.

'I've just found out he's in Dawnport, getting a report on the legion dispositions. Do you have half a day?' she added, 'or do you have important Master-General duties to attend to? Because I've got the afternoon off, and I've had an idea.'

Ril grimaced. 'Well, there's probably weeks of paperwork piled up, but I find that if I leave it for long enough, someone takes it away again, so it can't have been important in the first place. What's this idea?'

Basia threw him a grin and pulled a soft leather bag from her pouch. 'Look what I've got.' She tipped a handful of cracked and scorched jewels into her palm. 'I'd forgotten I had these: remember I was asked to help Cordan tune his periapt? The boy has a three-second attention span and burned out a small fortune in periapt-gems. They're worthless now, of course, but I'd not yet thrown them out.'

'Yes,' Ril said, 'so what?'

'Well, they'll have a gnostic-trace preserved in the crystals – not much, but even a partly tuned periapt will take on a bit of the mage's trace. I might be able to use them to find Cordan.'

Ril brightened. 'That's fantastic – but why haven't you told Setallius?'

'I was about to, but he's not here. You know how no two magi are exactly alike, and even two people with exactly the same affinities can end up using those affinities in unique ways? For me, it was always periapts.'

'I remember, after ... you know, your legs ... you used to lie on the bed for days on end, tuning and retuning stones, and amber and wooden carvings ... in fact, anything you could get your hands on.'

'There wasn't much else I could do,' Basia said, her eyes faraway, 'and they helped make the hours just disappear – I *needed* them to disappear then. After I lost my legs I wanted to vanish myself.'

They shared a look, then Ril asked, 'So what do you need me for?'

'Because apart from me, you spent the most time with those two loathsome piglets, so you might be able to pick up some of the slack if I run out of energy – we've always worked well together. And some-one will need to lead me and keep me safe if it works, because I'll be all but blind.'

Ril grinned – it sounded much better than paperwork, and it might even work. 'Makes sense – but I want some blades with us too, in case we end up in a bad place.' He sent a mental summons to Gryff and Larik, and within half an hour they were all gathered in the rear courtyard from where the kidnappers had driven away.

'This is the last known place Cordan stood,' Basia told Ril and the

Joyces, and quickly explained her theory to the brothers. They sipped from their hip-flasks and nodded as if they understood. The courtyard was empty but for two guards at the rear gates, who were staring at them curiously.

Basia pulled out one of the cracked gems. 'The theory is this: wherever a mage goes, he leaves a gossamer trail of his aura, like the tail of a shooting star. It's too little to trace, normally, but a periapt contains a concentration of their aura, so if someone like me, who's especially sensitive to the way periapts work, has their periapt, then they should be able to discern that residual aura trail: Cordan's "comet tail", so to speak.'

'Let's call it his "slime trail",' Ril suggested. 'Like a snail.'

Basia snorted. 'Works for me. Now listen, this mightn't work – it's been four days, after all – so no teasing if I can't do it. But I've done something similar before, I'm half-blooded, so I have the raw energy, and I'm good at this sort of thing. I *can* do it!'

She sounded to Ril like she was trying to convince herself, so he put a hand on her shoulder and kissed her cheek. 'I know you can.'

She shot him a glance full of memories of 909 and the well, so long ago. 'See,' she said, 'that's why I wanted you here.'

'Aw, pooty,' Larik drawled. 'Let's start a rumour—'

'Don't you dare,' Basia snapped with surprising heat, then she raised the gem. 'You won't see much,' she warned.

Ril and the two knights waited while she worked. It took a minute to raise a faint glow in the cracked gem and still she didn't move, her concentration total, eyes unfocused . . .

'Yes,' she breathed, then, '*Come on!*'

Ril took her arm and she began to walk slowly towards the locked iron gates. The guards looked at Ril curiously, but when he gestured for them to open up, they did so with alacrity. Basia led them into the narrow lane that led to a busy thoroughfare, but to Ril's surprise, she turned into a path barely wide enough for a carriage.

'Why would they go that way?' Ril asked.

'Because the City Guard have a station at the mouth of that lane,' Gryff speculated, pointing, 'marking where jurisdiction changes between Bastion and City – they take it pretty seriously.'

'Who knows about this alley, though?'

'Us,' Larik grinned, 'and anyone who likes to live the low life.'

'It's not a big secret,' Gryff added. 'If you weren't the high and mighty Prince-Consort these days, you'd know it like your own warts.'

Basia tugged at Ril and teetered off down the rough track and into a maze of alleyways between the packed-in two- and three-storey buildings, all of them barely wide enough for any carriage.

Ril's main role in this slow, strange progress was to keep Basia from tripping on the cobbles or walking into the piles of refuse as they followed the dirty little lane winding southwards through the backstreets of Highgrange, far away from the big manor houses, through meaner dwellings tenanted by menial labourers clustered about the open sewer that took the effluent from the Bastion. Basia led them through a pair of squares that functioned as butcheries, the air rancid with decaying meat, where brawny men in leather aprons hacked at enormous haunches of cattle and skinny youths loaded offal into barrows. That was followed by an equally noisome tallow-market, then a fish-market round a dirty fountain stinking of rotting river-fish.

'I reckon we're heading for Crumbly Way,' Larik commented.

'How well do you know these streets?' Ril asked, surprised.

'We've been here five years and backstreets are our natural habitat,' Gryff answered. 'Old Crumbly's the road folk used to take down to Kenside from here, before the Bastion was built and the new roads dug in. You can still use it, if you've a small, light carriage.'

As the periapt burned out and Basia stopped and blinked, looking around, Larik said suddenly, 'Lemme try something,' and ran into a rough-looking tavern.

He reappeared, grinning. 'Success,' he said. 'I know that tavern; I've stood a good few rounds there. So I tossed some coin around and folk remembered a carriage came through that day, on account of it stood out: a two-horse lighter, no insignia, with lacquered dark-green panels. The horses were Ventians. The driver was a big fella, brown beard – and they reckon he had the riverreek.'

Ril looked at Basia. 'Another Reeker: Jenet and Lamgren also had it.' None of them had any idea why this should be a recurring theme.

Basia tuned another of Cordan's discarded periapts, then led them blindly down a winding road following an ancient, very crumbly wall, while Larik ducked into shops he knew; he didn't find anyone else who'd seen the carriage, but passing one sharp bend, he whooped softly, pulled out his dagger and prised some splinters of wood from the wall. Some were lacquered green. 'Couldn't take the turn,' he guessed, pocketing the splinters carefully. 'I can use these later on.'

The next periapt got them all the way down Crumbly Way to the edge of Kenside before Basia sighed and tipped away the residue, powdery flakes of ash. 'I love being right,' she smirked. 'I've got four left. We should tell Dirk what we've found.'

'Later – there's hours of daylight left,' Ril replied. 'Let's keep going.'

Basia relented, so they bought some bread to sustain them and wolfed it down, then she tuned the next periapt and led them through Kenside. The place reeked of dead fish and rotting wood and rats lurked in every dark corner, waiting for the night. The crowds were constant, the poor busy doing whatever kept them fed. Gulls scrapped for morsels, children ran amok and rivermen trawled for whores and grog. But four magi wasn't a group anyone was going to take on.

'What a shit-heap,' Ril muttered.

'That's Kenside for you,' Larik grunted. 'I prefer Tockburn myself. Your Tockers are a better class of ruffian.'

They reached a square of clamouring street-vendors, presided over by an ancient fountain featuring the mould-encrusted image of an old Rimoni water god. Rows of cooking stalls offered skewers of mostly unidentifiable roasted meats. The thick haze from the cooking-fires made it hard to breathe.

'This is where Fisheart blends into Kenside,' Gryff told them as Basia stumbled on round the fountain and into a road that curved down towards the river. 'This is Scuppers Lane, takes you to the docks. Mage or no, keep a hand on your belt-pouch.'

'Got it.' Ril chucked a pair of coppers at a stall-girl and grabbed a skewer. 'Mmm, roast pork,' he murmured. 'That's what the day's been missing.'

'Roast rat, more like,' Larik smirked. 'An' you overpaid her. Leave the buying to me.'

Ril spat out the meat and scowled. 'Sure, always happy to do that.'

Scuppers Lane was redolent with the scents of roasted meat and roots, baked herb-bread and fresh piss. The shops were now mostly ironmongers, rope- and sail-makers, all servicing the riverboats. The air got colder as they headed towards the Bruin, and increasingly fishy. Most of the men they passed sported the distinctive pigtails, short jackets and narrow breeches of boatmen – everything tight so nothing got snagged on ropes – and they looked at the group with disdain, until Larik's hand signals soothed them.

'What's all that about?' Ril asked him.

'Just the Handspeak the rivermen use. If you know a bit of it, folk here pretty much let you be. Picked it up years ago, from an old riverman who settled in Coraine.'

They arrived in the middle of the docklands, where a sea of masts bobbed close by the wooden wharves. 'The river's running high,' Ril noted.

'Aye,' Gryff said, 'it's been raining upstream – turns the Bruin dirty and the Aerflus fills up.'

'I thought that was 'cause you took a huge dump this morning,' Larik snickered. 'We're coming into the Sunsurge, lad,' he went on to Ril. 'Because of the Leviathan Bridge, the empire thinks mostly about the Moontide, but the Sunsurge is *way* more important to the waterfolk. Come winter it's gonna pour and the lowlands'll flood, then the snows will come and freeze your bloody tits off. You watch; they'll be hauling the boats ashore on giant rollers pretty soon – that's why all commerce grinds to a halt every Sunsurge. Two lean years, that's what's coming.'

Ril had been in his twenties, chafing under Takwyth's leadership in Coraine, during the last Sunsurge. 'I do remember snowdrifts taller than horses in 922,' he admitted. 'Will it get so bad here?'

'It'll be bad, but the rivers never fully ice over, not like in the north,' Gryff said. 'Folk are soft here, not like home,' he added wistfully. 'The winters I've seen . . .'

'Don't even start,' Larik grumbled. 'Come on, Gryff, we've got some folks to see.'

Basia was looking tired and drawn; the concentrated gnosis-use was clearly taking it out of her. Ril got some char-roasted fish fillets wrapped in thin bread and a tankard of cider from one of the dozens of tiny trolley-stalls lining the dock.

'Ghastly place,' he muttered, feeling very alien here. Magi seldom used the riverboats, generally preferring windships. Kenside might be only a couple of miles from where he slept, but it was a whole different world, a desperate scrabble for coin and security. 'It's a den of thieves,' he added under his breath.

Basia laughed. 'That's what they say about the Bastion.'

'They think *we're* thieves?'

'Land-owning, tax-collecting, toll-extracting, debt-foreclosing thieves. They may even have a point, darling.'

Gryff and Larik returned; they'd found food and beer, but no fresh information, so Basia tuned another periapt and they made their way along the docks to the Fisheart end, where she swerved and walked out along a pier. Halfway along, the trail ended with a turn to the right so sharp that Basia almost stepped off into the river before Ril grabbed her. That broke her concentration, and the periapt crumbled in her fingers.

She cursed, then looked around. 'Kenside docks—!'

'Aye,' big Gryfflon said, patting her shoulder. 'Well done, lass!'

Ril gave her an admiring grin. 'You're pretty special, Fantoche. But now what?'

Basia was staring out across the waters of the Aerflus. 'There are ferries and private vessels that could go anywhere local – Emtori, Southside, up the Siber and down the Lowater.' She licked her lips, then sighed. 'I'm not sure I can do this on water. The traces don't linger so long, and they're almost gone as it is.'

'Then this is where I take over,' Larik said. He pulled out the tiny splinters he'd scraped from the wall. 'Same game, different rules. See, I'm mostly a sylvan-mage; you know, plant matter and the like. Splinters of wood can be used to find the rest of the same timber – they were all one tree once, right? There's a "sympathy" – like Basia's work with the periapts, only it works different – you'll see.'

He drew them into the shelter of a chandler's to shield the shards from the stiff river winds, then he set one splinter hovering in the air, cradled in a web of green light. It spun slowly, jabbed a few inches northwest, towards the warehouses, then flared and burned up. Larik murmured in satisfaction. 'We've got two more shots,' he announced. 'Come on!'

Larik took them along the docks to a road leading up to Fisheart and tried again in the lee of a tavern. People peered at them until Gryff discouraged their attention, but Ril was fairly sure some of those watching from a distance had been following them for some time, probably since Kenside, but there was little he could do about it.

I just hope none of them are going to run ahead of us and warn anyone.

The next splinter led them along the riverside, past the giant marble statues sunk into the Bruin; the sixty-foot-tall representations of past emperors stood on fluted pillars some fifty yards off shore. From a distance they looked spotless, but closer up, Ril could see they were thickly coated in bird-shit and river-slime. He hoped it would be a long time before a statue of Lyra was erected. *If it ever is . . .*

Finally, the last splinter led them to the transporting business of Lans Yensson, who ran both land- and water-based freight and passenger services from a large stables and yard near the base of Delta Pier, a small but well-preserved dock east of Pilum Hill. In the yard stood a rank of green carriages and they shared a satisfied grin.

Yensson was Hollenian, with blond hair and a reddish stubble, a genial smile and furtive eyes. He quickly recognised who he was welcoming and dropped to one knee before Ril. 'I saw you joust, your Grace, four days prior. So near, yes?'

'Mmm,' Ril replied, not welcoming the memory. Pearl was on the mend, but he wasn't sure the pegasus would ever fully recover. He let Larik describe the carriage, horses and driver, then asked, 'Was this your carriage?'

They watched the man's inner debate, which quickly resolved in favour of not antagonising four Bastion magi, one the Prince-Consort. 'It was: I can show it to you.' Yensson took them to a stable where a carriage was being repaired. 'The panels were damaged,' he said, pointing to the grazed side. 'Good thing I take a bond payment; these lacquer panels don't come cheap.' He cuffed the young man sanding down the timbers and sent him away. 'What else can I tell you, your Grace?'

'Who hired it?'

'A man calling himself Shel Thibou. Big man, plump, soft hands with three gold rings. Brown hair but a grey goatee. Hazel eyes and a cinnamon scent. Gold buckle.'

'You've got a good memory,' Ril remarked.

'You need one in this job. I've not met him before, but he spoke like a Pallacian from Gravenhurst. He said he needed the carriage on a one-night hire, to pick up and deliver a passenger from Highgrange to the docks.'

'When did this Thibou return it?' Basia asked.

'The morning after the tourney,' Yensson responded. 'We argued: he'd damaged the carriage, but he disputed the amount of the bond I withheld.' He scowled. 'I don't wish ill of folk, but we didn't part as friends. He struck me as having the Reek.'

Ril frowned. 'We understand he took the carriage to the last pier on Kenside docks. Why wouldn't he use Delta pier – it's right here?'

'That morning we were loading a grain barge for the Lowater – took all morning, so the ferries all left from Kenside that day. But he purchased his passage with us.' Yensson wavered. 'Normally it ain't right to give information on a man's passage, your Grace.' He saw Larik reach for his purse and added, 'Nay, it's not the money.'

'We suspect Master Thibou of involvement in child-kidnapping,' Basia said.

'Ah . . .' Yensson looked skywards. 'Well, he did have two children on the ferry with him. They took passage to Aerside Docks, in Emtori.'

Ril and his companions glanced across to the distant western shore of the confluence, where Emtori Heights brooded under grey skies. 'Thank you, Master Yensson,' Ril said. 'Thank you very much.'

Emtori, he mused. The day was almost gone by now, but finally, this felt like progress. There was real money in Emtori Heights, and connections to many of the Great Houses. Argundian and Hollenian refugees had settled it originally, people who'd sided with the empire against their own people in the many border wars that had raged for centuries between Rondelmar and her vassal-states.

Emtori Heights is where Cordan is being held. We'll find him in the morning.

27

Riverreek

Disease

*Where humans gather, disease thrives. Our cities are cesspits, breeding grounds for
every sickness and lurgy to plague our benighted lives. Yet still we flock together.*

JOVAN TYR, HEALER, 783

*Dupenium, Rondelmar, Yuros
Junesse 935*

Garod Sacrecour settled into the Sacrecour family throne – not the
Gnostic Throne of Pallas, but the *real* throne: that of the patriarch of
the Sacrecours in Dupenium. For centuries, whoever ruled Dupenium
also ruled Pallas and the empire.

He was the first Duke of Dupenium who wasn't also Emperor of
Rondelmar, and that destroyed all pleasure he took from either the
throne or the ducal title. *I am the rightful ruler of Rondelmar – I should be
emperor.* He'd already chosen his ruling name, close enough to his own
that there could be no mistaking who it was who had arisen to rule
the known world: Emperor Garodius Dupeni I, first of a new ruling
Sacrecour dynasty.

But the paths that would lead to that moment were still murky, as
treacherous and shadowy as the swirling darkness creeping into this
room. Though he knew to expect this, it still turned his mouth dry as
suddenly the shadows surged and *changed*.

The four chairs facing his across the table in his private chamber
were filled – well, not really *filled*, of course, for these weren't *actual*

people but their projected souls, thanks to the affinity known as spiritualism. The semi-transparent images were each cloaked and wearing a Lantric mask. He wished again that he didn't need them.

'Greetings, Lord Garod,' Tear said, her mask dripping ruby droplets from her eyes.

Her voice resonated in his mind, not his ears; any other person present wouldn't have heard anything. But he could see them, and sense their impatience. Greetings were exchanged, then Twoface asked, 'Do you agree to march when we tell you?'

Garod sat taller, wanting to assert himself. 'I'll march when I have guarantees that you really do have Cordan and Coramore, and that you'll release them into my hands at the gates of Pallas as promised.'

'You have our promise,' Angelstar intoned.

'Perhaps you feel that isn't sufficient?' Jest added, the leering, jovial mask sinister in the shadows.

'No, it's not sufficient! I don't even know that you really have the children. I don't know that they're *alive*. You tell me that Canossi and Klief will support me, but I have no word from them. You tell me there'll be a new grand prelate, but I hear nothing to support this.' He pointed at Jest. 'Give me something that's solid, damn you!'

'Perhaps this will convince you.' They all spoke together as a pair of rings clanked dully on the table surface. He gasped – spirits couldn't cause objects to simply appear. Then he followed the lines of force and understood: these spirits had flown the rings from Pallas – or wherever the children were being held – to this room, three hundred miles away. It was simple kinesis – except it wasn't simple, if they'd done it in an evening, nor easy. It would have taken great power and precision.

He examined the rings: they were either the genuine royal signets or extremely good copies. He touched them, and got a vision of Cordan and Coramore, asleep in different cells. It wasn't conclusive proof, but he could detect no illusion . . .

'Very well,' he said. 'Assuming I agree, what do you ask of me?'

'That every mounted fighting man you command set out for Pallas towards the end of Junesse,' Tear answered.

'Have them arrive on the second day of Darkmoon, the day after the Synod begins at the Celestium,' Angelstar clarified.

'But riders can't storm the city gates,' Garod protested.

'They won't need to,' Jest smirked. 'You'll arrive to find the Bastion and Celestium in our hands already.'

'And the city gates will be flung open for you,' Twoface concluded.

Garod leaned back on his ancestral throne, considering their words. *The Bastion and Celestium captured? The gates of Pallas open? Could it be?* 'What about the other dukes?' he asked.

'Klief have promised they won't interfere,' Jest replied.

'Canossi and Aquillea also,' said Angelstar.

'And the Dukes of Midrea, Andressea and Brevia likewise,' said Twoface.

'Garod,' Tear said quietly, 'all you need to do is ride into the city and restore order. It'll be 909 all over again.'

He clenched his fists as visions of a triumphant return swelled behind his eyes. 'And the children?'

'Will be delivered to you at the city gates,' the four masked figures replied. 'You have our promise.'

He stared at the phantoms, wondering if their promises were as substantial as their current forms. But they'd delivered so much already: the names of Setallius' agents in Dupenium; the allegiance of the men commanding the legions blocking the road to Pallas, and access through their people to Lyra Vereinen's inner court. He fingered the rings they'd brought him: solid, real . . . gold.

Mater-Imperia Lucia always said that some risk was inevitable when great decisions had to be made, and though he'd hated the bitch with a vengeance, she was usually right. 'Very well,' he said. 'We'll be there.'

Pallas, Rondelmar, Yuros
Junesse 935

When the tides were right, dozens of ferries could be found on the Aerflus, navigating the treacherous swirl of water that poured in from the Bruin and the Siber respectively. The Bruin's headwaters were in the mountains of Brevia and the forests of Andressea and Schlessen and the river was often filled with logs and storm wreckage from weeks-old weather. But the Siber came tumbling down from the higher lands to the south around Lac Siberne, flowing clearer and cleaner and faster, striking the confluence in a white tumult and causing the powerful surges and whirlpools that made being an Aerflus ferryman as much a calling as a job.

It was also a good place to dump bodies: catch the right whirlpool and they might never resurface. Ril learned that morsel of local knowledge from the ferryman taking them across, the morning after their discoveries in the docklands of Kenside.

The ferryman, a rangy man with a long forked beard, constantly fingered an amulet of Shaermuth, the pagan god of the Aerflus: a green-skinned giant with the head of a squid who supposedly lurked beneath the largest whirlpools, sucking the unwary under the waves then rending them with his tentacles and devouring them. The ferrymen drizzled frequent libations of alcohol to appease him.

'When He's drunk, Shaermuth dun't feel hungry,' the ferryman explained. 'He'll vomit ye back up if ye fall in!' He poured another mouthful of wine over the side, ignoring Larik and Gryff, who clearly thought it a shocking waste.

Basia, sitting beside Ril on the narrow wooden bench, was still drained from the complex trace-spells she'd been using the previous day. Ril had an arm around her to keep her steady as he admired the skill of the ferryman taking them confidently between the whirlpools and waves.

All river commerce in Pallas operated in the two-to-three-hour windows between low and high tides, and the river was crowded this morning with all the vessels that had been waiting patiently upstream.

'What's the plan?' he muttered to Basia.

'Dirklan's meeting us over there – he's bringing a skiff. I've got two more scrying attempts with Cordan's broken periapts,' she said, as their ferry swooped through the debris, scraping against a submerged log and knocking aside a drowned cow before catching the edge of a whirlpool and being pushed on their way. Inside another quarter of an hour they were clambering onto the solid wooden docks at Aerside below the eastern slopes of Emtori Heights. The docks were anchored by massive tree-trunk piles and sylvan, Water- and Earth-gnosis, to bind the wood and stone and repel the damp. Waves were hitting the sea-walls hard and the rest of the city – Pallas-Nord on one side and Southside on the other – was hidden by the spray.

Setallius was waiting for them on the pier, his silver hair blowing in the wind. Behind him was a burly man, bald, but with a thick beard, twin throwing axes scabarded across his back: Mort Singolo, his bodyguard. He patted Basia fondly on the arm before bowing, the minimum degree, to Ril. 'What have you got, Basia?' he asked.

She repeated Yensson's description: 'Shel Thibou; plump, with soft hands and three gold rings. Brown hair and a grey goatee, hazel eyes. He had the children with him, and possibly had a ginger-bearded driver. I think they came here.'

Singolo nodded. 'I grew up in Emtori. All the passenger ferries come here, to Pier Seven – the other piers take the river-trade.'

'It's the rich who use the ferries and they were all at the tourney,' Setallius mused. 'The water-traffic would have been light. Hopefully they'll have stood out.'

Singolo took the Joyce brothers with him, to ask questions of the wharfmen, while Ril and Basia sat on the pier and brought Setallius up to date, watching the tide change on the Aerflus and the confluence emptying of shipping as the risks increased. The spray from the waves striking the docks obscured the far shores, but it was still sunny above. The sixth day-bell chimed: midday.

'Why would the kidnappers come here?' Basia wondered. 'If I were them, I'd have gone straight to Dupenium.'

'They might have feared I'd intercept them if they risked the journey to Dupenium,' Setallius said. 'We started watching the skies and roads between here and the northeast from the moment the children vanished. And I have men inside Garod's household; his spymaster will know that.'

'If it's not the Sacrecours, who is it?' Ril asked. 'Opportunists, as Wurther suggested the other day?'

'Someone who feels that they can control the Sacrecours?' Basia suggested. 'People who see Cordan as means to an end, rather than the rightful ruler?'

'Using him to displace Lyra, while setting up a second coup afterwards leaving them in control?' Setallius pondered, then admitted, 'We don't know enough.'

A soft swish behind them heralded Singolo, who rumbled, 'We have something. The name "Shel Thibou" meant nothing, but one of the ferrymen remembers the fare: it was unusual, because it diverted to the old docks in Surrid – that's in southern Emtori, a poor area. A party of five, including two children.'

'Then that's where we should go,' Ril said.

'Aye,' Singolo said, 'but the reason the fare was unusual was that it went straight into the new quarantine area in Surrid: the one set up for the riverreek outbreak. People are dying in there, so no one goes there by choice.'

'Unless they have no fear of the riverreek,' Setallius said. 'Let's take a look.'

The closer to the quarantine zone, the deader the streets of Surrid became. The air stank: the horrible wood-and-roasted-meat stench of mass cremation. When they reached the enclosure they found hurriedly constructed walls blocking the street, though the barricade was solid, bolstered with Earth-gnosis. The moans of the ill carried from within. They found a vantage point upslope where they could look down into the square: it was full of debris, but no one was sitting in the sunshine; the only people moving were a dozen monks of Kore, who were burning corpses in one corner of the enclave.

When they went down to the northern entrance, the only way to reach the Surrid docks without going by boat or windskiff, they found a full cohort of Kirkegarde. As they stepped into view, the twenty Church soldiers stopped and stared at them in exactly the same way; it was uncanny and unnerving, the way they all moved at once – and it convinced them all they were in the right place, for it was *very* wrong.

Then a wagon rolled by, an open-framed animal cage on the back, stuffed with another dozen or more infected men, women and children, all shaking, pale and red-eyed with streaming noses and bloodshot eyes. Ril held his breath as they passed, and shuddered as a young boy with pleading eyes reached out towards him through the bars: an impotent, useless gesture.

'Riverreek was *never* this bad,' Basia muttered.

Setallius nudged Ril. 'Let's go somewhere we can talk.'

They found a near-deserted tavern, the only other person present the old woman behind the bar. Her hands shook as she poured for them; her nose was streaming and she kept wiping her hands through the trail of mucus – by the time she'd brought their drinks, not even Larik and Gryff wanted a drop.

'What do we do?' Ril asked.

'The way I see it, we have two options,' Setallius replied. 'We go in soft or we go in hard. We could do it subtly, creep in and look around, but the problem with that is that if we're noticed, messages will be swiftly passed and the children hidden again. The quarantine area is a mile long and half as wide; it's a veritable maze of ramshackle buildings wedged together. The chances of just the four of us finding anyone there is minimal – but if I bring in the Guard, whoever's got them will get plenty of warning.' He sighed heavily, and looked around the table. 'Any thoughts?'

'I still have a couple of Cordan's old periapts, enough for one more scrying attempt,' Basia offered. 'The trouble is, we don't know where to start from. So I can't do my "snail-trail" trick; whatever I do will be a short, sharp jab, just to try and punch through any wards and scry him.'

'The longer we go without finding them, the more chance we never will, in my view,' Ril said. 'If we've only got one shot, then let's try it now.'

'I agree with that,' Singolo said. 'We have to move fast: scry the boy, locate him, even roughly, then flood the area with men and tear it apart.'

'One chance . . .' Setallius mused. 'It's a lot to place on one spell, but I think I agree.' He leaned in. 'Listen. Here's what we'll do . . .'

Setallius and Singolo left to set up arrangements and Gryff and Larik went for a look around, leaving Ril and Basia alone with a bottle of wine which had arrived corked and waxed, so they could trust the contents. Ril looked at Basia admiringly. For someone who'd lost all that she had, and missed out on so much more, she constantly amazed him. 'You, Singolo – you're not ordinary people, are you?'

'Dirk recruits among the overlooked,' Basia replied. 'Ordinary magi end up as knights, battle-magi, clergymen or scholars. It's misfits like me who join the Volsai.'

'I don't know any other Volsai,' Ril replied, 'but I'll take your word for it.'

'You might be surprised who you know,' Basia said with a smile. 'One of Lyra's ladies; one of your personal guard, a few servants – most of our people aren't magi, just ordinary people who supplement their pay by passing on information.'

'What, secrets and the like? Who's screwing whom?' Ril wrinkled his nose. He despised tattlers and sneaks.

'They risk their lives for your safety, O Mighty Prince,' Basia replied. 'But actually, it's mostly just statistics: the number of travellers through the city gates, a few names if they're prominent citizens – so that Dirk can see the patterns. We'd love to know more, but we don't have the resources.'

They sipped the wine – it was *very* average – then Ril asked softly, 'Do you still dream about the well?'

Basia exhaled heavily. 'I used to, but Dirk used mystic-gnosis to filter the memories. Before that, I'd wake up screaming every night.'

'I couldn't stand enclosed spaces, not for years,' Ril admitted. 'No closed curtains – I had to be able to see the sky, every second. I still won't go underground.'

Basia looked at him, her eyes filled with empathy. 'What a pair we are.' She unstrapped her legs and rubbed the joints through her breeches, wincing and sighing at the pain-pleasure. 'By evening, I'm a wreck,' she said.

'And healing, morphic-gnosis, still can't do anything more?' Ril asked. 'There's nothing new come up?'

'We've tried *everything* – every trick in the book, and a few more besides – but the truth is, the energy needed to make something from

419

nothing is so *unbelievably* massive, and the pain is *excruciating*. Even trying to extend my thigh-bones a little – I just couldn't do it. I accepted what I am a long time ago, and now I just make the best of it. Dirk taught me how to do that. He was very gentle with me.'

Gentleness wasn't something Ril associated with Setallius. 'Do you love him?' He'd never dared ask that before, but this felt like the right moment.

'Of course – but not in the way you mean. He's twice my age, Ril, and his passion is his work. And I've come to terms with living without that sort of thing, you know that. Look, can we talk about something else?'

'Holy Kore, Fantoche,' he sighed. 'One day things will be better.'

Other patrons came in from time to time while they chatted, but not enough for a small tavern to survive on. Then Setallius and Singolo reappeared, wraithlike in the mists that rolled in late in the afternoon. 'It's nearly dusk, and I've got three centuries of City Guard moving into position outside the quarantine zone,' Setallius told them. 'They'll be ready in an hour, when the second night-bell rings. A few minutes before that, Basia will cast her scrying so we can get a sense of where they need to be, then we'll get them inside as swiftly as possible.'

'What if there's resistance?' Singolo wondered.

'I've told the centurions I want no casualties, but if swords are drawn against them, they must protect themselves.' He stood up. 'There's a church on the edge of the quarantined area; the steeple overlooks the whole place: we'll cast the spell there so Basia has a chance of aligning her scrying with visible landmarks.'

They took to the streets, six cloaked figures wrapped up against the night. There were guardsmen on patrol but few others out, as if there was an undeclared curfew. Saint Chalfon's Church was built into a block of shops, barely distinguishable except for the religious icons over the door and the steeple above. Setallius opened the doors with a spell and they stole inside, shivering at the dank air. There was a crossed-keys-and-tree motif on a bronze plaque before the altar, Ril noticed in passing, and grilled openings in the floor partially illuminated the catacombs below. He wondered where he'd be buried, then banished that morbid thought and followed the others up the bell-tower stairs.

At the top, there was just room for them all to sit, legs dangling into the belfry, facing a heavy bronze bell. Moonlight shone down through the slates, carving bars in the darkness. The sea of roofs stretched north and south; the dimly lit bulk of Emtori Heights blocked out the west. Eastwards, the Bastion and Celestium cast glowing reflections into the turbulent Aerflus. Pallas looked positively Imperial tonight: a prize worth defending.

'There have always been close ties between Emtori and the Celestium,' Setallius commented. 'Argundians take their religion seriously. During the Canonical Crisis of 818, the grand prelate preached against Emperor Voscarus and demanded Scripture-based laws for the entire empire. Voscarus regarded this as an attempted coup and blockaded the Celestium, trying to starve the clergy into submission. Many in Emtori supported the Celestium and at night they ran the blockade from here in Surrid. The clergy held out for nine months, by which time there wasn't a rat or toad left in Fenreach Swamp. Then Voscarus seized the Surrid and Aerside docks and arrested a number of families, and that finally broke the smugglers.'

Setallius didn't give history lessons for nothing. 'Where are you going with this?'

'Well, if I were a grand prelate who'd never forgiven the Corani for stealing both the royal children and Lyra Vereinen from under my nose, recovering the children and restoring them might be something I wanted to do. But the Celestium is a cesspit of treachery, and Wurther knows I have many agents there. So in many ways, hiding them in Emtori until he's prepared the ground for a coup makes sense.'

'And,' Basia added, 'the prelates are gathering in Synod at the end of Junesse, less than two months away.'

Ril ran his fingers through his hair. *Could this be true? Church versus Crown?* The looks on Setallius and Basia's faces told him they believed it possible.

Basia pulled out the last of Cordan's failed periapts. It was time to cast her spell. She conjured a swirl of light, cupped it in her hands and began muttering – not *magical* words, as the ignorant thought, just a litany of reminders to engage all her senses. Moments crawled by; a difficult scrying was never an instant thing. While Gryff and Larik kept watch, Ril, Dirklan and Mort held their breath, waiting.

Then a small lance of light shot away south; Basia threw her hand out in the same direction and kept it extended. 'That way; perhaps half a mile,' she panted, then the light fizzled away in a cloud of tiny sparks and she sagged against Ril, who was staring in the direction she'd pointed.

'There . . . see that tall building among the roofs? *There!*'

'I know the place,' Setallius said, conjuring light of his own now. A face appeared: a helmed man. 'Centurion, seal off the blocks either side of the Shipping Inspector's Offices on Washgate Road.' He dismissed the image and already heading for the stairs, conjured another. 'Washgate Road,' he cried, 'move in!'

By dawn, it was apparent that Setallius and his men weren't going to find the children easily. Ril had carried Basia down to a pew and watched over her as she drowsed until eventually he slept too, so that when the cleaners arrived in the predawn gloom to prepare for the sunrise mass, they were startled to find their Prince-Consort asleep with a strange woman.

More fuel for the gossips, Ril sighed as he and Basia left to meet the spymaster at the northern gates.

'Nothing,' Setallius told them. 'We've found *nothing*.'

Ril cursed silently. 'Was there any trouble?'

'None. The Kirkegarde stood aside and let us in. The people inside – Kore's Blood, it's pitiful in there. We need to get many more healer-magi in here. These quarantines are being woefully neglected, and that was never the intention.'

'So what now?' Basia asked.

'We keep looking. We're still uncovering cellars and below-ground basements that even the homeowners claim to have been unaware of, so something could still turn up. But for now, you two might as well return to the Bastion.'

It felt like a defeat, to return to Lyra and admit that the axe was still hanging over their heads.

*

'Did they come close?' Angelstar asked in his flat, menacing voice.

Ostevan, masked as Jest, wasn't alone in the Vertonius chapel; Jenet Brunlye and Bruss Lamgren were lurking like statues in the shadows. It was too risky for them to be seen abroad, but he still had uses for them. His fellow Masks were just projected images. 'They came close,' he admitted.

'I was near enough to Cordan to sense the scrying,' Lady Tear said pensively. 'I have no idea how a scrying could penetrate the combination of wards and solid stone, but *someone* did – I took the children deeper and sealed the tunnel behind me. No subsequent attempt was made.'

'Something personal to the prince?' Twoface suggested.

'Possibly,' Tear agreed, 'but the crisis is over. We still have our prizes, and the day we strike approaches.'

Ostevan had theories about his fellow conspirators' identities and motivations, but in truth, he wasn't certain of any of his guesses. Angelstar was clearly a knight, and he was only interested in the Celestium, so a Kirkegarde man, then, or Inquisition. Twoface also had the bearing of a knight, but his personality seemed *uneven*, as if he were conflicted within. *Twofaced indeed*. And Tear was a puzzle: definitely a Corani, like himself, but very much against Lyra – someone of ambition who saw herself as wife of an emperor, perhaps? He thought she was young, maybe thirty or so, but that might be illusion; what was clear was her shrewd callousness.

'Let's talk about that day,' he suggested.

'Yes,' said Twoface, 'we know the plan, but some details are unresolved.'

'Very well' – Tear spoke tersely – 'on the first day of Darkmoon, the last week of Junesse, we'll strike at both Bastion and Celestium. Our "Reekers" will create disorder and keep the Guard busy. Queen Lyra will be taken and sent to the Master. The senior Corani supporting her will be slain, and those we control installed in their place. Cordan will be presented to Garod Sacrecour at dawn when he arrives to restore order.' She paused, then said, 'I have my own plans for Coramore.'

'She's yours,' Angelstar said. 'Only Cordan matters.'

'The time has come to choose our roles,' Twoface said. 'There are two targets, and four of us: two of us need to be in the Bastion, and two in the Celestium. Both are formidable objectives – we can't favour one over the other.'

'My place is in the Bastion,' Tear said. 'I'm indifferent to the Celestium.'

'As I am to the Bastion,' Angelstar replied. 'Once Wurther is deposed, I will secure the Rymfort.' That aligned with Ostevan's suspicions about his identity. 'What of you, friend Jest?'

Behind his mask, Ostevan bit his lip. He'd been delaying his choice, seeking a sign – not an actual 'sign', of course; he wasn't a Sydian shaman! – but some small event that would tilt his decision. His bitterness towards Dominius Wurther had drawn him back to Pallas, and that hadn't faded. But Lyra Vereinen intrigued him: she *mattered*, and he was increasingly sure she could be of immense value to *him*. The rapport he'd cultivated with her made him ideally placed to be the one who took her.

But to be Grand Prelate is why I started on this path in the first place . . .

He glanced at Twoface, who was also undeclared. 'You first?'

'The Bastion,' Twoface said shortly.

'Then I shall take the Celestium,' Ostevan decided, wondering if there was some way of fulfilling both desires. 'Brothers, Sister: I strongly believe Queen Lyra should be captured intact, not infected.'

Tear rounded on him. 'My understanding is that the Master insists she be infected that night, and she shall be.' The malice in her voice conveyed very personal feelings toward Lyra Vereinen.

Twoface remained silent.

'But if she is, as we suspect, a dwymancer, infecting her may destroy her ability to use the dwyma—'

'We don't know that,' Tear interrupted. 'We will proceed as the Master desires.'

Ostevan bowed his head, feigning concession. 'You're right, of course. Let's get busy then. The chosen date is approaching swiftly and we have much to prepare.'

'Where are we with the prelates?' Angelstar asked.

'I have "persuaded" fourteen to join us. You?'

'I have eleven, and the rest will be thinking our way, come the time. Wurther will stand alone.'

Soon after the meeting broke up, but Ostevan left his awareness lingering in the aether, just on a suspicion . . . and sure enough, another presence duly reformed.

Twoface turned his genial half-face towards him. 'Brother Jest, why should the queen matter to you?' he asked. 'I thought your goals were aligned to the Holy City?'

Ostevan considered, then carefully asked, 'Have you noted that in all our dealings, the Master has never shown the slightest fear of anything or anyone – except the dwyma. And here we have someone who could be the first dwymancer in five hundred years and he wants her enslaved and potentially ruined.'

Twoface's mask seemed to smile more floridly still. 'And you worry that one day, when we have won the world for our Master, that he might not feel so benignly toward those who won him his throne? So you desire a weapon against him?'

Ostevan was impressed. 'I've underrated you, Brother Twoface.'

'Brother Jest, when you win us the Celestium, you'll control access to the heart of dwyma on Urte: the Shrine of Saint Eloy. I will ensure that it is I who takes the queen, not Tear. After that, I believe we may find much in common.' He half bowed his head and departed, and Ostevan returned his awareness to the darkened chapel.

He removed the Jest mask and basked in the unfolding of a new dream: *Emperor-Pontifex, with daemonic powers in one hand and a dwymancer queen beside me . . . a partnership none could withstand . . .*

28

Spirit-Caller

Hermetic: Animism

It may sound trite to say that becoming a beast for a while changes you, but it does: you're never the same after you've eaten grass or raw flesh or flown or run or crawled with limbs that are not human. Your whole perspective of life changes. What did it teach me? That we are, all of us, both predator and prey.

HERARD RAMOSEZ, ESTELLAN BATTLE-MAGE, 901

Mollachia, Yuros
Maicin 935

Sacrista Delestre drifted through churned snow and charred timbers, prodding at the bodies of men whose faces she vaguely recognised. The scout who'd found them said he'd heard fighting and seen the flames, but the fray was over before he could intervene. She doubted he'd tried too hard.

He heard them chant 'Sarkany' – so Kyrik, or Valdyr?

There had been similar raids all over the kingdom, men appearing like phantoms around dusk and killing savagely, but this was the first time they'd killed a battle-mage. Of course, few of the battle-magi even went on patrols – they were far more likely to be found anywhere the drink flowed and the fires were warm, depleting her brother's wine cellar and making whores of the daughters of Hegikaro. No one wanted to be out on frozen nights like this – it was supposed to be spring, but it felt more like winter. *What a Kore-bedamned place!*

She found the body she sought and tried reading the gnostic traces.

Halbertyr's corpse was in two pieces, his torso, still in bloody silks, lying three feet away from the head. She crouched down, touched his frozen flesh to remind herself what his gnostic trace felt like, then tried to sort through the residues of the other spells. Someone had killed a half-blood mage: surely that meant another mage?

Halbertyr's body had a great many stab wounds, the result of a frenzied attack. She noticed something clutched in his right hand: a knot of black hair, burned at the ends, and she stroked them, trying to draw out traces . . . The gnostic aura clinging to the hair was strangely blank, but she knew it: *Valdyr Sarkany.*

She straightened, frowning. Halbertyr had been an arrogant ass, but he'd been one of *her* legion, *her* people. She glanced over her shoulder at the small group of centurions watching her. *Father entrusted his legion to Robear and me. We've got to strike back.*

'Clean up this mess,' she snapped and stalked away. Robear would have clapped the survivors around the shoulders and told them they were heroes, but she'd never been able to do that, especially not when most of them leered at her whenever she turned her back. *Damn them all. They don't deserve praise.*

It would be so much easier if the governor would actually commit his men to helping subdue the rebels, but Inoxion was just milking the situation, waiting for them to fail. *He can go to Hel too.*

She reclaimed her mount and packhorse and led them to a cliff-top overlooking the scene. For a while she stared out over the sea of trees, wondering how to end this aggravating guerrilla war. The Mollach insurgents were proving dangerously elusive. Normally finding a non-mage was relatively easy, but this kingdom was a nightmare, with its deep forests and mountains riddled with caves. And who knew snow could block scrying just as water did?

Her magi had tried using birds controlled by animagery to find their fugitives, but outside a mile or so they lost control of the creatures. Scryings were repelled by stone, water, snow and darkness – and anyway, you needed to know who you were looking for. The forests were teeming with life, so tracking-wards designed to trigger when trodden upon were set off by everything except their quarry. Hunting hounds were foiled by rivers and streams, and it was perilous using skiffs in this horrendous, unpredictable weather – and anyway, the forest gave ample cover. The enemy knew every hidden path, and they knew none. And the populace refused to be cowed.

We've only got a year left here, but we've extracted barely a tenth of the wealth Father's demanding. The mines are only just coming back into production and the river traffic's only now beginning to flow. We need a breakthrough, or we'll have those bastard Augenheim bankers at our throats.

But now she had some of Valdyr Sarkany's hair: an amateur's mistake, and she was going to make him *pay*. Her affinities were in Theurgy – mind to mind – and Fire, but she had some strength in wizardry. That was a dangerous art, not to be used lightly, but it was also the best way to exploit what she'd found. She was working through her options when a gnostic call tickled at her mind. *<What?>*

<Tetchy, Sis!> Robear was drunk. *<Did you find anything?>*

<Yes. Halbertyr's dead. We've lost fifty-six rankers in three days and you've not even left the castle—>

<Hey, someone has to charm the investors, and you're useless at it. I've got Midrean traders crawling over me. All the bastards do is drink me out of wine, then sell me more.>

<If I can't stop these raids, those traders are going to take fright and leave us with empty purses.>

<Your purse has always been empty, that's half your problem,> Robear sniggered.

<Rukk you, arsehole!>

He fell silent, then replied in a meek voice, *<Sorry, shouldn't have said that. Let's just each do what we're good at, huh? It's how we've always worked.>*

<Yes, fine – go away, and don't call again.> She broke the connection so abruptly it started a headache, which took a few minutes of rubbing her temple to ease. Then she opened her eyes again and stared into space.

Oddly, it was the bleak loneliness of the vista that calmed her. She sat and shivered as the clouds streamed by overhead and the wind in the pines moaned below. She'd climbed high enough to not be overlooked and she felt like some pagan hunter-goddess, sniffing out her prey. The bleakness crept into her soul and soothed it.

I could live here – but Robear couldn't. Her brother was desperate to return to Midrea, where he and his backslapping cronies and licentious ladies scavenged the courts like crows on a carcase. She'd always hated it, the gossip and the backstabbing and the constant assumption that she was a whore or a safian, when she was neither.

Rukk him. After this, I'm getting out and living in the wilds for a while. But first, we need to capture and kill these bastards. Her men were getting more and more frustrated chasing ghosts and her father was demanding they start butchering innocents to drive out the guilty – Robear was lean-ing that way now too. She was the only one advocating more rational methods so that the investors didn't take fright.

These Mollachs don't understand that I'm the one keeping the hounds leashed.

Which brought her back to Valdyr's hair. She checked again that no one else was around, then marked out two summoning circles with silver dust from her belt-pouch, burning them into the rock with Fire-gnosis. She pulled saddlebags from the packhorse's back and arranged the grisly contents in one circle, then stepped into the other, the circle that would protect her, and began her summoning . . .

The aether was partly of this world and partly of *elsewhere*. The dead passed through it, but there were other spirits that dwelled *within* it: invisible, timeless observers of human life, largely unable to intervene, unless a mage used Sorcery to interact with them. Some were reve-nants, the spirits of the dead – and not just human dead – but these were usually transitory, most dissipating or passing on after a brief time. Necromancers specialised in dealing with such spirits. The other ones, the daemons native to the aether, were weak, mostly, and easily controlled, of limited use, but the eldest had existed for millennia, and were much more dangerous – and *useful*.

'*Ajakhiaemus,*' Sacrista called, softly in this world, but loud in the aether, '*Ajakhiaemus, come to me!*'

Her cliff-top perch remained silent and empty, but her heightened perceptions told her that the aether was watching her now and spirits were racing in, attracted by the call. Her body and mind were a prize to them: a weak-minded mage could be destroyed, their psyche fed upon and drained . . . and then refilled. Wizardry destroyed its practitioners more than any other Study: the spirits could leave her an empty husk, a puppet to dance to their tune or a broken madwoman.

The cold wind stung her skin, but she ignored it and concentrated on her gnostic sight, which showed her more than a dozen man-sized pillars of darkness, daemons in their unformed state, swirling around her, testing her wards. She held them at bay, ignoring the harmless distractions of the wind spirits, and concentrated on her call. 'Ajakhiaemus, speak to me.'

'*Sacrista,*' a voice hissed, inaudible to human ears.

'*Sacrista,*' the others echoed, picking up on her name, '*Sacrista! Open up to me!*'

'*Let me in – I will give you pleasures beyond imagining!*'

'*Power – cleave to me and I will give you might beyond reckoning!*'

'*Your ancestors rest inside me – do you yearn to speak to them, Sacrista?*'

She clung to the first voice, reached through her wards and pulled it into the other summoning circle, then swept the others away with an aetheric wind, leaving just her chosen daemon, a pillar of dark swirling inside the circle.

'Ajakhiaemus, thank you for coming.'

The pillar reformed into a male torso of black marble, visible from the waist up, wearing a blank white Lantric mask instead of a face, and flowing black curls.

'*It's my pleasure to serve you again, Sacrista.*'

Ajakhiaemus was an ancient being – maybe no giant among his kind, but his memories extended back to the Lantric city-states. She was proud that she, a mere half-blood, had mastered so old a daemon, but she remained wary: such a one was never truly subjugated.

'Ajakhiaemus, I have a task for you. There's a mage I wish you to find.'

'*I have sensed energies here,*' Ajakhiaemus hissed sibilantly. '*Not often, not sustained, but close.*' He pressed his face to the edge of the circle. '*Thou art lovely, Sacrista. Do you have a lover?*'

'Not everyone is obsessed with love.'

'*Without love, human life is meaningless. I have heard this so often, from so many.*' Ajakhiaemus altered his appearance a little, showing her hips and a solid phallus. '*It saddens me that thy needs are unfulfilled.*'

'My needs are fine,' she muttered. Her life had permitted few liaisons, and they had been mistakes, leaving her feeling soiled and repelled by notions of intimacy. She saw it as a blessing, because it left her mind clear.

'I weep for thee, Lady.'

'Don't bother. I've left the hair of your prey inside the circle: use it to find him.'

She watched as Ajakhiaemus lowered himself to the ground and sucked Valdyr's hairs into his masked mouth. When he straightened, he *was* Valdyr, but only for an instant, before becoming something shapeless.

'Yes. Yes, I'll find this one.'

'You'll need a body to wear in this world,' she said, gesturing towards the gory mounds of animal parts laid out inside his circle. 'Here is flesh for you to wear.'

She made herself watch as Ajakhiaemus inhabited the bloody remains of the beasts, using morphism, animagery and healing to pull together a form to wear. Sinews sprouted from the severed joints and melded with others, pulling and tugging and heaving until it had become something that could stand. The result was a bear's torso and forearms, the haunches and hind-legs of a stag and the head of a wolf with an eagle's eyes. Ajakhiaemus placed the stag's antlers atop his skull for good measure, then made the wounds close and the fur blend.

When he stood, he was well over nine feet tall. He stared at her through the distorting haze of the protective circle. He tried to speak, shaping his mouth until words came out. *'Hnngh-unghhh, da . . . vaz . . . sti . . . Sa . . . Criszz . . . Taaa . . .'* His voice was like stones grating against each other. Then he mastered it: *'Sacrista!'*

She shivered involuntarily at the blood-rimmed eagle-eyes, the corded muscles that bunched and flexed, the bloody claws on its paws. For a moment, blank hatred and lust shone from the daemon's gaze and pierced her through.

'Avaunt, Ajakhiaemus! Be still!' She sent a shimmer of energy through the warding, like lashing him with a whip.

'Peace, Witch! I will not assail thee.'

Carefully, cautiously, she loosed the wardings on his circle. She was still inside her own and unreachable, unless he broke the geas and then found the power to break her defences – that was possible, but unlikely. His physical presence here on Urte would be limited, in twenty-four hours or so her gnostic-bindings would break and his soul would be flung back into the aether.

You will not harm me or my people. She ensured he understood that meant her soldiers. *You will hunt Valdyr Sarkany and take him alive if possible. Kill him only if that is not possible. You will remain open to me throughout, and you will obey my commands.* She had to be able to follow his progress and adapt to new threats. *You will hunt by stealth, until you see the opportunity to strike.* 'Do you understand?' she asked the terrible giant towering over her.

'*I understand.*'

It's moment of truth time ... She dispelled the wards penning him inside the circle and Ajakhiaemus stepped cautiously onto the wet grass and yowled at her hungrily. But after a momentary contest of wills, he turned and bounded away into the forest. She sat within her own protective circle and opened her mind, seeing through his eyes as he crashed through the woods, following an intangible spore. In the first stream, he washed the gore from his body to lessen his scent, then went north and east into White Stag Land.

An ancient daemon like Ajakhiaemus was no single mind, more like a floating spiderweb of intelligences controlled by one central intellect that could be in many places at once. That core of intelligence now resided in the skull of the construct-beast, but the rest could sense and scry on many levels: already he was picking up resonances no mage could ever have detected, while his beast-limbs ate up the miles, pausing only to drink, and then to savage and eat a wild boar.

By dusk, she could sense the daemon's excitement as it closed in on its prey; she could feel the dreadful lust and hunger that filled its chest: a shiver of appetite that ran the length of her spine to wet her cleft and hollow out the marrow from her thigh bones. She opened her eyes, grinning savagely, drool running down her chin in rivulets as she pushed her fingers into herself and began to rub.

Links to such a powerful daemon never went just one way.

*

Three raiding parties, around a hundred men of the Vitezai Sarkanum, met up in southern Feher Szarvasfeld, or White Stag Land. The raids had been successful and they had plenty of plunder, even cattle from the Reztu Valley. The tunnels of the Rahnti Mines weren't suitable for livestock, so they planned to use the Magas Gorge route, a tough path, but their only option to get their plunder back to Lake Jegto.

The backslapping Valdyr was getting over killing the Rondian battle-mage was making him uncomfortable. Yes, he'd struck the killing blow, but it was Iztven and Ghili's victory more than his – although the two old Sydians didn't seem to care.

He joined Dragan Zhagy and Tibor Siravhy at their fire, where they were sipping palinka and exchanging war stories. The two men touched their hearts respectfully as he joined them: they'd faced death together now, and new bonds were being forged. More than that: these were quite possibly his future subjects, if anything – *Kore forfend* – happened to Kyrik. At least he'd shown them that he could fight.

The gnosis will come, he told himself, *and I'll be Kyrik's right hand.*

'We've got thirty head of cattle,' Dragan was saying. 'Once we get them north to Jegto, we'll slaughter them and cure the meat. There'll be enough for the entire campaign. We've made a good start.'

'Where do we strike after that?' Valdyr asked.

'I'm thinking we go south of the river and hit the silver traders as they leave Rejezust. They won't expect that.'

'But wouldn't we be cut off afterwards?'

'Plenty of caves in the south too,' Tibor replied. 'We could spend the whole summer there and never run out of boltholes.'

'But when Kyrik returns, it'll be to Jegto—'

'I'm sure he could find you in a blizzard, lad. But we'll leave some of our people at Jegto to meet Kyrik and guide him to us.'

'I'll take your advice,' Valdyr said. He really wanted to be the one making the decisions, but Dragan and Tibor were far more experienced, so he contented himself with trying to understand their reasoning. They'd been talking for hours and were all yawning—

—when something out in the darkness gave an unearthly yowl, the hunting cry of something between wolf and a much larger *other*, that froze his blood. Dragan paused, eyes narrowing in puzzlement, and that set Valdyr's nerves to trembling . . .

He came to his feet, reached over his shoulder and drew his zwei-handle. All round him, the others were also rising, drawing blades, stringing bows and checking quivers, all looking about apprehensively.

Darkmoon was only days away and Luna was just a crescent. A few drifts of dirty, hard-crusted snow lingered – which was how he caught the movement of something large lumbering across a clearing on the far side of the valley. 'There!' he said, jabbing a finger, but it had already vanished into the trees.

Valdyr was bitterly envious as Iztven and Ghili lit shields, faint trac-eries of pale blue light that cocooned them, then faded from sight. As they hobbled forward he could almost feel the eyes of *something* across the valley swivel and focus fully on him. The sensation reached every one of his senses: like a claw caressing his skin. A low growl resonated inside his eardrums.

'Wolf?' Dragan asked, his voice throaty.

It's more than a wolf . . .

There were four monsters that peopled the tales of Mollachia. The most reviled was the *strega*, an evil witch (who could be male or female); as children, Kyrik and Valdyr had grown accustomed to finding rusted knives under pillows or cloves of garlic bound to their doors, for the castle staff had struggled to accept that their lord had married a mage, not a strega. Such a one must be staked into their grave – a 'witch's grave' – to prevent their spirit from plaguing their enemies after death.

Then there was the *sarkan*, the draken-like creature who protected the realm, but demanded sacrifice in return – Valdyr's family took their name from that very beast. The *strigoi*, the unquiet dead who fed on the blood of the living, were the reason evil men and women were burned in Mollachia, not interred. And finally, there was the *vrulpa*: someone who took beast-shape to kill; legend had it that to despatch a vrulpa, you had not only to hack the head from the body, but the teeth must be turned into windchimes to drive off their kin. *Stronger than Oakhearts, swifter than Night*, the old verse went, *Wild as the Wind, hungry as Fire.*

'Vrulpa,' he whispered now, and Dragan stiffened.

The beast howled again, louder now, from somewhere at the base of a rocky, steep-sided gully maybe two hundred feet from where he stood. All round him, men poked torches onto the fires and lifted them to pierce the darkness as others nocked arrows to taut bowstrings.

'Form up,' Dragan growled. 'Protect your prince—'

As the men began to move, the beast yowled again, the maddened shriek of something goaded to the chase, and a huge shaggy shape broke from cover. Bows sang and arrows flickered, then light flared and the shafts shattered on gnostic shields. The beast raised itself on its hind legs and raced into the clearing, flames crackling along its arms. Its shape was nothing of nature: a stag's hind-legs, a bear's chest, a wolf's head, antlers on its crest: every inch shrieked of *wrongness*.

Kore's Blood! Valdyr gripped his zweihandle, standing his ground even as his legs screamed at him to run.

'*VRULPA! VRULPA!*' the Vitezai men shouted in alarm, firing again, but shields flared and their arrows fell uselessly to the ground – then twin streams of scarlet fire blazed across the dark beast and two men fell, screaming in agony as their clothing ignited.

The vrulpa bounded up the slope roaring, '*SARKANY!*'

29

The Vrulpa

Sorcery: Wizardry

There are beings who inhabit the aether, that shadow-place halfway between this world and the next. They have always been there, or so they say. Most are simple, stupid things, no more dangerous than the birds of the air. But some are as complex and perilous as the greatest magi, and they must be approached with great caution. 'Daemon', we call them, a term that in Frandian implies evil; which is apt, considering the perils in dealing with them.

LORJA LAMACH, VERELONI WIZARD, 856

Mollachia, Yuros
Maicin 935

As the vrulpa crested the slope, its head swivelled until it found Valdyr. Its amber eyes lit like small stars and it screamed in hatred, then ploughed into the first row of men who ran to heroically interpose themselves between the beast and their prince. The vrulpa raised its giant paws and a sheet of flame tore into them, hurling them backwards, hair and clothing ablaze. The creature smashed a spearman's spine on a boulder, then caught another in its antlers, spearing him in half a dozen places, before tossing him aside.

As the men reeled, it fixed its eyes again on Valdyr and screeched, '*SARKANY!*'

'Holy Kore, be with me,' Valdyr prayed. He saw Iztven and Ghili try to block it, chanting something and lighting a mesh of fire, but the beast tore through it and just a heartbeat later had ripped Ghili's head from her shoulder with one great paw-swipe. Then it stamped on Iztven, its hooves caving in the Sydian mage's ribcage, roaring as arrows thudded into its torso. It barely paused to snap them off before it was bounding onwards. Then Dragan stepped in front, his sword drawn, and Tibor took up position on his left, while more of their men converged on the vrulpa, charging in with weapons raised.

Another rolling wave of flame broke over them, sending more men, Tibor among them, rolling to the ground, beating at their clothing – then in a blur of claws and antlers, the vrulpa reared up in the middle of the conflagration and hurled Dragan thirty feet through the air, its gnostic shields effortlessly deflecting all their weapons, swords, spears and arrows alike.

'*SARKANY!*'

Nilasz ran towards it, but the beast's claws struck him, pushing him aside, and he went down in a writhing heap – and then the vrulpa was on Valdyr, swiping at his head with bear-sized claws. Valdyr ducked and swung and the beast caught his blade in its left hand, losing three claws, but closing its palm about the steel, not even flinching as blood sprayed from the lacerated flesh. The other claw swept around; Valdyr tried to wrench free his trapped blade, but succeeded only in tripping backwards down the slope.

The vrulpa laughed, a horribly human sound, and followed, almost contemptuously grabbing the spear someone was trying to skewer it with and planting the weapon in its owner's chest. Then it leaped at Valdyr again and Valdyr dodged sideways to avoid being crushed, but in the dark, he'd lost his bearings and there was no sideways, only down, and he tumbled headlong into the darkness. The air was knocked out of him, his head cracked on a fallen tree trunk that could have broken his neck and he slammed back-first into a half-buried rock, only his armour saving his spine.

The vrulpa appeared at the top of the rise and blazed blue fire at Valdyr, who somehow managed to twist away just in time; instead of incinerating him, the blast struck the rock and smashed an inch-deep furrow, sending stone chips flying. *My sword?* He'd lost it in the fall, but there it was, lying just a few feet away. He reached for it, but the vrulpa gestured and instead it spun to the monster's hand.

'*SARKANY!*' It leaped, effortlessly swinging Valdyr's sword, as Valdyr fled down the slope. Above them, the Vitezai were bellowing his name. Torches appeared on the rim above as the vrulpa came bounding at him, yowling like a wolf. It hacked at him, the sword afire; he dodged behind a tree trunk – and the blade stuck eight inches deep in the timber. The pine shook and its bark kindled as the beast pulled the blade free, then a flurry of arrows sleeted down. Most snapped on the creature's powerful shielding, but one got through and buried itself in the beast's back – it barely noticed.

Valdyr turned and ran again, dodging mage-bolts as he zigzagged down the slope, until a ball of fire blazed over his left shoulder and burst into the bush he'd been making for. He veered the other way, leaped down the bank and into a tiny stream, but he misjudged, caught his foot on an unsteady rock and stumbled, howling in silent agony as his ankle gave way and he came crashing down into a few inches of icy water.

He peered around to see the Vitezai were far above him – it was alarming how far he'd dropped in the last few seconds – then rolled over and tried to rise, but his ankle screamed and he fell to his knees. He had no time to get to his feet because the vrulpa had landed a dozen feet away, his blade raised, howling triumphantly.

This is it . . .

But *something else* answered: a bellowing growl, a stag's roar, from somewhere close enough to make the air shiver as it resonated through the gully. Valdyr looked around, terrified, expecting to see another vrulpa, but the monster chasing him had stopped and was sniffing the air. It was raising its blade again, ready to launch its final attack, when something blurred through the trees and launched itself through the air. Whatever it was slammed into the vrulpa's shielding and carved straight through – and now Valdyr could see it was a massive white stag, with antlers that pierced the vrulpa's torso in a dozen places, then the stag planted its hooves and viciously ripped the points sideways, sending the vrulpa hurling through the air . . .

. . . just as the tree it was spinning towards seemed to move – *impossible, surely?* – and with a sickening crunch, the monster's back slammed into the tree and a thick branch burst out the front of its chest.

Valdyr stared as smaller branches – *he would have sworn it was new growth* – erupted from the tree-trunk at an impossible pace before turning like tentacles and slamming their tips into the vrulpa's eye-sockets, ears, nostrils and mouth and flesh. The tree somehow *engulfed* the beast, then ripped it apart – blood spurted, and was immediately sucked into bark and soil. The earth at the base of the tree base boiled with beetles, and in a few moments there was nothing left but a few ripped shreds of dried-up fur and a shattered set of mismatched bones.

Holy Kore be with me . . .

Something snorted behind his ear—

—and he turned and looked up at the white stag silhouetted against the faint moonlight – and shining *through* the creature. Then flaming torches lit the gully, he blinked and in that instant the stag was gone, as if it had never been there. He sat up in the frigid water as the Vitezai streamed down the slope. The monster had vanished too, leaving little more than those few scraps of desiccated hide. His sword lay discarded by the stream.

Rothgar Baredge was the first to arrive, his cloak smouldering, his side soaked with blood, swiftly followed by Dragan Zhagy, directing a stream of abuse at the old gods of Mollachia – until he saw Valdyr, when he fell to his knees, half in the water, crying, 'My Prince! My Prince—!' He seized Valdyr and held him as if he were a child – then he looked around. 'Where's the vrulpa?'

'It's gone,' Valdyr panted, wincing as he tested his ankle.

'*Gone?*'

How in Hel do I explain when I don't really know what I saw . . . 'The White Stag,' he muttered in Dragan's ear, still panting as the *Gazda* helped him rise, keeping his shoulder under Valdyr's arm to steady him. 'It came and . . . well, the beast is gone.'

'The White Stag? You saw it? The land itself protects you, Valdyr Sarkany,' he said, reverent awe in his voice.

Valdyr looked, but found no hoof-prints in the gravel.

Sacrista Delestre lay trembling in her protective circle as wind and rain lashed down. She'd been oblivious to the weather, the pines tossing in the storm, the sliver of Luna lost in clouds, but now she shook herself violently and sat up, pulling her cloak around her.

What the Hel was that?

She kindled her wards, imagining a thousand terrible things. More important than trying to figure out what had destroyed the body of the daemon was where its spirit might now be – if Ajakhiaemus got loose in a human body, what might it not do?

She didn't panic, not yet: daemons did sometimes fail; that was a risk of the trade. Other wizards could break the geas and send the creature back, or some other mischance could free a daemon. A good wizard was always prepared. Ajakhiaemus might have found another body, but more likely it was simply dissipating into the aether. Either way, it only had a few minutes to try and harm her. The daemon would be steaming back along their link . . .

The first priority was always defence, and she rekindled her circle, while trying to work out exactly what had happened: *Valdyr Sarkany was at his mercy, and then . . . What? What did I see? A pale blur?*

Something had struck Ajakhiaemus from behind, punching through the beast's skull, and the daemon's spirit had been ripped from the body. The power she'd glimpsed at that instant was puzzling, but it could simply have been a boar-spear, perhaps wielded by another mage – she'd not seen Kyrik Sarkany . . .

That must be it: Kyrik slew my daemon while it was focused on Valdyr.

She was careful to remain inside her protective circle, drawing on the gnosis to keep from freezing. Now she sensed Ajakhiaemus – not hunting her as a freed daemon might, but disoriented and torn. Once she felt ready, she called him the rest of the way. <*Ajakhiaemus – come to me—*>

<*Lady Sacrista,*> the daemon wailed. In a few minutes, it was back in the summoning circle, a pallid wisp of itself. It formed its mask-face, but failed to manifest further. That her daemon was in this state told her much – but at least it made control simple.

She reached in and re-established her bindings, then asked, 'Did you kill the Sarkany?' It had been hard to tell in the blur of shadows.

The masked face was bowed, its expression bitter. '*Lady, I failed. I had him, but something like a stag – a white stag, appeared and then – I was struck down and cast into nothing.'*

'Damn.' She put her hands on her hips, wondering. It took a lot of time and danger to break in a powerful daemon, and she'd spent several years on Ajakhiaemus. He'd be of no use to her for months after this. She sighed, and let him go. 'Dismissed, Slave.' Then she sank to her haunches, fighting her disappointment. She'd really thought this would solve all their problems.

It should have worked. What went wrong?

Magas Gorge, Mollachia
Maicin 935

Valdyr Sarkany sat on a ledge overlooking a thundering waterfall in Magas Gorge. It was dusk, and the raiders were strung out along a series of small campsites, all with covered fires and concealed tents. The weather was mild now, by Mollachian standards at least, and they'd seen Rondian skiffs in the air, trying to pick up their trail.

He'd been thinking about Iztven and Ghili, wondering how a legend could bring two people across such distances, and why they would abandon their quest to die protecting him. Barbarians though they were, he'd almost liked them. Only a few days ago they'd saved his life against the battle-mage, and now this ... He'd buried them himself, given them a proper Kore burial, even though they were pagans.

May Kore forgive them their sins ...

Since the monster's attack, Dragan had abandoned the notion of raiding south of the Reztu, fearing that if one such creature could find them, others could too. The men still spoke of the beast as a *vrulpa*, but Dragan had a more realistic name.

'They say Robear Delestre's frigid sister is a daemon-caller,' he growled.

Valdyr still couldn't explain the white stag, and Dragan had told him to keep silent about it. 'White stags were seen when Zlateyr died – they're an ill omen.'

One new recruit told them Robear Delestre had hanged the family

DAVID HAIR

of a Vitezai man on suspicion alone, no proof – although most of the secret order were single or widowers, they all had ties to *someone*. Anger was growing among them, and it felt wrong to be retreating north.

'Where do we raid next, Prince Valdyr?' called Dimi from across the fire. The young man with a thin beard reminded Valdyr of a young Kyrik. 'Banezust?' Dimi had family there.

Valdyr was flattered that such a question might be directed at him; it was a sign of growing acceptance and status. The men clearly saw something more in him than he did himself; they'd seen the brutal scars on his back from the floggings he'd endured in Dhassa and equated them with courage, not with weakness and captivity, as he did. And they were all convinced he'd slain the vrulpa.

But he couldn't deny his kinship with them, and the land. Mollachia was hard, yes, but She was his Mother, and She cared for Her children, gave them sanctuary in places where outsiders wouldn't survive. *Perhaps She sent the white stag?*

Valdyr made a noncommittal gesture. 'Dimi, the redcloaks are thick as fleas around the mines. Rothgar's been down there; he's seen them.'

'I've a cousin who's a forester in the lower Magas,' Sandro, one of the scouts, put in. 'He told me the Imperials only patrol the main roads and settlements. They're not helping the Delestres in the upper valley at all.'

'Robear the Red is offering gold for local trackers to guide his patrols,' Nilasz put in. He had his arm in a sling, but refused to rest.

'No true man would accept,' Dragan rumbled.

'I heard the Grzdy brothers had taken it on,' Nilasz replied. 'And some of the Rimoni gypsies from the camp outside Rokafaj. They've got no reason to love us.'

'The Grzdy brothers are scum, and so are gypsies,' Dragan growled. 'My point stands: no *true* Mollach would betray us.'

'I heard it was Matez Grzdy who betrayed the Goldoni family, them who Robear hanged,' Dimi put in, his eyes simmering. 'I'd like to stick a sword in Matez's belly.'

'Where do the Grzdy family live?' Valdyr asked as the men fell silent.

'Are you sure you want to take that path, lad?' Tibor murmured.

Valdyr looked away, thinking, *Kyrik would take a moral stand, but he's*

442

not here. 'If the Rondians can hang our people, Matez Grzdy deserves no less.'

'I'm in,' Dimi said instantly.

Half a dozen other hands went up, then Tibor reluctantly raised his. 'I'll lead this. Someone needs to keep these young hounds on the leash.' He would take his party back south, a circuitous route that would eventually get them to Ujtabor – a week there, a week back, he predicted. Meanwhile Valdyr and Dragan would take the rest of the men back towards the camp at Jegto, as planned.

Valdyr farewelled Tibor, then he and Dragan led the men northwest, but they'd gone barely a mile when a man trotted down the riverbank and hailed them.

'Hai, Larin,' Sandro called, embracing the newcomer. 'What are you doing here?'

The newcomer went straight to Valdyr. 'My Prince, I have news: your brother has returned to Jegto.' His voice was neutral, hinting at problems.

'Is Kyrik well?' Valdyr asked anxiously. 'Did he bring riders?'

'Ysh, ysh: he arrived four days ago, at the head of a mighty column. He despatched me immediately to find you.' Larin looked at Dragan, his face still troubled. 'Five thousand riders, every one of them a deadly bowman!'

The Vitezai looked at each other uncertainly. This was good news, certainly, and yet Larin clearly had more to say. They urged him to speak on.

'Prince Kyrik says they're just the vanguard,' Larin said. 'Come autumn, the rest of the clan will arrive. Thirty thousand men, women and children, all up.'

Valdyr felt his jaw drop. *He went east to buy a few riders ... What in Hel is he doing?*

Even Dragan looked stunned. 'How will we feed them all?' he wondered, though that was the least of their unspoken concerns.

How will we control *them?* Valdyr wondered.

'Kyrik has brought magi also – eight of their Sfera in the vanguard alone—' Larin shook his head in wonder. 'He said between us and them, we could likely go head to head with the Delestres.'

They all nodded at that, but no one was smiling now. Valdyr remembered the Vlpa camp all too well: the dark faces with judging, demanding eyes, the chest-beating men and fierce women.

Gods, what are we doing to our homeland, letting these savages in? Thirty thousand! Once they're here, we'll not be Mollachia any more . . .

Dragan raised a hand for silence. 'Brothers, we must march north to support our Prince.' The gravity in his voice infected the men. There were no more cheers, just a solemn touch of their right hands to their hearts.

They can sense the dangers here as easily as I can. Kyrik, what are you doing?

While the men prepared to move off again, Valdyr drew Dragan aside. 'What do you make of this?'

'A full Sydian clan? We can't hide that many people. It's going to be open war, Prince.' The *Gazda* looked at Valdyr, his eyes hooded. 'We must force conflict quickly, while only this vanguard group are here: win the victory swiftly, then persuade Kyrik to forbid the rest of the clan entry. Otherwise we'll be swamped.

'How did Kyrik convince so many to come?' he wondered.

'I don't know,' Dragan replied, 'but I doubt we'll like the answer.'

They climbed the gorge for three more days, moving fast between mountain storms that closed in, sealing the skies and drenching them. They were well used to such weather, though, and took heart knowing such conditions would blind their enemy, while they were fit and strong, able to trot for hours without rest, despite the weight of their packs. Hardship was their friend.

Mid-morning on the fourth day, they broke from the Magas Gorge onto the high plateau above Lake Jegto. It was spring now, and where the snow had already retreated the land was coming alive, grass and wildflowers filling the air with a dreamy scent, but ice still clung to the high places.

Before the lakeside camp came into view, they could see hundreds of smoke plumes streaming into the air, and on the hills ahead there were mounted horsemen silhouetted against the skyline.

Dragan was right, Valdyr thought, *there'll be no hiding them.*

Another hour of hard walking brought them among the horse herds, and several dozen rangy horned cattle which were wandering freely and feasting on the new growth like there was no tomorrow – the grass had already been chewed down to the dirt, which was churned and covered in dung.

Riders shadowed them, but none waved or called a greeting until a party of horsemen came trotting towards them, bristling with readied bows. The Vitezai stopped, hands going to sword-hilts, but Valdyr stepped to the fore. 'I'm Valdyr Sarkany,' he called. 'I'm looking for my brother—'

'—and you've found him,' came a joyous call, and Kyrik galloped in, his blond hair streaming in the wind. He vaulted from the saddle and swept Valdyr into a bear-hug, pounding his back, and for a moment Valdyr let himself forget his unease at all these savages.

When Valdyr let him go, Kyrik embraced Dragan, Tibor and many others, while Valdyr looked around him. The Sydian riders were watching, making low comments to each other, their faces unreadable.

There's a few dozen of us, and five thousand of them . . . with many thousands more to come in a few months.

Kyrik returned to him, putting an arm around his shoulder. 'Damn, it's good to see you, Brother!'

'And you,' Valdyr replied cautiously. 'How many men?'

'Five thousand riders: enough manpower to match the Delestre legion.'

'How can we feed them?'

'They'll feed themselves – these cattle? Food on the hoof. All they need is decent pasture.' Kyrik looked animated, positive. 'Remember Thraan? He's aligned to our goals. They needed new land – they were being squeezed out of the plains – and we need people. This is good news, Brother.'

'But we don't have lands for outsiders.'

'Outsiders? They believe as Iztven and Ghili do, that they're our kin—'

'But they're not,' Valdyr said flatly.

Kyrik frowned, finally realising that his younger brother wasn't overjoyed. 'Either way, Val, we need each other. Mollach will die without their aid. We just need to find them grazing land. I'm thinking the Domhalott is perfect for them: plains, open skies, at least eight hundred square miles—'

'That puts them right by the trade routes,' Valdyr noted. 'One raid, and they sever our links to the outside.'

'They won't need to raid. And regardless, that's for the future. There's a battle to fight first.'

A prince must always think ahead, Valdyr thought. *Father always said so.* 'Are they Amteh now? Are those damned missionaries still with them?'

'No, Brother. Paruq's people stayed on the plains.'

'Thank Kore for that.' Valdyr looked away. *This isn't right. Mollachia is our land. We don't just give it away.* But suspicion was blooming. 'What else was required to get them to fight?' he asked.

Kyrik gave him an enigmatic look, then said, 'I married one of them.'

'*You did what?*'

'That was the price required, Brother.'

'You *married* one of them? *Kore's Blood, Kyrik!* What were you thinking?'

Kyrik glanced about. 'Drop your voice, Brother. These men speak our tongue.'

Valdyr swallowed, feeling physically ill, and more than that. He felt *betrayed*. 'Did you get a taste for dark cunni at the breeding-houses?' he spat.

Kyrik gripped him with a gnostically strengthened hand and hissed, 'Be silent, Val: we need allies and I found them – be thankful it's me paying the price, not you.'

'But it's *not* just you, Brother, is it? You're going to breed *mongrel children* with your dunghill bride and they'll inherit our kingdom!' Unwanted images rose from his forcibly repressed memories: women long forgotten with copper skin and ebony-tipped breasts, riding him while grunting like beasts. He locked eyes with his brother, fighting an anger so deep it gripped his spine.

But the eyes he was glaring into were the same eyes that had pulled him through in the dungeons at Hegikaro when water and food were gone. *My brother's eyes* . . . and Kyrik so clearly believed he was right.

Be thankful it's me paying the price . . .

Dragan had seen that something was amiss; he came striding up and placed a hand on either brother's shoulder. 'Lads? Is aught amiss?'

'Ask him,' Valdyr rasped, and stomped away.

30

What Price a Kingdom?

The Tides of Urte

If there is one thing that has shaped Urte, it is our impassable seas. Our two moons – mighty Luna and distant, wandering Simutu – have rendered the continents of Yuros and Ahmedhassa strangers to each other, and perhaps made inevitable the conflicts that eventuated when finally the two land masses were joined.

Always, everything comes back to the divide between East and West.

ORDO COSTRUO ARCANUM, HEBUSALIM, 856

Mollachia, Yuros
Maicin 935

Kyrik Sarkany stood at the rim of a low basin with the two hundred men of the Vitezai Sarkanum seated around him. The Sydians were preparing a formal feast for their new allies, their cooking-fires sending plumes of smoke streaming across the high plain skies, streaks of grey on grey. It was meant as a welcome, but Kyrik wanted to speak to his men well out of earshot of the tribesmen before bringing the two parties together.

He had to make them understand that this wasn't a foolish bargain, but a way forward, the only hope the kingdom had. Valdyr had absented himself, which hurt, but Dragan was here, and most of the senior men; Tibor was still in the south. First he told them of his deal with the Vlpa, and the reasons why.

'We wanted warriors,' he concluded, 'and I was offered five thousand, or none. So let's deal with that first: who here thinks I should have said "none"?'

The basin fell silent and the men shifted uneasily. Then Nilasz stood. 'We've been raiding against Robear's lot and we've hurt them – some more losses like this and these Rondians might just leave.'

There was a small murmur of agreement, but not many; Kyrik took heart from that. 'I've heard the reports and you've done well ... but we lost eight men when Sacrista Delestre sent a daemon against us, and another seven in the raids.'

'We've killed more of them than we've lost—'

'—but they can afford to lose men; they've got ten thousand of the bastards! The Vitezai are what, three hundred, spread over five camps?' He pointed to the Sydian camp. 'Now we're five thousand, three hundred men.'

Nilasz wasn't ready to back down. 'If we armed every man in the valley, we could take the fight to them.'

'If we armed every man in the valley, sure, but we don't have the weapons to do that – look, I don't doubt that when we rise openly, men will come from their homes to join us – but I don't think Ansel Inoxion and Robear Delestre are going to stand by and simply watch that happen. They've got our people under their thumb – they're hanging anyone they suspect of being Vitezai with absolutely no proof whatsoever. There are frightened people down there, and the longer we raid, the more damage Robear will inflict on them, until they begin to break ranks with us. We need to openly confront Robear, and for that we need the Vlpa riders.'

Nilasz shook his head sullenly and sat down.

Kyrik turned back to the group. 'So, if I was right to accept the offer of warriors, there were two prices I had to pay. One, we harbour their *entire* clan. We have unused land in Domhalott – high plains, bad for farming, but they're not farmers. We get warriors, they get land. Your views?'

'Just the obvious one,' Rothgar called, not bothering to stand. 'What if they decide they'd rather pasture their herds in our grain farms at Lapisz or Hegikaro instead?'

'Then we have a problem,' Kyrik admitted, 'but that's a problem we can deal with when it happens – and who knows what our circumstances will be then? First, we have two legions of Rondians to get rid of, and I think we're all agreed we can't shift them on our own.'

A mutter went around the dell, but there was no further dissent.

'Right then, here's the second thing: I agreed to tie myself to them in marriage. You all know that I pledged my father I would marry another mage, and no one's ever objected to that – the mage-blood is both sacred and potent. Well, my new wife carries the mage-blood: she too is a quarter-blood.'

A mutter went round the circle and he raised a hand to forestall questions for a moment. 'We all know we don't have the money to do as Father did and buy a quarter-blood wife in Augenheim – especially not if we fail to dislodge Robear Delestre. And I don't think Sacrista likes me,' he added with a grin that brought a chuckle or two. 'But my new wife comes with a dowry of warriors, and she doesn't weaken the Sarkany bloodline, so I ask you all, *have I erred?*'

He let the murmurs swirl about, picking up the undercurrent of acceptance forming. Then someone called, 'A few of the lads are worried at bringing their blood to our royal line, Prince.'

'I'm sure there were plenty unhappy when Rondian mage-blood was brought into the Sarkany line,' he countered. 'I'm a child of that union, and I love Mollachia as well as any of you. The children my wife and I bear will be born in Mollachia, and raised in Hegikaro Castle, Kore willing. They will be Sarkany, and Mollach.'

'Kore willing,' Nilasz echoed. 'We hear these pony-boys grovel to the Amteh—?'

Valdyr must have been talking of what he'd seen, Kyrik realised. 'The Amteh did send missionaries onto the plains, but they *aren't coming here* – and I'm sure Kore missionaries can be found to speak to the Vlpa in time,' he improvised. *If an Amteh missionary could turn heads, perhaps Kore could also?* 'Anything else?'

Dragan raised a hand and everyone fell silent. 'Tell us about "Zillitiya".'

'Ysh, let me speak of Zillitiya,' Kyrik replied. 'A hero among the Uffry-kai, who took his Foxhead warband into the mountains and became an immortal demi-god. Two Sydian ancients came here seeking him, and gave their lives aiding us.'

'We've grown up with tales of our Zlateyr,' a hunter named Juergan Tirlak called out. 'In our stories he's an *Andressan.*'

Kyrik raised his voice above the chorus of agreement. 'Ysh – but the tales say he used a horn-bow at a time no Andressan did. Either way, have you ever met an Andressan who wasn't a stingy prick?'

'Hey,' Larin snickered, 'I'm part Andressan.'

'My point stands,' Kyrik replied, winking, and getting a general laugh. 'With all respect to Larin, I don't care whether I'm descended – through however many generations – from an Andressan or a Sydian. I'm here, and I'm a Mollach. That's what matters. If the Sydians want to claim a Mollach as their hero – well, good for them. Especially if it makes them feel that they're our kin.'

That drew a mixed reaction – the men took pride in their heritage. But the basic sentiment sounded acceptable.

Dragan spoke again. 'There are families here who trace their ancestry to members of Zlateyr's warband, however thin that blood might now be. It's part of who we are.'

'And if Zlateyr's warband were really Sydian horse archers, not Andressan longbowmen, are you suddenly ashamed of your heritage?' Kyrik countered. 'Does it diminish Zlateyr's deeds?'

The Vitezai grumbled and muttered, but after a bit he saw mostly nodding heads and grudging agreement.

'Would your father have blessed your marriage?' Nilasz called.

Kyrik felt a flash of irritation. 'My father left us with a massive tax-debt and gave the vultures from Augenheim a chance to swoop! He's still my father and I respect his memory, but he's not here and I had a decision to make.'

'Is she pretty?' Rothgar asked cheekily, drawing another laugh.

A mental image of his wife flashed before him. 'Ysh, Roth, she's a fine mare!'

'Is it true what they say about Sydian women?' someone else called as some levity entered the gathering.

'It's better than you think!' He rubbed his groin while pulling a pained face. More laughter. 'Any other questions?' When no one raised a hand, he altered his voice to a tone of command. 'We're going to need to move south, lads. The pastures here are too thin for so many cattle and horses. It'll be hard to conceal the march, but my hope is we can make it to Domhalott unchecked. After that, it'll be war – but it'll finally be war on an even footing: we'll have a chance. Are you up for that?'

'We are,' a few shouted, and then to his utter relief, the rest took it up.

He had to stop himself sagging as Dragan stood and bared his yellow teeth. 'Our Prince has done well for us: he has brought us the allies we need and he has my loyalty and respect, as always.' He touched his right hand to his heart. 'And I congratulate him on his nuptials,' the old wolf added. 'May his marriage be fruitful!'

More cheers: the tension was broken and finally their smiles came out, especially when the wind blew cooking smells through the dell and their stomachs turned to more pleasant matters.

Kyrik went to find Valdyr.

Lake Jegto, the Icewater, was at its most beautiful: a dish of deep blue-green clasped in the bosom of the snow-capped Valadons. North of the lake, pine-clad hills rose sharply into the sky. The sunlight was gleaming down, toasting the rocks on the shore.

Valdyr, locked in his own anger, barely noticed. He'd walked far enough away that the alien chatter of the riders wouldn't reach his ears, but the reek of the campfires and the sour fragrance of the cattle carried to him. Cowpats plastered the ground here where the cattle had watered.

They're already smearing their shit all over our lands.

A boot crunched in the gravel behind him and Kyrik called, 'Brother?'

Valdyr didn't want to talk, but this moment was inevitable. He faced his sibling, because he didn't want this to be one of those arm over the shoulder sit-down talks. Kyrik had to earn that right anew.

Kyrik sighed. 'What would you have had me do, Val? It was the only logical course.'

'*Logic,*' Valdyr spat. 'Logic is what creates breeding-houses: doing what *can* be done, without thought to what *should* be done. What have you signed up for, Brother? To fill every quim in the tribe? How many wives did you marry? And how many will you just breed with anyway?'

'Valdyr, I—'

'Shut up – I'm not finished!' Valdyr bunched his fists, unable to not shout. 'Don't they make you sick, Brother? How can you stand to even touch them! They're like beasts – can't you even see that?' Images of dark skin swirled in his mind, and the echoes of humiliations.

Kyrik read that in him and said softly, 'Val, these people aren't the ones who hurt you. They're like us – they use our words; we likely share their blood.'

'And if I could, I'd bleed it out!' Valdyr turned away, mustering his arguments, remembering the centurion from the slave-camps who'd spoken of racial conflict, and how eloquent he'd sounded. 'We have to stay pure, for our *homeland!*'

'Purity?' Kyrik asked. 'What does that mean? What's an Andressan or a Midrean anyway? What does "white skin" even mean?' Kyrik grabbed Valdyr's shoulder. 'Don't tell me you still believe that shit you spouted fresh out of the slave-camp?'

Valdyr swung on instinct, his right fist smashing into his brother's jaw and sending him sprawling on his back. His knuckles screamed as if broken, making him hunch over, cradling his fist in agony.

Kyrik moaned as he struggled to a sitting position, holding his jaw.

'*Rukka-te*, animal lover,' Valdyr rasped, then a wave of pain shot up his arm. *Shit, I think I've broken my hand.*

He closed his eyes against the pain, barely hearing the sound of Kyrik's boots. He looked up as a fist smashed into his face, his nose cracked and blood sprayed as he flew back, the sky arcing over him and the gravel smashing into his back.

He came up seconds later, blood in his eyes and waded in, throwing a flurry of jabs at his brother's *oh so wise and knowing* visage, while Kyrik weaved and ducked and kept hammering steely blows into his midriff. But Valdyr had been in pick-fights in the chain-gangs, while Kyrik had only ever sparred, and after a flurry of feints, he smashed a left-handed blow to Kyrik's jaw, his elder brother's head cracked sideways and he went over the edge of a small drop and crashed through the thin ice, landing in the water – face-down, and not moving.

'Brother – oh Kore—!'

Valdyr leaped from the bank, fell into a hole beside Kyrik and went under himself. He came up gasping and thrashed towards him, got him on his back and dragged him to the bank, where he started hammering Kyrik's back until he convulsed and vomited, then lay shaking on the cold stones.

Kore's Blood, I could've killed my own brother . . .

All his anger turned to shock and remorse, and even more so when he realised that Kyrik could have used the gnosis against him and hadn't. His eyes closed, he sensed people closing in, then Dragan was there, hauling him to his feet and throwing a fur cloak over him before leading him back to the fires, where someone poured heat down his throat. He didn't lose consciousness but drifted, clinging to the sound of Kyrik's voice as he had in Hegikaro's dungeon, letting it draw him slowly back to life. When he was truly aware again, he was still wet but warmer, and steam was rising from his sodden clothes. His nose was blocked with dried blood, so he sucked in air through his teeth.

Kyrik was sitting a few yards away, also wrapped in furs, talking to someone clearly female. They hugged quickly, almost stealthily, lips touching and eyes intent. Then she turned and looked at him.

He married Hajya? But she's Sfera . . . I thought they couldn't marry?

She glared at him coldly while he recalled that dance and the way she'd tried to entice Kyrik to her bed. I guess she brought you to heel after all, Brother.

She walked away, and for a second he was admiring the way her hips swayed as she went, then he mentally slapped himself and looked back at Kyrik. His brother's jaw was swollen on the left side, he had a blackened right eye and a cut cheekbone. Then he realised that his own hand was wrapped in bandages, but when he tried to flex, movement and feeling had returned. Someone, Hajya maybe, had healed it using the gnosis – nothing else explained the rapid recovery.

'I'm sorry,' he croaked.

'That's okay, Brother. Families fight. It's expected. And I just dumped a Hel of a lot on your shoulders.'

'But I almost killed you—'

'Never got close.' Kyrik winced. 'You should see the other guy . . . oh, hang on—' He chuckled at his own wit, then ladled out some stew and passed it over. 'This is from Hajya's own fire, so it'll be damned good. I assume you'll eat food prepared by a *savage*?'

Valdyr flinched, then nodded.

'And I heard Iztven and Ghili saved you?'

'Ysh, they did.' *Okay, point taken.*

'Val, when I was learning from Godspeaker Paruq, he told me of the Great Hatreds. One of those was called *Naslavad*, which signifies the hatred of others based on their race. To be tainted by Naslavad is shameful, because it denies whole peoples any worth. Think about it: even these Sydians have virtues you might envy: their horsemanship and archery, for example. All nations have worth – even the Keshi.'

Valdyr listened dully. He'd met all kinds in the slave-camps, even kindly guards among the Dhassan, though they'd been exceptions. 'Brother, the Noorie women in the breeding-house *raped* me.' He held his head in his hands. 'Even though it was my cock in them, they *raped* me, over and again. I can't see brown skin without remembering that. Your pretty words might be true, but what I *feel* doesn't come from my head. It's a response I can't control. *They* did it to me and one day, *they'll* answer for it.'

'Brother, hate poisons the mind—'

'*Don't quote your Godspeaker friends at me – I'm sick of it!*'

They stared at each other, the hostility flaring again between them. Finally Kyrik shook his head and said placatingly, 'Perhaps a skilled mystic-mage can heal your pain, Val. They can do a lot to soothe bad memories.'

'No one is getting inside my head, Brother. No one.'

Kyrik gave him a sad look. 'Then at the least, Val, keep your feelings for my wife's people inside. It might not be the marriage I wanted, but sometimes life makes our choices for us.'

Valdyr swallowed, remembering the kiss he'd seen Kyrik and Hajya share. 'You looked happy enough earlier.'

Kyrik's face brightened. 'You, know, surprisingly, I am. I think we're becoming friends, and that's far more important than anything else between us.' Then he smiled. 'Though the "anything else" is pretty damned good too.'

'She looks like hard work. Something between a dancer and a . . . a sarkan.'

Kyrik laughed. 'Ysh, she's a sarkan. She's married a Sarkany . . but I think she was a draken all along.'

Hegikaro, Mollachia
Maicin 935

A sullen crowd gathered at Kapuviza, the Water Gate, where the bridge crossed the moat of Hegikaro Castle. Robear Delestre had erected a massive gallows on top of the arch so anyone who entered did so beneath the dangling legs of his latest executions.

Heavy-handed and ill-judged, Sacrista thought, *like all my dear brother does.*

The crowd was angry, but not violent: there were plenty of legionaries here, and they knew Robear didn't issue idle threats: if he said skulls would be cracked, then skulls were cracked. The hundreds watching were silent, their hatred expressed in cold stares and sinister hand-gestures; the Finger Curse, first and last fingers pointing at the object of their antipathy, was everywhere. Many were jabbed at her.

Barbarians.

She was standing surrounded by her officers on a wall overlooking the plaza, where she could see Robear on a higher balcony across the square, making extravagant gestures with a gold goblet amongst a laughing group of Midrean merchants and their families. The women wore richly coloured velvets and jewels in their elaborate hairdos piled atop their heads like extravagant hats; the young men, all lace cuffs and plumed hats, were strutting like conquerors.

'Shouldn't you be up there, Milady?' Gaville, her most senior battle-mage, asked.

'Was that a jest, Gaville?' she asked. Because if he was insinuating that she belonged among those trollops and fools, she'd be damned if she'd let it pass.

He stiffened, and said, 'Milady, I meant nothing, I just—'

'Forget it,' she snapped, even more annoyed.

She and Gaville had never got on, not since he'd tried to get into her bedchamber some ten years ago and she'd broken his arm. But he was their most experienced commander, even though he was a bully and an abuser of rank. Her father's legions weren't high-quality: they'd never gone on Crusade or campaign and the ranks were mostly filled up with thugs. Their battle-magi were no better: ambitious, conniving and spineless.

'Let's get this done,' she snapped. 'Bring out the prisoners.'

Gaville gestured to someone below, drums rolled and the men were led out, hooded and stumbling as they were goaded by the spear-butts of their captors. She scanned the crowd, seeking troublemakers, but though hatred floated in the air like mist off the lake, the only gesture of protest was that damned finger-curse. Ten feet below her, she saw a young girl, maybe sixteen, emitting a shrill wail, her fingers stabbed right at her.

Sweet Kore, shut her up, she thought.

The noise grew as the prisoners were led onto the platform. Their hoods were torn away, revealing battered faces, bruised, scabbed and swollen – she'd had a hand in questioning them herself, after Gaville's men had caught them near Ujtabor. Her men had killed four of the collaborators and captured these six, who included two young people from the town who'd apparently been trying to join them.

As each hood was raised, the wailing cries rose: they obviously had kin here, friends too. 'This could get feisty,' Gaville noted.

'No one reacts to provocation without my express order,' she warned. He just sniffed and carried on seeking dissent. *Incredible: he still thinks I'm soft just because I'm a woman.*

She looked down the line of captives. She'd seen that look before: glazed eyes, unable to credit that this was real, that they were about to die. Then she focused on the older man, Tibor: the commander, sober-faced, self-contained, the hardest to break. She'd had to get involved closely in his interrogation and his glassy stare was down to the damage she'd done smashing his psyche. Now he was barely aware of where he was. He'd had a lot to tell . . . *a lot, but not enough. I need to know more about this Vitezai Sarkanum.* She'd already sent men to round up Tibor's associates. The barbarians' secret order was led by one Dragan Zhagy, and the Sarkany brothers were involved. They were hiding in the foothills of the Valadons, somewhere called 'Jegto'. You had to follow the Magas upstream, beyond where she'd thought it passable. *That's where the Sarkany brothers are, with a few hundred men. We'll trap and crush them there.*

She signalled to the hooded executioners on the platform and they placed the nooses and shoved the prisoners out into space. There were six sharp *snaps*, some thrashing and a foul stench as bowels were voided. As the criminals swung on the creaking beams, a sea of eyes and fingers turned her way. The notion that she might one day live here vanished. *Damnable place! When can we leave?*

She found herself looking at that girl below her in the crowd, forcing herself to meet those blank eyes. *Rukka-te, honey. Curses mean nothing.* She made her eyes flash with light, to remind her who was who.

The girl shrieked even louder, a chilling, grating sound that made her shiver suddenly, and she tore her eyes away and looked up at Robear, who was clapping one of the merchants on the back as he led them back to their negotiation table. Her brother, feeling her gaze, paused to silently toast her, then swaggered away, accompanied by his flock of admirers.

'Finish this,' she snapped at Gaville. *I need a bloody drink too.*

The drink came with a price: Sacrista had to attend Robear's stupid soirée and mingle with his guests. She was out of sorts, her ears still ringing with the wails of that damned girl in the crowd, and she had to compose herself before going in.

Parties! I hate them. She marched into the celebration as if she were going to war.

'Sister!' Robear shouted in greeting above the wall of laughter and chatter filling the small chamber. There were easily eighty people packed in – the latest batch of investors come to monitor their Mollachian venture – and the air was thick with perfume and sweat. Some of her legion magi were trying to charm the merchants' daughters, others were just drinking, hard. In the corner was a small group of grey-clad men with sombre faces: the Governor's aides, freshly arrived from Augenheim.

She endured volley after volley of names and handshakes with a stream of men who couldn't work out whether to kiss her hand or shake it. 'Get me palinka,' she snapped at a servant, 'and make it a big one.' The local fruit brandy was the only redeeming feature in this Helhole; only once she'd gulped down a glass of the stuff did she begin to feel she could cope.

The next hour was torture, interrupted only when someone touched her arm. 'A word, Lady Sacrista?'

Ansel Inoxion's smug face was the last thing she wanted to see. His men had done *nothing* to help stop the Mollach raids. 'Governor. Please excuse me, I'm just going.'

'I wish to discuss the military situation.'

'Then talk to Robear.'

'But he doesn't really have a clue, does he? I understand you're rather stretched, both for money and men.' He took her arm as if about to promenade her about a garden. 'It distresses me to see an attractive young women in straits. Let's see how I can help, yes? Your brother's office is – where?'

He was the governor – one didn't tell him no, not if one expected any kind of aid. Her heart sank. 'I'll show you.'

She let him lead her to the administrative wing, pulling from his grip the moment they were alone to break into a military stride, to the governor's amusement.

'I've heard that of all the Delestre magi, you're the most capable, Lady,' he said.

'Then you heard right.'

'Excellent. I despise false modesty.'

She showed him into Robear's office, found a decanter of red wine and poured two goblets, then pointedly sat on a sofa opposite him. She took a sip of the wine; at least it was a good one, sweet berries with a leathery suppleness. 'Midrean merlo,' she said.

'A '28, yes?' he replied, crossing his legs and lounging. 'A Moontide year: dry – and with a better finish than the Third Crusade, eh?' He leaned forward. 'Tell me how you see things here, Sacrista.'

She didn't like his attempt at intimacy. 'I'm sure Robear's told you everything.'

'I'd prefer to hear truths from you than your brother's drunken blandishments – especially if I am to commit my soldiers to helping you.'

Perhaps if I lay it out straight, he'll see that it's in his interests to help us, she decided. 'All right: there are insurgents, but we're closing in on them. Those men you saw executed today? One of them was a ringleader, and before I had him hanged, I extracted information about the rebels' strength and positions. They will be dealt with as soon as the weather clears.'

'I understand there have been battle-magi slain.'

'Yes,' she admitted.

'And the Sarkany brothers escaped incarceration and now lead the rebels.'

'Yes.'

'They have the legal right to contest your presence, Lady.'

'You were there when we locked them up to die – you sanctioned it—'

'Did I? I don't remember.'

Oh, it's like that, is it? she thought bitterly. 'One legion is not enough to garrison this valley and hunt down these rebels,' she growled. 'Two would be plenty, but your men are *idle*, sir. If they took their share of the patrols, things would be greatly eased.'

'But you're the tax-farmers, Sacrista. My men are purely here to guard Imperial possessions.' Inoxion steepled his fingers. 'Your father sided with the Vereinen empress in 930 and in return was granted this tax-farming contract – but it is finite, and at the end of your term, you're out. August Delestre paid Treasurer Dubrayle a great deal of money for the contract and he expects you to make a whole lot more – and Dubrayle will take half of what you pay me, for he is *desperate* for revenue from any source. Your father and Lord

Dubrayle are two people you don't want to disappoint. Everyone is demanding a return.'

'The mines are about to reopen, the harvest is coming – we'll strip Mollachia this summer. If you help us crush these rebels, it'll guarantee your profit—'

Inoxion was looking unimpressed. 'I've learned there are few guarantees in life, Sacrista. The Imperial Council are prepared to let August Delestre farm taxes because his support has real value. He appointed you and Robear to do his dirty work. But if you fail to control this insurrection I will intervene, and you'll have to go home and explain yourself to August.' He licked his lips, undressing her with his eyes. 'What price a kingdom, Sacrista?'

It was strange how a beautiful wine could suddenly taste like acid.

Inoxion tapped a finger against his goblet. 'Now, I know your legion is stretched. I know you can't afford any more unforeseen costs. But there are other ways to win my aid, and I'm not unreasonable. Am I clear?'

She went cold. 'Perfectly, my Lord.'

'Excellent. Now, take off your clothes.'

She stood, trembling in fury. 'No, Governor, I will not. I'm a battle-mage, not a whore. You can keep your soldiers and go rukk yourself, because you're not coming near me.'

31

A Forest of Masts

Windship Travel

Before magi discovered that wood could be made to hold Air-gnosis, enabling the construction of windships, a person could travel no more than a dozen miles a day on foot, maybe double that if mounted. Windships can move such distances in an hour, untroubled by terrain. Truly, Air-gnosis and the windship opened up Yuros to trade – and to the legions.

ORDO COSTRUO COLLEGIATE, PONTUS

Sagostabad, Ahmedhassa
Akhira (Junesse) 935

Nock. Draw. Aim. Release. The bow leaped in Latif's hand, and the shaft sped away, striking the target thirty yards away, near the edge.

Nock. Draw. Aim. Release.

An arrow flew every five seconds – he could shoot faster, but that sacrificed depth of draw and the aim, and Ashmak demanded each shaft be capable of killing.

Ashmak demanded a lot of things.

His last arrow struck near the centre and Latif flexed his fingers painfully. Archery practise had never been so hard in Salim's retinue.

'Retrieve!' the instructor screamed, and everyone trotted out towards the targets, running at two-thirds speed, no one trying to stand out. It hadn't been that way at first, but more recently they'd reached a silent, un-negotiated agreement that all worked at the same pace.

'Move faster, you *moorhks!*' the instructor bellowed.

'One day I'm going to shoot that *ghatiya* in the throat, Ahm willing,' the man beside Latif muttered.

'Get in line,' another replied, but they worked quickly, ripping shafts from targets, smoothing damaged feathers and seeking the few that had gone astray. They were permitted a minute; those returning with less than a full quiver were flogged. That had stopped happening pretty quickly.

The Keshi bow was made of wood and buffalo-horn and leg sinews. The wood formed the core, but adding horn to the belly or inside panel facing the archer and the sinew to the outer side made it more powerful. From close range, an arrow could even punch through a steel breastplate . . . just like the one the instructor wore.

Latif had been fantasising about such a shot.

'Ten seconds!' the instructor hollered and they picked up pace, arriving back together. A whip flickered around Latif's ear, just a reminder, and he'd learned not to react. His brand had stopped weeping, though it still hurt; wearing armour chafed it.

'Ready, draw!' And the cycle began again.

Is it only a month since we were conscripted? he wondered. He'd forgotten any notions of escape – this was still a better life than dying on a Sagostabad building site. He was now a kamangir, an archer of the Piru-Satabam III, the third elephant contingent. Rani had been outfitted with a howdah made of wicker and dried hide and hung about with boiled leather and chain armour. The howdah had two levels: Sanjeep rode above the elephant's head in a fortified perch, while Latif and Ashmak rode in the tower on her back, more exposed, but with a superior field of fire.

Latif drilled in archery, spear- and sword-fighting every morning; in the afternoons, he drilled with Ashmak, Sanjeep and Rani, negotiating courses while firing at targets, rampaging over wooden man-shapes and smashing them to bits. Slaves were forbidden to leave, so evenings were spent in camp.

The question of which enemy they were to face was never answered, and Latif doubted that even Ashmak's commanders knew. The archers gossiped; most thought Lakh, others Gatioch or Mirobez. Some even mentioned Javon.

Nock. Draw. Aim. Release.

Most of the time his brain was focused on the routines, which was better than remembering all he'd lost: he could sink into a void and forget everything for a while.

Nock. Draw. Aim. Release.

They were returning from another volley when another man joined the instructor and Latif felt his throat catch, because this was someone he knew: Selmir had led the Hadishah at Riverdown during the Third Crusade, where he'd been outmanoeuvred by better-trained, stronger Rondian magi. Latif had been impersonating Salim then, while the real Salim took the main army north, and he'd had a run-in with Selmir. Today he was richly attired, the hilt of his scimitar gleaming gold, so clearly that had been just a minor setback in his career.

'Kamangiri, prepare!' the instructor shouted, while Selmir wandered behind the ranks. He chose to stand behind Latif.

'Now!'

Nock. Draw. Aim. Release.

Latif struck the target, nice and central – a good effort considering he was dreading recognition. *Move on, please,* he prayed.

'Wait!' Selmir's smooth voice cut across the training field, and the archers paused.

Latif's belly churned: *Has he recognised me?*

'How many of these men are slaves?' Selmir enquired.

'All of them, Hazarapati,' the instructor replied.

Hazarapati? So he commands a hazarabam – that's, what, a thousand men. Latif remembered Salim's military briefings. *But our unit of forty elephants has also been designated a hazarabam ... meaning Selmir is our new commanding officer.*

'They're all Lakh or Keshi,' the instructor said. 'Good Amteh men. If we freed them, they'd stay.'

Selmir made an amused noise. 'Is that right, *slave*?' He paused, then said, 'Well?'

Latif realised Selmir was talking to him. Head down, mind blank, he said, 'Ai, Hazarapati.' He kept his focus on the target as the brush of the man's mind touched his. The queasy sensation passed quickly, though. 'They do seem single-minded enough,' Selmir commented as he withdrew, 'but then, I always found archery practise hypnotic myself.'

Latif bit his lip, wary of a sudden strike, like a mouse passing the lair of a cobra, but the hazarapati paid him no further attention and moved on down the line as the archers resumed shooting.

That afternoon Selmir carried out a full inspection of the unit, all forty elephants with their crew of three armoured and armed. The magi captains all appeared to know Selmir personally, and departed with him afterwards for a briefing.

The following morning Ashmak announced, 'We're moving into the countryside, away from the city.' The rest of the day was spent dismantling their camp and loading carts, ready to be hooked up behind the elephants the next morning. That night, most of the men gathered to discuss the move, but Latif didn't care for company; instead, he spent the time practising the mental exercises to kept magi out of one's thoughts and thinking of escape. But dawn found him still there.

The hazarabam rode out, watched by thousands of curious citizens. As they wound their way into the desert, Latif thought, *So, my personal Shihad has begun.*

Lokistan, Ahmedhassa
Akhira (Junesse) 935

The trading-dhou floated at an altitude of nine hundred feet, affording Waqar Mubarak a view that left him and his friends dumbfounded and staring open-mouthed. Rashid's mission was to take a dozen windships south into Lokistan; four days out of Sagostabad and fighting vicious cross-winds, they'd traversed the mountains, all the while fearing for life and limb. But now here they were, flying over a valley where the forest that had once filled it had been replaced by acres of timber.

'Ahm on High,' Lukadin repeated, 'there are *hundreds* of windships here!'

'Not all have keels or sails,' Tamir pointed out.

'Not yet,' Baneet grunted, 'but look, over there.' He pointed to acres of sailcloth laid out in the sun. It looked like the cloth was being dyed by dozens of tiny figures.

'Is the whole of Lokistan here?' Fatima wondered. 'Look at all the people—'

'Several tribes, at least,' put in a voice of oil and syrup, and Saarif Ibram glided to Waqar's side, silencing the group. There was something about the plump merchant-mage that suggested some vast jest that only he understood, but he was the sultan's liaison. 'We've been working here for more than a decade. One of those warbirds takes three years to complete, did you know?'

'How can we fund this?' Waqar wondered aloud.

'Oh, these people have next to nothing except their timber, and now they don't even have that,' Saarif chuckled. 'A Keshi riyal is worth hundreds of their dinar. I can feed these animals for a pittance.'

'Where were these fleets during the Third Crusade?' Fatima asked.

'Right here, although only half as many, with too few keels and barely any crew. It was too soon to use them: the Rondians would have destroyed us. But now the Lokistani and Ingashir are flocking to us – they hate the Lakh with a passion beyond even ours. They're like rabid dogs, aching to bite again.'

'Uncle says you're behind schedule,' Waqar said.

'Indeed. We've never got enough workers – but the real issue has been the pilots. We have crews, and we have many times the archers we need, but each vessel needs an Air-mage. Only a third of all magi have Air-affinity, which makes our main challenge getting airborne.'

'That's a pretty big issue for a windfleet,' Tamir commented.

Saarif laughed. 'We have but four dozen Air-magi here and none are more than quarter-blood, but we've more than three hundred ships, so it is indeed a problem. But it is not as bad as you think, Prince Waqar. The breeding-houses grew between the Second and Third Crusades and many young magi are even now completing their training. The real breakthrough is *this*.' He produced a large glass-like gem from a pocket of his flowing robes. 'These were an Ordo Costruo innovation: they can be tuned to convert raw energy to a specific type of the gnosis – not very efficient, maybe, but it works well enough that with one of these, *any* mage can power a windship's keel.'

He offered the gem to Waqar, who studied it. 'Impressive,' he admitted.

'Such a gem burns through the gnosis at many times the natural rate, but it will enable many more vessels to fly than without,' he explained. 'We're bringing in hundreds of these gems, as well as more than five hundred low-blood magi – children really, fresh from the breeding-houses and with minimal training – but they'll have the power to get every windship here airborne.'

Dear Ahm, Waqar thought, *this is real. This war is really going to happen.*

'When will the Shihad begin?' asked Lukadin, much the most war-like of them.

'When our Glorious Sultan commands,' Saarif replied.

Irritating prick, Waqar thought. 'I'm your prince, and I also wish to know!'

'Your uncle is the sultan,' Saarif laughed, 'and he commands me to be silent.'

'He's in Sagostabad—!'

'He is everywhere,' Saarif replied evasively – even when the harbadab demanded that he should obey a prince. 'All will be revealed when Rashid wills it, no sooner.'

Waqar turned away to mask the unsettling effect the merchant-mage had on him. They were dropping into a vast open space near the centre of the valley where the forest had been erased as if by giants with shovels. Their fleet of twelve windships, heavy with cargo, followed them in, creaking timbers filling the air as they came to rest on their landing stanchions. It was a powerful feeling, to fly as the Rondians flew, and despite his irritation with Saarif, Waqar hadn't lost his wonder at the sensation.

Then the hot, dusty, smoky fug of the giant camp filled their lungs and brought them very quickly back to earth. Waqar had thought the mobs on the streets of Sagostabad ragged and filthy, but the Lokistani were something altogether different: the women, wearing full Amteh dress despite the punishing heat, were encrusted in dirt, their bekira-shrouds just cloth and dust. The bronze-skinned children were mostly naked. The men were bigger than typical Keshi, with hatchet noses, intimidating eyes and bushy beards, but when Waqar disembarked they fell to their knees in waves, as if he were the Prophet Himself returning at the End of Days.

'They believe you have come to lead them to victory,' Saarif murmured.

After the stony-faced chieftains had come forth to give homage, the cargo was finally revealed. Apart from the gems, the fleet carried enough gnostically crafted keels, already fully charged with Air-gnosis, to lift a third of the craft here into the air.

'You are to remain here and supervise the assembly of the war-fleet. The supply fleet will return thrice more,' Saarif told Waqar. 'By the end of Junesse, Sultan Rashid wants the entire fleet assembled and ready to fly.'

Tamir was running his eyes down the sheet of paper Saarif had given him: 'Three hundred transporter-craft, light and heavy, a combined capacity of nearly forty thousand men – the holds are huge, but there's no weight wasted on defence or weapons. With this fleet, we could drop an army anywhere we wanted—'

'You still have to feed them,' Baneet said dourly.

'Ai, Baneet would need a whole transporter of cattle to feed just him,' Fatima laughed.

'A clever general would fly to where food awaits.' Saarif's eyes were twinkling.

So he does know where the fleet is to be sent.

'The Rondians brought two hundred thousand men to Ahmedhassa in the last Crusade,' Lukadin enthused. 'A single sailing of this fleet could transport a fifth of that. How many fleets are being built?' he asked Saarif.

'Another six,' Saarif replied. 'We could put a quarter of a million men at an enemy's gates.'

That the Shihad would go to Lakh was now widely assumed, though Waqar still wondered about Javon, which led him to think about the intriguing Tarita. But seeing this fleet brought home to him that *anywhere* in Ahmedhassa was a potential target. Perhaps it was destiny that Kesh unite Ahmedhassa as the ultimate deterrent to invasion from the west. Perhaps this holy war really was blessed . . .

They had a day to settle in, then their work began in earnest. Waqar busied himself coming to grips with their role, which was mostly organisational, to ensure that his workforce saw a leader in him. He assembled the painfully young and fresh-faced magi and read them a letter from his uncle, praising their work and promising glory to come. Then he described the function of the gnosis-converting gems before distributing them.

He also ratified formal appointments, on Saarif's recommendations, and inspected each vessel. Most were crudely built; the niceties like carved and polished timbers, pretty bowsprits and the like were of less import than a craft that could fly. The building crews descended on the new keels and as the first craft rose into the air, so did loud cheers, followed by mass prayers and celebrations as a tide of exhilaration energised the camp. The Lokistani workers, caught up in the fervour, laboured even longer and harder as days became weeks.

Waqar buried his grief in the task at hand. He tried to contact his sister, but the mountains were blocking his calls; Jehana had been unreachable in Sagostabad before he left too, and that was troubling – but he had little room for brooding.

Once Saarif Ibram flew the first fifty craft away, Waqar felt they could speak more freely. 'Rashid must have every Air-mage and sylvan-mage in Ahmedhassa working on those keels,' he observed, as his friends shared a late-night sharbat.

'I expect he has,' Tamir commented, 'since the last Moontide.'

'*Shuban-Ahm*,' Waqar breathed, 'you're right – of course he's been building this fleet instead of viaducts and aqueducts, or restoring farms and all the other things he told Salim he was doing. People are starving throughout Ahmedhassa for this fleet.'

Such thoughts made these birds of war much less beautiful.

'Sacrifices must be made for the glory of Ahm,' Lukadin argued.

'Uncle *lied* to Salim,' Waqar breathed. 'He must have been secretly abetting the Shihadis all along.'

'There is no glory in a shameful peace,' Lukadin replied, quoting the *Kalistham*.

'Tell that to the dead,' Fatima scoffed.

When they were all gone to their separate tents, Waqar pulled out a relay-stave, left with him so that he could contact Sagostabad in emergency, but his mind was on Jehana, and the mysterious Tarita and her Javonesi friends. After much consideration, he took up the stave and sent out a call, augmented sufficiently to clear the mountains.

Hebusalim, Dhassa

Tarita left Sagostabad in early Akhira and rode the night skies for three days. The two-hundred-mile journey, several weeks' travel by road, was a relatively easy flight for a wind-pilot, even if the winds were contrary. She spent the night in the wilds, hiding her craft and setting birds to watch for intruders, then sleeping in the hull. Wind-travel was still a novel thing in Dhassa and she didn't want to draw attention – there were still many who thought magi were afreet, despite the role of Keshi magi in defeating the last Crusade.

Tarita might be young, and her education incomplete, but growing up in the servant halls of the royal palaces in Javon had given her plenty of experience in how the world worked. She'd seen ruthless people exploit status and power without conscience, and she was certain the masked assassins would be traced back to that sort of person: an emir; a sultan, a mage . . . Somehow, she had to pull their masks away.

It was her own safety that was uppermost in her mind, though, as she guided her craft to a certain rooftop in the shadow of the Domus Costruo, the headquarters of the Ordo Costruo, the Builder-magi, on the outskirts of Hebusalim. The city was a dark blur under a new moon, with the curved marble dome of the huge Bekira Dom-al'Ahm shining serene as a matriarch over the high walls and close-packed streets. Unlike Sagostabad, the city had been under constant repair since the Moontide and was now restored to its full glory.

The skiff crunched down and servants appeared to help lash down the sails and take charge of her small pile of baggage while she wearily climbed to the ground.

'Tarita Alhani,' a cool voice called and a willowy figure emerged from the shadows, moonlight gleaming on pale curling tresses, illuminating a dark, captivating face: Odessa D'Ark of the Ordo Costruo.

'Sal'Ahm,' Tarita replied, bowing respectfully. 'Capolio contacted you, Magister?'

'Of course – I hardly greet all new arrivals,' the Ordo Costruo's senior female mage replied dryly. 'He asked that you be permitted to examine the Ordo Costruo breeding records: you think our records might identify a Gatti-born mage involved in the death of Sultan Salim. We'll assist you, of course – but I expect a full report of your findings.'

Tarita bowed respectfully. 'Is it expected to be a big task?'

Odessa snorted. 'Girl, the records are incomplete, and encrypted.' When Tarita groaned, she added, 'However, I have a young scholar who loves puzzles.'

Tarita was given a room and access to the students' dining hall and introduced to a plump, soft young woman with a pale, dogged face. Gianna was twenty-six, and had no apparent ambition to use her gnosis for anything but research. Tarita couldn't imagine a life so *dull*, but she found Gianna's enthusiasm for scholarship likeable.

The Ordo Costruo had three departments: the Arcanum educated young magi; the Collegiate was a research library, devoted primarily to the gnosis, but also to the history of Urte, and the Magisterium housed the administration and builders: those who created the mighty aqueducts, bridges and buildings the order was famous for.

'The recovered breeding-house records fall under our jurisdiction in the Collegiate,' Gianna told Tarita. 'After we escaped the Hadishah, we managed to acquire a lot of the records.'

Tarita heard the 'we' and took the girl's hand sympathetically. 'You were a prisoner? I'm so sorry.' *Dear Ahm, she can't have been more than eighteen when they captured her . . .*

'I had two children, but of course I've never met them.' Gianna replied, gently but firmly removing her hand. 'Don't touch me again.'

Tarita flinched. *At least she didn't call me 'Noorie' or 'mudskin'.* 'I'm sorry.'

'I doubt it was your fault,' Gianna said tersely, then she sighed. 'No, I'm sorry – it's still . . . you know, *fresh*.' The scholar didn't ask about Tarita's origins – in fact, she actively appeared *not* to want to know

– and instead launched into a diatribe about the breeding-house records. 'They're intact, but they're coded. We've not yet deciphered them, but we've been meaning to: you've given us an excuse.'

Their first week was spent just organising and cataloguing, and the second week was spent decoding the shorthand of the Hadishah record-keepers, who'd decided to save parchment by inventing hieroglyphs to denote who was mated with whom and when, and the outcome. They varied as new staff replaced old and implemented their own preferences, until even Gianna was left scratching her head.

Every evening, Tarita reported to Capolio via a narrow-focus relay-stave call, complained of the lack of progress and was persuaded into persisting. She also tried to contact Waqar Mubarak, but got no response. After she'd burned out all six of her staves, she requested more from Odessa, who'd been checking on her from time to time to monitor progress. Between days spent scribbling and nights alone, Tarita felt like she was back in the Merozain monastery where she'd learned to use the gnosis.

It wasn't until her third week in Hebusalim, the penultimate week of Junesse, that Gianna finally identified a symbol that she was certain meant that the breeder, male or female, had Gatti blood, after they matched a 'ᘔ' sign, very occasionally dotted through the shorthand, to a name they *knew* to be Gatti: someone called Ptofaz, which narrowed their search considerably.

By the end of that week, with Darkmoon approaching, they had three men who might be of the right age to be the man Tarita sought. There were many breeding-houses, and not all had shared information, but Tarita was feeling hopeful as she passed those names on to Capolio.

Capolio replied the next day. *<They're all high-blooded and well-enough known in Hadishah circles, and only one of those men can't be accounted for.>* He told her the name of that man. *<Keep it to yourself. Tell Odessa you found nothing of value. I suspect this information is very dangerous to know.>*

She had no sooner broken the contact when another contact came, an unexpected one. Waqar Mubarak said urgently, *<I can't tell you what I'm working on or where I am, but I'm expected back in Sagostabad very soon.>*
<When?>

<Soon,> he replied, sounding tired and stressed. <Have you found anything?>

She remembered Capolio's warning. <Not really. I've been in Hebusalim, but it's a dead end.>

He went silent, and she was about to wish him goodnight, when he added, <I would appreciate you visiting my sister – I can't reach her, and I'm afraid that those who took my mother's life will come for her.>

<I will,> she promised, then broke the connection.

'What do you think of this?' Odessa D'Ark asked, gesturing down the rows of marble statuary and ornamental walls that ran out of sight into the dark. Tarita felt like a child beside the statuesque beauty, and somewhat overawed: according to Gianna, Odessa had also been a Hadishah prisoner, bearing a son to Rashid Mubarak's younger brother Narukhan – whom she'd killed before escaping the breeding-house.

Outside, it was early evening, and had it not been for Odessa's invitation, Tarita would have already left Hebusalim. But her request to see Jehana had resulted in this meeting in the Cryptorium.

'Honestly, Magister?' Tarita replied, 'I find it barbaric.'

Odessa looked taken aback. 'But it's the most beautiful Cryptorium in the world.'

'I think it's morbid. I'm from Javon – we have both Western and Eastern customs. The Eastern way is best: fire is purity, burning away the flesh and letting the soul fly free. Gnostic teachings about the soul support this. And necromancy wouldn't be so dangerous if people didn't leave bodies all over the place.'

'Returning bodies to the earth is important—'

'—for worms, maybe,' Tarita quipped, then, 'Look at this: marble busts, silver gates on the tombs, and behind every seal someone rotting – yeurck! It's creepy. The Gatti kings used to build whole cities of the dead while their people starved – who's more important, the living or the dead?'

Odessa looked amused. 'Having a place to come to talk to the departed is healing.'

'Perhaps ... But why are *we* here, Lady Odessa? Not to talk to the dead, I hope.'

'It's about your request to meet with Jehana Mubarak,' Odessa replied.

A thought struck Tarita. 'She's not in *here*, is she?'

Odessa answered with a question of her own. 'Why do you wish to see her?'

Suddenly there was a tension in the air. Tarita measured her reply. 'While investigating the death of Sultan Salim, I befriended Prince Waqar. He's been unable to reach his sister, and he asked that I make enquiries.'

Odessa looked at her, considering. 'So Waqar *knows* she is in Hebusalim?'

'He assumes she is,' Tarita replied, unsure why this conversation felt like a duel.

'Mmm,' Odessa murmured, turning a corner and walking down a row of gloomy sarcophagi, a globe of conjured light revealing relief statuary of heraldic beasts and the images of the dead. They might be underground, but the large chambers were well ventilated. 'These crypts date to the Ordo Costruo's first arrival here in Dhassa,' the Magister commented, then she stopped. 'Tarita, the Order have placed Jehana in protective custody since the death of her mother, Sakita. Did you know that?'

'No. I presume Prince Waqar doesn't know either.'

'Naturally. He refused to join us, you know, even though his mother invited him personally.'

Tarita didn't know that, and filed the information away. 'Then I suppose you're not going to let me see her.'

Odessa threw her a measuring glance. 'If it were up to me ... but it isn't.' She turned and asked, 'Did you unmask Salim's killer?'

Tarita recalled Capolio's instructions. 'No, Magister.'

Odessa studied her face. 'You're lying, Tarita.'

Tarita began to calculate distances. The Ordo Costruo woman wasn't armed and neither was she, but that hardly mattered: Odessa D'Ark was renowned as a formidable battle-mage.

'I d-don't un-understand,' she stammered, feigning distress to mislead the other woman, while preparing to move fast.

'Tarita . . . or Nakti, or whatever your real name is,' Odessa drawled, 'I can read any face on Urte and know if they speak the truth. I know you're lying.'

Tarita's spine crawled. *I only used 'Nakti' when tending Sakita.*

'You've identified the man you sought, haven't you?' Odessa said, stalking towards her as Tarita backed away. 'I'd have burned those records if I could have. Capolio used your findings to deduce the name, didn't he?'

"*If I could have?*" Tarita backed away. *Does that mean Odessa couldn't persuade the Order to destroy the records . . or she couldn't access them . . . is this really Odessa? And how does she know about Capolio . . .?*

'People who learn such names must die, "Nakti",' Odessa said. She twisted her wrists and conjured purple fire in both hands: necromantic-gnosis. 'And if you don't know where Jehana is, you're no use to me.'

A virulent bolt of violet energy shot towards Tarita, one that should have turned her to a skeletal husk where she stood, but her shield did enough – *just* – although the spill of *unlife* that did get through was enough to kill every layer of skin on her left cheek as it passed, splitting it open in a bloodless tear, like an old scar. The sheer power took Tarita's breath away – but she was Merozain-trained *and* an Ascendant, one of the few who could stand up to it.

First though, she needed space to ward – and to *think*. She darted sideways and shot along a narrow passage, using Air-gnosis and kinesis to fly a foot above ground. She was just a blur in the shadows – but Odessa was already blasting at her again, and as she spun up and away, the livid bolt lit up the massive chamber. Odessa flashed towards her as if space and time meant nothing and Tarita dodged again, furious at letting herself be drawn into this trap. She fired back, a livid blue mage-light that burst on Odessa's shields, lighting up her face – and Tarita saw that she'd put on a Lantric mask, one Tarita had seen in Salim's palace at Sagostabad.

Heartface.

Tarita threw herself away from a counter-blast of white-hot flames and shot down a side-aisle like a darting sparrow, making for a distant glimmer of light – an exit – but even as she spotted it, the lid of a sarcophagus thirty yards ahead slipped aside and shattered in a great crash of stone, sending chunks of rock flying.

A woman rose from the uncovered tomb, a silhouette against the darkness, and stepped into her path. Tarita skidded to a frantic halt as the figure rasped, 'Nakti . . .' Her voice was chillingly familiar.

32

Common Ground

Magi and Battlefield Supremacy

The Blessed Three Hundred, the Chosen of Kore, against the Rimoni Empire. There is a romance to it, of legends created and prophecies fulfilled: a small band of brethren, empowered by their god to overthrow a tyranny.

In reality, the Rimoni Empire never stood a chance. Without archery, cavalry and ballistae, the legions that tried to stand against the Ascendant Magi were incinerated from the safety of the air, destroyed without mercy or risk. It was nothing less than mass murder.

ORDO COSTRUO ARCANUM, HEBUSALIM, 542

Lake Jegto, Mollachia
Junesse 935

Drums rolled and thundered, a cacophony that boiled up into the skies over Jegto. The clouds over the valley were like an inverted dish; lightning flashed sporadically in the north and drizzle hung in the air as if too light to fall, clinging to the hides and furs and hair of the gathered Sydian riders swarming around the men of the Vitezai Sarkanum as they readied themselves for the march through the press to the chieftain's tent.

Like the rest of the Mollachs, Valdyr was clad in the only clothes he owned – but at least they were now clean, however inadvertently. He was feeling shaky still, shocked at the anger that had burst loose inside him and almost killed the brother he loved. That anger was getting harder to restrain, as if the tethers were becoming increasingly worn.

When I was locked up in chains, I had no choice but to hold it in. It's when I have choices that I lose control: that's a disturbing thought. But tonight of all nights, the formal presentation of the Vitezai to the tribe – delayed by his fight at the lake – meant he had to rein himself in.

Kyrik walked out in front of his men. His wounds, like Valdyr's, had been healed by Hajya's healing-gnosis, the bruising smoothed away. It was disturbing to feel a twinge of envy for his brother, for his formidable wife, Hajya of the Vlpa. But at the same time, the revulsion he felt for brown skin wouldn't go, and he sensed that Hajya knew that. Oddly, he was ashamed; her unspoken opinion shouldn't matter, but it did.

Kyrik stepped to the front of the Vitezai and his voice rang out. 'Embrace the strangeness, lads! Few outsiders are privileged to see what you will. You'll tell your children's children of this night. But please – *please* – be calm, be coolheaded, and don't do anything foolish. Indeed, do nothing at all! There is drink – be restrained! Some of these men have egos as big as you lot: don't let them provoke you. You're bigger and stronger than them and you don't need to prove anything. Remember, these are our allies, and if we want our lands back, we need them.'

Dragan Zhagy, speaking for his men, replied, 'My lord, we're not legionaries or mercenaries but an ancient order who have been persecuted down the years. We've had to hold our tongues while being slandered, imprisoned and tortured. We're not just chosen for prowess as fighters, but for character. We know what's at stake.'

There was a murmur of assent in the circle of men and Kyrik looked pleased. Then he made a point of coming up to Valdyr. 'Brother, I know you don't want to know these people, but you're my brother and they're kin by marriage now. Can you do this for me, please?'

Valdyr nodded mutely and let Kyrik hug him. The views of the Vitezai were closer to his own than Kyrik's – his brother's ideas sounded too much like one of his Noorie priest's sermons – but if he showed support, it might help them accept. 'I'm with you,' he reassured Kyrik. 'It'll be fine.'

Their bond might be shaky, but it was holding. It was time to go. Kyrik led them between the thickly packed warriors, each with a fox-sigil painted in the centre of their forehead, like a brand on a horse. *I*

DAVID HAIR

am Vlpa, it said, and they wore it with pride. But for allies, there was a lot of blank hostility, too.

'They stand tall for runts,' Larin muttered.

'Shut it,' Dragan drawled, but winked to show he appreciated the spirit of defiance.

Valdyr, the tallest man here, fixed his eyes on the back of Kyrik's head as they made their way down the narrow channel towards a line of fox banners, until they emerged into an open space before the Sydian leaders.

Brazko, his muscular torso bared to the chilly wind, was impossible to miss: a younger, fitter version of his father, Thraan, the nacelnik. His long hair and beard were braided, and he exuded a belligerent uncertainty, as if this were the biggest thing he'd ever done without his father's presence. *I hope he's not the sort to overreact under pressure . . .*

Hajya was a somewhat comforting presence on Brazko's left – not that she looked at Valdyr with any friendship. Her weathered face was stern, the Sfera markings rendering her as alien as the rest. To her left stood seven other Sfera, younger men and women.

Then suddenly the drums thudded, fire-dust burst on either side and as the Mollachs stiffened, a near-naked man in a fox-mask bounded into the space before them, ululating an impossibly long cry which made Valdyr's skin crawl. He started yowling, and others joined him as the warriors clapped rhythmically. More like him appeared, barking, and went down on their haunches, creeping forward like spiders.

Kyrik kept insisting these people were more civilised than he credited, but he couldn't see it. The Vitezai men just stared, and Valdyr thought, *They're just animals.*

'These are the shaman's people,' Kyrik called. 'Face it, respect it. It's a challenge: they're warning us of their power.'

You don't scare me, Valdyr thought, facing the dancers. *You make me laugh.*

But all the same, there was something unnerving about this 'fox dance', the way they snarled and spat as though possessed, and the display reached a crescendo amidst a thunder of drums – which suddenly fell silent. The dancers slapped their thighs with the palms of their hands thrice, yellow teeth bared and each pair of eyes locked

478

on one of the Vitezai, utterly still, until the lead dancer lifted his hand.

Valdyr wasn't the only one to sway as his senses adjusted. There was a collective intake of breath as the dancers backed away and the first one straightened and took his place on Brazko's right, opposite Hajya.

'Missef,' Kyrik murmured in Valdyr's direction. 'The shaman.'

The triumvirate of Sydian authority now stood before them; the chieftain's son, the shaman and the Sfera. 'Kirol Kyrik,' Brazko called, 'Clan Vlpa greets you, and welcomes your people! Please, bring them forward.'

'Prince Brazko, I thank you, and pay you host-homage,' Kyrik replied loudly. He dropped to his right knee, gesturing for the Vitezai to do the same. Valdyr was last to comply, but loyalty to Kyrik held. Looking up, he saw Hajya nodding at him faintly. That she thought her approval mattered annoyed him.

'Rise, be welcome,' Brazko said, his voice loud, formal. He stepped forward and embraced Kyrik, then said, 'Where is your brother?' All eyes went to Valdyr. As he advanced, he reminded himself of all he'd been through, taking heart from that. He embraced the strongly built Sydian, then allowed him to steer him towards Hajya. 'Come, meet your new sister.'

The weathered face of the Sfera leader twisted into a wry smile as she stepped forward and let him awkwardly kiss her cheeks. 'Greetings, Brother,' Hajya whispered. 'Take better care of my husband, ysh?' Then she stepped back, every step a little masterpiece of grace.

The senior Vitezai were introduced, Dragan first, after which the formality of the occasion subtly dissolved and Brazko, after a glance at Hajya, said, 'Come, let us speak together.'

The leaders, Vitezai and Vlpa, made their way into his pavilion and sat, Sydian-style, on large cushioned seats made from saddlebags stuffed with cloth. Food was laid out before them on shields covered in cloth; the only utensils were knives.

The men outside were also being served food and drink and Valdyr hoped there'd be no serious violence – a few fights were inevitable, given the nature of warriors, but as long as no blood was shed, they might just get through this intact.

Valdyr sat beside Kyrik, Dragan and half a dozen senior Vitezai. Opposite them sat Brazko, who looked a little intimidated, his eyes going constantly to the periapts the Sarkany brothers wore; beside him were Missef, Hajya, and a clutch of older Vlpa clansmen. There was some small talk as they drank and ate, then they set to the real business of the night. Brazko, as host, opened the discussion. 'So, Kirol Kyrik, what are your plans?'

Kyrik outlined his scheme to take the Vlpa down the Magas Gorge. 'So far, we've seen no indication that the Imperial Legion encamped around Lapisz is actually going to aid the Delestre legion – if we concentrate on defeating Robear, it's possible the Imperials will just leave. But our first priority is forage for your mounts.'

'Where will we find that?' Hajya asked, her voice a throaty purr. 'In a few months the rest of the clan will come with all our herds.'

Dragan produced a map. 'Here, in the Domhalott, there's good grazing, Kirolyna.'

Hajya glanced at Kyrik. 'What is this "Kirolyna"?'

'Queen,' Kyrik replied, with a faint smile.

The Sfera woman coloured slightly. 'Oh.' She looked hard at Dragan, then said, 'Very well. Tell me more.'

Dragan inclined his head. 'The Domhalott borders forest land that is rich in game. Other stores can be traded for. The lands up here, around Lake Jegto, will quickly become untenable.'

'Then we must ride soon, to secure the pastures and bring the Rondians to battle,' Brazko declared. 'We came to fight, not graze cattle!'

He's never fought a Rondian legion, Valdyr realised. No one talked big when they knew the realities of that.

'Once you're in the Domhalott, they'll have no choice but to come to us,' Rothgar said. 'Otherwise we could raid the river-trade with impunity. Getting there is the problem: in Magas Gorge we'll be strung out below high cliffs – we can't afford to be caught there.'

Brazko studied the map, then grunted his agreement. 'We must move quickly, as you say. How long to reach these lowland pastures?'

'The gorge is a hard path even on foot; for riders or cattle, it's very slow,' Rothgar answered. 'You'll do well to traverse it in less than seven days. We're about to enter the week of the waning moon – I'd hope to reach the Domhalott during Darkmoon.'

'The Vitezai will secure the line of march,' Dragan said, 'and half of us will guide your riders through the gorge and help with the trickiest of the river crossings. I'll take the rest through the Rahnti Mines, to secure the uplands overlooking the gorge and keep any Rondian patrols away.'

That agreed, they moved on to where and when to seek open battle, and how to win, which proved more contentious. 'My people do not fight in enclosed spaces, Kirol Kyrik,' Brazko said in a troubled voice. 'We must meet them on the plains.'

'The gods of our people ride the plains,' Missef agreed.

The Vitezai looked uneasy; they'd always fought from concealment. 'You can't defeat a Rondian legion in open battle,' Dragan said. 'Their battle-magi will carve you up.'

'We have eight of my Sfera here,' Hajya put in.

'With respect,' Kyrik replied, 'Rondian battle-magi are not something you would want your people to face. It's not simply a matter of having the gnosis: they are trained in gnostic warfare.'

'You are Kirol,' Hajya conceded, her tone suggesting a lot of aggressive pillow-talk later that night.

Valdyr didn't speak, but watched his brother manage the bullish pride of the chieftain, the defensive jabs of the shaman and Hajya's probing. He never contradicted his hosts, even in their outlandish claims about the prowess of their warriors – 'One rider is worth ten redcloaks,' Brazko boasted at one point, but Kyrik just moved on, keeping the debate as factual as he could.

Finally, it ended, and Kyrik asked, 'So, what did you make of that?' as he led the Vitezai back to their camp. It was late and the place was largely quiet – a few of the larger fires illuminated circles of drummers and dancers, but without the tribe's women and children, it was subdued.

'I thought Brazko and Hajya spoke soundly,' Valdyr admitted, 'but that shaman is mad, and he hates us.'

'He's not mad, but you're right, he doesn't love us. He knows that once the clan has settled here, many of his people will drift into the towns, seeking a better life. He knows Kore is strong here, and how impressive stone buildings can look to people raised in tents. He's afraid.'

'He should have stayed on the plains,' Valdyr sneered.

'He would have, given the choice. He voted for the clan to stay and take their chances, but he was overruled.'

'Can we trust him?' Dragan wondered.

'To do well by the clan, certainly,' Kyrik said, 'but he will always put his gods first. He may see defeat and migration home as preferable to victory and staying. We'll need to watch him.'

As they split up to find their tents, Kyrik turned and said, 'Well done, Brother.'

Valdyr ducked his head. 'If you say so. I don't envy you.'

Kyrik laughed. 'One day all this will be yours.' He waved a hand and turned away, heading into the heart of the Sydian camp, where his own pavilion waited. And Hajya.

'Keep it,' Valdyr called after him. 'I don't want any of it.'

Upper Osiapa Valley, Mollachia
Junesse 935

Robear Delestre stood in the saddle and massaged his buttocks. 'Gods, but I hate riding,' he groaned.

'Then take a skiff,' Sacrista told him. 'Or stay in Hegikaro.'

'I need to show these traders I'm a man of action,' Robear declared, pulling a heroic pose. Against her mood, Sacrista had to smile. That was the one thing Robear could always do. She didn't know why – he wasn't especially funny, and Kore knew she'd heard all his jokes before. Maybe each quip or comic face reminded her of an earlier, happier time. *I love my brother, more fool me.*

They glanced back at the merchants riding into White Stag Land as if this were some picnic outing in Bricia. 'Are we still on the right trail?' he asked.

She showed him the rough hide map she carried. 'See here: the larger river is the Osiapa – the Oldfather – which flows down from

the northeast. The smaller one coming in from the west is the Anya –
the Mother. That's the one we need to follow, all the way into White
Stag Land.'

'I hope the road is better,' Robear moaned.

'Sorry, it's worse – but think how these lard-arsed Midrean Lowlanders are feeling.'

'I'm a lard-arsed Lowlander myself, Sister. So were you, until recently.'

'I've been in the saddle more than you lately, Brother dear.' She
threw him a mocking salute. 'I need to find Gaville and check our
dispositions.'

Robear groaned and waved her away as she spurred her mount up the
trail. It took her only twenty minutes to find her battle-magi, watering
their horses where the two rivers met. They saluted grudgingly – she
might win respect, but not affection. Gaville, drinking from his flask,
finished before acknowledging her, though he was clearly well aware
she was waiting.

Her father would have dressed him down, barking orders and spittle in his face for his slackness, but she knew they'd only snicker, and
make remarks about *the time of the moon* behind her back. 'Gaville, are
we on schedule?'

'Aye. The vanguard are already ten miles upriver. There's a staging
camp there, and a trail into this "White Stag Land". From there, it's
all woodland, not hard.'

'Any sign of the enemy?'

'None. We've got skiffs in the air and ranging patrols marking out
campsites. We've got fifty miles of hard slog ahead of us just to reach
the Magas Gorge. That'll take us five days or more over this terrain,
and even then we're only halfway to this Jegto place.'

She looked up at the sliver moon, clearly visible even in the late
afternoon skies. 'Robear wants us at Magas Gorge on the first day of
Darkmoon, and at Lake Jegto by the last day of Junesse.'

'I'll make sure we keep to that.'

Gaville might be a stiff-backed swine, but he gets things done, Sacrista
admitted to herself. 'It seems to me the worst-case scenario is that
we ourselves get penned in the gorge,' she said.

'It's possible, but if that happens we'll just overfly the ambush and turn the tables.'

'Okay – do we know what awaits us at this lake? Have you scouted it?'

'Too risky, even from the air: we don't want to let them know we've found them.'

She scratched her chin uneasily. 'Fair enough. We've got four maniples on the march – that should be plenty. I just wish we knew what's to the north of this gorge. We might need to change plans quickly.'

'No plan ever survives contact with the enemy,' Gaville admitted.

As if you'd know, she thought, as she rode away. *At least he didn't say we needed Inoxion's men . . .*

33

The Time Has Come

Gods and Daemons

The aether is full of daemon spirits who (according to them, at least) originated in the aether and not here on Urte. Most are simple beings, but some are vast, as if thousands of these daemons had banded together to become one great entity. They are wise and knowledgeable beyond comprehension. And if that is not disturbing enough, some share the names of 'gods' of the ancient world.

Are they gods? Or the ghosts of gods? Or deceivers, telling us what we want to hear?

ORDO COSTRUO ARCANUM, PONTUS

The Celestium, Pallas
Junesse 935

The room was gloomy, the stately riches of the Church shrouded in shadow, the golden fixtures lit only by two candles on the desk which illuminated the faces of three men and barely anything else. One was a lowly friar from Tockburn and the second was a grizzled knight of the Kirkegarde – although you had to know him personally, for there were few clues in his garb.

The third was Kore's representative on Urte.

The role of grand prelate meant many things to different people, but most of all, it signified continuity. Dominius Wurther had filled the role for more than a quarter of a century, and he brought all the consistency and predictability that being the Voice of Kore required. Kore was changeless and eternal, and so must His Voice be.

But he knew it wouldn't last for ever. His hope was that he would die in his sleep, knowing that a successor of his own choosing was poised to carry on his work, but he wasn't so naïve as to think it'd be that simple. Everything he ate or drank was gnostically tested and tasted, and he had spies in every corner of the Church, sniffing out the stink of dissent – which meant dealing with men like this friar.

'It's not enough,' the friar said, looking at the heavy purse on the table.

Wurther scowled, glanced at the knight beside him, then pushed a second bag across the table to join the first. 'This better be good, Deshard.'

'Well worth it,' Friar Deshard boasted, flashing worn teeth as he swept both into a pocket. He was perhaps forty, and looked like he spent every day in a ditch. Quite how he'd become a friar Wurther was unsure, but the man had surprising knowledge of scripture, as well as of less savoury things. 'These people are very choosy about who they approach.'

'Then why would they come to you?' Lann Wilfort asked. The Supreme Grandmaster of the Kirkegarde had gained his rank not through politics but through leadership in the field; he was a tried and tested commander who'd got his men out of the mess that was the Third Crusade. Wurther trusted him far more than the snakes who usually ruled the Rymfort.

'Because I'm the real power in Tockburn Parish,' Deshard replied. 'My dithering superior, the Prelate of Pallas-Nord, does nothing without my approval. He's been approached by a secret group trying to tie down some votes among the prelature before this week's Synod.'

The Synod, now just five days away, was heavy on Wurther's mind, but he wasn't overly concerned – such rumours weren't uncommon. 'Deshard, on major matters, the Synod can only act if the prelates vote unanimously. I own the souls of most of them. Unanimity is a wonderful thing – it's why masterly inactivity is the prevailing doctrine of the Church.'

'Some things are worth more to a man than gold.'

Wilfort grunted. 'Don't tell Treasurer Dubrayle – he'd have an apoplexy.'

Deshard laughed. 'I'm rather appalled myself. But the threat of murder can make even gold pale in value. I understand threats have been made, *credible* threats, Grand Prelate: they want to force you to name a successor of *their* choice.'

'And then poison me, no doubt.'

'That's the inference. It's been done before.'

'I'm far from finished, you'll be pleased to know,' Wurther said.

'Your health, indeed,' Deshard grinned, raising his goblet but not touching it.

Needless caution – it was a good vintage, and there was no poison. Wurther had another swallow, to make the point, then bent closer. 'Who's behind this? There must be a name to rally support. Not just any idiot can be put forward as my successor.'

Deshard dropped his voice. 'I've heard that a *Comfateri* leads the meetings, and the man they whisper of as the future Voice of Kore has a *southern hue* to his skin.'

Although confessors were ten-a-pfennik and the Church was awash in Estellan zealots, Wurther knew exactly who was meant: *Ostevan and Rodrigo . . . predictable.* 'Do you have proof? Witnesses?'

'Proof can be found for anything if we try hard enough.'

'Not in these cases, Deshard. Conspiracy against a grand prelate is considered Grand Treason: such cases are heard by the Gnostic Keepers and the burden of proof is onerous. Witnesses are questioned under the gnosis.'

Deshard *tsked.* 'That does make it harder. These people have been careful. But if you were to incarcerate one of the attendees' – he grinned – 'my erstwhile superior, for example . . .'

'He's one of my supporters—'

'For now. I'm sure his replacement would support you just as earnestly.' Deshard attempted to look pious.

'You? A prelate?' Wurther snorted. 'You're no use to me dressed up as a festival decoration. I prefer you lying in the muck with your ear to the ground.'

Deshard looked mildly disappointed, but unsurprised. 'Another thing, Grand Prelate: it's been noted that there were deaths in the palace around the night of the Finostarre tournament: servants, guards, a certain knight and lady, all of whom spent much time attending upon the queen's young relatives. If the people knew those relatives were at large, there would be great fear and uncertainty.' Deshard scowled. 'Investments do poorly in such times.'

They shared an empathetic look: both had a lot of money in a lot of places.

'Your silence on that matter,' Wurther said, and threw him another bag of gold. The friar had earned it. He trusted Deshard enough to not disseminate these facts. He had a reputation for staying true to those who bought him.

When his spy had gone, Wurther poured Wilfort another drink and refilled his own goblet, then asked the Kirkegarde commander to bear with him. He turned and gazed through the window, thinking hard. A sliver of moon shone over the Aerflus: in a week it would be Darkmoon and the Synod would begin. Perhaps then his enemies would step out of the shadows.

A confessor and a prelate leading a new cabal, just in time for the upcoming Synod – and now the fact that the Sacrecour children have been sprung is being whispered. Both of these represented a threat to him. Then another thought struck him: might these two knives be wielded by the same hand?

If they were, it meant that Ostevan was actively working on a Celestium-based coup – but also against the queen he'd helped place on the throne. Could that be?

But Lyra never recalled you, Ostevan, did she? She tried, but I've played this game far longer and I wouldn't let her. Had that rejection been enough to make Ostevan abandon Lyra for other allies? He knew the man, all that cunning, ruthless ambition he himself had nurtured. Being a mere confessor – even one with the queen's ear – wouldn't satisfy him for long.

Suddenly the wine didn't taste so good. He could almost imagine a slow venom beginning to burn inside his gut. With a sudden jerk of the head, he spat it out and snarled at the darkness, 'Come and try me, Ostevan. You'll see I don't go easily.'

He turned to Wilfort. 'I sense a very large rat, my friend. This Synod will go ahead – I can't prevent it – but I can prepare.'

'Prepare for what, exactly?' the grandmaster asked.

'I'm not sure. The politics I can handle, and they'll know that. But I sense there is more here, something more ... *physical*. How many men can you get into the galleries overlooking the debating chamber?'

Wilfort raised an eyebrow. 'You suspect violence in the chamber?'

'They're magi, Lann. You should always expect violence.'

The grandmaster contemplated. 'Well, the reception hall adjoins the gallery and that can hold several hundred at a press. I could flood the gallery overlooking your debating chamber with crossbowmen in moments.'

'Then make your preparations.'

Dupenium, East Rondelmar, Yuros
Junesse 935

Garod Sacrecour, Duke of Dupenium, walked to the door of the maid's room, three doors down from where he slept, and almost choked at the stench of shit and iron. A small-boned woman lay on the floor, sprawled on her back, her ribcage shattered inwards, her blood and bodily wastes splattered on the walls and pooled between her spread-eagled limbs. Her face, miraculously untouched, was frozen in a silent howl.

'My wife's handmaid was a Corani spy?' he muttered to his spymaster. 'How the Hel did that elude you until now?'

'A skilled operative can be nigh impossible to detect, even with the gnosis,' the tall, priestly man at his side replied. Jasper Vendroot had been a Kore mage-priest, but he'd lost his faith and found his true calling many years ago. His face could turn from avuncular charm to chilling menace in a heartbeat.

'So she's the last of the spies on the list?' Garod scanned the remaining servants, lined up against the wall by a contingent of House Guards. They were understandably frightened: to them, the maid, a colleague, had been brutally slain for no reason.

But are they all as innocent as they look?

Vendroot folded his arms and listed those he'd apprehended or killed that evening: 'Two of your knights, one of your lady's train, three footmen and seven house-servants: all of them low-blooded magi, all installed by Setallius in the past two decades. This has been a grievous day for the Corani, my lord, their worst since 909. But One-Eye will have more people here – most informers aren't magi. We can't hope to find them all.'

'I want the Corani blind to what happens here! Are you saying that's impossible?'

'Yes,' Vendroot answered calmly. 'But if these were all the magi they had here, any informers left must rely on slower means to contact Setallius. You must proceed before that news can reach him.'

Garod looked down the corridor to Brylion Fasterius, waiting impatiently for his command. They'd reorganised all their mounted maniples into one legion of cavalry: five thousand riders with two horses each, and fifty mage-knights to spearhead the attack, all ready to pound down the back roads to Pallas.

Cavalry could travel hard and fast for an hour or two, but that wasn't sustainable. Five miles an hour, with breaks, was the collective wisdom. With remounts, he could expect fifty miles a day: so six days to cover three hundred miles. It was already the first day of the waning moon, and he had to get his men to Dawnport in Pallas, at dawn on the second day of Darkmoon.

It was time to act: to commit irrevocable treason.

'And the commanders of the Imperial legions guarding the approaches to Pallas have been paid off?' he asked, seeking reassurance.

Vendroot's voice was calm. 'They'll stand aside. I've spoken to them myself.'

Still Garod hesitated, conscious of all the eyes on him: the impatient Brylion, the anxious guardsmen, the terrified servants. 'It's this masked cabal . . . I don't trust them, Jasper.'

'Nor should you,' Vendroot replied. 'But for the moment, our purposes align.'

Garod pressed his lips to Vendroot's ear. 'This is a gamble, Jasper: we both know that. House Sacrecour might look strong, but between our debts and our losses in the Third Crusade, failure now is not acceptable.'

'I know, your Grace. But the longer the Corani hold Pallas, the more secure they become. How long can we wait? Each day they get stronger and we grow weaker.'

Garod rubbed his chin and took a deep breath. He raised his voice and ordered, 'Brylion, the time has come: we must be in Pallas at dawn, six days hence: on Torsdai-Darkmoon.'

Brylion's scarred face lit up and he pounded his right fist against his breastplate. 'As you command, Uncle.'

And so it begins. I pray our children will bless this day. Garod turned back to the servants. He knew all their names and faces, as he'd known the dead woman in the tiny room behind him. Some had been in service since before 909, like Jonas, his footman, who'd been with him since childhood. He'd trusted them with his life, the dark intimate places only family went.

'Jonas,' he called, and the old man raised his head hopefully. 'Pack my travel chest: I have an important journey to make.'

The old man bobbed his head gratefully and shuffled off to Garod's room. The duke surveyed the rest, then whispered, 'Jonas I trust. Give the rest merciful, discreet deaths.' He walked away. He'd seen enough blood for one day.

The Bastion, Pallas, Yuros

Lyra plodded heavily through her private garden, making her way slowly to the trickle of water from the fountain where her sapling Winter Tree grew. It was the sixth month of her pregnancy and her belly was well beyond her breasts now, her gait changing as the weight of her growing child shifted her balance. Domara had consented to giving her healing-gnosis on her back, though she was far less skilled than Ostevan. She missed his touch, but she knew outsiders would not approve, so they had reverted to more traditional lady-and-confessor relations. Those conversations were still one of the best parts of her day.

Despite the discomfort of her condition, there were consolations. Her marriage felt renewed, though it was harder to feel amorous in this condition. Ril understood though, and he was still attentive. Best of all, Domara had declared the danger of miscarriage over, and her child's movements brought tears of joy to her eyes.

My baby is going to live – thank you, Kore; preserve us, Corineus!

It was dusk, and she'd used a headache as an excuse to get some time alone – a relative term, when Basia waited at the gates of the garden, her watchful gaze following her charge through the twilight. The moon was rising – the merest sliver; tomorrow Junesse would enter Darkmoon: six days of empty sky, when the dead were said to walk and daemons could step into the material world. Setallius assured her that was nonsense.

She broke through the maze of the wild roses and dreamily passed the Oak Grove into the circle of elms around the pond and the Winter Tree sapling. The young tree was thickening, but its strange counter-seasonal cycle meant its leaves were turning gold and beginning to fall. In the darkening garden, the tree's pale splendour filled her with peace.

She knelt awkwardly beside the pool that fed its roots, reaching over the old moss-covered stones and dipping her fingers into the cold water, then raising them to the skies in offering to Aradea. A silvery lustre gathered in the droplets running down her arm as she whispered a wish, that her child be blessed and protected. It had become her daily ritual.

'Aradea, watch over what is mine.' She saw no irony in praying to both Kore and the Queen of the Fey. Both were real to her. She finished by touching the wet hand to her forehead, and a sense of *regard* shafted through her awareness. She blinked her eyes open and for a moment was sure there was a vast face, formed by the autumnal leaves, staring down at her. She felt no sense of threat, only of being *noticed*.

Then the wind shook the boughs and the moment was gone. She smiled quietly to herself, feeling a precious, fleeting tranquillity as she filled her silver jug. The water from this fountain was the nicest she'd ever tasted, and she was certain it had some virtue for her and her unborn child.

Then footsteps thudded and Ril ran into the garden, alarm on his face. 'Lyra? What was that light?'

She hadn't been conscious of any light. 'What did you see?'

'A faint greenish light, sylvan-gnosis perhaps, and I was worried . . .'

She let him enfold her, touched by a fond warmth. *Ril was worried*, she thought, basking in his protective bulk. 'It was the dwyma,' she told him. 'It touched me.'

'Should you be using it, in your condition?'

She rested her head against his chest. *Typical mage: "using it" you say, as if it were a handy tool, like your gnosis. It touched* me, *not the other way around.*'

'Whatever – Domara would have a fit if she knew.'

'Then don't tell her.' The dwyma was a secret known only by those closest to her: Ril, Basia, Dirklan – and Ostevan, though she'd not told the others she'd confessed her heresy during yesterday's Unburdening. As always, Ostevan – bless him – had taken the revelation in his stride, and sworn secrecy over it.

Ril kissed the top of her head. 'It's a beautiful garden, anyway. Very private.' He gave a wicked chuckle and slid one arm up to cradle her breasts. 'Don't the Sollans like to strip off and dance under the full moon?'

She slapped his hand away playfully. 'Not in this place . . . it wouldn't be right. Not here. Sometimes I feel Saint Eloy is watching me here.'

'Kore's Blood,' Ril muttered, 'first Fey Queens, now Ghostly Hermits. It's getting crowded in here.' He shivered. 'Let's go in, it's getting cold. I've sent Fantoche off to get a bite. I told her I'd help you undress tonight.'

He'd been sleeping with her more and more often. Their marriage was finally maturing into what she'd thought it would be. He was warmer now, less flighty. *Sometimes love takes time*, Ostevan often said – five years was a long time, but: *Love is patient*. That was from the *Book of Kore*.

'I've been reading something Setallius gave me,' she told Ril, looking up at the sliver moon through the branches. 'The writer says our world exists in a middle place, a world of perfect harmony between ice and fire, land and sky. Remove one, and the other will destroy us.'

'Sounds true enough.'

'He also says that dwyma was created at the same time as the gnosis – that one is the counter-balance to the other.'

'But dwyma is basically extinct,' he pointed out. 'There's only you.'

'Do you think so? When groves like this are dotted all over the empire, and some nights I can almost hear the man who preserved them talking to me?'

'Ha! Sounds like a rich-food dream.' He stroked her belly mischievously. 'You should cut back: you're getting fat.'

'Cheeky! The phrase you're looking for is "big with child".' She felt a surge of confidence and twisted in his grip to kiss him, and that seemed to melt another tiny layer of separation. She felt so close to him. *Our love is alive and growing, like my garden.*

Then the narrow crescent moon fell behind a cloud and the wind grew cooler, chilling her skin. She huddled closer to him. 'Take me upstairs. I'm hungry – not for food, though.'

Ril chuckled deep in his throat and kissed her again, more hungrily. 'As my Lady commands.' Then he paused. 'What's that?' He pointed to a mossy old stone: one of those from the border of the pool.

'I must have dislodged it,' she said, though she didn't remember doing so. She was puzzled to see him distracted; the prospect of lovemaking usually made him quite single-minded.

He picked it up and frowned. There was a pattern carved into its surface: a tree, and crossed keys. 'Look, I've seen this before, somewhere . . . Is it something to do with Saint Eloy, d'you think?'

'I wouldn't think so – until I planted my sapling, this garden had nothing to do with him. Dirklan will know: ask him tomorrow – you're *busy*, right now.'

'But where . . .?' he muttered. He bent and wedged it back into the border of stones, then threw her a grin and they walked hand in hand through the garden and back up the stairs to her suite. Geni was dismissed, most of the candles extinguished and they slipped between the silken sheets to tend this new spark and to make it grow.

An hour later, Ril jerked awake and sat up. Lyra rolled over blearily, wincing as the weight in her belly shifted. 'What is it, love?'

'That sigil, on the stone – I know where I saw it: at Saint Chalfon's, in Surrid.' His fine-chiselled bronze face was lit with concentration. 'There was a plaque – I saw it when I knelt.'

She looked up at him and yawned. 'I'm glad you've remembered – maybe you can sleep now?'

He hesitated, then said, 'I'll talk to Setallius in the morning.'

'Cordan?' Coramore whispered timidly as the lock clicked. The sound resonated dully. The only thing she was sure of was that they were underground. She'd been left alone for so long, it felt like *years*: a year of shrieking angrily for help, then a year of broken weeping, that she – *the Princess of the World* – could be so treated. Then another year of empty waiting. Food and water was left and her waste bucket changed, always while she slept – *how did they know?* The stone walls were smooth and dry; the air was stale but vented in through a grille above the door. Another year of bored fidgeting passed, lying on the hard mattress counting the bricks in the ceiling, and another year of tears.

'*Cordan?*' she called hopefully, but it wasn't her brother. It was one of her 'rescuers' – if this was rescue. The woman wearing the Lantric mask was robed in deep green velvets, with matching gloves: Tear, the soul of Tragedy.

I'll make your life a damned tragedy when I'm out of here, she promised herself silently as she glowered at the newcomer. 'What do you want? Where's Cordan?' she demanded, trying to hide her fear behind anger.

'He's safe,' Tear replied. The mask did strange things to her voice, a metallic echo that was slithery and unpleasant. 'The less you know the better, Princess.'

'I want to see him!'

'Soon,' Tear told her. She sat on the bed – *her bed* – staring at her through that menacing bronze-and-lacquer mask. The mask's tears looked like real blood, they were so perfectly rendered. 'Soon you'll be rewarded for all your patience.'

'It's not good enough,' Coramore told the masked woman, trembling in rage.

'You have no gnosis yet,' Tear mused, ignoring her complaint. 'But the potential might be enough, combined with the ichor, to trigger something . . .?'

Coramore didn't know what that meant, but it didn't sound good. But she was afraid to ask for an explanation.

Tear fell silent, staring at her for so long Coramore wanted to scream. Abruptly the masked woman asked, 'What would you like to do to Lyra and her husband?'

'*Them?*' she spat. 'We're going to lop off their heads and put them on spikes for the world to see.' Cordan liked to say such things, and in her imagination it sounded rather splendid.

'You'll do this yourself?' Tear sounded amused.

'Cordan will do it. It's his right.'

Her eyes narrowed inside the mask and the air grew cold. 'Come here, Coramore.'

The girl sensed the mood change and it was as if someone had shown her an hourglass containing the sands of her life, and most had already fallen. Suddenly, she was very afraid. 'I can't,' she whimpered. 'I'm only twelve.'

'*Come here.*'

'No.' She retreated until her back hit the wall. Tears stung her eyes. Something bad was going to happen, something *awful*. 'Cordan – *Cordan!*' she screamed.

'*Come here.*'

'No!' She fell to her knees. 'Leave me alone, *please* – I'm just a little girl – I want my brother—!'

'*Come here.*'

By now, that *horrible* voice wasn't one she dared disobey. 'What do you want?' Coramore begged, as she shuffled towards the masked woman.

Tear lifted her mask, and she recognised her: one of the court ladies, that gaggle of nobodies who clung to the powerful like ticks. Then the unmasked woman bared ivory teeth like small knives, snake and wolf in one, and Coramore tried to scream, but Tear had already wrenched her head sideways and she was lost in a blaze of agony as those terrifying incisors punctured skin. Her legs gave way.

What rose from the floor some time later wasn't her any more – though it remembered that once it had been.

'Come,' Tear told her. 'Outside, tomorrow is the first day of Darkmoon, the last day of the usurper. We have work to do if our so-called Empress is to fall.'

'The Empress of the Fall, she won't last at all,' not-Coramore sing-songed, her eyes dripping blood. She took Tear's hand and they left the light, and walked into the waiting darkness.

34

Draug-Witch

Sorcery: Necromancy

The Codex Arcanum, *the laws governing gnostic workings, has more pages govern-*
ing necromancy than all of the other crafts combined. It is the most maligned and
misunderstood power of the magi, and the most feared. Yet the peace in communing
with a lost loved one is worth any price to the bereaved, and that is the gift I bring.
CRAELIA LYNDRETHUSE, ARGUNDIAN NECROMANCER, 842

Hebusalim, Dhassa
Akhira (Junesse) 935

Tarita had never seen a human draug – a walking corpse – before. Merozain training did include the theory on how to destroy an animated
corpse, but they used dead lizards for practise, which was unpleasant
enough. But as she realised what she faced, appalled at seeing the visage
of someone she'd known and admired, all theory went out the window.

Sakita Mubarak's face had collapsed, her grey, desiccated skin sunk
into the skull, and she walked with joint-cracking stiffness. Her aura
was a tell-tale pale violet and her dry-rot stink sucked the air from
the vast chamber. Only her eyes retained lustre as her piercing gaze
stabbed at Tarita.

'Nakti,' Sakita rasped, raising a claw-like hand, 'why are you here?'
Her voice was nothing like what it had been in life; it was dull and
sullen, resentful. Tarita backed away, conscious that Odessa would be
closing in behind. If she was to get out of this, she needed to make
use of her full array of gnosis: so if necromancy was where Earth and

498

Sorcery intersected, she needed the opposite: Thaumaturgy and Air: which meant flight.

Run like Hel, in other words, she thought, wrenching herself free of Sakita's lunging kinesis-grip and diving sideways between two tombs. She poured out illusory darkness to mask her; then sent that darkness one way while darting another, terrified that at any moment one of those hunting her would appear above. She found a niche and melted into it, trying not to breathe.

Ten seconds – a lifetime – passed, then she heard Heartface – Odessa D'Ark or whoever it really was – closing in, her shoes tapping crisply on the tiles. She glimpsed the masked face, framed by the flowing mane of blonde hair, as she sashayed past her crawl-space, and in a few seconds, she heard a frustrated sigh. She'd managed to elude her, for now, but Tarita had only a vague idea of where her pursuers were. And her cut cheek refused to bleed; when she touched it, the rent flesh felt scaly . . . *dead*.

Sakita's corpse-voice scratched through the darkness. 'Who are you, *Nakti*? You're no healer. Your aura is like those accursed Merozains . . . Are you one of them?'

Tarita couldn't stop herself wondering how she'd fallen into this trap. Her sealed note to Odessa had been given to Gianna, who was supposed to give it to Odessa's secretary to pass it to Odessa: so at least one of those three was a traitor to the Order – though she couldn't imagine Gianni being part of this masked group. If these masked magi could use any of the affinities, then that might not have been the real Odessa who'd met her today . . . but equally, she could also be the *real* Odessa D'Ark.

And how is it that Sakita's here, and like this? It was the Ordo Costruo who took her body away . . . She thought of Waqar; it would destroy him if he knew. *And why is his sister Jehana so important?*

This wasn't the time to ponder these problems. There was no one close she could reliably call for help, and anyway, the energy flash of a gnostic call would instantly betray her position. She'd have to get out of this on her own. So she crept sideways, her aura tamped down to a wisp and wrapped in illusion. Two on one was too many, and these women had *decades* of experience she didn't have. She ought to be a match for them in raw power, but in skill they were likely far deadlier.

She'd been a servant most of her sixteen years, though, and she was no stranger to being on knees and haunches in places that finer people wouldn't even think to go. So she took to the cobwebbed corners and narrow spaces of the giant mausoleum, squeezing between mildewed walls and old tombs, crawling noiselessly through the rat- and gecko-droppings while her hunters stalked the wide aisles, occasionally sending bursts of fire washing down, seeking to flush her out. Then Heartface took to the air, floating erect above the tombs, her dress rippling as she passed, necromantic-gnosis still sparkling in her hands. Tarita pressed herself to the far side of an ornate sarcophagus and waited until she'd passed, then she crept across to the next aisle and risked peering out, checking left and right.

The entrance she was making for shimmered with a gnostic barrier: such spells took time to dismantle, more than she'd have. The other doors would be similarly warded, she was sure ... but she was a *servant*. She scanned the vast chamber, thinking like a cleaner: those who did the drudge work were always given discreet ways to come and go so they didn't offend the nobility with their presence. She picked a direction and melted through the darkness. Heartface was at the far end, but dead-Sakita could be anywhere; so she'd have to trust to fortune, because she couldn't hide for ever. She reached the main aisle and flitted across, making for a place where the shape of the ceiling indicated a recess, praying she was right.

And there it was: a small wooden door, deep in the shadows and cunningly disguised by the architecture: her escape route. She shimmied towards it, using all her skill and patience. *I have to get out – and then I have to warn someone about this . . .*

She'd almost reached the door when Sakita Mubarak stepped from the shadows, barely ten feet away. Tarita froze as a rictus-grin spread across the dead woman's decayed face. 'Nakti,' the draug breathed.

That continued ignorance of her real name gave Tarita hope and she stalled, trying to position herself for a lunge at the door. Heartface was doubtless on the way. 'You can't be Sakita – she's dead,' she called.

'Dead? Whatever do you mean, girl?' Sakita's skin flowed and a sweet-sour wet aroma flooded the air . . . then Sakita was young again, a studious-looking mixed-race woman – though her eyes were still venomous. 'I've never felt more alive.'

Tarita realised she'd allowed herself to become transfixed by the change: her foe was far too close – then Sakita lunged at her with a purple blade of necromantic energy.

The blade just missed spearing Tarita's arm. She feinted left and conjured her own spiratus blade, parrying the draug's blows and slashing back at her. Sakita howled in agony as the blade whipped across her shoulder, opening up cloth and skin, and her illusory beauty fell away, leaving her a draug again. Yowling with rage, she used her gnostic blade to batter Tarita's aside while her taloned left hand clawed at her face.

She felt her shields tear again. Her instincts screamed a warning; she arched her back, sprang into a flip and cartwheeled skywards as magebolts exploded where she'd been standing a heartbeat before. Heartface swooped in, her robes fluttering like bat-wings. Tarita landed, threw herself feet-first against the wall and catapulted herself back towards Sakita, reaching inside her robes.

She'd just remembered the elixir Capolio had given her for research – the recipe Sakita herself had devised to fight the venom in her body. She grabbed it with one hand as she threw a cross-body slash at her foe and batted her blade aside. She risked Sakita's violet-limned talon raking at her to get the elixir vial inside the draug's shields, shouting in pain as Sakita's nails dug into her right shoulder and she felt the beginnings of a life-drain that could rip her soul out – but with her left hand she smashed the vial against Sakita's face.

The draug screamed, her life-drain spell died and she reeled away, a livid blotch opening up on her face. Tarita pulled her spiratus blade back into line and could have thrust . . . but this was Waqar's mother. There had to be some way back for her . . .

Then her wards screamed, she shielded a kinesis-blast from Heartface and the moment was gone. Sakita staggered away into the blackness and Tarita went the other way, smashing the little oak door ahead of her apart and pushing herself through on a blast of Air-gnosis.

She landed in a narrow, lightless corridor and ran. She had to break through another door before hurling herself aside just in time as flames roared down the hall behind her. She was in an office – without pausing, she wrenched the curtains aside, threw herself against the shutters and crashed through onto a stone balcony overlooking a rocky slope and the desert below. She'd not realised the back of the hill fell away so far. A sound behind gave warning and she whirled to see Heartface at the office door. This time it was Tarita who struck first, blasting back at the masked woman with all her strength. Shields crackled red and Heartface jerked out of sight.

And the skies were open before her.

Tarita leaped from the balcony and dropped like a stone, her skin screaming with the agony of sprouting feathers, her back muscles rippling and skin tearing, limbs twisting as she fell . . . then nine-foot-wide wings burst from her back and unfurled, caught an updraft and she soared into the moonlit darkness.

She looked back, as one shape then another peeled from the balcony she'd left and followed her out into the night. Lowering her head, she hurtled onwards, seeking altitude, elevation and *speed*.

Southern Kesh

Waqar called, clutching the relay-stave, but no one responded and suddenly the searing heat in his hands was too much. He dropped the stave, which burst into flame and crumbled to black embers. Another one gone. He cursed, his worry for Jehana a knot of anger inside him. His cabin in the after-castle was the largest on the windship but it was still barely large enough to squeeze him and his friends inside. The timbers of his flagship, a giant transporter craft, were thrumming from the Air-gnosis in the keel and the winds blowing the craft steadily towards Sagostabad.

The order had come within hours of his brief contact with Tarita: every available windship was summoned to Kesh. The vast camp had been preparing for this moment and the loading got underway swiftly and smoothly, but it had still been one of the most exhausting days of Waqar's life. He was responsible, which meant he had to ensure every craft that could get airborne did so. There was no grand lifting of the fleet; each craft left as soon as the men and gear were aboard. His was the last to leave; the place looked like the devastated remains of a camp after battle, complete with the wailing of women and children left behind without food or supplies. He couldn't fix that; all he could do was pray to Ahm they had some place that would take them in until their men came home. He sighed, imagining similar scenes all over Kesh and Dhassa.

As they'd crossed the Rakasarpal, the tongue of water that separated Lokistan from southern Dhassa, he'd caught up with half a dozen of his fleet, straggling northeast. Their first stop was a staging camp where they'd pick up supplies; he'd find out their next destination there.

This is the Holy War, he thought wonderingly. *The Shihad is actually happening – and we don't even know who we're going to fight . . .* The enormity of it was staggering. *I hope you know what you've started, Uncle.*

But right now what he needed to know was not their enemy, but if Tarita had found his sister. He stared at the burnt-out stave, wondering what on Urte he should do: Jehana wouldn't respond and Tarita was unreachable. Then a memory popped into his head and he jumped up and scrabbled among his possessions for his belt-pouch. He searched it until he found the tiny copper toe-ring.

Tarita had worn it for most of her life, she'd said. With renewed enthusiasm, he pulled out another relay-stave and began the call, this time using the ring as a focus . . . *<Tarita! Tarita—>* He felt the contact, heard the strangest strangled snuffling, and then a gurgling noise. *<Tarita?>*

Her voice gasped into his skull, *<Waqar? Ahm on high – I've been praying you'd call—>*

<Tarita? Are you all right?> He was puzzled by the way she sounded, and the accompanying sense of fear.

<I had to shape-change to take your contact,> she breathed, *<I still don't know if they're out there.>*

He could see her through the link now – she was in some kind of hole and though he could see only her face and shoulder, both were damaged, and smeared in filth. An animal stink reached him. *<What's happening? Why are you hiding?>*

Then she was babbling in his ear, a dreadful narrative that he didn't want to – *couldn't* – believe. *Mother? No—! And Jehana . . . where* are *you?*

By the time Tarita was done, he was speechless with worry. They stared at each other through the link as the stave smouldered in his hand. *<Ahm be with you,>* he sent. *<Be safe. I'll try to send help.>*

He broke the link, wondering if he'd ever see her again – then the enormity of what he needed to do hit him. He raised his head and shouted gnostically for his friends.

'Waqar,' Fatima said, hugging him, 'whatever you need, we'll do it.'

Waqar had no idea how he'd have managed without his comrades. Luka, Tamir, Baneet, Fati: right now, he loved them all beyond expression. It had taken him half an hour to tell them everything he'd learned: his mother's body had been revived as a draug, his sister was missing, and those behind the murder of Salim were somehow involved.

'I have to go to Hebusalim,' he told them. 'I have to learn the truth – but Uncle Rashid wants me here to direct the fleet. So I've got to be in two places at once.'

'Then you have to get permission from Rashid to go,' Fatima advised.

'In the middle of the launching of a Shihad?' Lukadin said sceptically. 'I know you're family and all, but this is the *Shihad* – he won't allow it.'

'Luka's right,' Baneet rumbled. 'Step aside now and Attam and Xoredh will destroy your reputation in seconds. You might as well fall on your own sword.'

'Jehana is Rashid's niece, too,' Waqar insisted, then he sighed. 'But you're right, he'll never give permission.'

'Why not?' Fatima asked. 'You said these masked people have penetrated the Ordo Costruo, but they haven't yet found where the Order have hidden Jehana. Rashid doesn't trust the Ordo Costruo: if he knew Jehana was in danger, he'd want to protect her. So tell him you *know* where Jehana is . . .'

Waqar bit his lip. *'Lie to the sultan?'*

'Sure.' Fatima grinned. 'Tell him your spy-friend knows where Jehana is but will only speak to you. He'll let you go, I'm sure of it.'

'But I don't know where Jehana is—'

'She's your sister – a really powerful scryer could use your blood to find her, as long as you're close enough. This spy-friend of yours might be able to help.'

Lukadin went to argue, but Waqar hushed him. 'But what about my mother? Do I mention that?'

'I wouldn't,' Tamir said. 'A missing sister is one thing, but a draug is another thing entirely – that breaks all the Gnostic Codes. Your uncle wouldn't just send you, he'd send a whole army, which would force the Ordo Costruo to oppose him, then you'd have no chance of going in quietly and finding them both.'

That would be catastrophic, Waqar thought. 'Very well, I won't mention her.'

'Only an *idiot* would lie to the sultan,' Lukadin started, but Waqar had made up his mind.

'No – I hear you, Luka, but I have to do it.'

<*Uncle? I mean, Great Sultan?*> Waqar had cleared his cabin so that he could concentrate on the difficult conversation he had to have. With his last remaining relay-stave he focused on the Mubarak family sigil and sent out his call. He'd half-expected some delay, or to be ignored, but Rashid responded almost instantly.

<*Nephew? Is all well with your fleet?*> Waqar had an impression of his uncle's face and could sense that he was surrounded by bustle.

<*Yes, Uncle, we're about a day south of Sagostabad. The winds are favourable and we'll land close to dusk, on the last day of Waning Moon.*>

<*Excellent. Well done for getting so many airborne. The men you're to collect are more or less ready. Now, I need to confer with my generals, so unless there is other news, I must—*>

Waqar dared to interrupt, before Rashid cut him off. <*It's about Jehana—*>

Rashid's face became surprisingly intense. <*What about your sister?*>

Waqar launched into his tale, sticking as close to the truth as he dared. *<When I investigated Salim's death, I met a Javonesi agent, a woman named Tarita. I won her trust and she promised to inform for me.>*

<You 'won her trust',> Rashid said, his voice somewhat sceptical, somewhat amused. *<I hadn't thought my nephew a seducer of foreign spies – but go on.>*

<This evening Tarita contacted me from Hebusalim: she'd made discreet enquiries about Jehana, and was told that the Ordo Costruo have her in hiding. I'm worried for her – I think she's in danger.>

He swallowed, waiting to see if this almost-lie was something that Rashid would take at face value. The sultan had fallen silent; Waqar could feel he was drumming his fingers. *<What are you asking, Waqar?>* Rashid asked eventually.

<Tarita says she knows where Jehana is being held, but she'll only tell me, in person. I wish to go to Hebusalim and meet with her.>

<In the middle of the launch of the Shihad?>

Waqar gulped. *<Yes, Uncle.>*

The sound of drumming fingers came again and he feared the worst, but Rashid said, *<You have my permission, Nephew. Jehana is family, and I don't trust that cess-pit of scholarly ambition, especially after your mother's death. But be careful, and keep me apprised.>*

Waqar closed his eyes. *<Thank you, Uncle,>* he said fervently.

'—so we'll find Jehana, save Mother and maybe unmask these killers,' Waqar vowed, ignoring his friends' doubtful looks. 'Come on, we've got work to do: I have to appoint a new admiral to get this fleet to Sagostabad, loaded up and sent onwards – and obviously we can't take this transporter to Hebusalim; apart from the fact my uncle needs it, it's too slow. We need something fast – one of the war-dhous with the mounted ballistae. And I want you all with me, if you'll come?'

'Of course we'll come,' Baneet said firmly, answering for them all.

'Thank you,' he said, then a thought struck him. 'Listen, when we deal with Tarita, we have to remember that she's a Javonesi spy: we'll deal with her openly and honestly about finding Mother and Jehana – but we *cannot* tell her about the windfleet; for all we know, it's her land we're invading and Uncle would have our heads if he thought we'd given someone like her advance warning.'

They all nodded solemnly at that, then it was time to hurl themselves into the practicalities. Eventually a dhou drew alongside their transporter and they were able to cross over, replacing the pilot-mage and some of the archers, who'd swapped ships to make room. Rashid had contacted Waqar to ensure he knew their route and schedule, insisting once again he be kept up to date every step of the way.

Beneath the crescent of the waning moon, Waqar passed on the baton of the fleet to Neniphas, an experienced ex-Hadishah commander who knew more about flying than he did anyway, then the dhou was uncoupled and with Luka at the tiller, sped away. Fatima, like Luka an Air-mage, called wind to their sails.

'Four hours until sunrise,' Tamir noted. 'Let's see what this bird can do.'

They swung around and surged towards the north.

At dawn in the wilderness, a lone she-jackal cautiously sniffed the air. Birds screeched in a distant copse and a bull bellowed from somewhere towards a nearby village. The air was cool, but the pale pastel disc rising in the east was already radiating warmth.

The jackal yawned and peered about it. It'd spent the night in a small wriggle-space beneath a pile of boulders, the abandoned lair of some burrowing animal, cringing as hunters passed overhead – they came close, but they never sensed her and now they were gone, leaving swiftly in the hour before sunrise. Sunlight was the bane of necromancy, so she wasn't surprised.

The jackal sat up, then with an ugly twisting and pulling and morphing of bones and flesh, it straightened onto hind legs, fur sloughing away until a skinny black-haired girl emerged, naked, with ugly scarring all down her spine and dead flesh peeling from her left cheek and right shoulder. She sniffed the air one last time as her beast senses faded and decided that she was alone and safe for now.

'Praise to you, Great Ahm,' Tarita croaked, as the concept of speech returned. She shuddered in memory of the night just gone; she'd quickly realised she couldn't outrun her pursuers, but she had enough of a lead

to go to ground, to change shape and blend into the night. That had
been no small challenge, for Heartface and Sakita, realising her ploy,
started killing anything that drew breath. The pulses of death-gnosis
slew hundreds of birds and small reptiles, as well as larger beasts like
the cattle that grazed this harsh land. They'd almost found her, but
she'd found a den and burrowed under stone. She'd killed a slumber-
ing snake as she'd passed and devoured it; the unpleasant tang of the
flesh was still in her mouth.

Thanks to her toe-ring, Waqar had managed to reach her there –
he'd initiated the contact so she'd not had to expend energy, which
might have drawn the hunters. But she couldn't count on his aid – she
had to assume that she was on her own. Capolio was in Sagostabad,
too far away to call, as was her mistress in Javon. Going to the Ordo
Costruo was fraught with risk. The Merozains had a shrine here, but
it was possible her pursuers had realised she had Merozain training.

She was undecided when a contact pricked at her. She dithered – was
this Heartface's attempt to find her? – but she took the risk, opening
up to the call.

<Tarita? Ahm on High, where have you been?>

<Waqar—> She sagged in relief. *<Where are you?>*

<We're nearing the Hebb Valley; we'll be in Hebusalim in less than an hour.>

They must have flown here immediately after we spoke. Tarita's heart
thumped with excitement – then his words sank in. *<Dear Ahm, don't
go there – you're coming up from Sagostabad? There's a village called Kushtadi,
near the southern edge of the Hebb Valley. Land west of the fields and I'll find you.>*

She broke the contact and took jackal form again, and bounded away.

Two hours later, Tarita was padding through the broken lands at the
southern edge of the Hebb Valley. Out here, herders guarded their flocks
with bows, and jackals were shot on sight, so she travelled low to the
ground, both canine and gnostic senses engaged. To the north, Ordo
Costruo-built aqueducts had turned the plains a pale green, while to the
south, barren hills shimmered in the haze: a stark and vivid reminder
of how much the magi had done for this region.

She topped a rise and scanned the dell below, then backed away and, with careful, slow expenditure of power, she undid the shape-change. Then she walked back to the ridge, naked and dirty, her hair a tangle, still breathing hard.

Below her was a windship, and someone was furling the sail. Waqar stood beside the hull with the four friends she recognised from Sagostabad.

<*Sal'Ahm, Prince: I'm here. Can you bring clothes? I've got nothing at all.*>

Waqar spoke to the young mage-woman, who scampered back onto the dhou, then reappeared with an armful of material. She made her way up the slope, looking about warily, but didn't spot Tarita until she stepped from hiding. She flinched when she saw Tarita's state.

'Dear Ahm,' she exclaimed, wrinkling her nose, then, 'These will be too big for you. Wash them before you give them back.'

Tarita raised her chin, refusing to play the subservient maid to this mage-born princess. 'I'll buy you a nicer set when I can.' She was right – the clothes were so big she had to knot them tightly to stop them falling off.

The woman looked at her dubiously. 'So you're the girl Waqar talks about. You'd better not be lying to him, or we'll show you how gutter-born wretches like you are treated.'

'I know exactly how the likes of you treat the likes of me,' Tarita told her. 'I'm just lucky that my days of crawling around at your feet are behind me.'

'I doubt that. Once a crawler, always a crawler, I find. Just don't get any ideas that you can take advantage of Waqar's good nature. I'll be watching your every move, and I'm nowhere near as nice as he is.'

'You're right,' Tarita said, 'you're definitely not as nice as he is.' They glared at each other, then Tarita said, 'So, you're protecting him. I respect that. But you're wasting your aggression on me: I'm not your enemy, or your rival.'

'You, a rival?' she scoffed. 'I don't think so.' She stopped and peered. 'What's wrong with your face?'

Tarita touched her left cheek. 'A necromancy wound. I think it'll heal – well, I *hope* so: I'd hate to ruin my *incredible* beauty.' She breezed past the other girl before she could reply, sashaying towards the wind-dhou as the rest of the prince's companions watched her approach with uniformly suspicious expressions.

Then protocol took over: she dropped to her knees, touched her forehead to the dust and waited.

'Tarita!' Waqar said, hurrying towards her. 'Get up, get up – we're not at court.' He helped her rise, which made the woman snort irritably. 'Thank Ahm you escaped!'

'Can we speak freely?' she asked in a low voice.

'Of course – I've known Fatima, Luka, Baneet and Tamir all my life.'

'And the crew?'

Waqar looked surprised. Clearly paranoia was a new game for him. 'They're just a random crew,' he assured her, 'they had no notice of the change of plan, or why they're here.'

'Then let's just assume at least one is a spy.' Tarita waved to his friends to join them, ignoring their expressions, and led them well away from the dhou. 'So this is the situation,' she told them, enjoying being able to lecture royalty. 'Last night I was attacked by two women. One was wearing the Heartface mask that one of Sultan Salim's killers wore. The other was a draug: dead Sakita Mubarak. They cornered me in the Cryptorium of the Ordo Costruo, having lured me there in a way that makes it clear they have infiltrated the Order – but they've not tested my scrying since dawn: and necromancy is affected by sunlight.'

Waqar had clearly told them about Sakita already, because his friends all looked angry, not shocked. Waqar had put his head in his hands at her words, but Tarita ploughed on – there was no time for squeamishness. 'Heartface *might* be Odessa D'Ark of the Ordo Costruo – but equally, it could have been someone pretending to be her. She tried to kill me after she'd established two things: first, that I didn't know how to find Jehana, and second, that I know the name of the man who wore the Beak mask in Sagostabad.'

'Who?' Waqar asked.

'I'll tell you later,' she replied.

The small skinny one with the owlish eyes – Tamir? – spoke first. 'We think using Waqar's blood might lead us to Jehana and Sakita – do you know someone with the right affinities to do that?'

Tarita put her hands on her hips and stuck her chest out a little. 'If you ask nicely, I'll do it myself.'

Tamir looked at her sceptically. 'I tried to call both Jehana and Sakita on the way north using Waqar's blood and got nothing and I'm a half-blood. You're what? A breeding-house girl? What do you have that we don't?'

She liked his lean frame and cheeky-serious look, so she winked and said, 'I'm a Merozain trainee.'

She watched five jaws drop with considerable satisfaction.

Tamir licked his lips. 'Ah ... so ... Holy Ahm ...' Then he regained his composure and looked around the circle. 'A gnostic call has a longer range than scrying, but it can be refused and you'd never know whether it was actually *received*. Both Sakita and Jehana could be rejecting contact. But a scrying *forces* contact. It's difficult to penetrate wards if the subject doesn't want to be found, but Tarita as a Merozain might be able to find them, whether they're willing or no.'

The rest were exchanging worried glances, clearly nervous about discussing their fears before her, so she stepped away and let them huddle together. While she waited, she closed her eyes, listening to the aether. Her wards were untouched: no one was scrying her or seeking contact, and that was both a relief and a worry.

Capolio, why haven't you called? That Heartface knew his name terrified her.

Then Waqar waved her back into the circle. 'We accept your offer. I have to find my mother and do what's required to put her to rest – and I *must* find my sister. Please, help us. There will be rewards, many rewards, if rewards are required.'

Tarita had never expected to be able to tell a prince that rewards weren't necessary. 'Consider this a token of friendship between Kesh and Ja'afar,' she told him. 'I'll need a metal bowl, a map, a compass and some of your blood.'

It took time to position the map; Tamir did that in the end, making devious calculations to ensure it was correctly aligned. Then Fatima – who hadn't met Tarita's eyes since her revelation – brought water, and Waqar bled a few drops into it.

He and Jehana weren't twins, which would have made the spell easier, but they were brother and sister of the same parents. Tarita cast her mind into the spell, using the imprint of Waqar's blood to seek traces of his sister . . . to no avail.

'I'm sorry,' she said at last, 'but Jehana is beyond my reach.'

She saw the pain, anxiety and frustration on Waqar's face, but he contained it impressively. They tipped out the water, its efficacy now gone, and tried again, this time scrying for Sakita, which was easier as Tarita had tended Sakita on her death-bed and knew her gnostic trace. The breakthrough came quickly: all the blood in the silver bowl flowed to one edge and Tamir carefully plotted the line on the map.

It ran through Hebusalim.

'Do we go there now?' Waqar wondered.

'They could be anywhere along that line,' Lukadin pointed out. 'My suggestion would be to circle the valley, east or west, makes no odds, and take a new reading. Unless they're on the move, that would give us a more precise position.'

'Triangulate their position?' Tamir approved. 'I agree – but can they sense your scrying?' he asked Tarita.

'Ordinary scrying can be sensed and blocked,' Tarita replied, 'but this runs deeper. It depends how skilled I am, and how sensitive they are.'

Tamir met her eyes. 'What do you think, honestly?'

Tarita recalled the casual power of Heartface. 'Honestly, I doubt we've gone undetected.' Then she winked. 'You have nice eyes, Skinny. We could be friends.' Tamir blushed pleasingly.

Waqar frowned. 'Let's get on with this. You think they're shunning the daylight, so let's make the most of it ourselves. We've around six hours left.'

She was beginning to seriously worry about Capolio. He must surely know by now that something was wrong. But there was nothing to do but move on, so she followed Waqar and his friends onto the dhou, sitting awkwardly apart from the close-knit comrades and missing the time in her life when she'd had room for friends. As the dhou rose and swung into the wind, Tamir smiled at her, and that nudged the emptiness inside her just a little.

It was mid-afternoon before they found a village that was on their map – which none of them fully trusted – and could take a new reading. They still couldn't reach Jehana, but scrying for Sakita gave them a new line on the map: one that crossed the first one north of the city, somewhat out of line with their earlier fix. Tarita tried to actually see Sakita, but all she got was darkness.

'She's beneath the earth, maybe in a tomb,' she guessed. 'Perhaps Heartface has released her?'

'I hope so,' Waqar said fervently, as they studied the new line on the map. 'But according to this new fix, she's not in Hebusalim any more?'

'That map's only marginally more accurate than a finger-drawing in the sand,' Tamir muttered. 'But they could have moved her.'

They came to a hilltop west of the Holy City where the Domus Costruo and the Bekira Dome were silhouetted against the eastern sky. This time the blood ran to the northeast, and the line crossed the earlier fixes north of the intersection point by four or five miles.

'I think you're right,' Tarita said to Tamir, 'they're moving her.'

They took the dhou up again, while Tarita fretted, wishing she had a relay-stave, but Waqar had apparently run out. *Capolio*, she prayed, *please, call me!*

Her next scrying indicated an emir's palace on the road north, but they found it empty for the summer, tended only by a small group of servants who claimed to have seen no one that day. The next scrying took them still further north into the setting sun, a full sixty miles from Hebusalim.

'They must be flying too! I think they've sensed us and they're trying to run.'

'If they're running, they fear us,' Waqar declared. 'Let's try scrying again.'

Fatima protested; he'd been bled many times that day and it probably wasn't helping with the stress he must be under. But he brushed aside their concerns.

Tarita conjured again, misty light forming as the blood swirled in the bowl, and this time the contact was faster and stronger. The sun was gone, but twilight lingered, illuminating the face that appeared in the bloody waters of the scrying bowl: Sakita's face, not marred by death but smooth-skinned and perfect, like a mask of herself in lacquer. Waqar gasped softly, and the image turned its eyes his way. There was no recognition, no warmth.

A sensation like being slapped by a cold, wet hand made Tarita reel. The image winked out and the blood stopped running up the side of the bowl. But not before they saw the line it made: running northwest.

Tamir voiced the obvious. 'The only thing that way is the Leviathan Bridge.'

34

Watcher's Peak

Hereditary Traits

I have my mother's eyes, and my father's nose. I have the gnosis, passed down in my blood. I worship Kore as my parents did. But I was not born with my father's perversions!

TOMAC GRAVIN, DEFENCE TESTIMONY, BRES, 853

Feher Szarvasfeld, Mollachia
Junesse 935

Valdyr was among the first to emerge from the Rahnti Mines, on the south side of Watcher's Peak. Dragan Zhagy was with him, and Juergan Tirlak. They were all in gloomy spirits – Juergan had met them halfway with news of Tibor Siravhy's execution. *I encouraged that mission*, Valdyr reproached himself, over and over. Knowing that they all knew the risks was no consolation.

Dragan Zhagy's voice dragged him back to the present. 'Juergan, get to the look-out and see if there are redcloaks in the valley. We'll send scouting parties south while our main body goes west to the Magas Gorge.'

Right now, Kyrik was guiding the Sydian riders into Magas Gorge, leading horses and cattle along the wet, mossy stone tracks and across perilous fords beneath towering cliffs. The number of things that could go wrong was immense, but the worst of those was to be trapped in the gorge with Rondians on the cliffs.

'I'll go with Juergan,' Valdyr volunteered. 'I've not seen the shape of the land here from up high.'

515

Juergan seemed to consider Valdyr's company an honour. The scout led the way up a long goat-track to the nearest watch-point, a spear-head of stone with a difficult approach. At one point the path forked and Valdyr glanced upwards, seeing a silhouette of antlers – but they were old and weathered, a skull nailed to a tree-stump. 'What's that?'

'That's a marker for the trail to Watcher's Peak,' Juergan replied. 'The summit is above the snowline, except at high summer. They say that when Zlateyr stood on Watcher's Peak, he could see the entire kingdom.' He indicated the main trail. 'But we're going this way.'

Reaching the watch-point left them breathing hard, but the reward was a wide vista overlooking all of northern Feher Szarvasfeld. They lay panting at the top, careful not to break the silhouette of the horizon as they peered out. The land spread before them was an undulating mass of outcroppings and bare slopes broken by pine and brush thickets, crisscrossed with hundreds of tiny streams that seeped into the porous rock and vanished.

'How can we ever hope to see Rondian patrols from here?' Valdyr asked. 'The ground's too broken.'

'The main trail crosses open ground, *there*,' Juergan told him, point-ing down to a clearing about a mile southeast. 'Anyone traversing the valley on horseback has to go that way.' He pointed. 'There are other places too, where the paths climb out of the tree-line. Just let your eyes run from point to point and you'll be able to make out anyone who's there.' He touched his skull. 'Mollach knowledge, Prince.'

'I have a lot to learn, but I have good teachers,' Valdyr replied. They settled in to watch as the sun meandered towards its zenith. Then a tiny line of dots emerged from the pines and crossed the clearing. Juergan pulled out a metal tube capped with thick glass and peered, then showed Valdyr. 'It's a Rondian spyglass, like their windships use,' he said. 'Put your eye to the narrow end.'

When Valdyr did as he was did, he sucked in his breath: what had been black spots became a blurred column of red-cloaked riders. He couldn't pick out faces, but they were legion cavalry, not just scouts, and there were a lot of them.

'Where does the trail they're on lead?'

'Magas Gorge.'

Right where Kyrik's taking his savages . . . 'When will they get there?'

'Day after tomorrow, I reckon: about the same time the Vlpa emerge from the Narrows onto Neplezko Flat. There's a place there where we've carved a climb – we call it the Gazda's Stair – where you can get a man and a horse up to the eastern cliffs. If these redcloaks reach the top of the Stair while your brother is below, he'll be in trouble.' He pointed to a fresh line of riders on the far side of the distant clearing. 'Look, another column. They're moving in force.' Then he stiffened and pointed to three dots in the skies, moving swiftly. 'Windskiffs!'

Is it just bad luck, or do they know what we're doing? Valdyr wondered. 'Stay here, try to estimate their numbers. I'll go and tell Dragan.'

Valdyr found Dragan with the main body, preparing for the trek west to the Magas and drew him aside to tell him what he and Juergan had seen. 'How many riders do the Rondians have?' he asked.

'A standard legion has two maniples of cavalry,' Dragan told him. 'That's a thousand men.'

'We only saw a few dozen, but Juergan was still counting them when I left. We saw skiffs too.'

Dragan grimaced. 'We have two hundred men here, not enough to stop them.'

'Juergan says if they catch Kyrik below the Narrows, it'll be a massacre.'

'Ysh, it could.' Dragan stared out across the valley. 'It all depends on how far through the gorge Kyrik's got. If they can deploy on the cliffs above Neplezko Flat, they could fight, but if the Rondians reach those cliffs first, they'll be trapped below.'

Valdyr felt the lack of the gnosis more keenly than ever – with it, he could at least have tried to contact Kyrik and warn him. 'We'll have to send runners,' he said.

'But if the Rondians have skiffs in the air, that will be perilous – a running man is far easier to spot from above. We'll send men, certainly, but they'll need to stick to cover and that'll slow them considerably. I'll not have my boys risk themselves needlessly for those Sydian riders.'

Valdyr swallowed. 'My brother is with them.'

'And he's a mage – if anyone can get out of a trap, a mage can. The

Vitezai Sarkanum was formed by our forefathers to protect the realm, not to be thrown away protecting foreigners. We can harass the Rondians for as long as we like, with or without the Vlpa. Getting them here was a feat, but we must think first of our own kind. You see that, don't you? Even though your brother doesn't.'

Valdyr looked away, face burning.

'He's a decent man, Kyrik,' Dragan went on, 'but decency is for priests. A tabula player obsessed with protecting all his pieces will lose the game. That's Kyrik.' Dragan touched Valdyr's shoulder. 'You take after your father more than he does.'

He means it as a compliment, Valdyr reminded himself, though he had few happy memories of Elgren Sarkany. But losing Kyrik, for all their disagreements, would be unendurable. 'Surely your runners could beat these riders to the gorge?'

'Lad, it takes three hours just to reach the clearing below, and by then it'll be dark.'

'They could run through the night—'

'Holding torches to light our way, or simply running off cliffs? It's Darkmoon tomorrow night, my Prince. There's as good as no moonlight for the next seven nights. I'll send runners, but their first priority must be to stay alive and uncaptured. Beyond that, your brother and his Sydians are in Kore's hands.'

Magas Gorge, Mollachia
Junesse 935

Kyrik hauled steadily on the reins while panting out calming words to the restive beast. Braced against one rock, his feet planted on another, he tried once again to haul the horse out of the swift water, but the stallion was big-eyed with fright and shuddering at the fierce cold of the mountain river. Then Rothgar Baredge, the big, bearded Stonefolk hunter, added his muscle and together they got the struggling animal up and onto the bank. Kyrik groaned as he sagged against the rock wall.

'There,' the hunter panted, 'told you it weren't a hard crossing.'

'Last time I believe your lies,' Kyrik laughed. Then the stallion nudged him indignantly: it had been through this dozens of times in the past three days and knew the drill by now. 'Sorry, boy,' he apologised, pulling out a cloth, still soaked from the last crossing, and rubbed the horse down. If he didn't get the legs dry, chances were it'd go lame. 'Poor animal.'

As the most potent mage present, it had become Kyrik's duty to blaze the trail for the Vlpa, making each crossing first. He was thankful he had the best hunter in the valley to guide him. He found Rothgar good company; he was around thirty, of an age with Kyrik, though with his grey-streaked beard and weathered skin he could have passed for fifty.

They finished rubbing down the stallion, then Rothgar led the horse away while Kyrik waved at the next to cross: Brazko, the chief's eldest son, with another two dozen riders. The cliffs above caught the constant roar of the tortured water and funnelled it down the gorge, all but drowning out their voices. He glanced at the sky: it was an hour or so before they lost the light and they still needed to make camp. The Sydian column was spread out for miles on either side of the river. At no point since they'd entered the gorge had he been able to see more than three dozen riders.

Five minutes per man to cross, and we need to allow half an hour to set up camp . . . He held up both hands, three fingers raised on each, splayed so they could count. *Six more men across, then make camp*, was the message he hoped to convey. Then he and Rothgar helped Brazko haul his pony up the slope. The Sydians rode superbly, of course, but river crossings like this were beyond their experience. They'd adapted swiftly, though, with Brazko invariably third to cross, after Kyrik and Rothgar. They were all diligent in tending their mounts – the Vlpa men treated their horses better than their women, Kyrik thought.

Thinking of Sydian women sent his eyes roving across the ford to the far bank, seeking Hajya's shock of black hair amidst the tightly top-knotted warriors. Her strong face was marked with a thick blue stripe running across both eyes and the bridge of her nose, the same face-paint as the warriors in a warband ritual Brazko had led. It accentuated her exoticism and emphasised her penetrating gaze.

<Make sure you're one of the six to cross,> he sent. She didn't reply, but he knew she'd heard.

He left the warriors to deal with the rest of the crossings and hurriedly assembled his own Sydian tent, a semicircle of hide over three poles forming a cone. It was cosy enough when shared by two.

'When will we reach the path up to the cliff-tops?' he asked Rothgar.

'Tomorrow evening,' Rothgar estimated. 'We're still six miles north of Neplezko Flat and we're only making three miles a day so far, but the crossings are easier from here on, at least until we strike the narrows – there's some tricky climbs around the rapids, but after that the river forms a lake, about three hundred yards across. Neplezko Flat is beyond the lake. We call the path up top the eastern cliff the Gazda's Stair – getting a horse to the top is a feat, but no worse than some of the fords.'

'Will Dragan and Valdyr be there before us?'

'Probably – they should have cleared the Rahnti Mines yesterday evening, and it takes about a day and a half to get from Watcher's Peak to the Magas.'

'Then let's hope the Delestres have no inkling we're here.'

'On that count, we're in Kore's hands.'

They got back to the river in time to haul Hajya and her horse from the water. Kyrik went to rub down the animal, but Rothgar took the cloth from his hands. 'Your lady's soaked to the waist,' the hunter noted wryly. 'You might want to help her with her leggings. Leather's a bitch to get off when it's wet.'

Kyrik snorted, slapped the man's shoulder and went to help Hajya as best he could.

An hour later, he emerged from the tent, wrapped in a blanket to protect his modesty, and waved thanks at the man who'd cooked that evening. A small pot had been left at his tent flap. As he kindled a small fire to reheat the stew, he noticed Brazko and Rothgar talking intently, the other six warriors listening respectfully as they huddled around a larger fire. He contemplated joining them, but in truth, he just wanted one person's company tonight.

Hajya joined him soon after, wrapped in the fox-fur wedding cloak

he'd made for her. She sniffed ruefully at her armpits – she'd been disbelieving when he told her that Rondian women plucked out armpit
hairs – then kissed him and swayed away towards the river. She returned
soaking and shivering a few minutes later, dried herself on a blanket,
then hung it to dry, unconcernedly naked. 'Those men have seen me
before,' she remarked when he gestured towards the others, but she
did wrap the fox-fur about herself again.

He looked at her admiringly. Perhaps most men would have found
her unremarkable, and in stillness, she didn't stand out. But she did
everything with vigour and conviction. Her weathered face had never
been pretty and her muscular, fleshy body was ageing, but when she
moved, when she danced, when she spoke, no one else mattered.

She swivelled and caught him staring, and he fancied that pleased
her. 'What?'

'I'll tell you later,' he said, then turned his mind to logistics – there
were things he needed to know about her Sfera. 'I was talking to Rothgar earlier. We have to get enough men to the top of the eastern cliffs
above Neplezko Flat tomorrow to shield us in case an enemy patrol happens by. We'll not reach the flat until tomorrow afternoon, and if there
are Rondian scouts, we'll be hard to hide. How can your Sfera help?'

She considered. 'I'm primarily a hermetic mage so I can help calm
the beasts for the climb. Most of the others have similar gifts. I chose
the ones to travel with us for their abilities to hunt and fight – in
truth, almost all of our affinities are of elemental and physical magic.'

'Don't you have a diviner among you? Torzo?' He recalled a tall,
skinny man, a little older than Hajya. He'd never seen him move from
the shadows of the Sfera pavilion, but he'd foreseen Kyrik's advent last
month. 'A shame we didn't bring him. We could use someone who can
give us a view of the bigger picture.'

Hajya shook her head. 'Torzo's frail – and blind. A hard ride as we
did wouldn't have been possible – and anyway, Thraan needs him,
back on the plains.'

'I hadn't realised he was blind.'

'When it was realised that his strongest affinity was divination, the
Sfera leader – the one before me – had him blinded, so that his body

would be forced to rely on his mind. We've found such things can accentuate an affinity.'

Kyrik felt his eyes go round. 'That's *barbaric*!'

'Ysh, but it works,' Hajya said softly. 'I felt bad for my friend, but it was the way of it. Korznici, his granddaughter, has the same potential – if she is revealed to be a diviner, I will do the same to her.'

He swallowed. 'But—'

'We are all of us in the Vlpa Sfera low-blooded. We have learned little tricks to transcend our limitations. It's called survival.'

Every day brought him a new challenge. *She's an animage . . .* 'What did they do to you?'

Pain flashed momentarily in her eyes. 'Nothing you truly wish to know.'

He swallowed, and decided she was right: he didn't want to know. So they talked of neutral things for a time before returning to the tent to enjoy each other's bodies, then let sleep settle on them like a mantle and soothe away their fears.

Watcher's Peak, Feher Szarvasfeld, Mollachia

Dragan's runners were gone, but there were likely Rondian riders between them and the Magas Gorge. The *Gazda* had sent Juergan and a dozen other scouts south to get a better feel for the strength of the enemy and the news wasn't good: there were footmen too, advancing through the valley behind the cavalry. A small army lay between them and Magas Gorge.

The morning and afternoon crawled by. With so many fears and frustrations churning inside him, Valdyr couldn't rest. All his fretting and pacing finally took him to the trail to the watch-spur again, but on a whim, he took the peak trail so he could put his back to the blackened stump with the rack of antlers nailed to it and try to think.

We can't warn Kyrik and we can't fight a force that size. We're useless! I'm *useless.* He buried his head in his hands, screaming inside his head, *Kyrik, Kyrik, can you hear me?*

But his call never became a *call*. It never left his skull, just rattled inside it. He prayed to Kore that *someone* would get through in time. If they failed, then unless Kyrik found a way to contact him – and he'd said he wouldn't even try, in case it alerted the Delestre magi – then there was nothing he could do. The implications of his brother dying weren't lost on him: he'd be king – but he hated himself for thinking of it.

The crunch of boots below wasn't really welcome, but it was Dragan himself, climbing the steep track with an easy lope, like the wolf whose pelt he wore. He threw himself down beside Valdyr. 'The first scouts are in,' he said without preamble. 'The valley floor is crawling with redcloaks: cavalry and footmen. They're strung out over almost seven miles. We estimate two maniples of cavalry and maybe four of rankers: enough to fight a battle, but not arrayed like they expect one. They mightn't know about Kyrik's column yet.'

Valdyr brooded on this tendril of hope for a long, silent time.

'Your father and I came here once, when you were a boy,' Dragan said eventually. 'We'd thought to climb all the way to the peak and see the world as Zlateyr did. But there's a ravine only a stag could leap and the bridge is long lost. We nearly froze – and that was in Junesse.'

'Do you think Zlateyr and his warband were Sydian?'

Dragan's reply was vehement. 'Never! Zlateyr was a great *Mollach* hero. He was Andressan – like you and me: dark hair, *white skin*. Your brother can believe what he wants, and he can tell those Sydians whatever he wants, but he's wrong.'

His conviction sounded defensive, but Valdyr let it pass. *It shouldn't matter, but it does. Like the fact that just thinking of touching dark skin makes me ill.*

He looked up at the peak, its summit lost in cloud. 'I'd like to climb it one day.'

'Pick a hot day in Julsep,' Dragan replied, 'with clear skies. When the clouds drop past where we sit, there's a storm coming.' He clapped Valdyr on the shoulder and they were rising to leave when they heard a great snorting sound. Turning, they saw a giant stag barely a dozen paces away: an eighteen-pointer, built like a warhorse, with shaggy fur and the blackest eyes. Its coat was pure white.

Dragan slowly reached for his bow, but Valdyr caught his hand. 'No. It's sacred.'

'When did you become a priest, lad?' Dragan rumbled, but he dropped his hand. 'That fur, the velvet, the antlers – lowlanders pay deep in the purse for a white.'

'Zlateyr saw a white stag the day he died,' Valdyr breathed. *And one saved me from the Vrulpa-daemon . . .*

'Aye, and King Rodislan shot four in one season when he was twenty, and lived to sixty-seven. They're just animals, lad. There are herds north of Lake Jegto. Believe me, you don't want to get caught by those prongs.'

'I'd just said that I'd like to go up there, and it came.'

'You said "one day". That doesn't have to be today,' Dragan retorted.

Valdyr took a step towards the stag, which made a strange lowing and twitched its head backwards, towards Watcher's Peak. 'Look! It wants me to follow—'

'It's eyeing an escape route is what it's doing.'

But Valdyr was certain. He'd expressed a wish, and the stag had come. He didn't care if it was foolish: he needed to be doing something, and this was something. 'I'm going to follow it.' He took a step towards the massive beast, which tossed its magnificent head and moved a little way up the path.

Valdyr pursued as fast as he could, sucking in the cold, thin air that stung his throat. Dragan followed, telling him this was foolish, that losing Kyrik would be bad enough but losing him too would destroy the kingdom, but Valdyr, caught up in the stag's huge eyes, barely heard.

Then it bounded up another slope to the very edge of a wall of mist and Dragan called, 'Stop, lad!' He caught his arm. 'It's too risky – there's snow up there.'

The stag looked back and bellowed, trumpeting its strength and mastery, and the sound went echoing around the peaks, coming back in waves. The effect was stirring, setting Valdyr's heart drumming. 'No, I've got to follow.' He pulled free and trotted across the next dell, around a tiny grey tarn, and crunched up the slope.

Dragan came partway, then stopped. *'Please, lad!'*

The stag roared again as the mists closed in and it was just a silhouette at the top of the rise. When Valdyr looked back, Dragan was a forlorn figure beside the tarn, fading to a grey shadow, still shouting, *'Valdyr – come back!'*

The stag bounded off into the clouds, and Valdyr, afraid to lose it, ran after it until Dragan's voice was lost in the moan of the winds. He stumbled, grazed his hands and scrambled on as his field of vision dropped to two or three feet and the wind plucked and pulled at his cloak. The stag snorted on the slopes above. *That way? Or that?* He clambered up the rocky slope and almost ran into a giant boulder – and the picked-clean skeleton of another deer, a female, just a pile of yellowy broken bones and stubby antlers. It felt like a warning.

The air was colder. It'd been mid-afternoon when he left, but the light was fading into deep grey and it felt like he was climbing into night. But the white stag was before him again, stamping its fore-hooves and sending little rockfalls back down the slope.

Dragan wasn't wrong. I could die up here. He commended his soul to Kore, and the stag blasted air from its nostrils as if laughing, then with a flex of its huge shoulders it sprang into the gloom. Valdyr ran after it and darkness swallowed the world below. He staggered into old snow, crunching through the dirty skin of it, all his instincts shrieking at him to go back – but he refused, even though the wind was whining over the teeth of icy rocks, sucking at his vitality. The white stag was still ahead of him, always at the edge of vision. It no longer looked like a real beast but a wisp of mist, somehow visible despite the lack of moonlight, showing him paths where he'd seen none. The only light was the pallid glow of the mist.

He topped another rise and stumbled towards an area of flat ground – and suddenly realised the place was paved with broken slabs: a roadway, of sorts. The stag dashed through what might be a broken-topped arch sheltering some dead hagwoods, with Valdyr breathlessly following in its wake until he found himself inside the circle of a shattered keep barely ninety feet in diameter. The remaining walls were low, encrusted in ice and snow.

Wasn't there supposed to be some kind of ravine? He glanced back through the arch and almost fell: the ground behind him, the road he'd walked, was gone and there was only a precipice: a deep drop filled with swirling mist.

'Kore's Light!' he gasped, and this time it was the wind chuckling at his piety.

There was no sign of the stag as he walked into the stone circle. Surely this was a tower's foundations, he thought, wondering if he could find enough shelter here to wait out the night. There was an old fire-pit in the middle, and around it were huddled four mounds, like old folk in blankets trying to soak up the last of the heat from a burned-out blaze. He looked closer and realised that was exactly what they were: rime-coated bones encased in cloaks of heavy furs. How long ago they'd died, he had no idea. Two had armour and weapons; the other two were bare-headed, with tangled manes of dead hair. The skulls leered at him, teeth bared, frosted grey hair teased by the shifting air.

Though he was still sweating from the climb, the cold struck him and he began to shake, thinking of the dangers of frostbite, and worse. He looked back at the broken gates: the hagwoods were the first fuel he'd seen up here. They were long dead and it took no time to break off some branches and drag them to the fire-pit. He'd not worked out how to set fire to them, but somehow that problem solved itself: with a sudden terrifying whoosh, the branches caught alight and flames roared.

He almost ran, but it felt like death out there beyond the stones. His world had shrunk to this one last haven of light in the dark, so he hunkered down, frightened but watchful, between two of the dead and leaned into the flames, soaking up the heat rolling out of the pit. He had hard bread and dried meat in his pouch; as he began to thaw, he ate, the cavernous eye-sockets of the dead following his every move.

Nothing moved but the flames. Outside the stone circle, the wind was like the howling of the unquiet dead, but in here it was . . . *safe*.

He closed his eyes, drifting . . .

'Hey, boy, you want a swig?'

Valdyr blinked awake to find four faces peering at him: all black-haired, with narrow eyes and copper-skinned faces. *Sydians*. An old man with a top-knot – a shaman, he realised – was proffering a leather-wrapped flask. He went to refuse, then thought, *Why not: it's only a dream.*

He took a mouthful, and reeled as the liquor hit the back of his mouth, threatening to burn a hole right through to his brain.

The shaman chuckled. 'Good brew, ysh?'

Valdyr looked at him mutely as the fluid seared his throat.

'Tongue frozen, boy?' the woman tittered. 'Or burned off?'

'Dissolved,' the smaller of the two warriors laughed. 'Here, have a bite of venison, lad. We took down a white stag in the valley today.' He offered a stick with a hunk of roasted meat skewered on it. 'Go on, have some.'

Valdyr hesitated. *A white stag?* But he was only dreaming, so he took the meat and nibbled. Delicious juices filled his mouth and he wolfed the rest down ravenously.

'He's a handsome boy,' the woman commented. 'There's pain though, in here.' She gestured towards her heart. She wasn't pretty, but she had a confident frankness that was unsettling . . . a lot like Hajya of the Vlpa.

'Cautious,' the shaman said, dipping a wooden cup into a pail of water – snowmelt, he guessed – and handing it to Valdyr.

'Afraid,' said the young warrior. 'But no coward. He's faced death and taken lives.'

They turned to the one man who hadn't spoken: a tall, angular man, by far the biggest Sydian Valdyr had ever seen, though there wasn't a spare ounce of fat on him. He had a long, horse-like face and a black beard and ponytail. His cheeks were scarred and his rudder-like nose had been broken at least once.

'Is he the right one?' the woman asked him.

The tall man studied Valdyr coolly. 'I see a man at war with himself. I see bitterness and hatred. I see open wounds on his soul. But the potential is there.'

'But does he have the strength? I see brittleness,' the shaman commented.

The tall man peered at Valdyr, his eyes piercing. 'Do you know my name, boy?'

527

Valdyr shook his head, though a name occurred to him, one he wanted to deny.

'I brought my people here, made peace with the Stonefolk in the valley and settled the lands. Made a new kingdom.'

'Zlateyr?' Valdyr whispered.

'He does have a tongue after all,' the smaller warrior noted.

The big man smiled ironically. 'Yes, I am Zlateyr. I brought my clan from the steppes to the icy peaks, seeking a new home, a place where we could be something more than nomads. Now your brother has brought more.'

Valdyr looked around the circle. If this man was Zlateyr, then the woman must be his sister Luhti, the smaller man his son Eyrik, the shaman the legendary Sidorzi.

'But you reject your brother's actions,' Luhti said. 'You're too proud to accept the truth. You consider yourself "pure" when purity doesn't exist. All men are mongrels. You yourself are born of Stonefolk and Uffrykai. You know this in your heart.'

Valdyr looked around the circle, and shook his head. 'This is a dream.'

'It's no dream,' Zlateyr replied. 'You're more awake now than you've ever been.'

'Do you know what dwyma is?' Sidorzi asked.

Valdyr shook his head.

'You crave the gnosis,' Zlateyr said. 'We hear your anguish that you cannot reach it. In time, left to your own devices, you would stumble upon it – but there's another path open to you. All of life has energy and that energy has its own spirit: as a daemon harvests the souls of the dead, so does the Elétfa – the Tree of Life – draw life's energies into itself. The Elétfa can sense and reason, but its goals are not those of man or daemon. A *varazslo* can speak to the Tree and gain succour from it – as we can.' Zlateyr tapped Valdyr's chest. 'As *you* could.'

'A *varazslo*?' Valdyr didn't know the word. The Mollach word for mage was *vrajitoare*.

'One who can channel the forces of life. A dwymancer – a varazslo. The potential exists in all mage-born, but must be triggered before the gnosis is kindled.'

Valdyr had never heard of such a thing. 'Surely if this was real, then all of Urte would know?'

Zlateyr touched a finger to Valdyr's forehead. 'There have been varazslo for as long as there have been magi, but magi do not like rivals. We varazslo were never many, and we were hunted, but we've never vanished. The Elétfa sustains us, and I have felt the stirrings of a reawakening.'

'Even in Pallas,' Sidorzi added, 'at the heart of empire, we have lain concealed.'

'And now you've come,' Eyrik said. 'An answer to our prayers.'

Valdyr didn't feel like a prayer's answer. 'A white stag led me here – I thought it might be a sign. But signs and omens aren't real – the magi say so.'

'Not for magi,' Luhti answered, 'but dwyma is not like the gnosis. It is *life* – it moves through us. The gnosis is the axe in the hand of a woodsman. Dwyma grows the forest. It *is* the forest.'

'The gnosis is the surgeon's scalpel,' Eyrik added. 'Dwyma is the body.'

'The gnosis is a single word and the dwyma the voice of the world,' said Sidorzi.

Zlateyr leaned towards him. 'A mage uses the gnosis, but dwyma uses *us*: we paint in giant brushstrokes and take our strength from the vastness of the natural world. We must persuade the dwyma to hear us. Our power is slow to rouse and impossible to turn aside. It is eternal, and sees with the eyes of aeons.'

'Then you are alive still?' Valdyr asked.

'Alive? Dead? Ghost? The words are meaningless. We are leaves of the Elétfa. If you accept your powers, so too will you be.'

Luhti touched his arm. 'But first, you must accept what you are, because our power is not the gnosis, it is not a *tool* – it is a bargain. The Tree of Life will let you drink of its sap, but those so blessed *belong* to that power – it doesn't belong to *you*. Misuse it, and it will leave you and strip you hollow in its passing.'

'But if it's not a tool, what's it for?'

Luhti laughed coolly. 'It's not *for* anything – it *is*. It allows us to touch it, so that we might ensure that it continues to be.'

Valdyr swallowed. It all sounded so enticing when he'd been raging against his impotence ... but it also felt like being offered a spoon when he needed a knife. 'What will the Elétfa ask of me?'

'For now?' Zlateyr replied: 'To accept what you are: rise above your illusions of tribe and clan. Your blood comes from everywhere, from the cold North to the warm South, the green West and even the arid East. The first Sydians migrated from Dhassa before the land-bridge fell into the sea, and before them, Yothic and Frandi. You are from *everywhere*, Valdyr. Let that knowledge guide you.'

Valdyr swallowed. *Then I'm the same as those people in the breeding-house ... I'm just like Asiv.*

'No, *not* like him,' Luhti said, as if he'd spoken aloud. '*Nothing* like him.' Her hand on his cheek was warm, so tender, it made tears well up and run down his cheeks. 'He hurt you but he didn't *conquer* you.'

'He did conquer me,' Valdyr whispered. He hid his face, ashamed to face the heroes of Mollachia when he was nothing but the catamite of a mudskin rapist. *I'm not worthy of being here ...*

'We know what he did,' Zlateyr said, his voice both angry and sympathetic.

'How can you?'

'Because it's written all over your soul,' Luhti whispered, putting her arms around him. He flinched, but didn't pull away. 'We can see what else he did too.'

'We know about the daemons,' Zlateyr added. 'We know about his experiments on behalf of *Naxius*.'

It was too much. Memories suppressed for so long flooded back, and all he could see was Asiv's hateful face. He had been bad enough to start with, a cruel breeding-house master, but everything changed when Ervyn Naxius had arrived in Asiv Fariddan's quarters one night. It became clear very quickly that the Yurosi was no rescuer, just another man possessed of inexhaustible curiosity and a moral void who found in Asiv a kindred spirit. From then on, Naxius mentored Asiv, and each visit took Valdyr into a new and fresh Hel.

And when Asiv wasn't experimenting on the limits of daemon-possession and soul-bindings, he was fulfilling his own ever-growing perverted lusts, fed by the creatures he summoned.

'He'd chain me in a circle, then summon those things into my body,' Valdyr whispered. 'It was like drinking sewage. I couldn't stand it – I begged to die. I prayed to Kore and Sol and Ahm – and *no one heard!* Kyrik never came – *no one came!*'

Eventually Asiv had discarded him as too old, too used-up for his needs. No one had cared; Valdyr was reassigned to another house, back to the breeding programme.

'Yet you *were* rescued,' Luhti reminded him. 'Prayers can be answered in strange ways. You are here, when and where Mollachia needs you.'

'But I can't stand the Vlpa. They're like animals—'

Luhti stroked his cheek. 'There, is my hand so repulsive? Am I so ugly?'

He shook his head. 'You're different.'

'No, I'm not – none of us are. Zlateyr, me, Eyrik and Sidorzi: we're Uffrykai, just as Clan Vlpa are. Imagine them clothed as you Mollachs are and see if you can spot a difference. See their souls. Look beyond the skin.'

Valdyr closed his eyes, unable to think in such a way. But her body against his felt warm and comforting, like the mother he'd lost, and he found himself sinking into her side, cradled and *safe*. Somehow her presence banished his sickening memories of Asiv to somewhere in the deepest recesses of his mind.

Zlateyr's voice washed over him: 'We're all just flesh and blood, equal in all but the tiniest details. I saw this when I fought the Stonefolk – so we made peace. The Mollach people are the result of that peace; that peace is what begat you, Valdyr Sarkany. It's not hate for the Keshi you feel. It's hate for Asiv Fariddan and his ilk.'

Luhti lifted his head and when he opened his eyes, her face was that of a girl he'd been forced to mate with many times: one he'd hated; he'd struck her and kicked her until they'd chained him up so she could mate with him. But suddenly he realised she'd been as scared, as abused as he was. *Many of them were*, he realised.

I'm so sorry, he whispered to the memory. *I lashed out at the wrong people – the only people I could reach, when they were the ones least deserving of hatred.*

Luhti kissed his forehead, then his mouth, and he kissed her back, his lips melting into hers, his soul bleeding into her eyes. *'If your heart is changed, you will become the one we seek,'* she whispered, her voice fuzzy and fading. *'If not, the dirt of the grave will choke you.'*

For aeons he floated in her gaze.

Then he fell from her grasp into the bosom of sleep.

35

Loekryn's Bridge

The Celestium

During his long reign, the power of Emperor Sertain lay in both the temporal and spiritual realm: he was emperor and head of the Kore Church. But when he died, his son and heir Gordian was persuaded to separate the two spheres of power, and so the title of prelate was born. This became arch-prelate and then grand prelate as time passed, and the power of the Church came to rival that of the Rondian Emperor himself. The Building of the Celestium, across the Bruin from the Imperial Bastion, was interpreted as a direct challenge to Imperial power.

ORDO COSTRUO COLLEGIATE, PONTUS, 847

The Bastion, Pallas-Nord
Junesse 935

Ril awoke pressed against his wife's back, her pale hair teasing his nostrils. He inhaled the fragrance of her, the rosewater she washed with alleviating the earthier smells of their bodies. He kissed her bare shoulder, ran his hand down her side to her hip, wondering if she'd be amenable to . . .

'Good morning,' Geni chirruped, startling him.

Rukking maids! Have they no respect for a man's privacy? The girl scuttled away when he gestured in annoyance.

Lyra was still sleeping, her face so peaceful it felt cruel to wake her, so he slid from the bed, threw on breeches and gathered the rest of his clothes. In the next room, Geni was setting breakfast; she blushed as she saw his bare chest and midriff, which made him smile.

533

'Is Domara about?' he asked, pulling his shirt on.

'Not yet, sir,' Geni answered, trying hard to look like she wasn't watching him. 'She'll be another ten minutes.'

'Best I get out then.' He hurried to the door, then paused. 'Do you disapprove of me being here too, Geni?'

'Oh no, sir. My ma had eleven bairns: she and Da were at it right up 'til birthing, an' she never lost a one.'

'Good. Tell Domara, will you?'

'Oh, I try, sir,' Geni said enthusiastically. 'My ma always said that her best "shudder-shakes" – that's what she called 'em – was when she was near to birthing. A good 'un could bring the child on, she said.'

'Er . . . thank you, Geni – that's far more than I needed to know.' He heard Domara's voice approaching and fled, trying to remember what he needed to see Setallius about . . . *That sigil, yes!*

He didn't succeed in tracking the spymaster until after the midday meal, when he finally reappeared in his office. 'There you are,' Ril said, waving away an aide. 'It's the third time I've passed today. I tried a gnostic-call but couldn't reach you.'

'A certain amount of elusiveness is expected in my role,' Setallius drawled. 'How can I help?'

Ril explained the stone he'd found in Lyra's garden and the sigil that matched the bronze panel in front of the altar in Saint Chalfon's church in Surrid. 'I don't know why, but it's nagging at me. Do you know what it means?'

If the spymaster was puzzled or impatient at the request, it didn't show. He and his small circle of Volsai mages had been conducting the futile hunt for the royal children; it had been three weeks since the dead end in the Surrid quarantine zone. The riverreek epidemic was worsening – hundreds were now penned in and they'd had to open new quarantine areas in Fisheart and Esdale. The Treasury had some kind of coining crisis and Wurther was distracted by the upcoming Synod. The governance of Pallas and the empire was stumbling, rather than striding on.

If this were a duel, Ril thought, *now would be the time for our enemies to strike.*

Setallius went to his bookshelves and leafed through one, then another. At last he waved Ril over. 'Here it is: the tree and cross of Loekryn.'

Ril studied the hand-drawn illustration. 'Yes, that's it. Who or what was Loekryn?'

'Do you remember I recently mentioned the Canonical Crisis of 818?'

Ril cast his mind back. 'The clergy wanted canon law to overrule secular law?'

'Indeed, during the reign of Emperor Voscarus. He blockaded Southside to starve the prelates into submission. Loekryn was grand prelate, and he was defiant – he even boasted that he'd bridge the Aerflus to get supplies into Southside. They resisted for nine months, thanks to devotees smuggling in food and supplies, until Voscarus occupied Emtori, strangling the smuggling operation, and Loekryn capitulated.'

'What happened to him?'

'He took his own life, the only grand prelate to do so.' The spymaster grinned and added, 'He was then found to have been a woman.'

Ril burst out laughing. 'Really?'

'Well, maybe. The Church denied it, but the rumour persists.' Setallius frowned, and his voice became serious again. 'During the blockade, his seal was used in Emtori as a sign of a safe house for clergymen – and smugglers.'

'That explains the plaque at Saint Chalfon's I suppose,' Ril said. 'But why would there be a stone with that marking in Lyra's private garden?'

'It might just be a coincidence – building blocks do get re-used,' Setallius said.

Ril sat back in his chair, pondering. It was probably nothing – but he'd found the stone in Lyra's garden, which had become an increasingly uncanny place. 'Did your people ever search Saint Chalfon's?'

'It was outside the quarantine area, so no,' the spymaster replied. 'Although now it's inside. We've had to extend the zone because of the increased number of sufferers. I could send someone, if you like?'

'I think I'll go myself. May I take Basia? I don't think Lyra is planning on doing more than reading some papers and spending time with her ladies today.'

'Be my guest. I'll have someone trustworthy stay with her.' With a twinkle in his one good eye, he added, 'Well spotted – we'll make a Volsai of you yet.'

Ril snorted. 'No wonder your career as a courtier never worked out, if that's the best you can do for flattery.'

It was mid-afternoon before he and Basia managed to extract themselves from other duties. Dressed in rough clothing so as not to attract attention, they walked down to Kenside docks, but the tides were against them so they wasted almost two hours in a tavern, waiting for the waters to settle before they could get a ferry to Aerside.

'It's a shame we've never asked the Ordo Costruo to build us a nice bridge,' he observed as they disembarked.

'We did, once,' Basia replied. 'Emperor Sertain II asked, a long time ago, but they refused – no idea why – and his people hadn't mastered the solarus crystals, so every bridge he tried to build collapsed.'

Ril pulled a face. That the Pallas magi couldn't do *everything* was both comforting and disturbing.

Ril thought the Aerside docks were bustling: several large river-barges had come down the Siber River with cargo from Canossi and Delph and dour Argundian traders were haggling with shrewd Pallacian buyers. But Basia was unimpressed. 'It's very quiet,' she remarked. 'The river-reek's scaring off the traders.'

Sure enough, as they walked south and inland, the streets began to empty – not just of the bustle of the docklands but soon of all life. They passed abandoned terraces, shutters flapping in the wind, doors smashed, looted furniture piled on the streets. The one patrol they saw didn't even approach them.

'That's really strange,' Basia muttered as the guardsmen backed off. 'What the Hel is going on here?'

Then they turned into a square and found their path barricaded with more furniture, piled into heaps and roped together, right across the street. At first they thought the place empty, then half a dozen men in Kirkegarde uniforms rose from the shadow of a stone wall. They all looked as sick as the people they were supposed to be penning in.

'Stop. You can't come this way,' they said, and Ril could have sworn they'd all spoken in unison.

Basia caught his sleeve. 'Let's try another way.'

The air of menace radiating from the guardsmen quickly persuaded him and he let her lead him away. 'Did you notice?' he said quietly, 'it's cold here, but none of those Reekers went into the sun.'

'We're going to lose the sun soon ourselves,' she said, pointing to where it was beginning to fall behind Emtori Heights. 'This is even worse than our last visit.'

Ril jabbed a finger at the grey-walled buildings topping the Heights. 'What are those pricks up there doing about this?'

'What's the emperor doing?' Basia added, in a complaining voice.

'Exactly!' Ril agreed, then he laughed. 'Very droll: the "emperor" is *investigating*, with his good friend, Fantoche. Come on.'

They skirted the extended quarantine zone, encountering barricade after barricade, some manned by Kirkegarde, some by the riverreek victims themselves, and all exuding a fug of sour malice. Ril and Basia didn't try to gain admittance.

Then the sun vanished behind Emtori Heights – true sunset was still an hour away, but the temperature plummeted. The streets emptied of even the few people they'd seen.

Ril turned to Basia. 'We're magi, Basia: let's stop messing around.' He selected a deserted-looking house, unlocked the front door with a spell and they slipped inside. It had been plundered and abandoned, with shattered crockery covering the hall and kitchen floors, but they passed through into a back alley that was inside the quarantine zone. Silent shapes passed the end of the path and they pressed back into the doorway, then crept to the mouth of the alley.

The Surrid streets were sullen and silent, devoid even of scavenging animals. They instinctively hid from anyone they saw, but the Reekers just shambled by, lost in their own misery. Ril recalled his one and only brush with riverreek, in his early twenties: a week or two of listlessness, a streaming nose and a headache that was like a herd of horses stampeding through his skull. What these people had looked much worse.

This is the capital – so who's helping these people? Where are all the healers?

They reached another alley and followed it deeper into the maze of houses, trying to avoid the piles of garbage and dead animals – rats and cats and dogs mostly – lying rotting in the streets; oddly, none of the scavenging gulls that infested the docks were eating them. The drains were clogged and filled with vile, scum-encrusted water and the stink of raw sewage was everywhere.

Then Basia hissed, and they shrank against the walls: someone was standing at the far end of the alley and they were upright, not shuffling. Ril almost called out, but Basia shook her head firmly and whoever it was moved on with purposeful tread.

Who was that? One of the healers we've sent in to help people? An official?

Whoever it was had gone by the time they reached the head of the alley. In the next street, they had to constantly press into doorways to avoid more and more of the shuffling Reekers, and each time it was harder to press on. Their confidence, even their courage, was being eroded second by second.

At the next turn, Ril found himself passing an open window. Despite Basia's cautionary look, he couldn't help peering inside. There was a woman, bare-chested, trying to suckle the child she was cradling – then he realised the infant's face was grey and lifeless and he couldn't stop his shocked gasp. The mother looked up, bloody eyes weeping, and he jerked his head from the sight and scampered to the next turning. He looked back to see her at the window, peering out into the night, but he couldn't say if she could see him.

<*Idiot,*> Basia admonished, and he didn't disagree.

They finally found themselves at the back of Saint Chalfon's and poked their heads round the wall – then jerked themselves back into cover.

'Holy Hel,' Basia breathed in Ril's ear. 'Did they see us?'

'I don't know.'

He listened hard, then pointed backwards and they retreated quickly, just before boots sounded where they'd been seconds before.

<*There were dozens of them,*> he sent silently. <*It looked like they were guarding the church.*>

Basia threw him a worried look. <*There were more than just dozens: they*>

were in lines, right across the square and down the main road.> They crept back another turn so they could talk properly.

'Why would they be lined up outside that particular church?' Ril wondered. 'I think we should call Setallius.'

'Are you sure? Calling across a large body of water like the Aerflus takes some energy – what if they sense us?'

'What if they do?' Ril replied. 'They're just Reekers.' But even he didn't believe that. 'Let's go back into the alley, find some cover and try.'

The gnostic call did make the aether shimmer, but Basia reached the spymaster almost instantly and kept the link brief. Ril strained his senses—

—and heard the tramp of boots echoing along the alley.

He spotted a doorway, tried the handle and it opened. He yanked Basia through, then pinned her against the wall, finger to her lips, as he eased the door closed again. For a long minute they stared into each other's eyes ... and he was in that collapsed well again, in 909, and they were going to die. His heart was pounding against hers and he was shaking and so was she because she felt it too. They held each other breathlessly as booted feet shuffled past – and someone *sniffed* around the door.

Then the patrol of Reekers – or whatever they really were – was gone and they sagged into each other.

And Basia kissed him, briefly but hard, so hard she almost bit him, then pulled away. It wasn't unpleasant, just unexpected. He blinked, startled. '*Huh?*'

'Just saying thanks,' she said, but her cheeks went pink.

His heart didn't stop pounding. 'Sure, no problem. *Sister.* Did you reach Setallius?'

She nodded and pushed him away, as if he'd been the one getting too close. He floundered, went to speak, then almost jumped out of his skin as they heard someone move somewhere deeper in the house.

They were in someone's front room – a craftsman's, perhaps, by the look. He signed to Basia to remain where she was, then began to creep towards the door. It led to a kitchen, and beyond that, another doorway revealed stairs going upwards.

Someone was silhouetted in the doorway.

He lit a mage-light in his hands, revealing a red-eyed, pallid woman with a bleeding, streaming nose. Streaks of brown stained her front. She stank of sweat and vomit and her eyes were full of misery. She opened her mouth to scream and he shut her down with mesmeric-gnosis.

She succumbed easily, and he pulled a name from her mind. 'Adith! Look at me, Adith, look at me. It's going to be all right.'

He sensed Basia behind him. As she closed the kitchen door, he gently led the woman to a seat by the stove and sat her down. By then she was calm enough that she could speak. 'Where's Nalf?' she whimpered.

Her husband, Ril read. 'We'll find him. What's happened here?' He used mesmerism to send her into a state of trance, then drew out the tale.

'Nalf, he's a tool-maker,' she said, in a drowsy voice. 'He caught the riverreek first: we hoped it was just a cold, but then it set in and I caught it too. At night we couldn't sleep because it felt like we were choking on our own snot and we couldn't keep food down. Then healer-magi from the Church came and brought us here, to the quarantine. They gave us hot drinks and used spells to clear our breathing passages for a time, and we began to feel we'd live. A prelate from the Church visited the Surrid docks, promising more healers, more help. There were more than four thousand people in here.'

Ril looked at Basia. 'Does Setallius know there's so many?'

Basia shook her head. 'What was the name of the prelate?' she asked Adith.

'Rodrigo, the Estellan,' the young woman replied. 'I kissed the hem of his robe and he blessed me. Just a few more days, he said, to be sure we were clear of contagion.'

Ril bit his lip and met Basia's eyes, both hanging on the woman's tale.

'The night after the Grand Tourney, everything changed,' Adith said. 'Nalf and I, we went to Saint Jul's Square to get food, and a man stumbled in – I saw him, up close. He looked diseased, and he was babbling, half-mad with the riverreek – but he looked *cunning* too. Some people laughed, and a guard tried telling him to quieten down.'

She shook her head, still disbelieving. 'Then the Reeker *bit* the guard, on the arm.' Her voice dropped to a shocked whisper. 'We all thought the bitten man was dying, because he was shouting as if he'd been poisoned. Then more like the madman charged into the square from all sides and everyone panicked, running this way and that, and these madmen started biting people too, more and more of us. I was shoved over and found myself next to that poor guard and I saw him go still – and then he sat up, and his face was as mad and cunning as that Reeker. He sat up and slashed the throat of a man trying to help him, then . . . *Oh Dear Kore . . .*'

Adith reached blindly towards Ril, who stepped away – he wouldn't have touched her for all the gold in Pallas – but Adith barely noticed. 'He looked straight at me, and I swear, he was going to kill me, then Nalf yanked me away, and we ran for our lives.'

'Where did you go?' Basia asked softly.

'We tried to escape quarantine, but the Kirkegarde on the perimeters refused to let us out, and they were *changed* – not raving, not mad like the Reeker, but silent and cold and they all spoke in exactly the same way, not like Emtori men, not even like Pallacians. They built those barricades to keep us in! Some people tried to get out and they shot them with crossbows and stabbed them with spears.

'We couldn't escape, so we've been hiding ever since. And every night, more Reekers go by, breaking into houses, looking for those who are free of their condition. We ran out of food two days ago and Nalf went looking for more . . . and he hasn't come back.' She hunched into herself, pulled her knees to her chest and began to rock back and forth, side to side, keening.

Basia touched the side of her head and sent her to sleep as Ril slumped to one knee, utterly stunned. 'How can this be happening here? How can we not *know*?' He cast his mind back to the most recent meeting of the Imperial Council. 'The Church has been running all the quarantine areas. Wurther's Secretary, Chaplain Ennis, told the Imperial Council that the danger was passing.'

'Kirkegarde soldiers, all infected,' Basia said, her voice incredulous. 'Holy Kore, if this condition spreads, the whole city is under threat – we've got to stop this!'

Ril swallowed. 'How far away is Setallius?'

Basia's eyes sparked with pale light, scrying. 'Ten minutes.' She whispered something into the air, a brief flurry of words. 'I told him to look for us on the rooftop. Come on.'

Ril carried Adith to a bedroom and locked her in, then slipped the key under the door. They climbed into the attic and found the hatch to the roof; in a place where summers turned upper floors into furnaces the rooftop terraces were a necessity. They clambered out onto the tiles and huddled together – but not too close; that kiss was still replaying in Ril's mind, the shock of it like a sudden candle-flame in gloom.

Basia was clearly still thinking about it too, because she said softly, 'Why was there never an *us*, Ril? In all those years?'

He didn't look at her. 'I don't know,' he lied.

'Was it the legs?' she probed.

'No, nothing like that.' He brushed back his hair, fiddled with his gauntlets, did anything but meet her eyes. *Because I could never have left you*, was the truth. *Because you matter too much, and I've always had to have an escape route out of a relationship, even with Jenet. But you and I, our souls got tangled together in that well in 909. And now there's Lyra, and the only way out is probably a coffin.*

Perhaps she understood that, because she just leaned in and hugged him, then straightened and pointed to a windskiff skimming the roofs towards them; in a few seconds more, the spymaster was throwing them a mooring rope, which Ril wrapped around a gable spire, while Mort Singolo hauled in the sails. Once the craft was secured – there was enough Air-gnosis stored in the keel to keep the craft aloft for many days – they all made their way back down to the ground floor, where Basia brought Setallius up to date while Singolo checked the perimeter.

'So there were ranks of them, outside Saint Chalfon's?' Setallius asked. He looked at Ril. 'The very place you came here to visit.'

'There were dozens, maybe hundreds,' Basia confirmed.

'Was anyone speaking to them, giving orders, marshalling them?'

'No,' Ril put in, 'they don't even speak to each other.'

The spymaster frowned. 'Perhaps they don't need to. Let's go and have a look.'

They all turned as Mort Singolo strode back into the room. 'No one

seems to have heard or seen us,' the axeman reported. 'I heard movement in the distance – a lot of tramping feet – but that's died down.'

'What about Adith?' Basia asked.

'She's probably safest where she is,' Ril said, and Setallius nodded
in agreement.

Ril guided them back to the church, Setallius ghosting along behind,
Singolo following with Basia some distance behind. They could hear
the movement of feet, strangely rhythmic, as if they were all following the beat of an unheard drum, but before they reached the square
a booming sound echoed about them, followed by a metallic rattle.

Then there was silence.

They reached the end of the street and peered into the square, but
the entire plaza, which an hour earlier had been filled with Reekers,
was eerily empty. All that remained were a few scraps of refuse.

'Where has everyone gone?' Ril whispered.

Faraway, the bells of the city chimed the hour, like a signal that
something – *something bad* – had just begun.

The Bastion, Pallas

It begins, Ostevan Comfateri thought exultantly. He stared into the eyes
of the old man facing him: Brother Junius had served six Royal Confessors with uncomplaining diligence. The ichor had settled into his
veins, his eyes had bled those little tears that for some reason always
came at the end of the struggle for possession, and now Abraxas gazed
back at Ostevan from the old man's rheumy eyes.

The daemon looked around curiously: on the desk lay a stack of
papiermâché masks, all of them of Jest, as well as the true mask accepted
by Ostevan in Janune. There were also two mirrors, a jug of water, a
candle, a lump of rock and a pile of feathers: the sort of things the
ignorant thought magi used in 'casting spells'.

'*What is that trash for?*' Junius – or rather, Abraxas – asked.

'Obfuscation,' Ostevan replied. 'Now, if you don't mind, I have work
to do.' He put his finger to his lips, willing the daemon's awareness to

depart, leaving just the potential for power. *Master Naxius is truly a genius*, he acknowledged silently. He would love to know how the old madman had managed to persuade – or force – Abraxas into this arrangement. *He's effectively reduced a master-daemon to a source of power and information and a conduit for communication.*

'Prepare,' he told Junius.

A mage's powers were derived from tapping into the 'soul' – the energies created and sustained by their bodies – but not all magi could detach the soul – the spiratus – from the body at will. The Gnostic Study of spiritualism was concerned with the art. A travelling spiratus could even possess another, just as a daemon did, but even a normal human had enough innate defences that such possession was very difficult, and impossible to sustain for long.

But Junius was now Ostevan's absolute slave and he had no such defences. An uninitiated watcher would have seen two men staring at each other – until Junius stood and Ostevan slumped in his chair, his eyes emptying.

A mage would have seen Ostevan's soul step into Junius' body and assume complete control.

Then Ostevan-inside-Junius rose. He stared at his own body, which had fallen into a catatonic state – it wasn't a comfortable sensation, especially as his next act was to cut his own body's throat, not deep enough to kill, just enough to make a mess. Then he conjured a Chain-rune to bind the gnosis of the abandoned body and conceal it from scrying. *This is just a contingency*, he told himself – he had no desire to *not* return to that precious vessel.

Then he lit the candle, charred the feathers, tipped water over the body, crushed the rock and sprinkled the shards, cracked both mirrors, smiling at the thought of what an experienced mage would make of such acts. *Obfuscation*, he thought with a smile, placing all the Jest masks into a bag.

Outside the sun was falling behind Emtori Heights. He took the stairs into the bowels of the chapel, striding with an energy and purpose that the real Junius has long since forgotten. The night was young, and there was much to achieve before he took the grand prelate's throne.

Emtori, Pallas

Ril indicated Saint Chalfon's church. 'I presume they're inside?'

Dirklan Setallius nodded in agreement as Mort and Basia joined them. They stared across the darkened plaza, waiting for signs of movement, but none came. The one stained-glass window facing the street – a giant rosette high on the walls above the twin doors – remained dark. 'We need a closer look,' Setallius decided.

The moonless sky was heavy with stars. Everything remained silent as they stole across the space to the church doors and pressed their eyes and ears to the cracks. Ril heard the measured tread of boots walking away from them, and a smell seeped through to their nostrils.

'Lamp-oil,' Setallius said, sniffing. They kept listening again, but all was silent now. The spymaster stroked the door lock and Ril sensed him reaching out, feeling out the shape of the locks and barricades, engaging kinesis – then he withdrew. 'There are wards . . . strong wards,' he reported. 'If I try to break them, whoever set them will know.' He looked around, then said, 'Let's try the other side.'

They crept around the building, finding all the alleys equally silent and forbidding, and emerged behind a small cemetery, the only open space amidst the press of buildings. All was silent, but Ril wondered how many there were like Adith here, cowering in fear of the disease within the sickness.

They bite *people . . . The world's gone mad.*

There was a small door at the back of Saint Chalfon's, but it was also locked. Ril looked up at the church spire where Basia had cast her scrying spell – was it just three weeks ago? 'We could get in through the slats in the bell-tower. I could fly up and prise them open, then—'

'I've a better idea,' Singolo interrupted, and as the axeman splayed his fingers, the nearest stone grave-slab peeled like cloth from the earth, revealing a narrow set of stairs leading down into the earth. The smell of damp rot rose to greet them. 'Mage-family crypt,' he grunted.

In Pallas, with land so valuable, only the magi were permitted to inter their families inside the city walls; the middle classes buried their dead in public cemeteries outside, while the poor were simply cremated. Magi were descended of the Blessed Three Hundred, so their memorials were sacred sites.

'Does it open into the church vaults?' Ril asked.

'No idea,' the axeman admitted, 'but I'm an Earth-mage. I'll get us in either way.' He scrambled down, gnosis-light illuminating the way. Setallius indicated Ril and Basia should go next, and Ril stared into the hole . . .

. . . and a thousand nightmares arose in his mind. He froze, and Basia gripped his hand, hard. His first thought was that she was trying to give him strength, but when he saw her face, illuminated faintly from below, he knew that she felt exactly the same as him. They were in that well again, as the walls caved in . . .

No, we're right here! 'Hey Fantoche, it's just a hole in the ground,' he whispered, putting his arm around her. 'We can handle it. We've done it before.'

She looked at him gratefully. Despite the hours they'd spent trying to cure themselves of this terror, it had never quite left. But it was a familiar fear, by now. 'It's only a little hole, isn't it?' she murmured.

He squeezed her hand and they did it together. The hardest moment came when Singolo pulled the slab closed behind them, but they made it through that too. The walls crowded in and the ceiling pressed down on them alarmingly, but if they concentrated, they could pretend the small chamber was just an inner room in the Bastion. Mort's mage-light showed stone shelves surrounding them, labelled with bronze heraldic plaques bearing names.

'It's the tomb of the Ulvensen family, Argundian half-bloods,' Setallius said. 'A bastard line of some Emtori pure-bloods. They're river-traders.'

The spymaster walked to a wooden door at the far end of the mausoleum and pressed his eye to a keyhole. It glowed as he engaged gnostic-sight to penetrate the darkness. 'Better and better: they've connected the crypts to a corridor that runs into the church vaults. Makes the funerals easier on a rainy day, I suppose.'

He pulsed energy into the lock and pulled the door open and they followed him into the low-ceilinged, narrow stone passageway – another test of resolve for Ril and Basia. Neither was willing to back down before the other, so they went together. The short corridor led into a wider chamber. Metal grilles above let in enough dim light for Setallius and Singolo to banish their gnostic-lights.

Ril remembered the ventilation holes he'd seen in the church floor: they were right beneath the centre of the church. The air absolutely reeked of lamp-oil.

Someone was walking around on the stone floor of the church above them, punctuated by splashing sounds. There was a glassy *crunch* as something was dropped, the oil-smell redoubled and Ril realised what it meant. He peered up through one of the ventilation grilles as the boots came nearer, and someone appeared, head and shoulders in half-profile, looking at something in the church. Ril caught his breath: there was no face, just a Lantric mask: Angelstar, the nemesis. Then it was gone, the footsteps receded, they heard a door rattle open and the room above fell silent.

Then there was a surge in the aether, the sensation of very powerful gnosis being unleashed, and he turned back to the trembling Basia, pressed his mouth to her ear and whispered, 'Did you feel that? Did you see him?'

Before she could respond, flames gushed through the chamber above and vivid orange knives of fire stabbed through the holes of the grille. There was a great roar and the air was sucked from the chamber. Filled with panic, Ril jerked Basia back the way they'd come as smoke poured into the catacomb. The flames were swirling like liquid; already they could hear beams cracking. He slammed into a door and reeled backwards, then Basia stumbled into him, crying out in terror.

I ran the wrong way – this isn't the way out!

Then Setallius was there, the gnosis-light glowing from the periapt at his neck illuminating his spectral face. He tried the door, wincing at the power of the wards, then he shouted with his mind and Mort appeared. <*This way!*> the axeman roared into Ril's mind.

The next few seconds were a blur as he pulled Basia along, petrified at the darkness and weight of the stone above and the flames, aware that every gulp of air might be his last. Heat drenched them as they crossed chamber after chamber, with Setallius conjuring air now, no mean feat as he pulled all that was breathable to their mouths while beating back the flames trying to burn the oxygen. Then they staggered into another door and this time there were no wards – and no exit.

Mort hurled Ril at a dark square in the wall and he fell, sliding, shouting in terror, before spilling from the sloped chute into pitch-darkness and hitting the stone floor *damned* hard.

Three seconds later a howling Basia hit him in the small of his back with her artificial feet, but he grabbed her and scrambled away from the exit. The two of them just lay there, half-hysterical with relief and terror, as Setallius arrived, feet-first and landing elegantly. He stepped aside before Mort shot through and crashed onto his tail-bone, leaving him writhing in agony.

'I *rukking* hate you,' Basia panted, glaring at the spymaster, the only one of them on his feet.

For a minute, they all just gasped for air, then Ril locked eyes with Basia. Her gaze was naked, all their shared fears reflected between them like two facing mirrors. He reached out and pulled her to him, kissed her cheek and said, 'Sister, I can do this if you can.'

She forced a weak smile and murmured, 'Me too.'

He helped her up. Her strapping was coming apart, but she engaged a little animagery, though it wasn't her strongest suit, to fix the leather, and tightened the whole harness. He looked around and decided the chamber they'd fallen into was a storage room. Singolo stood painfully and hobbled to the door. He worked at the lock, while Setallius examined something on the wall. He illuminated it with his glowing periapt and beckoned to Ril: the tree-and-key sigil of Loekryn had been carved into the stone.

'What does it mean?' Ril wondered.

'Remember what I told you about the Canonical Crisis and Grand Prelate Loekryn's boast that he'd build a bridge across the Aerflus? Perhaps it wasn't a boast? Perhaps he did build a bridge: an underground, underwater one: a tunnel from Surrid to the Celestium.'

'And it's still here . . .' Ril stared, his mind racing despite the claustrophobic pressure building in his skull. 'What if all those . . . those biting people, those "Reekers" – what if they got sent down here before that masked man burned the church – which he must have done to close the door behind him.'

Setallius frowned. 'It's not impossible ... but if you're right, that means this isn't aimed at you and Lyra but at Wurther: a secret army of these Reekers to take down the grand prelate?'

Ril tried to picture that – he could see how such a thing might cause chaos in a city street – but the Celestium was full of real soldiers, and magi too – a Hel of a lot of magi, some of the most powerful in Yuros.

'There's something more to this,' he mused aloud. 'I'm sure of it. It's not enough to unseat Wurther.'

His thoughts were interrupted by Mort Singolo, who had managed to open the lock. He drew one of his twin throwing-axes from his harness and stood. 'We can move on. Shall we?'

Setallius faced them all. 'We need to confirm that there really are secret tunnels under the Aerflus, and if these Reekers have been sent along them.'

They each drew light from their periapts and held them aloft as they crept out of the room. Overpowering heat and smoke was rolling down from the left of the sloped tunnel outside the door, and Ril groaned and held Basia against him. It was strange – they'd never really been close physically, as if those three days trapped in the well had given them a very specific phobia of touching each other – but the moment they were underground together again, they couldn't let go of each other.

And she'd kissed him.

It's Lyra I love, he told himself. His wife had changed since the tourney, opening up emotionally and physically. The more jaded, knowing part of him just laughed. But he had a duty to his queen, even if that had just got harder.

Setallius pointed to the right. 'I think we have to go that way.'

Basia looked at Ril miserably; if he was correct, this tunnel led under stone and water, deeper than they'd ever gone. 'I'll do it if you do,' she told him, the old mantra.

'I don't think we have a choice,' Singolo growled. 'Stay here, and you'll run out of air.' He threw them a sympathetic look. 'Come on, we need to move.'

Ril swallowed as the nightmares closed in again: to be below ground, truly in the depths . . . to be trapped, with fire behind them and who knew what ahead . . . that was bad enough – but another fear compounded it all. That what they'd seen was the beginning of the end, that the axe poised above their heads was beginning to swing, and there was no way he could warn Lyra.

He wavered, begging his brain for some clever way to get back to the surface, but another crash reverberated through the tunnel and the smoke and heat billowed in like some dark daemon reaching for them. As one, they began to run down the sloped tunnel as fast as Basia's artificial legs could manage – then Ril stopped her and lifted her onto his back and they redoubled their pace, rushing into the nightmare.

The Bastion, Pallas, Yuros

Solon Takwyth knew that someone had been in his room the moment he entered. The Corani knights had been housed in the giant barracks of the Bastion for five years, and although he'd only just arrived, he'd been given one of the finest rooms: a loyal knight had sacrificed his own comfort in honour of him, and he'd publicly thanked the man, praising him in front of them all.

No one should have been able to penetrate the wards on his doors and windows. But he concealed his unease, promising the man he'd been conversing with a pint downstairs in the hall, then he entered, locked the door and walked to his desk.

Two things lay there: a Lantric mask, a beautifully made bronze and lacquer depiction of Twoface – half of the face fair and serene, the other half a skilfully rendered expression somewhere between malice and sorrow. Twoface the unpredictable: the man with secrets that drove him to act against his nature. Such masks could be found in the markets, though seldom as beautifully rendered as this.

He stroked his own disfigured face while he examined the other item: a note, in an almost familiar hand.

Dear Solon,

Forgive me for taking the liberty of contacting you at this crucial juncture. I'm sure you've been guessing at who is who, just as I have.

I just wanted to say that I understand what drove you to this point, and I respect it. When we are victorious, and I remove my own mask, I'll know you understand me as well.

There was no signature, just a neat sketch of another Lantric mask: Tear, the spirit of Tragedy. He frowned, studying both note and mask. Then the Bastion's alarm bells began to ring.

36

Magas Gorge

Tabula

The ancient 'Game of Kings' was devised in Lantris and popularised during the Rimoni Empire as the favoured board-game of the nobility. On an eight-by-eight squared board, two armies of sixteen pieces with varying powers contend to take the opposing queen. Emperor Sertain claimed the game kept his mind sharp through his centuries-long reign. His queen was never taken, and he died in his sleep.

ANNALS OF PALLAS, 804

Magas Gorge, Mollachia
Junesse 935

The waning moon had already left the sky when Kyrik crawled out of the tent in the predawn, leaving only a fading band of stars above the gorge. Tonight would be the first night of Darkmoon, a month full of superstitions, and Luna wouldn't reappear for six or seven days. *No doubt Hajya's people have hundreds of beliefs about it too*, he reflected as he stretched, then strode to the river. Most of the riders were already awake, and Hajya too. Dozens of men were in the river, darting in and out, exclaiming at the cold, but she was actually swimming, drawing on raw gnostic energy to keep herself warm. He did the same and swam to where she floated in the eddies at the edge of the current, seized her from behind and kissed her firmly. She twisted in his grasp like a wet otter and pressed herself against him.

'Do you always wander around naked in front of your tribe?' he chided.

She chuckled throatily. 'These young bucks all have far prettier women – younger too. I expect they feel sorry for you.'

'Jealous, more like. But in Hegikaro, women wear seventeen layers, minimum.'

'Liar,' she laughed. 'Are you worried your savage wife will embarrass you?' Then she whispered, 'I bled this morning – Darkmoon is my moonblood time. I have no child for you this month, my Kirol.'

He couldn't tell if she was disappointed or not. 'With all we must face, I think I'm relieved,' he said. 'We're going to war. It would frighten me to know you were with child at such a time.'

'But it would strengthen me,' she murmured regretfully. Then she leaped on him and pushed him under, and as he thrashed beneath the surface, she kicked away. By the time he'd regained the surface and his breath, she was wading into the shallows, water streaming down her back and buttocks.

He grinned at the sight, thinking, *Who wouldn't be jealous?*

But the day wasn't going to wait. He strode ashore himself, dried off and girded himself for the journey. A rider brought bowls of hot, spicy gruel, which he and Hajya gulped down, then he prepared their horses while she reapplied her blue face-paint, a ceremony being mirrored by many of the riders. The line across her eyes re-emphasised their differences.

'Husband – would you like some paint also?' she offered. 'The men would appreciate it.'

'Your men might – mine would think I've gone mad.'

She gave him a meaningful look. 'You are among the Vlpa now: we must remind them that you are Kirol.'

He frowned, then he sighed and held still, despite his impatience, while she deftly daubed at him with her fingers from her jar of blue paste. 'How does a kirol relate to a nacelnik?' he asked when she was done, reaching up to touch the unfamiliar paste.

'Let it dry!' she snapped, slapping away his hand. 'Kirol is a foreign king; he is the equal of the nacelnik.'

'A kingdom cannot have two kings,' he said, a little troubled. 'My people will expect him to bow to me.'

'Ah, the famous "equality" you speak of,' she remarked, her husky voice neutral. 'A problem for tomorrow, mm?' She showed him his face in the reflection of her dagger blade. 'See, a crown for Kirol Kyrik.'

There was indeed a blue crown painted on his right cheek – and a silhouetted fox on his right, amidst a swirl of decorative lines. 'Once we can be crowned we will bear the Rondian titles "King" and "Queen" – although for all I know, Robear Delestre has sold my father's crown as well.'

They broke off the discussion as Brazko and Rothgar approached. As the four of them huddled together to plan the day ahead, Kyrik was interested and pleased to see that the young Sydian appeared to admire the Stonefolk hunter. 'We're still six miles north of Neplezko Flat and the Gazda's Stair,' Rothgar reminded them, after staring at Kyrik's warpaint with raised eyebrows.

'Our hope is that Dragan and his Vitezai will reach there today,' Kyrik replied. He turned to Brazko. 'I want to take forty riders on ahead, to climb the Stair as soon as possible. Rothgar will guide us, and I'd like you with us, Brazko.'

'I will come, and climb this Stair,' he agreed. 'If there are enemies, we will chase them away.'

'Good. Rothgar, we'll leave Vitezai at each ford, to show the following riders the best places to cross.' He turned to Hajya. 'How can the Sfera help us, my Kirolyna?' he asked, as if they'd not discussed it already.

'My people are positioned all along the column to help the riders cross the most treacherous of the fords; they will also provide mind-to-mind communication, so that we'll know if anything goes wrong. One of my young men can take bird form: I sent him south. I have heard nothing since, so I will try and reach him during the day.' There was a tinge of worry in her voice.

'Might he have got lost?' Kyrik asked.

'Following a river?' Hajya pulled a face. 'Though he's not a bright boy, and easily distracted. Bird-mage, ysh?'

Animagi can grow too much like their favoured shape, Kyrik thought.

'Can you fly to find him?' Rothgar asked – he sounded fascinated at being exposed to so much that was foreign and strange.

'I can take two shapes,' Hajya said; 'steppenwulf and vlpa – plains-wolf and fox. The former is for hunting and fighting, the latter for scouting. Neither is useful in this situation – the best thing I can do is help at the fords, and maintain communication. I will come with you to these Narrows and position myself there.'

'What about Valdyr?' Rothgar asked. 'Are you able to find out where he is?'

Kyrik licked his lips. 'I'm not a good scryer – clairvoyance-gnosis isn't an affinity – and as he's not found his gnosis, he doesn't know how to receive a gnostic call. Non-magi can be taught, but it takes time and it's short-range – so unless Hajya's bird-mage returns, we're blind until we reach Neplezko Flat.'

'Then the sooner we're out of this place the better,' Rothgar observed.

'Indeed. Let's move.' He mounted his horse and led off, leaving Rothgar's second to marshal the next groups. A long day awaited.

Feher Szarvasfeld, Mollachia
Junesse 935

The day had dawned bitterly cold and fresh snow, thick on the hills above, dusted the valley floor as Robear Delestre led his legions north-west through White Stag Land. He'd been trying to remember what the natives called it, but it was another typically tongue-knotting Mollach word.

Why do they bother with their ridiculous language when Rondian is so much easier?

The windskiff scouts on the northern flanks hadn't reported in, which was annoying him, but the massive peaks and the high winds were likely playing havoc with their ability to fly, let alone using gnostic-contact. But he felt somewhat blind as he led his escort along the trail through the woodlands. The only colours were the white of the snow and sky, the black of the exposed trees and rocks and the red of the legion cloaks. But they were making good progress; at this rate they'd reach Magas Gorge before dusk, in time to make camp.

He glanced back at the young men trotting along in his retine:

DAVID HAIR

the sons of Midrean merchants and bankers, some of them also magi. They'd been whining about saddle-sores all morning and Robear could sympathise, but at least his old endurance was returning. *And those pricks are getting to see what real soldiering looks like. Maybe they'll give us more respect – and better loans – after this.*

Then a thud of hooves told him that Sacrista was on her way in from wherever she'd been skulking. She did try hard to look like she was in charge, he gave her that. 'Brother!' she hailed, trotting up in a cloud of steam from her horse's nostrils. She was riding bareheaded, her shock of coppery hair unruly, and rather fetching. *If only she'd loosen up, she could be a real asset socially.*

'Crista! What news?'

She looked pleased. 'A windskiff flew high over Magas Gorge at dawn and saw people and horses moving south. They couldn't say how many because of the terrain, but they swear there were hundreds!'

'So they really are in this gorge?' Robear asked. 'Is that good or bad?'

Sacrista rolled her eyes. 'It's brilliant news, Brother – if we can get archers and magi on the cliffs above, we can slaughter them.' She glanced back at the investors' sons and added more softly, 'Even those fools couldn't miss.'

'So we should press on?'

'Yes, *absolutely* – as fast as we can. We have to keep moving while daylight holds, at the gallop – we're only ten miles from the gorge so we can reach them before dusk. I'll tell the units to the north; you tell the main body. Don't wait for the footmen, Brother—'

Before she'd even finished speaking she'd turned her horse and was spurring it hard, and for a moment he was captivated by her energy and excitement, wishing she was someone other than his sister so he could show her how to *really* live. Then his new 'friends' cantered up, their faces weary of the ride already, but curious. 'What's your mad sister doing?' one asked.

'We have news,' he told them. 'The enemy is at hand!'

Neplezko Flat, Magas Gorge, Mollachia

Kyrik splashed across the shallow ford and onto a wide strip of flat gravel dotted with sharp, tough grasses: Neplezko Flat. He pushed his beast into a canter around the shore of the small lake. Behind him, a low waterfall churned the waters: the water was a vivid icy-blue at the north end, turning deeper blue-green as it flowed south. His eyes went immediately to the eastern cliffs. The ledge was some seventy yards above, bare of trees – and devoid of waiting people too. He picked out the Gazda's Stair, a treacherous path winding up the rocky face.

Brazko's men thundered in behind him, kicking up the water into a cloud of droplets, and Kyrik reined in and awaited Brazko and Rothgar.

'Brazko, we must get men up there immediately – it'll be faster if we leave our horses, so let's get the first twenty men up there and have the stragglers tend the mounts.' He looked at the sun – it was early afternoon.

Kyrik dismounted, flung his reins to Rothgar and engaged Air-gnosis, soaring up the cliff-face and landing at the top in a few seconds. He glanced down and waved to the riders below, who were staring upwards in awe, then turned his attention to the landscape ahead. The cliff-top lay beneath a higher ridge some two hundred yards before him. He could see a few goat trails running into a thicket of hagwoods clinging to the slope below that ridge. He picked one and climbed to it, looking out east over White Stag Land.

To his left, low mountains arced away, culminating in Watcher's Peak, where the Rahnti Mines lay. He looked that way first, hoping for some sign that Dragan was on the way, but there was nothing. Then he followed the horizon, looking eastwards over a sea of undulating forests and occasional open spaces, a rugged land where only trappers and hunters lived; many of those were Vitezai men who had been forced to abandon their homes. There were higher peaks to his right, marking the boundary to White Stag Land, cutting the high woodlands off from the lower valley.

He was still watching and fretting when Brazko and Rothgar joined him, the rest of the riders following in at intervals as they climbed the stair. 'Let's set up a perimeter here,' he ordered, 'until we can get the horses up. We need enough men up here to hold off a Rondian patrol. Dragan shouldn't be far away.'

'And after here?' Brazko asked.

'The main column will continue down the gorge until the Magas River joins the Tuzvolg River, then we take an eastward path into the Domhalott hill country.' Kyrik was watching a far-away black dot in the skies right at the edge of his sight. *Is that a skiff, or just a mountain eagle?*

More and more men began to arrive and within an hour he had almost a hundred men up here. Those below set up camp on the Flat: there was water aplenty, and room to make a proper camp, for those few thousand who'd come this far. The rest of the column would have to make do with another night perched wherever they could find a place. Now that he'd seen the lie of the land himself, Kyrik was starting to think they should keep a sizeable force up here to shadow their march south and protect their flank.

'Let's send out scouts,' he told Rothgar. 'See if we can find Dragan.'

Mid-afternoon became late afternoon, Brazko went back down the Stair to coordinate the camp as he continued to marshal more men up. Yrhen, the Sydian's head scout, joined him as he began to seriously fret. *Where are you, Dragan, Valdyr? Where are you?*

Then a glint of light flashed where it shouldn't and his worry deepened. Dragan's men would never be so careless as to allow sunlight to hit metal. He narrowed his eyes and this time he did see something moving in a cleft between two broken outcroppings, too big to be anything but a mounted man, maybe half a mile off.

He turned to Yrhen. 'See that? Southeast, between those two high points?' His mind was racing. 'If it's a Rondian scout, we need to get out there and bring him down before he sees us.'

Yrhen squinted. 'A rider, ysh – he's wearing . . . red.'

'Scouts don't wear red. He's cavalry.' Kyrik hesitated, calculating.

We've got maybe two hundred men up here now . . . the camp below has twice as many. Retreating upstream will be impossible with everyone coming in behind – and where would we go? Going downstream only brings us to more Narrows . . . The conclusion was obvious: *We have to hold these cliffs.*

He pulled Yrhen down from the ridgeline. 'Tell Brazko to get as many men up here as possible – if there's cavalry here, then we've already been spotted. *The Rondians know we're here—*'

The minutes felt endless as Brazko arrived, breathing hard, then took his men to form a defensive line along the ridge. There were half a dozen Vitezai Sarkanum as well, who formed a small guard cohort around Kyrik. All the while, more riders climbed the Gazda's Stair; they now had three hundred or more here.

The sun was westering, about to kiss the highest peaks, but there would be a lengthy twilight. In the distance they heard the call of the wolves and the rutting bellow of a stag. The air grew steadily colder and the wind rose. Little wonder the skiff he'd seen earlier had gone; there were clouds churning in from the north and Watcher's Peak had vanished. This wasn't a night to be flying.

Then Yrhen pointed. 'Ufgar,' he said, mangling Rothgar's name, and Kyrik followed his arm: a small band of men had broken from the trees at the bottom of the slope below and were splashing through a tiny stream, Rothgar Baredge at their head. In a few minutes they were puffing and panting their way to the top of the ridge. Rothgar made straight for Kyrik, an urgent look on his face. 'Redcloak riders in the next valley – lots of them, perhaps a full maniple, coming our way.'

This day was turning worse. 'No sign of Valdyr and Dragan?'

'No. The redcloaks are likely between them and us now – in fact, it's likely they've been between us for a good few days, which would be why Dragan isn't here.' The Vitezai ranger patted the wolf-head pommel of his sword. 'It's unlikely they don't realise we're here.'

'Tell the men to prepare.'

After the endless waiting, the next twenty minutes felt terrifyingly short. The first Rondians were spotted: a bareheaded rider emerged from the treeline below, about three hundred yards away, the last of the sunlight glinting on coppery hair. Kyrik caught his breath: Sacrista Delestre. Memories of the dungeon in Hegikaro resurfaced.

She's likely their strongest mage, and I'm ours. He loosened his blade, anticipating the duel to come.

<Hajya,> he called with his mind, the time for secrecy gone. He couldn't be sure if she could sense him from where she ought to be, safe in the Narrows below, but he sent a message anyway: *<You make me proud. Stay safe.>*

Inside a few seconds, the far slopes were teeming with red-cloaked horsemen: three hundred, perhaps four hundred. His men were concealed all along the ridgeline, behind boulders and in the hagwoods, quivers full and arrows nocked. Kyrik opened his inner eye, seeking the tell-tale aura of magi, and found three more, pacing their mounts in Sacrista's wake as she led the horsemen down the slope and then stopped in a ragged line.

That confirms it: they know we're here.

Sacrista looked up at the next ridge, not liking this place at all. The slopes were treacherous, covered by the debris of a thousand tiny landslides. They'd already lost horses to falls and broken limbs that day, in just such places. But Magas Gorge was close, according to the scouts who'd mapped this area the previous week, and she fancied she could hear the thunder of rapids – although that could just be the rising wind. The whole of the north was being eaten up by grey clouds spewing down from the heights.

It's going to be a shitty night, and we can't stop here.

Her scouts had spotted men on the slope above half an hour ago: a dozen, maybe more, they thought. She was easily within an archer's range, but there'd been no sign of life from above: either the enemy had already fled, or they had some discipline.

Either way, I've got almost a full maniple here, and Robear is only twenty minutes behind . . .

At her side, Glan Fressyn turned to the head scout. 'Are you sure this is the place?' the battle-mage asked.

'Aye, saw 'em on the ridge,' the scout replied.

Sacrista told Fressyn to stay put, then made her way to Draius Neuston, the maniple's commander, a bastard son of a Augenheim noble. 'The scouts saw men on the rise above,' she told him. 'If they're still up there, we should attack on foot – that slope is a leg-breaker.'

'We're cavalry,' Neuston replied dismissively. 'I'll handle the details, Lady.'

She gritted her teeth. '*Battle-mage* Neuston, that wasn't a suggestion. Tell your men to—'

—and suddenly the air filled with a vicious hiss, her senses screamed a warning and her shields flared. An instant later, two arrows slammed into them and shattered while all around her, a sleet of shafts sliced through the air and plunged into horse- and man-flesh.

'Ware!' she shouted, too late, as her horse staggered, its legs wobbled and an instant before it fell she rolled free, before it could crush her leg. She crunched into a thorny bush, unable to shield everything, mouthing agonised curses as she was punctured by thorns all down her side. Another volley diced the air and she saw riders and horses dropping like flies with arrows in bellies and limbs, while the remaining horses stampeded about, a menace to all around them. She pressed against the back of a heavy boulder, looking up in disbelief as Neuston simply stood his ground, placating his mare.

'A commander never hides,' he declared. Then three arrows slammed into him at once, two tearing through his wards and the third taking him in the left eye.

<*Oh, bad luck!*> she told his dying mind.

Fressyn dropped beside her. 'There's hundreds of them – they've got us cold—'

'There's a few dozen firing fast,' she retorted, 'and we've got five hundred men – get them into cover in the trees behind and form them up.'

Fressyn looked like he'd sooner just wait out the storm and let someone else take the risks.

Must I do everything myself? She spat, screwed up her courage and broke from cover, shielding hard as she dashed across the scree, hurdling bodies of the dead and wounded. 'Pull back to the trees!' she shouted as she went, and enough heard her to create a wave of retreat, dropping towards the wooded far slope, stumbling and cursing as they sought new cover. The arrows continued to fall, more precisely aimed now, taking down another dozen in a few seconds, leaving more wounded and a whole bunch of men trapped behind boulders, under cover but too scared to move.

She hurled a mage-bolt up the rise at an archer she glimpsed, but the range was too great and it flew wide. '*DISMOUNT – FORM UP – ON ME – FORM UP ON ME*,' she cried. Ensuring she was behind a pine, she gestured left and right. '*SKIRMISH LINES – MOVE!*'

On her own, she'd never have got them to move, but enough of the cohort leaders took up her orders and a line formed three men deep, stragglers and rear-guard pouring in to boost them. She stole glances from her vantage and realised things weren't as bad as she'd thought: maybe sixty or seventy dead or wounded, though that was bad enough, but she had plenty left for an assault.

They can't have many more arrows left. A weird sense of excitement took over: finally, this was war – the shadow-fencing was over. *I hope the bloody Sarkany brothers are up there – let's finish this tonight.*

She took a deep breath, re-kindled her wards and stepped into the open. '*READY? ADVANCE!*'

With a shout, the soldiers broke cover and piled up the slope behind her.

The Sydian bows sang and more arrows flew – a rapid fire that defied sight – and punctuating those flights were the three-foot shafts from the bows of Mollach archers, singing a slower, deeper tune as they sent precisely aimed volleys down the slope into the charging press of Rondian legionaries.

Kyrik had been counting, and by his reckoning they must be down to their last half-dozen arrows – and the number of men below was growing, not shrinking. A maniple was five hundred soldiers: the Rondians would take losses in the charge, but they would still likely match his force in numbers, and there was nowhere to retreat.

'*SHOOT! LOOSE EVERY ARROW!*' he cried, and another storm of flying wood and steel ripped into the men below – but in the centre a gnostic shield was splashing pale blue light across the gloom, and inside that bubble he could see Sacrista, her face set hard and determined. The Rondian soldiers had locked their shields together – they weren't carrying the big infantry shields that covered half the body, but they were still an impediment to archery – and scrambling up the stony, uneven slope. His men ran out of shafts and unsheathed their bladed weapons. The Vitezai had boar-spears, thick, heavy skewers eight feet long, with wide flanged heads; while the Sydian had only their light scimitars. Most had a little armour – leather plates for their chests and shoulders – but that was nothing compared to the tempered steel the legionaries wore.

Things were about to get brutally ugly.

Twenty yards, fifteen, ten . . .

'*HIT THEM!*' he shouted, and as he leaped from cover, his people rose to their feet from behind bushes, rocks and the stunted hagwoods and used the slope to drive down on their foes, thrusting spears and swords at any exposed flesh. Kyrik went in with his sword in one hand and his left hand blazing mage-fire, livid gouts of energy that cut down one man, then another, and another. For a moment the Rondian advance wavered as those in the fore struggled to deal with the sudden attack and the challenges of fighting uphill. Kyrik used kinesis to set a boulder rolling, crushing at least one soldier and scattering a dozen more – then a mage-bolt from Sacrista Delestre slammed into his shields. He fended it off and hurled a counterblast that she easily swatted away.

Then the frontlines crashed together, weapons clattered, men screamed, and the real carnage began.

The first man to reach him took Kyrik's sword in the throat, the second and third he battered backwards, then lanced with mage-bolts, and all the while, thrown javelins were bouncing off his shields. When he drove his blade right through the chest of a cohort commander the rankers recoiled, screaming, 'Mage! Ware: *battle-mage!*'

'He's mine!' Sacrista shouted, her voice bell-like amidst the clamour, and her men gratefully gave way. Her gaze locked on his. 'I see you've gone native with your warpaint and furs,' she sneered.

She blocked his mage-bolt, then sent a mesmeric-thrust at him, which he batted aside with more difficulty than he'd have liked. 'Don't you get sick of ruining lives for your father's coffers?' he panted, seeking an opening.

She battered away his lunge in a clatter of steel. 'Never. It's my only joy.'

They circled, exchanging blows, feeling out each other's speed and style, while around them, the Rondian lines, broken by the rough terrain, had turned into an uncoordinated mêlée. Here and there, outliers were battling each other one-on-one. As far as Kyrik could see, his tribesmen and hunters were holding, but there was an unending stream of soldiers coming up from below.

Then Sacrista lunged and suddenly they were toe to toe and hammering at each other's guard. He threw a blur of illusory movement left and stepped right, seeking to deceive her into misstepping, but she followed his true movement easily; her longsword flashed in like a striking snake, steel clattered and shields flashed, cones of pale blue light slashed with scarlet as they carved at each other, seeking weakness.

His blade was heavier, but her arm was strong; he tried to batter her backwards and instead found himself parrying frantically. When he gave ground, he almost tripped. All round him, the redcloaks were pressing onwards as his men fell under them or gave way beneath their well-honed attacks. Brazko was holding the centre together, but he saw Yrhen stabbed through the belly, then someone hacked the back of his neck as he dropped. Rothgar's wolf-hilted sword carved open a man's throat, but another two drove him back. The disciplined professionalism of the Rondian soldiers was carrying the day.

Then he had no more time, for Sacrista went on the offensive, tearing at his shielding with jabs of mage-fire, while her longsword forced him to give ground. She never overcommitted; she was every bit as dangerous as he'd imagined.

But if I'm to go, she's coming with me . . .

Watcher's Peak, White Stag Land, Mollachia

Valdyr woke and thrashed to his feet, shaking snow off his hair and blanket. He had no idea what time of day it was, but the stiffness of his muscles suggested he'd slept a long time. The light was dim, and shifting rapidly. The fire had gone out and the four icy mounds kept silent vigil.

I spoke with Zlateyr. I kissed Luhti. It felt like a dream.

The sound that had woken him was a snuffling noise: a white stag stood on the far side of the fire-pit between the bodies of Eyrik and Sidorzi. There was a gaping hole in its chest, rimmed by frozen blood, and a pulsing heart – skewered, but raw – lay on a stone beside the cold fire. He understood.

Eat . . . or don't eat. Remain who I am . . . or become someone else. It wasn't even a choice. Luhti's words whispered in his skull, reminding him of the risks. *If I'm false to the Elétfa, it will destroy me.*

But Mollach needed him. He bit into the deer's heart, tearing off an icy chunk, chewed and swallowed, then wolfed the rest down—

—and a wind rushed through him and filled him and bore him onwards, on the back of a white stag.

37

Storming Castles

Castles

When the Blessed Three Hundred rose against the Rimoni Empire, the forts of the
Rimoni legions proved more trap than protection. The magi had so many means of
breaking them down that they were no safer for the legionaries than open ground.
But military thinking never stands still, and soon the Rondian magi found ways
to integrate such places into their new ways of waging war. Strongholds regained
importance, buttressed by spells as much as by stone.

Sir Wrolf Maghrey, Military Historian, Pallas, 812

Beneath the Aerflus, Pallas
Junesse 935

Ril Endarion, Dirklan Setallius, Basia de Sirou and Mort Singolo pounded
along the tunnel, which carried a strong whiff of smoke from the fire
they were fleeing. They'd not seen anyone ahead of them yet, but smoke-
less gnostic-lamps embedded in the tunnel walls lit damp footprints
in the gravel: the riverreek victims were definitely somewhere ahead.

Within the first few hundred yards, more stairways dropped down
to join the tunnel, from other places in Emtori like Saint Chalfon, they
guessed. Ril suggested climbing one, but Setallius was certain they
would all have been blocked, as the church had been, so best not to
waste the time checking.

Even had they wished to contact someone, they no longer had that
option: clairvoyant-gnosis, scrying and gnostic calls were all prevented
by large bodies of earth and water, and right now they guessed they

were deep under the Aerflus. Setallius had worked out the tunnel ran towards the Greyspire district in Southside, though for how long, they had no idea.

Singolo ran efficiently, breathing easily, looking as if he could keep it up for days. Setallius was showing his age: his breath was laboured, his gait uneven. But it was Ril who was really struggling: for all her slight frame, Basia weighed enough that carrying her was swiftly draining him.

Then Singolo stopped him and took Basia himself; she looked like a twig in his meaty hands. 'Can't have the "Prince of the Spear" arrive blown,' the giant axeman chuckled, and Ril, panting like a bellows, slapped his shoulder gratefully. He shared a look with Basia, but their mutual claustrophobia had receded, drowned by the other horrors they'd seen, at least for now. He didn't doubt it would return.

The smooth passage turned occasionally, maybe following the contours of the bedrock through which it had been punched by Earth-gnosis. The stench of the Reekers lingered, a mix of blood and vomit and weeks-old sweat.

They had to stop when they reached a point where the tunnel snaked right – and forked. Singolo put Basia down and they all drew weapons and approached the junction cautiously. But there was still no one to be seen, not in the pool of light from the gnostic-lamp above the fork, nor in the dimly lit passages.

'They went this way,' Singolo announced, coming back from the right-hand passage, still sniffing the air.

Ril tried the left, and confirmed, 'This way too.' He looked at Setallius, who was breathing hard. 'If we've been going east, then the Celestium is straight on ... and the left passage must go to Pallas-Nord—'

'—and the Bastion,' Basia breathed. 'The riverreek victims are going to both the Celestium and the Bastion!'

'I fear they are the foot-soldiers in a palace coup aimed at both Lyra and Wurther.' The spymaster cursed softly. 'And here we are, trapped beneath the Aerflus and unable to warn anyone.' He glanced in each direction, then said, 'The sooner we get to the surface, the sooner we can give warning.'

'So we go right?' Mort asked. 'We can't be more than a mile from the Celestium, but the Bastion's probably three miles away.'

'I don't give a shit about Wurther,' said Ril. 'It's Lyra we must protect!'

Basia nodded in support, but Setallius was shaking his head. 'The sooner we reach the surface, the quicker we can warn her – not to mention the other people whose lives might be saved.'

'I'm going left,' Ril snapped. Then he paused. 'I'll not make it a command.'

Because I couldn't enforce it anyway . . . but I'll remember . . .

The four of them stared at each other, then Basia said, 'I'd just slow you down. Let me go right and try to send out the warnings.' There was a sick look of fear on her face and Ril sympathised, but Lyra was in danger.

'We can't let you go alone,' he replied. 'Dirk, you take Basia down the right-hand path and try to warn Lyra. I'll go straight for her.'

'Then with your permission,' the axeman said, looking at Setallius, 'I'll go with Ril. The two of us can travel fast – and we're the best in a scrap.'

The spymaster nodded. They all clasped hands, then without another word, they split up and ran.

The Celestium, Pallas

Time. You can have so much of it, Dominius Wurther reflected, shifting uncomfortably on his throne in the Scriptorium Chamber, *then suddenly you're counting out the last few moments.* His brain had been trotting out such morbid thoughts all day. He surveyed the semicircle of prelates arrayed before him for the evening session of the first day of Synod. For the last half-hour they'd been hectored by Giovanni Prelatus, a Sacrecour man, in an increasingly tedious rant about sin.

Never my favourite topic.

'We have sinned,' Giovanni thundered, 'we have sinned by not opposing this usurper regime!'

Giovanni had a dozen backing him, which was puzzling Wurther. Synod had the power to displace a grand prelate, but the vote had to be unanimous, and that was surely impossible to engineer when even one abstention killed the motion. And Wurther knew he had votes in the bag already; he had letters of support from three absentee prelates in his scroll-case. This was all a waste of time.

'Do you have a *point*, Giovanni?' he put in. 'Our ears grow weary and supper awaits.'

'You had the royal children in your grasp,' Giovanni replied, 'and *you* lost them—'

That again? 'I think we all know the circumstances,' Wurther replied. 'The conclave agreed to shift allegiance to the Corani heiress: an indisputably legitimate claimant. Beyond that, our mandate is of the spiritual, not the temporal world.'

'Preventing evil reigning unchallenged is also our mandate,' Giovanni shouted.

Good grief, Wurther thought, *are we reduced to bogeyman stories?* 'Lyra Vereinen is not widely regarded as *evil*, to the best of my knowledge,' he observed, scanning the circle of faces. Yet again, he thought there was something very strange here: the prelates all looked . . . *ill*. They were pale and snuffling, bloodshot eyes, as if the riverreek was sweeping through them – and not just those with Giovanni either . . .

He felt a sense of real threat tonight: not to prestige or status: but to life and limb. *Was I right? Is the real purpose of this Synod simply to get us all into the same room?*

He glanced up at the gallery. During open debates like this, younger priests were welcome to listen. Tonight only one man was there: a big dark silhouette reclining against a pillar, his steel-cased shoulders glinting in the candlelight. <*Wilfort,*> Wurther sent, <*be alert.*>

The tall figure nodded faintly, then retreated deeper into the shadows. *I have to trust someone*, Wurther mused, hoping Wilfort really was reliable. *It's a Hel of a thing to get wrong . . .*

'We stand: the last bastion against the Lord of Hel,' Giovanni declaimed. 'You gave your oath to hinder his works with all your heart, mind and body, Grand Prelate.'

'And so I do,' Wurther sighed. 'Do you have a *rational* point, Giovanni? We're all getting rather hungry—'

'*Hungry . . . ?*' Giovanni's head tilted as if he was listening to unheard music. Eerily, all of the prelates on his side of the chamber mirrored his movement. He made a strange gesture, putting his hand inside his robes as if clutching at his stomach, and again the prelates behind him did the same.

Wurther peered at them uncertainly. *What is this?* He took up his rod of office and hammered it thrice, holding his breath. That was the signal for his honour guard, a dozen Kirkegarde mage-knights, to rise from their positions below and flank him left and right: an honour guard – but also a reminder that only one man commanded the swords here.

As they took up their positions, he said, 'Brethren, tonight's debate – such as it was – is over. We will reconvene tomorrow.'

Giovanni glared at him, then he produced a Lantric mask wrought of papier-mâché and placed it over his face. Behind him, every other prelate did the same. Each was identical: *Jest*.

I'll say it's a bloody jest, but it's not a funny one! 'What is the meaning of this?' Wurther demanded, his words resounding about the chamber.

No one said a word, but the doors behind them flew open and another entered, also wearing a 'Jest' mask, but this one glinted: metal and lacquer. He also bore the crozier of a prelate, which he tapped on the tiles as he walked toward Wurther's throne. The masked faces followed his entry as one, then turned to Wurther again. The effect of those ranks of masks was chilling.

Any time you like, Wilfort . . . Wurther glanced at the guardsmen flanking him, hoping they were up for whatever was coming next, because most of these prelates, while hardly warriors, were pure-blood magi.

The newcomer walked to the front of the benches housing the prelates, his movements filled with languid grace. '*Meaning?* Does anything really have meaning, Dominius? We preach that it does, but we're magi: we know the Truth, and the Truth is that there is no meaning. We have lifted the mask of Kore, the mask of God, and found nothing behind. There's no universal struggle of Divine Goodness against Eternal Evil – Kore and the Lord of Hel are phantoms, whimsies, no more real than Aradea and the Fey. We here know this, the fictions and half-truths, the sacred words we dress our lives in. The only thing that *matters* is *this—*'

Jest hammered his crozier into the tiles, the sound reverberating about the chamber. 'Wealth, might, and the power to control thoughts: *that's* what the Church is! We know the masses are stupid, so we simplify things for them: we dress up our desires as "Kore's Will" – how else could Johan Corin, a man so drunk on his own cleverness that he didn't see his best friend was poisoning his followers, become a Messiah? How else could an old harvest-god be recreated as the Supreme Being? *Religion is control*: we insiders know this, and we wield it. But you are unfit to do so.'

'*Unfit?*' Dominius snorted. 'How so?'

Jest pointed at Wurther, and the men of Wurther's honour guard flinched and raised gnostic shields. 'Because you failed to do what your role demands: as the Voice of Kore, you had the chance to become the ultimate power in Yuros and you failed. Had you done as advised that day, you would have been both Pontifex and emperor!'

Wurther's suspicions were confirmed. *Only one man knows about that conversation. It's you behind that mask, isn't it Ostevan? Jilted by the Corani, still clinging to the dream of ultimate power and betraying the empress out of spite.* He gripped his periapt and sent to Wilfort: <*Get your men in here – now!*>

For a moment there was no response, then Wilfort sent a shocked, <*What in Hel?*> back down the link.

Rukka! In an unfolding nightmare, the masked prelates raised their hands, darkness kindling about their fists. His guardsmen strengthened their shields and brandished weapons as doors burst open above and crossbowmen spilled in, but his eyes were on *the* Jest: Ostevan, he was sure. The bright lacquer flowed, moving like flesh as he shouted in the Runic Tongue. A maelstrom of light formed around him.

Wurther slammed his hand down on the Sacred Heart pattern on the table before him, triggering an old gnostic circle of protection set there for this very purpose. Walls of blue light encased him as outside it, jagged bolts of light flew and prelates and mage-knights flowed together, steel crashing on croziers. Shrieks and cries of injury and death filled the enclosed space.

*

The final stretch of the main tunnel took Basia and Dirklan up a short slope. A single lamp illuminated the point where the tunnel became a stair.

Basia looked wearily at Dirklan. He was clearly working damned hard just to keep moving, but she was in agony, both physically and mentally. The constant weight of her claustrophobia was beating down on her, and her stumps were grinding into the tops of her artefact-legs, making every step a torment. Without her healing-affinity to soothe them, she'd have been unable to move. But now, finally, respite beckoned.

Thank Kore . . . I don't know how much more of this I can take.

Despite the exhaustion and the fear, she was conscious that this was the first time she'd been able to function while underground. The ghosts of 909 were not entirely exorcised, but she felt as if she'd made peace with them at last.

I've beaten the fear. I've really done it . . . Well, Ril and I beat it together.

That she'd kissed him still haunted her; that was one mask she'd never meant to let slip. *But how could I not fall in love with the one who got me through that? And why did he never notice?*

A wiser part of herself replied, *Because you hid it, and he was only a boy. You were too frightened that he'd reject you if you told him how you felt. He was about to become a knight and you were a cripple, so much easier to not put him to that test, to instead play the devoted friend who was just too* ironic *to ever stoop to something so* gauche *as falling in love.*

She couldn't say what Ril had felt – but his mouth on hers had felt so *right*. But the thought of the next step was terrifying.

You've beaten the claustrophobia. So what are you going to do about that fear?

'How are you managing?' Dirklan's panting voice pulled her back to the present.

She threw him a wan smile. 'I'm just about all in.'

'Not long to go,' he told her. 'Do you need help?'

'No – let's just get it done. We'll get to the top and warn the city, then I'll crawl into a corner and sleep for a week.'

The climb was a hard one, the stairs gritty with the passage of many feet, and the stench of the Reekers lingering in the unmoving air. Dirklan went ahead, walking silently, to ensure they weren't about to run in to anyone; she clumped along behind him, using kinesis to haul herself, step by step – walking on the flat was hard enough, but slopes and steps were devilish.

Finally they reached a storage room, filthy with the passage of feet and the reek of the diseased. Dirklan found the way out and they emerged onto a crenellated rooftop overlooking the inner city of the Celestium.

The citadel of the Church of Kore was in uproar: bells were clanging and trumpets braying, while soldiers and priests and servants were charging in all directions. But their eyes were drawn to the massive dome of the Celestium Basilica itself – and the smoke pouring from the upper windows that rimmed the dome.

Basia gripped the battlements and dragged her eyes to the north, to the black silhouette of the Bastion, where flames licked the lower slopes. Back towards Emtori, the docks of Surrid were ablaze. 'We're too late,' she gasped.

The spymaster was silent, all his concentration on the periapt he clutched in his hand. As he sent warnings to his people in Pallas-Nord, a tremendous feeling of helplessness enveloped her. After all the effort, all she'd endured and overcome in the tunnels below – and they were in the wrong place.

'We should have gone with Ril and Mort,' she muttered, as he finished his call.

'We'd have only slowed them down.' He looked as tired as she felt.

'We might have made a difference—'

'We'll never know. I've been juggling with limited resources all my life.' He put a hand on her shoulder. 'When you take my place, you'll understand.'

'*Take your place?*'

'I won't live forever, Basia.'

She swallowed, staring at his face, well-beloved, despite the age and the scars, and trying to imagine life without him. And without Ril.

She looked away, biting her lip. 'Dear Kore, let us all come through this.'

The Bastion, Pallas-Nord

Lyra was standing at the window of her room, half-listening to Hilta Pollanou chatter about how *awful* this riverreek season was. 'Those poor people,' Hilta was saying, 'imagine being made to leave your home and forced to live among other sick people – how can you possibly get well in conditions like that?'

'The healers are doing sterling work, everyone says so,' Sedina Way-cross answered, plaiting her long flaxen hair. 'The poor get riverreek all the time.'

Geni, embroidering in the corner, was silent.

Lyra couldn't muster the energy to join the depressing conversation. She was wondering where Ril was – he and Basia de Sirou had gone somewhere, so a young female mage named Ascella was standing in as her bodyguard. She was outside her doors with the guardsmen right now. Dirklan Setallius was off somewhere too. She would have liked to have asked him about the hunt for Cordan and Coramore.

Why do I feel like everything is unravelling tonight? Then she saw an orange glow, some miles southwest across the Aerflus, at the foot of Emtori Heights. 'What's that?' she asked, pointing. 'It looks like fire.'

Hilta joined her, her soft hair catching the candlelight. 'It does, doesn't it?' she replied. 'Fire can be *awful* in the poorer areas: it's so hard to contain.'

Sedina joined them at the window, her face filled with vague concern. 'That's the Surrid docklands. My family have their House on the Emtori Heights. The docks are dirty and lawless,' she added. 'Better they burn.'

'Sedina,' Hilta reproved, 'the poor can't help their station.'

'All honest, hardworking men can improve their station,' Sedina sniffed. 'The poor are just lazy. Everyone knows this. I see them from my carriage – people sleeping through the day when they should be working.'

'My family give alms, and not just on Holy Days,' Hilta announced in her "I'm a better person" voice. 'Poverty is a failing, but they can be helped. I bet you've never even met a poor person.'

'Ha! I have servants – I know all about what lazy wretches poor people are—'

'Be quiet, all of you,' Lyra said. She liked Hilta and Sedina most of the time, but they could be such condescending snobs. She'd *really* seen poverty, in the convent, and she was determined she'd never forget what it looked like. She almost dismissed them both, even though it was only early evening. *I'd rather be alone than listen to them prattle.* Then she cradled her belly. *I'm never alone now, am I?* She smiled.

Geni joined them at the rail of the balcony. 'My family are from Surrid,' she said quietly, then she gasped. 'Look, another fire' – she pointed 'and another—!'

She was right: more fires were breaking out in Emtori. Then something caught Lyra's eye: much closer, in the alleys inside the Bastion's wall: not a movement, but an *absence* of movement in a place which was *always* bustling with people hurrying to and fro. Beneath a night-lamp was a person, a hundred yards away or more, who seemed to be staring straight at her. She was sure it was a child.

Then Hilta exclaimed, 'Look!' and pointed out another fire in Surrid. For an instant – no more, she was certain – Lyra took her eyes from the person below, and when she looked back, the child was gone. But the sense of being watched persisted.

Her feelings of vulnerability intensified. *I wish Ril were here.*

The fires were definitely spreading. There were more guards than usual on the battlements below, all pointing towards the distant spectacle – then an Imperial windskiff soared by, heading towards Emtori.

Hilta waved encouragement. 'See, Majesty? Our Fire-magi, off to save the day!'

'I hope it doesn't spread to the Heights where our people live,' Sedina remarked.

Lyra glanced back at Geni, whose mouth was a thin line. *Sedina is so thoughtless. I must speak to her.* But as she glanced back down, hearing a guard captain barking orders to the men on the wall, her thoughts froze.

In the shadow of the tall corner tower was a small figure in a hooded fawn cloak, looking up at her. She could have sworn it was the same person she'd seen far below. *How did they get there so quickly?* Then, *Cordan and Coramore had fawn cloaks . . .*

She turned to the woman beside her. 'Hilta—'

But when she looked back, the figure beside the tower was gone.

The shadows were dense and the moonless sky only emphasised the distant chill of the stars. She shuddered and took a step backwards.

'Majesty?' Hilta asked, her matronly face puzzled. 'Are you well? Have you caught a chill?'

'Look, there goes another skiff,' Sedina said, oblivious.

'I don't feel ...' Lyra almost said 'safe', but hesitated. *Am I jumping at shadows? Why would Cordan or Coramore be wandering outside, anyway?*

'It's too cold out here,' Hilta fussed, 'especially for a mother to be – let's get you inside.' Herding Lyra towards the doors, she added, 'Geni, get tea – at once.'

Lyra let herself be ushered inside, but Sedina stayed on the balcony. 'There goes a third skiff,' she called. 'I'm going to watch.'

There was a sensation Lyra got while in her Winter Garden some-times: a feeling of awareness, and she'd mutter to herself, *Aradea is awake*. She had that feeling now. Sometimes it was a feeling of comfort, of being nurtured.

Tonight, it was a *warning*.

'Sedina,' she called, 'come inside!'

'But it's *all* happening!' Sedina shouted back.

'*I said come inside!*'

The willowy blonde woman blinked at the sudden crack of authority in Lyra's voice. She hesitated, then bowed her head and began to walk back towards the door—

—just as a skinny white arm reached over the balcony, a cowled head appeared – and then a girl in a fawn cloak was standing on the balcony behind her. Lyra and Hilta choked as the hood dropped.

'*Coramore—*'

Coramore Sacrecour's face was ravaged by riverreek. Her eyes were red, her nose bloody and streaming; her drooling mouth was all scab and weeping sores. She stood there like the spectre of disease, staring at Lyra. Then she bared gleaming white teeth which looked somehow *elongated*, sharpened. *Predator teeth*.

Lyra and Hilta and Geni all gaped. Sedina stared at them, a question forming on her lips, then she realised they were looking behind her. She turned, her body blocking Coramore from Lyra's sight ...

38

The Heart of the Storm

The Draken

The draken is a chthonic beast: one that arises from the earth. The adoption of such beasts as a patron-spirit is usually an attempt by a ruler to lay claim to the land – and, of course, to associate the ferocity and power of the draken with their own myth. Such was the reasoning of Korestane Felz, who took the name 'Sarkany' – the Mollach word for draken – when he took the throne of Mollachia in 826

ATTIUS LEX, HISTORIAN, AUGENHEIM, 871

Magas Gorge, Mollachia
Junesse 935

Kyrik Sarkany had a good sword arm, but not good enough: Sacrista could feel the tide turning her way, and her confidence grew. Kyrik had reach on her, and good technique, but she had the upper hand, and the rabble of natives and weird tribesfolk Kyrik was leading were starting to break.

If I take down their leader, this will be my victory. She fuelled her blade and arm with more energy, compensating for her smaller build, and surged forward. Their blades crashed together, carving sparkling gouges in each other's shields, and he gave ground again, his face taut and bleak.

<*You're trapped, Sarkany,*> she sent, the barb wrapped with mesmeric-gnosis, meant to distract. <*The dungeons are waiting . . .*>

He reacted with a foolish lunge and her riposte almost took his right eye. He staggered back, tripped over a thorn bush and went sprawling. When he tried to rise, she smashed kinetic-gnosis down on him, leaving him winded, threw a burst of light into his eyes to blind him and closed in.

Then Fressyn appeared alongside her, his sword lifted in a killing blow. 'He's mine!' she warned the battle-mage, but he launched a double-handed overhead blow at the fallen Mollach—

—just as a boulder hurtled out of the gloom and flattened him with a wet crunch. Fressyn was so intent on his moment of glory he'd barely shielded – and he'd paid the price. When the boulder rolled on, all that was left was a boneless, bloody smear.

'No, Bitch, he's *mine*,' said a female voice in awkward Rondian, and Sacrista looked up in surprise to see a woman step into view from over the ridgeline.

The woman – a Sydian *savage*, with face and arms streaked with blue – was panting, as if she'd been running hard to get here. A cloud of black hair surrounded an ageing face; her solid body was clad only in a short leather smock. But she had an amber periapt, and pale shields woven about her. Four more like her, male and female, were standing along the ridgeline. Gnosis-light flared, the remaining defenders rallied, and the advancing legionaries recoiled uncertainly.

Sacrista realised her duel with Kyrik had isolated her a little. She gripped her blade and spun it casually: the picture of utter capability. She could kill Sarkany, right now – but she wanted him alive. *I need to use him to induce his brother's surrender and end this rebellion once and for all.*

'To me!' she shouted, and was answered by a clarion of trumpets. A glance backwards revealed that her men were still coming up the slope, and her heart sang as Robear's mental voice filled her head. <*Coming, Sister – to the rescue! Ha!*>

'Rescue' be damned. But she smiled her most evil smile at the Sydian woman. '"Bitch", is it? You have no idea.'

Kyrik's vision was doubly blurred, by the hammer-blow of kinesis and the blood pouring from the cut above his eye. There was no air in his lungs, but he inhaled desperately as he heard a voice he desperately didn't want to hear, not *here*.

No, Hajya! He rammed the heels of his hands into his eye-sockets, trying to counter Sacrista's blinding spell, while around him boots crunched, weapons clashed and people cried out, praying, and venting their pain. But all he cared was that the woman he loved was facing someone well beyond her—

He got his eyes open, just in time . . .

Sacrista advanced swiftly up the slope, closing the distance, as the Sydian woman's whole shape blurred into an impressively swift shape-change. Sacrista realised she wasn't trying to alter herself fully, but to enhance her fighting prowess: her chest swelled and her spine lengthened, her legs stretched and then snapped as the joints reversed and reconfigured, thin fur crawled like a shadow over her skin as her nose and mouth became a snout, and then a maw of teeth.

Sacrista lunged, and the woman's left arm flailed sideways, striking the side of her blade and battering it away, then her right *raked* and Sacrista, stunned at the speed of the riposte, barely managed to arch her back away. Then the woman was leaping at her, claws raking at her shields as she staggered back. The woman's face – still hairless, but contorted into a wolf-visage – split open and yellow teeth snapped at her.

But Sacrista's shields held . . . and she was a half-blood mage trained for war.

She slammed her right hand up, hammering kinesis-force into the Sydian witch and sending her hurling backwards. Then she followed up the blow by leaping to land over the woman as she tried to rise and smashed an overhanded blow at her shoulder. Though the witch blocked with shields, the force of the blow was enough to break the woman's left arm at the elbow and crush her to the ground.

'Who's the bitch now?' she snarled, sweeping another sideways blow at the woman that almost severed her right claw. She followed by stepping in and ramming the hilt, infused with gnosis-energy, into the side of the woman's head. The witch's shields stripped her blade of gnostic fire but the blow still struck her temple with bone-crunching force, dropping her in a heap. She spun her blade and raised it above the woman's breast to finish the job—

—as Kyrik howled in despair and erupted from the ground, his face transcendent with rage, power bursting from him and hammering into her. She was battered backwards, hurled down the slope. She crunched against a boulder, losing her blade – she'd have broken her back, too, if she'd not been able to keep her shields together. The legionaries who tried to stand against him were scattered as Kyrik blasted mage-fire at them, then again at her, anger lending him a speed and ferocity she could only defend against – and then he was on her, before she'd been able to retrieve her blade. She blocked with shielding, but blocking steel with kinesis was a fool's game. She tried to elude him, feinted left, darted right—

—and howled silently as his sword plunged through her right thigh, his weight pushing in behind. They fell together, his blade pinning her to the ground, her vision became a tunnel: one face, one man—

—then trumpets blasted, so close she was deafened, and Robear stormed up the slope on horseback, his steed's hooves borne by Airgnosis, riding the air, and his sword swiped around, taking Kyrik Sarkany in the side. The big Mollachian spun and toppled, landing on top of her in a horrific jolt that pushed the wind from her lungs.

They clutched blindly at each other in a blaze of convulsive agony, their faces inches apart, eyes glazed and draining of life, recognition fading as they tumbled into the waiting void.

The White Stag rode the winds with Valdyr clinging to its back as they plummeted down cliffs and crashed through forests, leaving splintered timber behind. They ripped along valleys like a mountain storm, clouds of snow-dust boiling in their wake, the stag a projectile of horn and fur, impossibly swift.

But his ears heard further than that: they heard the tumult of battle, and his brother's fierce need.

He dug his fingers into the stag's fur, tears icing up on his cheeks, his hair streaming out behind him. They triggered avalanches from the highest slopes of Watcher's Peak in their passing, sending snow and rocks tumbling into the forests of Feher Szarvasfeld thousands of feet below. A surging wave of black clouds followed behind them; white fingers of death cracked the tree trunks and splintered stone as they came. He felt like more than a man: he was an arrow carved from the branches of the Elétfa, the Tree of Life, and loosed upon the land.

Then he felt Kyrik cry out, and fear and rage flared brighter again inside his chest.

'*Onwards!*' he shouted, and the stag's massive limbs pounded harder and faster, and the world became a white blur.

Robear Delestre dismounted as the native scum finally realised they were beaten and fell back, rallying to a brown-bearded man brandishing a wolf's-head hilt and reforming in a ragged line near the top of the cliffs. His own men were scattered, so Robear paused to regroup them. He wanted this done properly. There'd be no gaps in the lines: he would hem these peasants in and hurl them all from the cliffs.

Kyrik Sarkany had landed on his sister, which offended him. He threw the Mollach carelessly aside and saw to Sacrista. Thankfully, she'd only blacked out, and the sword spearing her thigh had missed the bone. She'd live, *thank Kore!* Despite her imperfections, he couldn't imagine life without her. He removed the sword and quickly sealed the wound. He had an affinity to healing, although he didn't often utilise it – knights were warriors, not healers. But he had to admit, at times it was damned handy.

Kyrik Sarkany was still living as well. 'Take him, Chain him and put him in irons,' he told the nearest battle-mage. 'We'll work out what to do with him later.'

Then the crowd of merchants' and bankers' sons galloped up, looking flushed with exertion and excitement. 'I hope we're not too late,' they called.

Robear indicated the surviving enemy, silhouetted against the clifftops. 'The last few dozen are trapped – but our scouts reckon there are masses more in the gorge below, so once we command the heights, it'll be slaughter.'

'Lovely. I do enjoy a good slaughter,' one of the bankers chuckled.

'I say,' another said, 'your sister looks in bad shape. Best to keep girls from the battlefield, eh?'

Robear laughed as if it were a splendid jest. Then he saw her eyelids flutter open and she woke. He bent over her, whispering, 'Sister dear, the scrapes you get into!'

'Go to Hel,' she groaned. She'd be limping for weeks and she'd have the scar for life, but she'd recover, he decided. 'Thanks, Arsehole,' she added grudgingly.

'You're welcome, Bitch.' He pulled her into a quick hug.

'Yes,' she murmured, 'I showed her who's the bitch. Get me my sword back, Rob.'

He looked around and spotted her distinctive blade lying beside a corpse up the slope. He sauntered over, swept up Sacrista's blade and glanced at the female savage lying there. She looked halfway through some kind of shape-change – *or maybe these savages are just that ugly? It'll be a boon to the world to end her.* He lifted Sacrista's blade to finish her as an icy gust of wind rolled over them, making him shiver. He glanced up and realised the lower slopes had vanished and the valley to the east was somehow filling up with darkness. Lightning flashed through the mountains to the north – then thunder suddenly cracked and rolled, stunningly loud.

He turned back . . . and found the she-savage had crawled away to the feet of a giant with a bow. They stared at each other, he and the young tribesman, and he smiled to see that the ignorant savage was unafraid.

He's probably never even seen a mage-knight fight.

He kindled mage-fire in his left hand and was about to advance when one of his battle-magi approached. 'Milord, our scouts say when the clouds cover the lower slopes, you've got less than twenty minutes to find shelter,' he said.

Robear watched the way the storm was flowing straight along the valley towards him and decided the advice was sound. *Who cares if a few natives get away?* He didn't wish to get wet on such a cold night – and more importantly, Sacrista was in no shape for a night in the open.

'Agreed. Let's get under cover,' he said. 'We'll complete the mopping-up in the morning.' He threw the young giant a mocking salute; the young man returned the gesture—

—and he blasted the boy's face off with a mage-bolt.

The tribesman crashed like a falling tree and the she-savage at his feet cried out in pain and betrayal. He smirked and hurled her off the cliff with a burst of kinesis, then walked away, whistling cheerily.

Really, these savages are no challenge.

Then the lightning cracked again, the thunder rolled and light drained from the world as clouds raced towards him. *Twenty minutes to find shelter?* he thought. *I don't think we've got more than two—*

The White Stag bellowed, sounding his rage, and all through Feher Szarvasfeld the cry was answered as they careened down the snow-covered paths. Valdyr glanced left and saw another stag with a rider clinging to its back: Sidorzi, the dead shaman. The revenant was laughing like a fiend. Then two more shapes appeared behind him, shrieking madly: Eyrik and Luhti, all their gentle humanity subsumed in the lust of the hunt. They were somewhere between dead and alive, their skulls coated in cold blueish flesh, their eyes like pits. Behind them a misty horde of ghostly wolves and other frost-rimed beasts yowled.

Then Zlateyr ranged up beside him, his drawn sword flickering with lightning, and as their eyes met, fierce, bloody joy erupted from their throats.

Onwards!

They broke through the trees and onto the plains as Kyrik cried aloud and Valdyr's vision flashed forward to Robear Delestre, standing on a rocky slope in the midst of a crowd of Rondians a mile or so away and looking at him—

—and an instant later, they were *there.*

Sacrista, still dazed, looked about for her brother. There he was, coming towards her with a wry smile on his face, twirling her sword.

She tried to stand, and one of the bankers' sons caught her arm, his self-satisfied face aping sympathy. 'Can you ride, Lady Sacrista?' he said. 'If you've lost your horse, you can share mine—'

She slapped his arm away and took a step, but had to grab at him again.

'I've got you,' he said, with condescending concern.

The sun was gone and dark clouds were pouring down from the north.

The wind was shrilling, frigid air slapped her face – and she thought she caught a glimpse of *something* in the storm. *Something impossible.* She tried to scream a warning, but it was already too late.

Kyrik lay in an agony of physical and mental torment as a Rondian battle-mage bent over him.

Where's Hajya? God of All, let her have escaped—

There were well-dressed Rondians with pompous voices all round him. Sacrista was on her feet, clinging to a richly dressed lowlander. Her thigh was bloody, but she was alive, and the taste of defeat soured his mouth.

Not the dungeon again, he prayed.

Then thunder cracked again, building in intensity, and he shuddered at another sudden drop in temperature. All around, men were shouting about finding shelter.

'Right you, hold still.' The battle-mage standing over him shook him, making his head spin even more wildly 'Sooner we're done, the sooner we can get under cover.' He opened his palm, beginning a Chain-rune—

—when a shard of ice flashed through the man, piercing his left breast. He choked and crumpled to the ground, blood gushing from the wound – and instantly freezing.

Kyrik stared, stunned, as blackness flowed from the east. Beasts roared and howled and bellowed and the thunder in the sky became the thunder of hooves.

The White Stag roared and Valdyr saw the flash of a hated face and swung his sword. The head flew and the body crumpled as he swept past, and in his wake a blast of frozen air struck the ridge. To the left and right, the four Watchers were carving down any Rondians standing, but it was the storm that was dealing the real killing blows: in moments the whole of the Delestre force was engulfed and trapped inside a dark world where flesh froze and bones broke into slivers and steel shattered. He pulled his steed about to see wolves of ice and fog rend a horse; he heard Zlateyr's bow ring and an arrow slammed into a Rondian commander's chest; he saw a line of rankers lurch to a frozen halt; he saw men and horses freeze solid, fall and shatter on the rocks.

Onwards!

Hundreds of Rondians were fleeing across the open ground towards Magas Gorge. He swept towards them, mowing down all those he passed. The Watchers in his wake were revelling in the destruction as the soft, warm auras of the living winked out.

He craved more – then he sensed *thousands* of souls somewhere ahead. He led his ghostly band right to the lip of the cliff, stopping on the very edge of the precipice to survey the scene below. His stag snorted, the wolves howled and ice and snow ran like a frozen river over the rim.

Below were hundreds, maybe thousands of Sydians and their horses, gathered for the difficult climb to the cliff-top. A sea of faces stared up at him, frightened by all they could hear and feel, even more by what they *couldn't* see but could imagine.

Then he saw that there were still living men on the cliff-top around him: men he knew: Vitezai Sarkanum men. He stared at them and became – *just a little* – more himself and less the hunter.

He turned to Zlateyr. 'These people below are Vlpa.'

'Our people,' the folk-hero replied. '*Your* people.'

My People. Valdyr still felt the urge to continue the slaughter. His heart was thundering, his rage blazing – but other needs were now pulling at him, and the force that had borne him along suddenly wavered.

'The foe is destroyed,' he managed, and a wave of dizziness threatened. 'These *are* my people.' He looked around. 'Where's my brother?'

Zlateyr pointed back up to the ridgeline and Valdyr's preternatural senses showed him a mound lying unmoving on the frosted slope.

'*KYRIK!*' He leaped from the stag and ran – and suddenly he was there, right where his brother was. He barely noticed as a bitter wind swept in and the Watchers and beasts of the hunt began to fray until one final, massive gust tore the ghostly hunt apart and swept the glittering dust of their passing in a skywards spiral.

A curtain of white closed in.

39

A Broken Bastion

Imperial Owls

The owl is the chosen badge of the Imperial Secret Service or 'Volsai' – magi sworn to the throne and pledged to guard against treachery. Ironically, they have become synonymous with treachery themselves, as the degree of literal and metaphorical backstabbing among the Owls is legendary.

ORDO COSTRUO COLLEGIATE, PONTUS, 883

The Bastion, Pallas
Junesse 935

Ril and Mort called air to their lungs and kinesis to their legs to aug-ment their strength. Both were warrior-fit, used to drilling for hours, and they ate up the distance. The passage ran deeper and deeper at first, but after about ten minutes – perhaps a mile of the three or four they must traverse – it levelled. Another twenty minutes and they were climbing. Both were now sweating in pools, their lungs burning.

'Reckon we're under the docklands yet?' Mort panted.

'Can't be . . . far off . . .' gasped Ril. 'Those bastards must've run like the wind.'

'They had a good half an hour on us, probably more. But we can't be far behind now – smell that? The stink's much worse.'

They stumbled to a walk by mutual consent as the climb became steeper. 'If they were just sick people, they couldn't do this,' Ril noted, once he could breathe again.

'Aye,' Mort grunted. 'There were quarantines in Pallas-Nord too,' he added, and that thought was enough to make them lurch into a jog again.

They reached a branch, ignored the tunnel that lacked the stench of the Reekers and ploughed onwards until their own route ended in a stair that spiralled anti-clockwise upwards into the rock.

The stone was still too thick for clairvoyance to penetrate – Ril aborted his call to Lyra the moment he felt the aether shiver at his attempt. If their enemies sensed them, they could easily be bottled up in this stairwell.

'What're the odds we're right beneath the Bastion?' Mort muttered. He pulled an axe from his back and took the lead. 'Come on!'

They climbed in silence, gnostic-lamps lighting as they approached and fading as they passed. The climb was sapping, and whenever they paused to listen, they still heard nothing ahead. Then Ril felt the faintest touch of cleaner air and spotted a tiny ventilation shaft, just a slit in the stone – but more followed. They were getting closer. The walls changed from stone to brick, so they must now be climbing through the lower palace, hidden behind supposedly solid walls.

'We have Earth-magi,' he gasped to Mort. 'Why doesn't Dirk know about this tunnel already?'

'Spoken like an Air-mage,' Mort sniffed. 'You have no idea what you're asking.'

The climb ended abruptly at a door that had been left ajar, the lintel filthy from the passage of many feet. The trail led down a dusty corridor and through another entrance, this one built into the wall so cleverly it was near invisible from the other side. They made their way into a marble-tiled corridor hung with portraits. Oil-lamps guttered here and there, too few to do much to alleviate the gloom.

'The Gallery of Remembrance,' Ril whispered. 'Second level.' Carved and painted faces stared at them, but the passage was empty of life.

Mort indicated the trail of muddied feet running right and then veering left. 'This leads to the gallery above the throne room,' he murmured. 'Can we risk a call?'

But before Ril could start, the distant boom of a bell echoed out of the silence, getting louder as others joined in, and Mort clapped his shoulders, his face wide-eyed. 'We're too late – the alarm is raised – *the attack has begun!*'

The Bastion, Pallas

Solon Takwyth strode the high inner wall of the Bastion, a cohort of Imperial Guards in his wake, until he spotted a knot of men led by Oryn Levis – *Lumpy*, his former second. They all looked frightened.

'What's happening?' he called. 'Who's the foe here?'

'It's the riverreek sufferers,' Levis replied, shouting above the racket. 'There's a quarantine pen below us in Fisheart – there've been disturbances all week, and ten minutes ago a horde of them leaped the fences and tore into the perimeter guards!'

'Oryn, is this fuss just a bunch of rioting *Reekers*?'

'So we thought,' Levis replied, 'but look—' He jabbed a finger towards the outer battlements. 'The Reekers have broken out and they're scaling the Bastion walls!'

Takwyth could see the riverside areas of Pallas-Nord, where lantern-lit ferries bobbed in the distance. Southside looked serene, the Celestium shining above the river – but he could hear alarm bells tolling across the Bruin. And to the southwest, Surrid was burning.

Chaos is spreading . . . just as the Puppeteer said it would . . .

The second curtain-wall where they stood was separated from the lower outer wall by a two-hundred-foot-wide killing zone. There was another empty space between the curtain-wall and the palace behind them. Takwyth looked around: they were right below the royal suite, and lights were glowing from the balcony window of Lyra Vereinen's rooms five storeys above them. There were no outside steps other than the narrow stone staircase that wound around a buttress to the Queen's Winter Garden.

So two walls and a sheer climb . . . 'How are they reaching the battlements?'

'They're climbing,' Levis said incredulously. 'Look! Bare-handed – it's unbelievable!'

Movement on the battlements of the outer wall below caught their eyes. The soldiers stationed there had been jabbing downwards with pikes and spears, presumably knocking the climbers off the walls, although they'd not heard anyone cry out. But the first of the assailants had reached the top: the ragged woman swatted a man so hard he was thrown wailing from the wall to crash, broken, in the killing zone. Another guard speared the woman through the chest – but unbelievably, *she didn't fall*. Instead, she gripped the man's spear and held it inside herself. The guard was drawing his sword when another Reeker emerged over the top and hurled himself at him, sending both guard and woman spiralling into the killing zone below.

'What the Hel?' Levis exclaimed, pointing to where the fallen Reekerwoman had stood up and was shaking off the crushed body of the man who'd fallen with her. Then she walked to the inner wall and began to climb, hand over fist.

Levis looked at Takwyth with a growing look of desperation, his eyes imploring his friend to make sense of this: to be the knight, the protector.

Lumpy's not made for nights like this. Time to take charge . . . Solon drew his sword. 'Steady, Oryn. We're magi of Coraine.' He turned to the senior man of his guard. These were ordinary men, not magi. 'Form up on these walls – swords, not spears,' he ordered calmly. 'You saw what happened below – don't let that be you. A man can't climb if he's got no hands, eh? Think about it—'

Below them, the outer wall was now engulfed. Rolven Sulpeter had appeared on a buttress tower, surrounded by mage-knights, men of his retinue, together with the Joyce brothers and Jos Bortolin. They were holding, blasting the attackers on the battlements and sending fire and lightning down on the climbers, but the ordinary guardsmen were being overrun; they were conceding the battlements. There was no way they could cover the whole of the walls. They needed more men here, and especially more magi.

Where are Ril Endarion and Dirklan Setallius? he wondered.

More and more of the Reekers were pouring unopposed over the top of the outer wall, but they weren't turning on the towers. Instead, they dropped straight to the killing ground below – then immediately began to scale the sheer walls, scrabbling like insects, their upturned faces pallid and deathly. They barely needed to grip: traces of kinesis were visible to his gnostic sight. They were making directly for him – and the royal suite, right behind.

'Draw weapons,' he shouted, 'protect the walls!'

The guards had barely a moment to ready themselves. The bells were tolling furiously as the Reekers came on – dozens now, almost a hundred, Takwyth reckoned as he slammed a mage-bolt into a middle-aged burgher with a paunch – who yowled, his chest all but burst open, *and kept climbing.*

Beside him Levis blasted another with fire and kinesis, knocking him from the wall – but they were the only magi here. Takwyth glanced to his right and saw the first of the horde reach his cohort: his men were busy hacking off hands, and the first few riverreek victims were knocked back down the walls.

Then a woman who looked like a fishwife grasped the sword one man was using and pinned it to the stone, then slammed her fingers through the guard's eye-sockets, using the leverage to pull herself onto the battlements. Her silence was as terrifying as a berserker's roar. Someone discharged a crossbow, the quarrel slammed into her chest and she recoiled against the battlement crenulations . . . then attacked again.

'*Holy Hels,*' Levis gasped, then they both waded in. Although they blasted climber after climber, combining fire and kinesis to clear a small swathe in the hordes below, their men were clearly wavering as people who should have been stunned or slain fought on with terrifying strength. Levis looked as pale as the diseased, but he torched another man and sent him spinning out into the void. Then with a clatter, a contingent of half a dozen battle-magi swept in and four windskiffs soared out of the darkness, everyone on board blasting away simultaneously with mage-fire.

'Spread out!' Takwyth shouted to the newcomers, experienced mage-knights, he was relieved to see, led by Jorden Falquist. 'Plug the gaps – stand firm!' He paused to send a diseased, half-naked woman with a crossbow bolt already through her left breast spinning away from the walls, then a Reeker launched himself at him, while two more grabbed the guard beside him.

He parried and kicked away another attacker, buying a second, and knocked his foe off-balance, then thrust, feeding mage-fire along his blade as his sword slid between the man's ribs and into his heart – and the organ exploded—

—making the burgher snarl with fury. He raked at Takwyth's face, so he kicked him off his blade and swept it into a roundhouse two-handed blow. Gnosis-sharpened steel cleaved neck-muscles and tore through the spinal column and the head and body separated. The man dropped – *and didn't rise.*

'Behead them!' he shouted. *'Behead them!'*

But there was no respite: another wave was breaking over the top, diseased men in filthy Imperial Guard uniforms who shrugged off the storm of mage-bolts and other spells, hammering their weapons into the midriffs of four defenders before they could even blink. Solon saw Jorden Falquist tumble from the battlements and the young lad next to him went down in the grip of three Reekers, who were biting at his neck and thighs until his veins started running black, like roots spreading through his flesh.

They were being swamped.

Then his attackers left the wildly flailing lad and launched themselves at him. With his left hand and kinesis he hurled one away and hacked the arm off another, then crunched his blade into the man's neck – but the angle was wrong. Instead of lopping the head off, the blade buried itself in the Reeker's collarbone. He had to hurl more kinesis at the third before kindling raw energy in his blade and kicked the second away, to give himself a moment's respite so he could finish the job, almost burying his sword in the stone as he decapitated the attacker, and only then was he able to check on the fallen guard—

—who snarled and rose from the battlements, his eyes blazing amber. For a moment, Takwyth was stunned into immobility, and the man launched himself at him—

—and was hurled away by Oryn Levis, who grabbed his arm as he teetered on the edge of the drop into the inner grounds, then hauled him to safety. But they were breached: the few survivors were staggering back along the battlements as a sea of attackers came swarming onwards, dropping from the wall and then climbing the side of the inner bailey . . .

. . . *towards my Empress* . . .

Windskiff riders were closing in and his head buzzed with the calls of the incoming battle-magi and knights. They now understood the need to decapitate – that was spreading through the aether like wildfire – but there was nothing between Lyra's suite and the fresh onslaught . . .

'Oryn,' he shouted, 'come with me!' and took to the air with a rush, his comrade – an Earth-mage, but at a press able to draw on kinesis, at least for very short distances – wobbled upwards in his wake.

Time slowed to a trickle for Lyra, each separate second imprinted on her soul. On the balcony Sedina Waycross was blocking Lyra and Hilta's view of Coramore – until she suddenly jolted and rose six inches, dangling—

—from a bloody rod of bone that had punched through her left breast and out through her upper back. Blood sprayed across the windows and through the half-open doors as Lyra, Hilta and Geni gasped in concert. The teapot Geni was carrying crashed to the floor and shattered as Sedina's willowy form fell as well, but something smaller remained standing.

Then Coramore, or something wearing her form, stepped over the body, covered in blood, her right hand a skeletal claw dripping with gore. Geni stood petrified. Hilta backed away – but Lyra lumbered forward, caught the door handle and slammed it shut in the girl's blood-splattered face. She felt the locking-ward catch and the frame flashed with pale light: the locking-spells Setallius had bound into every door and window-frame. Sedina's blood on the glass obscured all but a blurred view outside.

Then a little tongue licked a circle in the smeared blood and an eye peered in. 'I'm the rightful empress,' Coramore crooned. 'You're wearing my crown, Lyra!'

The women backed towards the other door – then Coramore's bony fist smashed through the glass panel in a spray of glass and a flash of light, effortlessly snapping Setallius' wards.

Lyra felt the breath freeze in her throat. Beside her Hilta went rigid, gnostic shields forming around her.

A mage-bolt of vivid blue burst from Coramore's left hand and slammed into Hilta, and her shields crackled and instantly went from blue to scarlet. Hilta reeled at the impact, then tried to marshal her defences as Lyra backed behind her, calling for her stand-in bodyguard. 'ASCELLA!' she screamed, '*ASCELLA!*'

Before Hilta's shields could reform, Coramore gestured and the pure-blood noblewoman was hurled like a doll into a cabinet, shattering the front and collapsing motionless among the pile of smashed wood and glass and porcelain fragments. Blood began to flow from a dozen cuts and Coramore stalked towards her, looking at the blood with savage intent, a trickle of drool running from her mouth.

Lyra pulled Geni from Coramore's path. *We're too far from the door.* 'ASCELLA!' she screamed again, but it was as if they were in a bubble of silence, because no one responded.

With a soft whimper, Geni straightened. She was quivering, but her jaw was set. 'Get behind me, Majesty,' she squeaked with heart-breaking courage.

Lyra grabbed the girl's arm. 'No, you get out!' She pulling her backwards with her, towards the bedroom. The only exit led to the Winter Garden.

Coramore turned in their direction and Lyra and Geni froze, caught in her red-eyed gaze. 'No one leaves without my permission,' she growled.

Then the girl was suddenly thirty feet away and bending over Hilta as she tried to get to her feet, clearly dazed and scarcely aware of what was happening. Coramore's mouth grew snake-like incisors and she *bit* Hilta – not a tidy nip, but a wind-piping crushing crunch, like a wolf taking down a doe. Dark amber fluids visibly flowed into Hilta's neck and spread through the veins.

'Watch,' the princess crowed, hunched over and licking the fresh blood from her lips. As if to emphasise her mastery, she flung out her arm, light flashed and the entrance wards re-sealed, locking out the rest of the world. Outside, the bells were clamouring with ever-greater urgency and they could hear shouting, and fearful cries.

'Do you hear that, "your Majesty"?' Coramore asked. 'That's the sound of your world ending!' She made a 'reveal' gesture, as a stage-performer might make . . .

. . . and Hilta sat up.

Her face and chest had turned ochre and blood was running from her eyes and streaming from her wound – which sealed as she saw Lyra and Geni. She snarled like a rabid dog and began to crawl, then rose onto her haunches and came stalking towards them while Coramore tittered happily.

Lyra grabbed Geni again and backed towards her bedroom door, her heart racing, her mind churning as she tried to *reach-reach-reach* for the power she'd brushed against in her garden below – but it was too far. Nothing answered.

Hilta lurched closer as outside, a guardsman was hammering on the door, calling, 'Majesty? Are you safe?'

'All is well,' Coramore sing-songed in Lyra's own voice, winking extravagantly.

The child in Lyra's belly moved and she felt her own limbs unlock. With strength she'd never known she had, she snatched up a chair and threw it into Hilta's flank, smashing her sideways. Then she grabbed at the petrified Geni to haul her back into the bedroom—

—but Coramore had already flashed across the room and caught the maid's neck in her right hand. Her left became a spearhead, but Geni caught her wrist the moment before it stabbed, fighting with all her strength against the twig-thin girl.

For an instant she held . . .

. . . and Lyra groped blindly, found a candle-stand and hammered it at Coramore's skull. Bone crunched and the girl's body convulsed, her grip on Geni slipping – until Hilta slammed into Geni's side and bore her to the ground, tearing at her with clawed fingers.

Lyra cried out, raising the bloodied candle-stand again, when Coramore suddenly straightened, laughing delightedly. For a brief moment, Geni's face was clear amidst the confusion of bodies, and she shrieked, '*Get out!*' at Lyra. Then Hilta tore out the girl's throat and all Lyra could hear was the sound of guzzling. She fell backwards through the bedroom door and tried to pull it closed, but Coramore caught the handle and hurled it open again.

They stared at each other, the girl's feral eyes transfixing Lyra where she sprawled.

'*Oh, the Master's going to have* wonderful *fun with you,*' Coramore crowed.

Then the door to the suite burst open and a guardsman stumbled into the room, a second behind him. As one, Coramore and Hilta whirled, the first guard blanched and levelled his spear and they both stared at the bloody fiends before them, unable to reconcile what their eyes were telling them.

Coramore pointed at Hilta. 'She's gone mad,' she howled, '*kill her!*'

The two guardsmen wavered, then Hilta shrieked and hurled herself at the first, who set his spear by reflex, and a moment later the head burst through Hilta's back. The second guard took an involuntary step towards Coramore, his left hand reaching to sweep her into his protective reach, not understanding that Lyra was shouting a warning.

Coramore slid under the guardsman's arm, then her left hand contorted and plunged straight through his chainmail, leather jerkin and ribcage. The guardsman stared down at the limb sticking out of his torso, then his legs gave way. Beside him, the first guard was gaping as the impaled Hilta hauled herself along the spear-shaft towards him, yowling and mewling. He let go of the weapon as a swiping hand almost took his head off, but it was a brief victory, for in the next minute, Hilta had pulled the spear from her own body, reversed it and with inhuman strength, slammed it through the guardsman, throwing him into the far corner of the room.

Then a horde of shambling, ragged figures brandishing cleavers and knives and clubs swarmed over the balcony railing outside, pounded over Sedina's body and burst through the balcony windows in a shower of glass and broken timbers.

Lyra threw off her paralysis and screamed for Ril, for Setallius, for *anyone* – but the only ones who heard were Coramore, Hilta and their ragged host of a dozen or more Reekers oozing with disease and madness stalking towards her.

'What?' Coramore leered, cupping her ear. 'I can't hear you. No one can hear you!' She cackled in cruel hilarity. 'After all these years, you still haven't learned to use the gnosis? You deserve to die!'

Lyra scrabbled backwards to the foot of her bed as Coramore kicked Geni out of the way. The maid rolled onto her side – and then her eyes fell open. They were amber, like Hilta's, and she bared her teeth when she saw Lyra.

'She's mine,' Coramore warned, as the Reekers behind her started reaching, snarling, towards Lyra. She heard a sound and from the corner of her eye saw more of them on the bedroom balcony, blocking off the stairs to the Winter Garden. They were rattling the doors, making the locking-wards flare.

'So this is your inner sanctum?' Coramore chirped. 'You know, I might redecorate – with your blood.' The Sacrecour princess held out her hand and all her minions stopped advancing and watched. 'Do you know my name?'

Lyra whispered, 'Coramore . . .?' although she truly had no idea.

'Wrong! I am Abraxas – and all this will be mine!'

Lyra was beyond fear. Her guards were gone, her ladies somehow possessed and Ril and anyone else she might have hoped to save her were nowhere in sight. The sanctuary of her garden was too far – and even then, it would likely avail her nothing.

There was only pride left. 'Do your worst,' she said, lifting her chin.

Coramore giggled. 'Oh, Lyra darling, we certainly shall.'

Then with a massive crash, something struck the side of the building, the bank of windows shattered, stone and timber splintered and cracked and the bedroom balcony fell away, bearing the riverreek victims with it, all howling in shock. Fire blossomed in the sitting room and as the remaining diseased yowled like beasts, gnosis-energy shivered through the air.

Coramore cast a surprised look backwards as Solon Takwyth's voice belled out like a clarion, 'LYRA! I'M COMING!'

The Bastion, Pallas

Ril looked at Singolo, wavering between his need to send a gnostic call to Lyra, even though the alarm had already been raised, and following the Reekers' trail. Then trumpets resounded through the passages and his heart leaped in fear and hope.

It was the Imperial fanfare.

Kore's Balls – Lyra must already be in the throne room with these poor bastards!

Ril was about to start tearing along the corridor screaming her name when Mort grabbed his shoulder. 'Ril, no! Sometimes it's best to arrive at a party unannounced.'

He realised the axeman was right. They had no idea what was going on. Any call to Lyra would likely alert whoever else was with her. He took a deep breath to centre himself, then followed Mort through the Gallery of Remembrance to a huge atrium with a giant staircase, ten flights leading from the ground floor and the throne room to the upper reaches of the palace. Hundreds of courtiers were pouring down the stairs, heading for the throne room, their fearful voices babbling amidst the tolling bells and the trumpeting fanfare. He saw their terrified faces and realised most were unarmed – not that many would know how to fight anyway, for these were the bureaucrats and their wives, their skills social or administrative. In an emergency, they'd flock to the throne room, expecting to be reassured by their ruler.

And it's a trap.

He almost broke cover, but Mort hauled him back in, hissing, 'These masked bastards are preparing something, otherwise the fight would be all-on by now. Let's get close enough to decapitate the snakes before they bite, eh?'

But my wife is here somewhere, Ril thought, then shook himself and began to think. 'You're right ... it looks like the Reekers are in the rooms around the throne hall – there's no upper gallery, but there are vantages for crossbowmen on this level. This way – let's go!'

At first they saw no guards, until a straggler hurtled around a corner, fretting over the lacing of his breeches. Ril caught the man's arm. 'You, do you know who I am?'

The guard stared, then gulped. 'Prince Ril, sir! I'm so sorry, I'm just going to my post now! I was—'

Ril wrenched off his signet ring and thrust it into the man's hand. 'Your name?'

'Henrik, Imperius III, Maniple—'

'Whatever! Listen, Henrik: take this ring to your commander and tell him he's commanded to come *here* – right now – this is an emergency! You'll be the saviour of the realm, Henrik – *go!*'

Henrik looked again at the ring, then sprinted away.

Ril watched him go, then turned. *If I remember rightly . . .* He grunted in satisfaction as he pulled a heavy velvet curtain aside, revealing a narrow doorway. He flicked it open with the gnosis and found an antechamber with an arrow-slit overlooking a lit space. There was even a crossbow and a dozen bolts in a rack on the wall. 'Yours,' he told Mort, then raced along to the next vantage point.

He'd just settled and loaded his weapon, barely able to hear himself think above the babble of voices and the blare of trumpets and bells, when the trumpets ceased and a clear, cold voice cut across room.

'Welcome!' the voice called. *A woman's voice*, Ril realised in surprise. It was slightly distorted, with a metallic ring, but still penetrating. He craned his neck and saw a petite hooded shape, most definitely feminine, on the stage where the court herald would normally stand. 'Welcome to the dawn of a new age!' she shouted.

She was flanked by two figures he knew only too well. Sir Bruss Lamgren stood like a statue, a giant Schlessen zweihandle held tip-down between his feet. But the figure that stole Ril's gaze was his one-time lover, Jenet Brunlye, in her red dress. He stared at her in anguish. She held an iron rod mounted with a ruby, the sort of periapt necromancers used, though that had never been one of her affinities.

The masked woman's bold proclamation caused the crowd of dishevelled courtiers beneath the dais to go silent, until one drunk yelled, 'What new age?'

'The Age of the Masquerade,' the woman replied, flicking her hood away from her face. She had a mane of brown hair, tight curls rippling down her back, but her face was hidden behind a Lantric mask: *Tear*.

The lacquered white of the disguise contrasted sharply with the scarlet lips and dripping tears.

The crowd looked at one another, confused. 'What masquerade?' someone shouted. 'Why are the bells tolling?' another called. 'Where's the queen?' another bellowed, and many took up the call.

'*THE QUEEN HAS GONE*,' Tear cried aloud. '*SHE IS NO MORE!*'

There was a sucking in of collective breath and Ril felt the ground beneath him spin away. Lyra's face flashed before him and almost he tried to *call* to her, but that was drowned beneath a wave of fury as Tear gestured and a small, familiar figure stepped from the wings of the dais and walked to her side.

Cordan Sacrecour: clad in the regalia of the emperor. All that was missing was the crown. The young prince – still only twelve – looked frightened.

Faces went pale, and many were noticing that the doors had stealthily been closed, shutting them in.

'What's happening?' a woman wailed. The older Corani courtiers, those who remembered 909, began to huddle together as Lamgren and Jenet stepped to the edge of the stage and raised their weapons.

'We have called you here to enlist you in a great deed,' Tear proclaimed, her metallic voice cutting through the babble. 'You see before you Prince Cordan Sacrecour, the Imperial heir. Do you wish to see him rule you?'

The courtiers looked at each other uncertainly. But a few were bold enough to call, 'Not bloody likely!'

Ril finished winding his crossbow, placed his bolt and sighted, first upon the masked woman's chest, then Cordan's. But it was to Jenet Brunlye his eyes kept moving. *What are you doing here, Jenet? What have you become?*

Focusing on the boy-prince enabled Ril to see that he alone of those onstage was as scared as anyone in the crowd. *He's terrified of this Tear bitch*, Ril realised. He shifted his aim back to her, his finger quivering over the release.

'But who are you?' an old man, a minor Corani noble, demanded of Tear.

'Me? I am a loyal Corani—'

The old man pointed an accusing finger at her. 'Then why would you support Cordan *bloody* Sacrecour?'

Tear drew herself erect. 'Because Lyra Vereinen has betrayed the trust we placed in her. She's failed to keep the peace, or to enrich her people! She cast off the best man in Koredom in favour of a lecherous mudskinned Estellan!'

Cheers, Ril thought, struggling not to shoot, but what she said and did next could tell him a lot about how deep her plans went, and how loyal the court was to Lyra.

'How is what you're doing any better?'

If an immobile mask could be thought to smile, Tear smiled. It was evident in her posture and her voice as she walked behind Cordan and placed her hands on his shoulders. Cordan visibly quailed at her touch, while Ril cursed as his shot became harder. He re-sighted at the only part of her that was clear: her head and neck.

'Because tomorrow,' Tear shouted, 'Garod Sacrecour's people will march into the Bastion and reclaim it, brought by the lure of this boy, just as you were lured by the promise of riches five years ago. And when they arrive, we will *crush* them, as Lyra should have done five years ago – and Solon Takwyth will take the throne!'

Cordan twisted in Tear's grip: this was clearly news to him too. But her fingers were like vices, clamping him in place.

Ril stared as the pfenniks began to drop into place.

They're going to kill Lyra. He swallowed. Tear had claimed she was gone already. *And when Garod arrives, they'll kill him too – and* Takky's *behind it?* He wished there was someone here who knew the game better than him – Setallius or Dubrayle or even old Duchess Radine – to advise him, to tell him if this was plausible, or just fantasy. *Do they really have that kind of reach?* But there was just him.

The noise of the room below rose again, confusion apparent, then a younger man, a portly official from Treasury, stepped forward. 'I've no great objection to Takwyth, if the queen is dead. But where is he?'

'Aye, and what did you mean by "enlist"?' someone demanded. 'We're not fighters here!'

Bruss Lamgren and Jenet Brunlye simultaneously raised their left hands and gestured, and the doors to the hall flew open. The crowd whirled, then recoiled in alarm. Ril didn't need to be able to see to know what was there: rank upon rank of filthy riverreek victims, bloody mucus drooling from the corners of their mouths.

'Anyone has it in them to fight,' Tear told them, 'if given the right weapons.'

The shambling mob entered the throne room, baring their teeth to reveal snake-like canines, as the courtiers started wailing for help.

40

The Storm Queen

The Creation of Urte

When the Seraphs saw Kore's new creation, teeming with life and full of beauty, they said unto Him, 'We wish to go forth from Paradise, to dwell in your creation, and know it and through knowing it, know you.'

Kore warned them, 'This Creation is imperfect, and it will taint your own perfection. When the time comes to return, you may no longer be worthy of Paradise.'

Despite this warning, the Seraphs left Paradise and became Man. We are their children, imperfect, and longing to return to our Creator.

BOOK OF KORE

Southpoint Tower, coastal Dhassa
Akhira (Junesse) 935

The Ordo Costruo windship drew alongside the landing platform, a small railed balcony a third of the way up the massive cylinder that was Southpoint Tower. Less than two hundred yards from the foot of the tower, massive cliffs fell into the churning sea. The last rays of a pallid, grey-shrouded sun were gone and the night was closing in. The windship's sails were flapping briskly in the rising winds: a storm was coming from the southwest and the captain was anxious to be off.

Brother Yash of the Merozain Brotherhood stood by the gangplanks, fidgeting.

'All that monastic training and you still can't stand still?' Rene Cardien teased. The big-framed Ordo Costruo mage laughed at his own jest and clapped him on the shoulder warmly.

602

'We're running late,' Yash fretted. 'We have to get to Midpoint tonight too: that's another hundred and fifty miles—'

'Midnight, we'll be there,' Cardien interrupted. He turned to the woman beside him. 'You've had the best of the journey, my dear Ancelia.' He bowed extravagantly.

Ancelia, a stooped, bookish woman, had a tiny white cat on her shoulder. She, like Rene and Yash, was travelling to the towers to take over watch-duties. 'You know, Rene,' she was saying, 'these week-long shifts on the thrones are taxing for us older folk.'

Yash might not be old, but he couldn't say he was happy to be here either. The five massive towers on the Bridge needed constant vigilance as they harvested the energy of the sun, capturing it in giant clusters of solarus crystals, converted it to raw gnostic energy, then again into Earth-gnosis, which they pumped into the foundations of the Bridge to sustain the structure. A mage enthroned in any of the towers of the Leviathan Bridge could hurl energy-bolts capable of blasting a windship from the sky, even one hundreds of miles away – Constant Sacrecour and most of his court had met their deaths this way at the end of the Third Crusade. Now the mere threat prevented unwanted airborne traffic over the ocean, but the duty wasn't popular – the Ordo Costruo was, after all, an order devoted to peace and scholarship. Now they were leaning heavily on their new allies, the Merozain monks, to aid in the task.

Right now, that meant Yash. The air inside the towers always felt draining, and it was well-known that prolonged exposure to the solarus crystals could be fatal. But whether he liked it or not, he was bound for Northpoint once they'd deposited Ancelia at Southpoint and Rene Cardien at Midpoint, the nexus of the Bridge's power. Separate windships were flying replacements to Dawn and Sunset Isles.

Once Ancelia had safely disembarked, they were off again, on the outriding winds of the oncoming storm. Their pilot conjured a fresh tailwind, sweeping the windship along the line of the Bridge – invisible, and almost a mile below the sea – towards Midpoint. Rene Cardien went below to sleep, while Yash joined the pilot, Draim Wrenswater, a veteran Rondian Ordo Costruo man, to watch the sunset and share a flask of coffee.

They were an hour from Midpoint when the aether crackled and the brass panel beside the tiller, used for communicating with a specific windcraft, began to glow. The only lights were the lamps on the deck and the stars above – it was the first day of the Darkmoon, and Luna was hidden.

The tired Air-mage was so fixed on his tasks that he didn't notice the panel's light, so Yash reached out and touched it, completing the link. 'Hello, this is the Windship *Cloudwatch*,' he said.

<Greetings, Cloudwatch,*>* a thin voice sounded from the brass. *<This is Midpoint. Magister Brovanius has the throne tonight. He scries you at eighteen miles south-southeast of Midpoint. Please confirm.>*

The towers constantly scryed the skies above the Bridge for illicit traders and more tangible threats. Yash glanced at Draim, who said, 'Yup, that's our position.'

<Are you alone?> the voice in the panel asked.

'I believe so,' Yash said, 'but it's dark out here.'

The Midpoint mage wasn't amused. *<Are you travelling with any other vessel?>*

'No – why?'

<Magister Brovanius has detected other vessels, about a mile astern of you and higher up. They may be trying to use their proximity to you to avoid detection.>

Yash and Draim shared a troubled look. In the years since the Third Crusade, there had been dozens of windships – from both continents – deliberately flying into the airspace controlled by the towers, which encompassed all of the ocean between Yuros and Ahmedhassa and many miles inland, testing their vigilance and resolve.

'Let's hope they're just trying to see if we're awake,' he replied.

There was silence for a few minutes, then the tower called to them again, *<They're still not responding.>*

Yash frowned. 'Should we intercept?'

<Not in this weather. Just get out of their sector of the sky and we'll deal with it. It's been too long since we demonstrated our power.>

Demonstrate our power: a mild euphemism for sending a beam of gnostic energy, too powerful for even an Ascendant to resist, against what could be a lost vessel seeking shelter. Yash glanced at Draim, who rolled his eyes. 'We're happy to intercept,' Yash sent back. 'There're a thousand innocent reasons for why they might not respond to your call.'

There was a long silence, then the voice came again. <*Magister Brovanius grants permission, but be swift. The closer they get, the more difficult it is for us to react.*>

'Of course.' Yash broke the connection, shared a pregnant look with Draim, then walked to the stern, using gnostic sight to pierce the darkness. It revealed nothing except a yawning emptiness.

If you're out there, where are you?

Draim nudged him and pointed to the southwest, where cloud was beginning to shift across the skies. He heard distant thunder and saw pale flashes on the horizons.

'That mess is comin' in like a pack of rabid dogs,' he shouted, 'and faster'n the weather-watchers said! Going to be touch and go to get down on Midpoint.'

Yash ground his teeth. 'How did they get it so wrong?'

'Because we lost Lady Sakita is why,' Draim pointed out. 'She was the best. Damned shame she's gone.'

Yash had met the Ordo Costruo's best weather-mage several times and been impressed by her passion and zeal. But he trusted Draim Wrenswater to get them home. His own attention was on the skies behind them. There was a patch of gloom up there that seemed too dark, but he couldn't pierce it. It could be nothing, but . . .

Soon, though, the storm clouds covered the sky, the stinging rain became a torrential downpour and lightning flashed in sheets across the skies. He was startled by someone touching his arm, but it was Rene Cardien.

'We've got to get down before the lightning finds us, Magister!' Yash shouted.

'Aye, but I sensed something up there—' Cardien shouted in his ear, pointing southwest. The clouds parted momentarily and they glimpsed a dark bulk, startlingly close, and others behind it. 'There!'

The Pontic Sea

'Look at it,' Tamir exclaimed, 'it's always changing – always in motion. Incredible.'

'It's just water,' Baneet muttered. The Earth-mage looked very uncomfortable to be in the air over the ocean.

'A Hel of a lot of it, though,' Fatima added. 'Look at the way it batters the cliffs!'

Twilight was fading to deepest grey as they peered over the railing at the coastline of northern Dhassa and watched the giant waves shatter into spray and foam on the towering walls of the coast. 'We're entering the period the Rondians call the Sunsurge,' Tamir shouted above the din. 'In some places, the waves will breach the seawalls and wash across the land – because it's salty, it'll kill more vegetation than it succours. See how high the waves are even now – so imagine them in a year's time!'

Waqar couldn't – but his mind was wrapped up in other matters. They'd tried another blood-scry and again got a tiny contact before it was savagely repulsed. But the direction was clear now: his mother was somewhere over the ocean, above the line of the Leviathan Bridge.

The brass panel beside the tiller flashed and the pilot squeaked nervously. They were some five miles from Southpoint Tower; its beacon was gleaming in the hazy gloom of the sea-spray. Waqar glanced at Tarita, who was gazing into the sky intently, her eyes glowing as she probed the darkness.

He touched the panel, praying they had the right passwords. He'd contacted his uncle by relay-stave an hour before and told him they'd traced Jehana to a windship, that they might need the trading code for that day. The Ordo Costruo, now policing the skies over the Bridge, had instituted a complex, secretive system of codes for legitimate windtraders, and they changed every three days. It was far from foolproof, but a smuggler would have to make some considerable effort to get those codes.

Rashid had been able to supply a code without breaking contact. <*Are you sure it's Jehana you're following?*> he asked, sounding puzzled.

That was an odd question to ask, but when Waqar replied, <*To the best of our knowledge,*> Rashid had gone silent for a time before supplying the pass code. Now they'd find out if it was correct.

'Sal-Ahm,' Waqar replied to the brass panel. 'This is the dhou *Al-Talib* from Hebusalim.'

The responding voice was a woman, speaking formal Keshi. 'This is Southpoint, *Al-Talib*. You're a late addition to my roster: do you have trading codes?'

'Abou-17-Lokus,' he replied.

There was a pause, then the mage from Southpoint replied, 'Thank you, *Al-Talib*. You have permission to pass, but there's a storm coming in from the southwest. We suggest you turn back and find shelter until it blows by.'

That sounded sensible, but Sakita was somewhere north of here. If he let up now, he might never find her again. 'Thank you, Southpoint, but our mission is diplomatic and urgent. We must press on.'

'Then go like Hel, *Al-Talib*,' the woman replied.

'Sal-Ahm, Lady—?'

'Ancelia. May both Kore and Ahm be with you, *Al-Talib*.'

The contact was cut as the winds whined through the rigging. The windship slewed across the sky, and they all cried out aloud, grabbing at anything solid. Clouds swarmed across the sky and thunder crashed overhead.

The Pontic Sea

Yash grabbed Draim Wrenswater's arm and pointed to where he'd seen that dark windship. 'Get us up there—'

Draim looked appalled, but Rene Cardien agreed, 'Take her up, Draim—'

'It's into the teeth of the gales, Milord – those winds are climbing to hurricane strength . . . I can't risk it!'

'You must – I need to see what's up there. I tried to scry, and was blocked.' The Ordo Costruo Arch-Magus looked calm, even though the

winds were lashing them ferociously. 'Yash, you have Air-gnosis ...
Ha! You're Merozain – you've got everything! Help Draim, will you? I'll
liaise with Brovanius. It takes ten seconds to uncouple the energy from
the tower so that it can be used defensively – we're only a couple of
minutes from Midpoint and we'll be closer before we intercept. There
is a genuine peril here.'

They threw themselves into their tasks, the crew performing miracles in keeping the remaining sails trimmed while Draim not only
kept the tiller steady but also manipulated the winds as much as he
could. They were rising fast and flying almost blind until Rene Cardien
sent a funnel of light ahead of them. He'd been constantly scanning the
darkness, a cone of light carving through the glittering sheets of rain,
and all the while scrying – Yash could sense the expenditure of power.
Then Cardien's light caught on something hundreds of yards away but
hurtling towards them and Yash stared as he boosted his own vision
with scrying, his Ascendant-strength punching through the wards.

He was stunned to see a Keshi dhou, a large one, swarming with
crew clinging to the ropes and rails with what must have been preternatural strength. Even in that brief flash of vision, he could see that
these were not normal crewmembers.

They were draugs.

In the prow, her arms spread wide and screaming at the storm, was
a woman he knew: Sakita Mubarak, her dead face was blackened by
decay, her desiccated limbs wrapped in rags, her soaked hair streaming in the gale as her craft hurtled towards Midpoint. She was in the
throes of some kind of ecstatic conjuration, energy crackling through
her, her aura a storm within the storm.

In the space that it took to register the sight, it was gone – and three
more vessels went soaring past, all identical, except that a different
mage rode in each prow, all of them clad in shredded Ordo Costruo
robes, their faces barely more than skin on skulls. They howled at
Yash's vessel as they passed.

It's Sakita's *storm! It's their storm! They're assaulting the tower with draugs!*

The *how and why* had to wait. Yash gathered energy, grabbing at his
options, and settling on fire. Cardien had clearly also seen, because he

breathed, <*Sakita!*> in a horrified whisper, then bellowed down the link to Midpoint, <*Brovanius, defend yourself – bring the intruders down!*>

'What's that?' Tamir shouted. He had the best eyes among them and he'd been scanning the darkness from the very tip of the prow. Now he was pointing due north, where a glimmer of light pierced the darkness.

'It's Midpoint Tower,' Tarita responded. 'Each of the towers has a beacon.'

The *Al-Talib* rode the winds in crazy surges, lightning flashing above illuminating the bowels of the storm in boiling, swirling flashes. The deck was rain-slick and treacherous, and the captain kept begging Waqar to let him turn back. Only the Mubarak name was keeping him from outright mutiny.

'Wait, see that?' Tamir cried, jabbing a finger into the north: a cone of light, burning through the rain, closer than the tower. He turned to the captain, clinging to his post beside Lukadin at the tiller, and cried, 'That way!'

The wind-dhou lurched as Lukadin fought the storm. The crew, huddled against the railing, were glassy-eyed; they'd never flown in such conditions before and they were past praying. Most of the sails were in, but the vessel was still screaming along, the speed threatening to tear it apart.

'What's happening?' Lukadin demanded of Tamir.

'I don't know, but it can't be good— Look!'

Something was caught in the flash of the light beam, now only half a mile away: a giant Keshi dhou, running before the storm. Waqar didn't need to bleed into a bowl to know this was his mother's ship. Three more such vessels flashed in and out of sight in its wake, and he even glimpsed a tiny triangular-sailed windskiff flashing by. He ran to the side and looked about frantically, but there was only the storm.

'Waqar?' Fatima called. 'What is it?'

'I thought I saw—' He staggered as another blast threatened to tip them over and grabbed at Tarita's arm. He shouted, 'I saw a skiff come up behind us – and Mother's on that lead dhou – we have to—'

He choked on his words as two of the ships lit up like fallen suns

– a beam of light blasted from the beacon of the tower and one of those lit-up vessels just *ceased to exist*. The blast all but blinded them, even though the beam had passed more than half a mile from their position.

Waqar stared at the darkness, trying to interpret the images burned on his retinas. He saw a grid of light coming in from four points of the compass: the satellite towers feeding the nexus of Midpoint. He called into the aether, <*MOTHER – MOTHER!*>

For a second he thought he sensed her, a flicker of contact, but something clawed at his mind and slapped his awareness away. Then a second blast from the tower erased another of the lit-up windships – but he'd divined their purpose now.

They're just a distraction . . . He looked downwards and saw the third of the ships suddenly light up: it was heading straight for the tower and the surface of the ocean was rising like a funnel, being sucked upwards in its wake. The beam of the tower was flickering impotently, as if it couldn't find its target in the darkness and chaos of the storm. Then it found its mark, light flashed—

—and passed *behind* the onrushing windship.

With a brilliant crack, lightning forked from all directions, centred on the giant dhou as it skimmed the giant waves, heading for Midpoint, lit up with a blinding crackle of energy.

Then the beam from the tower found its mark and struck the ship, which exploded in a concussive burst of energy barely a hundred yards from the tower.

Thank Ahm, Waqar breathed, staring about him. His friends were clinging to the rails of the vessel, eyes wide and terrified. He turned to Tarita, shouting—

—when his words were drowned by a sound like a goddess heralding the end of time.

Yash saw the moment the storm imploded. He was still reeling, half-blinded by the three explosions that had brought down the attacking windcraft, but he knew there was a fourth somewhere and was looking in all directions, panic rising when he saw that Brovanius had overcommitted, through panic or inexperience. The tower beacon was too dim, the energies too low.

Then he saw the final wind-dhou, with Sakita Mubarak's deathly form shrieking aloud from the prow, her voice *becoming* the voice of the storm. This was beyond any form of the gnosis – she was an elemental force and the skies were her plaything.

Rene Cardien grabbed his shoulder. '*Dwyma – she's calling upon the dwyma!*'

The words meant nothing to Yash.

Then Sakita's voice eclipsed the storm entirely. For a second the dhou and all aboard were just dark smudges against her vivid form. All of time froze: the raindrops all crystallising where they floated. Then with a tremendous rush that sucked all of the energy from the wind, every drop of water in the air rushed inwards and enveloped Sakita's ship as it began to plummet towards Midpoint Tower.

Sakita's vessel was now encased in a massive ball of ice and was falling like a meteor. His brain fed information, half-forgotten lessons as a young monk: a cubic yard of ice weighed over half a ton . . . a windship weighed hundreds of tons on its own . . . and this one was encased in ice many times its size, and it was falling at almost terminal velocity towards a tower that had burned out and was right now just a pile of bricks and shaped stone . . .

Then his brain ceased to calculate and he, Rene Cardien and Draim shouted as one: <*Brovanius, the ice boulder* – bring it down!>

Midpoint Tower, half-immersed in the turbulent seas, gleamed and pulsed through the suddenly clearing air. The solarus crystal flared and the light went from pale blue to sullen red, turning the night scarlet and illuminating the giant ball of ice. For a moment, Yash could see the shape of the wind-dhou, frozen within the ice ball and lit from within, a vivid, swirling rainbow that hinted at immense energies. He rose to his feet, willing the blast of light to strike . . .

The air had crystallised and for a moment no one aboard *Al-Talib* could breathe. The young magi and the crew staggered, gasping for breath, then wind swirled in to fill the sudden void in the air. But they were still miles from the tower and the momentary effect caused the ship to suddenly list and drop. A few panicky seconds later, the pilot had righted his craft and all the men who'd lashed themselves to the sides were thanking Ahm for his protection and their forethought.

Waqar swallowed cold air and almost wept. His comrades joined him at the rails as they all tried to understand what they were seeing. It was as if a giant unseen mouth had sucked the clouds away, for the night was suddenly crystal-clear, the stars a blanket. Midpoint Tower, some two miles ahead, pulsed scarlet, turning the churning seas around it the colour of blood.

Waqar stared at a ball of light, falling towards the red beacon at blinding speed, coming right out of the empty sky. 'What's—?'

Yash saw the falling ice-boulder encased around the draug-ship strike the tower, around a hundred feet from the top. The sight burned across his retinas: an explosion beyond experience. The concussion rippled through the air, and for a moment, thin white beams of light flashed, linking the solarus cluster atop Midpoint to the other four towers, and he thought, *It'll hold, it'll hold – it's held—*

Then as their own craft shook and began to come apart, he saw the mid-section of the tower collapse, the beacon shaking, then crashing down into the waves, exploding into a suddenly boiling sea. Then sight was gone, burned away, and he screamed in agony, clutching his face as he fell from the spinning deck. He heard wailing cries, Rene Cardien and Draim Wrenswater both cut short amidst the sickening sounds of their windship disintegrating . . . He reached for something – *anything* – as scalding steam washed around him and a heaving wall flew towards him: the surface of the ocean. Bodies and timber hammered into the boiling sea and lives winked out.

Then the wall of water struck, and erased him.

41

Twoface

Pallas

The tale of Pallas, a tiny village on the Bruin River that became the greatest city of the world, is also the story of Rondelmar and our Rondian Empire. We have brought light to the darkness, vengeance against the oppressor and wealth to the needy. We are the centre of this world, the nexus, the place to which all roads lead. To be a citizen of Pallas is to be a Prince of Urte. To rule Pallas is to rule the world.

FAINE SYNDICUS, KORE SCHOLAR, PALLAS, 889

The Queen's Suite, The Bastion, Pallas
Junesse 935

Solon Takwyth and Oryn Levis, pure-blood magi trained for battle, struck hard and fast. Levis smashed the bedroom balcony, breaking it from its pillars and sending it and two dozen riverreek draugs crashing down the side of the inner bailey walls, while Solon slammed Air-gnosis lightning into the press of stinking figures on the main balcony, then scattered those still standing with kinesis as he landed.

'LYRA! I'M COMING!'

Then it was all hack and slash, double-handed blows coming down on necks and skulls – a sailor, still rising from being blasted off his feet; a pretty fishwife disfigured by disease; a youth no more than sixteen—

Lumpy landed behind him and they started chopping their way inside, battering away everything that reached for them, lopping off limbs and heads in a blood-splattered frenzy. The sheer horror of it, of seeing ordinary men and women turned into these depraved things, could have frozen his brain if he let it, but he refused to engage with any emotion except the desperate will to survive and reach *his* queen.

Then Hilta Pollanou was in front of him and thrusting a spear at his breast. He twisted and staggered as the spearhead grazed his breastplate, then hacked at her and her face spun away as her torso fell towards him in a gush of blood, soaking his tabard as he stormed on towards the queen's bedroom and finally saw the one he sought—

—and realised he was too late.

Takwyth's voice still echoed in Lyra's ears, and for all their past, it resounded in her heart and mind and gave her something to cling to as she backed away from Coramore. But hope wasn't power, and the gnostic energy radiating from Coramore was debilitating. Her child was writhing inside, as if it too could feel the presence of such malice.

She reached behind her, seeking her silver water-jug, filled at sunset from the pond below as usual – she had no plan, just the need to go down fighting. But Coramore gestured and kinesis slammed Lyra backwards, hurling her against the bed, her lungs jolted empty by the force of impact, and she convulsed, blind instinct folding her into herself to protect her unborn.

Coramore's hand cracked across her face and her head rocked sideways. Her brain went as numb as her cheek as the girl straddled her and bent down. She twisted Lyra's head aside and her gore-tangled hair parted like a curtain, revealing a mouth stretched around fangs dripping black ichor.

Lyra flailed, but Coramore was as immoveable as granite – then her left hand caught the handle of the water-jug and even as Coramore reared up like a snake, ready to plunge those fangs into her throat, she tipped the water from the Winter Garden onto Coramore's head and back—

—and Coramore instantly went into some kind of seizure, wrenching her head away and screaming as if she were dissolving in acid. She fell off Lyra, howling in a frenzy, her whole body in spasm, her head battering the floor and legs kicking, as the most inhuman wail filled the room. Blood sprayed with each impact of her head on the floorboards. Around them, the other attackers staggered as if they too were afflicted.

Lyra crawled away, her breath laboured and her unborn child kicking frantically, painfully. She reached for the jug: there was still a mouthful left, caught in the curvature of the handle, and without conscious thought, she tipped it into Coramore's mouth. The princess choked and thrashed, then rolled onto her side and vomited out a thick blackened mucus before sagging motionless on the floor.

Lyra looked up to see an armoured man burst through the door, then big, strong arms enclosed her, folding her against a bloodied breastplate. 'Ril,' she gasped, as tears blurred her sight, *'take me to the fountain . . .'*

Solon held *his* queen against him, still not sure what he'd seen. The attackers had been like draugs, the dead, reanimated by necromancy, but he'd not sensed necromantic-gnosis, and surely no necromancer could create and master so many – he'd seen hundreds tonight, and that was impossible, especially as they'd clearly been animated by *one* directing mind, whose goal had been the young woman he held to his chest.

My queen. The woman I should have been allowed to marry. That she carried another's child, and had called that man's name in her delirium, only mocked his loyalty further. *Where were you, Endarion? Where were you when she needed you?*

She was trying to speak, something about a fountain, and he stroked her hair, wishing he could kiss her. Seeing her so vulnerable tore at him. She'd been his obsession for his entire exile. He had to see her safe.

His faithful Lumpy was standing in the midst of the carnage in the living room, sword still dripping, head bowed as he sucked in air, listening to a guard captain while his men prodded at the bodies. Oryn became aware of his gaze and came to the bedroom door. 'We're holding outside. The attacks are no longer reaching the inner wall, and we're counter-attacking along the outer. The Reekers are in confusion – like sheep without a shepherd, the captain says.'

Takwyth exhaled in relief, then gently eased Lyra to her feet and sat her in a chair where she could cradle her stomach. He knew precisely what she feared – that this would trigger something terrible inside her womb. He sent one of the men to find her midwife, and had another take Coramore away, with strict instructions to ensure not just her safety, but that she didn't endanger others. She was part of this, somehow.

After ensuring Lyra was calm, he walked to the edge of the bedroom. The glassdoors had shattered when Oryn had collapsed the outside balcony. He could see the stair to the garden below, but to reach it one would have to leap five feet across the drop and he wasn't certain the steps were stable. The air was still again, just a faint breeze filled with ripe smoke and oily blood. He turned back. Queen Lyra was looking at him with round eyes, and he felt a powerful stirring inside. *She's realised that I mean her no ill.* That gave him hope for the future.

He shared a grim look with Oryn as he joined him in the living room. The guards who'd burst in were milling about, obviously still frightened by a foe who would not die, and the queen's young bodyguard, Ascella, was visibly shaken. He knew the remedy for that: a simple task. He directed her to reset the door-wards once the men had dragged the bodies away. Most were burghers of the city, but he felt a pang as he saw Sedina Waycross among them; and Hilta Pollanou, whom he'd slain himself. Even the queen's maid was among them.

How did this infection reach members of the queen's own household?

He turned to Oryn, but the main door opened and Ascella staggered back into the room and fell—

—in half, her body parted at the waist, and his brain, which had witnessed plenty of carnage in the south over the last five years, momentarily froze.

An armoured man entered the suite behind her: big, wearing black-and gold-chased armour, a gore-coated battle-axe in his left hand. He was wearing a bronze Lantric mask: that of Twoface.

Memory of the mask and note left on the desk in his room flashed before his eyes.

Tear . . . Tear thought I was this man . . .

Then survival instincts obliterated the processes of logic and he shouted, 'Oryn! Watch out—' even as the newcomer's fingers splayed and five mage-bolts blasted out, each one so vivid it sucked the light from the room, and crackled through the squad of guardsmen before they'd even registered his presence. Each was thrown into a contorted dance, then hung suspended in the air, linked to Twoface as if he were the hub in a spoked wheel made of light. Then they collapsed bone-lessly, clattering to the floor, dead already. Only Oryn Levis still stood amidst the scattered bodies.

'*Lumpy!*' he bellowed again, his own shields crackling into place.

Twoface's axe whipped around as Oryn threw up a desperate block; sparks flew as weapons clanged, half a dozen blows flew backwards and forwards, then Twoface's axe caught Oryn's sword and twisted it aside, and the masked man *chopped*.

Takwyth was charging into the fray, already – *again?* – too late.

The axe crunched into Oryn Levis' midriff, broke his shielding and chainmail and plunged into his belly. Lumpy bent over the blow, his sword dropping from his hands, then Twoface grunted and threw the knight into Takwyth's path. He caught him, staggered, reversed his footing, grabbed his friend about the chest with his left arm, extended his sword arm towards his foe and backed towards the bedroom.

'*Lyra,*' he shouted, praying she was alert enough to hear and act, '*run – get out!*'

Twoface chuckled darkly. 'Hail, Solon Takwyth, Knight of Coraine.' He spun his axe theatrically. 'The Puppeteer wishes to renew his offer to you. Join us, he bids me say – and I endorse it ... You have no idea what you've refused, Solon.'

He thrust Oryn behind him, just in time to meet Twoface's savage assault. He angled his blade to block the axe-head, then thrust and scoured against shielding that sparked a brilliant blue: stronger wards than he'd ever seen. He gave ground as Twoface bobbed his head in some semblance of respect.

'You're good, Takwyth – I was always in your shadow, but now I'm invincible!'

Something in his voice, his stance, was familiar, but it was elusive.

You talk too much. He counter-attacked, blow after blow, but to his astonishment the other man wielded the massive axe as if it were weightless, and his shields and parries never faltered. He found himself driven back until he struck the doorframe and ran out of room.

'Step aside, Solon. I want the queen alive. Let me pass, and you'll both live.'

It was move or die: so he moved, thrusting – just a feint, but Twoface went to block, giving him the room to dart sideways through the bedroom door and slam it shut. An axe-blow hammered into the timber even as he added locking-spells to the door-wards.

Oryn Levis was slumped against the side of a chest of drawers, blood pooling from his stomach. A healer-mage might be able to give him a lifeline, but he had no such skill. Lyra was bending over him, but she too looked helpless. He had no idea what affinities she had, but clearly healing wasn't one of them.

'What's happening, Sir Solon?' she asked. 'Who's attacking us?'

She was scared, but he heard self-possession as well. She was still thinking, still rational: still *his* queen.

'It's just one man,' he told her. 'Help will come, Majesty! We just have to hold on.' He began to look for exits all the same, but the only way out was the broken staircase on the outside. Then Twoface's axe crunched into the door again and the timbers began to splinter, despite Takwyth's wards, and that show of strength chilled him. *Those are pureblood wards! How can he be so strong?*

CRASH! The axe struck again, and the door shook. Oryn groaned, his eyes glassy, a look he had seen on many a battlefield. 'Oryn,' he said, grabbing his friend's arm, 'stay with me – help's coming!'

'Solon,' Oryn gasped, blood running from his mouth, 'he knows you – what's the *offer* he is renewing?'

'Save your strength, Lumpy,' he begged him.

'You're right ...' Oryn slurred, 'En ... darion ... must ... go.' Then his eyes emptied.

CRASH!

He threw all of his power into renewing his failing wards. 'Lyra,' he shouted, 'you have to run – *please!*' He pointed to the stairs. 'Go – get out of here—'

She was staring at him. 'What was he saying? *What was that about Ril?*'

CRASH!

Solon fed the wards again, then realised that Lyra was refusing to leave without hearing an explanation. 'While I was in exile, I was approached by a man who claimed he could help me "regain my place". I met with him—'

CRASH!

'What man?'

'I don't know! He wore a bronze Lantric mask: the Puppeteer. It was in Becchio, midway through last year. *I turned him down, Lyra!* I would never act against you – I love you, as I love Coraine!'

Her face contorted at his words, but not with any gladness. 'You never warned us?'

'By telling who? *Setallius?* For all I knew it was him!' He was blinking back tears, because he'd come so close to regaining her trust and now everything was broken again. 'Lyra, I will protect you with my last breath.'

'*Then inhale it now, Takwyth!*' a metallic voice boomed, and the door came apart in a hail of splinters. The masked knight came through snorting like a bull, caught his first blow effortlessly and battered him backwards. He gave ground, overmatched in strength, seeking only to confine his foe in the narrow entrance, but Twoface's sheer power drove him even further back.

It occurred to Solon Takwyth that this man really was his better – but his self-belief never wavered. He'd pull something out – he always did. But Lyra was only a stray mage-bolt from death.

'*Get out,*' he begged her, '*run!*' Lyra finally seemed to understand, and heaving herself up, one hand clasped around her distended belly, made for the shattered balcony. Then Twoface came at him again and all he could do was parry and parry and parry, keeping the masked knight from the fleeing queen.

The Throne Hall, The Bastion, Pallas

As the Reekers poured into the room below and the courtiers herded together, Ril kindled gnosis-fire on the head of his crossbow bolt and squeezed the release. The bow jerked in his grip and the glowing bolt flew.

He'd not fired one in years, not since 930, during Lyra's rescue – he wasn't an especially good shot and anything *could* have happened.

What *did* happen was that his bolt flashed a hair's breadth past Cordan's head and slammed into Tear's right shoulder. The impact of a heavy flanged bolt fired at forty yards on a hundred-pound pull, enhanced by gnostic-fire to shear through shielding, did the rest. She *was* shielding, which coalesced with eye-blink reactions, but the fires he'd placed on the tip allowed it to rip through and strike home. The bolt spun her around, ripping flesh and splintering bone, and as she reeled and fell, Cordan howled, then ran. Then a second bolt – from Mort's position – hammered through Tear's pain-frayed shields and slammed into the meat of her left thigh. She jerked back and forth, then rolled to the back of the dais and fell from view.

In response, Bruss Lamgren leaped from the stage, his two-handed sword held high, and swept it in an arc that beheaded a portly courtier while Jenet Brunlye randomly blazed death-light spells into the press, her face contorted in glee.

No! Ril leaped forty feet from his vantage to the floor below, landing between the courtiers and the advancing Reekers, who'd been thrown into confusion by Tear's injuries. Some came straight at him: the first he slammed aside with kinesis, the next he blasted with a mage-bolt as Mort crashed to the floor beside him, his twin axes flashing. The advancing Reekers recoiled, and the courtiers spilled towards them.

'Get out of the damned way,' Ril shouted as he stormed towards the dais. He saw Cordan up there, his arrogant young face white with shock, and shouted, '*Cordan! To me!*' as he hacked down one Reeker, then another, painfully aware that these were his own people, no matter what was currently driving them.

Then Lamgren was upon him, that immense zweihandle whistling past his head as he ducked and almost smashing his sword from his hands with the back-stroke. Ril fired mage-bolts and then kinesis at him, all of which was shielded as if the blows meant nothing – but for all its power, the zweihandle was a slower weapon than his, and somehow he managed to deflect it high, then stab his sword-tip into Lamgren's chest, punching through shields and breastplate . . .

To his amazement the man didn't even acknowledge the blow; he just grabbed Ril's gauntlet, and baring impossibly long fangs, tried to bite his wrist. His strength was hideous, and Ril almost lost his sword—

Then Mort's battle-axe severed the man's neck and Ril almost over-balanced as the headless torso collapsed. He wrenched his blade free, darted in behind the whirl of the axeman's blades and ran towards Cordan again, while Mort took his back against half a dozen Reekers who came at him.

Cordan was transfixed by the horror before him. Jenet was still standing on the stage above, blazing violet light at the nearest courtier-mage, ripping away his shields and crumbling the man's hand to the bone. As he howled and dropped to his knees, Jenet saw Ril and for a second he was sure there was something that went beyond recognition to empathy, to *remembrance*.

Then her eyes blazed and an intense bolt of purple light flashed towards him—

—but Ril was already moving and conjuring – necromancy might be a blind spot for him, but illusion wasn't, and he feinted left with a blur of himself while really darting right, and Jenet's blaze of death-magic washed over the men attacking Mort instead. They fell lifeless to the ground, allowing Ril to reach the stage in a flowing leap that placed him between Cordan and her.

She's not Jenet any more, Ril's brain screamed – but he still couldn't bring himself to unleash a fatal blow. They'd invested so much in shared dreaming and planning, even though their paths had led dif-ferent places . . .

He drove in and wouldn't let her escape him, battering aside the iron rod with his left hand as it unleashed a blaze of energy that wasted itself scouring the painted ceiling. For a moment she was at his mercy

– her shields were as strong as he'd ever encountered, but a thrust from a pure-blood's blade could punch through steel plate. She might have raw power beyond him now, but combat was also about speed, skill, precision and experience, and whatever *owned* her couldn't quite transcend her own limitations in the arts of war. He tore her shields open, then thrust—

But combat was also about choices: he couldn't kill *Jenet*.

His brain caught his reflexes in time to divert his own blow and pierce her shoulder instead of her left breast – and a flash in her black eyes told him she recognised what he'd done. For a moment, the *thing* inside her was blinked away and he believed she could be redeemed.

She lurched sideways, staggered and fell, calling his name.

Then her face changed and he knew he'd lost his chance, wasted on misguided mercy, forfeiting himself for a memory. She lifted the iron rod, the ruby blazed—

—as Mort's axe crashed through the back of her shielding in a burst of sparks and clove through her neck. For a moment he was stunned immobile, his heart pounding, but Mort's furious roar brought him back. '*Fight or die, boy!*'

Then Mort was surging on, hacking down another attacker, clearing a path towards Tear and the boy-prince.

'Cordan – come to me,' Ril called. '*Come here!*'

Then Tear, one arm hanging limp and her shoulder and thigh transfixed by crossbow bolts, rasped, '*Come to me, Cordan.*' Her words were heavy with mesmeric-gnosis. '*Only I can save you now.*'

'Cordan,' Ril shouted, 'stay here—' His back was unprotected, but he sensed Mort behind him, and at the fringes of his awareness, the battle cries of the Imperial Guard as they stormed into the room, scattering the Reekers before them.

Henrik, you really did save the realm, Ril thought wildly, but he never took his eyes off Tear. 'You heard what she said before, Cordan,' he called. 'You're just a disposable piece in a game to her. Come back here, to me.'

The Sacrecour prince wavered, then with a wail, he hurled himself at Ril, who swept the boy behind him and raised his shields.

Tear straightened, her wounds turning purple and bones popping back into place. 'Bad choice, Sacrecour,' she snarled, stalking towards them.

The Winter Garden, The Bastion, Pallas

The balcony was broken, but the stair was anchored by the pillar it spiralled around. *I have to get to my garden* – but the top stair hung in space, five feet from the edge of the stonework.

Anyone with a little athleticism could have leaped the gap without difficulty, but Lyra's belly was heavy and fear had turned her legs to jelly.

Behind her, the two knights crashed together, snorting like rutting stags. Sparks flew from gnostic shields, steel crashed on steel and stray mage-bolts shattered in dazzling sprays of light. Takwyth was being driven back. The gulf loomed before her, pulling at her, the drop yawning like a giant's mouth.

Then her unborn child kicked, and adrenalin and need broke her paralysis. She backed up, took three rapid steps and leaped. Her front foot landed on a step, her back one swished in the air; she teetered and grabbed at the broken handrail—

—and for a dreadful moment she swung over the empty space, just clinging on, then she pulled herself back and hauled herself safely onto the stairs. For a moment she lay gasping and shaking. *Corineus my Saviour, thank you!*

She clambered to her feet, still wobbling, and looked back to see Takwyth and Twoface smashing their weapons together, then staggering apart, both off-balance. A mage-bolt caught Takwyth in the chest, but he lurched upright again and repositioned himself again between her and the masked knight.

He really is loyal. He's prepared to die for me . . . But where's Ril?

Urgency re-imposed itself and she wobbled down the stairs as fast as she dared, clinging to the rail as she went round and round, until, dizzy, she stepped onto the lawn at the edge of the rose-bower – just as a great crunching blow and a cry resounded from the room above.

She looked up and saw an armoured shape at the edge of the hole in the wall.

The duel lost all pattern amidst a sight-defying swirl of blows and counter-blows, physical and gnostic, instincts honed by decades of drills and the 'kill or be killed' chaos of the mêlée. Solon Takwyth was no longer thinking, just acting and reacting, caught up in the dance of death.

Twoface was too much for him, that was becoming clear as every fleeting second revealed a new twist to his powers: a death-light blast of necromancy; a spiratus-blade thrust from a phantom dagger that flashed in and out of existence in his right hand. Solon was bleeding from a dozen places now, slowing, hurt. *Losing.*

He'd never lost a fight. He *refused* to. Anger sustained him, driving him to ask more and more of himself. He was leaping and twisting like a far younger man, calling on outrageous movements he'd lost years ago, his spine and his tendons screaming, his lungs moving like forge-bellows. Beneath his armour he was soaked in sweat; perspiration stung his eyes, his sight blurring . . .

But there were soldiers closing in – he could hear voices, and the aether crackled with calls: <*Milord, I'm coming! We're all coming!*> All his captains, all his aides, the mage-knights he'd led for so long, those who'd stayed loyal to him in his exile, were only moments away . . .

KRANG! He blocked Twoface's axe, and again, defending now, just holding on for help. They'd been going at it like this for – what? Two, three minutes? An age in combat. The ballads that sang of day-long combats were drivel, as any real fighter knew. Duels lasted half a minute, seldom more. This was an *epic.*

But it ended seconds later . . . He blocked three blows that would have levelled houses and their weapons locked, gauntlets entangled. He tried to head-butt Twoface away and their eyes locked – mesmeric-gnosis slammed through him, ripped at his mental defences and speared his vision, and then—

—he was in the Celestium, he'd just punched Endarion and Lyra was staring at him in shock as his world collapsed . . .

Twoface's axe-haft swam through the vision and slammed into the gorget that protected his throat, crushing the metal and caving it in, ripping flesh and smashing his left collarbone. He went over backwards, still fighting for balance, but then he was treading air as he went spinning away, too numbed to shield. He smashed into the branches of a tree and splintered them, heard three limbs snap, felt his back pierced in two places as blood burst from his mouth and nose, then darkness poured in.

The Celestium, Pallas

In the first seconds of the assault, Dominius Wurther couldn't tell if all was lost or all was won. As the masked prelates rose to their feet, surrounding the man in the lacquered Jest mask, the amount of gnosis-energy that boiled around them was truly daunting. That he was standing before his throne, like a target, made it all the more frightening. But his guards, no doubt motivated as much by self-preservation as loyalty, were fighting with desperate courage.

A storm of gnosis-fire slammed into the circle of protection about him, turning them from translucent pale blue to an opaque scarlet as it wavered and began to fray.

'Kore be with us!' he bellowed, and threw his own not inconsiderable powers into the wards at precisely the moment they began to fail.

In mass mage combat, where any kind of attack could come from any direction, defence was imperative; fortunately, defensive gnosis was stronger and easier than attacking – but an overwhelming attack; or of a sort that wasn't expected, could still get through. Amidst the torrent of fire and projectiles, a finger's-wide flash of purple light lanced through and one of the man at his side collapsed, his whole face turning to a flaking skull, then crumbling inwards. His defenders closed ranks and deepened their defences, but unless they countered, it was just a matter of time ...

Then Wilfort's men, led by his marshals, burst through the doors of the upper gallery. The Kirkegarde mage-knights were fully shielded and armed for battle, while the soldiers behind them were carrying crossbows, chosen for their penetrating power. A sustained volley burst the bubble of energy around Jest's corrupted prelates and at least four went down. For a moment, Wurther believed they'd turned the tide.

Then those prelates who'd gone down simply stood again – and a devastating wall of flame and lightning burst over the gallery, with horrifying results. Black smoke engulfed the area, and apart from a few of the marshals who'd kept their personal shielding tight, the rest were burned to nothing. One of the marshals summoned Air-gnosis, trying to make the air breathable – which allowed him to be singled out: a dozen blasts slammed into him and he went up like a spilled oil-lamp.

The chamber was filled with smoke and flame, throwing everything into confusion. Wilfort was pouring men in from all sides, and Jest's prelates were being struck from all sides – *but they kept on getting up.* Wurther backed to the edge of his Circle, not quite scared yet, but very, *very* nervous.

Then a third wave of Kirkegarde burst in from the opposite side, more crossbows cracked, more bolts flew and though most were shattering on the shielding, some punched through, and more of Jest's people went down, some with three or more bolts sticking out of their flesh.

And still they kept getting up.

Draugs? Can they be draugs? 'Necromancy!' the grand prelate shouted, aloud and into the aether, knowing the Kirkegarde magi would pick it up and use the appropriate counter-spells.

Then a fourth wave of men smashed into the chamber, into the lower reaches, and at first he thought they were Wilfort's men – although there had to be more than three hundred in the galleries already – but he quickly realised that instead of assailing Jest's people, they were swarming *up the walls*, adhering like spiders, then pouring into the upper seats and engaging Wilfort's men. They looked like draugs, but they moved *fast*. The ordinary soldiers, already caught up in a gnostic maelstrom, were panicking, for the hordes were refusing to fall. Then Wurther's guard came under direct attack as the draugs turned on them.

His own affinities were rooted in Earth and Sorcery; necromancy was something he practised, obviously within the very strict guidelines of the faith. A draug was a corpse inhabited by the spiratus of a dead man:

a spirit which still lingered, reluctant or unable to leave this world. Most spirits couldn't inhabit a body – the energy of the living was too strong, and they didn't have enough energy to reanimate a corpse on their own. A necromancer could facilitate that – or cancel it.

Violet light formed around his hands, he shouted aloud and sent a necromantic spirit-banishing rippling towards the clustered attackers, fully expecting them to collapse lifeless. Instead they kept coming, tearing at his knight-protectors, and at last he began to feel real fear.

They're not draugs – so what the Hel are they?

The Scriptorium Chamber had become a slaughterhouse, but the attackers wouldn't stop coming, and they wouldn't die. It was Wilfort's men who were going down and staying down.

'Retreat,' Wurther shouted, 'to the Sanctum—'

In the gallery above, Wilfort was nowhere to be seen, but his men were already falling back in disarray. The chamber was lost, but there was a narrow corridor behind his plinth that led to the Grand Prelate's Sanctum. He tried to keep his men together as they shielded and gave ground, but the *not-draugs* stepped aside and then it was Jest and his masked prelates before him, driving them backwards with a torrent of mage-fire. The lacquered mask heightened the apparent indestructibility of the man behind it.

Then there were just two men left to protect Wurther, and they must have realised they were doomed, because they wailed despairingly and threw themselves into one final assault, only to be met by a storm of kinesis-blows that broke their limbs and then their necks. The power used was simple and devastating, and delivered with terrifying efficiency.

And now there was no one between Wurther and his foe as he fell backwards through the Sanctum, barely able to counter the mage-bolts and gnostic fire that crackled around him. His robes were charred, his hair singed, his eyes blurring. Disbelief left him stunned: he'd never quite believed that he wouldn't die in his bed.

Jest advanced, flicking his crozier, and another blast of kinesis hurled Wurther against the defensive barrier he'd been trying to create, shattering it and smashing him into an iron grille that gouged his back – but the padlock shattered and the door opened: a passageway to somewhere, *anywhere*. Wurther took it, hurtling at a speed he'd not been able to manage for decades, and found himself pelting through old catacombs he'd never realised existed, his enemy trailing him, blasting the stonework of ancient sarcophagi and memorials, until he burst through a forgotten doorway and into the space before a low mound topped by a single tree.

The Shrine of Saint Eloy.

He turned, caught at bay as Jest emerged like a stalking wolf. Behind him, the tunnel filled with more figures: masked prelates and diseased commoners, many bearing wounds that should have killed them. They filed into the open behind Jest and fanned out, facing the grand prelate.

'For dignity's sake, Dominius,' Jest called, 'stop running. Die with courage.'

Wurther had always thought courage and dignity overrated, but right now he could see nowhere else to go. Above him was the small hillock surmounted by the Winter Tree, standing stark and bare. In the mound's base was the cave where Saint Eloy had lived almost his entire life: the heart of Koredom on Urte.

A decent place to die, he decided.

Apparently Jest thought so too. 'It's good that you've come here, Dominius,' he remarked. 'The place of vigil: a fine place to end your reign and begin the new age.' He gestured with his crozier. 'Kneel.'

'I'm Kore's voice on Urte, Ostevan,' Wurther wheezed. 'I don't kneel.'

Kinesis-blows hammered him front and back, pummelling him until he crumpled to his knees, his face slamming into the stones. His vision blurred and blood and snot splattered on the tiles. He tried to rise, but he felt like he was clamped in irons.

'Of course you kneel, Dom. We all kneel to someone.'

Jest walked slowly forward, transmuting his crozier into a reaper's scythe.

42

The Winter Garden

Empires

The Yoths of northern Yuros, the Persei of Lantris, the Rimoni: every empire of the past has fallen, leaving only the dusty memories of old glories, hubris and evil. Why do you believe the Rondians will be any different?

THE BLACK HISTORIES (ANONYMOUS), 776

The Winter Garden, The Bastion, Pallas
Junesse 935

Lyra saw Takwyth fall, crashing off the wall of the garden and slamming into a tree, where his body was caught in the branches. Wailing silently, she looked up again to see Twoface dropping from the hole in the wall. Impelled by kinesis, he floated towards her.

The night air was full of shouting and the distant sounds of fighting on the walls in the south corner, but here, there was only her and the masked knight.

She turned and ran deeper into the grove, making for the pool. 'I'm not your enemy,' Twoface called, his voice hollow and metallic, echoing as if he were an empty casing of bronze and steel. 'The Master wishes you to join us.'

The Master? A glance backwards showed the hulking metal figure striding towards her. The rose bushes seemed to shrink from his path, but the birds were shrilling fit to waken the dead.

'*Only my Master can secure your realm for you,*' Twoface called.

She staggered through the last veil of roses into the Oak Grove, heard

629

the crunch of boots and spun around to see Twoface only a dozen paces behind. He stopped as she raised a hand, his wards flaring to protect himself – then lowered them when she failed to do anything.

He still thinks I have the gnosis . . . He fears . . . something. She felt a stirring, a thrill that ran through her. Wind came whipping at her skirts, stinging her bare shoulders. *Aradea is awake*, she thought giddily. 'Get out,' she shouted, 'you don't belong here!'

The wind hit him and Twoface staggered momentarily, but came on, raising his axe. 'I'm not here to kill you but to save you.'

'Save me? You're insane!' she retorted. She turned, cradling her belly, and lurched towards the thicket of elms and her Winter Tree.

She heard Twoface curse and felt the wind slap him as he crashed after her. At times she felt him reach for her and grip her with unseen force, only for that force to shred, but he was only a few feet behind, his gauntleted hand reaching for her – then a branch from an oak tree slammed down and struck him, hard enough to make him stagger sideways. Another came at him, but his axe swung, blue fire on its edge, and it hacked the branch in half.

She heard something like a scream, and the oak quivered and recoiled.

He slowed, more cautious, and she ran on, across the magpie lawn, through the elms to the pond where her Winter Tree grew. She didn't stop at the edge but stumbled into the water, where she fell to her knees, briefly going under. She struggled to her feet as the armoured figure reached the edge. He stretched towards her, his hand impotently groping the air, but he wouldn't enter the pool.

Her heart in her mouth, she turned her back on the hulking knight and focused on the Winter Tree above her. There was a berry on the lowest branch; without thinking, she plucked it, thrust it into her mouth and swallowed. It was like biting on light: a golden glow that bloomed in her belly and spread. She exhaled, gulped down the clean air of the grove, and an incredible sense of nurture filled her.

Aradea is here . . .

Eloy is here . . .

Twoface felt it too: she could see it in the way he moved, warily stalking the edge of the pool. He tried a mage-bolt, but it died on the air, so too a fire-spell. He lowered his axe and his voice. 'Lyra, I know what you are – we can help you unlock it.' He extended a gauntlet to her. 'Join us, and we will be invincible.'

She ignored him. Invincibility? What was that, when she could feel a silent avalanche in the air, a hidden inferno, drawing closer and closer . . .

It's here.

The nearest of the oaks suddenly ripped free of the earth, *changing* as it moved. As Twoface turned to face it, the tree became a giant twig- and moss-encrusted vaguely human form, but the aura that shone about it, encased in and encasing the wooden form, was human-like: a leafy-visaged woman with barked skin: just as Aradea, Queen of the Fey, had been depicted in the edition of the *Fables* Lyra had grown up with.

Twoface looked paralysed in awe. 'A *genilocus*?' he gasped. 'I've never—'
Then he leaped, his axe a blur as he went at the creature.

Lyra froze . . .

. . . and the oak tree's branches hammered in from all sides on the masked knight's shielding and armour, smashing into him and tearing aside his defences. Then a single shaft of wood exploded up from the ground and through his back. He convulsed on the spike – and a cloud of darkness erupted from his mouth, a foulness that sprayed across the lawn. Aradea stamped him to the ground, then looked back at Lyra.

The Throne Hall, the Bastion, Pallas

What Ril was doing made no sense to himself.

He was dimly aware that the men of the Imperial Guard were grappling with the waves of Reekers, and that Mort Singolo was behind him, performing miracles of butchery to keep them both alive. But his world was focused on only two beings: the masked woman, Tear, and the boy-prince, Cordan, who clung fearfully to his leg. He pushed the boy behind him again, raised his sword and prepared to do what was necessary to keep the *Sacrecour heir* alive.

I can't believe I'm about to die protecting this little turd.

Tear seemed to grow in size and menace as she stalked forward, a blade of purple shadows forming in her right hand. He kindled gnostic-light to ward his blade, swallowed and dropped into a crouch.

Then something like a bell chimed, and in a rush of shadows, Tear staggered, stumbled backwards and fell through the curtains behind the dais. Ril went to follow, but Cordan was still clinging to him, and it took him a few seconds to extricate himself – and by then, the space behind the stage was empty and the doors at either end were open. He guessed at one, got it wrong and took the other.

He found nothing but an empty corridor, and a Lantric mask hanging from a picture hook, as if to taunt him.

The Celestium, Pallas

Dominius Wurther felt Jest's hand cup his chin to bare his throat for the sickle. Helplessly, he allowed his gaze to be drawn up to the mocking mask of his killer—

—as amber light blasted out of Saint Eloy's cave and scythed through Jest and his people. The masked man's wards went from scarlet to crit-ical and he was hurled into his followers, who shrieked and collapsed. Wurther pressed his face to the ground and prayed as he'd never prayed before: in fervour and in certainty that these prayers were perhaps the only prayers he'd ever uttered that had an iota of being heard.

As the golden light faded, only one man moved: Jest.

Wurther felt the moment of hope wink out and despair reclaiming his soul: *Is he indestructible?*

But Jest was no longer even looking at him. Around him, his diseased minions stood motionless. There was an eerie silence before they all sagged to the ground at exactly the same moment.

'*Saint Eloy?*' Jest said, his voice finally uncertain. '*Impossible*—' Then he threw a look over his shoulder, towards the Bastion, as if hearing something from faraway, and murmured, '*How could she . . .?*'

Then he too collapsed.

The grand prelate stared, not quite believing the evidence of his eyes. The night had fallen almost silent, then he heard a ragged, distant cheer, from the direction of the tunnel through which he'd fled. He *really* hoped that meant what he thought it did.

Looking back at the shrine, the golden glow was fading so fast it wasn't hard to believe he'd imagined it. But for a moment he fancied he saw something in the amber: a face, a *woman's* face – one he knew.

"How could she . . .?" Jest's dying words . . . Wurther stored them, certain they were the key to understanding what he'd just seen.

But he had more pressing concerns. He staggered to his feet and went to the fallen Jest. He pulled off the mask – and stared, because it *wasn't* Ostevan Comfateri.

'*Brother Junius?*' he breathed, faintly incredulous. '*How can this be?*'

Then Lann Wilfort and a handful of his Kirkegarde knights arrived, picking their way through the tunnel. 'Grand Prelate?' Wilfort called. 'Are you here?'

Wurther looked back at the shrine, but the glow was gone and only the bodies remained. Wilfort was striding towards him, his face filling with what looked like unfeigned relief as he saw Wurther. The Supreme Grandmaster of the Kirkegarde looked like he'd gone through a battering: his left eye was all but closed, and his right arm was bleeding and limp. 'Good to see you, Lann,' Wurther told him, waddling forward and embracing him.

I don't think I've actually hugged anyone in twenty years . . .

'You too, your Holiness,' Wilford said fervently. 'You too! They had us,' he muttered in Wurther's ear. 'Half the spells we tried didn't work – they could survive anything except beheading or total destruction, and they fought like berserkers. Then they all just dropped dead.'

His eyes held a question: *Did you do this?*

While claiming credit for a miracle wasn't outside Wurther's moral code, right now he wasn't sure this was a miracle he *wanted* to claim. 'I don't know. Maybe Saint Eloy? A Seraph? Maybe the Winter Tree itself? But a miracle it was. I was about to die and Kore saved me.'

They both turned to stare at the stark, rocky mound that housed the cave and the tree above. The leaves were withering, a sign that summer was on the way. 'What did you see?' Wilfort whispered.

'A golden light that blasted the life from our attackers.'

'And the masked man, their leader?'

'Gone.' Wurther indicated the fallen Brother Junius. 'It was him.'

Wilfort cocked an eyebrow. *'Junius? Really?'*

'Exactly,' Wurther rasped. 'Junius was a servant, with no ambition and no thoughts beyond his duties. He's not a traitor, much less some kind of super-magus!' He stepped close to Wilfort, and whispered, 'Someone came *very* close to destroying us today, and I have no idea why they didn't succeed. They made slaves and monsters of our prelates – pure-blood magi every one – and they turned a horde of sick citizens into berserkers and loosed them in our midst. This was almost a disaster.'

Wilfort didn't look like he needed to be told. 'There has been an assault upon the Bastion also, Holiness. Reports are sketchy at this point, but apparently a horde of people – *just like those who assaulted us* – broke out of a quarantine zone and stormed the walls.'

'They held?'

'It appears so, but there's visible damage to the Imperial apartments. There's no word of casualties, but the queen's banner still flies.' Wilfort pointed back towards the destruction in the throne hall. 'The prelates are all dead – many without a death-wound. Whatever destroyed Junius appears to have slain them as well. As for the rest of the attackers who burst in – those citizens who came from Kore-knows-where – they're all milling about in confusion, no idea what happened or what they did. We're locking them up.'

Wurther didn't care much for the peasantry. 'The prelates are all dead,' he echoed, as his nose for opportunity twitched: *I thought some of those old bastards would never die. Now I can fill their ranks with my people . . .*

But there were more pressing concerns. He grasped Wilfort's shoulder. 'If a threat remains, as I'm sure it does, we must reach out to the Bastion – but they *must not* know how close we came to death today.'

He and Wilfort shared a silent, shaky look, filled with shared fears.

'Our first step on that front is to contact someone – anyone in authority – and have them seize Ostevan Comfateri – he must be interrogated, for that was *him*, not Junius. I *know* it was him.'

The Winter Garden, The Bastion, Pallas

Aradea's face was never still, never just one thing: it changed from young to womanly to old from moment to moment, but the expression remained the same: not fond or empathetic, but *curious*, an animal's wonder at seeing another creature. Lyra saw hunger and fury, matched by something more human: a desire to *understand*. Her senses felt stretched, as if she occupied the whole grove and could sense every twig and root and blade of grass, every crawling insect, all the squirrels and the birds nesting here, all the burrowing secrets . . . and a man teetering between life and death in the branches of a tree. She felt timeless, old and young, weary and renewed. This was only a small place . . . but it belonged to *her* . . . and the Queen of the Fey.

For a long moment they just stared at each other, then the young-old face creased into a smile and her big, alien eyes softened. Together, they made a wish.

Then voices called, men shouting for the empress, pounding closer, fearful and furious, and Aradea was gone. The tree she'd inhabited slammed roots back into the earth, her branches retracted from the dead knight and reached again for the night sky. The owls took to the air and something rushed out of the grove. The sense of being bloated with energy receded, leaving Lyra feeling relieved, thankful and deflated.

A mass of Corani knights arrived, brandishing torches to light their way. Some of the tree branches swayed away from the flames, but she was the only one to notice. 'My Queen!' the first man shouted, the cry taken up with relief as her guards found her alive. Then she heard more voices, from men who'd found Solon Takwyth and were easing him gently from the branches. 'He's alive – get the healers!'

They wanted to herd her to safety, but she stopped them. 'The danger's passed,' she told them. 'Where's my husband? Where's Prince Ril?'

'We don't know, Lady – we're under orders from Lord Sulpeter to stay with you.'

They were all Corani knights, and they looked . . . *wholesome* . . . but there was something she had to know first. 'I'll join you shortly,' she told them. 'I'm safe here.'

She waited until they had reluctantly retreated to the other end of the gardens, where Domara was tending Solon Takwyth, then she bent over the broken body of Twoface and lifted the mask.

Sir Esvald Berlond.

But he was Takwyth's man . . . he must have taken up the offer Solon refused?

She shivered, then replaced the mask and walked away, making a small wish, that by next morning, the earthworms and the roots and vines would have consumed him, flesh and bone.

The Bastion, Pallas-Nord

Ostevan Comfateri came awake through the rough jostling of a gaunt-leted hand on his shoulders. He looked up to see a circle of grim mage-knights; Corani all, led by an even grimmer-faced Ril Endarion.

'What . . .?' Ostevan slurred, not feigning his disorientation.

What the Hel did that? It came from Saint Eloy's shrine . . . Then the answer came: *Pandaemancy . . . it nearly destroyed me . . . it would have, except that my soul regained my body in time . . .*

The nearness of his escape took his breath away.

Thank . . . whoever . . . for the impulse that led me to switch bodies with Junius!

'My Prince! What's happening? Why—?' Ostevan was in control of his faculties now, and made sure to infuse his voice with panic. 'Junius – you must find him! He did this—'

One of the other knights bent over Ostevan, his eyes lit by gnostic-sight. 'The Comfateri's gnosis is under a Chain-rune. I'll see whose.'

Ostevan held his breath: this was the biggest test. He'd cast the Chain-rune using Abraxas' powers and his own intellect, but channelled the spell through Junius, so some residual trace of the hapless brother should remain. He waited, tensing . . . and then the knight grunted. 'It's Junius', I think. Not a good reading, but it's there. I've worked with the old coot at times in the healing bays – I know his trace.'

Ril Endarion stared down at him, his dark-toned face battered and bruised, his eyes suspicious. 'We have information out of the Celestium that you're involved in the night's attacks. You have questions to face, Confessor. The queen is on her way.'

Ostevan closed his eyes to mask his thoughts. *So Lyra survived* . . . He was surprised by how much relief he felt. Then the deeper implications struck him: *Then we all failed – Bastion and Celestium. We* failed*!* He feigned dizziness while reaching out to Abraxas, the link undisturbed by the Chain-rune. *<Master,>* he called.

Naxius' Puppeteer mask filled his inner eye and in moments he learned what had transpired in the Winter Garden that night. Somewhat chillingly, Naxius had been following everything they did – including his own movements.

Ostevan expected admonishment, perhaps even punishment, for the failure to attain their goals, but instead Naxius made an ironic gesture of blessing, as if he were the priest, and vanished from the link. Ostevan opened his eyes again as Queen Lyra Vereinen swept into the chapel, escorted by a cluster of knights.

But no Dirklan Setallius. No Solon Takwyth. And no Esvald Berlond . . . that wasn't who I'd expected . . . Nor who Tear thought, I suspect . . .

Lyra looked utterly exhausted, her eyes bruised, black circles beneath. Her face foreshadowed how she'd look in a decade's time. There was fear in her voice as she anxiously asked, 'Ostevan? What happened here?'

Her voice told him her mood: *She wants to believe I'm innocent.*

'Majesty,' he babbled, 'thank Kore you're here – Junius did this . . . he took me by surprise, and . . . and he *bit* me, Majesty, on the neck. It was ghastly – I thought I would die—'

Lyra's eyes went wide, but caution took over. 'Dominius Wurther swears you led the attack on the Celestium tonight. He is adamant.'

'I've been unconscious all night,' Ostevan protested. 'And under a Chain-rune. Junius did this.'

'It was Junius' Chain-rune,' Endarion confirmed reluctantly.

'After he bit me, he taunted me: how he would use me as a slave,' Ostevan said, pitching it to pluck on Lyra's heart-strings. 'I truly don't know how I survived.'

That was the weakness of his tale – he *should* be a slave – but Naxius had seen certain things in the queen's suite, through the eyes of all

Abraxas' minions – including Coramore. There must be a tale he could spin – but nothing came.

The looks on everyone's face, even Lyra's, said that if he had truly been bitten, he couldn't be trusted. Endarion was clearly unwilling to let him off the hook. 'What about all this rubbish?' he said, indicating the empty water-jug, the burnt-out candle and the shattered mirrors. 'No one uses this shit for the gnosis, so what is it doing here?'

Ostevan floundered, unable to find a rational explanation, cursing himself for leaving these trinkets here at all.

Then inspiration struck. 'Majesty, I have a confession,' he said, fixing his gaze on Lyra. 'I was curious about your Winter Garden. I went there uninvited and collected fallen feathers, a stone and some water. I know it was forbidden, but it seemed to me there was some power – some *benevolent* power – in the place. I wanted to understand it, the better to help you. I was examining these items when Junius attacked me.'

Lyra stared, her eyes narrowing in recognition. She'd confessed about the dwyma just days before, after all. 'Go on,' she encouraged, while Endarion glared.

'After Junius left, I was struggling, and my leg kicked the water-jug and it spilled on me.' *Just as water from your pool seems to have aided Coramore.* His tale was solidifying. 'I felt myself rallying so I seized the jug and drained the rest. Then I fell into darkness ... until Prince Ril found me.'

Ostevan risked a glance and saw that Lyra's eyes were bright with excited wonder, while Endarion was rocking back on his heels, scowling. 'I feel ... somehow *renewed*,' he told the young queen. 'It's a miracle.'

When Lyra laid her hand on his, he knew he'd won. 'Oh, Ostevan, it's not a miracle, it's something so much more – I have so much to tell you—' She actually embraced him, and he basked in the scent of her, the brush of skin, a preview of how she would feel when he finally possessed her.

But that would have to wait, for now.

She straightened and turned to her knights. 'Remove the Chain-rune and see to my Confessor's comfort. He's been through an ordeal, just as we all have. But he is my true and loyal servant – Grand Prelate Wurther was mistaken.'

Ril Endarion made one last try. 'Why would harmless old Junius do this?'

Ostevan looked up, feigning sorrow. 'Brother Junius was a troubled soul,' he lied. 'He came to me for Unburdening not long after I returned. He confessed to sordid things, Majesty, dreadful acts with children. But he swore he'd forsaken such crimes, and the confidentiality of the Unburdening prevented me from acting.' He hung his head as if dismayed at himself and the dreadful machinations of Fate. 'Clearly he found a patron willing to tolerate such vice and fell into their toils.'

As he'd hoped, a wretched look crossed Lyra's face. She took his hands. 'What a dreadful position to be in. Ostevan, I know you're exhausted now, as am I, but we must talk, as soon as possible.' Her eyes poured out her soul.

She's desperate to believe well of me.

'Milady, I am forever your servant,' he told her, bowing his head to hide his relief and exultation.

We failed tonight, he admitted silently, *but perhaps we've also sown the seeds of victory.*

43

The Broken Tower

The Leviathan Bridge

The Ordo Costruo, dissident magi, were the first men of Yuros to 'discover' Ahmedhassa, a land whose splendour far exceeds the barbarism of their own homeland. Presenting a fair face, these agents of Shaitan caused a Bridge to be made, linking East and West. Only hatred, greed, deceit and sorrow has ever journeyed across it. All the world longs for this travesty to be unmade.

ALI BEYRAMI, MAULA OF SAGOSTABAD, 934

Midpoint Tower, Pontic Sea
Junesse 935

Waqar and his friends stared open-mouthed, trying to take in what they'd just seen.

'I think something hit the tower . . .' Fatima managed to say.

'A meteor?' Tamir guessed.

Waqar scryed his mother, but there was nothing. He looked at Tarita but she was standing motionless, uncomprehending.

'The Bridge is *damaged*,' Lukadin – more than any of them a Shihadi – cried out, waving a triumphant fist. 'May it be swept away!'

'There were *people* in that tower,' Fatima gasped.

Lukadin snorted. 'Ordo Costruo heathens.'

'The people who rebuilt Hebusalim,' Tamir replied, his clever face slack with disbelief. 'Ahm on High! It was a meteor, wasn't it? A meteor?'

'Meteors don't hit the one inhabited place in an ocean,' Waqar said, thinking of that last glimpse of his mother's mind. 'Mother was inside that blast – she *caused* it . . . just before it, I sensed her—' He slammed his fist down on the railing. 'It has to be the same people who killed Salim: these masked people – *but who are they?*'

No one had any answers.

The air was clearing swiftly now, the rain and clouds for miles gone and the wind was dropping by the second as the storm simply faded to nothing. The waves were still gigantic, but that was probably normal. Then Tamir pointed. 'Look, there – there's a skiff, going to the tower.'

'I think I saw it earlier,' Waqar remembered. 'Follow it in – there may be survivors!'

Their captain and crew, operating in a kind of fatalistic daze, navigated their craft towards the stump of the tower. As they got closer, the swathe of stars in the rapidly clearing skies above illuminated the scene faintly. Midpoint was just a broken cylinder, the top only just above the largest waves. It was about three hundred feet across, stairs and rooms built into the outer walls and a hollow core where the solarus energy had flowed from the beacon down to the sea-floor far below. They pulled alongside the wrecked stump, seeking a place to moor. Their crew no longer feared for their lives from the storm, but they were clearly still terrified to be here.

Lukadin guided them into the top of the tower, only a few dozen feet above the waves when they swelled up. The skiff they'd seen was already there, moored to the wrecked pinnacle. It was empty.

Lukadin brought them in alongside. 'Sal'Ahm!' he called.

Fatima smacked his shoulder. 'Hush, idiot – we don't know who they are.'

'What do we do now?' Baneet asked.

Waqar glanced at Tarita, who was pale as a ghost. He'd become used to leaning on her in the past month, but now she looked like the young maid she used to be, stunned and out of her depth. It was up to him to take charge. 'Right,' he said, 'let's go inside, and see if anyone can be saved. We'll all go in – the captain and his crew can't leave without Lukadin to pilot the dhou. Our goal is to find survivors – but be on guard: we don't know who the skiff-rider is, and the survivors may be hostile. And the energy from the tower might still be dangerous.'

'Then we get out,' Tamir added. 'The Ordo Costruo will send people and anyone they find around here will be blamed.'

Waqar was first to leap to the rim of the broken tower, shining gnosis-light to illuminate the way, followed by Baneet, Fatima, Tamir and, after a pause, Tarita. He wished he had time to ask what she was thinking, but people could be dying below.

The stairs descended in a spiral inside the outer wall of the cylinder. Sea-water was running through cracks in the walls whenever a wave crested, cascading down into the structure. There was no light – all the gnostic-lamps on the walls were dead, and collapsed interior walls revealed smashed offices and a guardroom. There were bodies lying against the inner walls, but none moved.

'Watch out!' Tarita called as another wave topped the stump and a bitterly cold wall of water swept down the stairs. They clung to each other until the water had passed, gurgling downwards and out of sight.

'The bottom's going to fill eventually,' Tamir observed, 'assuming the whole thing doesn't collapse on top of us. Can we hurry, O Prince?'

Waqar sped up, descending as fast as he dared, leading them through a section of stairs where the inner wall had fallen against the outer, choking the stairwell – but there was room to get through, and on the other side the stairs were drier – the next wave to flood down was diverted by the blockage into an inner room, through a broken wall and into the tower's core. Waqar couldn't guess if that was a good or bad thing; he just knew the stairs were drier and unblocked, so he picked up speed until he found a landing where a pasty-faced middle-aged woman in pale blue Ordo Costruo robes was lying in a pool of her own blood. Her throat was cut, the flesh still warm.

They looked at each other grimly and drew their weapons.

The next inner door revealed an office and the iron reek of fresh blood was heavy in the air. Three more Builder-magi lay charred and motionless amidst smouldering parchments and collapsed bookcases.

Waqar was not alone in going rigid at the slightest sound. An inner room opened onto a library and a back stair leading downwards.

Then a discharge of strong gnostic-energy from below shivered through the aether.

If my mother truly did this at the behest of the masked ones, then odds are it's another masked assassin down there. Tarita might be a match for them, but the rest of us aren't . . .

He wavered, torn between fear and duty, then Tarita pointed to the back stair and indicated that he take the main stair. He saw in her a fierce resolve to strike back, and found a kindred emotion inside himself.

These people didn't just kill my mother, they corrupted her corpse into a tool for their plans . . . I'm going to kill one of them, or die trying.

He touched Lukadin's arm. 'Go with Tarita.'

Without a backwards look, he led the others to the outer stair, Baneet behind him, Fatima and Tamir, the weaker fighters, in their wake. They descended another turn of the stairs and found another landing, and a door. The steps continued, but the door was ajar, revealing a large circular chamber. He crept to the doorway and peered in.

Another body was lying in the middle of the floor, crushed beneath a massive chandelier, the tiles shattered around it, the air still murky with discharged spells. Around it were three stone plinths with glass tops. The whole room still had some residual energy, because the gnostic-lamps were still working.

A grey-robed man was standing beside the fallen chandelier, facing away from Waqar, intent upon one of the glass-topped plinths. Energy sparked from his fingertips and fizzed around the edges of the casing: an opening spell against locking-wards. Usually there was only one winner: the opening-spell – unless the lock was cast by someone of far greater power than the opener. The glass casing reflected the man's face: a copper mask of a cat. Since Salim's assassination, Waqar had been reading a lot about Lantric masks, so he recognised this one: *Felix*, the spirit of luck.

The glass shattered, and Felix reached in and pulled out a spearhead mounted on a broken wooden shaft only about two feet long. He held it up, examining it, then put it aside and walked to the next plinth. More sparks flew.

This must be some kind of Ordo Costruo treasure-house.

A previously concealed hatch on the far side opened and Tarita slipped through. Felix was concentrating on his task, but Waqar's heart went to his mouth, especially when Lukadin followed the Jhafi girl through. There was nowhere for either to hide, and any second now, Felix would become aware . . .

Waqar didn't think so much as react, stepping inside and calling, 'Who are you?'

It was gratifying to see Felix stiffen and look up – *so they're not omniscient!* – but when that metal face fixed on him, his bones drained of marrow.

Felix completed opening the second glass and pulled out a gleaming scimitar, made in an ancient style but glistening as if newly forged. He flourished it and said, 'Prince Waqar, I hoped you would come.'

His voice was distorted, but Waqar realised it was also familiar. *Dear Ahm, I think I know this man—*

'You're one of those who murdered the sultan,' Waqar said through gritted teeth, clinging to his courage. Baneet, Tamir and Fatima also stepped into the room and fanned out, weapons raised.

Felix snorted. 'Wrong, dear boy.' When he spoke, his mask moved as if it were a second skin. 'My business that night was with your mother.'

Waqar felt his heart skip a beat. 'You . . .' Almost, he raised his blade and charged, but he knew that the moment he took that step, there was every chance he and his friends would die. 'What did you do to her?'

Felix waved a dismissive hand. 'I think you know what we did, Prince Waqar. The better question is: *why her?*'

Behind the masked man, Tarita was ghosting in from one side and Lukadin the other, but neither were yet close enough to strike. So Waqar swallowed and asked, 'Why, then?'

Felix drew himself up like an orator. 'Because she had a power unlike any other mage. You know, surely, that she was considered the greatest weather-mage of all, yes? But do you know why? I'll tell you – and not just because I enjoy talking, but *because you are her son.*'

Waqar felt his throat close as the implications of Felix's words hit him. *He's completely confident he can kill us all and then do to me whatever he did to Mother . . . But he thinks he can persuade me, and forego the killing. He actually thinks I'll join them . . . Mother said that I have a power . . . and so does Jehana . . .*

He swallowed again, and motioned all his friends to remain still. *I want to them all hear this . . . in case any of us escape . . .* Those at his side complied, and behind Felix, Tarita and Lukadin froze as well.

'The Ordo Costruo have researched many things,' Felix said smugly. 'One of those research projects concerned a branch of magic unlike the gnosis, useless for combat and small tasks, but able to be employed to massive effect – like manipulating vast weather patterns. Your mother was the foremost of those the order bred or created.'

My mother was 'bred or created'? Waqar's mouth dried up completely.

'She had three apprentices,' Felix went on. 'I think you know they left her to fight against the Third Crusade – it was their storm that ravaged the Rondian army at Shaliyah. Tonight they rode the other three windships – those that were sacrificed to weaken the tower's defences and enable your mother's ice-bolt to strike.'

'You killed my mother so you could resurrect and use her?'

'No, no, Prince Waqar,' Felix responded smoothly, 'that she died was regrettable. It was a potion she took – a mix of silver and other elements to fight what she saw as an infection – that killed her. She killed herself – or rather, the person who fed her that potion did . . .'

Waqar swallowed. *The elixir she made me bring . . . and Tarita . . .*

Felix took a step towards him, spreading his hands as if in invitation. 'Waqar, your mother wasn't slain by *us* – we gave her a *gift*. Only when she died were we forced to do the unthinkable, to utilise her as we did. Had she but understood, she would have received a great *awakening* – as you will, if you join us.'

He calls the venom he put inside Mother a 'gift'? 'Why would I ever join you?'

'Because war is not just coming, Waqar, *it's here*. The world is about to be plunged into chaos, beyond even what the Crusades wrought. No one thought you'd inherited your mother's powers, but in her final days, she revealed that the potential is still inside you – which is why I awaited you here.' Felix stretched a hand towards him. 'Join us, and you'll be embraced as a brother. You'll become one of a small elite group, shaping a better world. We are gods among men, Waqar, shaping the destiny of nations – join us!' His voice became sly. 'Your sister already has . . .'

Felix's voice had become more and more persuasive, more resonant, more melodic, soaring as he spoke, and Waqar felt his friends' eyes swivel towards him. They were actually worried that he was tempted.

But the last lie was one too many; it had snapped the spell.

'My sister would never join the people who killed our mother.'

Felix laughed. 'Think you not?'

'And I will never join you – you destroyed her, then turned her against everything she loved!'

'"Loved"?' Felix snorted. 'You think she *loved* the Ordo Costruo? A prissy order of men with quills for cocks who used her for their own gratification? *She loved power* – and that's what we gave her. *She died laughing*—'

Waqar lifted his blade as rage all but swallowed him. Beside him, his friends took the cue and kindled gnosis-fire. Then he stopped. *If I attack, he'll kill everyone in this room . . . except me.*

'Still can't decide, little Prince?' Felix purred. 'You think too much.' The silver scimitar in his hands came alive with gnosis-light. He bared his teeth – thin, pointed cat-teeth with incisors that dripped a dirty amber fluid. 'You'll join us, willing or no.'

Tarita moved, darting in with a dagger held double-handed, intending to drive it into Felix's side.

But the moment she broke cover, the masked man half-turned and an explosion of power surged from him in all directions; Tarita and Lukadin went spinning away and struck the far wall, Waqar was thrown backwards, hammering his back against the stone, Fatima pinned beside him, and Tamir vanished head-first out of the door.

Felix's second assault was directed at Tarita, as if he recognised her as his main threat. A torrent of fire swept at her, but she recovered in time to shield, and the fire-burst splashed around a body-length translucent disc. Felix followed her, slashing at her with the silver scimitar; his first blow shattered her blade and the second almost took her head off – it was as if her gnostic shields didn't exist.

Fatima managed to break free and charged, closely followed by Baneet, but Felix whirled and slammed a mage-bolt into Fatima's chest, sending her reeling backwards, her shields fused and fading. Waqar put himself between Felix and Fatima as Felix hurled Baneet away again. Tamir tried to re-enter the room, and was almost engulfed in fire.

Waqar launched himself at the cat-masked man in desperation at seeing his friends struck down with such contemptuous ease, but his sword snapped in half on the silver blade Felix wielded. The masked assassin made a gripping motion with his left hand and something like an invisible hand gripped him, bent him backwards and held him immobile. Felix leered at him, and as Tarita tried to reach him, he launched a torrent of mage-bolts at her. Waqar thought she'd go under, but her shields held – *just* – and for an instant, all of Felix's attention was on the tiny Jhafi girl.

Just as the one member of his group so far overlooked took his shot.

Lukadin had stolen in on the masked assassin's blind side. In his hands was the two-foot long spear-shaft topped by the dull-bladed spearhead Felix had retrieved from the first of the glass cases. As he raised it, the spearhead blazed with light, a fallen sun in spear form—

—which plunged unimpeded through Felix's shields and buried itself in the man's chest. Energy – a brilliant blast of darkness like polished coal – blasted his torso apart in a bloody eruption, hurling Lukadin backwards even as Felix collapsed in a charred heap, limbs splayed. The silver scimitar fell from the body and rattled to the floor, still aglow with heat and light, but fading.

Waqar fell to Lukadin's side as around him his friends groaned and staggered towards them. 'Luka! *Luka!*' he shouted.

Lukadin's whole body looked desiccated, as if he'd walked days in the desert without water, but his hand reached for and found the cooling spearhead and he clutched it like a child, his eyes burning in exultation, his breath coming in joyous swallows as he cried, '*I got the bastard, I got the bastard!*'

He certainly had. Felix had been reduced to charred flesh and bones covered by scraps of cloth. The sight was utterly sickening, and Waqar recoiled from the thought of touching the corpse, but he had to know if his guess was correct. He pulled the mask from the dead man's face as the others crowded around.

'*Dear Ahm . . .*' Fatima breathed. 'It's Saarif Ibram . . .'

DAVID HAIR

Waqar's brain whirled. *Saarif Ibram: one of the richest men in Ahmedhassa, and the man Rashid had me reporting to in Lokistan . . .*

If this is Felix, who are Ironhelm, Heartface and Beak?

But there were more pressing matters. He looked down the silver scimitar, remembering how it had broken his and Tarita's blades like they were sticks. He glanced up at the Jhafi girl, and he could tell she was tempted, but wouldn't take it ahead of a prince.

'This belongs to the Ordo Costruo,' he said, picking up the fallen blade. 'We're not looters.' He glanced at Lukadin, thinking how dreadful he looked.

'If this spear is the only thing that can kill these masked people, we'd be stupid to leave it behind,' Lukadin muttered, clinging possessively to his prize.

Waqar sighed, then nodded in assent. But he reversed the scimitar and offered it to Tarita. 'For all you've done.'

She met his eyes. <*Did Cat-mask lie about the elixir?*> she sent silently.

<*I don't know,*> he answered, <*but Mother gave us both the recipe – she was determined to either beat that thing inside her, or die.*> The implication chilled him. Aloud he said, 'I must return to Rashid's service; I'm a prince of the realm. But if you remain in pursuit of this man's colleagues, you'll need a weapon like this.'

She inclined her head and accepted his gift. 'My Prince,' she said, with a reverence she'd not shown before. Their gazes lingered on each other, and for a moment he wished they were alone, in a place that death hadn't found.

Tamir's robes were still smouldering, his skin blotchy with burns, but he clapped Waqar on the shoulder. 'If the rest of this tower collapses, we're dead. The stairwell is filling from below and I swear it's going to tear apart any minute. Can we *please go*?'

'Yes – *yes*.' Waqar stood, then glanced into the one unbroken glass case. It held a book: *Daemonicon di Naxius*. He was wondering whether to try and unlock it when Tarita slammed the hilt of her new blade down on the glass and it shattered in a concussion of gnostic energy. She reached in, removed the book and stowed it in a satchel. 'I know people who will be able to interpret it,' she said briskly.

648

'Come on,' Tamir cried, 'there are things *breaking* all around us – *come on—*'

Baneet helped Lukadin to walk and they hurried upwards as fast as they could. Tamir was right: the tower had been fatally damaged, and with each wave that slammed against it, they could hear stone cracking. Clambering through the semi-blocked section, they were almost engulfed by seawater pouring down the stairs. When they emerged they were soaked in salty water, although the seas were visibly calming and the skies were almost clear. Waqar was shocked to realise dawn was near. The dhou captain was frantically gesticulating that they really, *really* had to leave: the wind was blowing up from the south now, and there was darkness on that horizon deeper than the night.

Another storm? If it's headwinds all the way back, we'll never make it.

Tarita took Felix's skiff, threw her gear aboard, then deftly unfastened the sails. As the rest of them clambered onto the dhou, Waqar leaped to her side, waited until she was at the tiller, then untied the mooring-rope. As the prow swung about, he leaned in, threw the coil of rope into the bottom of the hull, grasped the skiff with one hand, and went to kiss her cheek.

She turned to meet his movement and their lips touched and for a moment, mashed together. He blinked, drank in her thin, determined, vibrant face and managed a smile. 'Thank you, Tarita. Thank you for everything.'

'Please, my Prince, she said demurely, 'I'm a dirt-caste orphan.'

'You're much more than that. I can never repay you.'

'Don't let that stop you from trying,' she advised. 'I need to go.'

He leaned in and asked, 'What name did you learn in Hebusalim?'

She considered, then whispered back, 'I guess you've earned that. But if Saarif Ibram was at court, so might this man be: *Asiv Fariddan.* Be careful who you tell – my advice would be "no one".'

Then she released the sails. They billowed in the wind, and she sped away eastwards, towards the palest part of the sky – the east, the direction of Javon.

'Hey, Prince of Love!' Fatima snarked. 'Now you've seduced the *enemy spy*, can we leave?'

649

He leaped aboard and gave the captain permission to release the moorings. Lukadin was too battered to fly, but Fatima took the tiller, released Air-gnosis from the keel and they rose, turning in the breeze to head back to the south. Steam was now venting from the central core of Midpoint and the waves had almost engulfed the broken stump of the tower.

Do I go to Uncle and confront him – and risk hearing things I never want to know?

Or do I got to the Ordo Costruo and tell them what I've discovered? What would they do to Jehana and me if I did? Did Felix lie about Jehana . . . surely *it was a lie?*

And who is Asiv Fariddan?

He contemplated his choices, his eyes on the distant south, as the sun rose and lit the skies – including the band of darkness on the southern horizon. He tore his mind free of his reverie and stared.

It wasn't a stormcloud coming up from the southeast: it was a *windfleet*, following the line of the Leviathan Bridge. Skiffs, dhous, transporters, even warbirds – and all of them were triangular-sailed, all of them bearing the crescent moon and scimitar. There were hundreds – no, *thousands* – of windcraft, and he finally realised what he was looking at.

The Shihad was never meant to invade Javon or Khotri or Lakh. It was always exactly what it claimed to be: a Holy War against the Crusaders. The Leviathan Bridge was destroyed, or soon would be, unless this damage was repairable, and either way, the wind-paths were open and the Shihad was flying to Yuros.

Rashid always knew the timing of this attack – the masked ones told him. They've been playing him as a puppet, or acting for him all along . . . Or he's one himself.

Tamir touched his arm. His face said he'd already worked all that out. 'What will you do now, Waqar?'

'What can I do? My fleet awaits, and I must resume command of it. I must do my sultan's bidding.' He dropped his voice and added, 'If I find Rashid ordered my mother's death, I'll kill him myself.'

Epilogue

An East Wind

The Value of Life

*Nothing is more valuable than a human life – to the possessor of that life. For
the rest of us, it's more complicated. What can they do for me? Do we like them?
What are the consequences?*

I like to assign a monetary value to the options and work with that.

GUY FULBRUCKE, ARGUNDIAN MERCHANT AND SPY, 898

*Dawnport Gate, Pallas, Rondelmar
Junesse 935*

Ril and Lyra watched the horsemen shuffling anxiously before the east-
ernmost gate of Pallas-Nord. Their vantage in the gatehouse afforded
them views over the Bruin and the ramshackle, indefensible village of
Dawnport, just outside the city walls. It also enabled them to enjoy the
sight of Duke Garod Sacrecour, floundering before the closed gates while
his knights fidgeted. Finally Garod came to a decision and advanced
under a flag of parley.

'Do you think he'll try anything?' Lyra asked. While it might have
been satisfying to see another enemy struck down, she was still too
shaken by the betrayals of the night to crave more drama.

Ril indicated the battlements, left and right, lined with Imperial
Guard and Corani legionaries and battle-magi. A dozen of the largest
military windships – warbirds feared throughout two continents for
their firepower – hung in the skies above. 'I don't think so.'

They'd learned of Garod's approach only an hour before, but that
had given Dirklan Setallius time enough to deploy soldiers and ensure

the gates remained closed. The spymaster had returned from the Celestium a few hours before dawn, anxious and berating himself for not seeing this coming.

Should he have? Lyra wondered. *Have our enemies been clever, or have we been blind?* These were questions she needed answered, but they were issues for tomorrow. *Today it's about mourning . . . and this . . .*

Lyra took Ril's hand and they stepped to the rim of the gatehouse tower. 'Duke Garod,' she called, 'what a surprise – I didn't know you planned a visit?'

Garod must have realised that whatever he'd been expecting would no longer be happening, so there was no histrionics, or even surprise. He had informants in the city, no doubt, because when he spoke, his reply was smooth, his tale somewhat plausible.

'Your Majesty, it is a joy to see you,' he shouted, somehow contriving to sound sincere. 'My spymaster insisted there was a danger to you and I immediately decided I must ride to your aid.'

Lyra felt a surge of temper at this bare-faced lie, but she contented herself with rolling her eyes, confident he'd not be able to see the details of her expression from this distance. 'We're grateful, your Grace – although a simple warning would have sufficed. We must learn to exchange information more freely.'

'Majesty, we decided our *unexpected* arrival would enable us to better aid you.'

Ril snorted. 'Kore's Balls, the man has a nerve.'

'While you're here, would you like to see your nephew and niece?' Lyra offered, her voice guileless. She turned and waved Cordan and Coramore, who'd been standing quivering behind them, to come forth. 'Look, here they are.'

Garod's face was a picture as he took in the two pallid, ginger-haired children squirming on the battlements, so close, yet out of reach. 'It gives me joy to see you both,' he called to them weakly.

So you see, Garod, we're still alive, we still have our hostages, and the city gates are closed, Lyra thought with grim satisfaction. *Turn around and go home.*

What she actually said was, 'Would you like to come up and visit them?'

She watched the thoughts crawl over Garod's face: the knowledge that a violent assault Lyra knew he was involved in had failed. *Would he place himself into her reach?* She doubted it, and so it proved.

'It would be a joy,' Garod called back, 'but unfortunately this precipitous ride was taken with little thought to the well-being of my own lands. I really must return, if the danger here has passed—'

'What a shame,' Lyra answered. She saw Cordan and Coramore glance in her direction, and there was no sign of their normal arrogance. They were both still terrified by the events of the previous night, not to mention what was to be done with them. In truth, Lyra hadn't fully decided. Cordan was cowed into silent compliance, and mercifully, Coramore appeared to remember little of what she'd done.

Garod made his bows and fled, and in a few minutes his riders were a dust-cloud passing through Dawnport and heading back home. She hoped it rained all the way.

'It's not too late to hit them with the windships,' Ril muttered hopefully.

'But I like Garod,' she said, 'he's predictable and fallible.' She turned to Setallius. 'Dirklan, we've much to learn about what happened tonight. We must discuss it as soon as possible. In the meantime, take Cordan and Coramore to Redburn Tower and make sure no one can reach them. They've seen evil at close hand, and we must tread carefully.' She and Ril turned to the two children, unsure whether to expect fear or fury, but wordlessly, they went down on one knee, Coramore to her and Cordan to Ril, and that felt just. Then Setallius led them away.

'What of the surviving attackers?' she asked Ril.

'When the Masks fled, they lost all will to fight. We've got several hundred penned up, but the guards are terrified of them – I've had to deploy magi to watch them. Those who can talk claim to have no memory of what happened. They say they don't even know how they got here.'

Lyra shuddered. 'Study them, and learn the truth. We must fix things, and go on.' Then she felt something and grabbed his hand and laid it against the swell of her stomach. Her unborn was kicking her ungently, and she felt a sudden burst of relief, mirrored in Ril's face when he felt it too. 'We have much to live for.'

His expression still carried a shadow – Jenet Brunlye was among the dead, and Lyra knew she'd meant a lot to him. He seemed worryingly distant again and wouldn't catch her eye.

They were halfway down the steps when Setallius hurried back to meet them, his robes fluttering. He didn't bother with formalities, just waved away her retinue and bent his head in close between them, his expression stony. 'Your Majesties, there is serious news out of Pontus.'

'Pontus?' Lyra echoed. 'What news?'

'There are reports of an attack on the Leviathan Bridge itself, and thousands of Keshi windships in the air over Pontus. It appears that the East is invading Yuros.'

Lyra looked from the spymaster's face to Ril's and back again, scarcely believing her ears.

Dear Kore, all this, and we're at war after all.

The Pontic Sea

Smoke and steam were still pouring from the stump of Midpoint Tower as the windfleet sailed serenely above. To Latif, clinging to the rails, the sight was a tragedy, but he suspected he was the only one in the whole fleet who thought so. He wondered if any of the Ordo Costruo or Merozain monks he'd met had died here, and muttered a prayer for their souls.

When the fleet had appeared in the air above the vast camp of the army of Sagostabad, the men of his hazarabam had scarcely believed their eyes. They'd been told they were to go to war, but not the means, or the destination. No one suspected that Sultan Rashid had so many windships, and Latif felt again the sense of crushing betrayal: Rashid had clearly been preparing this fleet for *years*, diverting money intended to rebuild houses and schools and hospitals.

The more he thought about it, the more his belief that Rashid had ordered Salim's death intensified – but all around him, tens of thousands of men were chanting praises: to them, Rashid was the new Prophet.

Even when the fleet had risen into the Sagostabad skies, the soldiers praying like frightened virgins, they all assumed it was to fly south to Lakh, and when the windfleet turned north, they guessed at Javon. Two days later, they'd landed in a staging-camp in the southern Zhassi Valley, but next morning, instead of going north and west towards Javon, they'd swung northeast and flown out over the roiling sea.

When they saw the destroyed tower at Midpoint, realisation dawned: *they were waging Holy War on Yuros itself.* And the skies filled, more and more fleets joining them, Latif understood: this wasn't a raid, it was an invasion.

Rashid Mubarak, Latif thought, *you are a worker of dark miracles.*

Sultan Rashid Mubarak I sat on a throne on the forecastle of his flagship. He'd sent his retinue below, for none of them – *none of them* – understood what this moment meant to him. Attam and Xoredh only were permitted to stay, for both had contributed, but it was *his* moment.

When the Ordo Costruo had first refused to destroy their own creation and allowed the Crusaders to cross the Bridge, they truly believed that the Rondian Emperor would see the folly of war and repent.

So naïve, to think that an emperor would care about the sufferings of lesser beings. And now I too am an emperor, and I understand: my only concern must be ruling. To rule, one must stay enthroned. To stay enthroned, one must crush all enemies. One must grow stronger, or perish.

I'm doing this for you, Attam. For you, Xoredh. Even for you, foolish Waqar and naïve Jehana. I'm doing it for our futures.

'Look on this, my sons,' he murmured, 'our war has begun.'

Feher Szarvasfeld, Mollachia

Kyrik Sarkany faced the massive pyre on Neplezko Flat as the Sydian drums rumbled in a climactic flurry of beats and then fell abruptly silent. For three days they'd played unceasingly, the sound rising and falling in remembrance of the fallen. Among the Sydians grief, like love, was done with *intensity*. The Vlpa riders were in a ferment of loss, anger and dread. One hundred and fifty-three of their dead were laid out on the long pile of brushwood and dead pine branches awaiting the torch in his hands, waiting for him to light the pyre.

Over these three days of mourning, the tales of that night had been shared among the clan, growing and changing. Horned riders, white stags, vengeful storms; the best part of a Rondian legion dead in the most inexplicable circumstances ...

The clansmen walked around Valdyr now as if he might at any moment turn and shatter the ground beneath their feet. Gifts were left at his tent anonymously, by men too frightened to come near him.

For his part, Valdyr had said nothing about how he'd come to appear in the midst of a storm, let alone one of such *magnitude*. Something about a mountain peak? That was the most Kyrik had been able to chisel out of his brother.

Dragan Zhagy had arrived the following day, staggering across the ice; he'd not been able to offer any explanations either, just, *Valdyr went up the mountain after the White Stag.* What that meant, Kyrik still didn't know.

The dead Vitezai had already been lain in the ground, as was their way, and cairns built. The dead Rondians were mostly entombed below a massive sheet of ice, out of reach. Burying or burning them would have been the labour of weeks, and there wasn't the time. Nor did they much care.

The Vlpa will ride on to the Domhalott, to the pastures. Then we'll plan our campaign to drive the rest of the Rondians out of the valley. But first we must burn our dead.

He turned to the woman at his side. Hajya, cloaked in her wedding fox-furs, was far from well yet. Her face was gaunt, there was more grey in her hair, her left arm, broken in two places, was splinted and in a sling, the other, burned and grazed almost to the bones in places, bandaged shoulder to finger. Somehow she'd conjured just enough kinesis-energy to cushion her landing when that bastard Robear had hurled her from the cliff. Only Robear's carelessness in not seeing it through – and her own tenacity and healing skills – had kept body and soul together. His relief was beyond expression.

'Help me,' he said quietly. 'We'll do this together.'

She had to cling to his arm – and he knew how much his wife *hated* that – as they went forward to the pyre. He was hobbling himself, and deeply thankful he could still move at all; he'd badly needed the Sfera's healing-gnosis. Together, they brandished the torch, holding it high for a moment, before touching the flame to the brushwood. He watched it catch slowly, then roar to life, fuelled by Fire-gnosis, surging hungrily over timber and dead flesh.

Out loud, he murmured, 'Farewell, Brazko, son of Thraan.' Names and faces came to his mind: Yrhen, the Vlpa clan's chief scout, and others he'd exchanged a few words with, who'd followed his dream and paid with their lives.

As the flames took hold, it felt symbolic: *We're going to set fire to the land and burn the Rondians out.*

At last the pyre had burned down, and he and Hajya could finally rest. He held her hand as she slept. Valdyr sat beside him, dazed and subdued. Kyrik had been surprised and pleased to see how concerned his brother was for his wife.

'Do we know who leads the Rondian retreat?' Kyrik asked him. The scouts had reported a few hundred Rondian infantry, stragglers late to the battle, were retreating to Hegikaro as fast as they could move.

Valdyr shook his head. 'Dragan says they've found Robear Delestre's body, but not Sacrista's. She's likely buried under six foot of ice, he thinks.'

'We can hope,' Kyrik said, thinking, *Val's changed – but how? It's not just the battle . . .* If this fragile alliance between Mollach and Sydian was to survive, he and his brother needed to be united. 'What happened that night, Val?'

'I don't know,' his brother replied. 'It was like a dream, and I'm forgetting more and more of it, the longer time passes.' He didn't sound like he wanted to remember.

'The gnosis doesn't work like that, Brother. Even Ascendant magi can't call up ghostly storms that freeze one army while sparing the other! I don't understand any of this, and that frightens me.'

'You think it doesn't scare me too?' Valdyr replied, sounding a little like his old, truculent self. 'It's done now – I think that part of me has been emptied out. I hope so.' They fell silent again, staring at the embers, and for once Valdyr didn't flinch when Kyrik put an arm around his shoulders.

'Brother,' Valdyr began awkwardly, 'these Sydians ... I believe you're right: they're our people too.'

Kyrik stared. 'What changed your mind?'

'Something I heard in the wind on Watcher's Peak.'

After all they'd been through, this felt like a breakthrough. He embraced his brother warmly, trying to pretend he wasn't close to tears.

Valdyr went to seek his own tent, and not long afterwards, Hajya woke. As Kyrik fed her soup, she whispered, 'I heard your sending, in the Narrows – you make me proud too.'

Day One was spent huddled in the lee of a pile of snow-covered boulders, kept alive by the body-heat of a dying horse. Sacrista was amazed to still be breathing. The Mollachs and their allies came close, several times, but even as the sun blazed across the skies, lighting up the ice-field below her, she remained silent and unseen. She caught a snow hare and gorged on the hot raw flesh, melted snow to drink and slept, scared she'd never wake – but the storm had passed.

The impossibility of what she'd seen still bewildered her. She'd blasted spectral wolves that were hunting her, driven off a giant white bear and played hide and seek in the storm with a wild-eyed archer riding a white stag – they were all gone now, but the deadly cold remained.

Perhaps this is a dream I'm having as I die alone in the snow?

But dawn on Day Two felt all too real as her battered body protested even the slightest movement. Before the Sydians returned she managed to crawl away, not realising how close she came to a pair of hunters and a scout who was assiduously checking for fresh trails.

Normal autumn weather began to return, and the slight lift in the air temperature got her through Day Three. The Sydians burned their dead that night: she could see the roaring bonfire from afar.

Day Four, she killed a scavenging wolf with a mage-bolt and filled her belly with raw flesh, not able to expend any more energy to cook it, nor willing to risk a fire. She spent Day Five sleeping and letting her wounds stabilise. According to the *Book of Kore*, Urte was forged in five days, after which Kore had rested, making the sixth of the week holy – she had no idea what day it was; the nearest church was too far away to hear the bells, but on Day Six she truly felt renewed. Her thigh still pained her – she was using a broken branch as a staff – and she felt like a wild beast herself, but she was *alive*. During the day she crossed the ice that encased her men, praying for the salvation of Robear's soul, and for revenge.

'Who goes?' a sentry called as she stumbled from the tree-line.

It had taken another three days to reach the wooden palisade of the legion camp on Lake Drozst and Sacrista was famished and bone-weary. Her thigh was agony, the skin damaged so badly she doubted the scars could be healed away. When she tried to call out, her voice cracked.

'Who goes?' the sentry shouted again.

She swallowed water from her flask, then rasped, 'Who do you think?' *Idiot.*

Then she noticed the banners: not Delestre, but Imperial. She was still taking that in when a squad of men trotted from a postern and surrounded her. 'Is she one of those damn Mollachs?' one asked.

Another replied, 'She looks like that Delestre bi— Uh, Robear's sister.'

Then an officer strode through the rankers and ordered, 'Sheath your weapons. Lady Sacrista, it's good to see you. Governor Inoxion sent us up the valley when the news came of your defeat. You were feared dead.'

It's a miracle I'm not, she thought numbly. 'Where are my men? I had two maniples camped here.'

'They've gone to Hegikaro to secure the castle, Milady,' the officer replied. 'I presume you'll want to bathe and change before seeing the governor?'

Her throat tightened. 'See him?'

'Aye, Milady. He's right here. He's come to give what aid he can.'

She looked past him, to a cluster of men in Imperial robes on the walls, watching. She could almost picture the smirk on Inoxion's face. 'What price a kingdom?' he'd once asked her.

My soul . . . It's going to cost my soul.

In the Aether . . .
Junesse 935

Ostevan Comfateri was the first of the masked faces to slowly wink into existence. Moments later, Tear and Angelstar appeared at his side – but not Twoface; no surprise – he'd sensed the man die.

Only three appeared among their Eastern brethren: Ironhelm, Heart-face and Beak. No Felix? Interesting that he'd not sensed anything there. It suggested that distance did matter in the link.

What was noticeable was the way the six of them were arrayed: there was a distinct divide between East and West. No one spoke for a long time, until Ironhelm said, 'We have won a great victory against the Ordo Costruo. The Leviathan Bridge has been fatally damaged and Holy War has been launched. The Convocation has resolved that for every city sacked in the Crusades, a Yurosi city shall be razed.'

Ostevan was grateful that the incredulity on his face was hidden by a mask. *They've attacked the Bridge? They're invading? Is this part of Naxius' plan?*

He recalled that the Ordo Costruo had expelled Ervyn Naxius; it was doubtful that he had ever forgotten that, let alone forgiven. But the invaders were too far from Pallas to threaten his world. In fact, an invasion from the Ahmedhassa presented the perfect opportunity to further unsettle the empress and the grand prelate . . .

'How did your own plans fare, Yurosi?' Heartface, hovering close to Ironhelm, asked. 'Did you succeed?'

The three western magi exchanged a glance, and Ostevan answered, 'We met with unexpected resistance: the empress and the grand prelate remain on their thrones.'

'For now,' Angelstar muttered.

'What "unexpected resistance"?' Beak enquired.

'Pandaemancy,' Tear replied, though Ostevan felt she ought to have remained silent. 'Dwyma.'

'Ah.' Ironhelm's voice was smug. 'It was the dwyma which gave *us* our victory.'

That brought Ostevan another internal lurch. *They have pandaemancers?* Suddenly the distance from Pallas to Pontus felt a lot shorter, and their so-called 'holy war' a much more real threat to his own interests. *How far, realistically, could an Eastern invader get across Yuros?* he wondered.

And how essential to my own eventual survival is gaining sole control of Lyra?

He was still digesting this when the Puppeteer appeared, positioned between the two groups. 'Greetings, brethren,' he said blithely, as if unaware of the tension in the air. 'You've exchanged news? Excellent. I am of course fully aware of all that transpired. Yes, in Pallas we were checked – but we now know the full nature of what we face, and can act accordingly. And in the East, war is unleashed. It will spread across the known world, and in that chaos we will strike down all rival powers.'

'Just who are our *real* rivals?' Ostevan said, eyeing the three masked Easterners, who gazed back, shimmering with unsubtle menace.

'Any who stand against us,' the Puppeteer said mildly. 'I see you fear that you will find yourselves in opposition. Put that thought aside. The left hand of Abraxas does not plot against the right. We are one body, my Brethren. Together, we *are* Abraxas.'

That notion was more troubling than reassuring, but Ostevan bowed with the others. 'What of the fallen? We have lost two of our number: if we are one body, we have been crippled.'

'Not for long.' The Puppeteer's hand appeared, dangling a handful of blank masks. 'That is the magic of masks,' he replied. 'Anyone can wear them. Anyone at all.'

THE SUNSURGE QUARTET
continues with Book 2:
PRINCE OF THE SPEAR

ACKNOWLEDGEMENTS

Thanks firstly to Jo Fletcher for the faith to let me play some more in this world we've created. Your judgement, experience and encouragement get me through when the epic journey feels a little too epic for my weary feet. Thanks also to Sam Bradbury, Olivia Mead and the rest of the JFB/Quercus team, Emily Faccini for the fresh maps, Patrick Carpenter and Rory Kee for the cover, and everyone else involved.

Thanks also to my test readers: Kerry Greig, Paul Linton, Heather Adams and Catherine Mayo. When my instincts fail, they're the ones who pull the story back on track, and each brings their own strengths to the game. Kerry, Paul and Heather test-read *The Moontide Quartet*, but Catherine is new to the team: she's another New Zealand writer, specialising in stories set in the Ancient Greek period, so if that's your thing, I encourage you to seek out her work.

Heather (with her husband Mike Bryan) is my agent, and it's through her efforts in putting my work under Jo's nose that I have this opportunity to write this series: I could not be grateful enough.

Biggest hugs to Kerry, who manages to be cheery about having a husband who writes, and therefore struggles to disconnect from his imaginary friends, wakes up in the middle of the night to jot ideas down, and otherwise lives the madness. I couldn't do any of this without her support and tolerance.

Lots of love to my children, Brendan and Melissa, my parents Cliff and Biddy, and all my friends, especially Mark, Felix and Stefania, Raj, Andrew and Brenda, and Keith and Kathryn. And a big shout-out to the

.aff of Immigration New Zealand in Bangkok, Thailand, for welcoming us to our new transitory home.

Hello to Jason Isaacs.

David Hair
New Zealand and Bangkok, 2016